CONDENSED BOOKS

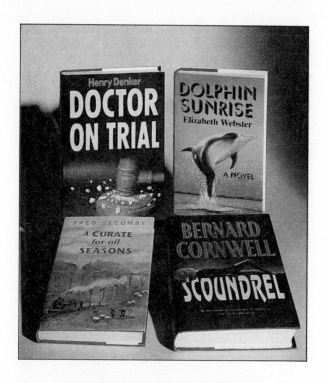

THE READER'S DIGEST ASSOCIATION LIMITED
Berkeley Square House, London W1X 6AB

THE READER'S DIGEST ASSOCIATION
SOUTH AFRICA (PTY) LTD
Reader's Digest House, 130 Strand Street, Cape Town

Page make-up by MS Filmsetting, Frome, Somerset
Separations by Magnacraft, London
Printed by BPCC Magazines (Leeds) Ltd
Bound by BPCC Hazells Ltd, Aylesbury

For information as to ownership
of copyright in the material of this book see last page

CONDENSED BOOKS

SCOUNDREL

Bernard Cornwell

PUBLISHED BY MICHAEL JOSEPH

DOLPHIN SUNRISE

Elizabeth Webster

PUBLISHED BY SOUVENIR PRESS

DOCTOR ON TRIAL

Henry Denker

PUBLISHED BY PIATKUS

A CURATE FOR ALL SEASONS

Fred Secombe

PUBLISHED BY MICHAEL JOSEPH

CONTENTS

SCOUNDREL

Bernard Cornwell

For years Paul Shanahan has led the life of a scoundrel—he has run arms and struck deals for some of the world's deadliest terrorist groups. Now he wants to turn his back on the past and retire in peace to his Cape Cod home. So when the IRA approach him once again and ask him to transport a boatload of gold to America, he accepts, his eye firmly set on the prospect of a secure retirement. But in the murky world of terrorism nothing—not even gold—is ever quite what it seems . . .

A riveting new best seller from the highly popular Bernard Cornwell.

DOLPHIN SUNRISE

Elizabeth Webster

After the tragic death of his mother, fifteen-year-old Matthew Ferguson is confused and lonely—until kindly neighbours offer to take him on holiday to Cornwall. During a long, happy summer Matthew makes new friends, among them wise old Captain St George with whom he shares a special bond. But it is his encounters with an extraordinary dolphin that bring about the most remarkable transformation in the quiet boy.

A spellbinding story about one of the earth's most beautiful but threatened species, which celebrates the healing power of life's simplest joys.

DOCTOR ON TRIAL

Henry Denker

All her life Kate Forrester has wanted to be a doctor. Showing a dedication second.to none, she has earned herself a residency at one of New York's finest hospitals, and is coping admirably with all the challenges it presents. Until one night, a young patient—the daughter of a ruthless real-estate tycoon—dies mysteriously while under her care. Suddenly it is a matter for the lawyers, and Kate's lifelong dream seems sure to collapse around her.

Henry Denker, author of *The Choice* and *A Gift of Life*, has written another remarkable novel highlighting the challenges of the medical profession.

page 291

A CURATE FOR ALL SEASONS

Fred Secombe

How does a young, inexperienced curate win the respect of an unruly flock? Especially when, like most novices, he demonstrates an uncanny talent for landing himself in the most bizarre situations. Fred Secombe provides the answers in these reminiscences of the hair-raising, hilarious, and sometimes heart-rending, moments during his years as a curate in a sleepy Welsh village after the close of the Second World War.

These glowing fictionalised memoirs, steeped in atmosphere and humour, are a sheer delight to read.

page 435

SCOUNDREL

BERNARD CORNWELL

ILLUSTRATED BY PETER MENNIM

Paul Shanahan has led a tough and dangerous life. Working in the pay of various international terrorist groups, he has learned to survive in a world where no one can be trusted and where life comes cheap.

Now, after spending four years on the sidelines, quietly running a yacht-broking business, Shanahan is about to be pitched back into the action. Kathleen Donovan is on his doorstep demanding to know the truth about her sister, Roisin, the only woman Shanahan ever really loved. And his old IRA paymasters are seeking his services for their latest audacious plan to transport five million dollars in gold across the Atlantic. Shanahan is wary, but the call back to his old ways seems too strong to resist . . .

1

August 1, 1990 was my fortieth birthday. Sophie, my lover for the past three years, left me for a younger man, the cat fell sick, and the next morning Saddam Hussein invaded Kuwait.

Welcome to the best years of my life.

Three weeks later Shafiq asked if I could deliver a boat from the Mediterranean to America. Hannah, my part-time secretary, had taken Shafiq's telephone call and late that afternoon she came to the fishing harbour to give me the day's news.

At first I thought I must have misheard her. I was working in a trawler's engine room, with the motor going. 'Who called?' I shouted up through the open hatch.

'Shafiq.' Hannah shrugged. 'He said you know him.'

I knew him all right, knew him well enough to wonder just what the hell was coming next. 'He wanted what?'

'He wants a boat delivered from the Mediterranean.'

'When?'

'He doesn't know.'

'From where in the Mediterranean? France? Spain? Italy?'

'Just the Mediterranean. He said he couldn't be more specific.'

'And I'm to deliver it where?'

Hannah smiled. 'Just America.'

I shut off the engine, waited for the noise to die away, and then looked up at Hannah. 'What kind of boat?'

'He doesn't know.' She laughed. Hannah had a nice laugh, but since Sophie had taken off, every woman seemed to have a nice laugh. 'I shall tell him no,' she said, 'yes?'

'Tell him yes, yes.'

Hannah adopted the patient look she used when she was trying to save me from myself. 'Yes?'

'Yes, *oui, ja, si*. That's what we're in business for.' Or at least that was what my letterhead said: Nordsee Yacht Delivery, Services and Surveying, Sole Proprietor, Paul Shanahan, Nieuwpoort, Belgium, though in the last few years the servicing and surveying had taken over from the delivery.

'But, Paul! You don't know when or how or what or where! How can I commit you?'

'When he phones back, tell him the answer is yes.'

Hannah uttered a very Flemish noise, a kind of glottal grunt which denoted a practical person's scorn for an impractical fool. She turned a page in her notebook. 'And a woman called Kathleen Donovan called. An American. She wants to see you.'

What is this? I thought. A man turns forty and suddenly his past comes back to haunt him, and I had a swift filthy image of Roisin's blood on the yellow stone, and I thought of betrayal and unhappiness and love, and I hoped to God that if Roisin's sister was looking for me she would never, ever find me.

'Tell her I've never heard of her and I don't want to see her.' I could not explain any of it to Hannah who was so very practical. 'And tell Shafiq I want to know why.'

Hannah frowned at me. 'Why what?'

'Just why!'

'OK! I'll ask!' She threw up her hands, turned and walked away along the quay.

I went back to work, surveying a trawler that was being sold across the North Sea to Scotland, but my mind was hardly on the boat; instead I was wondering why, out of nowhere and on the very same day, the ghosts of danger past and love betrayed had come back to haunt me. And, if I was honest, to excite me too. Life had become dull, predictable, placid, but now the ghosts had stirred.

I had waited four years for Shafiq to remember me, to summon me back to the darker paths. Four years. And I was ready.

'IT HAS BEEN a long time, Paul!' Shafiq, indolent, thin, kind, sly and middle-aged, sat on a deep sofa. He had taken a suite in the George V in Paris and wanted me to admire his opulence. He was also in an ebullient mood, for Shafiq loved Paris, loved France, and the more the French hated the Arabs, the more Shafiq approved of Gallic good taste. Shafiq was a Palestinian who lived in Libya, where he worked for Colonel Gaddafi's Centre to Resist Imperialism, Racism, Backwardness and Fascism. At first I had refused to believe any such organisation existed, but it did, and had probably given Shafiq his taste for European decadence. At first sight he seemed an unlikely secret agent for he was too childlike, too flamboyant and too likable, but they were perhaps the very qualities that had let him survive so long.

'So what do you want?' I asked him sourly.

'I have never known Paris so hot! Thank God for the invention of air conditioning.' He opened a small, brightly enamelled tin of cachous and slipped one under his tongue. 'I am pretending to be a Greek. I have a diplomatic passport even, look!'

I ignored both the fake passport and Shafiq's delight in possessing it. His contribution to resisting imperialism, racism, backwardness and fascism was to act as a messenger between Libya and whatever terrorist groups were the flavour of Colonel Gaddafi's month.

'You would like a Gauloise? Here! Take the pack, Paul.' He tossed the cigarettes to me.

'I've given up.'

'You've given up smoking! That's wonderful, Paul, really wonderful! The doctors say I should give up, but what do they know? You'd like some tea?'

'What the hell do you want, Shafiq?'

'I want you to deliver a boat to America, of course, just as I told your secretary.'

'What kind of a boat? From where? To where? When?'

'I'm not sure.' He lit a cigarette, then waved it vaguely about as if these details were of no importance. 'How is your love life?'

'It doesn't exist. I've just been junked for a married French pharmacist. I got custody of the cat. Whose boat is it?'

'You lost your girlfriend?' Shafiq was instantly concerned.

'Whose boat is it, Shafiq?'

'It belongs to friends.' Again he gestured vaguely. 'How long will it take you to deliver the boat to America?'

'That depends on what kind of a boat it is and how far it's going and at what time of year you want it delivered.'

'A sailboat,' he said. 'With a big lead keel.' He smiled, as though that answered all my queries.

I cast a beseeching look towards the ceiling's ornamental plaster-work. 'Three months? Four? How do I know? The bigger the boat, the quicker. Maybe.'

'Three months? Four?' He sounded neither pleased nor displeased. 'Why did your lover leave you?'

'Because, being an American, I want to retire to America one day and she doesn't, because she says I'm too secretive, because she finds life in Nieuwpoort dull, and because her Frenchman gave her a Mercedes.'

Shafiq shook his head. 'No wonder you are unhappy.'

'If I'm unhappy about anything,' I assured him, 'it's this meeting. For God's sake, Shafiq, you ignore me for four years, then you drag me to Paris to tell me you want me to deliver a boat, and now you can't give me a single detail about the job.'

He shrugged, then tapped his cigarette ash into a crystal bowl. 'You know why, Paul, you know why.' He would not look at me. 'They said you were CIA.'

'Oh, hell.' I leaned back in the chair, disgust in my voice.

'We know it isn't true, of course.' Shafiq tried to reassure me. 'But we can't be too careful, you know that. And it wasn't our side that accused you, it was the girl! What was her name? Roisin?' He even pronounced it properly, Rosh-een, proving that he remembered her well enough. 'Your girl, Paul.'

'My girl? She was anybody's, Shafiq.'

He chuckled, then made a dismissive gesture. 'So you understand, eh? You see why we could not trust you? Not me, of course, I never believed you were CIA. But they wanted to make sure. They said wait, wait and see if he runs home to America. I guess you didn't run home, eh?' He smiled at me.

'So this sailboat,' I asked coldly, 'is it to do with Iraq?'

'Iraq?' Shafiq spread hands as big as oarblades in a gesture suggesting he had never heard of Iraq or its invasion of Kuwait. 'It's just business.'

'The business of smuggling?' I asked. 'I don't smuggle things, Shafiq, unless I know what I'm smuggling, and why, and who it's going to, and who might be trying to stop it, and how much they propose paying me to get it past them.'

'I told them you'd say that!' Shafiq sounded triumphant.

'They?' I challenged him.

'The people who want you to go to Miami tomorrow,' he answered coyly. 'Your old friends.'

12

'They're in Miami?' That did surprise me.

'They're expecting you there tomorrow. I have your ticket. First class even!' He made it sound like a red carpet into the lions' den. Not that I needed such an enticement. I had waited four years for someone to rescue me from hydraulic systems and Fibreglass osmosis and rotted keel bolts.

So I telephoned Hannah at her Nieuwpoort home. It was a Sunday afternoon. 'Cancel this week's appointments,' I told her.

'But why?'

'Because I'm going to Miami,' I said, as though it was something I did every month.

Hannah sighed. 'Kathleen Donovan phoned again. She says she's visiting Europe and she promises she doesn't need much of your time . . .'

'Hannah!' I interrupted her. 'Make sure the cat takes its pills, will you?' Then I put the telephone down gently.

LITTLE MARTY DOYLE was waiting for me at Miami Airport where, despite the heat, he was jumping up and down like an excited poodle. 'It's just great to see you, Paulie! Just great! It's been years, hasn't it? I was saying as much to Michael last night.'

Marty is a nothing, a lickspittle, an errand boy. Officially he works for the Boston School Committee, while unofficially he gophers and chauffeurs for Michael Herlihy, who never learned to drive because he suffers from motion sickness and his mother always insisted he had to sit in the back of the family car. These days Marty is his dogsbody and driver.

'So what are you doing in Miami?' I asked him.

'Looking after Michael. Is that all your luggage?' He gestured at my sea bag. 'I'll carry it for you.'

I lifted the sea bag out of his reach. 'Just lead on.'

'It's been years, Paulie, but you don't look any older, not a day! That beard suits you. So how are you? The car's this way. Have you heard the news?' He was skipping around me like an excited child.

'The war has started?' I guessed.

'War?' Marty seemed oblivious to the American-led build-up of forces in Saudi Arabia. 'It's about Larry,' he said finally, 'they reckon it's healed, see? He'll be as good as new!'

'Who the hell is Larry?' I asked tiredly.

'Larry Bird!' Marty was astonished at my obtuseness. 'He missed the end of last season because of a growth on his heel.'

'Oh.' I might have known that the most important thing in Marty's world would be the Boston Celtics. The Celts were a religion in Boston, but somehow, perhaps because I now lived in a small harbour town on the Belgian coast, my devotions had lapsed.

Yet it felt good to be back on American soil, even in Florida's unfamiliar tropical heat. I had been away seven years. I had never meant the time to stretch so, but there were no family reasons to go home for my parents were dead and my sister was married to a buffoon I could not stand. These last years I had worked in Nieuwpoort and nursed my dreams of one day going home to a long, easy retirement in the Cape Cod house I had inherited from my father. I was saving up for that retirement.

'Michael's waiting for us.' Marty led me out of the terminal to a waiting limousine. 'And there's a fellow come over from Ireland to meet you. Brendan, his name is. Brendan Flynn.'

'Brendan Flynn?' That chilled me. Brendan was one of the Provisional IRA's top men, maybe third or fourth in the movement's hierarchy, and such men did not travel abroad for trivial reasons. I had walked into the deal eagerly enough, but the mention of Brendan's name gave the whole business a real smell of danger.

'It must be something big, Paulie, for a fellow to fly all the way from Ireland.' Marty was fishing for news. 'So what do you think it's about?' he asked as the limousine swung clear of the airport traffic.

'Just shut up, Marty.'

But Marty was incapable of silence and, as he drove north, he told me how he had seen my sister just the week before, and that Maureen was looking good, and how her boys were growing up, but that was the way of boys, wasn't it? And who did I think would be up for the Superbowl this year? The Forty-Niners again?

Marty paused in his stream of chatter as we neared the Hialeah Racetrack. He was looking for a turn-off among a tangle of warehouses and small machine shops. 'Here we are,' he announced, and the softly sprung car wallowed over a rough patch of road, turned into a rusting gateway through a chain-link fence topped with barbed wire, and stopped in the shade of a white-painted warehouse that had no identifying name on its anonymous façade. A stone-faced man sitting in a guard shed beside the main door must have recognised Marty for I was casually waved forward without any query. 'You're to go straight in,' Marty said, 'and I'm to wait.'

I stepped into the warehouse's shadowed, vast interior. Two forklift trucks stood just inside the door, but otherwise I could see nothing except tower-blocks of stacked cardboard boxes. The air smelt of machine oil and newly sawn timber, or like machine-gun oil and coffin wood. I was nervous.

'Is that you, Shanahan?' Michael Herlihy's disapproving voice sounded from the darkness at the far end of the huge shed.

'It's me.'

'Come and join us!' It was a command. Michael Herlihy had little time for the niceties of life, only for the dictates of work and duty. He was a scrawny little runt of a man, nothing but sinew and cold resolve, whose idea of a good time was to compete in the Boston marathon. By trade he was an attorney and, like me, he came from among Boston's 'two-toilet Irish': the wealthy American-Irish who had houses on the Point and summer homes on the South Shore or on Cape Cod. In his spare time he was the Chairperson of Congressman O'Shaughnessy's Re-election Committee and President of the New England Chapter of the Friends of Free Ireland. Michael preferred to describe himself as the Commander of the Provisional IRA's Boston Brigade, which was stretching a point for there was no formally established Boston Brigade, but Michael nevertheless fancied himself as a freedom fighter and kept a pair of black gloves and a black beret folded in tissue paper, ready to be placed on his funeral casket. He had never married, never wanted to, he said.

Now, in Miami's oppressive heat, he was waiting for me with three other men. Two were strangers, while the third, who came to greet me with outstretched arms, was Brendan Flynn himself. 'Is it you yourself, Paulie? My God, but it's grand to see you!' His Belfast accent was sour as a pickle. 'You're looking good in yourself! It must be all that Belgian beer.' He half crushed me in a welcoming embrace, then stepped back and gave my shoulder a friendly thump that might have felled a bullock. He was a tall man, built like an ox, with a bristling beard and a voice that erupted from deep in his beer-fed belly. 'And how are you, Paulie?'

'I'm just fine.' I had meant to reward four years of silence with a harsh reserve, but I found myself warming to Brendan's enthusiasm. 'And yourself?' I asked him.

'There's grey in my beard! Do you see it? I'm getting old, Paulie, I'm getting old. God, but it's grand to see you!'

'You should see me more often, Brendan.'

'None of that now! We're all friends!' He put an arm round my shoulders. 'But, my God, this heat! It's like living in a bread oven.' It was no wonder that Brendan was feeling the heat for he was wearing a tweed jacket and a woollen waistcoat over a flannel shirt, just as if Miami had a climate like Dublin. Brendan had lived in Dublin ever since he had planted one bomb too many in Belfast. Now he dragged me enthusiastically towards an opened crate. 'Come and look at the toys Michael has found us!'

Michael Herlihy sidled alongside me. 'Paul?' That was his idea of a greeting. We had known each other since second grade, yet he could not bring himself to say hello. 'You had no problems reaching us?'

'Why should I have problems? No police force is watching me.' I aimed the remark at Brendan. If he had travelled here with his usual flamboyance it would be a miracle if the FBI and the Miami police were not inspecting us at this very moment.

'Stop your fretting, Paulie.' Brendan dismissed my criticism. 'You sound like an old woman, so you do. The Garda lost my footprints days ago.' He began excavating mounds of corrugated cardboard-and-foam packing from inside an opened crate. 'I took a flight to Holland, a train to Switzerland, a flight to Rio, and then another plane up here. Besides, it's worth the risk for this, eh?' He turned, lifting from the opened crate a plastic-wrapped bundle. Even Michael Herlihy, who was not given to expressing enthusiasm, looked excited.

'There!' Brendan laid the bundle on a crate and pulled back its wrapping. 'Would you just look at that wee darling?'

'A Stinger,' I said, unable to keep the reverence from my voice.

'A Stinger,' Michael Herlihy confirmed softly.

'One of fifty-three Stingers,' Brendan amended, 'all of them in prime working order, still in their factory packing, and all with carrying slings and full instructions. Not bad, eh? You see now why I took the risk of coming here?'

I saw exactly, because I knew just how highly the IRA valued these weapons. The Stinger is an American-made, shoulder-fired, ground-to-air missile armed with a heat-seeking high-explosive warhead. The missile and its launcher weigh a mere thirty pounds, and the missile itself is quick, accurate and deadly to any aircraft within four miles of its launch point. Brendan was gazing at the unwrapped weapon with a dreamy expression and I knew that in his mind's eye he was already seeing the British helicopters tumbling in flames from the skies above Northern Ireland.

The Provos had tried other shoulder-fired antiaircraft missiles. They had used Blowpipes stolen from the Short Brothers factory in Belfast, and Russian-made Red Stars donated by Libya, but neither was a patch on the Stinger, which worked every time. Fire a Stinger

and every newspaper in Britain, Ireland and America would sit up and take notice of the IRA.

'It will be the most significant arms shipment in the history of the Irish struggle,' Michael Herlihy said softly, caressing the olive-green firing tube which concealed the missile itself. Bombs or bullets had yet to budge the Brits from Ulster's soil, but Stingers, Herlihy and Brendan fervently believed, would so shock the forces of occupation that Ireland would be freed.

There seemed just one snag. Or rather two: both of them thin, tall, dressed in pale linen suits and with dark smooth faces. Michael Herlihy made the introductions. 'Mr Alvarez and Mr Carlos.' They were not names to be taken seriously, but merely convenient labels for this meeting. 'Mr Alvarez and Mr Carlos represent the consortium that acquired the missiles,' Michael said unhappily.

'Consortium?' I asked.

The one who called himself Alvarez answered. 'The fifty-three missiles are currently listed as US Government property.' He spoke without irony, as though I would be grateful for the information.

'And the consortium's price?' I asked Alvarez.

'For fifty-three weapons, señor, five million dollars. Of course, señor, if you are able to buy the same quality for less elsewhere, then we shall understand. But our price remains five million dollars.' He paused. 'To be paid in gold coins, here, in Miami.'

'Oh, naturally,' I scoffed. The price had to be extortionate. I had been away from the illegal arms business for four years, but I could not believe the cost of a Stinger had escalated so high, not since the United States had been giving Stinger missiles to the Afghan mujaheddin, which surely meant there had to be others available on the black market.

Brendan took me by the arm and steered me out of the Cubans' earshot. 'The cost isn't your business, Paul. We already have the gold! It's all agreed. All we need do is bring the gold here.'

I understood at last. 'In a boat? From the Mediterranean?'

'That's right.' Brendan's grip on my arm was hurting. 'The point of bringing you here was so you could see the Stingers for yourself. Shafiq said you'd not help us unless you knew just what it was all about, so now we're showing you. You always were a careful man, Paulie, were you not?'

'Except in women, Brendan?' I asked the question sarcastically, probing a four-year-old wound.

'She was more trouble than she was worth, that one.' He spoke of

Roisin, but his casual tone did not entirely disguise the old hurt. He let go his bone-crushing grip and slapped my back instead. 'So will you fetch the boat over? Because it'll be just like the old days!'

'Sure,' I said, 'sure.' Because it *would* be just like the old days.

IN THE OLD DAYS I had been the Provisional IRA's liaison man with the Middle East. I was the guy who made the deals with the Palestinians and who listened for hours to Gaddafi's plans for worldwide revolution. I was the Provo's sugar daddy who brought them millions in money, guns and bombs until, suddenly, they decided I could not be trusted: there was a whisper that I was CIA, and the whisper had finished me. At least they had left me alive, unlike Roisin who had been executed on the yellow hillside under the blazing Lebanese sun.

The Provisional IRA's leaders claimed that Roisin had betrayed a man. Roisin had tried to shift the blame onto me, and that brush of suspicion had been enough. The IRA had used my apartment once or twice as a hiding place for men on the run, but for four years they had not shown me any of their old confidence, until now, when suddenly they wanted a boat delivered across the Atlantic.

'We would have asked Michael to bring the boat over,' Brendan explained, 'but he gets sick just looking at the sea!' He laughed, and Herlihy gave him his thin, unamused smile. Michael did not like being teased about his chronic motion-sickness, which seemed an unsuitable affliction for a black-gloved soldier.

Brendan poured me a whiskey. We had gone back to his room in a waterfront Miami hotel where, bathed in blissful air conditioning, he was explaining why it was necessary to bring the yacht from Europe to America. 'The Cuban bastards insist on gold, and Michael tells me it would be next to impossible to find it over here.'

'Treasury regulations,' Herlihy explained. He was drinking mineral water. 'Any transactions involving more than ten thousand dollars must be reported to the treasury department. The legislation was enacted to track down drug dealers.'

'So the Libyans are giving you the gold?'

'Your old pals, the Libyans, obliged us with the money.' Brendan was standing at the window, puffing at a cigarette and staring down at the pelicans perched on the seafront pilings below. 'We don't have that kind of scratch ourselves,' he said happily, 'but we did manage to raise the half-million deposit. Or Michael did.'

'You raised half a million bucks?' I asked Herlihy in astonishment.

The folks in Boston, New York, Philadelphia and the other cities where the Irish-Americans lived were not usually wealthy, and even their small donations had been shrinking, thanks to the politicians from the Irish Republic who had been touring America to preach that the IRA was an enemy to the south, just as much as it was to Britain. 'How the hell did you do it?'

'It's none of your business,' Herlihy told me sourly.

'Your business, Paulie,' Brendan said, 'is the five million in gold. The Libyans are putting it up, God bless them, but they're insisting we make the arrangements for moving the gold here, and that's when we thought of you. Can you do it now?' He sounded genial enough, but many men had died misunderstanding Brendan's open, happy face and bluff, cheerful manner. Beneath it he was implacable, a man consumed by hatred whose every moment was devoted to the cause. If I turned down this job he would probably kill me.

I took a sip of whiskey. 'Has anyone found out how much five million bucks in gold weighs?'

'A thousand pounds, near enough,' Brendan said, then waited for my response. I had worried about what the weight of the gold would do to a sailing boat, but a thousand pounds of extra ballast would be nothing to a decent-sized cruiser.

'I can carry that,' I said.

'And of course, Paulie, there'll be a good wee fee in this for you.'

'How much?'

'The half-million deposit that we'll get back when the gold arrives. Does that sound good to you?' Brendan glanced at Herlihy. I saw him blanch at the amount and for a second I thought he was going to protest, then, reluctantly, he nodded.

'The point being,' Brendan beamed at me, 'that I know a boat filled with gold could be a hell of a temptation, even to a man as honest as yourself, Paulie, but I look at it this way. If you try to steal the gold then you'll have made an enemy of me, and one day I'll find you and I'll make your death harder and slower than your worst nightmares. Or you can keep the faith and walk away at the end of the job with a half-million dollars.'

'Half a million sounds good to me,' I said as equably as I could.

'Not that we're utter fools, Paulie'—Brendan was still smiling—'because we'll be giving you some company on the trip.'

'To be my guards, you mean?' I asked sourly.

'To be your crew.' Brendan was keeping the tone of the conversation light, because he knew I could not turn him down. 'Two of my lads will be your crew,' he went on. 'Work them hard, eh?'

I shrugged. 'Fine.' Why, I was wondering, if the Libyans had insisted that the Provisional IRA transport the gold, had Shafiq approached me first? And why had Brendan, with his usual enthusiasm, suddenly decided to quote a much higher fee to tempt me? I suspected that the half a million dollars were nothing but bait to make me take the job, and that Brendan's two guards would chop me down the moment the voyage was done. Indeed, the whole affair seemed oddly ragged. The Provisional IRA did not launch half-baked schemes these days, which suggested that this operation was being planned hastily—perhaps in the single short month since an Iraqi army had stormed across the defenceless frontier of Kuwait.

'The important thing now,' Brendan went blithely on, 'is to get the right boat.'

'If I'm going to sail it across the pond,' I said, 'then I want to choose it.'

'So would you mind flying right back to Europe?' Brendan asked. 'The Libyans are in a hurry to ship the gold.'

Michael Herlihy added another reason for the haste. 'Next Easter is the seventy-fifth anniversary of the Easter Rising and we'd like to give the British a memorial to mark the occasion.'

'You want me to fly back tomorrow?' I asked Brendan. I had hoped for a chance to fly north and visit the Cape Cod house that I had not seen in seven years.

'Not tomorrow,' Brendan said, 'tonight,' and, like a conjurer, he produced the air ticket from his tweed jacket. 'Paris, then on to Tunisia. First class, Paul!'

They were trying too hard, I thought. Surely they should be treating me like a volunteer? The discrepancy was just another unlikely ragged edge to add to my disquiet, but also to my curiosity. A lot of people were going to a lot of trouble to make me accept this job, and that much effort suggested there could be a huge reward hidden among the details, so I said I would fly out that night.

Brendan went with me to Miami Airport. 'It's grand to be working with you again, Paulie, just grand.'

I ignored the blarney. 'You couldn't find anyone else with the right qualifications, was that it? So you're forced to trust me again?' I could not keep the bitterness from my voice. Little Marty Doyle was driving us and his ears were pricking with interest at our conversation.

'You know the rules, Paul,' Brendan said awkwardly. 'It only takes a touch of suspicion to make us wary.'

'Wary!' I protested. 'Four years of silence because Roisin accuses me of being in the CIA? Come off it, Brendan. She invented fairy stories like other women make up headaches.'

'We know the girl lied about you,' he admitted sombrely. 'You've proved it. You could have betrayed us any time in the last four years and you haven't. And besides, Herlihy had a word with his people in Boston and they said the girl was fantasising. There was no way the Yanks were running an operation like she said. All moonshine.'

I wondered who Herlihy's people were, and supposed they were Boston police who could tap the FBI who, in turn, could call in a favour from the Central Intelligence Agency. So someone had run a check on Roisin's allegations, and I had come up snow-white. 'Did Herlihy's people check on Roisin as well?' I asked. 'Was she CIA?'

'Just a troublemaking bitch, that's all.' Brendan was silent for a few seconds. 'She had a tongue on her like a flamethrower! But she was a lass, wasn't she?'

I had always thought that Roisin and Brendan had been lovers, and the wistfulness of his last words brought the old jealousy surging back. Roisin had been a gunman's groupie, a worshipper of death, yet still I loved her. I had thought the world revolved about her, that the sun was dimmed by her, the moon darkened by her and the stars dazzled by her. And she was dead.

I caught the night flight to Paris.

2.

Shafiq was waiting for me at Tunisia's Skanes-Monastir Airport. He was wearing a suit of silver-grey linen with a pink rose buttonhole which, on closer inspection, turned out to be plastic. I was a shabby contrast in my crumpled, much-travelled clothes. 'So how was Miami?' Shafiq asked me.

'Hot.'

He escorted me to the car park where his rented white Peugeot waited. Out of sailing habit I cocked an eye at the weather. The day was cloudless, while the wind was in the north and cool enough to make me glad I had brought a sweater. 'Where are we going?'

'The marina at Monastir.' Shafiq unlocked the car. 'We are going to meet someone.' He accelerated out of the car park, spitting a stream of Arab profanities at a taxi driver who had dared to sound a protesting horn at the Peugeot's irruption into the traffic stream.

'I thought we were buying a boat?'

'We are, we are, but you are going to meet someone first. His name is Halil! He's in charge of this end of the operation. Just as Mr Herlihy is in charge of the other. Halil is a great man, you should know that before you meet him.' He lit a cigarette and grinned conspiratorially at me. 'You saw the Stingers?'

'I saw one.'

'What a weapon! Now you understand about the gold, yes?'

'No! What's the point of stuffing a boat with gold and sailing it across the Atlantic? Haven't your people heard of bank drafts? Or wire transfers?'

Shafiq laughed. 'Paul! Paul!' He spoke as though he was chiding me for a familiar and lovable cantankerousness, then he fell silent as the Peugeot approached the harbour.

Above us towered the turrets and castellated walls of the Ribat fortress, while next to it, from loudspeakers installed in the minaret of the Grand Mosque, a tape recording called the faithful to prayer. We turned a corner and there, spread beneath us in the autumn sunshine, was the marina. The Mediterranean sailing season had not yet ended and so the pontoons were thick with boats, many of them flying elaborate race flags so that the ancient harbour looked as if a fleet of medieval war vessels had gathered under its gaudy banners.

'Halil is waiting on the boat,' Shafiq said, suddenly nervous.

'The boat? I thought I was choosing the boat?'

'Halil has found something he thinks is suitable. It might be best if you agreed with him.'

Shafiq was palpably anxious. Clearly Halil, whoever he was, had the power of life and death, but I was determined not to be impressed. 'Halil is an expert on crossing the Atlantic?' I asked sarcastically.

'He is an expert on whatever he chooses to be. So come.'

We walked down one of the long floating pontoons. Shafiq led me towards the far end where a handsome sloop was moored. 'That's the boat! You like her?'

'How can I tell?' I said irritably, yet in truth I did like the white-hulled *Corsaire*, whose name was painted across her sugar-scoop stern. She looked a handsome boat, expensive and well-equipped, some forty-four foot long with a centre cockpit and a long low freeboard. The design, I grudgingly admitted to myself, did not look like a bad choice for a transatlantic voyage, so long as she was in good condition.

'Why is she for sale?' I asked Shafiq.

'Her French owner left her here last winter. But he's since fallen ill and he needs to sell her.' Shafiq raised a hand in greeting to the two young men who sat in *Corsaire*'s cockpit. He spoke to them in Arabic, gesturing at me, and they grunted back brief replies. I had seen such men before: thugs plucked from the Palestinian refugee camps, trained to kill, then given guns, girls and the licence to strut like heroes among their exiled people.

'Halil's bodyguard,' Shafiq said in a low voice, then smiled obsequiously as the two young men gestured us aboard. While one stood guard, the other ran quick hands across our bodies to make certain neither of us was armed. He relieved me of my sea bag, then pointed me towards the main companionway.

'Be respectful, Paul!' Shafiq hissed at me. 'Please!'

I ducked down the steep stairs. To my right was the chart table and instrument array, to my left the galley, while ahead was a spacious saloon with comfortable sofas. It seemed very dark after the bright sunlight, but I could just see a young man sprawled on the furthest sofa. At first he looked so unprepossessing that I assumed he must be a third bodyguard, but then he took off his sunglasses and leaned his elbows on the saloon table. 'I am Halil. Sit.'

It was a command rather than an invitation. Behind me the hatch slid shut, imprisoning me in *Corsaire*'s belly with the man called Halil. It was stuffy and humid in the boat. I sat down on the starboard settle. My eyes were slowly adjusting to the gloom, yet I could still see nothing noteworthy about the man who raised such fears in Shafiq. Halil looked to be in his middle thirties. His black hair was brushed straight back from a dark-skinned, unremarkable face, and his only idiosyncrasy was a thin moustache like a 1940s bandleader. He was wearing a white shirt, no tie and a black suit. He looked strongly built, like a peasant, while his left hand, the only one visible, had short square fingers. A burning cigarette rested in an ashtray on the table and beside it was a packet of Camels and a gold lighter.

'The owner wants six hundred and fifty thousand French francs for this boat,' Halil said unceremoniously, 'is that a fair price?'

'If she's in good condition,' I said, 'she's a bargain.'

Halil brought his right hand into view to lift the cigarette, and sucked deep on the smoke. The hand, I noticed, was shaking.

'I shall offer six hundred thousand,' he said flatly.

The dark eyes flicked towards me, and I began to understand Shafiq's nervousness, for there was something almost reptilian in the blankness of this man's eyes.

'You'd best make no offer till I've inspected the boat,' I told him, 'and I'll want her hauled out of the water so I can see her hull.'

'She has already been inspected,' Halil said, 'and declared fit for your journey. She is thirteen and a half metres long, four and a quarter metres wide, and has an underwater depth of one and three quarter metres. Her keel contains three thousand five hundred kilos of lead. What more do you need to know?'

'A lot,' I said, noting how heavily *Corsaire* was ballasted, which suggested her builder had been a cautious man.

'There is no time to be particular,' Halil spoke with an unmistakable menace in his voice. He seemed utterly sure of himself, yet his next question showed how much he still needed my expertise. 'How long will it take you to cross the Atlantic with her?'

'Leaving from here?'

He paused, as if unwilling to admit anything. 'From near here. To Miami.' Where, I thought, her delivery skipper would be murdered.

'When will the voyage be made?' I asked.

'That does not matter,' Halil said disparagingly. In fact it mattered like hell. Any Atlantic passage undertaken before the trade winds had established themselves would take much longer than if I waited till the new year, but I sensed this man was not amenable to detail and so I made a crude guess.

'Three months.'

'That long?' He sounded horrified. 'Why not use the engine? Can't you put extra fuel on board and motor across?'

'A boat like this one will only go as fast as her waterline allows. A big motor yacht would cross much faster.'

He lifted the cigarette to his lips and this time I saw that the fingers of his right hand seemed crooked, as though they had been injured and had never healed properly. The hand shook, and suddenly he changed the subject, asking me whether I believed America would fight to liberate Kuwait. It seemed an odd question in the context, but I nodded and said I was sure America would fight.

'I hope so,' Halil said. 'I hope so.' He spoke softly, but I sensed how badly this man wanted to see a great Arab victory in the desert. Was his query somehow related to this boat, to my recruitment and to a Stinger missile in a Miami warehouse? The truth of this operation, if it ever emerged at all, would appear only gradually.

Halil took a folded sheet of newsprint from his suit pocket. 'Your politicians are already trying to escape the horrors of defeat,' he said. 'Look for yourself!' He pushed the scrap of newspaper across the saloon table. It was a recent front-page story from the *New York Times* which told how House Representative Thomas O'Shaughnessy had introduced a bill to Congress which, if passed, would forbid the employment of American military forces in the Gulf for one whole year. O'Shaughnessy was quoted as wanting to give economic sanctions a chance to work before force was used. 'You see,' Halil's voice was mocking, 'even your legislators want peace. They have no courage, Shanahan.'

I shook my head. 'O'Shaughnessy's a clown, Halil. In Boston they say he's too dumb to succeed, but too rich to fail. He's only in Congress because his daddy is rich.' Thomas O'Shaughnessy was less than thirty years old, yet he was already serving his second term in Congress. Michael Herlihy was one of his staff, helping him cultivate the IRA sympathisers in his Boston constituency. I suspected Michael had been behind one of Tommy's early crusades which demanded that the British government treat IRA prisoners according to the Geneva Convention. The campaign had collapsed in ridicule when it was pointed out that the Geneva Convention permitted combatant governments to execute enemy soldiers captured out of uniform, which meant Tommy's bill would have given American sanction for the Brits to slaughter every IRA man they took prisoner. The proposal had never been seriously meant; it was only a proof to his constituents that Tommy's heart was in the right place, even if his brain was lost somewhere in outer space.

I offered the cutting back to Halil. 'Congressmen like O'Shaughnessy will make a lot of feeble noises, but the American public will listen to the President and, if Saddam Hussein stays in Kuwait, you'll get your war.'

'May God prove you right,' Halil said, 'because I want to see the bodies of the American army feeding the desert jackals for years to come. In the sands of Kuwait, Shanahan, we shall see the humbling of America and the glory of Islam.'

I said nothing, but just held the cutting across the table until Halil leaned forward for it. He reached with his good left hand and, as he did, I suddenly knew just who this man was and why Shafiq was so terrified of him, and I felt the same terror too, because this man, this unremarkable man, was wearing a woman's Blancpain wristwatch.

He was il Hayaween.

The Blancpain watch was enshrined in a thin case of gold and platinum. Except for its small size the watch did not appear particularly feminine, but simply looked exquisitely elegant. It was also very expensive. I knew, for I had bought the Blancpain myself.

I had bought it five years before in Vienna where Shafiq had met me, one spring afternoon, in the café of the Sacher Hotel. He was lingering over a *sachertorte* until it was time for him to leave for the airport. Suddenly he dropped his fork and cursed. 'I am supposed to buy a gift! Oh God, I forgot! Paul, help me, please!'

There had followed a desperate few hours as we searched Vienna for a jeweller who might stock watches. I had derided Shafiq's urgency until he explained that it was the legendary il Hayaween who had demanded the watch, and Colonel Gaddafi himself who wanted to be the watch's giver, and then I understood just what the price of failure might entail for Shafiq. Yet our search seemed hopeless. Blancpains are old-fashioned, handmade Swiss watches, powered by clockwork and without a scrap of quartz or battery acid, and such rare timepieces needed to be specially ordered. The shops began to close and Shafiq was nearing despair until, in one of the little streets close to St Stephen's Cathedral, we found a single specimen. It was beautiful, but it was also a woman's watch. 'Do you think he'll know?' Shafiq asked me nervously.

'It doesn't look especially feminine,' I said, 'just a bit small.'

'If it's the wrong watch, Paul, he'll kill me!'

'And if you take him no watch at all?'

Shafiq went quite pale.

'We'll take it,' I told the shopkeeper, and proffered my credit card.

Now I had seen that same watch on Halil's wrist, and I knew who he was. Il Hayaween was not his real name, any more than Halil was, or even Daoud Malif, which was the name ascribed to him by the Western press. The nickname il Hayaween was an Arabic insult meaning 'the animal' but no one would dare speak the word into Halil's face for, in all the shadowy world of terror, he was reckoned the most famous, the most dangerous and the most daring of all the deadly men who had ever graduated from the refugee camps of the Palestinian exiles. Il Hayaween was a ruthless killer who gave hope to his dispossessed people. In the gutters of Gaza and the ghettos of Hebron, il Hayaween was the leveller, the man who frightened the Israelis and terrified the Americans. Children in refugee camps learned the tales of il Hayaween's fame: how he had shot the Israeli Ambassador in a tea garden in Geneva, how he had bombed American soldiers in a Frankfurt nightclub, how he had ambushed an Israeli school bus and slaughtered its occupants. Whenever a misfortune struck an enemy of Palestine, il Hayaween was reputed to be its author. Some Western journalists doubted his very existence, but he lived all right, and I was talking to him in the saloon of a French yacht in Monastir's marina.

Where I was not thinking straight; not yet. Terrorists live in a skewed world. Their view is overshadowed by the cause, and every single thing that moves or creeps or swarms on the earth is seen in relation to the cause, and nothing is too trivial to escape the cause. Thus, to a man like il Hayaween, a game of baseball is evidence that the American public does not care about the monstrous crime committed against the Palestinian people, evidence that the American people do not want to consider that crime, preferring to watch a game of bat and ball. Therefore a scheme to kill baseball spectators would be a justifiable act because it could jolt the rest of America into an understanding of the truth.

So perhaps, in such a skewed world, paying for weapons with a boatload of gold makes sense. And risking the gold by sailing the boat across the Atlantic makes sense. And allowing a Palestinian terrorist to choose the boat makes sense. And involving Palestine's most notorious killer in the purchase of Stinger missiles destined for Northern Ireland makes sense. Or maybe not.

Halil pushed the folded newspaper cutting into his pocket and stared into my eyes. 'Shanahan,' he said, with a tinge of distaste. 'You moved to Ireland when you were twenty-seven. Is that right?'

'Yes.'

'You lived in Dublin for one year and in Belfast for two?'

'Yes.'

'You joined the Provisional IRA?'

'That was why I went to Ireland.'

'And the Provisional IRA asked you to live in Europe?'

'Because it would be easier to liaise with foreign groups.'

'Yet six years later they ceased to use you for such liaison. Why?'

I understood that this man already knew the answers and that this catechism was just to make me feel uncomfortable. 'Because of a woman,' I told him.

'Roisin Donovan.' He let the name hang in the stifling air. 'An American agent, they say. Do you believe she was CIA?'

I shook my head. 'No. Roisin was impulsive and angry. She had a hair-trigger temper. She was not a person anyone would choose to keep secrets.'

'And you?' Halil asked.

I laughed. 'No government would trust me, I'm a rogue. Civil

28

servants choose people like themselves; dull, predictable and safe.'

Halil raised the trembling cigarette and inhaled. 'But these agents she spoke of, they were different. They were not predictable.'

I said nothing. I could hear the halyards beating on the metal mast. I could even hear the slight noise of the chronometer's second hand ticking away above the chart table.

'These agents'—Halil broke the silence—'would be sent from America and would have no ties to home. They would stay away for years, never talking to their headquarters, never reporting to an embassy, never behaving like an agent, but just watching and listening until, one day, they would disappear. They would go home with their secrets and never be seen again.'

'That was Roisin's fantasy,' I said. 'She made things up.'

'She accused you of being such an agent—an agent who does not exist.'

'I told you, she made it up.'

Roisin had indeed accused me of being one of the agents 'who did not exist', one of the secret secret agents. It had been a clever and compelling idea. She claimed that the CIA had sent agents abroad who had no links with home. They would receive no salary, so that no payroll could betray their existence; they would have no field controllers, no letter drops, no codebooks, nothing that would link them with the CIA. They were simply men and women sent to trawl the world's darkness in the hope that one day they would carry a rich haul of secrets back to the CIA at Langley, Virginia.

'She made it up,' I said again. 'She made the whole thing up.'

Halil watched me, judging me. I could understand the terror that such a concept as the agents who did not exist would hold for a terrorist. Terrorism works because it breaks the rules, but when the authorities break the rules it turns the terror back on the terrorists.

'Your woman claimed the CIA had infiltrated a long-term agent into the Provisional IRA with the specific intent of exploring the IRA's links with other terrorist groups.' He paused. 'That could only be you.'

'She was desperate. She wanted to blind her own accusers with a smokescreen. And how the hell would she know about the agents who don't exist? You think maybe she read it in *Newsweek*?'

'Maybe you told her in bed.'

I laughed. It was not wise to laugh at Halil because he was a man whose pride was easily hurt, but this time he let it pass. 'She blamed you for Seamus Geoghegan's betrayal.'

That was an easy accusation to rebut. 'I didn't know where Seamus was, so I couldn't have betrayed him. I was in the Lebanon when it happened, and he was captured in Belfast.' Seamus was the Provisional IRA's star, the il Hayaween of Ireland, and Roisin had given him to the British. Or so the Brits had said, and that accusation had finished Roisin. Her response had been to blame me, but she was the one who died.

'So the girl was lying?'

Halil wanted to believe my denials. Not that I would have been allowed within ten miles of him if he seriously believed Roisin's story, but he wanted to make sure.

'Roisin saw plots everywhere. She was also a very destructive woman, and that was why she betrayed Seamus Geoghegan.'

He frowned. 'I don't understand.'

'Seamus is frightened of women. He's the bravest man ever born in Ireland, but he doesn't have the courage to ask a girl for a dance because he thinks all women are the Virgin Mary. I suspect Roisin tried to seduce Seamus, failed, and so she punished him.' I could think of no other explanation. Seamus had been one of my closest friends—and perhaps still was, though it had been four years since I had last seen him. He had been betrayed, arrested, tried and sentenced, but a year later, in a brilliantly staged IRA coup, he had escaped from the Long Kesh prison camp. He was now in America, a fugitive from British vengeance.

'You saw Roisin die?' Halil asked.

'Yes.' She had died in the Lebanon, where she had been attending the Hasbaiya terrorist training camp. It had been Roisin's keenest ambition to have the IRA send her on that course, and her eagerness had given rise to a suspicion that she planned to betray Hasbaiya as well as Seamus. Thus, as a favour to their Irish allies as well as to themselves, the Palestinians had arranged her execution.

'You didn't try to stop the killing?' Halil asked me. 'You loved her.'

'She betrayed my friend,' I said, and I saw, in the sudden poisonous recurrence of memory, the split second when the vivid blood had spurted from Roisin's punctured skull to splash among the yellow stones. I had been wearing a red and white checked kaffiyeh which I had wrapped about my face and which, mercifully, had prevented Roisin from recognising me. For a few moments I had suspected that I too was about to be shot for the heinous crime of being an American, but instead I had been curtly ordered to bury her. Afterwards the Palestinians had questioned me about Roisin, trying to determine how much she had known and how much she might have betrayed to her masters in Washington. I had given them what reassurances I could, and then, cleared of her accusations but still not wholly trusted, I was cast into the outer darkness and given nothing but trifling jobs.

Till now, when it was Halil's turn to assess my guilt or innocence, and, as he stared at me, I wondered why a man of his reputation was caught up in such a small matter as Northern Ireland. The death of a few Brits on that wild damp island could hardly count for much, certainly not at a time when the Arab world had found a new champion to flaunt Islam's banner in the face of the hated Americans.

Halil suddenly waved a dismissive hand. 'Look at the boat,' he said offhandedly, 'and tell me your opinion.'

So, under the silent gaze of Shafiq, Halil and his two bodyguards, I clambered about *Corsaire*. I did not have nearly enough time to make a proper survey, but I decided she was a well-made and well-maintained craft. Her hull was Fibreglass and her deck was teak. A sturdy inflatable dinghy was folded away in an aft locker, together with an electric-powered pump to inflate it. I poked and pried through the accommodations below, and lifted the main-cabin sole to find the bilge filled with flexible water tanks. The only feature I disliked was her engine which, though capable enough at sixty horsepower, was fuelled by petrol, but at least the motor banged into healthy life as soon as I connected the batteries and turned the ignition key.

'You like the boat?' Halil asked me.

'I'd prefer a diesel engine.'

'Why?'

'Petrol fumes explode. Diesel is safer. But she's not a bad boat.' The engine compartment was well ventilated and equipped with an automatic fire-extinguisher so that, even in the unlikely event of a fuel-fire, *Corsaire* would probably survive. 'She'll do—as long as she's prepared properly. For a start I need to get her out of the water and have her hull scrubbed down. She'll want a couple of layers of good antifouling paint. Then she's got to be equipped and stocked for a three-month voyage.'

'Make a list. We will send for you when the boat is ready.'

'Why can't I prepare the boat?' I asked. 'I'm sailing it!'

'We shall prepare it.' Halil answered, flat and unyielding. 'Make a list, Mr Shanahan.'

So that night I slept on board *Corsaire* and next morning made a huge list, encompassing not just the victuals needed to carry three men across the Atlantic, but also the safety equipment and chandlery that would complete *Corsaire*'s inventory.

Halil came and glanced through my handwritten pages. Most of the items were obvious, but some made him frown. 'Fibreglass mats? Resin? White paint?'

'That's how I hide the gold. By making a false floor under the cabin.'

'Water tanks? Three-inch flexible piping?'

'We'll be hiding the gold where the present water tanks are placed, so we'll need new ones specially shaped for their areas. You don't want a customs officer wondering why we've got tube tanks in a square locker. And I need the tubing to run the water aft.'

'Lead weights?'

'We're altering the boat's trim, so she'll need rebalancing.' I mixed the lies with the truth so easily, but then I was as practised at that game as il Hayaween, maybe more so. We all have our secrets.

'It will be done,' he promised. 'I shall send you a message when the shipment is ready. It might take a month to collect the coins, maybe more, maybe less.' He spoke carelessly, but I remembered Brendan Flynn implying that the gold was already safely collected. Halil's offhand words only added more dissonance to the cacophony of strange noises that surrounded the Stingers.

Yet the nervous world was already full of discordant sounds. In Iraq and Saudi Arabia the sabres rattled, and on the West Bank and in Jordan the Palestinians ululated for their coming victory beneath the crescent flags of Islam. Everywhere, it seemed, the world was preparing for war. I flew home to Nieuwpoort.

3

Once back in Belgium I slept off the jetlag of two Atlantic flights, then told Hannah that I was closing down Nordsee Yacht Delivery, Services and Surveying.

'I'm tired of working, Hannah. I need a rest. I've decided I'll buy a boat and become a sea-gypsy.'

'But what of the Rotterdam surveys?' The Flemish mind could hardly encompass such irresponsibility.

'I'll do the trawlers.' They were two boats in Rotterdam that I had agreed to survey, and I needed work while I was waiting for Halil's summons, but once that summons arrived I had to leave instantly.

'And what about that Mr Shafiq?' Hannah asked suspiciously. She was dying to know who he was, and why I had flown halfway round the globe for him, but the world of IRA men, the Libyans and midnight boat deliveries was something she knew nothing about, and I intended to keep it that way. I also intended to make my fortune in these next few weeks. I really was retiring, I really was going out of business, but I could not tell Hannah any of it.

Instead I gave her custody of the cat, closed down my bank accounts and began searching for something very specific: a forty-four-foot boat, registered in America but for sale in Europe. I faxed messages to yacht brokers in half a dozen countries and searched the advertisements in every European yachting magazine. I thought I had found what I wanted in the German port of Langeoog, but the boat, though owned by an American, lacked either a state registration certificate or any coastguard documentation. 'Does it really matter?' the broker asked me. 'Over here we're not so particular.'

But I was being very particular, and so I went on searching until, just before Halloween, a brokerage in Cork, Ireland, sent me details of an American cutter moored in Ardgroom Harbour off the Kenmare River.

I gave Hannah my apartment keys and made her promise to check the answering machine each day, then I flew to Cork where I hired a car and drove west to Ardgroom Harbour. I borrowed a fisherman's dinghy and sculled myself out to the yacht.

Rebel Lady was an American-built, American-owned, forty-four-foot cutter with a dark green hull that had been battered by rough seas. Gulls had streaked her with their droppings and weed grew at her black-painted bootline, yet, despite her shabby condition, *Rebel Lady* looked almost brand new. A 'For Sale' sign was attached to her starboard shrouds, while her hailing port, lettered like her defiant name in elegant black and gold, was Boston, Mass. *Rebel Lady* even had her Massachusetts registration number still painted on her bows, which meant that if her papers were intact then, for my purposes, she was perfect.

I found her keys hidden in the locker where the broker had told me to look and let myself into her saloon, which smelt of stale air. Arched across the coachroof's main beam was a row of handsome brass instruments, including a chronometer still ticking obediently away to Greenwich Mean Time; over the chart table there was a depth-sounder, a VHF radio, a wind-speed and direction indicator, and an expensive loran receiver. I also saw the familiar yellow jacket of *Eldridge's Tide and Pilot Book* and I could not resist turning the well-thumbed pages with their tables of high and low water at Boston, the current table for the Cape Cod Canal and the charts of the tidal currents in Nantucket Sound. The book reminded me that I had been away from my home waters for much too long.

I sat in the swivel chair of *Rebel Lady*'s chart table and thought how she would make a fine boat for Cape Cod. I closed my eyes and heard the water splash and ripple down her flanks, and the sound somehow reminded me that this would also be a lonely boat. Damn Roisin, I thought, for all the dreams she had broken, because forty-four foot was too long a boat for a lonely man.

I called the broker from a bar in Ardgroom and learned that *Rebel Lady* belonged to an American doctor who, taking a summer's sabbatical, had sailed with his three sons to search for their family's Irish roots. However, sailing in sun-drenched Boston Harbour had not prepared him for a stinging force-nine gale in the mid-Atlantic: seasick, terrified and with a broken wrist and a fractured rib, the good doctor had made his Irish landfall and sworn he would never again set foot on a boat. 'He'll take whatever you've a mind to give,' the Cork broker told me with a refreshing honesty, 'but it would be a criminal shame to give the man less than seventy-five thousand pounds. She's a fine boat, is she not?'

'You're sure you've got all her papers?'

'Every last one of them. The boat's a mere two years old and she's only ever had the one owner: O'Neill. Dr James O'Neill. A grand man is the doctor, but a better physician than a sailor, I should think.'

'I'll be paying you cash,' I said. 'Say seventy thousand?'

He paused for just a second, then accepted. 'It's a bargain, Mr Stanley.' I had given my name as Henry Stanley.

I took myself back to *Rebel Lady* and chucked the 'For Sale' sign overboard. Then, using my rigging knife, I prised away the manufacturer's plate from the side of her coachroof. I copied the hull identification number from her transom and the serial number from the engine and then drove back to Cork, where I treated the broker to a pint of stout and paid him seventy thousand Irish pounds for the boat. It was a steal, but undoubtedly Dr James O'Neill would be well pleased to be rid of the cause of so much of his discomfort.

The broker counted the pile of notes happily, then he watched as I counted another stack of notes onto the table. 'And what would they be for, Mr Stanley, if I might ask?'

'I'm paying you to look after her. I want the mast off her, and I'd like her brought ashore and scrubbed down. I'll send you word when I want her launched and rigged again, but it may not be till next summer. And I want a new name painted on her stern.'

'Changing a boat's name?' He sipped his stout, then wiped the froth from his moustache with the back of his hand. 'That means bad luck, Mr Stanley.'

'Not where I come from.' I pulled a beer mat towards me and wrote the new name and hailing port on it. ' "*Roisin*, Stage Harbor",' I said aloud. 'And no "u" in harbor. You can do that?'

'It shouldn't be a problem.' The notes vanished into a pocket.

As I left the bar I scorned myself as a sentimental fool for painting a dead girl's name on a boat. I caught a glimpse of my bearded face in a mirror in the bar's hallway and I frowned at the reflection as though I was looking at a stranger. I did not like what I saw. The face was hagridden, redolent of too much bad conscience. Mirrors made me think of myself, which was why I owned so few of them. It was better not to think, not to remember, and not to wonder what I had made of my life.

That night I phoned Belgium and left a message for an old friend called Teodor, and the following morning, with *Rebel Lady*'s papers safe in my sea bag, I flew to Barcelona to see a shipping company. My business there took two days. I telephoned Hannah to discover if any summons had come from Tunisia, but there was no message. 'Except that American girl, Kathleen Donovan, is still trying to reach you,' Hannah said. 'When will you be back?'

'Late tomorrow. And I've told you, I don't want to meet her. I'll see you on Thursday.'

Next morning I flew to Brussels, collected my car from the long-term car park, then drove to the town of Namur where Teodor was waiting for me. He needed to take photographs; one for the false Massachusetts driving licence and another, with different clothes and lighting, for the false American passport. Teodor was the finest counterfeiter in the Low Countries and had been supplying me with false papers for over ten years. He was an old man now.

'You're going on a journey, Paul?' he asked me as he worked in his shirtsleeves under a bright magnifying lamp.

'Yes.'

He reached for tweezers and a can of spray adhesive. 'Why do I sense this is the last time I'll see you?'

'Because you're an emotional and maudlin old fool.'

He chuckled, then sprayed a tiny jet of adhesive onto one of the photographs. 'You're going home, aren't you?'

'Am I?'

'You've had enough, Paul, I can tell. You're like an athlete facing his last and biggest race. You want to win, but you want to stop competing even more.' He shot me a glance from under his thick white eyebrows. 'You've been in Europe how long now? Almost ten years? Not many people last ten years in your kind of work.'

'You don't know what kind of work I do, Teodor.'

He laughed softly. 'I have deduced you are not an accountant. Nor are you one of those bureaucrats who live in Brussels off the taxes I take care not to pay. No, you are a man who keeps secrets, and that can be a very tiring profession.' He straightened up from his work. 'Now come here, I need Dr O'Neill's signature. Three times, and with different pens. I have even made you a Visa card, see?'

I peered at the card under Teodor's strong worklamp. 'How the hell did you manage the hologram?' I asked in genuine admiration.

'Genius, Paul, mere genius. Now, practise the signature before you sign. You're a doctor, remember, so you scribble, you don't write. Good. Again!' Teodor was a perfectionist. 'It will all be for nothing unless you collect a few items to support the fiction. Buy some medical journals and send yourself a couple of letters addressed to Dr O'Neill.'

I left him two hours later with a whole new identity safe in my pocket, then I drove across country to Nieuwpoort. The rainy autumn wind had gone into the northeast to bring the Low Countries a foretaste of winter. I drove fast, but even so it was almost midnight before I parked the Opel in the alleyway opposite my apartment house. I locked the car, ran across the road and pushed open the apartment block's unlocked front door.

'Is that Mr Shanahan?'

I reeled back from the shadow that suddenly rose inside the dark hall. Someone was waiting for me, someone who knew my name, and I remembered my old training which had taught that, before making a kill, it was prudent to identify the victim.

'Mr Shanahan?' It was a girl's voice, American and unthreatening, which was no proof she was not holding a gun in the shadowed hallway. I crouched in the porch, holding my sea bag up to protect my chest from the half-expected bullet.

'I'm sorry. I didn't mean to frighten you. It's just that the light bulb was broken in here, so I had to wait in the dark.'

'Who the hell are you?' I straightened up.

'Your secretary said you'd be back tonight. Gee, I'm sorry, it's just that I had to see you because I've got an Apex ticket and I have to fly back to the States tomorrow and this was my last chance. I didn't mean to scare you.' The girl seemed to be more upset than I was. She had come to the doorway so that the streetlight lit her face and I knew who she was, oh God, I knew who she was. She looked so like Roisin, so achingly like Roisin.

'Who are you?' I asked again.

'My name's Kathleen Donovan,' she said, Even her voice was like her sister's, like enough to bring a mocking ghost to shadow the rainswept darkness. 'I just wanted to see you,' she explained.

'What about?' I asked harshly. 'Do you know what time it is?' I pushed past her into the hallway. I did not want to talk to her, but she looked so like Roisin that I could not say no. 'Let's at least talk where it's warm.'

Kathleen Donovan followed me up the uncarpeted stairs and edged nervously into my apartment.

'Coffee?' I asked her. 'Or something stronger?'

'Just a glass of water, please.'

I fetched her a glass of water and poured myself a whiskey, then drew the curtains against the chill Belgian night and lit the gas fire.

She perched herself on the sofa's edge. She looked to be in her late twenties and was dressed in a sober tweed suit, a high-necked blouse and a string of plain blue beads. Kathleen had the same dark red hair as Roisin and the same hesitant expression that suggested she was perpetually puzzled by the world. Indeed, Kathleen looked so horribly like her sister that it hurt just to be in the same room. 'Doesn't my name mean anything?' she asked. 'I had—have—an older sister called Roisin. I think you knew her.'

Knew her? My God, but they were hardly the adequate words. The first moment I saw Roisin in a Dublin pub I knew I would never be happy until I loved her, and when I loved her I suspected I would never be happy again. A friend said there was such a woman for every man, but most men were lucky and never met their fate. I had, and Roisin and I had loved in a sudden incandescent blaze of lust, until, just as suddenly, she had stalked away from me. Later, I had watched her die, and her ghost had haunted my life ever since.

'I'm sorry,' I said, 'but I've never heard of her.'

Kathleen Donovan stared at me. 'She lived in Ireland for a while,' she said, 'in Belfast. Just off the Malone Road.' She began searching through her handbag and I watched her, marvelling at the resemblance. Roisin had been thinner than Kathleen, but the two sisters had the same Irish green eyes and the same pale, vulnerable skin, though Kathleen seemed much calmer, more at peace with herself. Her eyes seemed to hold wisdom where Roisin's had held nothing but an unpredictable wildness. Indeed, I suddenly thought with a pang, Kathleen was just what I had hoped Roisin might become.

'Here's a picture of her,' Kathleen held out a snapshot.

I glanced down at the photograph. It showed a younger Roisin than I remembered, but the camera had perfectly caught the blazing intensity of her hunter's eyes. 'I'm sorry,' I tried to sound careless, 'but I've never seen her.'

'You lived in Belfast, didn't you?' Kathleen asked me.

'Yes, but that was ten years ago. Sorry,' I said again, and tossed the picture down.

Kathleen momentarily closed her eyes. 'Mr Shanahan,' she said at last, 'I know what Roisin was, and I know that means you can't tell me everything, but I want you to understand that our mother is dying and she wants to know if Roisin is alive or dead. That's all.' She stared at me with eyes that were sheened with tears. 'Is it so very much to ask?'

I swallowed whiskey, feeling foully uncomfortable. 'Tell me about your sister,' I said, 'and I'll see if anything jogs my memory.' I knew I should dismiss this girl, but another part of me wanted to keep her here.

Kathleen took a breath. 'We grew up in Baltimore, but our parents were born in Ireland. They emigrated in nineteen fifty. Mom and Dad wanted to forget Ireland, really, but Roisin was obsessed by it. I don't know when it started, back in High School, I guess, but she was really mad at Mom and Dad for living in America. She wanted to be Irish.'

'I know the syndrome,' I said.

'She learned Gaelic, she learned Irish history, and she learned Irish hatreds. Then she went to live in Ireland.' Kathleen frowned up at me. 'You know all this, don't you?'

I shook my head. 'I wish I could help, but I know nothing.'

Kathleen began to cry very softly. 'You can help!' she insisted. 'She mentioned you in her letters! She said you were a yachtsman and had a house on Cape Cod!' She sniffed and wiped away her tears. 'I'm sorry. I'm just so tired.'

'Paul Shanahan isn't such an unusual name,' I said.

She dismissed that feeble evasion with an abrupt shake of her head.

38

'I've spent three weeks in Ireland, talking to people who knew Roisin. They kept mentioning you. They said you might have had links with the IRA.' She spoke defiantly. 'They said that's why Roisin wanted to be with you, because you were her introduction to the IRA.'

'Me?' I sounded wonderfully astonished.

'And one person I spoke with,' Kathleen pressed on, 'said you were in the IRA for sure. He said you were one of their best-kept secrets.'

'Oh, the Irish love to gossip, Miss Donovan, and they do it better than anyone in the world, but it's only in Dublin bars and bad novels that Americans play heroic roles in the IRA. I went to Ireland to learn about traditional boatbuilding skills, and I stayed there because I liked the country, but I moved on here because I couldn't make a living in Ireland. I'm a marine engineer and surveyor. I'm not in the IRA, I never was, and I never knew your sister.'

Kathleen stared at me, her eyes huge, and I wanted to cross the room and hold her tight and tell her all the truth and beg her forgiveness for that truth, but instead I stayed where I was.

'I heard another story,' she said. 'I heard a rumour that Roisin was executed for betraying the IRA. I spoke to a policeman in Dublin and he said he'd heard she was working for American Intelligence and that it was Roisin who betrayed Seamus Geoghegan. You've heard of him, haven't you?'

'He's the fellow the British are trying to extradite from America, right?'

'He's a friend of yours,' Kathleen accused me.

I laughed. 'Let's be serious! I'm a boat surveyor.'

'I met Seamus Geoghegan's brother, Mr Shanahan, in Derry. He was the one who told me about you and the IRA, and that wasn't bar gossip. He told me his brother stayed in your apartment!'

I shook my head wearily. 'I'm sorry,' I said, 'but I don't know Seamus Geoghegan or his brother and I don't know your sister.'

Kathleen dismissed my denials with an abrupt gesture. 'Maybe it's all true, Mr Shanahan! Maybe she was in American Intelligence and did betray Geoghegan! Does that make you a member of American Intelligence too? Is that why you can't talk to me?' She paused, eyes bright, desperate for an answer. 'For God's sake,' she went on, 'my mother's got less than a year to live! All she wants is to be certain. Do you know what it's like to grieve for a child, but not even to know if you need to grieve? Mom keeps thinking Roisin will come home, that she's alive somewhere. For the love of God, Mr Shanahan, I'm not a security risk! Just give me a nod, that's all!'

The gas fire hissed. Kathleen stared up at me. I took a deep breath. 'I really can't help you,' I said.

'Oh, you bastard!' Kathleen Donovan said tiredly.

'Can I drive you somewhere?' I asked gently.

'You can burn in hell.' She snatched up her coat, turned and walked away. The front door of the apartment banged as she stormed out and, a moment later, I heard her footsteps clatter away on the pavement outside.

I sat on the sofa, leaned my head back and closed my eyes. I could have told Kathleen everything, but I had long schooled myself against the truth. The truth makes a man vulnerable. Lies are a shield, a fog, a maze in which to lose the curious. I told myself Kathleen Donovan could have been a stooge for British Intelligence, or even for the Provisional IRA. Maybe Brendan Flynn had sent Kathleen to see if I would betray my membership of the IRA, thus marking myself as not to be trusted with the Libyan gold.

So, I reassured myself, I had been right to tell Kathleen nothing, because the first rule was to trust no one and the second rule was never to tell the truth. They were good rules, even if they did mean having to send a girl away in tears into a wet windy night, and even if it did mean drinking the rest of the bottle of Jameson's to smear away the memory of Kathleen's hurt face.

I HEARD NOTHING from Tunisia in November. December came and in the streets of Nieuwpoort the Christmas lights struggled to shine through the winter rains. I lived frugally and wondered if the whole deal had collapsed. When Shafiq had first contacted me everything about the Stinger deal had been urgent and exciting, while now the whole scheme had slowed to a crawl, if not utter immobility. Perhaps, after all, this was proving to be just another operation gone sour in the planning. But I waited patiently and hoped that I had not destroyed my surveying business for nothing.

The winter nights drew ever longer and still I heard nothing from either Tunisia or Dublin.

Then, just before Christmas, I was woken in the middle of a cold night by the chatter of the fax machine. I was requested to make a survey of a cruising yacht presently laid up in Marseilles. Would I please send an estimate of my travel costs and a statement of my fees to Monsieur Jean Piguet. That name was the key, the ciphered message which meant *Corsaire* was ready.

I felt a pulse of excitement, a surge of adrenalin I had not felt for a long time. It was the seductive kick of danger and the anticipation of risk. The time had come to vanish.

I did not sleep any more that night. Instead I packed my sea bag with what few belongings I wanted to carry into my new life, then waited for the winter dawn. At nine o'clock I went to one of the fishing-harbour cafés and used its public phone to call the shipping company in Barcelona, then I made a long call to Brussels. The dice thus irrevocably thrown, I threw my sea bag into the back of the car and left Belgium for good.

4

Shafiq was waiting for me at Skanes-Monastir Airport, jittery with excitement. 'Did you think we had forgotten you?' he asked archly.

'I thought you'd found someone else to do the job,' I said.

'Paul! Paul!' He chided me. 'It just took longer than we expected to assemble the gold, nothing else.' He led me out of the terminal. 'So what did you make of Halil?'

'A dangerous man.' I spoke with a careful neutrality.

'Dangerous?' Shafiq threw my sea bag and heavy yellow oilskin jacket into the boot of his car. 'Is a tiger dangerous? Does a hawk kill? Ha! Dangerous.' He mocked the inadequacy of my description, then accelerated into the airport traffic. 'He is a great man.'

'What happened to his right hand?'

'He was shot in the wrist. The bullet severed some nerves and tendons. He can still use the hand, but clumsily.'

'Lucky it was his right wrist,' I said blandly, 'and not his left. It would have been a shame to lose that pretty watch.'

Shafiq roared with laughter. 'That's good, Paul! You are not so blind, eh? But you will say nothing. You understand me? Halil has a long reach and a lethal grip.' I noted how Shafiq still used the pseudonym 'Halil' rather than the nickname il Hayaween. Both of us might know Halil's identity, but it would be risking fate to admit it openly, even to each other.

'Am I going to meet Halil today?' I asked.

'Not here. He will bring you the gold at Ghar El Melh. It's on the north coast and will be safer. Not so many eyes watching.'

'Do I pick up my crew there?'

'No. They came yesterday.' Shafiq sighed and I suspected he was glad that I was taking Brendan's two gunmen off his hands. 'It is a pity,' he went on, 'that we could not have sent Palestinians to help you, but such men would surely have raised suspicions on their arrival in America.'

'Have you met these two before?'

'Never.' He gave a brief shake of his head. 'It isn't like the old days, Paul. I don't deal with Ireland any more, and I hear nothing from anyone. These days I just run a few errands.'

His mood had plunged as he made the sad confession and I supposed that he must have been tarred by Roisin's accusation that I was one of the deep-penetration CIA agents; poor Shafiq had been relegated to the minor leagues. Then, when it was decided that I was the perfect man to sail Halil's gold across the Atlantic, Shafiq must have been reactivated as the person most likely to recruit me. No wonder he had seemed so pleased to be in Paris; it must have been his first visit in four years.

'Just errands,' he added in a self-pitying echo.

'But you must be important, Shafiq,' I flattered him, 'if they trust you to work with Halil. What I don't understand is why a man as important as Halil, and a man as experienced as yourself, should be dealing with a matter as trivial as Ireland. Nothing that Brendan Flynn is doing will bring the destruction of Israel one day nearer, yet your movement is devoting its best men to his ambitions! It is all so unsophisticated, Shafiq!'

I had known the accusation would goad Shafiq who, sure enough, shook his head angrily. 'What we are doing is just one tiny part of a massive operation. What do you call it? A cog! You only see a cog while all around us, unseen, great millwheels are turning.' He was pleased with the metaphor and embellished it by taking both hands off the wheel and churning them vigorously in the air. 'Halil is the planning officer for the worldwide punishment of Iraq's enemies! And the enemies of Iraq are the enemies of Palestine! And wherever those enemies might live, Halil's work will be seen!'

'Stingers? In Ireland?'

Shafiq waved a dismissive hand. 'Everyone knows that Britain does America's bidding, and that America is Israel's master, so Britain must be made to suffer. It is only a small part of the pain the West will feel as a punishment for opposing Iraq.'

'Oh, I see now. We had to wait for the gold to arrive from Iraq! What is it? Gold captured in Kuwait?'

Shafiq waved a hand in an affirmative gesture.

'What I still don't understand,' I said, trying to tempt Shafiq into further indiscretion, 'is why Halil sends money by boat when he might just as well send it electronically.'

'Ha!' Shafiq exclaimed. 'Everyone knows that the Americans can now monitor every electronic transfer of money in the world! So instead we shall be old-fashioned and smuggle gold like a pirate! I thought that would please you, Paul. Does it not please you?'

'Oh, it does,' I said. But it pleased me even more that I had been given a glimpse of the truth, that the Stingers were part of the worldwide campaign of terror that Saddam Hussein had sworn to unleash on his enemies. Brendan Flynn had not been dealing with Tripoli, but with Baghdad, and Baghdad's urgency would explain why the price of the Stingers had gone so high; because a worldwide terror campaign would hugely increase the demand for illicit weapons. It all made sense.

Shafiq was suddenly scared that he had been far too indiscreet. 'I have said nothing you can repeat, Paul! Nothing!'

'Shafiq!' I said earnestly and with a hurt expression in my voice. 'Shafiq! You and I are old friends. Do you think I am the kind of man to betray an old comrade? I have heard nothing today that I will ever repeat to another soul.'

'Thank you, Paul, thank you.'

We turned into Monastir's marina. It was winter, and the pontoons looked drab. Most of the yachts were under wraps, waiting out the winter months until the Mediterranean spring fetched their owners south again. Only *Corsaire* looked fully ready for the sea, even to the extent of having two crewmen sprawled in her cockpit. 'Are they my guards?' I asked Shafiq.

'Your crew.' He sounded hurt that I should be so distrustful.

I plucked my oilskin and sea bag from the boot, then went to meet the two men who, I still felt sure, Brendan had sent to kill me when my usefulness was done. My God, I thought when I got aboard *Corsaire*, but was this the best the Provisional IRA could drag up? Liam was a skinny youth with a starved wan face, red hair and jug ears. By contrast, Gerry was a beefy, red-faced man whose shirt strained across his plump back and bulging stomach. He greeted me with a surly nod, as though trying to establish a pecking order at our very first meeting.

I chucked my sea bag into the after cabin and ordered them to tell me about themselves. 'We can't be strangers and shipmates,' I said cheerfully, 'so tell me your stories. How old are you, for a start?'

They were both twenty-three, born and raised in Belfast, and both now living in Dublin. They pretended to be battle-hardened veterans of the Irish troubles, but their boasting was unconvincing. Liam and Gerry had the restricted vocabulary of deprivation and the thin minds of ignorance, they were the cannon fodder of riots and revolution, and they were supposed to be my shipmates for the next three months. I asked if either had ever sailed before. Liam shook his head, though Gerry claimed to have spent some time aboard an uncle's lobster boat. He was vague on the details, but bridled indignantly when I asked if he was competent to steer a simple course. 'I can look after myself, mister!'

Liam was far more apprehensive. 'We're crossing the Atlantic in this wee boat? But I get seasick, mister!'

'You what?' I asked in horror.

'I told Mr Flynn that, but he said it didn't matter! He said this would be like a cruise, so he did.'

'The aeroplane was real good,' Gerry said accusingly, as though *Corsaire*'s accommodation was a disappointment after their charter flight from Dublin. For both boys it had been their very first aeroplane flight, but they were neither of them looking forward to their maiden yachting voyage with quite the same excitement.

Shafiq gave me Halil's written instructions. They were simple enough. I was to take *Corsaire* to the north Tunisian port of Ghar El Melh where we should wait for the gold. Once the coins were concealed aboard *Corsaire* we were to sail for Miami. 'And who do I contact when I reach Miami?' I demanded.

'They know who to contact.' Shafiq pointed to the two Irish lads.

'What a way to run a revolution,' I said unhappily. 'So let's get on with it.'

I stowed my few belongings, put my sextant in a drawer of the chart table, then checked through the supplies which il Hayaween had arranged to be put aboard. Everything seemed to be present, including thirty feet of flexible plastic tubing that I thrust out of sight in a deep cockpit locker. Then, with nothing to hold us under the battlements of Monastir, I started *Corsaire*'s engine and singled up her mooring lines. Shafiq had taken care of all the time-consuming bureaucratic procedures that usually accompanied a Tunisian departure, so, after bidding him farewell, I cast off, reversed from the pontoon and motored towards the open sea.

At the very first surge of the waves Liam turned a whitish green. I told him to stay on deck and he lay flat, groaning and unhappy as we plugged head-on into the persistent north wind.

'Have you ever heard of Michael Herlihy?' I asked Liam, who shook his head miserably. 'He's much worse than you,' I said cheerfully. 'He gets seasick just looking at a boat.'

'How long till we get to wherever we're going?' he moaned.

'Two days to Ghar El Melh, then two or three months across the Atlantic.'

'Months?' Liam crossed himself. 'God help me.'

The morning turned cold as we headed north into the Gulf of Hammamet. Liam's seasickness got no better, yet he insisted on sharing Gerry's enormous midday fry-up, which he fetched back up in seconds.

Liam soon became almost comatose, but Gerry was talkative during the afternoon, and I heard the all-too-familiar Belfast story of children born into bleak housing estates and growing up into the hopelessness of chronic unemployment. Uneducated, unskilled and bitter, they were good for nothing except to be the foot-soldiers for Ireland's troubles, but even that calling had turned sour: their names had been given to the security forces, and so Liam and Gerry had been forced to flee south to the Republic of Ireland. There, in what they called the Free State, they had found a refuge in a Dublin housing estate every bit as bleak as the Belfast ghetto from which they had fled.

I put up the sails, heading into a steep sea that threw up great fountains of salty spray. The boat seemed clumsier than her lines had suggested, riding low in the water and making heavy work of seas that a boat of her length should have soared across. Her previous owner had over-ballasted her, perhaps out of nervousness. Doubtless he had wanted a safe docile boat for a fine summer day; *Corsaire* was ill-suited to this choppy, windy work and I dreaded to think how she would behave with an extra thousand pounds of weight in her belly.

IT TOOK THE LUMBERING *Corsaire* three days to reach Ghar El Melh, which turned out to be a small harbour surrounded by ancient fortifications. My pilot book told me that this dying port had once sheltered the feared Barbary pirates, but Liam and Gerry only cared to know whether the village might shelter a pub.

'Probably not,' I said.

'No booze?' Liam, recovered from his seasickness by being safely anchored in port, asked in a horrified voice.

'Not a drop.'

'So how long are we going to be here?'

'Till the gold arrives,' I explained.

'Have you really nothing to drink on board?' Gerry wheedled.

'Not a drop,' I lied. In fact, I had hidden two bottles of Jameson's Whiskey that I was saving for Christmas Day.

I had hoped we would be at sea by then, but Christmas came and the gold had still not arrived and so we stayed at anchor in the deserted harbour. Our Christmas dinner was Spam fritters, tinned peas and French fries. Afterwards I brought out the Jameson's and the three of us sat in *Corsaire*'s saloon and, with tongues freed by the whiskey, Liam and Gerry spoke of their own heroic exploits, but I easily punctured their bombast when I told them I had lived in Belfast myself, and had given shelter to Seamus Geoghegan when he was first on the run from Derry.

'You knew Seamus?' Liam asked incredulously.

'Sure. Very well.' I saw my reputation soar in their eyes.

'You really knew him?' Gerry asked.

I crossed two fingers. 'Like that.'

Gerry smiled at me, then frowned, and I wondered if he was contemplating the difficulty of eventually killing me. He took a long drink of whiskey, then poured himself another mugful. 'It's funny you being an American,' he said at last. 'If I had the chance I wouldn't leave America, not to go to Belfast! I'd stay in America, make some money, eh?' He suddenly frowned at me again. 'Is it really five million dollars we're waiting for?'

I nodded. 'In gold,' I said.

'Brendan said it was the most important mission we'd ever perform.'

'I'm sure it is,' I said, 'I'm sure it is,' and, the very next morning, in a cold north wind, the gold arrived.

IL HAYAWEEN ARRIVED in a black-windowed Mercedes, accompanied by his two dark-suited bodyguards, who commandeered a fisherman to ferry the three of them out to *Corsaire*. Il Hayaween sharply ordered Gerry and Liam to stay out of earshot below, then sent his two bodyguards to wait on the foredeck. He looked at his precious Blancpain watch. 'The trawler should be here by noon.'

'Good,' I said.

He sat on the cockpit thwart after fastidiously wiping it with a linen handkerchief.

'Is she suitable?' He waved his good left hand around *Corsaire*.

'She wallows like a pig. She's too heavy. But I can get her to

America.' I shrugged. 'There's a chance the Stingers will reach Ireland by April twenty-fourth, but I wouldn't bet on it. Not unless someone makes arrangements to ship them before the gold gets to Miami.'

'April twenty-fourth?' Il Hayaween frowned at me.

'The seventy-fifth anniversary of the Easter Rising. Don't Flynn and Herlihy want to give the Brits an Easter headache?'

He blinked as if he did not really understand what I was talking about, then shook his head. 'The war will come sooner than that.'

'In Kuwait?' I asked.

'Of course.' He paused. 'We have already received pledges of support from Ireland. But will they keep their word?' He glared at me as he asked the question.

'I'm sure they will,' I said truthfully. I was hardly surprised that the Provisional IRA had promised to support Iraq with a campaign of violence, because for many years now the Arabs had been the major supplier of the IRA's needs, and the Army Council could hardly turn down such a request from so generous a benefactor. What did surprise me was that il Hayaween was telling me this.

'We shall be relying on your organisation to support Iraq's defence against the imperialist aggression.' He laboriously raised his maimed hand to light a cigarette. 'Reactionary forces in Damascus and Tehran have suggested we should wait and see how effective Iraq's armed forces prove before we launch a worldwide campaign of terror, but we have refused to condone such timidity.' He sucked on the cigarette as though taking strength from its harsh smoke. 'We expect action, Shanahan.'

'I'm sure you'll get it,' I said.

Moments later a trawler crept across the harbour's outer bar and anchored just inside the sheltering sandbank. She carried no flag and bore no identifying number on her bows, but il Hayaween confirmed that she was the vessel carrying the gold. I hoisted *Corsaire*'s anchor, went alongside the ancient, rusting fishing boat and put Gerry and Liam to work carrying the heavy bags of coin from one ship to the other. As the first bags arrived I cleared *Corsaire*'s cabin and lifted her floorboards to reveal the empty belly of the boat, which looked like an elongated Fibreglass bowl studded with the chunky bolts which held her massive lead-filled keel in place. It was into that long bowl-like trough that we poured the gold coins, settling *Corsaire* even deeper into the water.

It took two hours before the transfer was finished and the trawler's skipper put back to sea. Il Hayaween satisfied himself that the coins had been bedded down in *Corsaire*'s bilge. 'They will be well hidden?'

'I've hidden a score of cargoes this way,' I reassured him. 'I'll glass the gold into the boat and no one will be able to tell the new floor from the old. Stop worrying.'

'I am paid to worry,' he said, then snapped his fingers to summon his two bodyguards, holding out his hands for their two submachine guns. 'These are for your crew. Throw the guns overboard before you reach Miami,' he ordered Gerry and Liam.

'We will, sir, we will.'

'If you fail me,' il Hayaween said to the three of us, 'then I shall pursue you to the last hiding place on earth, and when I find you I shall kill you, but not quickly, not quickly at all.' He grimaced at us, perhaps meaning it to be a smile, then turned towards the fisherman's boat that had been summoned from the quay. None of us moved as he clambered over the gunwale, raising his maimed hand in a gesture of farewell.

I put Gerry and Liam to work again. I inflated *Corsaire*'s dinghy and sent Gerry ashore to collect buckets of fine sand that I poured to fill the gaps between the gold coins. Then, when the sand and gold were riddled firm and smoothed over, I covered the mixture with layers of glass-fibre mat-and-cloth strips. Liam helped me, but his capacity for even such a simple task was short-lived. 'It's boring,' he complained, then retreated to the cockpit where he lit a cigarette and stared balefully at the grey-green harbour water.

I finished the job myself; first mixing the resin and its foul-smelling hardener, then brushing the mixed liquid onto the prepared fibre mat. That job done, I went back to the cockpit to wait as the Fibreglass hardened and dried. I made idle chatter with Liam and Gerry, but my thoughts were on the sheer amateurishness of this operation. How was it, with all the resources of Iraq and the Palestinians behind us, we were still reduced to this laborious method of smuggling gold?

As darkness fell I mixed the white gelcoat with its hardener and brushed it onto the original cabin floor. By midnight the new work had dried hard and the gold was hidden beneath a false floor. I laid down the floorboards, covered them with the saloon carpet, then hoisted *Corsaire*'s anchor and motored across the shallows of the harbour entrance. Clear of the bar and with the weight of the gold making her even more sluggish than before, *Corsaire* plunged her bows into the open sea.

I raised the yacht's sails, shut off her motor, and took my ramshackle enterprise into the night.

5

We sailed into the winter Mediterranean, a sea of short grey waves, spiteful winds and busy sea lanes. My two guards, realising that their responsibilities involved wakefulness, imposed a crude watch system on themselves which meant that, on our first afternoon out from Tunisia, Gerry was trying to sleep in the forecabin while the seasick Liam was slumped in the cockpit, trying not to show his misery.

'I can cure your seasickness,' I told him.

'How?' he groaned.

'A bottle of cod-liver oil and a bottle of whiskey, both drunk straight down, followed by thirty-six hours of absolute agony, but after that I promise you'll never be seasick again.'

'Oh, my God.' He leaned over the side. I had once made the same offer to Michael Herlihy, who had similarly turned it down. When we were teenagers, I had cruelly forced him into a small cat-boat and brought him ashore two hours later looking like a wet dead squirrel. I doubted he had ever forgiven me.

Liam flopped back on the thwart and watched as I opened the engine hatch and took a wrench to the boat's exhaust system, disconnecting the outlet pipe from the muffler. We were under sail, so the engine was cold. Then I took the thirty feet of flexible tubing from the cockpit locker and connected it to the top of the muffler with a jubilee clip. I fed the pipe's free end through the engine compartment's forward bulkhead and thus into the starboard lockers of the saloon. Liam, recovering from his last spasm of sickness, frowned at the serpentine loops of tubing that filled the engine hatch and cockpit floor. 'What are you doing?'

'Running a blower through the bilges to dry off the gelcoat we put on top of the gold.'

'Will it take the stink out of the boat?' he asked. 'Because it stinks down there, it does.'

'That's the resin-hardener. It'll pass.'

I put the boat under the command of the autohelm, then went down to the saloon where I opened the lockers, pulled the tubing through and introduced it into the boat's bathroom where a shower tray had a water-activated pump under its outflow. A grille in the bathroom door allowed fresh air to circulate from the saloon to keep mildew from growing too thickly in the shower stall, and the grille made the bathroom perfect for my purpose. I cut off the excess

50

tubing, which I carried back to the cockpit and tossed overboard.

Liam, his face pale as milk, watched in misery as I unfolded a chart. 'Where are we?' he asked.

'There.' I pointed to a spot just off the Tunisian coast. In fact we were much further north, but I could have sailed the *Corsaire* down the throat of hell and he would have been too sick to notice.

My two guards ate sandwiches that night, washed down with instant coffee. I gave Liam four powerful sleeping pills to help his drowsiness overcome the stench of the hardener, then sent him to his bunk in the forecabin. Gerry sat with me in the cockpit for a while, but soon became bored with the darkness and went below.

'I'm going to have to close the companionway,' I called down after a while.

'I need the fresh air,' he whined.

'The light's wrecking my night vision. So either switch the lights off, or close the hatch.'

He shut the companionway. I waited till my eyes had adjusted to the darkness, then went to the foredeck where I tripped the catch on the half-open forehatch. As I softly closed the hatch I could hear Liam's rhythmic snores. I went back to the cockpit and waited.

I was beating northwest, taking *Corsaire* into the open waters between Sardinia and the Balearics. It was a dark, chilly night, and the heavy boat's choppy motion seemed to reflect my mood. I was nervous. My heart felt raw and sick, an actual feeling in my chest that I suspected was the physical manifestation of conscience. I wondered if, over the years, I had become careless of death, and that sense of a skewed and wasted past made my whole future seem as bleak as the seas ahead.

At midnight I turned on the engine. The starter whirred, caught, and the motor steadied into a regular and muffled beat. I left it out of gear as though I was merely running it to charge the batteries. I heard nothing from the saloon and suspected that Gerry, like the half-drugged Liam, was asleep. After a while the water-activated pump beneath the shower tray clicked on and spewed water outboard for a while. Still no one woke below.

I let the motor run as *Corsaire* thumped and dipped into the Mediterranean night. The stars were shrouded by clouds so I steered by compass, taking *Corsaire* and her dying cargo northwest towards Europe. I was supposed to be racing along the North African coast to the Straits of Gibraltar, and from there southeast to the Canary Islands from where we were supposed to let the trade winds carry our cargo of gold across the Atlantic, but instead, in this choppy darkness, I was committing murder. I had routed the engine's exhaust into the main cabin and now its fumes were filling the boat; the exhaust system's cooling water was collecting in the shower tray and being expelled, but the poison gas was staying below.

At four in the morning, while it was still dark, I shut off the engine. I steeled myself to open the companionway and was greeted with a belch of foul, gaseous air. I gagged and backed away as the smoky gas streamed out of the saloon. I could just see Gerry slumped on the table, his fingers curled either side of his cropped hair.

I took a deep breath of fresh air, then went down into the saloon and put a finger on Gerry's neck. There was no pulse. I went into the forecabin where Liam lay on his back with his open eyes staring sightlessly at the closed hatch, his pale skin reddened by the effects of the carbon monoxide. I put a finger to his neck to find that, like Gerry, he was quite dead. I then pushed the forehatch open to let a gust of welcome chill air into the boat's fetid interior.

When the air had cleared I manhandled the bodies into the cockpit, and then weighed them down with the lead ballast weights that il Hayaween had so thoughtfully provided. I heaved them overboard. There was just enough wolfish grey light in the dawn sky to show that the two bodies sank instantly. I fetched their two guns and hurled them into the sea, then disconnected the flexible tubing and threw it overboard.

Afterwards, exhausted, I made coffee and ate some breakfast. I reconnected the exhaust and then, with the sunlight streaming between a watery chasm of the dissipating clouds, I began to jettison the materials I had used to hide the gold: the resin, the hardener, the mats and the brushes. I kept two brushes and the can of white gelcoat, but everything else went overboard.

I cleaned the exhaust deposits from the shower tray, then searched the boat for every last trace of Gerry and Liam. I tossed overboard their tawdry plastic holdalls and their changes of clothes, after finding a slip of cardboard that had been folded into the breast pocket of Gerry's suit jacket. On it was an Irish telephone number which Gerry had doubtless been told to call once he reached America. I memorised the number, then threw the cardboard scrap overboard. Afterwards, with the boat rinsed clean, I tried to frame a prayer to atone for my night's work, but no prayer would come.

I had murdered two men, solely for my own gain. I had killed Liam and Gerry for five million dollars. My story would be simple: that the badly overloaded boat, wallowing in rough seas, had been pooped by a bad wave and had sunk. That I had tried to rescue Liam and Gerry, but failed. That the gold, with the boat, was lost. That I had survived in a life raft, alone. When I reached America I would hide for a few weeks then, when the IRA found me, I would brazen the story out.

I tried to justify the murder by telling myself that they would have killed me if I had finished the voyage. I told myself that if you sup with the devil you need a very long spoon, and that Gerry and Liam should have known what dinner table they were sitting at. I tried to justify their murder, but it was on my conscience as I sailed on to Barcelona. That too was part of the plan.

It was a hellish journey. I was single-handed in a busy sea, so I dared not leave the cockpit. Instead I cat-napped at the helm and snatched the odd hour of sleep whenever it seemed safe. One night I was startled awake to hear the throbbing of a steamer's engines pounding in the darkness and, when I turned in panic, I saw the lights of a vast ship thundering past not a hundred yards away.

The next day, during a lull from the cold winter winds that were sweeping south from the French coast, I buckled on a lifeline and put *Corsaire* on self-steering. Then I crouched on the swimming platform built into her sugar-scoop stern and painted out the name and the French hailing port, Port Vendres. I then took all *Corsaire*'s papers, shredded them, and committed them to the deep.

On the following day, when the second coat of white paint was dry and the old lettering completely hidden, I unrolled some transfer names I had ordered by mail in Belgium and rubbed them onto the fresh paint. Thus *Corsaire* became *Rebel Lady*, and Port Vendres became Boston, Mass. Then I fastened the old *Rebel Lady* maker's plate onto the side of *Corsaire*'s coachroof and, using commercial stick-on letters and numbers I had bought in Nieuwpoort, I put *Rebel Lady*'s Massachusetts registration number on either bow. I finally replaced the French tricolour with the Stars and Stripes, and thus *Corsaire* ceased to exist and in her place was Dr O'Neill's forty-four-foot boat, *Rebel Lady*, ready to go home.

Two days later I delivered *Rebel Lady* to the shipping company in Barcelona. I spent a busy day knocking down her topworks: taking off her sails and craning out her mast. Then, with her spars safely lashed to her decks, she was hoisted out of the water.

Once she was safely cradled I borrowed an electric drill and, using templates I had brought from Nieuwpoort, I etched *Rebel Lady*'s hull identification number onto her transom. Then I locked her hatches, signed her over to the shipping company, paid the balance of my account in cash and walked out of the docks to find a taxi. In a day or so *Rebel Lady* would be loaded onto a container ship, and then, with her secret hidden in her belly, she would be carried west to America.

And I too was going to America, but not across the Atlantic. Fear of il Hayaween made me circumspect and so I took a train to Nice, and another to Paris. I telephoned Brussels again, then caught a plane for Singapore. I was vanishing, going east about the world, but running for the refuge of home.

I STAYED ONE NIGHT in a hotel near Singapore's Changi Airport then, in a hot humid dawn, still groggy with sleeplessness and jetlag, I flew north to Hong Kong where I waited two hours before catching a plane to San Francisco. From there, using my false American passport and carrying a stained sea bag and my bright yellow oilskin jacket, I came home.

My flight to Boston was delayed, and we did not land at Logan Airport till the small hours of the morning. It had been snowing and the temperature was way below zero. The last sleep I had enjoyed had been somewhere over the western Pacific, and I should have stayed the rest of that night in a Boston hotel, but all I really wanted to do was reach my house on Cape Cod and so I rented a car and set off down the snowy Massachusetts roads.

The drive took just over two hours, and the thought of the waiting house filled me with a feverish expectancy; like a hunted beast seeking a secret lair, I wanted the safety and reassurance of home. There was a small risk that my enemies might be watching the Cape Cod house, but I had not seen the place in seven years, and Shafiq and his friends did not even know it existed. As I crossed the Cape Cod Canal the clouds slid apart to reveal a clean-edged moon cut sharp as a whistle in a sky of ice-bright stars. A big illuminated sign outside a hardware store asked God to bless our troops. The radio, even at four in the morning, was filled with the threats of war, then it played 'God Bless America' and I felt tears prick at my eyes. It had been so very long since I had been home.

It was ten past four in the starbright morning when I turned onto the track that led east towards the ocean and, as I breasted the pine-clad sandy ridge that edged the marsh, I could suddenly see for miles. The far Atlantic was silver and black while the nearer waters of the bay glistened like a sheet of burnished steel. I braked the car to a stop on the ridge's crest and, with the radio and lights turned off, I sat and stared down at the view in which, dead centre, my waiting house lay silent. The house and the seeping beams of the Cape's lighthouses were the only new things in this view since the days when the wandering Indian tribes had dug for clams in the shoals of this sandy promontory that stuck so deep into the Atlantic.

I rolled down the car window to catch, on the surge of freezing air, the shifting sound of the distant ocean breakers. The sound brought with it a sudden rush of love for this place. It was home, it was safety, it was mine. Here, I told myself, I could at last live honestly. No more secrets. I had come home. I felt no fears. This place was too far from the hatreds of the Middle East or the bitterness of Ulster to bear danger. This was the refuge where I would hide until *Rebel Lady* reached America, then I would give myself up to the government for questioning. My telephone calls to Brussels had been to warn them of Stinger missiles, il Hayaween and my conviction that a terrible series of airliner massacres was planned as a revenge for America's thwarting of Saddam Hussein's plans. I had given the CIA as much information as they needed to stop the Stingers being deployed, but they would want more. They would want all the information I had gathered since first they had sent me out twelve years before.

For Roisin had been right. I was one of the CIA's agents who did not exist, who would leave no tracks and make no footprints. I had been turned out into the world and told to stay out until I had something worth bringing home; I would be paid nothing, offered nothing. Even then, Simon van Stryker, who had recruited me to the programme, called us his 'stringless agents' because there would be no puppet strings to lead our enemies back to Langley, Virginia. Now I was going back there of my own accord, but in my own time and I would not give them everything. *Rebel Lady* and her cargo were mine, to keep me in my old age.

I rolled up the window, let in the clutch and drove towards my house which had been built a hundred and fifty years before by a Captain Matthew Starbuck. Retiring from the profitable pursuit of whales in the Southern Ocean, he had come to this Cape Cod marsh and built himself a home snug against the Atlantic winds. My father had bought the Starbuck house from the estate of the captain's great-granddaughter and had dreamed of retiring to it, but the dream had never come true. Now I would make it home. I remembered how I had once dreamed of bringing Roisin to this house; I had even dreamed, God help me, of raising our children on this shore.

I drove slowly up the driveway of crushed clam shells that

splintered loudly under the tyres, and stopped on the big turnaround in front of the house where my headlights shone stark on the silver-grey cedar shingles. It was a classic Cape Cod house; a simple, low building with two windows either side of its front door, a steep staircase in the hallway and two snug dormer rooms upstairs. It was a home as simple as a child's drawing, a home at peace with its surroundings, and the thought that it was mine was wondrously comforting as I killed the headlights and climbed out of the car, holding the house keys that I had kept safe these seven years.

My key scraped in the lock as it turned. There had never been electricity in the house, and I had no torch, but the moon shone brightly enough to illuminate the hallway. My sister Maureen, who used the house as a holiday home, had left some yellow rain-slickers hanging on the pegs by the door, but otherwise the shadowed hall looked just as I had left it seven years before. The antique wooden sea-trunk with its rope handles still stood under the steep-pitched stairway, and on its painted lid was a candle in a pewter holder. I fumbled in the holder's dish, hoping to find a book of matches.

At which point an electric light dazzled me. I started back, but before I could escape something terrible struck my face and I was blinded. The pain made me want to scream, but I could not even breathe, and, with my hands scrabbling like claws at my scorching eyes, I collapsed.

6

The police arrived five minutes later, their two cars wailing down the track then skidding ferociously as they braked on the clam shells. A young excited officer, his pistol drawn, burst through the open front door and shouted at me not to move.

'Oh, grow up,' I said. 'Do I look as if I'm about to run away?'

My sight had half returned and, through the painful tears, I could just see that the girl who had attacked me was now sitting on the stairs holding an antique whaling harpoon that used to hang on my bedroom wall. She had not used the vicious harpoon to cripple me, but a squeegee bottle that now stood beside her on the steep stairway.

'He broke in,' the girl explained laconically to the three policemen who now piled excitedly into the hallway. 'He says his name is Dr O'Neill.' She sounded scornful.

In the last few moments I had learned that this was one very tough lady. An older officer knelt beside me and gently pulled my hands from my face. 'What did you do to him?' he asked the girl.

'Squirted him good.' The girl showed the officers the liquid soap bottle that she had used to lacerate me through the banister rails. 'It's ammonia and it's legal,' she added defensively.

One of the policemen fetched a saucepan of water from the kitchen. My breathing was more or less normal now, but the pain in my eyes was atrocious. The officer poured water on my face while outside the house the police radios sounded unnaturally loud in the still, cold night air.

'We'll take him away in a moment, ma'am,' the older policeman, a sergeant, reassured the girl. Then he looked at me curiously. 'I know you!' he said suddenly.

I blinked at him. My sight was still blurred, but I recognised the sergeant as Ted Nickerson, a guy I had last seen in twelfth grade. Damn it, I thought, but this was not what I had planned! The last thing I needed was for the word to spread that I had returned to America.

'You're Paul Shanahan!' Ted exclaimed. 'Which means . . .' he stopped, glancing at the girl.

'Which means this is my house,' I confirmed.

'It's not his house.' The girl insisted. 'Guy's a lying scumbag. I rent this place! I've got a five-year lease!' She was shivering in a nightdress and an old woollen dressing gown. My old woollen dressing gown. She had bare feet, long black hair and an oriental face.

'This is the Shanahan house.' Ted Nickerson confirmed the ownership uncomfortably.

'No way!' The girl protested. 'The house belongs to a guy in Boston, a guy called Patrick McPhee.'

'McPhee's my brother-in-law,' I told her, 'and he's married to my sister, Maureen. Maureen holds the keys to the place while I'm away, that's all! She uses it for summer vacations and odd weekends.'

The girl stared at me. I guessed that by using Maureen's name I had convinced her I might be telling the truth.

'How was I to know?' She was on the defensive now. 'He doesn't knock, he just comes into the house . . .'

'Like he owns it?' I finished for her.

'Then why the hell are you calling yourself Dr O'Neill?'

'None of your business,' I snarled, then struggled to my feet. My eyes were still streaming with tears, but I was recovering. 'Who put electric light in here?'

'I did,' the girl said defiantly. 'I'm a painter. I need light to work.'

'Did you put in a telephone as well?' Ted Nickerson asked her. 'I need to make a call.'

'Help yourself. In the kitchen.'

The girl edged tentatively down the stairs that Captain Starbuck had built as steep as the companionways on his old whaling ships. 'Can we close the front door?' she asked. 'I'm kind of chilly.'

'Sure, ma'am.'

I went through into the living room, from where I could hear Sergeant Nickerson grunting into the telephone in the kitchen.

Apart from the electric light and the paintings, the room had not changed much. It was panelled in old pale oak and its low-beamed ceiling was formed by the pine planks of the dormer storey upstairs.

'Do you really own the house?' The girl had followed me into the living room.

'Yes.'

'Hell!' she said angrily, then, with arms folded, she walked to one of the small windows that stared eastwards across the ocean. 'The mailman told me he didn't think Patrick McPhee was the owner, but I thought that was just troublemaking gossip.'

'McPhee's a creep,' I said savagely. 'Marrying him was the worst day's work Maureen ever did. So how long have you been here?'

'Three years, but I don't live here permanently. I've got a place of my own in New York.' She turned to glare at me, as though the night's misadventures were all my fault. 'I've invested in this place! I put in the electricity and the phone! I was dumb, OK, but I like this place. It's the light.'

'I know,' I said, and I did know. In autumn and winter the light on the Cape is so clear and sharp that it seems like the world is newly minted. Thousands of painters had been drawn by that light, though most of them merely wasted good paint and canvas trying to capture it. Whether the girl was good or not I could not tell, for my eyesight was still smeared, though in the electric light her canvases seemed full of anger and jaggedness.

'My name's Sarah,' she said in a placatory tone, 'Sarah Sing Tennyson.'

'Paul Shanahan,' I said, and almost added that it was nice to meet her, but that courtesy seemed inappropriate. 'Sing?' I asked instead. 'That's an odd name.'

'My mother was Chinese.' Sarah Sing Tennyson was tall with very long, very straight and very black hair that framed a narrow, almost feral face. She had dark slanted eyes above high cheekbones. A good-looking trespasser, I thought sourly.

'When did you put the electricity in?' I asked her. 'I didn't see any wires outside.'

'Two summers ago. I had to bury the cables because this is all National Seashore land so you're not allowed to string wires off poles. It was very expensive.'

More fool you, I thought. 'How much rent are you paying Patrick?'

'Is it your business?' she bridled.

'It's my house,' I bridled back, 'and if my brother-in-law lets my house, then it is my business!'

We were saved from further argument when the kitchen door opened and Ted Nickerson, still holding the telephone handset, stared at me oddly. 'Paul? I'm talking to a guy named Peter Gillespie. Does that name mean anything to you?'

'Nothing at all,' I said truthfully.

'He says he expected to see you in Europe. Does that make sense?'

Nickerson had been staring oddly at me ever since he recognised me; now his puzzlement only seemed to deepen.

My God, I thought, the CIA had been quicker than I had expected. They had responded to my warning call by putting out an alert.

'We got a warning to look out for you two days ago, Paul,' Ted Nickerson said.

'Tell Gillespie I'll call him in a few weeks.'

Ted shook his head. 'I've got orders to hold you, Paul. Protective custody.' He moved his free hand to his holstered pistol, making Sarah Sing Tennyson gasp.

I half raised my hands in a gesture of supplication. 'OK, Ted, no need for drama.'

'You're not under arrest, Paul,' Ted said carefully, 'just under police protection.' He spoke into the phone, telling whoever was at the other end that I was safely in the bag.

I MET PETER GILLESPIE next morning. He came to the police station with an agent called Stuart Callaghan, who was to be my bodyguard.

'You've had breakfast, Mr Shanahan?' Gillespie had very puncti-liously showed me his identification.

'Sure.'

'Then, if you're ready?' Gillespie was plainly eager to begin my debriefing. I was carrying, after all, over a decade of secrets. 'We have a plane waiting at Hyannis Airport.'

'Hold on!' I protested. It was not yet eight in the morning, I had snatched two hours' indifferent sleep in a holding cell and I felt like death warmed up. 'I've got to see someone before I leave. I want to use the telephone, then go back to my house.'

Gillespie was plainly unhappy, but he was uncertain how best to handle me. I was no prisoner, despite being locked up overnight, yet I came from the shadowy world of international terrorism. Gillespie himself was very straight, tall, punctiliously courteous and businesslike, and clearly reluctant to let me use the phone, but he seemed to recognise my determination and so waved me towards a desk.

I needed to talk to an old friend. I would have much preferred to have talked with him in private, but Gillespie's presence gave me no choice. I would have to risk the CIA knowing about Johnny Riordan. We had been friends since childhood, when his father used to look after the Cape house for my father. Old Eamonn Riordan had been a good fisherman, but his son was an even better one. Johnny had a natural talent for boats, the sea and for living. He was a great muscled lump of goodwill, common sense and kindness, a man I was loath to involve in any trouble, for Johnny Riordan was a father, happily married, and without a mean fibre in his body. He tried to scrape a bare existence from lobstering, scalloping or tub-trawling the seas about the Cape, but in the lean months he was forced to take on other menial jobs. I had not spoken with Johnny in seven years but I knew, if I did call, he would not blink an eyelid.

Nor did he. 'So you're back at last, are you?' He laughed. 'Which means you'll be wanting a meal.'

'No,' I said. 'I want to meet you at my house. Can you make it?'

'Sure I can make it.'

Johnny's pick-up truck was already parked in the driveway when Gillespie and Callaghan drove me home. Johnny himself I found ensconced before Sarah Sing Tennyson's hearth where he was telling my tenant tall tales of prohibition; how the Cape Codders used to run rings round the federal agents, and how there were still forgotten caches of Canadian whiskey in some of the cranberry bogs.

'Well now, look who it is!' He greeted me ebulliently. He was a big man, with a shock of black hair, a broad black beard and an open cheerful face.

'You've met my tenant?' I gestured at Sarah.

'It's good to have an artist living here, isn't it?' Johnny waved towards Sarah Tennyson's paintings which were mostly of the Nauset lighthouse, but rendered so gloomily that they might have depicted a watchtower in hell. 'I was telling her how they tried to teach me to do art at school! What a waste! And good morning to you!' This last greeting was to Gillespie who had followed me into the house.

I hurried Johnny into the kitchen. 'This is family business,' I said firmly to Gillespie, and slammed the door shut.

'What's going on?' Johnny asked me. 'She told me she's renting the place! I knew she was here off and on, but I thought she just borrowed it from Maureen at weekends. I know Maureen's husband is here sometimes, but . . .'

'It doesn't matter,' I cut Johnny off. I knew I would have only a few moments before Gillespie interrupted us and I dared not waste a minute. 'Listen, I'm having a boat delivered to you. It's coming from Barcelona, and a customs agent will call you from Boston in about six or seven weeks. There shouldn't be any customs duty to pay on her, because she's registered in Massachusetts. These are her papers.' I took the original *Rebel Lady* papers from my oilskin pocket and shoved them into a bemused Johnny's hands. 'If there are any problems, this will help.' I began peeling hundred-dollar bills from the roll I had collected when I closed my bank accounts in Belgium. 'I paid for her carriage to the Cape, but you'll need to hire a crane to get her off the truck. Her new owner's name is on those papers, and your story is that he asked you to store her here for the winter.'

Johnny riffled through the hundred-dollar bills, then gave me a very disapproving look. 'This isn't drugs, is it, Paulie? Because if it is, I'm not helping.'

'I swear to God, Johnny, this has nothing to do with drugs. There's gold aboard her,' I told him reluctantly, 'which is why I don't want anyone to know about her. If anyone asks what we're talking about in here, you're agreeing to look after this house while I'm gone. You understand, Johnny? The boat's a secret.'

'Gold! In her hull?' Johnny seemed cheered by that, then watched in amazement as I slipped the rest of the hundred-dollar bills inside my false passport, added Teodor's other false papers, then reached up to raise one of the spare-bedroom floorboards that comprised the kitchen ceiling. Johnny supported the floorboard while I fumbled along the top surface of one of the kitchen's old black beams. Eventually I found the cavity I had long ago hollowed into the beam, and into which I now dropped the passport, papers and money.

'There shouldn't be any problems with the boat,' I told Johnny. 'Her papers are in order and I'll probably be back before she arrives anyway. But listen!' I rammed a finger into his chest. 'There might be some real bastards looking for this boat. If anyone wants to argue about her, back off. These are friends of Michael Herlihy, so if Michael asks questions, just tell him I asked you to look after the boat and you don't know any more about it than that, and if he wants the boat, just let it go! You understand me? I don't want you or your family to be hurt.'

My mention of Mick Herlihy had made Johnny very unhappy. 'This is IRA business, isn't it?'

I was saved from answering because a very suspicious Gillespie pushed open the kitchen door. 'What's going on?'

'Paulie's just telling me what he wants done with the house while he's away.' Johnny, bless him, told the lie with all the conviction of a guileless man. 'Are you sure you don't want aluminium siding?' he asked me. 'The salt plays havoc with shingles.'

'God no! No aluminium. Keep the cedar.'

'If you're through?' Gillespie invited me to accompany him.

'And for God's sake, Johnny,' I went on loudly enough for Sarah Sing Tennyson to overhear me, 'make sure the girl gets out of here.'

Sarah Tennyson's anger flared. 'Don't you dare come here again, Shanahan!' she shouted over Gillespie's shoulder. 'I've already talked to my attorneys this morning and they say I signed the lease in good faith and I've paid the rent on time, so this place is mine.' Her voice was crackling with spite. 'This is my house for as long as the lease lasts, and if you break in here once more I'll sue you. Do you understand me, Shanahan?'

'What I understand,' I said, 'is that your lawyer can play let's-get-rich with my brother-in-law's lawyer, but I don't care to be involved. Get your money back from Patrick McPhee and send me the bill for the phone and the electricity, and then you can take away your finger paintings, give me back the front-door key and vanish.'

She pointed to the front hall. 'Get the hell out of my house, Shanahan. All of you!'

'Let's just do as she says,' Gillespie muttered. We scuttled ignominiously out to the driveway where Stuart Callaghan waited in the car. The hire car I'd rented at Logan Airport was also there. I had used the fake credit card to rent it and I guessed its owners would eventually get it back.

I looked back as we accelerated up the clam-shell drive and I saw Sarah Tennyson, her face a mask of outrage, watching to make certain we really did leave my property. I blew her a kiss, then we were over the sandy ridge and into the scrub pine, and gone.

'I DON'T LIKE SARAH TENNYSON,' I told Gillespie, 'but someone should warn her that she's in danger if she stays in that house.'

'I'll look after it.' Gillespie glanced out of the aeroplane window at the monotonous cloudscape that unreeled beneath us. We had driven to the small municipal airport at Hyannis where our six-seater plane had taken off into a sudden flurry of wet snow. Gillespie had already told me that the Agency intended to keep me out of harm's way for as many weeks as it would take to empty me of secrets. 'We're kind of excited to have you back,' he coyly confided. 'Not everyone thought that the Stringless Program would work.'

At Hyannis Airport I had bought a newspaper that told of war preparations on either side of the Kuwaiti frontier. The paper also reported on last-minute bids to prevent the fighting. Congressman O'Shaughnessy's bill forbidding the use of American armed forces for one year had failed, yet the congressman was still urging the President to give economic sanctions a chance. On an inside page was an article about the worldwide precautions against Iraq's expected terrorist onslaught; there were armoured vehicles patrolling European airports, and air passenger numbers had fallen drastically.

The plane suddenly banked and dropped. Raindrops streamed sternwards on the windows as we sliced into the clouds. The plane buffeted, dropped hard in an air-pocket, then we were out of the clouds and flying just feet above a snow-streaked countryside. Wet tarmac appeared beneath us, the wheels bounced, smoked and squealed, and we had come to earth.

The aircraft did not go near the small terminal, but instead taxied to where two cars waited. One was a limousine with black-tinted windows and the other a police car; two state troopers holding rifles stood by the limousine. The CIA clearly believed il Hayaween had a long reach.

We took Interstate 84 eastwards into the snow-streaked forests of the Pocono Mountains. We drove fast, our way cleared by the state troopers. Deep in the mountains we turned off the interstate and twisted our way up ever narrower roads until we reached a big painted sign that read 'US Department of Agriculture, Rabies Research Station, Absolutely NO Unauthorised Entry'.

I grinned. 'I'm your mad dog, am I?'

Gillespie shrugged. 'It keeps out the inquisitive.'

The limousine stopped at a checkpoint manned by uniformed guards. A high fieldstone wall topped with coils of barbed wire stretched into the forests either side of the gates. The guards peered at me, examined Gillespie's credentials, then the steel gates were mechanically opened and the limousine accelerated into a wide parkland studded with snow-shrouded rhododendrons. We passed across a stone bridge and into view of a massive, steep-roofed house that looked like some French mansion unaccountably marooned in a North American wilderness.

The grand portico led into a palatial, panelled entrance hall. I suspected the house had been donated to the government by the bewhiskered magnate whose portrait hung above the stone fireplace. It was lavish and comfortable.

Leading off the entrance hall was a library, its shelves, I later discovered, crammed with the collected writings of the founding fathers, which was just the sort of dutiful yet unreadable collection one would expect of a patriotic millionaire. There was also a dining room, a kitchen and an exercise room. My quarters comprised a bathroom, a kitchenette and a bedroom, which held a wide bed, a sofa, a desk, rugs, a bookcase full of thrillers, and a television set.

'We expect to be holding conversations with you most days and for quite long hours, though there will be some evenings when you will be unoccupied,' Gillespie told me. 'The refrigerator is stocked, and the television works.'

'And the telephone?' I gestured at the phone beside the bed. 'Is it bugged?' I teased him.

'I couldn't truthfully tell you either way.' Gillespie actually blushed as he half admitted I was under surveillance, but only a complete fool would have assumed otherwise. 'We have a lot to do, Mr Shanahan, so shall we go downstairs and begin?'

To unpick the past. To tell a tale of bombers and gunners, heroes and lovers. Confession time.

7

I was tired, dog-tired. 'We won't take a lot of time today,' Gillespie promised, 'but your messages to our people in Brussels were kind of intriguing.' He was being very tactful, not asking why I had appeared in America when I had promised to walk into the Brussels Embassy, nor asking why I had used a false name. 'You talked about Stingers? About a meeting in Miami? You suggested a connection with Saddam Hussein? With il Hayaween?'

I told Gillespie everything about the meeting in Florida where

Michael Herlihy and Brendan Flynn had introduced me to the two Cubans. I described how the Provisional IRA had negotiated the purchase of fifty-three Stinger missiles for one and a half million dollars.

Gillespie wrote the sum down. I was certain that the library, where we were sitting with Stuart Callaghan, must be wired for sound and that, somewhere, tape recorders were spooling down my every word. But Gillespie was the kind of man who liked to make notes. 'And why were you invited to the meeting?' he asked.

'Because I used to be the Provisionals' liaison officer with outside terrorist organisations. I was their money man.'

Gillespie's head came up from his notebook. 'You liaised with all outside terrorist organisations?' he asked.

'So far as I know, yes, although in effect that was mainly the Palestinians and the Libyans. We did some business with the Basques as well, but they were never as important as the Middle Eastern guys.'

Gillespie was impressed by the Middle Eastern connections, though I rather deflated the good impression by telling him how the IRA had ceased to trust me several years before, which meant that much of my information was out of date.

'Why did they stop trusting you?'

'That's kind of a long story.'

'We'll get to it. But if you were inactive, why didn't you come home?'

'Because I always hoped they'd reactivate me. They never cut me off entirely.'

'We're fortunate they didn't.' Gillespie was chasing a commodity as rare as rainbow's gold, the truth, and he wanted to make sure I was not bringing him fool's gold. Maybe my return at this critical time had happened because the enemy had turned me? Maybe I was telling lies to make them look in one direction while il Hayaween attacked from another? I might be a hero of the Stringless Program come back from the world's darkness, but that did not mean they would trust me. Nor did I intend to trust *them*. I had my secrets, chief of which was the existence of five million dollars in a renamed yacht.

'How were the Stingers paid for?'

'The usual method,' I said, 'is electronic transfer. I never handled the money, just the request. I requested the payment from Shafiq, he told me it was all OK'd, and then I phoned a number in Ireland to say that everything was on line and the money would be coming.'

'You have the telephone number in Ireland?'

I gave him the number that had been in Gerry's suit pocket, but warned him that it would almost certainly belong to a message-taker who would have no inkling of what the messages were about.

'Do you imagine that the Stingers are on their way to Ireland?'

'I'm guessing that il Hayaween never did mean to send all the Stingers to Ireland, but to deploy some in the States. If we attack Saddam Hussein's forces in Kuwait then he may well bring down planes in Washington and Miami and New York and anywhere else he can. I suspect the IRA are just being used by il Hayaween. The Palestinians weren't in a position to travel to Miami to buy the missiles; the Irish were. But now the missiles are paid for, then God knows what il Hayaween has in mind.'

Stuart Callaghan had lit a fire in the library's big hearth. Now, at Gillespie's bidding, he took away the new details of the Stinger trade, doubtless to telephone them through to Langley so that the search for the missiles could be intensified. Gillespie still worried at my story. 'You say the money is usually transferred by wire?'

'Almost always. It's heavy stuff to carry around in a suitcase.'

He smiled. 'And where would the half-million deposit have come from?'

'Boston, I guess. Herlihy must use a dozen banks.'

Gillespie looked up at me. 'One last question before we break. Why did you use a false passport to enter the country? And what about the credit card for your hire car?'

'Habit,' I said. 'I guess I wanted to use false papers one last time.'

'You still have the passport and credit card?'

'I tossed them. I won't need false papers again, will I?'

'No, you won't.' Gillespie pretended to believe me. 'I guess that's the immediate business taken care of. What I'd like you to do now, Paul, is take a rest. You look bushed. Maybe we'll pick up this afternoon? There'll be someone with me by then.'

'Van Stryker?' Simon van Stryker had recruited me into the Stringless Program and I had liked him. I had spent years looking forward to meeting him again, hearing his congratulations.

'Van Stryker's rather exalted these days. But you will meet him in due course. He takes an interest in you.' Gillespie paused. 'We've asked one of the Agency's psychiatrists to sit in on future sessions. It's normal practice.'

'To find out if I've gone mad?' I asked lightly.

'Something like that, yes.' He replied just as lightly. In fact the shrink would be there to detect my lies.

'Fine by me!' I said. Just great.

THE PSYCHIATRIST'S APPEARANCE suggested someone who ought to have been knitting baby socks for a grandchild rather than monitoring a debriefing about terrorism. She was a middle-aged, motherly black woman who smiled pleasantly at me, then shook the snow off her overshoes and settled in the bay window at the far end of the long library table. 'Terrible weather,' she said cosily. 'Do you mind if I call you Paul? I'm Carole Adamson.'

'Paul's fine.'

'Don't you mind me, Paul. I'm just here to listen.' Carole Adamson was wearing a thick woollen cardigan and had a comfortable smile, but I was certain that every little lie and evasion would telegraph themselves to her shrewd and watchful eyes. I could not see her without turning in my chair, but I was very aware of her scrutiny.

Gillespie began the afternoon session by saying FBI agents had begun their search for the Stinger missiles and their Cuban vendors. In the meantime, he said, he wanted to explore my history of terrorist connections. 'I want to go back to the very beginning,' he said. 'Who introduced you to the IRA?'

'A guy called Joey Grogan.'

'Was that in America?' Gillespie asked. 'Or in Ireland?'

'In Boston,' I said, and felt a flicker of annoyance that Gillespie wanted to plough this old field. 'Why don't you just look it up?'

'All we know about you is what we can read in police records but, as far as the Agency is concerned, you have never existed. So we have to begin at the beginning. Where does Mr Grogan live?'

'He's dead.' Poor Joey had died of emphysema in 1986 and Peggy, his widow, had immediately absconded to a trailer park in Florida with sixteen thousand dollars collected from Boston's Irish bars by the Friends of Free Ireland. The Friends ostensibly collected money to support the widows and orphans of IRA soldiers, but everyone assumed the donations were for buying guns anyway. In fact, what little did reach Ireland was a hundred times more likely to end up in a pub's cash-till than with a gunman's widow.

'You were recruited into the IRA before you met us?' Gillespie asked. 'Before you met van Stryker?'

'I was supporting them, sure, but I didn't join the IRA proper till I went to live in Ireland.'

'Why did you support them?'

'Because the Irish are my tribe! Because I learned about Wolfe Tone and Patrick Pearse long before anyone in my family thought to tell me about George Washington. Because I swallowed stories of the famine with my mother's milk. There probably isn't a family in South Boston that doesn't claim ancestors who were put to the sword by Cromwell, or massacred in the rising of ninety-eight, or beaten up by the Black and Tans!'

Gillespie wanted to know about my childhood, but there were no dark secrets there. I had been a happy child, dividing my time between our family's Boston house, my father's Cape Cod retreat, and his various business premises. Those premises ranged from the Green Harp Bar in Charlestown to a marina in Weymouth, but my father's real fortune was made from his brothels in Scollay Square.

'Brothels?' Gillespie asked painfully. 'And what was your mother's attitude to your father's businesses?'

'She endured my father and adored her three children.'

'But you must have been a trial to her?' Gillespie probed. 'We took the trouble to find your old police records.'

'Mom believed women were born to suffer. That's what the priest and the nuns told her, and that's how she wanted it.' I had first been in court for beating ten kinds of living hell out of a man who had insulted my sister, and two years after that I did four months for receiving stolen goods.

'And your father died while you were in prison?'

'Yes. He was in the back room of a Southie Bar when some bastards decided to burn the place down. They shot him first. We were told it was an insurance scam.'

Gillespie stared thoughtfully at me. 'It must have been upsetting for you. You were only twenty-one. That's young to lose a parent.'

'What are you trying to prove, Gillespie?' I challenged him. 'I thought I was here to help you guys, and instead you're trying to make out that I'm some kind of basket-case because my pa died?'

'What happened to your father's killers?' Gillespie was entirely unmoved by my protest.

'Beats me,' I shrugged, 'they were never found.'

'Two of the suspected killers were found in the Charles River, strangled, and a third man was found with his head thrust down a toilet in a Roxbury bar. He had drowned. The police believe that you and your brother were in that same bar on that night, but could find no witnesses.'

'I thought you said I was in prison?'

'The parole board had released you on compassionate grounds before the funeral. Your brother was on leave from the Marines.'

I shrugged and spread my hands as though I knew nothing.

Gillespie looked at his notebook. 'Your brother died in Vietnam?'

'Yes. And no, his death didn't make me angry at America.'

Gillespie ignored the irrelevance. 'So how did you earn a living after your father's death?'

'I took over his businesses. I kept the marina at Weymouth and the Green Harp Bar in Charlestown. I sold everything else.' I had been twenty-one, rich as a dream and cock of the Boston walk, but the money had slipped away like ice on a summer sidewalk. I let cronies use the marina slips for free, I ran a slate for friends in the Green Harp. On one day alone I dropped two hundred thousand dollars on a horse which started at a hundred to one and finished as dogmeat.

Eventually I had to sell the marina and a half-share in the bar to pay my debts. My half-share in the Green Harp still made money, but the money trickled away on girls and booze and horses. My mother wanted me to marry some good Catholic virgin, but I needed the spice of danger, and Joey Grogan brought it me.

Joey was a passionate man, drunk with Irish myths and obsessed with liberating his ancestral home. I had first met him when he arrived at the Green Harp Bar to empty the Friends of Free Ireland collecting box; later he recruited me to help him assemble an arms shipment for Ulster. The shipment was small stuff, mostly old handguns that we bought on the street corners of Boston, but five years later Joey and I were sending big stuff: Armalites and even a pair of M60 machine guns that had been liberated from a Massachusetts National Guard armoury.

There was silence. A log spat angrily in the fire. 'Was it the death, in seventy-six, of your mother,' Gillespie asked mildly, 'that gave you the freedom to enter the drug trade?'

'I was never in the drug trade,' I snapped. The debriefing had turned hostile because I resented this harrowing of my past. I had always been uncomfortable in the confessional because I hated to reflect on my actions: I was impetuous, generous and foolish, but not reflective. I had small patience for my countrymen's love of self-analysis. My dad had taught me to live life at full throttle and not to worry about the rearview mirrors, but these sessions with Gillespie promised to be long, uncomfortable bouts of mirror-gazing.

Gillespie turned a page in his folder. 'In nineteen seventy-seven you were arrested in a boat called the *Fighting Irish* off Boca Grande Key in Florida, and the boat was carrying half a ton of marijuana.'

'I was charged?' I challenged him.

'Of course not.'

Because instead of going for trial I had gone underground, saved by a codfish aristocrat named Simon van Stryker and his Stringless Program. I had become legitimate.

SIMON VAN STRYKER WAS A Wasp superstar. He was a tall, elegant man born to inestimable privilege, with immaculate manners, a gentle manner and eyes as cold as the water off Nova Scotia. The moment I first saw him I knew his type, just as he knew mine. I was two-toilet Irish and he was the codfish aristocracy. His kind had never liked my kind for we were the incontinent, Papist immigrants who had fouled up their perfect Protestant America in the nineteenth century, but van Stryker still became my recruiter, my master, my friend.

I had faced God knows how many years in a federal prison in the depths of the Everglades. Instead van Stryker had taken me to a house in Georgia, not unlike the house where Gillespie now took my secrets apart. There, surrounded by camelias and azaleas, van Stryker and his team had probed me and analysed me. 'Are you a patriot?' they had wanted to know, but I had only to hear 'America the Beautiful' for the tears to start. We Shanahans had always been emotional, and America was my country: my love for it was laid down like the sediments of the seabed, dark and immovable however hard the wind blew or high the seas broke. To me patriotism was bred in the bone, a part of the blood, etched till death.

So what did I feel about Ireland? That was easy, Ireland was smiling eyes and shamrocks and the road ever rising to meet you and the St Patrick's Day parade when all South Boston went gloriously drunk. Ireland was good talk and warm hearts and fellowship.

Did I collect money for the cause? they asked.

Sure I did, and if the money went to buy guns and bombs it was for expelling the English from Ireland. Hadn't the English been slaughtering the Irish for centuries?

Had I ever seen a child eviscerated by a bomb? Simon van Stryker asked me.

I had shrugged the question away, but Simon van Stryker had photographs of the child. She had been three years old, waiting with her mother at a bus stop in Belfast. The mother had died too.

And here was a picture of another man, also a Catholic, whose kneecaps had been shot through. He had owned a hardware store, selling penny nails and epoxy glue, but he had refused to pay the IRA their protection money so one night they had come for him with a loaded gun and taken him into his backyard and shot him through

70

the kneecaps while his wife screamed in the kitchen. Then they shot his dog to stop it barking and burned his shop down.

And this was a woman shrunken to the size of a ventriloquist's dummy by a firebomb. She was a Protestant who had done nothing wrong except be in the wrong place at the wrong time, but no terrorist had ever apologised for her death because they reckoned she should have known better than to go shopping in Belfast City Centre.

Look at the photographs, Simon van Stryker had ordered me. Look at them. We were walking along a damp path between the glistening leaves of the magnolias. I remember how it was drifted with fallen petals, the petals turning brown and curling at the edges.

Terrorism, he told me is a means, not a cause. By its very nature it is random: it must kill the child if it is to shock the adult, hurt the helpless if it is to gain the world's attention. Terrorism, he told me again and again, is evil. It did not matter how noble was the cause that the terrorist served, the methods were evil.

'They have no choice!' I tried to argue with him.

'They choose evil,' he said. A terrorist chooses to use the bullet and the bomb because he knows that if he relinquishes those weapons then he is reduced to the level of ordinary politicians who have to struggle with the mundane problems of poverty and unemployment. Terrorists, having no answer to those matters, talk in transcendent terms, claiming their bullets and bombs will make a perfect world, but in the end it is still just terror. If I wanted one creed to cling to over the years, van Stryker told me, then I should remember that no matter how good the cause, it was wrong if it used terror as a means.

'What years?' I had asked.

'The years,' he said, 'that you would otherwise have spent in prison. I saved you from those years, so now you will give them to me. And to America.'

He explained that the CIA's division of counterterrorism used the usual weapons of espionage against the various terrorist and insurgent groups which threatened American interests, but that those weapons were rarely useful. Terrorist cells were wonderfully designed to resist intelligence operations: their secrets were protected by a wall of rumour and a moat of disinformation. Some terrorists did not even claim responsibility for atrocities they performed, preferring that the West should never learn who had inflicted the hurt.

'But we in the West have one terrorist organisation that is all our own, and which is trusted by the others,' van Stryker told me. 'If we can insert one good man into that organisation, then it's just possible that he can travel far and deep into its darkness and one day, in his own good time, bring back news from that journey.'

'You mean me?'

'I mean you.'

'You want me to betray the Irish?'

'Which Irish?' He had rounded on me scornfully. 'The IRA claims to detest the Free State's Dublin government as strongly as they hate London. The Irish electorate doesn't vote for the IRA, and most of it wants nothing more than to see the IRA disappear! Besides, my enemy is not just the IRA, but their friends too: the Libyans and the Palestinians.'

'So how do I reach them?'

'Let the IRA work that out. We'll merely equip you with the skills that will suggest to them that you might make a perfect courier. IRA activists can't move in Europe without the police of a dozen nations watching, but the Garda and the British Special Branch won't take any interest in an American yacht delivery skipper.'

'And what do I make from it?' I had asked truculently.

'You're free, Paul. You'll be taught a trade, given the capital to start your own business, and a ticket to Ireland.'

'And when will you be finished with me?'

'When does a fisherman come home? You bring me back a rich catch in your own good time.'

'Why me?' I asked him.

Van Stryker laughed. 'Because you're a scoundrel, Paul. I can hire any number of straight-arrows, Rhodes scholars every one, but how often do I find a rogue who runs guns to Ireland and who murdered his father's killers? No, don't deny it.' Van Stryker gave me a quirky, almost affectionate smile. 'When you sup with the devil, Paul, it is prudent to use a very long spoon and you're my spoon.'

'And suppose I never come back?'

Van Stryker shrugged. 'I didn't say there was no risk. Maybe you'll leave here and do nothing? Maybe you'll betray this programme? All I can do is offer you a new life and what you make of it is up to you. You aren't the only one I'm sending into the darkness, and if just one of you comes home it might be worth it.'

And now I had come home to tell my secrets. All but one.

GILLESPIE SPENT THE FIRST FEW DAYS constructing a framework of my years abroad. Names, places, dates. Then, when he had the chronology straight and a rough idea of just what secrets I could tell, he brought in the experts to pick my brains. They were the Agency's specialists on the Middle Eastern terrorist groups.

Gillespie took me through the Irish years himself. I told him how I had gone to live in Dublin and then, at Brendan Flynn's request, to Belfast where I had started a yacht surveying-and-delivery service that acted as a cover for the smuggling of weapons, explosives and gunmen across the Irish Sea. I described how I had planted two bombs in Belfast, purely to show the IRA I could be trusted.

'Did anyone die in the explosions?' Carole Adamson asked.

'No,' I said. 'We phoned in warnings.'

'We?' Gillespie asked.

'A guy from Derry called Seamus Geoghegan led the unit.'

'We know of Mr Geoghegan,' Gillespie said. He told me Seamus was now in Boston, fighting off a British attempt to extradite him. Seamus's defence was that he was a political refugee entitled to the protection of the American Constitution, while the British argued that he was a common murderer.

'How did you feel about the two bombings?' Gillespie asked.

Outside it was snowing gently, covering the already snow-heaped bushes with a new layer of glittering white.

'I was doing what van Stryker wanted me to do. I was infiltrating the IRA.' I said it defiantly.

'But did you enjoy it?' Gillespie probed.

'It was exciting,' I allowed. 'You take risks when you plant a bomb, and you don't want the excitement to end, so when the job's done you go to a bar and drink. You boast. You listen to other men boasting.' That was true, but I could just as easily have said that we got drunk because we did not want to think about what we had just done. Because we knew that nothing had been achieved by the bomb and that nothing ever would be achieved by it.

'You have a conscience about what you did?' Carole Adamson asked.

'I was doing it for America, wasn't I?'

And for America I had triumphed when, in 1980, the IRA asked me to be their liaison officer with other terrorist groups. They saw me as a man who could move about the world without attracting suspicion, and suggested I moved to Europe where my existence would provoke even less attention. I took the marine business to Nieuwpoort where I hired Hannah as my part-time secretary, rescued a cat from the alleyway opposite my house, and began trawling the dark seas for van Stryker's profit.

'What sort of business did you conduct with these other terrorist groups?' Gillespie asked in his mild monotonous voice.

I spread my hands as if to suggest the answer could go on for ever, but then offered a short version. 'The Basques were after our bombing expertise, especially our electronic timers, while the Palestinians got a kick out of providing us with weaponry. I was a kind of procurement officer with them. Most of the weapons came from Russia and the explosives from Czechoslovakia, but the Kremlin didn't want their involvement to be too obvious so they used Gaddafi as a middleman.'

'And that was the extent of Gaddafi's involvement?'

I shook my head. 'Whatever the IRA wants, Gaddafi will give them, because he hates Britain.' Gaddafi's hatred had intensified following Prime Minister Thatcher's permission for the American bombers to use British bases for their attack on Tripoli. After that raid nothing had been too good for the Provisional IRA. They had become Gaddafi's chosen instruments of vengeance.

'He gives more than weapons?' Gillespie asked.

'Weapons, advice, refuge. I know they've sent at least two guys to Tripoli to learn interrogation techniques.'

The first CIA experts arrived from Langley. There was a small man with pebble-glasses who knew an extraordinary amount about how illegal immigrants were smuggled into the South of France, and wanted to know whether terrorist groups used the same routes. I gave him what help I could. Another man, dry as a stick, tried to trace the financial links between Libya and the various groups, while a third came to ask me about the East German training camp at Tantow which I had visited twice. Every day there were more photograph albums, more pictures, more identifications.

A dark-haired woman arrived to talk about Libya and its support of terrorism. She showed me a photograph of Shafiq and I told her about his elegant suits and his penchant for cachous and Gauloise cigarettes. She wanted to know about the methods Shafiq had used to contact me, the places we had met and the codes we had devised for our telephone conversations. I wondered how long it would be before some Western agent dragged Shafiq into a waiting car.

She was attractive, with a quick face and a sharp mind.

'Now let us talk about il Hayaween,' the CIA woman said.

I dutifully described his face, his clothes, his mastery of English, his sunglasses, his Blancpain watch, his injured right hand and his taste for American cigarettes. She also wanted some confirmation of the legends about il Hayaween, but I had only heard rumours, such as the stories of his massacre of Israeli schoolchildren.

Gillespie, who sat in on all the sessions, shuddered. 'How does a man live with the knowledge of a deed like that?'

'Maybe he has no imagination?' Carole Adamson suggested from her customary seat in the window.

I shook my head. 'The best killers have imagination. To be as cunning as il Hayaween you must have imagination. That's what makes him so good. But he also thinks he's doing God's work.'

'Do the IRA think they're doing God's work?' Gillespie asked without a trace of irony.

I shook my head. 'Religion in Ireland just defines which side you're on. The Troubles are about people who feel they have no control over their own lives, people who live in public housing and have no jobs and eat bad food and smoke themselves to death. There's no future, no hope, so all that's left is the pleasure of revenge. What else can the poor bastards do? They know the south doesn't like them, and that the Brits would like nothing better than to get the hell out, and so they fight back the only way they can; with bullets and bombs and the pleasure of knowing they're reducing other people to their own level of misery.'

Gillespie seemed about to reply, but suddenly, shockingly, a telephone rang. He hurried to a recess at the back of the library where he spoke a couple of words before coming slowly back to the table with a look of surprise on his face. 'It's the war,' he said aloud and to no one in particular. 'It started last night. We're at war.'

8

American and allied bombers were flying over the kingdom of Nebuchadnezzar. Tomahawk cruise missiles were hissing above the Land of the Two Rivers where Eden had once flourished and Babylon, the flower of all cities, had blossomed. Gillespie suggested we break off the debriefing to watch the television in the dining room. The news seemed impossibly optimistic, telling of incredibly accurate allied bombing and remarkably light aircraft losses. There was no word yet of an Iraqi response and no news of terrorist attacks.

When the news programme was over we broke for lunch. After the meal Gillespie courteously asked the dark-haired woman if she would mind waiting a few moments before resuming her questioning, and asked me one more time about the fifty-three Stingers.

Gillespie's problem was that neither the FBI nor the CIA could find a single substantiating fact for my story of the meeting in Miami and the sale of the missiles. Gillespie brought me photographs of warehouses close to Hialeah Racetrack, but even when I identified the building in which I had seen the Stinger, it had led nowhere.

As Gillespie took me back to the library for the afternoon session, he told me that the telephone number in Ireland had proved to belong to a sixty-eight-year-old spinster who sold religious statuettes, while Brendan Flynn, questioned by the Irish police about a meeting in Miami, blithely retorted that he had been attending a conference on the future of Ireland at the University of Utrecht.

'Michael Herlihy has two Boston lawyers willing to testify that he was taking depositions on that day, while Marty Doyle claims to have been driving Herlihy around Boston.' Gillespie looked at me with silent reproof. 'I also have to tell you,' he went on, 'that the British and Irish authorities have heard nothing about Stingers!'

'I saw one.'

'We'll keep looking,' he said, though without enthusiasm, and then he turned to the dark-haired woman. 'You wanted to raise a particular matter with Mr Shanahan?'

'Hasbaiya,' she said bluntly.

I turned to her. Of course they wanted to know about Hasbaiya, but the very thought of the place made me go tense, and I was aware of Carole Adamson's scrutiny. 'I've been to Hasbaiya,' I said as easily as I could.

'How often?'

'Often enough.'

Hasbaiya was the most notorious of the Palestinian training camps, a graduate school of death. It was not the biggest terrorist-training camp in the world, but Hasbaiya was the star in that dark firmament of evil. 'Did you attend training courses there?' the woman asked.

'No. My visits were just to introduce trainees.' I explained that no one could attend Hasbaiya without being vouched for by someone the Palestinians trusted, and I had been the person who verified that the trainees I took to the camp were who they claimed to be and not some American or Israeli agent. 'I introduced four IRA men, one woman, and three Basques.'

'Tell us about the camp.'

I described it. Hasbaiya was built in the grounds of an old winery on the upper slopes of the Lebanon's Beqa'a Valley. Most of its

76

territory was used as a training ground to turn Palestinian refugees into storm troopers, but at the top of the camp was a more secret area where terrorists came to perfect their skills. Hasbaiya used death as an integral part of its syllabus. Every trainee went to Hasbaiya knowing that men and women died there, and that to be squeamish in the face of that slaughter was to demonstrate unworthiness.

Gillespie broke in. 'You're saying trainees died?'

'Sometimes, yes.'

'For what reason?' he asked in his precise manner.

'They didn't have to have a reason.' I hesitated again, wondering how to explain the inexplicable. 'Were you ever in the army?'

'The Marine Corps.'

'Well, I'm told that sometimes the army or the Marines will give a recruit a live rabbit and tell him it's dinner, but if the recruit doesn't have the guts to kill the rabbit then he goes hungry.'

I talked of an American girl, a Harvard graduate, who had gone to Hasbaiya full of the fervour of one who would change the world. 'I saw her strangled with copper wire, just as a demonstration.'

'So who was the demonstrator?' Gillespie sounded horrified.

'Another trainee was ordered to kill her, and if he'd have hesitated or disobeyed, then he'd have been the next to die. It was their way of making the trainees rethink their attitude to death.' I paused, knowing I had not given the real flavour of Hasbaiya; the febrile excitement that infected the place, the enthusiasm for killing and the triumph of mastering its dangers.

'Did you kill anyone at Hasbaiya?' Gillespie asked.

'I told you, I wasn't a trainee. I just escorted people there.'

'That doesn't answer the question,' Carole Adamson said with an unaccustomed asperity.

'I did kill a man, yes,' I admitted.

'Were you ordered to?'

I shook my head. 'It was a fight. A guy called Axel picked the fight with me. God knows why.'

'When was that?' Gillespie asked.

'On my last visit, in nineteen eighty-six.'

'How did you kill him?'

'With a heavy blow,' I said. I had told only a tiny shred of the truth. The rest of the tale was my nightmare and not to be shared.

Gillespie was consulting the early pages of his notebook. 'Eighty-six,' he said, 'was when the IRA stopped trusting you. Was that anything to do with Hasbaiya?'

I hesitated again. Outside the window the snow was dazzling, glinting with a billion specks of light. 'Yes,' I admitted, knowing that in the end I would have to tell a part of the story. 'I took an American girl to Hasbaiya, and she accused me of being a CIA agent.'

'The girl's name?' Gillespie was writing in his book.

'Roisin Donovan,' I said as casually as I could. 'I think she spelt her first name R-O-I-S-I-N.'

'American, you say?' He frowned at me.

'Like me,' I said, 'tribal Irish. But she came from Baltimore.'

'So tell me about her.'

I feigned ignorance. 'To be honest I didn't know too much about her, except that she'd moved to Northern Ireland and was very active in the women's section of the Provisional IRA.' I could feel my heart thumping and I was sure Carole Adamson must be registering my discomfort. I myself was horribly aware of everything in the room; the crackle of the fire, the creak of my chair, the scrape of Gillespie's pencil on the pages of his notebook.

'Why did she accuse you?' Gillespie asked. 'Describe the circumstances to me.'

I took a breath. 'I took her to Hasbaiya. We reached the camp and I took her to the commandant's quarters. She went inside, spoke with Malouk, the commandant, and ten minutes later he asked me to stay on in the camp for a few days. Malouk wasn't a man you argued with, so I said sure, and that night he arrested me.'

'Because Roisin Donovan had accused you?'

'Yes. She knew about this programme,' I said accusingly, 'and she said I was one of van Stryker's agents.'

'She knew his name?' Gillespie sounded horrified.

'No. But she knew the broad outlines of his idea.'

'So what did they do?'

'They sent a message to Ireland to discover whether anyone there suspected me, and that message saved me. Seamus Geoghegan had taken refuge in Roisin's apartment, and on the very day she'd left for the Lebanon he'd been arrested by the Brits. They claimed to have been given information by an informer, and it could only have been Roisin. So it seemed that she was the traitor, not me, and that she was merely trying to spread the guilt to confuse everyone.' I made a rueful face. 'But even so she'd tarred me with suspicion, and that suspicion was enough to make them cut me out of the game.'

'What happened to Miss Donovan?' Gillespie asked.

'She was shot,' I said bleakly.

There was silence. Carole Adamson had scribbled a note which she now leaned forward to slide down the table. Gillespie unfolded the scrap of paper, then screwed the note into a ball and tossed it at the fire, but the ball bounced off the mantel and rolled onto the hearth rug. 'How much time did you spend in her company? I mean, on the way to Hasbaiya?'

'Three days. We met in Athens, flew to Damascus, then drove to the Lebanon.'

'What did you talk about on your journey?'

'Nothing much,' I said. 'She wasn't very sociable.'

'Did you like her personally?' Gillespie pressed me.

'Like her? I don't know.' I was feeling excruciatingly uncomfortable. 'Hell! She isn't important.'

There was silence again. The light was fading outside, and the dark-haired woman looked at her watch. 'I should be going, Peter.' She spoke to Gillespie. 'I hate driving in the dark.'

'Of course.' The spell was broken. People round the table moved, stretched, made small talk. The woman thanked me for my time, said I had been helpful, then followed Carole Adamson into the hall to find her coat. Gillespie said he needed to visit the bathroom.

They left me alone in the library. Seamus had once told me that conscience could be diluted in alcohol, and now I helped myself to a bottle of rye whiskey kept in the drinks cabinet and carried it back to the deep library window. There I watched the snow, drank, and watched the snow again. Then I remembered the ball of paper lying on the hearth rug, so I turned and picked it up, uncrinkled the paper, and read Carole Adamson's urgent words. *He's telling lies!*

And no wonder, by God, no wonder.

ROISIN HAD BEEN LUCKY in one thing only; she had died swiftly.

I later heard that Brendan Flynn had himself requested this act of mercy. He claimed that Roisin had been given neither the time nor the opportunity to betray the Palestinians, only the Irish, and that the Irish should therefore set the manner of her death. I had always wondered if Brendan asked the favour because he too had been one of her lovers. Whatever, Roisin was taken to a dry gully beyond the camp and shot. She took one bullet in the head and her blood had splashed onto the yellow, sulphurous rocks. I remembered her look of outrage and defiance as she had died.

I was ordered to bury her there on the hillside. A German called Axel offered to stay with me, though he did little to help as I hacked a shallow grave with a long-helved spade. I wondered why he had volunteered, and only began to understand when he stopped me from rolling Roisin's thin corpse into the stony earth. 'I want to look at her,' he said in his heavily accented English, 'she was very pretty.' And then he leaned down and ripped Roisin's flimsy shirt open.

'Cover her up!' I said. 'It isn't right to bury her half-naked.'

Axel had squinted up at me. 'I think you have American bourgeois inhibitions. You should deal with that. It isn't healthy.'

'I said cover her up!' I snapped.

'OK! OK!' But instead of pulling the torn shirt over her body he caressed her and it was at that moment I hit him with the edge of the spade. He remained alive all the time that I took to bury Roisin and to cover her shallow grave with a heap of stones. In the end he died. I did not bury him. I left him to the wild-winged creatures that screamed in the night, then I carried my bloodied spade back to the camp where I confessed my deed. No one in Hasbaiya cared that Axel had been killed.

Outside the window the snow fell with the coming night.

THE AIR WAR IN THE GULF blazed on, yet still no reprisals seared America. No planes tumbled from the sky, no bombs slashed at city centres. Gillespie still questioned me about the Cubans in Miami, but I sensed he no longer believed a word of my tale.

The days passed in a dull rhythm. I turned the pages of photograph albums and dredged up memories of meetings years before. I watched the breakfast television news every morning, and one day a news bulletin told of a bomb attack in London. The Provisional IRA had parked a roofless van in Whitehall, and the van had concealed a battery of mortars that had launched their bombs against Downing Street. The new Prime Minister and his cabinet had narrowly escaped injury. Later that morning, Gillespie asked me about the attack. I could only offer my strong suspicion that the operation had originally been planned as a strike against Margaret Thatcher, but that the plan's execution had been delayed to become a part of Iraq's worldwide terrorist revenge. Two more bombs struck London, both at train stations. One commuter was killed. I suggested to Gillespie that the Provisionals had been driven to such crudities by their eagerness to convince Saddam Hussein that they were cooperating.

In the days following the IRA attacks Gillespie pressed hard about my knowledge of IRA active service units, but I knew nothing. The only top IRA men I knew were Brendan Flynn and Seamus

Geoghegan. The rest were already dead, or else I had never met them.

I knew the debriefing was coming to an end when Gillespie asked about my future, offering to give me the benefits of the Federal Witness Protection Program. 'We'll give you a new name, a new social security number, a new job, and a settlement grant somewhere far away from your old haunts. No one could possibly trace you.'

'You'll make me a school janitor in North Dakota? Thank you, but no. I'm going back to the Cape.'

He frowned. 'Is that sensible? You'll have made enemies. They'll know where to find you.'

'I don't want to hide.'

He half smiled. 'You need the risk, is that it?'

'I like the Cape, that's all. It's home.'

'Then so be it.'

NEXT EVENING, AT LONG LAST, Simon van Stryker came to offer me his blessing. I received no warning of his coming, but when we gathered in the library before dinner I found a tray had been placed on the table with an ice bucket, crystal glasses, a soda syphon, two kinds of Scotch and a bottle of sherry. 'Is this a celebration?' I asked.

'In a way, yes,' Gillespie said, then he turned to the window as the sound of a helicopter thumped through the library's double glazing. A brilliant beam of light swept across the darkening snow, then shrank as the helicopter descended in a sparkling white cloud and settled onto the snow-covered lawn. None of us spoke.

Moments later the heavy front door banged hollowly and there was a mutter of voices in the hall. Then the library door was thrust open to reveal a tall, smiling man clothed in faultless evening dress and it was suddenly hard to imagine Simon van Stryker dressed in any other way. His hair was whiter than I remembered and I guessed he must be in his sixties by now, but he looked very fit and his face was still lean and animated. He strode across the room. 'Paul Shanahan! You kept the faith!' He held out his hand. I shook it awkwardly.

Van Stryker greeted Carole Adamson. He held out his hand to Gillespie. 'You've had a long task, well done.' He smiled at us, filling the room with an air of vibrant intelligence. He held his hands to the fire, then nodded acceptance of a whisky. 'But a very small one, Peter. I'm expected at a dinner at the White House tonight. I shall be late, but that's better than not showing up at all.' He stood in front of the fire, staring about the high-ceilinged library with its rows of indigestible reading. 'Some extraordinary men have told us their life-stories in

this room, Paul. I like to think of it as America's confessional.'

'Do I get absolution now?'

Van Stryker laughed at my question. He was clearly not staying long, but I was glad he had made the effort to come to this snowbound mansion. I needed to see him. For twelve years he had been my mentor.

'So what on earth happened to your Stingers, Shanahan?' van Stryker asked me now. 'Maybe they never existed?'

I shrugged. 'Maybe, but I held one of them. Perhaps maybe it was an operation that went sour.' I did not add that it might have gone sour because some clever bastard had purloined the purchase price.

Van Stryker's gaze was steady. 'What's happened to the rest of Saddam Hussein's revenge?' he asked. 'Has that gone sour too?'

'Maybe,' I said.

'Of all Saddam Hussein's allies only the IRA have drawn blood,' he said bitterly. 'One dead civilian on London's Victoria Station. Is that the very best il Hayaween can produce?'

'They almost got the British Prime Minister,' I pointed out.

Van Stryker shook his head. 'Our analysis shows the Provisionals had that attack planned for months. There has to be something more!' He sounded angry. 'Have you told us everything, Paul?'

'At least three times, it seems.' I told myself that all I had held back was the real price of the missiles and the method by which the Iraqis or the Libyans had tried to pay that price. The gold was mine. Yet I still felt guilty for hiding it. Van Stryker inspired loyalty.

Now he looked at his watch before turning to Gillespie. 'What's your evaluation of Shanahan, Peter?'

'I think the debriefing's been very useful,' Gillespie said, though without enthusiasm. 'We haven't solved the Stinger story, and maybe never will, but what he's told us about the Palestinian groups and Libya has proved most valuable.'

'Dr Adamson, what is your judgment of Paul Shanahan?'

'I'm not sure I have one yet. He's been protecting himself because he resents being questioned, which is why he treated this debriefing like a contest.'

'And who won?' van Stryker asked lightly.

'I lost count of the score.' Carole Adamson was suddenly no longer motherly and comforting, but sharp. 'He's hidden his real self behind a mask of flippancy.'

'You mean he's a deceiver?' Van Stryker was still equable. 'But isn't that why we chose him in the first place?'

'But who is he deceiving? He's hiding more than his personality. Whatever Mr Shanahan sees as being in his own best interest will be kept good and private from us.'

'Paul?' Van Stryker turned courteously towards me.

'I've hidden nothing,' I said with wondrously feigned innocence.

Carole Adamson gave me a disinterested glance. 'I'd ask him a few hard questions about Miss Roisin Donovan. That should lift a corner of his mask.'

Van Stryker held his hands towards the fire. 'We know she lived with you in Belfast, Paul. Yet you claim not to have known her.'

'Aren't I allowed some privacy?'

'Not in America's confessional, no.' He smiled, glanced at me, then looked back to the fire. 'You were lovers?'

'Yes.'

'She had a lot of other lovers. Did you know that?'

I wondered how much they knew about Roisin, but I did not want to ask. Instead of answering van Stryker I challenged him instead. 'Was Roisin one of your Stringless Agents?'

He looked at me with surprise. 'No.'

'Then how the hell did she know so much about this programme?'

He shrugged. 'Did she know so much? Or did she just invent the outlines? It isn't a difficult concept to invent, is it? If what you say about her accusations is right then she only ever talked about generalities, and named no names.'

'Except mine,' I said bitterly.

'And you're alive, Paul, and she's not. You always were a survivor. A rogue and a scoundrel, but a survivor.' He smiled at me. 'I came here to thank you.'

'To thank me?' His gentle courtesy took me by surprise.

'You're my first stringless puppet to come home, and I thank you for it. And we owe you money,' he held up a hand to still my exclamation of surprise, 'I know we said you would not be paid, and officially we owe you nothing, but I'll make sure the Agency diverts some funds in due course. And, of course, we may have more questions for you. Questions are the one thing that never end. Peter knows where you'll be, does he?'

'I'm going back to the Cape,' I told him.

'I envy you. Nancy and I have a summer cottage on the Vineyard, but we never manage enough time there. Life is too busy. We do some sailing when we can.'

'You've got your own boat?' I asked him.

'A Nautor Swan,' he said casually. 'A sixty-one-footer. She's ashore for the winter, on jackstands in our yard.'

It would be a Nautor Swan, I thought, and doubtless Nancy was beautiful and their children successful and the summer cottage on Martha's Vineyard a waterfront mansion. This was the codfish aristocracy. Whereas I had been the poor bastard who dared the Beqa'a Valley and the backstreets of Tripoli. I deserved that gold.

Van Stryker took a business card from his breast pocket. 'If you do dredge anything up from your subconscious and want to talk, then that number will always reach me. And thank you, Paul, for taking the risks you did. Now I really must go!' Van Stryker smiled a courteous farewell to Gillespie and Adamson, shook my hand one more time, and then was gone. Outside the window the helicopter lights dazzled us as the machine hammered up into the darkness.

They let me go next morning, with five hundred dollars in cash and an air ticket to Boston. It was a cold still morning and a new fall of snow glittered under the wintry sun. I pulled on my yellow oilskin and stepped into the bright new day, a free man again. And going home.

9

I knew how badly Michael Herlihy would be wanting to discover the truth of the missing gold; he would be wanting it badly enough to have its location beaten out of me. Yet, at the same time, I knew I could not avoid a confrontation with Michael for ever, because if I was to live the rest of my life on Cape Cod, then Michael and his henchmen would need to be faced down or bought off. I would also need to make sure that Sarah Sing Tennyson was evicted from my property, which meant I had to twist the tail of the bombastic ape who had married my sister.

The bombastic ape was called Patrick McPhee. He was a big-bellied man with a hair-trigger temper; a drunk, a failure, and a bully and a lout. Everyone had warned Maureen against marrying him, but in McPhee my sister had seen a tall handsome young baseball player who boasted of his glorious future in the major leagues. When she became pregnant my father raged at her, provided her generously with a dowry and then walked her down the aisle of Holy Redeemer. Maureen had worn a lace-edged frock of glorious white, and within days she had the first black bruises to show for her trouble. 'The screen door banged into me when I was carrying some shopping,' she told our mother, and a month later she had tripped across a kerbstone, then it was a fall she took while stepping off a bus, and so it had gone on ever since.

Patrick had duly gone to the minor leagues and there failed. He came home to Boston where he drank, put on weight and lived off past glories and Maureen's money. As the taxi drove me down the rain-sodden street to where the family lived, I reflected that all Maureen had to show for her impetuous romance was a crumbling house and five sullen sons who took after their father.

Maureen herself opened the door to my knock and for a moment she just stared. 'Oh, my little brother,' she finally said. She had put on weight and there was a bruise next to her right eye.

'Can I come in?'

'You've come this far, so why not the last step?' She pushed the screen door open and stepped aside to let me into the kitchen. In the corner a television blared.

'Where are the boys?' I asked when she had switched off the set.

'Probably at Roscoe's, playing pool. His lordship's at the Parish, of course, where else?' Maureen sat down at the table and lit a cigarette. The ashtray was overflowing with butts and her fingers were the colour of woodstain. 'You look good. Where in God's name have you been for the last seven years?'

I dropped my sea bag by the door and sat down. 'Mostly in Belgium. Here and there. I really came to see Patrick about that girl, Sarah Sing Tennyson.'

She shrugged. 'I told his honour not to rent the house to her, but things have been tight these last few years.' She studied me across the table. 'You're in trouble, aren't you? I can smell it like the smoke off a bonfire. You know they've been asking about you?'

'Who has?'

'Herlihy and his friends. Are you going to tell me why?'

'No.'

'Why do I even ask?' She struggled to her feet, and reached into a high cupboard for glasses and a bottle of Jameson's. My God, I thought, she was only forty-two yet she looked twenty years older. Then she sat and pushed the whiskey bottle towards me. 'Help yourself.'

'Patrick's going to have to get rid of that Tennyson girl,' I said. 'How much rent is he taking off her?'

'Five hundred a month, and even then he gets to use the house when she's not there. God knows why she lets him.'

'Five hundred?' I was astonished. Sarah Sing Tennyson had to be crazy to pay that much for part-time occupancy.

'Not that I get to see any of the money,' Maureen said bleakly, 'his eminence takes it all for himself.'

'Is he in work?'

'Not so you'd notice. A bit here and there.'

I poured myself a generous finger of my brother-in-law's whiskey. 'When were you last at the Cape?'

'It must be all of four years. His lordship doesn't approve of my going down there. He takes his Parish friends if the girl's not there, but not me.' She drew on the cigarette. I had given Maureen the keys to the Cape house so she could have an escape hatch, but I had never intended Patrick to take the place for his own amusement.

'He won't be going there any longer,' I said, 'I'm moving back in. Have you seen Johnny Riordan lately?'

She shook her head. 'Not for three years. The last time he came here Patrick picked a fight with him and Johnny hasn't visited since.'

'What was the row about?'

She sighed. 'Patrick had just got back from Ireland, so he was sounding off about the Brits, how they were worse than the Nazis, and Johnny wouldn't take him seriously.'

'Patrick went to Ireland!' I could not hide my astonishment.

'The Friends of Free Ireland arranged the trip. They had one week in Dublin and one week in Belfast. Father Shea went from Holy Redeemer, and Michael Herlihy travelled, of course, and some young fellow from the congressman's office went with them. Patrick was full of himself when he got back. He was ready to fight England single-handed! So now he's on the committee. He's planning wars against England when he isn't drinking whiskey or losing money on the horses.' She lit another cigarette from the stub of the first. 'Are you really moving back home?'

'Yes.'

'So what are you going to do?'

'I don't know. Maybe run after the tuna? I could make a good living with a tuna boat.'

'Sure you could.' Maureen knew all about dreams that never came true. She was probably the expert.

I picked up my bag and went to the door. 'You say Patrick's at the Parish?'

'All day. I wish he'd stay there all night, too.' She got to her feet, and put her arms round me. I sensed she was crying inside, whether at her wasted life or for relief at my homecoming, I could not tell.

I kissed her, then drew back slightly and very gently touched the yellow-edged bruise beside her right eye. 'Look after yourself,' I said.

I let the door bang shut and walked away.

THE HALL WAS ALWAYS CALLED 'the Parish', though in fact it was not the parish hall at all, but belonged to one of Boston's many fraternal orders who were happy for their big brick buildings to serve as social clubs where the local Irish community could vent its joys, sorrows and political passions. Those passions were evidenced by two enthusiastic slogans which were painted in green letters on the Parish's side wall: 'Brits Out of Ireland!' and 'Support the Provos!'

The Parish was also where men came to watch the Celts on a giant TV projection screen, and when the Celts were playing even the politics of old Ireland took second place. Yet, that Sunday, when I pushed through the Parish door, the crowd was watching a news channel. The land war in the Gulf had at last begun, and Saddam Hussein's mother of battles was at last being joined.

I pushed through to the bar. The place was crowded and noisy and filled with smoke. I glanced round, saw no sign of Patrick, so instead cocked a finger towards Charlie Monaghan behind the bar. Charlie stared at me, grinned, then abandoned his customers to march down the bar with an outstretched hand. 'Is it yourself, Paulie?' He reached across the bar to embrace me. 'I thought it was a ghost, so I did!'

'How are you?'

'I'm just grand! Just grand! No complaints, now. Have a Guinness on the house, Paulie. My God, it's just like old times!'

I managed to check the ebullient flow long enough to ask where I would find my brother-in-law.

'He's busy in the snug, so he is.' The snug was a back room of the Parish, much given to private business. Charlie slid the Guinness across the bar with a conspiratorial wink. 'He's got Tommy O'Shaughnessy in there.'

'The congressman?' I sounded astonished.

'Aye! The dumb guy who wanted to give Saddam Hussein a whole year to get his army ready.' However dumb Congressman O'Shaughnessy might be, he was still mighty exalted company for Patrick McPhee. Thomas O'Shaughnessy was a thousand-toilet Irish, a Boston aristocrat whose family was one of the richest in Massachusetts. Tommy's grandfather had been an immigrant from County Mayo who had made his fortune in cement manufacture. Tommy's father had more than doubled the family's wealth but, fearing for the company's profits if his son ever took over the family business, he had purchased Thomas a seat in the House of Representatives instead. Rumour had it that the safe Boston constituency had cost the family well over eight million dollars. 'So what's Tommy doing here?' I asked Charlie.

'Plotting, of course.' Charlie leaned across the bar and lowered his voice. 'You know Seamus Geoghegan?'

'Of course I know Seamus. We're old friends.'

'Well, you know he's right here in Boston? The Brits failed to extradite him, but now they're having another go in an appeal court. So we need money to defend him.'

'We being the Friends of Free Ireland?' I guessed.

'You got it, Paulie. Patrick's on the committee. Michael Herlihy really runs it, of course, but Michael needs someone to tally up the cash and keep the membership list in order, and Patrick volunteered after he visited Ireland.'

'So now he's touching O'Shaughnessy for Seamus's legal aid?'

Charlie nodded, then held up a warning hand as he saw me turning to leave. 'But he says he doesn't want to be disturbed.'

'To hell with that. He's family, isn't he?' I winked at Charlie, picked up the Guinness and my sea bag and went to the snug.

There were five of them in there. Two were strangers, but I knew the other three. There was Patrick, Tommy O'Shaughnessy and, to my surprise, the bright boy of Derry, Seamus Geoghegan himself.

'Who the devil . . .' Patrick started to protest when I pushed through the door, then he recognised me and his jaw fell open.

'Patrick. Congressman,' I greeted them with a nod apiece, then smiled at Seamus.

'Paulie!' He stood, arms spread, then came round the table, grinning, and embraced me vigorously. 'You're in dead trouble, you know that?' he whispered in my ear, then stepped back and raised his voice. 'You're looking grand, so you are! Just grand.'

'Watch my Guinness, you ape!' I protested, and placed what was left of my drink on the table. 'How are you doing?'

'We're in executive session here,' Patrick said pompously.

Tommy O'Shaughnessy, a dazzling, handsome youth, looked vaguely worried, but that was his usual expression for the congressman had always gone through life with only one oar in the water. 'You remember me, Congressman?' I asked him.

'Of course,' he said, though he did not use my name, which suggested he did not know me from George Washington. 'Might I introduce Robert Stitch?' Tommy went on with his customary politeness. He used courtesy as a defence against cleverness, and it worked, for he had a reputation, especially among women, of being an appealingly well-behaved boy. 'Robert is one of my congressional aides,' he explained.

Stitch was pure Boston Brahmin, a young codfish aristocrat, who offered me a curt unfriendly nod.

'And that's my lawyer, Chuck Sterndale,' Seamus cut in and jerked his head towards a wild-haired, bearded and bespectacled man. 'Paulie Shanahan was with me in Belfast, so he was,' Seamus told the room happily. 'The first time I did a runner from Derry and the bastards were all over my backside, Paulie put me up in his flat. We had a grand time, didn't we, Paulie?'

'We had good crack.' I used the old Belfast expression.

'You're Irish, Mr Shanahan?' Stitch asked cautiously.

'By ancestry, but I was born not a mile away from this room. Unlike some I can mention, I actually went to Ulster to do my bit for the cause.'

That got to Patrick, as I had meant it to. He glared at me.

'Tell me why you rented out my house, Patrick.' I walked to the back of his chair. 'A five-year lease, Patrick? Five hundred a month? That's thirty thousand bucks. You want to write me a cheque?'

'We'll talk about it later, Paulie.'

'We're talking about it now.' He tried to stand up, but I put my hands on his shoulders and held him down. 'How long has she been there, Patrick? Three years? That's eighteen thousand bucks you've taken already! Have you got it handy?' I reached into his inside jacket pocket and found his wallet that held a stack of twenty-dollar bills, maybe two or three thousand dollars' worth. 'I'll take it as a down payment, Patrick, but I'll be back for the rest. Meanwhile, just tell Miss Sing Tennyson that she's to get the hell out of my home.'

'You can't take that money!' Patrick pleaded. 'That's not mine.'

'But nor is the rent you take off Miss Tennyson.' I bent down and whispered in his ear. 'I'm back home for good now, Patrick, and if I find another bruise on Maureen I'll cut your head off and feed it to the crows, so help me God.' Then I straightened up and belted him across the right side of his head so hard that he squealed with pain and almost fell off his chair. 'Hey, Seamus, come and have a drink at the bar. We'll plan some fishing trips, eh?'

'Sounds grand, Paulie.'

I walked to the door. Robert Stitch was frozen, Patrick was shaking like a leaf while O'Shaughnessy looked terrified. Only Seamus and his lawyer were grinning. 'Keep Seamus out of the hands of the Brits,' I told Chuck Sterndale.

'I'll surely do my best, Mr Shanahan. But some of that money you just took off Mr McPhee would help me do it.'

'Mr McPhee owes me thousands more, and it's all yours, OK?' I looked at Patrick. 'I'm having another drink with Charlie Monaghan now,' I told him, 'and after that I'm catching a bus for the Cape. You'll know where to find me. See you in a minute, Seamus.'

I picked up my bag and went to the bar where Charlie Monaghan, who had a perfect sense for when trouble was brewing, gave me another Guinness and made himself scarce. Most of the room was still watching the big screen for war news. I saw Herlihy's sidekick, Marty Doyle, scuttle across the far side of the room and I guessed he was going to inform his master that I had appeared in Boston. I waved at him, but he ignored me like a healthy man avoiding the gaze of someone stricken by the Black Death.

After a few minutes Seamus joined me at the bar. He was a man as tall as myself, with black hair and scary pale eyes. Except for the eyes, it was a good face, bony and gaunt, a real portrait of a gunman. 'Give us a Powers!' he called to one of Charlie's bar assistants. He was not expected to pay for his drink; no real IRA man ever had to pay for a drink in the Parish.

Seamus lit a cigarette and squinted at me through its smoke. 'Either you're mad to come back here, or you're wearing bullet-proof underpants. Your brother-in-law's talking about you on the telephone and wee Marty Doyle is screaming that Michael Herlihy will cut you off at the knees. They're saying prayers for you already.'

I laughed. I liked Seamus. 'You know it's been the best part of ten years since we met,' I told him.

'As long as that?' He shook his head in disbelief, then shot me a wary look. 'But I'm hearing these stories about you, Paulie, that you did a runner with a lot of money.'

'Only five million in gold,' I said. 'Be reasonable, Seamus.'

He almost choked on his Powers. 'You're mad! They'll never let you get away with it!'

'Who said I had it?' I demanded. 'The boat sank.'

'And so it did, Paulie,' Seamus said, 'and the Brits are giving us back the six counties, and the Pope is giving me a cardinal's hat. Who do you think you're talking to, eh?'

I shrugged. 'It wasn't their money, Seamus. It came from the Iraqis. It had nothing to do with Belfast.'

'That's not what I hear. I hear they paid half a million bucks as a deposit on some Stingers. And that you told them you were bringing the balance!'

'Herlihy should keep his damned mouth shut,' I said.

'He didn't tell me!' Seamus said. 'I heard it from Ireland, so I did. I reckon Brendan Flynn wants your guts for garters.' Seamus had turned to watch the big room with his pale, wary eyes. 'You want me to talk to them? I'll say it was all a misunderstanding.'

'You don't know the half of it,' I said grimly.

'You mean those two who vanished? Liam and Gerry?'

I hesitated, then nodded. 'They're dead.'

Seamus just shook his head. 'Brendan doesn't give a toss about those two. All they did was collect protection money. He'll probably thank you, so he will! For God's sake, Paulie, let me talk to him.'

'Have a try,' I said, though only to make Seamus happy.

'What shall I say? That you'll bring the money in soon?'

'Sure,' I said, not meaning it at all.

'Five million, eh?' Seamus laughed. 'And I remember when you and I couldn't find a quid between us.'

'We were never that skint,' I said, 'but they were good days.'

'Aye, they were. Better than these.' He dropped his cigarette onto the floor and killed it with the toe of his boot. 'People are nice enough here, but it isn't home. The beer's freezing, the summers are hotter than hell, and they're always watching netball on the telly!'

'It's called basketball,' I said, 'and it's Boston's religion.'

He laughed, then shook his head. 'I miss Derry, Paulie. I mean, I know it's not much of a place, but I miss it.'

'I miss Belfast,' I said, and I did, too. It was a dirty, ugly, battered city but I had never been happier than when I had lived there. The brick streets crackled with wit and were warmed by friendship.

Seamus grimaced. 'And family, that's another thing! My dad died last year and I couldn't be with him. And my mam's not well. My brother wrote and told me, but what can I do?'

I remembered Kathleen Donovan telling me how she had met his brother and I suddenly wondered what use was five million bucks without someone to share it with?

Seamus shook his head sorrowfully. 'Hell, Paulie, I just want to go home. The younger lads can do some of the fighting now, eh? I've put a few quid away, so I have, and a scrap of farmland in Derry would do me just grand. A few cattle, some arable, and a tight little house.' He paused, his eyes far away. 'I was thinking of Roisin the other day.' He had reddened with embarrassment, and I wondered just how badly she had humiliated him.

'I often think of her,' I admitted.

'I had a letter from her sister a few weeks back. It came to my lawyer's office. She wanted to know what happened to Roisin, like. What was I to say?'

'The truth?' I suggested, though the word tasted like ash.

'Chuck said I shouldn't write back, in case it was a set-up by the Brits. And what could I have told her anyway? That Roisin was shot by the Arabs?' Seamus stared at the green cut-out shamrocks that decorated the bar's back-mirror. 'She never did betray me, Paulie. No one did. The Brits said they had the information off her, but they were just making trouble, and I reckon their trouble worked for they got her a bullet, right?' He frowned. 'And she was a rare girl. She had a tongue on her though, didn't she just? Never heard a woman speak like it.' He suddenly froze, his eyes staring at the mirror which reflected the far side of the room. 'Are those two boys after you, do you think?'

Two men, both wearing plaid jackets buttoned tight up to their necks, had appeared at the far side of the hall. They were young, broad-chested, and convinced of their own toughness, and neither was trying to hide their interest in me. 'They're looking for me, right enough,' I told Seamus.

'Why?'

'Personal. Patrick wants that money back I just took off him, and he doesn't want to ask me for it himself.'

'Are you sure it's not political?'

I shook my head. 'There wouldn't have been time to get the orders. Do you think Brendan would have me chopped up before he knows where the gold is? No, this is personal, Seamus.'

He grinned. 'Then I'm on your side, Paulie. Two of them and two of us, eh?' He drained the last of his whiskey. 'Do we finish them off?'

'We just frighten them.'

'You go first then. I'll be twenty paces behind.' He made a great play of shaking my hand and saying farewell, then I picked up my bag and pulled on my oilskin. The two men watched me go to the side door, saw that Seamus was ordering another drink, and followed me towards the winter afternoon.

10

In the old days the Parish's side door had opened into an alleyway that ran between the hall and an Italian bakery, but the bakery had long been pulled down to leave a parking lot which was hidden from the road by a high fence. The fence made the lot a fine and private place, in the middle of which an empty police cruiser was now sitting with its engine running, its front doors open, and its emergency lights whipping an urgently lurid glow across the handful of parked vehicles. The cruiser explained why the men had appeared with their plaid coats buttoned to their throats: it was not that the police uniforms would have scared anyone in the Parish, but the two men had wanted to take me quietly. Besides the police cruiser there were two trucks parked in the lot, a red Lincoln Continental and a black Mercedes sports car that must have belonged to O'Shaughnessy for it had a special congressional licence plate.

I cut right, going past the Mercedes towards the gap in the fence. There was a cold wind and a light rain in the darkening air. I heard the Parish side door bang open behind me and felt the adrenalin warm my veins. 'Shanahan!' someone shouted. I turned, but kept walking backwards.

'Freeze there!' The two youngsters were nervous, but were determined to play the scene tough. They fumbled under their tight-buttoned plaid coats for their pistols. They were still trying to extricate their guns when Seamus came out of the Parish door.

I had started walking towards them, feigning innocence. 'You wanted me, boys?'

'Don't mind me, lads.' Seamus sauntered down the steps.

'We just wanted a word with Mr Shanahan. Something private.'

'Private, is it? But Paulie and I are old friends. There's no secrets between us, are there, Paulie?'

'You can talk in front of Seamus,' I said. 'So what is it? A donation for the police orphanage?' I was six paces in front of them and Seamus was three paces behind, and the two cops were both sweating despite the chill wind, and no wonder, for Seamus had a fearsome reputation.

'It's nothing.' One of the two cops decided to back out of the confrontation. 'Nothing at all. Forget it.'

'You're disappointing me, boys.' I took a step closer, and suddenly the Parish side door banged open and an agitated Michael Herlihy appeared on the top step. 'Stop it! You hear me? Doyle, O'Connor? Back off, now, both of you!' Herlihy's voice was sharp as ice. He must have been close by, perhaps in the back room of Tully's Tavern, when Marty Doyle had told him of my appearance. Herlihy, hearing that Patrick was having me beaten up by the Parish's tame police, saw the small matter of five million dollars being complicated, and so he had come full pelt out of his lair to head off the trouble. 'Whatever you were doing,' he ordered the two policemen, 'stop it!'

'We were just leaving! It was all a mistake.'

The relieved policemen moved to walk past me towards their car, but I put out a hand to stop them. 'Hadn't you heard, boys? The Parish has got valet parking these days. Isn't that right, Seamus?'

'Right enough, Paulie.'

Seamus was not restraining the policemen, but neither cop dared move a muscle as I climbed into their squad car and shifted it into reverse. I smiled through the windscreen, then rammed my foot onto the accelerator. The police car shot backwards, smack into the brick sidewall of the neighbouring hardware store. 'Sorry, boys!' I shouted. 'I'm more used to boats than I am to cars.'

Seamus was laughing. Herlihy glared but did not try to stop me, while the two police officers just stood like whipped children. I pulled forward, hearing the tinkle of broken brake lights falling to the ground, then rammed the accelerator again, this time aiming the car at O'Shaughnessy's Mercedes. Herlihy closed his eyes as I rammed the police cruiser hard into the flank of the sleek black sports car. There was a horrible mangling noise.

A dozen men had come out of the Parish, attracted by the squeal and crash of tortured metal. Herlihy, tight with fury, turned and ordered them back inside. O'Shaughnessy and his aide were wondering if the world had slipped gears while Patrick McPhee, knowing he had started this madness, fled in panic from Michael's anger.

'Here goes!' I shouted. 'I'll get it right this time!' I shifted into reverse again, slammed my foot on the accelerator and crashed the car back sickeningly hard into the brick wall. I killed the engine and climbed out, to see that the boot lid of the police car was spectacularly buckled. The cruiser also had a crumpled bumper and had lost a headlight and the best part of a wheel arch, while the body panels of the congressman's Mercedes were horribly dented and gouged. 'Replace it with an American car, Congressman,' I called to him.

O'Shaughnessy's aide hurried the congressman back into the Parish as the two policemen stalked past me. 'Damn you, Shanahan,' one of them muttered, then they climbed into their wrecked cruiser and, with a foul scraping sound, drove out of the lot.

Michael Herlihy glared at me. 'That wasn't clever, Paul,' he said.

'It wasn't meant to be clever, Michael, just a scrap of fun.'

Herlihy picked his way through the puddles of the parking lot until he was standing close beside me. 'Where have you been these last few weeks, Shanahan?' He had waved Seamus aside, wanting to speak privately with me.

'I've been chatting to the CIA, Michael.' I smiled down into his thin, bloodless face. 'I got worried that the Arabs weren't sending the Stingers to Ireland, but planned to use them here. I knew you wouldn't have wanted that to happen, Michael, it would have been bad for the movement's image, wouldn't it now? So I played the patriot game.'

He ignored my blarney. 'Where in God's name is the money?' He was intense, hissing his words, his body tight as a whip.

I came out with my story, though it seemed a lot less convincing now than when I had first planned it. 'I should have told you, Michael, the boat sank. It was a rotten boat. It went down off Sardinia. I tried to save the two Belfast boys, but they panicked and the boat went down like a stone with them still inside. And with all that gold weighing the boat down, they never stood a chance.'

'Don't tell me lies.' The rain flecked his glasses as his voice gathered intensity. 'You've gone too far, Paul, and Ireland wants you to answer some questions.'

'You're the one who'll have to answer questions,' I said. 'That money didn't come from Libya, it came from Saddam Hussein, the bastard who's doing his level best to slaughter American boys right now. So what you're going to do now, Michael, is forget the money, forget the Stingers, and forget me.'

'You're insane!' Michael's voice rose to a shrill intensity.

Seamus crossed the lot to act as a peacemaker. 'I'm taking care of it, Michael,' he said soothingly. 'Paulie will find the money.'

'Leave this alone, Seamus!' Herlihy snapped, then looked back to me. 'I'll have you killed, so help me! You bring me the money, Shanahan, all of it, or you'll wish you'd never been born.' He turned and stalked across the parking lot, then stopped at the Parish's side door for a parting shot. 'There's a British Consulate in Boston, Paul. It takes one phone call, just one, and I can have the Brits on your back. I won't weep for you.' He went inside.

'The Brits wouldn't dare come here, would they?' Seamus asked.

'God, no! Michael's always seeing Brits under the bed. He thinks he's on their wanted list and it makes him feel like a hero. His biggest danger is that he'll get a shock off his electric toothbrush. He's a jerk.'

'But a dangerous one.' Seamus picked up my discarded sea bag and tossed it to me. 'Look after yourself, Paulie. And don't worry about Michael. I'll say it was all a misunderstanding and that you'll be bringing the money.'

'You're a grand man, Seamus.'

I said farewell, then walked away, and I hoped to God that the Brits did not have an undercover team in New England for I was already playing two sides against a third and I did not need a fourth.

But those worries could wait. Instead, through the spitting rain and with Patrick's money in my pocket, I walked to the bus and was carried home. To Cape Cod.

IT WAS DARK when the taxi dropped me off. I could not be sure that some nasty surprise would not be waiting at the house and so I had told the driver to drop me off at the convenience store close to the track which led over the sandy ridge. I bought myself some groceries and then walked back to the track which twisted through the pine woods to my house on the salt marsh. I stopped on the ridge and watched the marsh for a long time, but all seemed innocent under the high scudding clouds and so I walked down the driveway to discover that Sarah Sing Tennyson had changed the locks. 'Hell!'

I found a decent-sized stone, went to the kitchen window and broke through one of the glass panes. No alarm shrieked, no one called out, so I guessed Sarah Sing Tennyson was not in residence. I unlatched the window catch, then heaved up the sash window and crawled through onto the draining board. I pushed two cups and a plate off it to shatter on the kitchen floor, but at least I was home. I groped around the kitchen until I found the newly installed light switch.

I had made more enemies than Saddam Hussein in the past few weeks so my first priority was to defend myself. I went into the empty garage and found that most of my old tools were still under the bench. I took the crowbar back into the living room where Captain Alexander Starbuck had built a broad hearth out of four massive stone slabs. I lifted the right-hand slab, shifting it aside to reveal a deep hole, the best of the many hiding places constructed in the house during Prohibition. At high spring tides it could flood, but those rare tides had never affected the whiskey hidden in the hole, nor had they pierced the layers of thick plastic sheeting I had sealed round the long wooden box that I now wrestled up onto the hearth. I had last seen this box when I had hidden it seven years before.

Then I swore as the telephone rang. There was a loud click in the kitchen and suddenly Sarah Sing Tennyson's voice sounded. 'I'm sorry I can't speak with you right now, but if you'd like to leave a message after the tone I'll get back to you just as soon as I can.' Another click, and then a man's voice spoke. 'Where are you, Sarah? Listen, just give me a call, OK? This is William, just in case you've forgotten who I am.' I grinned in sympathy for poor William, then laughed as I thought of the FBI or the CIA trying to decode the lovesick fool's message. The phone had to be bugged.

I carried my unearthed box over to the long table and used a pair of Sarah Sing Tennyson's scissors to slash through the plastic wrapping. I levered the top off the box and found the contents just as I had left them. The US army issue Colt .45 automatic dating from the Second World War. Its magazine held a paltry seven rounds, but they were powerful. I cleaned the pistol meticulously, dry-fired it a few times to make sure that everything was working, then pushed one of its magazines home. Feeling a good deal safer, I dropped the gun into a pocket of my oilskin jacket.

I found some of my tenant's cardboard and masking tape that I used to make a crude repair to the window and afterwards used her coffee and grinder to make myself a pot of fresh-brewed. Then I lit a fire and made some sandwiches. Food had rarely tasted better. It was like the magic moment at the end of a freezing sea watch, when junk food thrown together in a pitching galley tastes like a banquet.

I turned off the electric lights and carried the coffee to the bay window. Over the wind's fretful noise I could just hear the roar of the distant ocean breakers. Closer, a thousand rivulets of salt water were creeping up from the bay, flooding the salt marshes and rippling the eel grass where the most succulent scallops grew. There were oysters too, and the best clams in the world, and mussels and lobsters to make an appetite drool. In the old days it was a rare house that did not have a deer carcass hung up at winter's beginning, and in the autumn there were ducks and beach-plums, cranberries, wild blackberries. It was a good place to live.

And to die, I remembered. I went back to the box and lifted out my second gun, a semi-automatic M1 Carbine. It was a simple battle-ready rifle dating from the Second World War, yet it fired beautifully. I cleaned and loaded the M1 which, like the Colt, had been stolen in Boston for eventual delivery to the IRA. I had kept both guns for myself, and now they would help protect Saddam Hussein's gold.

Thinking of the gold reminded me that in the morning I must find a public telephone to discover if Johnny Riordan had any news of *Rebel Lady*. In the meantime I carried the two guns upstairs, where I found my antique whaling harpoon on the bedroom wall. The harpoon was a nasty piece of work; its rusting iron head was six foot long, wickedly barbed, and socketed onto a wooden pole handle that gave it another six foot of reach. I used the harpoon to brace the door in case an enemy tried to surprise me in the night, then I undressed, laid the guns close to hand, climbed under Sarah Sing Tennyson's patchwork quilt, and slept.

I SLEPT LIKE THE DEAD. I slept through the dawn and into the morning, and I did not wake till the tide was pushing in again to the marsh channels. A bright winter sunlight streaked the yellow panelled wall and lit the stripped-pine chest of drawers. I could smell the ocean, and I could smell the scent of Sarah Sing Tennyson on her sheets and pillowcases. It had been so long since I had smelt a woman's smell and I immediately thought of Roisin.

Sometimes I told myself that I had romanticised Roisin's memory to protect myself from other entanglements, yet in truth I wanted entanglement. I wanted to wake to a house full of noise and children and dogs and muddle. I wanted a wife. I wanted what passed in this world for normality, and yet was such a rare privilege for it was only made possible by love.

I rolled over onto my back. My bedroom dormer faced east towards the sea and once, when the bay's tide had been unusually high, I had seen the water's dappled ripples reflected by the rising sun onto this bedroom ceiling. I had always dreamed of putting an old duck punt in the closest channel and, at the bay's deep-water edge, where a secret tideway wriggled past Pochet Island, I had planned to moor a small cat-boat that a child could sail, for this was God's adventure playground, a place where a child could play wild and yet feel safe. It was a place to romp with dogs along the tideline and to take a canoe across the bay to where the ocean beaches stretched empty.

Except I would raise no children here, and Roisin was dead. God, I thought, I was forty years old! In the trade of terror that made me an old, old man. And now I would face my enemies here. Like a beast seeking refuge, I had come home, but only to play for the biggest stakes of all. If I won I would be left here alone with all the money a man would ever need, and if I lost I would die, shot down like a dog. Now, in this light-flooded morning, I had to think where danger lay.

Brendan Flynn was dangerous. But Brendan was far away and he would be loath to set an operation on American soil.

Michael Herlihy was angry, for I had stung him, but he was not a fool. I knew he would make some effort to retrieve the gold, but the effort would be subtle and, in the end, like the lawyer he was, he would probably agree to a settlement.

Which left the most dangerous enemy of all, il Hayaween, but would he really come for me in America? This was not his turf. I dared not underestimate il Hayaween, but I had come to the one place that would give him pause for, though the Palestinians understood Europe, America unnerved them.

Then tyres suddenly crunched loud on the clam-shell drive and I flung back the bedclothes, pulled the harpoon away from the door and, taking the safety catch off the loaded carbine, ran down the steep stairs. I was crouched behind the front door before the vehicle had come to a halt, my heart pounding. I listened. The crunching sound of the tyres stopped and I heard a click as the vehicle's door opened, then I ripped open the house door and aimed the carbine straight at the intruder's chest.

Straight at Kathleen Donovan who stared at me, and I suddenly knew there was no one else I would rather have seen, for if my conscience was ever to be clear then she was as good a person as any to begin the process. Then I saw her eyes widening in alarm at the sight of the gun. 'No!' she said. 'No!'

'I'm sorry.' I made the gun safe and put it aside. 'I'm sorry,' I said again, and then I realised I had come downstairs stark naked. 'You just woke me. Come on in. I'll get dressed.' I ran back upstairs and prayed that this time I would not miss my chance. Not this time, not now that I was home at last, and now that I was so utterly alone.

SHE WAITED OUTSIDE THE HOUSE, refused my offer of coffee, but instead asked to walk towards the sea.

'How did you know I was here?' I asked her.

'I didn't. I was just hoping.' She walked ahead of me on the narrow track, staring down as she walked. 'If you must know'—she finally turned and looked defiantly back into my face—'I hired a private detective, and he found this address.'

'So you just came here?' I asked.

'Because I want to know why you lied about Roisin,' she said. 'Or do you still insist you never knew her?'

'I knew her,' I admitted.

We walked on in silence. The sand on the path had been bleached white as bone by the dry winter air and by the day's bright sun. The wind was light, coming cold from the northeast. Kathleen wore a black overcoat with red cuffs and a tall collar that stuck up to meet her tasselled woollen hat. 'Is she dead?' she asked persistently.

'Yes. Four years now.' We were speaking very stiffly.

'How?'

100

I could feel myself shaking, and I only trusted myself to answer with one word. 'Shot.' I sighed. My breath misted in the air. 'She died,' I said, 'in a Palestinian training camp called Hasbaiya. She'd gone there to learn about killing, but instead they killed her.'

'Why?' A terrible intensity in the voice.

'Because they thought she was a CIA agent.'

'Oh, my God.' I thought for a second that Kathleen was going to fall and I held out a hand to steady her, but she shook my help away and walked on alone. She turned after a few paces and raised her green eyes in a challenge. 'Why didn't you tell me this in Belgium?'

'Because . . .' I faltered, but I had promised myself that I would tell this girl the truth. 'I know it'll sound stupid, but I thought you might be working for the Brits.'

She laughed scornfully. 'First Roisin is in the CIA, now I work for the British?'

I tried to explain. 'Concealment's a way of life. I'm sorry, I really am. I wanted to tell you, but I dared not.'

'So why tell me now?' She had begun walking again.

'Because I'm out of it now. It's all over for me.'

'Out of what?' she asked derisively. 'The IRA?'

'I worked for the CIA,' I told her.

She glanced at me, looked away, and I saw that she did not believe me. 'And Roisin too?' Kathleen asked.

'She wasn't in the CIA.'

'Then why did they shoot her?'

So I told her about Seamus's betrayal, and that too sounded lame, and then I went back to the beginning, right to the very beginning in the smoky Dublin pub when Roisin had come in from the night with raindrops glistening in her hair, and on through to the day when I had piled the stones on her grave. I left Axel out of the tale, and I sketched over the end of our relationship, but the rest was truthful enough.

Kathleen walked in silence for a long time. To our right I could see my house across the bay's mouth while to my left the ocean seethed beyond the dunes. 'I always wanted Roisin to come and live here,' I confessed to Kathleen, 'I had this dream of raising children and of going shopping on weekends and of sailing on the bay.'

Kathleen looked up at me, surprise on her face. 'Roisin was never very motherly, unless she changed when she reached Ireland?'

I shook my head. 'She never changed. She was Cathleen ni Houlihan till the very day she died.' Cathleen ni Houlihan was the great fighting heroine of Irish legend.

Kathleen smiled in recognition. 'When Roisin was eight she offered to pay me her weekly allowance for the rest of her life, if I would just change names with her. She so wanted to be called Kathleen.' We had reached the innermost dunes and now threaded through them towards the sea. 'Did Roisin join the IRA because of you?'

'Not because of me, no, but I introduced her.'

'Did she kill anyone?' It was a hostile question.

'Not directly, at least I never heard that she did.' I walked in silence for a few paces. 'I tried to stop her getting involved, but it was no good. And after I left Belfast she stayed on by herself. But they didn't

102

really trust her, not like their own people. They used outsiders like us when we could be useful, but they never really trusted us.'

Kathleen still walked with her head down as we climbed the last line of dunes before the sea.

'Did you betray her?'

'Me?'

'You said you were CIA. So you must have informed on her along with everyone else.' Her voice was hostile, her accusations wild.

'It didn't work like that.' I knew I dared not describe van Stryker's Stringless Program. 'I didn't inform on her. I loved her.'

'Did you want her to live in Belgium with you?'

'More than I wanted anything else.' I walked past a dead gull's feathered bones and I spoke of a love's ending. 'Roisin thought my job in Belgium would be dull. It was too far from the armed struggle, you see. She desperately wanted to be involved at the heart of things, and so she refused to come with me. We used to meet whenever I could persuade her. I wanted to marry her,' I told Kathleen, 'but she wasn't interested.' I stopped at the crest of the dunes to see a ragged sea breaking and spewing a winter's spray along the endless sand.

'Were there other men?' Kathleen asked.

'Yes,' I said, then was silent for as long as it took for a dozen great waves to break and shatter along the empty shore. 'I'm sorry I didn't tell you any of this in Belgium. I guess I should have written to your family when she died.'

'I think we all knew she was dead. You can sense it, can't you? But we wanted to know, you understand? We wanted to be certain one way or the other.' A gull screamed overhead and Kathleen pushed a strand of dark red hair out of her eyes.

'What will you tell your parents?'

She shrugged. 'I guess I'll say she died in a car accident and that she was given the Last Rites and a proper Christian burial. I don't think Mom and Dad want the truth. They don't approve of terrorism. Nor do I.' She said the last three words very forcefully. 'I've had to think about terrorism,' Kathleen went on, 'because of Roisin. Even before she went to Ireland she believed in violence. But I don't think there's any excuse for murder.'

I didn't know what to say any more. 'For Roisin it was a cause,' I told Kathleen. 'That was why she wanted to go to Hasbaiya. She wanted to learn how to kill without flinching. She wanted to win Ireland all by herself.'

Kathleen stared at me for a long time. 'Roisin really hurt you, didn't she?'

How pale the sea was, I thought, and how cold. 'More than I ever thought possible,' I admitted, 'more than I ever thought possible.'

'I'll take that coffee now,' she said in a small forced voice.

We walked away from the sea, our shadows long and dark against the white winter sand.

We did not talk much as we walked back round the head of the bay. As we neared the house I asked Kathleen where she lived, and she told me in Maryland, not far from her parents. She said she had trained as a dental hygienist. 'But I'm out of work right now. I was

stupid enough to marry the dentist, you see, and now we're divorced.'
She sounded resigned. 'At least we didn't have kids.'

'Ah.' I was nervous, because I so wanted Kathleen to like me.
Indeed, I suddenly felt as though my whole future happiness
depended on Kathleen's approval of me. I saw in her a quieter,
gentler Roisin.

We reached the house and I pushed open the kitchen door, which I
had left unlocked because Sarah Sing Tennyson had not thought to
leave me a new key when she changed the locks, and there she was.
Sarah Sing Tennyson was standing in my kitchen with a squeegee
bottle in her right hand.

I began to twist away. I had the Colt .45 hidden in my oilskin
pocket, but Sarah Sing Tennyson was much faster than me. She
squeezed, and my hands flew to my burning face and I half heard
Kathleen scream with fear. Then something hit me viciously hard
across the skull. My knees began to give way, a man's voice grunted
as he hit me again, then all went dark.

11

I recovered consciousness in a moving vehicle. That it was moving
was about all I could tell for my head had been shrouded in a bag and
I had been thrust down on the floor. My eyes were in terrible pain, my
face was smarting and my nostrils were filled with the stink of
ammonia. I tried to stretch out, but found that I had been trussed
into immobility. For some reason, though, I had not been gagged.

'Who the hell . . .' I began the question then screamed terribly, for
no sooner had I spoken than a blow stabbed my kidneys. The pain
was terrible; a dreadful lance that seared through my abdomen. I
gasped for breath, half gagging, and then I remembered Kathleen
and had a sudden terror that she would be hurt. 'Please . . .' But as
soon as I opened my mouth the terrible pain sliced into my back
again and my screams sounded like the terror of a wounded animal.

Whoever these people were, they were experts: they had taken me
with a skill and efficiency that spoke of long practice. I was helpless,
and if they decided to kill me, there was nothing I could do to stop it.

The car pulled off the road, then I heard the tyres scrunch on
gravel. I had no idea how long we had been driving. I had no idea if
we were even on the Cape still.

The car seemed to drive into an enclosed space. I could hear its exhaust echoing loud, then the engine was switched off and I heard the doors open. A hand reached down, grabbed one of the ropes that pinioned me, and yanked me with extraordinary force out of the car and onto a cold hard floor.

I sensed someone kneeling beside me. Something cold touched my ankle, a knife blade I imagined, but the blade merely cut the bonds that trussed my legs. A hand yanked me upright. My wrists were still bound and the thick sack was still over my head, but otherwise I had been freed of the ropes.

A hand pushed me forward. I stumbled, hardly able to walk. My feet were bare on the concrete floor. I had been wearing boots and socks when I had been ambushed, but they, like my oilskin jacket which had held my gun, had been stripped off me. I was pushed again and I seemed to enter a thickly carpeted passageway. It was warm suddenly. A hand checked me. I heard a door open. The hand turned me to the right, pushed me very slowly forward, and I found my foot stepping down a flight of wooden stairs. I went down into what had to be a cellar. The footsteps of my captors were loud on the wooden stairs, then echoed from the bare concrete floor. At the foot of the steps I was pushed a few steps forward, then checked again.

I stood still. Then, suddenly, a knife sawed at my wrists and the ropes fell away. I rubbed my wrists, then raised my hands towards the bag tied round my head.

A club or cosh hit my kidneys. I screamed and half fell, but hands held me upright. I wanted to be sick. The pain swelled in me, receded, swelled again; a pain that came in red waves.

Hands gripped my sweater and jerked it upwards. Unable to resist, I raised my arms and they tugged the woollen sea-jersey off. The bag over my head had been tied at my throat and so stayed in place. Then the belt of my jeans was unbuckled, the jeans were unzipped. Hands pulled my jeans down, then my underpants.

I was naked and I was cold. I was hurting and I was frightened. Hands touched my throat and I whimpered softly, then realised that the warm fingers were untying the lacing of the bag that shrouded my head. I sensed the person take a backwards step, then the bag was whipped off and, though my eyes were dazzled and still smarting from the ammonia, I could at last see where I was.

Facing me was Sarah Sing Tennyson. She was holding my clothes. Standing beside her was a tall and well-built man wearing a black balaclava helmet, like those which the IRA favoured when they were photographed by journalists. The knitted cap hid all but his eyes and his mouth. He also wore black leather gloves, a black sweater, black shoes and black trousers. I sensed that there was at least one other person behind me, but I dared not turn round.

The cellar was stone-walled and completely bare of any furnishings except a coiled garden hose that had been attached to a tap which served a metal sink fixed to one wall. The wooden stairs were to my left, climbing steeply to a closed door. The cellar was lit by a single bulb and had a floor of bare cement with a drain in its centre, a feature which, in these circumstances, was as menacing as the hose.

Sarah Sing Tennyson had my clothes draped over one arm. She was also holding a pair of shears with steel blades a foot long. She said nothing, but, when she was certain that the sight of the shears had captured my attention, she began to slice my clothes into shreds. She worked slowly, as if to emphasise the destruction. The sound of the shear blades sliding against each other made a sinister metallic sibilance in the echoing cellar. Each slice of the blades reminded me that I was totally at the questionable mercy of Sarah Sing Tennyson and her companions.

'You're going to answer some questions,' the masked man said, and his voice gave me the first clue as to who my abductors were, for he spoke in the sour accent of Northern Ireland. 'Where's the boat?'

'What boat?' I asked, and then I screamed, because there was not one man behind me, but two, and both of them had hit me at once. I fell, and then all three were working me over, using short, sharp blows that terrorised me with pain. I could control neither my bowels nor my bladder and, when they had finished, I was weeping and filthy.

Sarah Sing Tennyson had not joined in the beating, but just watched with a half-smile on her face. The three masked men were all experts at pain and humiliation and I remembered the men who had gone from Belfast to Libya to learn the modern techniques of interrogation. I knew that I would have no choice but to tell these men what they wanted to know.

'Stand up.' There was no emotion in the man's voice.

I staggered to my feet, weeping and moaning, as one of the men uncoiled the hose and triggered a jet of water at me. By the time I was clean, I was also shivering and my teeth chattered.

'Let me lay down the rules of this interrogation,' the man said in his quiet, reasonable voice. 'You're going to tell us what we want to know. If you tell us, you'll live. If you don't tell us, you'll die, but you'll suffer a lot in the dying. So where is the boat?'

'She's travelling deck cargo . . .' I could not finish the sentence.

'Going to Boston?'

'Yes,' I said eagerly, 'that's right, going to Boston.'

'When will it arrive?'

'The shippers thought the voyage should take about six weeks.' I hurried the words, not wanting to be hit.

'Their name?'

'Exportación Layetano, Barcelona.'

Rivulets of water trickled away from my shivering body towards the drain. I noticed there was no blood in the water. These experts had hurt me without breaking my skin.

'The boat's name?'

'She used to be called *Corsaire*. I changed it to *Rebel Lady*.'

'Describe her.'

I stammered out a description.

'How much gold is on board?'

'Five million dollars.'

Was there a second's hesitation of surprise? The flat voice resumed. 'Describe how the gold is stored aboard the boat.'

So I described the saloon's false floor, and how the cabin sole lifted to reveal the Fibreglass concealing the mix of sand and gold.

'Does the boat have registration papers?'

'Yes. They're at my house.' I told the lie because I could not expose Johnny to these bastards. Then I screamed, because something thumped in my tender kidneys, and I was falling as another slash of pain seared down from my neck. I hit the wet concrete, whimpering.

'Get up.'

I slowly struggled up. I wanted to slash at the tormentors behind me, but they were fitter than me, they were better than me, and I was weakened, shivering and so horribly vulnerable.

'Lies will be met with pain,' the man said in a bored voice. 'The boat's papers are with Johnny Riordan, yes?'

So they had known all along and had just been testing me. 'Yes.'

'Why did you give Riordan money?'

'To hire a crane to get the boat off the truck.'

The questioner had been holding the black hood that had covered my eyes. He now tossed it to me.

'Put it on.'

I obeyed. I could hear my four captors moving about in the cellar. Footsteps climbed the stairs, then came back. Something scraped on the floor, the feet banged hollowly on the wooden stairs again.

'Take the hood off,' the voice ordered, and as I did so the door at the top of the stairs slammed shut and I found myself alone. A metal camp bed with three blankets had been placed by a wall with a zinc bucket at its foot. I just had time to notice those amenities when the light went out. I staggered to the cot bed, pulled the blankets about me and curled up.

I was no weakling, but I knew I could not fight these bastards. This team worked as a disciplined unit, without hesitation and without any need to speak to each other. They believed that their anonymity conferred menace, and so it did, but as I lay in the dark I realised that the only people who knew about the gold were those who had despatched it. The CIA did not know, the Brits did not know.

So either I had been taken by il Hayaween's men or the Provisionals and common sense, quite apart from the Northern Irish accents of my captors, pointed to the latter: no Palestinian or Libyan terrorist would dare try to enter the United States while the war in the Gulf raged. I had underestimated Michael Herlihy and I had misunderstood Sarah Sing Tennyson. She had to be a terrorist groupie, a hanger-on to the movement. I knew she was an acquaintance of my brother-in-law, who in turn was associated with Herlihy. Had she been left in my house expressly to raise the alarm when I came home? And she had met Johnny, which would explain their knowledge of his involvement. God, I thought, but let these bastards spare Johnny. And what had they done to Kathleen? Or was she a part of it?

I shivered under the thin blankets. By staying very still I could somehow hide from the pain. I just wanted to huddle under the blanket in the dark womb of the cellar, listening to the heartlike rhythm of the sea.

My God, I thought, but it was the sea I could hear. It was not the thunder of huge ocean rollers, but the susurration of smaller waves breaking on a soft beach, which suggested I was either close to Nantucket Sound or to Cape Cod. Weymouth, perhaps? The town, south of Boston and nicknamed the Irish Riviera, would be a good place for a Provisional IRA interrogation team to hide.

And the fact that this team was from the Provisionals held out one ray of hope: surely they would let me live, simply because they would not dare to kill me. They would know that I was not only a renegade and thief but also something far more dangerous: a legitimate American. If I was wrong, then my best hope was that they would not inflict a slow death, but would be rid of me quickly.

And so I lay in the dark, shivering, trying to remember prayers.

THE DOOR AT THE TOP of the stairs crashed open. There was no light. 'Hood on! Now!' The Northern Irish voice shouted from the stairhead. 'Put it on! Hurry! Hurry!' Feet clattered on the stairs.

Still half asleep, I frantically fumbled for the black hood, discovering it on the floor beside the bed. I pulled it on.

'Stand up! Move! Move! Move!'

I scrambled off the bed. More footsteps hurried loudly down the stairs. I sensed it was now night-time, and wondered how long I had been asleep.

'Step forward. Stop there! Hood off.'

I pulled the hood off, blinking in the light. As before, the unmasked Sarah Sing Tennyson faced me while, to her left, my questioner stood in his sinister head-to-foot black. I guessed the other two men had taken their positions behind me.

'What was the purpose of the five million dollars?'

'To buy Stingers.' My speech was thick with sleep.

'How many Stingers?'

'Fifty-three,' I answered. They knew the answers, but they would ask me questions to which they knew the answers just to keep me from guessing their identity.

'Who was selling the missiles?'

'A Cuban consortium in Miami.'

'The missiles were meant for Ulster?'

'Yes.'

'Was the trade arranged in America or Ireland?'

'Both, I think.'

'Explain.'

The Ulster accent was toneless. I assumed the questioner was running over known ground to lull my suspicions as he moved imperceptibly towards the questions he really wanted answered. I told him about Brendan Flynn and Michael Herlihy, and even about little Marty Doyle. I described Shafiq's part in the arrangements, and how il Hayaween had taken over the mission. I admitted that I had deliberately broken il Hayaween's instructions by renaming *Corsaire* and shipping her to America.

'Why did you break those instructions?'

'Because I wanted to return to America quickly to report on the missile sale to my superiors.'

'Your superiors?' Was there a hint of puzzlement in my interrogator's voice? 'Explain.'

I kept my voice dull and listless. 'Van Stryker and his people.'

'Who is van Stryker?'

'CIA, Department of Counterterrorism.'

There was a measurable pause, and a detectable uncertainty when my interrogator spoke again. 'You're CIA?'

I said hopelessly, 'Since nineteen seventy-seven.'

I could see Sarah Sing Tennyson's reaction clearly enough. Till now she had kept a supercilious and careless expression, but now there was a genuine worry on her face.

'Describe your mission in the CIA.' I sensed my interrogator was winging it, wondering where my surprising admissions would lead.

'To penetrate Middle Eastern terrorist groups.' I spoke dully, mouthing the words I had rehearsed in the cellar's creeping dark. 'I was instructed to use the credentials of IRA membership as an introduction to such groups.'

'The CIA ordered you to join the IRA?'

'Yes. I was already collecting money for Ireland and sending weapons from Boston, so the IRA knew and trusted me.'

'How did the CIA discover you?'

'I was arrested for running drugs into Florida.'

'And the CIA ordered you to spy on the IRA?'

'No. I was ordered to concentrate on the Middle Eastern groups, and my standing with those groups depended on my being totally trusted by the Provos, so I was ordered not to risk that trust by informing on them.'

'Have you reported back to van Stryker?' the interrogator asked.

'Yes. I was debriefed last month in the Pocono Mountains.'

'So van Stryker will collect the boat from Boston.'

I hesitated, and a foot shifted menacingly behind me. 'No! I was going to collect it.'

'You planned to steal the money?' My questioner sounded amused.

'Yes. I told van Stryker that money was being telexed from Europe.'

'And how much money does van Stryker think is involved?'

'One and a half million, of which a half-million has been paid.'

'Is Herlihy looking for the boat?'

'Of course he is.'

'Put the hood on.'

I pulled the hood over my face. I heard them go upstairs and heard the cellar door scrape shut. I dragged the hood off my head, feeling a sudden exultation. I had worried them! I had unbalanced them so much that on this visit they had not laid a finger on me!

111

I turned to see a paper bag had been left on the floor by my bed. The bag contained a cold cheeseburger in a styrofoam container, along with a cardboard cup of tepid coffee. I ate hungrily.

Then, suddenly, the lights went out. I lay down and waited. I dared to think I might live. I dared to feel hope.

I STAYED IN THE CELLAR for days. I lost track of the time as the meals came irregularly and my sleep periods were broken by sudden interrogation sessions. I received no more beatings.

The questions went on, mostly now about my debriefing and just what I had told the CIA about the IRA. I was given a pillow and thicker blankets, and my interrogators even let me ask a question of them without rewarding me with pain. What happened, I asked them, to the girl who had been with me when they abducted me?

'Nothing. She merely agreed to help us by taking you away from the house while we set up your reception committee.'

'She's with you?' I could not hide my disappointment.

'Why shouldn't she be, considering who her sister was?'

I thought what a fool Kathleen had made of me, and I almost blushed when I remembered my hopes as we walked back from the beach. I had seen her as Roisin's replacement and all the time Kathleen had been a part of Herlihy's attempt to get even with me!

The days passed. My mind became numb. Then came a long period during which no one came to question me. The house, it seemed, was oddly silent. The cellar light was off.

I rolled off the bed and crouched on the floor. There was something unsettling in the silence. I had become accustomed to the small sounds of the house; the squeak of a door, the scrape of a foot, the distant noise of a toilet flushing, but now there was nothing. With trepidation, I edged my way to the stairs and then climbed slowly upwards. I reached the top step. I stopped there, listening, but there was nothing to be heard. I groped for the door lever, pressed it down and, to my astonishment, the door swung open.

I stepped out of the door to find myself in a long, beautifully furnished and deeply carpeted hallway. A brass chandelier hung in the centre of the hallway, while a balustraded staircase curved away to my left; the wallpaper was a Chinese design showing birds of paradise among leafy fronds. To my right an open door led into a vast airy kitchen with a massive fridge humming in one corner. Two paper plates had been discarded on a worktop along with a pot of cold coffee.

I went back into the hallway, selected a door at random and found myself inside a lavishly appointed living room. The room was hung with delicate watercolours, the sofas were deep and soft while the occasional tables gleamed with the burnish of ancient polished wood. The shuttered windows were framed by curtains of antique tapestry corded with red velvet. I crossed the room and pulled back the wooden shutters.

I was suddenly, wonderfully dazzled by the reflection of a full winter sun streaming from a glittering winter sea. This house was built almost at the sea's edge: the small waves flopped tiredly onto a private beach not twenty paces from my window. Out to sea there was a red buoy with a number '9' painted on it and to my right a boathouse and an ice-slicked private dock. A yacht was berthed at the dock, and I suddenly noticed what name was painted on her sugar-scoop stern.

She was *Rebel Lady*.

I stumbled upstairs, flinging open cupboard doors as I searched for clothes. In the master bedroom, where the rumpled sheets suggested one of my interrogators had slept, I found some jeans, a shirt and sweater and a pair of blue and white boat shoes. I also took a slicker from the wardrobe and ran downstairs.

Then, before going out to explore *Rebel Lady*, I spotted a telephone on the kitchen wall. Remembering my worries about Johnny I picked up the phone and punched in his number. I could scarcely believe that the phone worked, but it rang and Johnny himself answered and I felt a great wash of relief pour through me. 'Oh, Johnny,' I said, and slid down the wall to sit on the kitchen floor.

'Paulie?' Johnny's voice was worried. 'I've been trying to reach you for two weeks!'

'Two weeks?' My mind was stumbling. 'What day is it, Johnny?'

'Sunday, of course.'

'Who's winning the war?'

'That finished days ago! It was a walkover. What the hell's happened to you, Paulie?'

'Did someone come for the boat papers?' I asked him.

'Sure, the pretty Chinese girl.' Johnny's tone suddenly changed. 'Are you saying you didn't send her?'

'In a way I did.' Not that it mattered now, I thought. The main thing was that Johnny was all right.

'Are you OK, Paulie?' Johnny asked.

'Not really.'

'So where the hell are you?'

'Big house, I'm guessing it's somewhere on the Cape shore of Nantucket Sound. Does a red buoy with a number nine mean anything?'

'Not off the top of my head.'

'Hold on.' I had spotted a pile of junk mail addressed to 'The Occupier'. I read the address to Johnny, who whistled.

'You're keeping rich company. Centerville, eh? That number nine buoy must mark the Spindle Rock. I'll come and get you in the truck. Be there in forty-five minutes.'

I put the phone down and tugged open the kitchen door, noticing that the alarm system which should have been triggered by the door's opening had been ripped out. I pulled the thin slicker round my shoulders and shivered as I walked gingerly along the frozen path to the private dock. I paused beside the boathouse, scrubbed frost from a windowpane, then peered inside to see a beautiful speedboat suspended on slings above the water. The boat's name was painted down her flank in huge green letters, *Quick Colleen*: a fitting accessory to this luxurious summer home that my captors had used as their temporary base. I walked on to where *Rebel Lady* fretted at her lines.

I stepped cautiously down into her cockpit and found that her companionway was unlocked. I pulled the boards free, slid back her main hatch and ducked inside. The saloon was a shambles. My interrogators had taken axes to the false floor, ripping and tearing away the Fibreglass to expose the gold beneath. Five million dollars worth of gold, all gone, all but one krugerrand that I found lost in a heap of sand and Fibreglass chippings. I picked the coin up, spun it on my palm, then pushed it into a pocket as a souvenir.

I climbed back to the dock and walked slowly towards the house.

Then I stopped because I heard a car's tyres grating on the gravel drive. Voices sounded. There was nowhere to hide, so I stayed still.

First round the corner of the house was a pretty young blonde woman in a long fur coat. She saw me and stopped. 'Darling?' She was speaking to Congressman Thomas O'Shaughnessy who followed her round the side of the house. He just stopped and gaped at me.

Then two men appeared. One was the congressman's aide, Robert Stitch, the other was Michael Herlihy. O'Shaughnessy still gaped at me, but Stitch was quicker on the uptake. 'Shall I call the police, Congressman?'

'I wouldn't, Congressman, I really wouldn't,' I advised him.

The congressman suddenly recognised me. 'You're Shanahan, isn't that right? This is my wife, Duffy. You already know Mr Herlihy?' O'Shaughnessy acted as if this was a meeting in his golf club.

'Just what the hell are you doing here?' Stitch intervened in the pleasantries.

'Do we really need to have this conversation in the yard?' Mrs O'Shaughnessy asked plaintively. 'I'm freezing!'

Stitch moved to confront me as O'Shaughnessy escorted his wife into the house.

'Can you give me one good reason why I shouldn't call the police?' he asked nastily.

'Yes,' I said. 'Try explaining to the police why the congressman allowed his cellar to be used by a Provisional IRA hit squad for the last two weeks.'

'He did what?' He backed away from me, not sure I was telling the truth, then decided he had better employ some quick damage-control just in case I was. 'It isn't true! We've been researching a trade deal in Mexico. We haven't been here.' He hurried into the house and left Herlihy glaring at me.

'What are you doing here, Shanahan?'

'There's your boat,' I pointed at *Rebel Lady*. 'That's what you wanted, isn't it?' I grabbed him by the collar of his coat, ran him along the dock and pushed him down into the cockpit. 'There! Look! That was where your precious money was!'

Herlihy looked astonished. Then a gust of wind shook the boat, a sluggish wave heaved up the wounded hull and he immediately paled and dived for the gunwale. He groaned. I had forgotten just what a terrible affliction his seasickness was.

I fished the single gold coin from my pocket as I stalked away. 'Here's the rest of your money, you bastard!' I tossed it to him. 'I'm going home how. And leave me alone, you hear me?'

I walked down the long gravel drive to the road. Johnny arrived twenty minutes later and we drove away.

12.

'So what happened to you back there?' Johnny asked as we drove away from the high-hedged mansion on the beach.

'I guess I was falling out with the IRA.'

'You shouldn't have had anything to do with them in the first place,' he said flatly. 'And the gold?'

'All gone.'

He laughed. To Johnny the only rewards worth having were those that had taken hard work, the rest was dishonest at worst and meretricious at best. Johnny and his kind were the backbone of America, the good heart of an honest country that somehow contrived to put men like Tommy O'Shaughnessy into Congress. 'You want the money back you gave me?' Johnny asked me. 'I haven't spent it.'

'Keep it,' I said. God, I thought, I would have to get a job now. I wondered how much money van Stryker planned to give me; not enough, I suspected, to pay for the years of lotus-eating idleness I had planned beside the Cape Cod waters. 'I had dreams of buying a tuna boat with that gold,' I confessed to Johnny. 'Now I doubt I could even afford a can of tuna.'

He chuckled. 'You don't want a tuna boat. There are too many of them already, and they're all using aeroplanes as spotters. Ten years ago you could harpoon a big fish every week, but now you're lucky if you see a decent-sized fish all summer.'

Another dream dead, I thought. Had the last twelve years been for nothing? 'Is there much of a market for boat surveying?' I asked.

'Not that I know of.' Johnny drove placidly on. 'But I need a crewman every so often.'

'Are you offering me a job?'

'I'm offering you freezing hands, a wet ass, hard nights, and maybe the chance of a penny or two if the government lets us catch a fish when we're not filling in forms.'

'You're on,' I said.

'But it isn't a career,' Johnny warned me. 'I can hardly keep my own family in bread.' He brooded for a few miles, then turned a frown on me. 'Did you really tell Sarah Tennyson to fetch the boat for you?'

I shook my head. 'She lied to you, but I guess it doesn't matter.'

'So who was she?'

I shrugged. 'I don't know, Johnny. She's probably a terrorist groupie. Some girls get their kicks by hanging around killers. I think the Provos put her in my house to act as a tripwire.' And she had played that part so cleverly! I had even asked Gillespie to warn her of trouble, and she was a part of that trouble all along.

'So the Provos got the gold.' Johnny sighed. Then, being Johnny, he found a silver lining to the cloud. 'But at least you got the electricity put into the house.'

'But why?' I asked that question aloud, suddenly struck by an incongruity. Sarah Sing Tennyson had been in my house three years already. That made no sense, not if she had merely been placed there as a tripwire for my return.

'Why what?' Johnny asked.

'God knows.' I was suddenly disgusted with myself and with everything I had done in the last few weeks. What did it matter whether Sarah Sing Tennyson had been in my house three months or three years? I had played the game and lost. It was over.

I stayed that night with Johnny, and next day went home and began clearing out my house. I took Sarah Sing Tennyson's paintings outside and burned them. I scrubbed the kitchen, dusted the stairway and aired the bedrooms. I had lost the Colt. 45 when I was snatched, but I found the carbine under the bed. I hid it away, then replaced the broken kitchen window and put new locks on the doors. When a telephone bill arrived addressed to Ms Sing Tennyson I sent it to Herlihy's law office, then had the telephone disconnected.

I lived spare. On the days when the tides were slack I went trawling for cod with Johnny, and he paid me wages from the pile of money I had given him for *Rebel Lady*. I used a chunk of my own cash to buy myself a cheap pick-up truck. I was one of at least a hundred people who applied for a mechanic's job at an Upper Cape marina, but at forty I was reckoned too old for the position. My remaining cache of money dwindled and it was painful to remember that, just a year ago, I had been sole proprietor of Nordsee Yacht Delivery; now, thanks to my own greed, I was down to my last few bucks, though I still owned the renamed *Roisin* in Ireland. Come the spring's revival in the boat market, I decided I would have her sold.

ONE FINE MARCH MORNING Sergeant Ted Nickerson, the policeman who had rescued me from Sarah Sing Tennyson's ammonia on the night of my return to the Cape, dropped by the house. 'Just keeping an eye on the place,' he explained as he climbed out of his cruiser. 'So you're home for good now, Paul?'

'Yes.'

'The CIA finished with you?'

'Ask them, Ted.' I was not feeling sociable.

Nickerson took a cigarette from a pocket and shielded the lighter with his free hand. 'We got a telephone call a while back, from a young lady called Kathleen Donovan. She was kind of distressed. Said she thought you were being kidnapped. Were you?'

117

'Yes,' I said.

'But we had orders not to interfere. If anything happened we were to talk to a guy in the Washington office of the FBI. So we did, and he seemed to think you could look after yourself. I guess he was right?'

'I guess so.' The FBI, I surmised, had acted for the CIA who had sensibly not wanted a small-town police force to tangle with international terrorists. But I noted that neither the CIA nor the FBI had seemed unduly worried by my disappearance. No one had enquired about me since, and I could only surmise that van Stryker or Gillespie considered that I deserved whatever mischief came my way. I had been useful to them, now I had been discarded.

'But I thought you ought to know about the young lady,' Ted went on, 'especially as she sounded kind of upset. She particularly wanted me to let her know if you were OK.' He took a scrap of paper from a pocket and held it out. 'That's her phone number.'

I took it. 'Thanks, Ted.'

'Just being neighbourly, Paul.' He hesitated. 'I suppose you're not going to tell me what this is all about?'

'One day, maybe.'

'Yeah, and maybe one day the Red Sox will win the Series.' He climbed into his car, waved goodbye and drove away.

I stared at the piece of paper. It felt like one last chance. Or, of course, it could be another trap to snare a fool, but my future was not so golden that I needed to take care of it. I drove the truck up to the main road and placed a call to Maryland.

KATHLEEN DONOVAN LIVED in a small house on the ragged outskirts of a one-street country town. The house had two storeys, a wide verandah and a windbreak of scrub pine. Behind it was a meadow with an old tobacco-drying shed decaying in its centre. 'None of it's mine,' she said. 'I just rent it.'

'It's nice,' I said with as much conviction as I could muster.

She laughed suddenly, knowing I had lied out of politeness. 'This was an experiment. I always wanted to live in the country, and I thought once David and I were divorced that it would be a real good time to do it, but it isn't all it's cracked up to be. Not one of my carrots came up, not one! And the deer ate all the lettuce and there were worms in the tomatoes.'

'That's why God made supermarkets.'

We were standing beside my pick-up. I had only just arrived, and I guessed she was regretting her impulsive agreement to let me visit her. I was nervous, and the ten-hour drive from Cape Cod had given me too much time to anticipate the failure of this meeting. I wanted to fall in love with Kathleen, and I had even half convinced myself that it was not simply because she was her sister's ghost.

She looked up at me. 'I'm sorry.'

'Why?'

'For agreeing to help those people. Who were they?'

'You didn't know them?' I asked.

'Not really.' She turned away. 'You want to walk?'

'Sure.'

She led me to the road and we walked towards the small town.

'It was the girl who came to me, Sarah Sing Tennyson,' Kathleen said. 'She said you'd thrown her out of the house, and that she wanted to get inside to rescue her paintings, and that if I took you for a walk then she knew she'd be safe.' Kathleen blushed slightly. 'She was very persuasive.'

'I can imagine.' I kicked a dry pine cone ahead of me. 'I wonder how she found you?'

'You remember I hired a private detective to find out about you? Well, he visited the house when she was there, and I guess he and she talked. But she never told me she was taking men with her, or that they planned to beat you up. I couldn't believe it!' Her voice rose in protest as she remembered the violence. 'I phoned the police!'

'I know, thank you.'

'So who were they?'

'They were from Ireland,' I told her. 'They locked me up for a while. They were looking for something, and when I told them where it was they let me go.'

She looked up at me. 'I felt badly. I agreed to help Sarah Tennyson, because you'd been a pig to me in Belgium and I thought I'd enjoy getting back at you. But you were different on Cape Cod.'

I walked in silence for a few paces. 'I wanted to tell someone the truth,' I said, 'and I'd decided to trust you. I thought that after so many years of lies it would be a change to tell the truth.'

'And is it a change?' she asked.

'It makes life less complicated.'

'Like I thought small town life would be, only it isn't really less complicated, there's just less of it. This is it.' She nodded at the main street. 'Two churches, a town office, a bank, feed store, convenience store, coffee shop and a post office.'

'And you like living here?' I asked.

'I hate it.'

We both laughed. 'And you're too stubborn to admit you've made a mistake,' I challenged her, 'because you're so like Roisin.'

'Am I like Roisin?' she asked. We had stopped in the main street and were facing each other. 'Am I really?'

'Yes. In looks, anyway.'

'Don't,' she told me. She was frowning.

'Don't?' It seemed the world trembled on an edge, and I knew it was not going to fall my way.

'I've got a guy, Paul,' Kathleen said gently. 'He teaches school in Frederick.'

'I didn't mean that,' I said, but I had meant it, and she knew I had meant it, and suddenly I felt such a fool.

'Let's have some coffee,' she said, and we sat in the coffee shop and she told me about her trip to Europe, and her adventures in Dublin and Belfast, but I was not really listening; inside I was desolate. Roisin was gone for ever. I had thought she could be clawed back from the past, but it was not to be.

'I hope you found out what you wanted to know,' Kathleen told me when we walked back to the truck.

'I did, thanks.'

She put her hand on my sleeve. 'I'm sorry, Paul.'

Me too, I thought, me too. 'Good luck with the teacher.'

'Thanks.' She smiled. 'Good luck to you too.'

'Sure,' I said, 'sure,' and drove back to Cape Cod.

IT WAS PAST ONE O'CLOCK when I reached the house. It was a dark night and the moon was hidden by high flying clouds. I was too tired to open the garage so I just left the truck on the clam-shell turnaround then walked to the kitchen door. I was weary and I was disgusted with myself. I had really believed I could fall in love with a ghost.

I unlocked the door, pushed into the kitchen and froze. I could smell tea. It was just an aroma, but unmistakable. My M1 carbine was hidden in the living room so I pulled out my fish-filleting knife and then, very slowly, I edged towards the living-room door.

It was jet dark in the house. Had Herlihy sent someone to kill me after all? I reached the living-room door. For a second I contemplated turning on the light, then decided that darkness was probably a better friend.

I pressed down the door lever, crouched, and pushed the door open.

120

It swung into the living room's darkness. I was crouched low, the knife in my right hand. The M1 was hidden four paces from me, held by strips of tape to the underside of the long table. I was gauging just how long it would take me to free the weapon when a man's voice sleepily spoke my name. 'Shanahan?'

My heart leaped in panic, but I managed to stay still.

'Shanahan?' the man said again, and this time I heard the fear in his voice. I suspected he had been dozing and was now scared of what the darkness had brought into this cold room. 'I'm going to turn a light on, OK?' the man said, and I suddenly recognised the voice of my CIA interrogator.

'Is that you?'

'It's me, yeah.' I felt the tension flood out of me. 'Did you have to wait in the dark? I could have filleted you.'

'To be honest I fell asleep. But I didn't want to leave a light on in case you thought the ungodly were waiting for you. Which is why we left our car up at the post office.'

'How did you get in?'

'Stuart Callaghan picked the lock of the front door. He's good at things like that.' Gillespie was moving cautiously across the dark room. He had been sitting on the old settee in the bay window and now he shuffled towards the main light switch beside the hall door.

'So what are you doing here?' I eased the filleting knife back into its sheath.

'We need to know about the boat, *Rebel Lady*. And about the money on board her.' He sounded very disapproving.

'How the hell did you find out about *Rebel Lady*?' I asked.

'It's our job to find things out,' he said in a pained voice. Then he found the switch and suddenly the room was filled with light. Gillespie must have been cold for he was wearing one of the yellow plastic rain-slickers that had been hanging in the hallway.

'I assume you're not alone?' I asked him.

'No. Callaghan is upstairs. I decided one of us would wait for you while the other slept. But I didn't mean us both to fall asleep.' He yawned, then walked to the table where he had left his cellular telephone. 'I'll just report that you've surfaced.'

I was still crouching against the kitchen door and Gillespie was pressing a number into the telephone when he suddenly coughed and looked up at me with a puzzled expression. At least I think he coughed. It was hard to tell because at the same time the whole room was filled with the sound of a gunshot and a splintering crash as the bullet shattered a pane of the bay window behind Gillespie. The CIA man jerked forward and I realised the cough was the sound of the air being punched from his lungs by the violence of the bullet's strike. I was taking a breath to shout at him to get down when a second bullet, fired through the broken window and thus undeflected and unchecked, struck him in the back, and this time Gillespie was hurled violently to the floor.

I edged back into the kitchen shadows. Gillespie was not moving. I could just see two bullet holes in his back and blood on the floor.

Callaghan was surely awake now? The sound of the gunshots was reverberating in my ears. The marksman had to be in the marshes beyond my terrace. Should I try to fetch the gun hidden under the table? But that would mean going into the light that had made Gillespie a target. I slid the knife free again.

A footstep sounded outside beyond the bay window. Someone was out there, and coming inside to make sure of his work! I edged back out of the wash of light which came from the living room and I thought I saw a shadow at the window. Please God, I prayed, but let this not be il Hayaween. Then the shadow moved, grunted. The gunman was looking through the window to see what his bullets had accomplished, but Gillespie's body was half hidden from the window by the heavy table.

I gripped the filleting knife's cord-wrapped handle. The killer was working with a high-velocity rifle, so what chance did I have if he came indoors? None. Maybe I should run for it? No, not with the killer still outside. Wait, I told myself, wait.

Footsteps sounded sudden and loud on the steep stairs from the bedrooms. 'Mr Gillespie? Are you there, sir?' Callaghan shouted.

I sat utterly still.

'Hell!' Callaghan had come into the living room and was staring at Gillespie. 'Hell!' he said again, and whirled round, dragging his gun from his shoulder holster. He saw the broken window and ran towards it, flattening himself against the curtains so that he could peer round the corner into the salt darkness. He stood there, muttering to himself. I took a breath, readying myself to speak to him, when suddenly he turned, gasping, and I heard the rifle fire, its sound dreadfully loud in the confines of the house, and in the very same instant Callaghan fired back and I saw the muzzle flame of his pistol bright against the dark window.

Callaghan fired a second time, but it was merely a reflexive spasm of his fingers as he went down. I had seen the rifle bullet jar his chest like a seismic shock, and I knew that the gunman was a marksman of genius for he had hit Callaghan's heart with a single lethal shot.

Callaghan slumped to the floor. There was silence.

The killer was in the house. In a second or two he would turn over Gillespie's body and find he had killed the wrong man. He had surely been after me, no one else.

Why had I not hidden the carbine in the truck? I tensed myself ready to move, but fear kept me still. If I gave this man a half-second to react I would be dead because this assassin was very good.

Then I heard an odd scraping noise from the far end of the living room. Was the man dragging Callaghan's body away? Next there was a terrible splintering crash, a moan, then silence.

I moved. Very slowly. First I stood, then I took a half-pace forward so I could see into the living room.

And there he was; slumped against the far wall, his rifle a couple of feet from his right hand. He was wearing a black sweater, black trousers, black leather gloves and a black balaclava helmet that showed only his eyes and mouth. The black sweater seemed to glisten at his belly, and I realised that Stuart Callaghan, with his first dying shot, had badly wounded the killer.

'Hello, Seamus.' I crossed the room and kicked his rifle away, then stooped and picked up Callaghan's fallen automatic.

'This is a bloody mess, Paulie.' Seamus made an enormous effort to reach up with his right hand and pull off the black woollen balaclava helmet. 'Bastard got me in the belly.'

'You were after me.'

'I thought that bastard was you.' He jerked his chin towards Gillespie. From the outside, with his back turned and wearing a yellow slicker he had found in my hallway, Gillespie must have looked very much like me. 'Who the hell are they?' Seamus asked.

'The law. They came to question me.' I crouched in front of Seamus and tried to assess his injury. I was no expert, but it looked bad. The bullet had struck Seamus low on his left hip. He was bleeding horribly. If I had used Gillespie's cellular telephone to call an ambulance Seamus might have lived, but he understood why I did no such thing. Those who live by the sword must die by it.

I looked at Callaghan. 'That was a good shot, Seamus.'

'I was always a good shot.' His speech was slow, but he was making sense.

'Who ordered me killed?' I asked.

'Michael Herlihy, of course. He said you'd nicked the money and you had to be punished.' Seamus drew in a terrible, shuddering breath. 'I wouldn't do it till I got confirmation, but it came, right enough.'

'From Brendan Flynn?' I guessed sourly.

'Aye. I'm sorry it had to be me, Paulie.'

'You're not given much of a choice in these things.' I squatted in front of him. 'Is it hurting, Seamus?'

'It's sort of dull now, Paulie. Not so bad, really.' He sat in silence, his head against the wall. 'I always liked you, you know.'

'I liked you, Seamus.' Already we were using the past tense.

'I remember Brendan Flynn telling me you were a dangerous one, but I reckoned you were all right.' He sighed. 'Why did you steal the money?'

'I didn't. I wanted to, but I didn't.'

'They say you did, but I suppose they're nicking it for themselves. Just like they always do.' Blood was puddling under him. He was weakening so much that he could hardly lift his right hand. 'There's some ciggies in my shirt pocket,' he said, 'would you mind?'

I held the automatic close to his face as I groped under his sweater. I found the cigarettes and a lighter, put a cigarette between his lips and clicked a flame.

'You used to smoke, didn't you?' Seamus asked.

'I gave it up.'

'Don't you miss it, Paulie?'

'Smoking? Sure I do. The day I get to heaven, St Peter's going to be waiting with a packet of twenty and a book of matches.'

'You think you'll get to heaven?' The cigarette twitched in his lips as he spoke.

'We'll all meet there, Seamus. You, me, all the boys. And the hills will be green as emerald and the streams full of salmon and the sun ever shining.'

'Like my wee house in the hills of Derry, eh?' That was a dream that would never come true. Seamus blinked rapidly, maybe because the smoke was in his eyes. 'There was even a girl in Lifford.'

'You? A girl?'

'I was sweet on her. Her dad said I could ask her out, so he did.'

'But you never did ask her?'

'Never had time, Paulie. I wasn't like you. I wasn't one for the girls.' He seemed to be aware that something had been amiss in his life, and I wondered what demons had chased him through the long dark corridors of his lonely nights.

'They said they'd give me a medal,' Seamus said after a long silence. 'They said there's a Massachusetts medal of freedom. They said they've given it to other IRA men. They said they'd pin it on my chest on the State House steps.'

'Michael Herlihy told you that?'

'Aye, but I had to kill you first. He said you'd betrayed the movement and that he'd give me money if I killed you, but I told him I didn't want any money. Then he said they'd give me the medal, like. My mam would have been pleased, Paulie, to see me with a medal. She was always nagging at me to do something in life, know what I mean?' He had gone very pale.

'How long were you waiting for me?' I asked.

'Since tea time. Herlihy had Marty Doyle drive me out here.'

'Where's Marty now?'

'Waiting up by the shops.' Seamus grinned weakly. 'He's driving a bloody flower van. Can you believe it?' He breathed hard. 'Did you ever know Father Brady? He told me it would be a bad end. Can you not get me a priest now, Paulie?'

'No, Seamus, I can't.' There could be no priests and no ambulance and no local police. That was the rule of the secret world and Seamus knew it.

He nodded acceptance of my refusal. 'Roisin said some things . . . she was a fearful strong girl, so she was. She got mad at me,' Seamus said sadly. 'How was she shot?' he asked suddenly.

'In that Arab place?' I knew I could not avoid the subject.

'Yes.' Seamus's pale knowing eyes looked at me. 'It was you, wasn't it?'

'Me, Seamus?' A thousand acts of contrition had not let me deliver those two words with any conviction.

'It was you that shot her.'

I hesitated, not sure whether I even trusted a man on the lip of eternity, but then I nodded. 'Yes. But she didn't know it was me. I was wearing a headdress, see, and they just gave me the gun.'

'And then you shot her?'

'Once through the head. Quick.' I wondered how Seamus had known, then guessed it was written on my soul for all the damned to read, and I wondered how I could ever have hoped for happiness with Kathleen after what I had done to her sister.

'You poor bastard, Paulie,' Seamus said, then he suddenly tensed with the onslaught of a terrible pain. He wailed and the cigarette rolled out of his mouth. I thought he had died, but suddenly he opened his eyes and twitched a hand towards me. 'Just tell me it's going to be all right, Paulie.'

'It is,' I said. I held his hand to give him the solace of human touch. He had known so little love, while his talent for rage had been used by lesser men.

'Tell me,' he demanded again.

'Ireland will be one,' I told him, 'united under God, and there'll be no division left, and no more tears, and no more dying.'

He tried to speak again, and his tongue seemed to rattle in the back of his mouth, but his will-power overcame the spasm of death to let him quote a line of verse. ' "Life springs from death",' he said, but he could go no further, and so I edged even closer to him and put my face down by his face and there was no breath in him at all, nothing, and so I touched his eyes shut with my right hand and finished the words for him. ' "And from the graves of patriot men and women spring living nations." '

Seamus Geoghegan, the bright boy of Derry, was dead.

13

I took Callaghan's automatic, the money and the passport from the hiding place in the beam, then left through the kitchen door. I climbed into the pick-up, rammed it into gear and accelerated up the track onto the main road.

I could see the white-painted van in the parking lot of the convenience store. Next door was a shed that advertised frozen yoghurt. I pulled up in front of the yoghurt shop where my pick-up's headlights illuminated the legend on the van's body: 'Shamrock Flower Shoppe. Blooms for all Family Occasions'. Then I killed the lights, left the engine running and ran across to the van.

I rapped on the driver's door, startling Marty who had evidently been fast asleep. He opened the door. 'Is that you, Seamus? I must have dropped off.'

I dragged Marty out of the seat. He yelped in panic as I spun him round to the dark side of the van, away from the road, and screamed as I rammed the muzzle of the pistol into his throat. 'Say a prayer, Marty.'

'Is it you, Paulie? Where's Seamus?'

'He's dead, Marty. Now listen, you bastard, you're not going to give me any trouble or else Mrs Doyle will be collecting the life insurance and you'll be nothing but a framed photograph on top of the television set. Is that what you want, Marty?'

'No, Paulie, no! I'll do whatever you want!'

'Then get in the back of the van.'

I pushed him through the van's rear door. The body of the van was filled with flower boxes fastened with lengths of green wire that I used to pinion Marty's wrists and ankles. Then I gagged him with a strip of cloth I cut from his sweater. 'Now just wait here, Marty, and don't make a peep or I'll use you for target practice.'

There was a telephone beside the frozen yoghurt shop. I pulled a visiting card from my pocket and punched in the numbers. It was an 800 number, a free call, and when it was over I called Johnny, who was asleep but roused himself quickly enough when I told him what I wanted. 'I'll meet you by the dinghy,' he told me, 'in half an hour.'

I went back to my pick-up.

I drove south on Route 28. As I arrived at Stage Harbor it began to sleet.

Johnny arrived ten minutes later and I followed him down to where his dinghy was tethered. 'Give me the boat keys,' I said.

'Forget it, Paulie, I'm coming with you.'

I did not argue. Everything had gone wrong this night and I needed help. So we rowed out to Johnny's trawler, the *Julie-Anne*, started her up and went to sea.

WE MOTORED WESTWARD, guided through the shoals of Nantucket Sound by the winking lights of the buoys in the glassy-wet darkness. The big diesel motor throbbed comfortingly away. It was warm in the wheelhouse. Johnny steered with one hand and held a coffee mug with the other. 'So what's it about?' he asked.

I did not answer. I just stared through the glow of the *Julie-Anne*'s navigation lights and I thought how many had died. Liam, Gerry, Gillespie, Callaghan, Seamus. And they were probably just the beginning.

'At least tell me whose side I'm on.' Johnny insisted.

'The angels. But don't go near my house for a few days. Someone wanted to punish me for taking the gold.'

'I thought you said the IRA had got their gold back?'

'I guess they wanted me dead as an example to anyone else who had a mind to rip them off. But just stay clear of the house, Johnny.'

We travelled on in silence. About three hours after we had left Stage Harbor I saw the lights of Martha's Vineyard, and the eastern horizon was just hinting at the dawn as we slid past Chappaquiddick Point. The water was smooth and slick, pocked with the rain and skeined with a thin mist that hazed the lights of Edgartown as Johnny, with a careless skill, nudged his huge trawler towards a pier. 'Do you want me to wait for you?'

'No. But thanks.'

'Look after yourself, Paulie.'

I jumped ashore, then walked into town. I was looking for a big house with a Nautor Swan parked on jackstands in her front yard. I had come for van Stryker's help.

'SHANAHAN.' SIMON VAN STRYKER opened his door and ushered me inside. He was dressed in an Aran sweater, corduroy trousers and fleece-lined sea-boots, but he looked every inch as distinguished as the last time we had met, when he had been rigged out to dine at the White House. 'I've got a team heading for your house.' The 800 number was the one on the card van Stryker had given me in the Poconoes: the call had been answered by a young man who had calmly listened to my description of three dead bodies. I had held on while he called van Stryker who, in turn, had ordered me to meet him at his summer house. 'Laphroaig?' he offered.

'Please.'

He led me into the kitchen and poured me a generous slug of whiskey. 'So tell me exactly what happened.'

I told him the story of the night, of Gillespie and Callaghan dying, of Seamus bleeding to death. 'I left the bodies there and called for help,' I finished lamely.

'That was wise of you, Paul.' Van Stryker began breaking some eggs into a bowl while I looked through his windows across the rain-stippled harbour to the low heathland of Chappaquiddick. Dawn was seeping across the cloudy sky, making the water look like dull gunmetal. 'So tell me,' he ordered, 'what you think this is all about.'

'It's about Stingers,' I said firmly. 'Il Hayaween loves to kill jumbo jets. He wants bodies floating in Boston Harbor, and across the perimeter roads of a dozen airports. He wants America to pay for Saddam Hussein's humiliation.'

'You don't believe the Stingers were meant for Ireland?'

'Some, yes, but only a few, as a reward for negotiating the purchase. It would have been impossible for the Arabs to come to America and negotiate the sale, so Flynn did it for them.'

'Why didn't you tell us about *Rebel Lady?*'

I coloured slightly. 'Because I planned to steal the money. That was my pension plan.' I paused, sipped his good whisky, then looked up at van Stryker's thin, clever face. 'How did you find out about *Rebel Lady?*'

He stirred the eggs. 'Gillespie found out. Good old-fashioned bugging. My guess is that there are microphones covering the downstairs of your house, and a voice-activated tape recorder concealed in the attic. That's how they usually do it.'

'They?'

'The FBI prefer using the telephone to carry the wiretapped signals away, but that's difficult if you're not operating legally. So I suspect your eavesdroppers used a tape recorder. Which means, of course, that they must have had access to your house to collect the tapes.'

'Sarah Sing Tennyson,' I said, and felt as a blind man must feel when given sight or, much more aptly, like a fool given reason.

'In fact her name isn't Tennyson. It's Ko, Sally Ko. Her father is Hong Kong Chinese and her mother's from London. Miss Ko is British Intelligence, though naturally the British say she's a cultural attaché.'

'Oh, God,' I said, and I thought what a fool I had been, what an utter fool. 'And she wasn't even after me,' I said, 'but after Patrick and his friends?'

'Your brother-in-law? Yes. I'm told he sometimes used your house to plot arms shipments, which the Brits rather gratefully intercepted. Gillespie only discovered all this when the CIA went to put in their own wiretaps and found the British microphones in place.'

Why else would a tenant pay to have electricity installed? It was necessary to power the hidden tape recorder. Every time my dumb-ass brother-in-law plotted another arms shipment to Ireland, British Intelligence had listened in. Then they must have heard me talking to Johnny about a shipment of gold, and suddenly their humdrum intelligence operation had turned into a triumph. And what a triumph it had proved! Five million in gold and fifty-three Stingers neutralised. 'The bastards,' I said feelingly.

Van Stryker took two plates from a dresser. 'It was clever of them to use Congressman O'Shaugnessy's house!' He laughed. 'That was a very elegant touch.'

'Elegant like hell. I thought they were going to kill me!'

'I'm sure Gillespie warned them against anything so drastic.'

And of course it was Gillespie who had set me up for the Brits.

They had snatched me on my first morning back home, and how had they known I would be there if Gillespie had not told them? And that would also explain why the FBI had told Sergeant Nickerson not to worry when Kathleen Donovan had made her protest at my kidnapping. 'You set them onto me, didn't you?' I said again, remembering my humiliation.

'Gillespie felt you had been less than honest with him at the debriefing,' van Stryker admitted, 'and your tale of Stinger missiles just didn't make sense, Paul. I could have made things much tougher for you, but we all thought this way would be much quicker. And so it proved. I needed to know what you were hiding, and I found out. You were hiding one million dollars.'

'Is that what Miss Ko told you?' I asked.

'She did more than tell us. She even shared the million with us, or rather we permitted them to take one half. Thanks to you, Paul, Her Majesty's Secret Service is now richer to the tune of half a million dollars.'

'No,' I said with relish, 'they're richer to the tune of four and a half million dollars. There were five million bucks on that boat, van Stryker, all in gold. Your allies have cheated you.'

'Five?' He was incredulous. 'Five! Isn't that rather a lot of money for fifty-three missiles? If the missiles even exist. Tell me everything, Paul, and this time make it the truth.'

So I told him the truth, the whole truth. I spoke of Brendan Flynn, Michael Herlihy, Shafiq, il Hayaween, Liam, Gerry, *Rebel Lady*, Sarah Sing Tennyson, the British interrogators, the gold and Seamus Geoghegan. Van Stryker listened to it all in silence until I had no more to tell, and then suddenly the telephone rang, startling us both. Van Stryker answered it, spoke softly for a few moments, then put it down. 'Your house is secure. My people are there.'

'What will you do with the bodies?'

'We'll take Gillespie and Callaghan a long way away and fashion a car accident. And Geoghegan will disappear. I rather suspect the British will be blamed.' Van Stryker tipped the omelettes onto the plates. 'Now, eat.'

He put an omelette in front of me and I devoured it as though I had not eaten in weeks. Van Stryker ate more fastidiously. 'I wish you'd told me about the five million dollars at the beginning, Paul. It's simply too much money! And why gold? Why not a simple bank transfer?'

'Maybe Herlihy demanded gold?'

'And why send two punks to guard you? Why not use two or three of their top men? And why Stingers?'

'Because they're the best.'

'But you don't need the best to knock down an airliner!' van Stryker protested. 'Airliners are lumbering great targets; they're not agile like a ground-support helicopter or fast like a low-level fighter-bomber. A cobbled-together Russian Red Star could knock out a Boeing 747, and the Palestinians must have hundreds of Red Stars! So why Stingers? And why you?'

He had utterly confused me now. 'What do you mean? Why me?'

'Why did they want you?'

'To bring the boat across, of course.'

Van Stryker shook his head. 'No! Why would they bring a boat to America with five million dollars' worth of gold they don't need, to buy fifty-three Stingers they don't want, and which probably never even existed? For God's sake, Paul, we have spent weeks looking for those missiles and there isn't even a whisper of confirmation that they exist! So forget the missiles. Think about why they wanted you.'

'To bring the boat across,' I said again, but this time in a different tone: a tone of slow revelation.

'Because the boat is hiding something.' Van Stryker carried on the thought. 'And they showed you a Stinger and they showed you money because they knew you'd buy that story because you of all people know how the IRA has been lusting after Stingers. But this isn't about Stingers, Paul, it never was! This is about the boat!'

'Oh, God,' I said. 'I left the boat at O'Shaughnessy's house with Herlihy!'

'So what's in it, Paul? What were they hiding under a coat of gold?'

'I don't know, I don't know,' but whatever it was, I had given it back to them.

'We'll find the boat.' Van Stryker snatched up the phone. 'Give me the description again.'

'Find Herlihy first,' I suggested, 'because he'll know where *Rebel Lady*'s hidden.'

It took van Stryker half an hour to ascertain that Herlihy had vanished. He was not at his home. FBI agents broke in to find his apartment empty. Neither was he at the Parish or Tully's Tavern.

'I can find him,' I told van Stryker.

'You can?'

I would have to. Because Saddam Hussein had sent America a present, and I had lost it. Now I would have to find it again.

'THE MONEY WAS NEVER IMPORTANT!' van Stryker shouted at me. 'The gold was a blind to disguise the truth! And that's why Herlihy sent Geoghegan to kill you. He'd retrieved the boat, after all, and your telling tales was the one danger left. Is that it?' He pointed down.

He was shouting because we were in a Coastguard helicopter that had been summoned to Martha's Vineyard on van Stryker's authority. We had flown fast and low across the wintry water of Nantucket Sound and were now hovering above the shop where I had left Marty Doyle.

'That's it!' I could see the white Shamrock Flower Shoppe van. I reckoned that if anyone knew where Herlihy was hiding, then it had to be Marty Doyle.

'Down!' Van Stryker gestured the order at the crew chief who passed it on to the pilot. We were in the rescue compartment, a cavernous metal space behind and below the control cabin. A winch and a rescue basket filled one side of the rescue chamber.

The machine settled down slowly on the empty parking lot.

'Be quick!' van Stryker ordered me.

I ran to the flower van, yanked the back door open, and there discovered a terrified and half-frozen Marty Doyle. I dragged him out and, because his ankles were tied with the green wire, I carried him like a child to the throbbing helicopter. I slung him onto the metal floor, then clambered in after him.

'Up!' van Stryker shouted.

As we rose into the air I saw the first blue flicker of a police car's light coming south to discover why a helicopter was disturbing the Cape's frosty morning, but we were already racing out towards the open Atlantic. We passed over my house and across the dunes where I had walked with Kathleen Donovan, and out across the tumultuous smoking rollers that hammered incessantly on the frozen sand.

I pulled the woollen gag off Marty's face. 'Morning, Marty.'

He was shivering. Both doors of the big helicopter were wide open and the morning was freezing. 'Where are we going?' Marty asked.

'To find Michael Herlihy,' I told him, 'so where is he?'

'I don't know, Paul. Honest!'

I smiled at him, then cut off his wire bonds. 'Put this on, Marty.' It was a safety harness. He was shaking with cold, but he managed to get his arms into the harness that I buckled tight across his chest. 'So where's Herlihy?' I asked again.

Marty looked at me with his doglike gaze. 'As God is my witness, Paul, I swear I don't know.'

I pushed him out of the door.

He screamed and flailed, then jerked as the safety line I had attached to the back of his harness caught hold. He hung beneath the helicopter, three hundred feet above the heaving grey seas.

I hauled him back into the helicopter's belly. 'I don't think you heard me, Marty. Where's Herlihy?'

'He's at the congressman's summer home. Oh, God, please don't do it again! Paulie! Please!'

I gave him a cup of coffee as the big rescue helicopter tilted its rotors west and sped us back towards Nantucket Sound and the last dark secrets of *Rebel Lady*.

VAN STRYKER AND I had flown to Otis Air Force Base at the inner end of the Cape, then driven to Centerville. It was still not yet nine o'clock and we were already parked close to Congressman O'Shaughnessy's beach house.

I opened the car door. 'I'll be back by eleven.'

'It takes longer than that to squeeze the truth out of a man.'

'Not really.' I smiled, and climbed out of the car.

The wind was cold. The street had the joyless, deserted feel of a resort out of season.

I clicked open the gate. The house appeared shuttered and empty. I walked round to the back, bruising the frosted grass beneath my boots. There was no one in the kitchen and, as I had expected, the door was locked. I knew there was an alarm system, which I assumed the congressman would have had repaired, but so long as there was someone in the house, then there seemed a good chance that the system would be switched off. In which hopeful belief I smashed through a pane of the door's glass.

The noise seemed appalling, but no alarm bell shrilled its hammer tone. I reached to the latch and let myself in.

I still had Callaghan's gun. I took it from the oilskin's deep pocket and stalked into the main hallway. The living room was deserted and its tall windows securely shuttered. I edged through another half open door into a huge dining room which held a table that could seat twenty guests. Another door stood ajar at the dining room's far end, and I edged it further open to see a book-lined den with one wall smothered in framed diplomas and awards. Michael Herlihy, still fully dressed, was fast asleep in a leather armchair.

I put the gun barrel under his nose. 'Morning, Michael.'

'What? No!' He woke, shaking.

'Be very still, Michael,' I said, 'and very quiet. Seamus is dead.'

'I don't know anything!' He tried to get out of the chair, but the gun persuaded him to stay still. I ran a hand over his rumpled clothes and found a small automatic. I put it into my pocket.

'You sent Seamus to kill me. Marty Doyle told me.'

Michael stiffened. 'I have no knowledge of these matters.'

'That's very formal, Michael, very legalistic. Where's the boat?'

'I don't know. The congressman arranged to have her towed away from his property. Why don't you ask him yourself? He's in Washington.' He pulled a telephone towards him, then gasped as I slashed the gun barrel across his bony nose.

'No telephones, Michael. So where's *Rebel Lady*?'

'I told you, Paul, I do not know!'

'Then let's find out if you're telling the truth, shall we?'

The room's heavy velvet curtains were tethered by tasselled silk cords. I slashed the cords free, then tied Michael's hands behind his back. That done, I picked a sturdy poker from the hearth, then pushed him out of the den and into the luxurious dining room. 'This is a comfortable hiding place, Michael. Tell me, have the Arabs sent you more money?'

'You'll regret these allegations!'

'The five million was your price, wasn't it? You and Brendan?'

'I don't know what you're talking about!'

I forced him to stumble on down the hallway, then out through the broken kitchen door and down the brick path to the boathouse. Michael was dressed in his lawyer's three-piece suit and began to shiver in the bitter wind.

'Where's *Rebel Lady*?'

'I have no idea. Can't we talk about this inside?'

'Why not in here, Michael?' The padlocked boathouse door soon yielded to the leverage of the poker. I pushed Herlihy inside and tethered him to a stanchion with the free end of the curtain cord.

'No, please!' He suddenly understood what I intended doing. 'I don't know what you're talking about!'

'I think you do, Michael.' I went to the far wall where two control boxes operated the twin hoists holding *Quick Colleen*. I pressed the green buttons and the machinery hummed smoothly as it lowered the sharp-prowed boat into the frozen dock. The ice splintered noisily under the hull's weight, then the speedboat settled in the frigid water, her bow facing inwards. 'Do you remember when we were teenagers and I took you out for a boat ride?'

135

'Please, Paul!' He was shaking.

'Where's *Rebel Lady*?'

'We sank her, out there!'

'I wonder why I don't believe you? But we'll soon see if you're telling the truth.' I stepped onto *Quick Colleen*'s foredeck, unbuckled the forward hoist strap and unclipped her cockpit cover to discover her ignition key was still in the dashboard. I tossed the cover onto the dock and then pressed the switches that tilted the big two-hundred-horsepower engines into the water. The batteries still had power and the twin engines whined down into the icy waves that lapped soft against the low racing transom. I checked the big fuel tank and found it full, primed the engines, advanced the chokes and turned the key. 'Fun Time,' I said happily as the engines caught and fired.

'No!' Michael clung desperately to the stanchion. I slapped his hands free, kicked his feet out from under him, then hurled him onto the white leather seats of *Quick Colleen*. 'No!' he protested again. His face already had a deathly pallor.

'Where's *Rebel Lady*?'

'I told you! We sank her.'

'Then let's go look for her!' I rammed the throttles into reverse and *Quick Colleen* slashed backwards through the boathouse entrance. I swivelled her, rammed the twin levers forward, and screamed straight out to sea.

'Isn't this fun?' I spun the wheel, forcing *Quick Colleen* to turn like a jet fighter. She skidded sideways as the huge engines tried to counteract the centrifugal force, then I wrenched her back, gave her full throttles, and let her run loose and fast towards far Nantucket.

Herlihy had already vomited on the leather seat and was still retching and heaving. The boat thumped on the waves, banging like a demented hammer as it bounced in the air and came down in an explosion of white water, and Michael was grovelling and sliding around as he desperately tried to keep his balance.

I turned the boat hard, accelerated again and rammed her back through her own wake. Michael stared up at me, a terrible look on his pale face, then shook his head as if to tell me he had taken enough torment.

I cut the throttles, letting *Quick Colleen* idle in the water. 'So where's *Rebel Lady*?' I asked him.

'In Washington DC. At the Virginia Shore Marine Depot.'

'Where's that?'

He retched and groaned. Even the small rocking of the boat was murder to him. 'It's at the northern end of Washington National Airport. Now, please, Paul! Take me back!'

'Who took her there?'

'I hired a delivery firm in Cotuit.'

I gave the engines a tad of power, throwing Michael back onto the cushions. 'What's hidden inside her, Michael?'

'I don't know. Truly! Nothing perhaps. You were bringing the money, that's all! Then she was to be left at that yard.'

'Il Hayaween ordered her taken to that particular yard, yes?'

'Yes!'

'And he sent you more money?'

He was reluctant to say, but I gunned the throttles slightly and he yielded immediately. 'Five million again. Wired to the Caymans . . .'

'And the five million is for you and Brendan to share, yes?'

'Yes.'

'And no one else knows about this, do they?' I suddenly saw it clearly. That was why Brendan had sent me two punks, because he dared not ask for good men. 'This operation was never cleared by the Army Council, was it?' I accused him.

Michael gazed up at me. He was too cowed and wretched to dare tell a lie and so he shook his head. Which meant he and Brendan were freelancing. None of this had been approved by the Provisional IRA's Army Council. 'There never were any Stingers, were there?' I asked.

'There would have been!' Michael pleaded. 'We could have bought every Stinger on the market! Don't you understand? We had to make money!'

'So who were those Cubans?'

'The Arabs provided them, they were genuine. We had to convince you that there really were Stingers.'

'Bastard,' I told Herlihy, then I gave *Quick Colleen*'s throttles a thrust, whipping her into some fast S-turns, spinning and flogging her through the merciless sea. Herlihy was screaming and sobbing.

I cut the throttles again, letting the sleek hull settle into the small waves. Michael was gagging and moaning; a man in anguish. 'Tell me,' I demanded, 'what is in that boat and worth ten million dollars of Saddam Hussein's money?'

'I don't know. We just delivered the boat to Washington.'

'And what were you to do with me?' I put a hand to the throttles.

'You were to be killed! You and the two boys.'

'Because *Rebel Lady*,' I said, 'was never to be associated with the IRA, is that it?'

137

'Yes!' He gazed beseechingly at me.

'And you and Brendan were willing to help Saddam Hussein attack America?'

'We didn't know what it was about!' he protested.

'Oh, you did, Michael. You may not know what's inside *Rebel Lady*, but you know damn well she isn't carrying a goodwill card for the President.'

'She brought us money,' he said, 'and I'll give the money to the cause.'

'Ireland doesn't need traitors like you.' And I pushed the throttles forward and headed hard for the shore.

And wondered just what lay in the dark belly of the *Rebel Lady*.

WASHINGTON DC LIES NINETY-FIVE MILES from the mouth of the Potomac River. *Rebel Lady* would probably have done most of those miles under power after her delivery crew had sailed her south from Cape Cod. Once into the Potomac, they would have motored her up to the nation's capital and, if they had remembered the old tradition that honoured George Washington, they would have sounded the ship's bell as they passed Mount Vernon.

Once in the city itself they would have taken the Virginia Channel where, just south of the Pentagon, the Virginia Shore Marina Depot lay. In winter the dilapidated yard was a storage place for cruisers and dismasted yachts. It was a dispiriting place, hedged behind by the expressway looping off the river bridges, and in front by the gantries and pylons that held the approach lights for Washington National Airport's main runway.

'Of course we're not as well known as the sailing marina to the south of the airport,' the yard's manager shouted to me as a passenger jet thundered above us, 'but we've got more depth of water than the Pentagon Lagoon.' I could see the Washington Monument across the river and beyond it, to my right, the last gleams of reflected sunlight from the Capitol Dome. The Capitol, like the White House, was a little over two miles away while the Pentagon was just one mile north. *Rebel Lady* had been brought like a plague bacillus right into the very heart of the Republic.

Once she had reached the yard, *Rebel Lady* had been craned out of the water and cradled by metal jackstands, her thick keel resting on big wooden blocks. On Herlihy's orders her new name had been painted out, making her just one more anonymous boat among the hundreds of craft stored during the winter months.

138

Now, at dusk on the day which had started with *Quick Colleen* in Nantucket Sound, I stood where *Rebel Lady* had been hidden. *Rebel Lady* herself had already been taken away to have her secret excised, but I had wanted to come to the boatyard to see for myself just where Saddam Hussein's revenge would have been triggered.

'Shame what they did to her,' the manager said. 'Wrecking an interior like that.'

'Wicked,' I agreed.

'Funny thing, though. She had a Florida manufacturer's nameplate on her coachroof, but she wasn't built in the States.'

'No, she wasn't.' The real *Rebel Lady*, now called *Roisin*, waited for me in Ardgroom. I had decided I did not like that new name. I would find another name. *Scoundrel* perhaps? Then I would go and claim my boat and sail her back across the Atlantic.

'One of my guys reckoned she was French built,' the manager told me, 'but she was a hell of a lot heavier than any French boat I've ever seen. So what was it all about?'

'Smuggling. Cocaine.' I offered him the answer which he would find most believable.

'I reckoned as much,' he said happily. 'I was here when they X-rayed her. They got excited, I can tell you!' He gestured towards the cumbersome X-ray equipment that was used to survey the health of hidden keel-bolts. 'You think we'll be on the TV news?' he asked hopefully.

I shook my head. 'You don't want to be on the evening news, believe me, not with that boat. But thank you for letting me see the place.' I climbed into the back seat of the government car and slammed the door.

It had all been so close. And so clever. Whatever it was. Now, through the city's evening traffic, I went to find out.

REBEL LADY HAD BEEN TAKEN to one of the military reservations close to Washington where, in a great empty hangar, she stood forlorn under massive bright lights. I found van Stryker in a glass-walled booth from where he watched the white-garbed team that worked underneath the jacked-up hull. 'It's in the lead keel,' he told me.

The huge bulbous keel had already been taken off *Rebel Lady*. Like most ballast keels it had been secured to the Fibreglass hull by long silicon-bronze stud bolts. Van Stryker's team had loosened the bolts and gently lowered the keel to the hangar floor. Standing beside the exposed keel, which was now hidden from my view by the men and women in their protective clothing, was a bright yellow flask as big as a small car, and decorated with the three-leafed insignia of the nuclear industry. 'It was a nuclear bomb?' I asked in horror.

'No. He doesn't have the technology to make a bomb, not yet.' Van Stryker looked tired. His job was to preserve the Republic from the attacks of terrorists and he knew just how close this attack had come to success.

'So what is it?'

Van Stryker sipped at a brown plastic mug of coffee. 'We think the Iraqis hollowed out that keel and filled it with around four tons of uranium-dioxide. That's the nuclear fuel you put in ordinary commercial power stations like Three Mile Island or Chernobyl. They chopped the fuel rods into pellets and mixed them up with powdered aluminium and what looks like ammonium nitrate, to make the uranium into a huge firebomb. Then they added a detonator and a timer. Simple, really, and comparatively cheap.'

'And what will that lot do?'

'The firebomb would have reached a temperature of over seven thousand degrees Fahrenheit, and once the nuclear fuel caught fire it would have spread a miniature plume of radioactivity just like Chernobyl.' Van Stryker offered me a sudden sympathetic glance. 'Don't worry, Paul, my experts say you probably weren't exposed to excessive radiation. By sheathing that horror in lead and keeping it under water they gave you protection. Then you made yourself even safer by piling the gold on top.'

I stared at the white-dressed figures. 'What would the bomb have done to Washington?'

'Their toxic bonfire might have made the Pentagon, or even the White House, unusable for years to come. What a revenge for Baghdad that would have been.' Van Stryker fell silent for a few seconds. 'Think of a city contaminated with radioactive isotopes. Think of the birth defects, think of the cancers. That's why they wanted the boat out of the water when the detonator triggered, so the fire could start properly. If she'd been floating it would have been snuffed out and at best just contaminated a few miles of river. On dry land, and with a good wind, they might have smeared a hundred square miles with lethal poisons.'

I said nothing, but just stared at *Rebel Lady*, wondering if she would ever sail again. She deserved one last romp through high seas with full sail and no unfair ballast slowing her down.

'The Garda arrested Brendan Flynn this afternoon,' van Stryker said.

'Will you extradite him?'

'No. The less the public know about this, the better. The Garda will find something with which to charge him, and a few years in Portlaoise jail should teach him to respect us.'

'And Herlihy?'

Van Stryker shook his head. 'There are too many lawyers round him to make a trumped-up charge stick, but I think the Internal Revenue Service could be persuaded to make his life a misery.'

'And what of me?' I asked.

'On the whole,' he said, 'you've been on the side of the angels. We'll give you some back pay, Paul. Say a hundred thousand? You can make a new start with that.'

'Yes, but it isn't five million, is it?'

'Which the Brits have suddenly agreed to turn over to us,' van Stryker said grimly.

A telephone buzzed suddenly. Van Stryker answered the phone and I saw one of the protectively clothed figures beside *Rebel Lady* speaking into the other handset. Van Stryker grunted a few times, thanked the man, then put the telephone down. 'July fourth,' he said slowly. 'The timer was set for noon on Independence Day. It's a fair bet Washington will be crowded that day. Maybe a victory parade for Desert Storm? Well, they're going to be disappointed.'

'It isn't over, is it?' I said. 'Il Hayaween won't stop with this failure.'

'He's lost the initiative, Paul, and we'll be setting traps for him and, thanks to the Gulf War, he's lost some of his old hiding places. This is a victory, Paul.' He gestured at the broken boat. 'We're going to make the bastards who sent us that present dance to Uncle Sam's tune and, who knows, we might even dance them into an early grave.'

'I suppose,' I said slowly, 'that I should thank you for keeping me out of an early grave?'

'You don't have to thank me.' Van Stryker did not look at me as he spoke. 'When I sent you out twelve years ago I never expected to see you again. We sent others, don't ask who, and so far you're the only one to come back. Two others certainly won't return and a third might have joined our enemies. It wasn't an easy job you did, and I don't suppose you feel clean about it, but you served your country, Paul.' He turned and held out his hand. 'As far as I am concerned, you can go with a clear conscience.'

It was a bright night, the sky ablaze with stars above a clean country that was safe from harm. I walked to the car, breathing the cold air, and I wondered what would happen now.

'The airport, sir?' the driver asked.

'Please,' I said, and we drove away. The sentries waved us through the guardpost, and the brilliant lights disappeared behind as we drove through the dark woods towards the small safe towns of America.

I would go home to my own small town, but I guessed, after all, that I would not stay there. There would be no peace for me there. Ghosts still stalked my world and I did not know how to exorcise them; nor would il Hayaween abandon me, for I had made a fool of him and he would want me dead. I thought of Roisin's eyes in the instant before I had pulled the trigger. Oh dear God, but the paths we choose so heedlessly.

I closed my eyes. In the spring, I thought, I would go to Ireland, and I would take my boat to sea and I would let her take me somewhere, I did not know where, I did not care where, just anywhere that a scoundrel might find refuge.

BERNARD CORNWELL

Inspiration for *Scoundrel* came from the headline-making mortar attack on 10 Downing Street during the Gulf War in 1991. 'It seemed plain that it was originally organised as part of a worldwide terrorist campaign,' says Bernard Cornwell. The incident set him thinking about the links between various terrorist groups around the world. He'd spent three years in Northern Ireland working as head of Current Affairs for the BBC, so the IRA was a subject he already knew quite a lot about. Now, with homes in Cape Cod and Florida, he is also familiar with life in the United States.

Although Paul Shanahan's story is at the heart of the book, 'hero' doesn't seem the best way to describe him. Bernard Cornwell admits that it was hard to develop a novel around a central character who has spent much of his life involved with terrorism. In the first draft of the book Paul Shanahan 'got the girl,' laughs Bernard Cornwell, 'but then I thought—no he can't, that's rewarding him too much, so I changed the ending.'

Vehement in his dislike of terrorism, Bernard Cornwell has some compassion for people who get caught up in a life of violence. 'I understand but I don't approve,' he says. The underlying theme in the book is that 'you can love the sinner but hate the sin. It doesn't matter whether you like the terrorist as an individual, or the cause, you must hate the method.' Although he feels sorry for Paul Shanahan, the only character he likes is van Stryker because 'he has an unequivocal hatred of terrorism.'

Bernard Cornwell met his American wife Judy in 1978, and they moved to the States to be close to her family. As he didn't have a work permit he turned to writing fiction and started with a historical military adventure, which grew into the phenomenally successful *Sharpe* series. Now, he writes two best-selling books a year, alternating between historical novels and modern-day sailing thrillers. He enjoys writing both because, 'one is a change from the other.'

Dolphin Sunrise

BY ELIZABETH WEBSTER

ILLUSTRATED BY PAT FOGARTY

No one knows quite what to do about Matthew Ferguson. After a tragedy that leaves him orphaned, the quiet, serious fifteen-year-old has become increasingly wary and withdrawn. So when kindly neighbours suggest the boy should go with them on a holiday to Cornwall, everyone agrees that a change of air might be just what he needs.

New surroundings and sunshine work their magic, but Matthew is to find true healing in a totally unexpected way— through a very special dolphin, a creature who utterly enchants him, and who teaches him to rejoice in life itself . . .

PART I

JOY AS IT FLIES

It was the smell of smoke that woke him. He sat for a moment where he was, head on arms, slumped across the table where he had been working. Fallen asleep again, he thought. So much for revision. What time was it? How long had he been asleep? And had the Farleys come in yet, or was he still supposed to be listening out for the kids upstairs?

He had heard his mother and Len slam out of the house earlier on, after the usual shouting and smashing match. They'd have gone down to the Green Man, he supposed. They usually did, after a row. But the Farleys? They were quieter than his mum or Len. And much more reliable. They had said they'd be in by eleven.

He looked at his watch. Half ten. So they wouldn't be back yet. Maybe he'd better check on the kids. And that smoke. His mum and Len smoked like chimneys but, if they were out, where was it coming from? Come to think of it, the smell wasn't exactly like tobacco, more like . . . What was it like?

He sprang to his feet. It smelt like burning foam cushions . . . it smelt like fire.

He went to the door and opened it cautiously. At once a billowing cloud of acrid smoke began to pour into the room, curling up the stairs from below. He couldn't see any flames anywhere, but the lower floor was thick with dense black smoke and the fumes were rising towards him in a choking pall. The living-room door was shut, but he

147

could see the dark fingers of lethal vapour creeping out from underneath it in ever-increasing volume.

'Mum?' he shouted. 'Len? You in there?'

There was no answer. But now he could hear an ominous crackling sound from within that closed door, as if flames were already beginning to take hold. 'Mum?' he shouted again. But it was obvious they weren't there. They must have gone off to the pub and left a cigarette burning somewhere. The idiots.

Then he thought of the kids upstairs. I'm the idiot, he told himself. Must get them out. Now. How long have I got, I wonder?

He raced up the stairs to the flat above, grabbing the key that the Farleys had left with him. The kids were all asleep and he had a job to rouse them. Danny, the oldest, lay sprawled in a tangled heap with Jampy, the two-year-old, curled up in a ball inside the shelter of one outflung arm. Seven-year-old Donna had the baby, Kirsty, cradled in a careful embrace.

'Wake up!' hissed Matthew, shaking them. 'Come on. Wake up! You've got to get out of here. *Wake up!*'

Drowsily, they looked at him with round, startled eyes.

'Come on!' he said again. 'Danny, get some towels and douse them in the sink.' Scolding and pushing, he got them up, draped them in the wet towels and dragged them out of the bedroom onto the stairs.

When they saw the smoke Danny and Donna looked at Matthew with a flick of fear, but they did not scream. They were too disciplined for that. The Farleys were fairly tough parents, but kind.

'Come *on*,' Matthew urged them. 'Never mind the smoke.' But as he spoke there was a whoosh of hot air from below, and his mother's living-room door fell outwards in a spurt of flame.

He looked down in horror. He could never get the kids through that. 'Into my room!' he shouted. 'You'll have to get out of the window. Like Batman. It'll be fun.'

The children obeyed him instinctively.

'We'll tie the sheets together,' he said, pushing them into his room. 'We're only two storeys up. You'll manage easily.'

He seized his bottom sheet, realising as he did so that the duvet on top was a dead loss. Have to get some more sheets off the kids' beds. Why didn't I think of it before?

'Tie this end to the leg of my bed,' he told Danny. 'Won't be long.'

He dashed upstairs, fighting now through even denser smoke and a rising heat from the flames below, seized some more sheets and plunged recklessly down the stairs again, eyes streaming and breath

148

coming in painful gasps in spite of a wet cloth round his mouth.

He saw, glancing down, that the flames were already reaching the bottom stairs. Once they took hold, the stairwell would act like a funnel.

'Quick!' he said, and began knotting sheets together with clumsy hands. 'Donna, you go first with Kirsty.'

Donna looked at the sheet-rope doubtfully and clutched the baby more tightly in her arms. Matthew saw her hesitate, and knew why.

'I'll tie her on, then she can't fall, and you'll have your hands free. Hold the rope and slide down. Understand?'

Donna nodded and waited while Matthew tied the baby on to her back. Kirsty seemed to think the excitement was all a big game, and gave Matthew a toothless smile as he strapped her into place. Then he shoved the bed-leg hard against the wall below the window and leaned out of the window to look at the dangling sheet-rope before helping Donna to clamber over the sill. It was dark outside, but he could see heads craning upwards from the pavement below.

'Help her down!' he yelled. 'Someone ring the fire brigade!'

He watched Donna and the baby disappear down the dark house wall. Was the rope long enough? Danny could probably jump the last few feet, but Jampy? He was only two and his legs were very short. On a sudden impulse, he seized the thick duvet off his bed and flung it out of the window. It would be softer to land on. Softer than the pavement anyway.

'Quick!' he said to Danny. 'Now you and Jampy!'

Behind him there was another ominous whoosh of hot air, and he saw the flare of flames rushing up the stairs outside his door. Fool! he thought. First rule of a fire. Shut the doors! And he rushed over, almost as fast as the flames came towards him, and tried frantically to slam his door against them. But he was too late. A wall of fire seemed to belly out at him through the doorway, and the wooden door simply blackened and buckled before his eyes and then suddenly crackled into edges of flame as well.

No good wasting time on that. He ran back to Danny and Jampy by the window. At least he could get them out. But the smoke was now appallingly thick and acrid and he found Jampy slumped in a heap on the bed, with Danny furiously shaking him and crying: 'Jampy! Wake up!'

'It's the smoke. We've got to get him out to the air fast,' Matthew ordered. Wildly, he flung off his shirt and knotted the sleeves round the two-year-old's thin wrists. 'Put him round your neck. Fireman's lift,' he instructed. 'That's it. *Quick!*' Already the doorway was alight, and the floorboards were getting too hot to stand on. 'Hold on tight!' he said, and heaved Danny out of the window, with Jampy hanging round his neck like a limp rag doll.

As Danny's head disappeared from view, a whole line of flames began springing upwards through the floorboards. The knotted sheet on the bed-leg began to smoulder before Matthew's eyes. 'Oh my God,' he muttered, grabbing the sheet to stop it giving way before Danny got down. But the flames were getting closer, and the heat was getting unbearable. Suddenly he felt the thin sheet give behind him and begin to run through his hands. He braced himself against the window frame and he clung on, eyes shut and streaming, until he heard a shout from below. He supposed they were down safely. It was just as well, for by now his end of the sheet-rope was a charred ruin and had slipped through his burnt hands out of the window. Got to get out fast.

But how? There was nothing left to hang on to now. His bed was alight and the bottoms of his jeans were smouldering. Also, the smoke was making him stupid.

He climbed out onto the windowledge and sat there, looking down. The ring of faces was still there, while a bit further away under a streetlight he could see two men struggling with a ladder. No time for that. No time at all.

'Jump!' shouted a voice. 'We've got a sheet. We'll catch you.'

Jump, he thought. Maybe if I hang on to the window ledge and slide down it won't seem so far . . . But the window ledge was now too hot to hold on to, and he could see flames below him, spurting out through the downstairs windows. I'll have to jump, he told himself. No time for anything else. No time to be frightened. Jump!

There was a rush of air on his face. His hair seemed to stand on end. Then there was a sickening, teeth-jarring thud and a white flash of pain.

His last thought was, The fools! They didn't hold the sheet tight enough! Then the world seemed to turn in a shower of sparks and clanging bells and go suddenly dark.

THERE WERE VOICES somewhere in the dark. Only, it wasn't dark any more. It was unbearably light. So light that it hurt his eyes even though they were closed, and it hurt his eyelids too. They felt stiff and naked under the light and he wanted to cover them with his hands. Only, he found that he couldn't move his hands. They seemed to be strung up in some sort of cage . . . The voices hovered over him, rising and falling, but the words didn't make sense.

' . . . some shock as well.'

'Not extensive, no . . . hands . . .'

Hands? He couldn't move his hands. He tried, and fierce sharp agonies seemed to shoot through them. Why?

' . . and feet. But the fractures will give them time . . .'

Time. For what? He tried to move his feet. They seemed to be held in some sort of heavy vice. He tried again, but the effort made his face hurt. It felt just as stiff and unworkable as his eyelids. Stiff and fiery.

Fiery? Suddenly, he remembered. He struggled to open his eyes and a sort of croak came out of his mouth. 'Kids . . .?'

'They're safe, Matthew. All safe. Thanks to you.'

'Oh . . . good,' he sighed.

'Coming round . . . another shot,' murmured a rather commanding voice.

'Just a little prick,' said another voice. 'Don't try to move yet.'

He lay still, and presently he floated off again into the merciful dark.

The next time, he did manage to get his eyes open a crack, and he found himself looking at his own legs strung up on a pulley in front of him. He seemed to be in a sort of side-ward on his own, but he could just see the main hospital ward stretching away beyond him. He turned his head a little, and met the eyes of a young nurse who was bending over him.

'Feeling better?'

'Yes.'

'Up to visitors?'

His heart gave a curious lurch of fear. What visitors? He didn't want his mother and Len arguing all round his bed. Or coming here drunk or something.

'What visitors?'

The nurse seemed a little wary. 'There are plenty of people who want to see you. Bit of a hero, you know.' She saw his reluctance and added gently, 'We'll have to ration you.'

The first to come were the Farleys. Madge Farley cried all over him and called him 'you poor boy', gasping out halting words of gratitude. It was unlike her to be gushing. Jim Farley just stood there, looking red in the face, and growling, 'Good lad,' from time to time between Madge's outbursts.

Matthew supposed it was the painkillers, but he kept seeing the faces before him in flashes of startling clarity. Madge's face was often tight and scraped-looking, what with the four kids to look after and a part-time cleaning job in the evenings when Jim got home. Her brown eyes usually looked flat and sharpish, but now they were bright with tears and her mouth was actually trembling. As for Jim, his faded blue eyes seemed almost puzzled by something—as if they could not think how to express what he felt.

'It was nice of you to come,' said Matthew politely, trying to dispel Jim's look of silent stress.

This innocent remark produced another tide of tears in Madge, and she began to babble something about 'when we've got everything, and you're on your own—'

But here Jim cut in sharply with one warning word, 'Madge!' and to Matthew's surprise the two of them hurried away, promising to come again tomorrow.

'Bring the kids,' Matthew called after them. 'I'd like to see they're all in one piece.'

Matthew drifted into a doze. But something was bugging him. *On your own* . . . And come to think of it, why had it been the Farleys who came first?

He opened his eyes and called Sister.

'Why hasn't my mother been to see me?' he asked.

The question seemed to hover in the air between them. Then Sister spoke hesitantly. 'I'm afraid she can't. I'll get the doctor to explain.'

'They're dead, aren't they?' he said dully. 'They're dead.'

Sister did not answer. But presently a grave young doctor came and sat down by his bed.

'I thought they were out,' said Matthew, in a voice of growing horror. 'I *heard* them go out.'

'They were asleep, Matthew.'

'But I called—I called and called.'

'I'm sure you did.' The serious, assessing eyes were kind. 'It was much too late then you see. They'd have been unconscious by then—or even dead. The smoke would have killed them.' He leaned forward and laid a friendly hand on Matthew's shoulder. 'They wouldn't have felt a thing, you know. They just—never woke up.'

'I thought they were out . . .' Matthew repeated.

'You did everything you could,' said the young doctor, filled with sympathy for this shock-ridden fifteen-year-old. 'You saved four young lives, after all.'

'You don't understand,' said Matthew. But it was hopeless to

152

explain. How could he say: I didn't like them. Not either of them. They were always drunk and always fighting. *But I never wished them dead.* 'You don't understand,' he repeated, and slow, shameful tears began to drip out of his eyes.

AFTER THAT, A WHOLE LOT more people came to see him. There was a friendly young policewoman who was quiet and patient and took down a careful statement. There was a woman from Pimlico Council Social Services department who tried to ask questions in a soothing voice that put his teeth on edge. And there was someone from the insurance who didn't make any sense at all.

But one day the Farley kids came on their own after school, Donna carrying the baby and Danny holding firmly on to Jampy who wanted to know why Matthew's legs were strung up to the ceiling. He was glad to see the kids. Somehow, their sturdy unconcern made him feel better. He was sick of all those hushed voices and sympathetic glances.

'Where are you all living?' he asked, realising all at once that they had lost their home too, and all their possessions.

'Bed and breakfast,' said Donna, in a matter-of-fact and absurdly adult tone. She made a face at Matthew and added, 'Till the council gets us a new flat. Mum hates it.'

'Can't swing a cat in it, she says,' agreed Danny.

'Swing a cat!' echoed Jampy, running round in circles beside Matthew's bed.

Danny grabbed him and turned back to Matthew with a hard and challenging stare. 'When you comin' out then?'

'When I can walk, I s'pose.'

'Better getta move on, then.'

Jampy was still jumping up and down. 'Getta move on!' he chanted. 'Getta move on!'

Donna was looking at Matthew as if weighing up something in her mind. 'Mum says we're all going to the sea,' she announced. 'Soon as you're ready.'

IT TOOK HIM SIX WEEKS to escape from the hospital. During that time, they took the cages off his burnt hands and the traction pulleys off his broken legs and taught him to walk again. It was a slow and somewhat painful process, and he got very cross with his own clumsiness. They gave him a walking iron on one leg and a pair of crutches, and told him he must keep the other leg off the ground for longer because it was a multiple fracture and his burnt foot was still not quite healed. So he learned to swing himself along in a lopsided fashion, and tried not to fall over too often.

They might have let him go at this stage, but the doctors were worried about him. They talked of delayed shock and a natural exhaustion, but they did not like Matthew's closed white face, his docile acceptance of idleness, and his silence. Then there was the problem of the boy's future. He was, it seemed, totally alone in the world, unless the Social Services people could come up with a distant relation somewhere. In the meantime, where was he to go? And was he fit to go anywhere?

At last, however, Madge Farley announced that the neighbours had all clubbed together, and someone had offered them all a free caravan on a site in Cornwall, and she was only waiting for the doctors to release Matthew. So what were they going to do about it?

They thought they might let him go if he would report to the local hospital for physiotherapy once a week. But then one of the doctors remembered that there was an aqua-surf club in that area, and it would have its own physiotherapist and swimming instructor to give Matthew all the right exercises on the spot.

At this point, Madge Farley put her hands on her hips and looked the doctors up and down with a stern and beady eye.

'Well then, what are we waiting for?'

SO THERE THEY ALL WERE, by the sea. It was early autumn by now, and the days were mild and sunny. The caravan was set a little apart from some others on a site among grassy dunes above the sea, and they could walk down across a sloping sandy cliff to the beach. Matthew found the caravan steps a bit tricky, but then they gave him a tent of his own and he only had to negotiate the steps for meals. At first the walk to the sea seemed long, especially over the shifting dunes, but he soon got used to it.

The beach itself was a long, curved stretch of flawless sand, and the surf pounding on it was simply beautiful. But Matthew knew, sadly, that he couldn't hope to stand up in those magnificent waves, let alone ride them like the surfers. He could only stumble along on his stiff, ungainly legs, and look at the sea from a safe distance.

The kids scampered and shouted in front of him, and Madge and Jim Farley plodded on behind with rugs and towels and a picnic. For them it was the holiday of a lifetime—they had never been able to afford one before—and they were determined to enjoy every minute of it. But for Matthew it was all strange and dreamlike, and he seemed to see the world through glass, as if he was on the other side and could not reach it.

The sea seemed real, though. You could swim in it and be part of it . . . He longed to swim. To escape the heavy drag of his legs, the gritty sand that was too soft to walk in. It would be cool in the water, he could lie floating in the arms of the wide sea-swell, and forget his own clumsy limbs, his heavy body, and his guilt.

'Are you Matthew Ferguson?' A voice broke into his dream.

He looked up. The man standing before him was young and smiling, with tawny gold hair that clung in wet tongues round his head, and very blue, farseeing eyes in a tanned, wind-scoured face. He was carrying a surfboard under one arm, and rivulets of seawater were running down his gleaming wet suit onto the sand.

'I'm Skip,' he told him, holding out his other hand in friendly welcome. 'At least, my name's David Alexander, but everybody calls me Skip because I run the aqua-surf club. I've been looking out for you.'

Matthew took the proffered hand. It was cool and firm, and seemed to generate strength and confidence.

'Come along, I'll introduce you to the others.' Skip was leading Matthew towards a dark line of rocks at one end of the bay.

'Now, just listen to me before we meet the boys. No surfing for you—yet. It's much too dangerous for damaged legs.' His smile was warm and encouraging as he turned his head to glance at Matthew. 'But swimming off the rocks is OK. If you *can* swim, that is?'

'Oh yes,' Matthew assured him. 'I was fairly good—before.'

Skip nodded, not wasting time on commiseration. Matthew was grateful for that. 'You can slip into fairly deep water from the rocks. No staggering about in the shallows with the surf knocking you down. Keep to calm water until you're stronger. Understand?'

'Yes,' agreed Matthew humbly. It made sense, after all.

'There's a heated pool at the club where you'll do your physio exercises. I'll see you through those. And I'll swim with you the first couple of times in the sea, just to make sure you don't get cramp or something.' He added, to Matthew's protesting face, 'These are dangerous waters. Mustn't be stupid. It puts other people's lives at risk.'

Matthew nodded, chastened.

Skip smiled. 'Right. Lecture over. Come and meet the boys.'

The boys seemed to be mostly young men of about Skip's age.

They didn't comment on Matthew's legs and for this he was thankful. They greeted him cheerfully with instant friendliness.

'Seals come in sometimes,' volunteered one.

'Seals?' Matthew looked startled.

'Grey seals—out there.' A brown hand pointed towards the distant line of rocks round the point. 'You can get quite close to them. They're quite happy unless you splash too much.'

'And unless the virus gets to them,' said Skip, sounding curiously proprietorial and anxious. Clearly, the little seal colony was yet another of his responsibilities.

Matthew looked out to sea. He thought there were small heads bobbing about close to the rocks, but he couldn't be sure.

'Here,' said Skip, holding out a wet suit. 'Try this for size.'

THERE BEGAN FOR MATTHEW a time of painful enchantment. The sea was always there, beckoning and calling, and he was always trying to keep up with Skip or one of the other aqua-club members who had been appointed to watch over him. His legs hurt and his back ached, and tears of frustration mingled with the salt sea-spray, but he loved every moment of it. Sometimes he just idled, floating and drifting, gazing up at the sky, feeling the lift and fall of the ocean under his tired limbs. Sometimes Skip gave him a snorkel and he turned on his face and lay looking down through translucent depths. And once or twice the dark bobbing head of a seal came up through a wave to have a look at him, and then disappeared again under the next sea-swell.

One day there was a storm and Matthew was not allowed to swim. Instead, he took the four kids along to the beach shop for ice creams, and then settled down to help them build an elaborate fort in the wet sand just above the tideline.

'Where's your shiny suit then?' asked Donna, who clearly thought Matthew was rather splendid in his borrowed gear.

He grinned at her. 'Wouldn't give it to me today. Too rough.'

'Shiny suit,' said Jampy, jumping up and down.

'Look out, you clot,' yelled Danny, seeing imminent disaster for his battlements. 'Now look what you've done!'

'Shiny suit!' repeated Jampy, still dancing in the sun and paying no heed at all to the ruin beneath his small brown feet.

Madge looked across at them from the safety of her deck chair and windbreak, and then turned to smile at Jim. They seemed happy enough, the kids—and Matthew was already beginning to look better. But she could not help noticing that the look of shuttered sadness was still on his face when the kids failed to distract him. So far, she had not tried to talk to him about anything serious.

'Jim,' she said doubtfully, 'oughtn't we to—?'

'No.' Jim shook his head in slow reproof. 'Leave 'im be.'

Madge nodded and said no more. Instead, she got up and plodded off through the blowing sand to the caravan, where she began to cut sandwiches. When you didn't know what to do for someone, you could always feed them.

THE OLD MAN SAT in the sun and watched the sea. It was sheltered down by the deserted lifeboat station, and the bench was set into the harbour wall with its back to the wind. Only, of course, there wasn't a harbour any more. Just the small, derelict quay where the fishing fleet used to come in, and the slipway for the lifeboat below the flaking lifeboat-station doors that were permanently closed now. Beyond that, up the hill a little and leaning into the headland, there were still some cottages occupied by the same old fisher-folk families. But for the most part, nowadays, it was holiday flats and caravan sites and bungalows, and the four-square hotel at the other end of the sea wall, looking out into the bay.

It wasn't a bad hotel, as hotels go, and the villagers still liked to use the smoky old bar with its low ceiling and polished brass ship's bell. It had its own deep-set windows embracing the view of the sea, but he liked to get out into the air and look at the passing world by himself. He was there every day, if the weather was fine and, if it rained, he climbed a little higher and went into the shelter outside the old seamen's union building. Today, it was fine and glittering after the storm, and he sat in the splintered sunlight admiring the surf.

The boy with the limp was there again. Not swimming today, of course, but playing on the beach with the rest of his family. Doing his best to be playful, thought the old captain, watching him—for he seemed to be a grave, somewhat shadowed boy who rarely smiled. A bit awkward too, on land, but in the sea he looked entirely different, almost happy, and much more graceful.

A sudden spurt of laughter came from the beach below him as the tide came in behind the children and quietly demolished the fortress they had so carefully built on the sand. The boy picked up the youngest child—that smiling baby—and whirled it above his head, and then deposited it safely beside its mother, who seemed to be busy handing out sandwiches to everyone. But the boy did not seem to want a sandwich. He was coming up the beach towards the harbour wall.

Matthew came up the steps and saw the old man sitting in the sun. He had noticed him before, several times, and now—for some reason that he could not quite understand—he smiled at him.

'Hello,' said Captain St George, smiling back. 'Too rough for swimming today?'

' 'Fraid so.' Matthew hesitated for a moment, and then sat down on the bench beside him. 'It's nice here in the sun.'

The old man nodded. 'I come here most days, from the hotel up the cliff.' He looked out at the sea with faded, tranquil eyes. 'Cuts you down to size, doesn't it?'

Matthew grinned. 'A pinhead in all that ocean.'

They were silent for a while; and then, greatly daring, Verney St George asked, 'What happened to your leg?'

'Legs.' Matthew shot him a half-smiling glance. 'Fell out of a window.'

'Oh. Awkward.'

'Very.' And then, in case he sounded self-pitying, he added swiftly, 'But they're improving.'

'I can see that.'

Matthew looked pleased. 'Can you really?'

'Oh yes. Definitely more mobile. Don't your family think so?' Verney St George waved an expressive hand at the cheerful little party on the beach below them.

For a moment the boy seemed embarrassed. Then he said in a carefully careless tone, 'They're not my family. Just—friends who brought me along.'

The captain did not enquire further. Instead, he said neutrally enough, 'They seem a nice bunch of kids.'

'Yes,' agreed Matthew, warmly. 'They are. Especially Jampy.'

'Instant joy,' murmured the old man, watching the antics of Jampy, who was trailing a long crimson ribbon of seaweed on the new-washed sand. 'Wish I had it.'

'So do I,' admitted Matthew.

The two of them—the old man and the boy—looked at one another in perfect understanding.

SEVERAL TIMES AFTER THAT Matthew climbed up the steps to talk to the old man. They watched the surfers, and smiled indulgently at Jampy and Donna chasing Danny across the sand. Sometimes

158

Matthew felt as old as Captain St George, watching the kids playing down below, and sometimes Verney St George badly wanted to know why anyone so young could be so sad. But he did not ask—not then—and Matthew did not tell him. They just talked idly of neutral things and let the unspoken sympathy between them grow quietly on its own.

One day there was another storm, and most people stayed at home. Captain St George did not come out, and Matthew missed him, especially as he was not allowed in the sea that day either. He spent extra time in the aqua-surf club pool, teaching his legs to behave themselves, and then surprised himself by calling at the square old hotel on the clifftop to ask after the captain.

They told him that the captain was resting today. Sometimes, they said, he was not well enough to go out, but they felt sure he would be all right again soon. Only half satisfied, Matthew turned away. He was much too shy to ask to see him.

The next day the wind dropped and Matthew was given permission to swim again.

'Be careful, though,' warned Skip sternly. 'There's still a bit of a swell. Don't go too far out.'

Matthew climbed round to the little deserted bay beyond the main beach, and slipped into the water on the sheltered side of the rocks. It was quiet there, deep and quiet. He was idling on his back when he suddenly became aware that he was being watched. He couldn't quite understand the sensation, but he was quite sure about it. Someone, or something, was watching him. He turned over and righted himself, treading water in the rocking sea swell.

A huge, dark face was looking at him. Two bright, intelligent eyes were fixed on his face, and a wide, welcoming smile was spread across the grey massive head beneath the thrusting nose.

For a moment, Matthew was terrified. But then a curious sense of reassurance seemed to wash over him. It came, he felt sure, from the creature in front of him—the beautiful, gleaming creature that was regarding him with such intense interest.

It's a dolphin, he thought. What am I afraid of? It's come to have a look at me. And why not? I must look a clumsy sort of object.

The dolphin seemed to be laughing in agreement. It dived under a wave, moved in a swift streak of glinting darkness round him, and then leaped out of the water in a graceful curve.

'Oh!' said Matthew, smiling. 'Aren't you beautiful. I wish I could leap like that.'

The dolphin turned in a wide arc and came swimming towards him. Matthew put out a hand, greatly daring, and touched the black-and-silver wet flank as it sailed past him. It felt smooth and firm, and almost familiar—like someone he already knew.

The great creature turned again in the translucent water, weaving patterns of liquid grace all round him, approaching and retreating, teasing and inviting, showing no trace of fear.

Matthew was utterly captivated. He swam close and tried vainly to imitate the dolphin's effortless movements in the water. It seemed to wait for him, moderating its own flashing speed to his slow progress, and its smile seemed to be tolerant and almost affectionate. *You aren't very quick,* it seemed to be saying to him. *But as humans go, you're not too bad.* Then it dived again and came up so close that its silken body brushed alongside his own, and Matthew laughed and clasped his arms round it in sudden delight. For a moment they swam together, until with a flick of its tail-fluke it shook itself free and leaped in the air again.

Instant joy, thought Matthew, remembering the old man on the bench, and Jampy dancing on the sand. Yes, instant joy!

The dolphin leaped in the air once more, dived deep and came up close, nuzzling against his body with its thrusting bottle nose.

'I shall call you Flite,' said Matthew. 'Because you can almost fly. Lord Flite-a-Leaping. You must be an aristocrat, with a nose like that.' He put his arms round the dolphin's sinuous body again and hugged it close. 'Flite,' he crooned. The dolphin smiled and flicked its tail at him.

For nearly an hour they swam and played together, growing in some strange way ever closer as they circled and dived in the clear green depths. Then at last Matthew's damaged legs began to tire, and he knew he would have to go in.

But the clever eyes seemed to know his reluctance—for suddenly the powerful body came close again, pushing him towards the shallower water near the rocks.

'All right,' said Matthew. 'I've got the message. It's time I went in. But I don't want to leave you.'

He stroked the smooth, gleaming head with one cold wet hand, and turned away to swim back to the rocks. Flite gave him one final, cheerful thrust with his beak, leaped high into the sunlight in a bright flash of ecstasy, and headed away out to sea.

'Well, he's gone,' said Matthew sadly, looking back at a sea that was suddenly grey and very empty.

'YOU STAYED IN TOO LONG,' said Skip severely, rubbing Matthew down with a rough but kindly hand. 'That's counterproductive.'

'I know.' Matthew gave him a lopsided grin. 'But—I was enjoying myself.' He didn't know why he was being secretive about the dolphin, but something made him keep quiet. What he and Flite had shared was a private, special joy, not to be exclaimed over, trampled on and spoilt. He knew about that. Oh yes, his mother had been good at that. He shivered, for those were the kind of thoughts he simply must not have—not any more—not after everything that had happened . . . But he sometimes felt that by dying in the fire, his mother and her latest awful boyfriend had put the final seal of destruction on his life—on all his dreams and visions. Just for a little while, out there with Flite the dolphin, he thought he had found them again, in the deep translucent spaces of the wild Atlantic.

'You OK?' Skip's clear, assessing gaze raked Matthew's thin body to the bone. 'Better get changed before you turn entirely blue.'

'I—I'm not cold,' chattered Matthew, trying in vain to explain.

'No?' Skip's hand came down on Matthew's shoulder, propelling him forward. 'No exercises today. Go and lie in the sun.'

THE OLD MAN WAS THERE again when he climbed up the steps to the harbour wall. He was sitting in the sun, his ruff of white hair sticking out under his seaman's cap, and his watery blue eyes fixed on the restless sea. His knotted hands were resting on the white bone handle of a thin black walking stick with a gold-coloured ferrule.

'Good swim?' The calm voice was friendly.

'Yes, thanks.'

'Sea's gone down a lot.'

'Mm. Just about right for me.' He sounded faintly contemptuous of himself, and the old man laughed.

'Most people wouldn't go in off the rocks at all in this swell.'

So he had seen him go in. What else had he seen? Matthew felt a flick of reluctance. He didn't want to talk about Flite. Not to anyone.

But the captain made no further comment. He went on staring at the sea and then said abruptly, 'You lonely?'

Matthew started. 'Lonely?'

'Yes. Lonely. I'm lonely. Are you?'

Matthew considered it. 'I don't know,' he said at last. 'I suppose . . . I've always been a bit—er—on my own. But *lonely*? I don't think so.'

'Other company?'

'There's the kids—' He waved a hand at the party on the beach.

'Boys your own age? Like Skip's surfers?'

Matthew's eyes opened wide. 'You know Skip?'

'Everyone knows Skip. He does a good job at the club.'

'Yes.' Matthew sighed. 'The surfers have asked me over for the evening a couple of times, but . . .'

Verney St George glared at him. 'You should go. No good mopin' about.'

Matthew opened his mouth to protest and then shut it again. At last he said mildly, 'You've been checking up on me.'

''Fraid so.'

'Why?'

The captain's glare was still belligerent. 'Wanted to know what's bitin' you. It's a waste of time, you know.'

'What is?'

'Guilt.'

Matthew stared. He was so startled he almost got up and ran. But he couldn't run, so he sat there, pale with shock. 'Guilt?'

Captain St George turned his head and looked straight at Matthew. 'What you did for those kids was only right and proper. Young lives are important. From all accounts, you couldn't have saved those other two. It's sad, but there it is.'

Matthew blinked. 'It's—not as simple as that . . .'

'Why not?' The captain's voice was crisp.

'It's difficult—' He drew in a painful breath. 'You see, I—I didn't like them much.'

'What's that got to do with it?'

The boy looked at him, amazed. 'I thought—'

'You thought because you didn't like them, you must have left them to die on purpose?' The blunt words were meant to shock.

Matthew put up his hand, as if warding off a blow. 'I didn't mean—'

'Of course you didn't. You'd have got your worst enemy out of there if you could. Anybody would.' The old man leaned forward and tapped him on the arm with an emphatic finger. 'Get the facts straight, boy. You thought they were out. They weren't. They were in all that smoke and fire, and they were dead, long before you even noticed the smoke. You were not responsible.'

Matthew's eyes were dark with memory. 'I still feel responsible.'

Captain St George grunted with exasperation. He paused, and then said, 'Tell me about your mother.'

Matthew sighed. 'What can I say? There was always someone new with her, and I was always in the way, cramping her style. She liked a good time, that's all.'

'What about your father?'

'Died in a car crash, so she told me. I never really knew him.'

'And—this latest one—did you know him?'

'Not really. They used to drink a lot, shout and throw things, and then they'd go down to the pub and start all over again. I thought that's what they'd done that night.' Matthew's voice was suddenly brittle. 'But I should have made sure . . . '

'If you'd gone down those stairs to have a look, you'd be dead too—and so would all those young kids.'

Matthew was silent. He saw the logic of that. 'It's all such a mess,' he said, in a sick and weary voice.

'It's over,' stated the captain. 'It's *over*, boy. No more looking back. Only a fool spends his life looking backwards. I should know.'

Matthew heard the bitterness in the incisive voice and wondered at it, but he was suddenly too tired to pursue his thoughts further. It was time to follow Skip's orders and lie in the sun.

HE WAS ALMOST AFRAID to go into the sea next day, in case it remained empty and cold. But the dolphin came again. He had not been swimming more than a few minutes, it seemed, before the blue-grey shadow cut through the water towards him.

'Flite!' he called, and held his arms out in welcome. 'You came.'

The dolphin's response was a series of clicks and squeaks and a couple of spectacular leaps in the air. *Come on*, he seemed to be saying. *Stop being so earthbound and slow. Look how high I can jump! Isn't life glorious?*

Matthew looked, and marvelled, and followed as best he could. And, Yes! he thought. *Isn't life glorious?*

For a long time they played together, turning and diving, gliding down into green depths and swimming up again into sunlight, to swirling bubbles and dazzling cascades of upflung water. Sometimes the dolphin made circles round him, but sometimes it came close and allowed him to hold on to its strong dorsal fin and swim beside it, and once or twice the great head came close and looked at him eye to eye, as if to say, *I know you now.*

Matthew wondered if he would ever dare to ride on the friendly sea creature's back as men were supposed to have done in the legends. It would be wonderful to try, but somehow he knew he must let the dolphin make all the overtures. So he swam peacefully beside it in a state of happy enchantment, joining in its games and leaps and lightning turns with all the skill he could muster. But then, all at once, a terrifying cramp assailed him in his damaged legs, and he curled up in a tight ball of pain and began to sink like a stone.

For a moment the dolphin seemed to be puzzled, but then some echo of his pain seemed to reach it in a strange telepathy, for the long, fluid body suddenly shot down below his helpless, stiff legs and began to nudge him upwards. Dimly Matthew felt the curve of the dolphin's back pushing up beneath him, until he was riding just behind its head as it knifed its way upwards through the surge and pull of the sea. The dolphin's nose broke surface very swiftly and air rushed into Matthew's lungs, but the dolphin did not immediately shrug him off its back. It went on, cutting through the water, entirely sure of its direction until it reached the shelter of the rocks where it had left Matthew before. Then, and only then, did it turn and roll gently in the breaking surf, depositing Matthew safely within reach of land.

The cramp was gone now, but he felt limp and very tired. Even so, he turned in the water and hugged the dolphin before he tried to climb up onto the wet rocks. 'Thank you, Flite,' he murmured, close to the dolphin's head. 'I was almost a goner there!'

Flite merely leaped in the air once more to show that life was still good. Then the dolphin shot away out to sea.

'DID YOU TALK TO HIM?' asked Skip, looking at the old man.

'Yes.' Captain St George nodded and pushed Skip's drink towards him. They were sitting in the bar of the hotel, with its big curved windows looking over the sunlit bay.

'Any—result?'

'Some.' The seamed brown face grew thoughtful. 'It's a difficult thing to dispel—a sense of guilt. I think he's coming out of shock a bit, at least.'

Skip nodded, and took a slow swig of beer. 'He came down to the club last night.'

'Good. How did he get on with the boys?'

'Fine. Especially when he got hold of a guitar.'

The old man started. 'Guitar? Can he play?'

'Like a real pro.'

'Pop music and the like?' The captain was a bit vague about such things.

'Oh no,' said Skip, shaking his head. 'Well, he did play a couple of songs for the boys to sing along. But for the rest, he simply sat down with the thing on his knee and forgot we were there. I've never heard anything like it.'

The captain stared at him in astonishment, then he said slowly, 'Well, one hidden talent uncovered. What else is he good at?'

'Computers. Mary's got one in the office. She's trying to keep tabs on the seal population, among other things. Got in an awful mess. He put her right in no time.'

The old captain whistled. 'That's a useful skill today. Any idea about his schooling?'

Skip sighed. 'He says he was taking GCSEs this summer. Did most of them, but missed a couple at the end.'

The two pairs of eyes met in a curious, bleak concern.

'Skip—what's to become of him? What did the Social Services people say?'

'They simply told me what to do for his physical recovery, and asked me to keep a general eye on him. I don't think they know what to do with him, really. They're trying to trace a relative, I think. And meantime, Madge Farley will do her best for him, I'm sure.'

'Maybe,' said Captain St George, with doubt in his voice, 'we ought to go and talk to her?'

'Maybe we should,' agreed Skip.

MADGE FARLEY, WHEN THEY FOUND HER, was almost as blunt as old Captain St George, and quite as concerned.

'See, I'd have Matt like a shot. He's a good boy, always was, and my kids adore him. But what can I do? Two rooms in a bed-and-breakfast they've given us, two bloody rooms for four kids and Jim and me. I suppose Matt could sleep on the floor . . . but it wouldn't be good for him.'

'No,' said the captain, with feeling. 'It wouldn't.'

Madge turned to Skip, her face full of helpless rage. 'They're so flippin' *stupid*,' she said. 'If they'd give us a new flat, it'd be all right for everyone. But they'll dither about until it's too late, and then put the boy into care because he's got nowhere to go.'

Skip exploded. 'They can't do that.'

'Oh yes, they can. He's got no relatives, see—no home—no possessions, neither. Nothing but the things he stands up in.'

'Is there any money?' asked the captain.

Madge snorted. 'When did them two ever save anything? It all went on the booze. I don't think they even fed Matthew properly. I used to ask him up to mind the kids sometimes just to get a meal inside him.'

166

She scowled in disapproval and then added as an afterthought, 'The insurance man did come round to have a look, though . . . there might be something.'

'Always on his own, was he?' asked St George.

'Oh yes, as long as I've known him, and that's ten years. He used to stay in his room mostly, and study. He was clever, see? I think he took to his books sort of early, to shut things out, if you know what I mean.'

'I know what you mean,' agreed the captain.

'What about his guitar?' asked Skip.

Madge brightened a little. 'Oh yes, he was always playing. Except when his mother yelled at him to stop.'

'Did he—did anyone teach him?' asked the captain.

Madge nodded vigorously. 'Someone at school, one of the masters, I think. I remember Matt telling me his mum wouldn't pay for lessons, so he took on an extra paper round.' She sighed. 'Of course, that's gone up in smoke as well, poor kid, and his computer. Months of saving, that cost him, I know.'

She suddenly stopped and looked at the two men with distress. 'But what I don't understand is, what's to become of him? I haven't dared talk to Matt about it yet. He seems so . . . so shut inside himself, somehow. We're going home in a couple of days—and I don't know what to do for the best.'

Skip said suddenly, 'He could stay on with us for a bit—if he wants to. Just till things are sorted out, I mean.'

'Could he?' Madge looked doubtful. 'Would they let him?'

'We'll see,' said the captain. 'Leave it to us. We'll find out.'

'But,' said Skip, 'we must find out what Matthew wants first.'

MATTHEW KNEW WHAT HE WANTED. He wanted to stay within reach of the sea, where he could play with Flite the dolphin all day long. Nothing else seemed to matter. Nothing else even seemed real any more. Except the feel of a guitar under his hands, and the magic that music could weave on the air.

Music and the sea. The dolphin's dance was like music—those intricate patterns of grace and beauty; and the sound of the surf was like music. They were all one, somehow, in his mind, and he did not think he could do without them, now.

'Would you like to stay on a bit?' asked Skip.

'Yes,' said Matthew. 'Please.' He looked at Skip with a wild hope leaping inside him. 'But will they let me?'

'I don't know. The captain's going to find out.'

167

Matthew looked puzzled for a moment. 'The captain? You mean the old man I've been talking to? Who is he, Skip?'

A strange expression crossed Skip's face. 'Don't you know? . . . No, I suppose you wouldn't . . .' He paused for so long that Matthew had to prompt him.

'Is he really a sea captain?'

'I think he was once—when he was young. That's how he began. Master of one small ship. Now Captain St George is head of one of the biggest shipping lines in Europe.'

'*What?*'

Skip was smiling at Matthew's astonishment. 'A real tycoon—and very rich, they say. Though he lives quietly enough down here.'

'But he—'

'Oh, I know. He wears a shabby seaman's jacket and a battered old cap on his head. But although he pretends to be just an old man idling the day away, he knows precisely where all his ships are, and keeps in touch with his London office every day with his own computer.'

Matthew whistled. 'What kind of ships?'

'Not the big liners any more—mostly tankers, freighters, ferries, tourist boats, caïques—you name it, he's got them all.'

'Does he live down here all the time?'

'No. But he comes to stay at the hotel every summer. Sometimes he stays on through the autumn, but he usually goes before the winter, somewhere south where it's warm. He's been very ill, they say, though he never talks about it.'

Matthew said slowly, 'He's been good to me.'

'So I gather. You're honoured.' His voice was dry, faintly edged with some hidden tension. 'He's not always good to people.'

'He said he was lonely,' said Matthew.

Skip's eyes narrowed and he seemed to go very still. 'Did he? You are honoured. He's never confessed that to anyone else, I'm sure.'

Matthew looked at Skip thoughtfully and caught a glimpse of anguish in his face which made him look quite different. Then the look receded, and Skip's face took on its normal contours. 'Well, we'll leave the captain to sort out your problems. In the meantime, the boys want you to play for them again. Will you come?'

'All right,' agreed Matthew. 'Why not?'

THAT NIGHT THE MEMBERS of the aqua-surf club greeted Matthew like an old friend. 'Look who's here!' they cried. 'Old Limpy-Legs himself!' and 'Fingers Ferguson in person!'

He had long since given up being touchy about his legs, and he found himself grinning back and accepting a shandy and a Cornish pasty before he settled down to play. He played everything they asked for, as far as he could. Pop songs, folk songs, old sea shanties, all the favourites they could remember, he didn't mind. He had a guitar in his hands and his fingers were happy. They had been stiff at first, and a bit painful on the strings, but it came back, and the more he played, the better they felt. So he played on, finding his way through every half-remembered tune and every shouted chorus.

But at last there came a small lull and one of them said, 'Well, what about the real stuff? Let's have some class around here.'

He began with Bach and by the time the neat, ordered pattern of notes came to an end, he had forgotten his audience. So he went on to Albéniz—something sad and savage, and then to Granados and those fierce, spiky chords. When it was over, and the applause had broken into the little astonished silence that preceded it, he saw that there was someone new in the clubroom.

It was a girl with short blonde hair that swung in a gleaming cap round her head, and she was staring at him out of strange, tawny eyes that were a curious mixture of brown and gold.

'Where did you learn to play like that?' she asked.

Matthew smiled. 'I had a smashing teacher.'

'You must have.'

Skip strolled up and stood beside her, laying a friendly hand on her shoulder. She looked up, and a gleam like summer lightning seemed to spark between them. 'I see you two have met,' said Skip.

'Not really.' She smiled back at Matthew. 'Introduce me to the maestro.'

'Oh, honestly!' protested Matthew. 'Give me a break!'

She laughed and Skip grinned down at him. 'This is Dr Petra Davison—from the Sea Mammal Research Unit. Anything you want to know about seals, or whales, she'll tell you.'

'You ought to play to them,' she remarked.

'Who?'

'The seals. They love music. They come quite close in to listen—especially if you sing to them. I've often done it.'

Matthew had a sudden picture of this vivid blonde girl standing on a rock singing wildly in the wind, and a whole lot of bobbing heads listening in the water.

'Magic!' he exclaimed softly. 'Do other creatures like it too?'

'Dolphins, you mean?'

The two of them were smiling at him, and he suddenly realised that they knew all about Flite—and had carefully not said anything about it to anyone. An enormous sense of relief came over him. He had hated deceiving Skip, even in the mildest way.

'You know about Flite,' he said.

'Is that what you call him?'

'Lord-a-Leaping Flite,' pronounced Matthew, smiling. 'I ought to have told you before, but I—'

'But you wanted to keep him to yourself. I don't blame you,' Skip finished for him.

Matthew turned to the blonde girl beside him shyly. 'Do you want to come out and meet him?'

She seemed to hesitate. 'I'm only here to monitor the seal colony at the moment.'

'Monitor?'

'Take a count—if I can. And see if any of them show any signs of the North Sea virus.' She turned to Skip enquiringly. 'You've had no casualties here, have you?'

'No. But someone reported a dead porpoise washed up on a beach further north.'

Fear clutched at Matthew. 'A *porpoise*? Could dolphins catch it?'

Petra sighed. 'We don't know yet. There have been reports of dolphins dying from a mysterious virus off the east coast of America, but we haven't seen it here.' She looked at Matthew with compassion, seeing his anxiety. 'That's only half the story, though. Other terrible things are happening to dolphins, you know.'

'Such as?'

'Well, for a start, there are the purse-seine nets used for tuna fishing. They get caught in them, hundreds of them, along with the tuna. They can't come to the surface to breathe, so they drown.'

'*Drown!*' He thought of Flite trapped in the nets, twisting and turning, desperate to get out, and he shivered. 'He saved my life yesterday, I think.'

'How come?' asked Skip, and when Matthew told him, he said slowly, 'You know what they say round here? "Dolphins only come to them as needs 'em!" '

'Do they?' Matthew was absurdly pleased.

'They cry in the nets,' said Petra suddenly, in a bleak, strange voice. 'You can hear them through the water.'

'That's terrible.'

She turned on him, almost in anger. 'You don't know the half of it!

170

That's nothing to what the Japanese do. They drive them into the bay with their boats, block the way out to sea with nets, and then they slaughter the lot.'

He was appalled. 'Why?'

Petra shrugged slim brown shoulders. 'Tradition, they call it. They always have. The dolphins eat their fish.'

'*Their* fish?'

She gave him a brief, acknowledging smile. 'That's the big question, isn't it? Who owns the seas?'

'I'm sure Flite only eats what he needs,' he said aloud.

'Yes.' She sighed. 'It's only man that is greedy. Before we started grabbing, the balance was perfect.'

Perfect balance, thought Matthew. That beautiful, joyous creature. How could we be so stupid? So senselessly destructive? How could anyone want to kill a gentle, unaggressive creature like Flite?

'Why didn't you tell me you knew about Flite?' he asked Skip shyly.

'To begin with, I didn't want to disturb you. The two of you seemed happy enough.' Skip grinned. 'And secondly, though it's the end of the season and there aren't a lot of visitors left, I didn't want them all plunging into the sea and splashing about and frightening your dolphin away. Petra and I thought you were best left alone.'

Matthew looked from one to the other of them. He doubted that they understood what a marvellous gift they had given him—that careful silence that left him and Flite free to meet and play together in the empty sea. 'Thank you,' he said humbly, and was surprised when they both smiled at him as if they knew his thoughts.

CAPTAIN ST GEORGE SPENT the morning on the telephone. Then he strolled down to see Skip.

'Some people are coming down,' said the captain briefly. 'In a day or two. Let you know when.'

'Good,' nodded Skip. 'Have you told Madge? She'll be glad to know something's happening.'

'I'll go there now,' offered St George. 'Where's the boy?'

'In the sea,' said Skip, smiling. 'Well out of the way.'

The captain grunted, and turned back up the beach, leaning on his white-handled ebony stick.

MATTHEW WAS INDEED IN THE SEA, and so was Flite. They met as joyously as before, but this time Matthew sensed that there was a certain protective watchfulness about the dolphin's attitude—almost

171

as if he were making sure that his clumsy two-legged friend didn't get into trouble again. The gentle smile was as wide and welcoming as ever, and the long, graceful body leaped in the air with the same ecstatic freedom but, while they played and dived round each other, the bright, intelligent eyes regarded him gravely, as if assessing how much his companion could do.

Presently Matthew noticed that someone was sitting on the rocks, watching him. He swam a little closer in and saw that it was Petra. She was wearing a wet suit, and dangling her legs in the water, but she made no move to leave the rocks and follow him. Her bright hair hung straight and glinting in the sun, and she sat very still.

'Don't you want to come in?' he asked, treading water.

She seemed to hesitate. 'Not if it will worry him.'

Matthew turned to look for the dolphin and saw him leaping through a wave only a few yards out. 'Nothing worries Flite,' he said, and found himself holding out his hand to her.

She slipped in off the rocks without a splash and swam quietly towards him. 'I'll stay here,' she murmured. 'Give him a chance to have a look at me. You go and talk to him.'

'He won't need an introduction!' Matthew laughed.

Petra thought in surprise, He looks a different boy when he laughs. But aloud she only said in the same soft voice, 'Better wait and see.'

Matthew leaned into a wave and dived, gliding down to look for that smooth grey-blue shadow. But he hadn't gone very far down when the dolphin's great head came towards him, thrusting joyfully through the clear water with his powerful beak. *Oh, there you are*, he seemed to say. *Where've you been?*

'Flite,' said Matthew, coming up beside him into filtered sunlight, 'there's someone here I want you to meet. You needn't be afraid.'

Afraid? The clever eyes looked at him and seemed to dance with reflected light. *Who's afraid? In the ocean, I am a king.* With a flash of silver, he leaped high in the air. Then he submerged, sank out of view, and came up suddenly very close to Petra, regarding her with the same questioning attention that he sometimes turned on Matthew. *And who are you?* he seemed to ask.

Petra stayed very still in the water and let him circle round her. 'I wish you could tell me where you've come from,' she sighed, and stretched out her arms to their full length either side of her in an attempt to guess at the dolphin's size and weight. 'Or where you're going to . . .' Greatly daring, she touched the gleaming flanks with one gentle hand.

Flite did not flinch at her touch, but he turned his great body round to look for Matthew, as if seeking reassurance, and seeing him there beside him curved round his friend in a fluid, protective arch.

Petra smiled. 'It's you he trusts,' she said to Matthew gently. Then she said, 'Goodbye, Flite. Thank you for talking to me.' Quietly, she turned in the water and swam away.

The dolphin watched her go, and then turned smoothly into the next wave, leaping with joyous abandon into the sun as Matthew released his hold. *Life is for living!* said Flite, in a cascade of foam, squeaks and clicks and effortless communication. *Dive deep! Leap high! Swim and fly! The world is all blue and gold! Rejoice, rejoice!*

Matthew rejoiced.

WHEN AT LAST HE CAME OUT, tired and happy, and Flite had headed out to sea, Matthew found Petra waiting for him on the rocks.

'I hope I didn't disturb him too much,' she said. 'But I thought I ought to have a look at him. We're supposed to report sightings, now that they are getting so scarce. And any details we can get helps our research.'

Matthew smiled at her serious face. 'So what can you tell me about him?'

She sighed. 'Not a lot. A young bottle-nosed dolphin, in prime condition. He is a male, by the way, though I don't know how you knew.'

'Nor do I . . . How do you tell?'

'They keep their sexual organs hidden—more streamlined, you see. But the male has a slit in his abdomen. And the male is bigger than the female—though we've no way of comparing that here.'

'How big is he, do you think?'

'Over ten foot, I should say.'

'He's very friendly.'

'Too friendly, perhaps,' mused Petra, remembering the extraordinary closeness between those two in the water. It could only lead to heartbreak of one kind or another and she felt compelled to warn him.

'He will go soon, you know—when the weather gets colder.'

Matthew nodded. 'I know.' There was sadness in his face, too—but he resolutely shook it from him, together with a shower of sea-spray as he stripped off his wet suit and lay back in the sun to dry off. 'I know it can't last,' he murmured, staring straight up at the limitless sky above him. 'But I'm going to enjoy it while I can.'

No one was in when the captain arrived. The caravan door stood open and, while he was standing there wondering what to do, the children came up in a scatter of laughter and stopped in front of him. The baby in Donna's arms smiled at him cheerfully, but the others looked at him wide-eyed with suspicion.

'Mum's out shopping,' said Danny helpfully.

'So I see.' There was a spark of amusement in the old captain's stern glance.

'Shopping, shopping,' agreed Jampy, hopping up and down on one leg. He saw someone else's dog sneaking under the caravan and made a dive for it, trying to crawl under the chassis. Danny hauled him back.

'Behave yourself!' he hissed.

Jampy laughed, did a pirouette that would have been a credit to Flite himself, and dodged under Danny's arm. 'Behave!' he chanted, dancing. 'Behave!'

Donna looked at the captain with pained apology. 'He's a bit of a handful,' she explained, sounding absurdly like her mother. 'Dad's gone for some water, but he'll be back in a minute.' She put on her best manner. 'Won't you come inside?'

'Don't mind if I do,' smiled the captain, and followed them into the yellow caravan. It was clean and neat as a new pin.

'All shipshape and Bristol fashion,' he approved.

At this point, Jim Farley's shadow fell on the doorway. The big man took in the situation at a glance, and set the two brimming buckets of water down on the floor. 'Hop it, kids,' he said, and they scattered like dew on the grass.

Captain St George cleared his throat. 'I've fixed up a meeting. Some people are coming down to talk about Matthew's future.'

Jim nodded. 'Madge'll be pleased. Fair out of her mind with worry, she's been.'

The captain grunted in sympathy. 'It's a difficult situation.'

Jim was silent 'We're fond of Matt,' he said suddenly. 'All of us.' He looked at Captain St George with painful honesty. 'Not just grateful, if you understand me?'

'I understand.'

'That Evie Ferguson—she never gave Matt nothing!' Then, with a sudden burst of courage he put his thoughts into words. 'It's not right—him being on his own. A boy needs affection, Captain. Like any animal. He starves, else.'

Captain St George nodded. 'Don't we all?' he said.

Dolphin Sunrise

THAT NIGHT WHEN MATTHEW started playing, he saw the old captain slip in at the back of the long clubroom. He did not try to come forward, but stayed in the shadows, so that he wouldn't be noticed. Checking up on me again, thought Matthew. I'll show him.

He also noticed that Skip and Petra were sitting close together in another shadowy corner, heads bent in earnest conversation. Skip seemed to be trying to convince her of something, and she kept shaking her head so that her hair sparked with muted gold.

Then one of the surfers noticed the captain and called for sea shanties, and soon they were all yelling about drunken sailors and yardarms and mizzens. He didn't quite know how he got into the 'Rio Grande', but all at once the sadness of that old, old song of departure seemed to get into his fingers and into all those young, careless voices.

> 'Then away, boys, away,
> 'Way down Rio—
> And fare you well, my pretty young girl,
> For we're bound for the Rio Grande.'

As he came to an end, he saw Skip's and Petra's faces under the light again. They looked riven, frozen in inarticulate anguish as they looked at one another across the shabby table, and Matthew saw Skip lean forward and lay a gentle, entreating hand on Petra's arm. But she still shook her head, still turned it away from the light to keep it hidden.

'Away, boys, away—' sang the cheerful young voices, not knowing or caring about the long history of voyages and partings in that ancient song. But Matthew cared. His hands faltered on the strings, and to change the mood, he plunged into the Spanish songs, the dances—de Falla, and Granados again. Then he leaped into a lively *jota* to cheer everyone up, and finally slowed down into a calm, rocking berceuse.

When he finally looked up, the old captain was still sitting at the back. But Skip and Petra had gone.

THE MOONLIGHT BEAT DOWN on the shore as they walked together across the sand. It cast deep shadows behind them and laid a long silver pathway on the sea.

'You could stay a bit longer?' begged Skip.

'I have to be in the Pacific next week,' Petra answered, sounding sad but resolute. Then she said, 'Of course, you could come too?'

There was a faint question in her voice, just as there had been in

175

Skip's. But his answer was just as resolute. 'You know I can't. There's this place to run. And the seal watch. And then Matthew might be staying on for a bit. I can't just walk out on everything.'

'Neither can I.' Her voice was bleak.

They walked on for a while in silence. At last he said, 'Maybe—in the winter—the surf club closes down then. And perhaps Matthew will be fixed up. Maybe I could follow you out for a holiday?'

She laughed. 'Monitoring the whalers? . . . Some holiday!'

He grinned back, and hugged her close. 'I'd be with you.' They were both laughing now, and he suddenly paused in his stride and drew her even closer, looking intently into her face under the white moon. 'Petra?'

'Yes.' Her answer was quiet. 'Yes, Skip . . . It's all right.'

They kissed then, quietly and deeply, with the sound of the sea in their ears, and the moonlight dazzling their eyes. But presently they were walking again beside the sea, and Skip was saying, 'I still think you should have told him.'

'I can't, Skip. I promised.'

Skip swore mildly under his breath. 'That was an old promise—about an old story. Isn't it time it was forgotten?'

She sighed. 'Maybe . . . But now is not the time.'

'If you leave it much longer, it may be too late.'

'I realise that . . .' She looked at him and added in a hesitant voice, 'But if I did, wouldn't it make things more difficult for us?'

Skip nodded briefly. 'Yes. It would.'

'So—' She tucked her arm through his, drawing him close again. 'When I warned Matthew about the dolphin going south, he said, "I know it can't last. But I'm going to enjoy it while I can." '

They looked at each other in the moonlight and smiled.

'Why not?' said Skip.

THE CAPTAIN CALLED his meeting at the clubhouse, together with Skip and the Farleys. At the meeting was the social worker who had visited Matthew in hospital, Margaret Wilson; a solicitor called John Harvey who apparently was representing Matthew and dealing with the insurance; and—to Matthew's astonishment and pleasure—Tudor Davies, his old friend and teacher who had taught him all he knew about the guitar, as well as a fair amount about maths and computer science.

Tudor Davies was a small, wiry Welshman with a shock of wild brown hair growing grey at the edges, a wide, flexible sort of grin, and very bright brown eyes that missed nothing. 'Matthew,' Tudor said, in his deep, lilting voice. 'Good to see you. How's tricks?'

'Pretty good,' said Matthew, smiling, and was surprised when the little Welshman put an arm round his shoulders and hugged him.

'Everyone's sent messages,' rumbled Tudor into his ear. 'Hope you're coming back to us—when you're fit.'

The captain wasted no time starting the meeting, addressing Matthew first. 'Since it's your future we're discussing, I think we'd better put our suggestions forward, and leave you and Mrs Wilson to decide what's best.'

Matthew nodded. He wasn't in the least sure that this wispy grey woman would know what was best, but he supposed she had the right to decide. That was what social workers did: decide. But he wished they would leave him alone and let him decide for himself.

'Mrs Wilson,' said the captain, with bluff courtesy, 'is that all right by you?'

Mrs Wilson attempted to smile. 'Of course.' The smile nearly reached her eyes which were permanently cautious, and Captain St George was almost inclined to revise his first opinion of her. See how she reacts later, he thought. Still looks a bit hidebound to me.

Aloud he said: 'Skip—you'd better give your physio report first.'

Skip winked at Matthew and held up a sheet of paper from which he read in a crisp, clear voice. Blind them with science, the captain had said and, by the time he had finished, they were all looking at him with awe.

'So,' he concluded, 'the visiting hospital doctor suggests another three to four weeks at least to complete the treatment. He can, of course, stay here at the club if he likes.'

There was a silence while everyone waited for everyone else to speak. At last Margaret Wilson said in a dry, unconvinced voice, 'I'm sure it's all *technically* correct. But if he stayed on here, what *domestic* arrangements do you have?'

I wish she wouldn't talk in italics, thought Skip, exasperated. 'Domestic?' He sounded totally uncomprehending. 'Oh, you mean food and so on? We have a resident cook and a cleaner who comes in from the village.'

'I *see*,' said Margaret, in the kind of tone that saw nothing.

'I couldn't stay here, Skip,' Matthew said, 'unless I could do some kind of work to pay my way.'

Skip grinned his relief at the diversion. 'That could be arranged. There are plenty of winter chores.'

'Speaking of *winter*,' pursued Mrs Wilson, 'what about the swimming? Won't it be too cold in the sea?'

'We have a heated pool here,' said Skip patiently. 'Matthew often uses it when the sea is too rough—and he always does his exercises there every day. That is how I can check his progress.'

'I *see*,' said Margaret again, but before Margaret Wilson could raise any more objections the captain turned to Madge with an ill-suppressed twinkle. 'Mrs Farley, tell us what you would like to do.'

Madge's pebble-bright glance flashed with scorn. She had taken the measure of this social worker, and what she saw she didn't much like. But Jim shot her a warning glance, and she drew a long breath before she spoke. Be careful, she told herself.

'I'd like Matt to live with us, if he's willing. We're all fond of him, and we'd try to give him a good home. That is,' Madge pursued with intent, 'if the council will give us a new flat.' She looked at Margaret Wilson squarely. 'Can't do it, else, see? Not in bed and breakfast.'

Margaret Wilson nodded slowly. 'That sounds reasonable.'

'Can you give 'em a push?'

She hesitated. 'I could try. It would be a case of *fostering*, then. I would have to report back to the authorities as to your *suitability*.'

There was a moment's stunned silence, and then Jim suddenly spoke. 'Good with kids, Madge is.'

'I'm sure, Mr Farley. I'm *sure*.'

'Works hard. Not much time for fun and games,' he added, with sturdy loyalty. 'But she cares about 'em, see?'

If she says, 'I'm sure' again, thought Matthew, I shall scream.

But she said something much worse. 'Can you tell me, Mrs Farley, exactly *why* you were out on the night of the fire?'

Madge went white—and Matthew spoke—in a clipped, brittle voice of anger that nobody recognised. 'I can tell you, Mrs Wilson. I will repeat my police statement, if you like.' His glare was icy. 'Mr Farley works as caretaker in a big office block and Mrs Farley also works there in the evenings as an office cleaner. Normally, Jim comes home for his tea at six, and Madge—Mrs Farley—goes out at seven.' He glanced coldly at the flustered social worker. 'But that night there happened to be an office party, and Jim Farley had to stay on till the last guest had gone. Mrs Farley had to start her cleaning two hours late, so Jim decided to wait for her and see her home. It's a bad part of town to walk in alone at night.' He paused. Everyone was listening intently. 'Madge put the kids to bed that night, and came down to ask me to keep an eye on them. They were all asleep before she left—at about nine. I went up to check once, but there was no sound, so I went back to my homework. Just as well I did, really, instead of sitting in their lounge watching telly. I mightn't have smelt the smoke soon enough.'

There was a tingling silence. 'I can't think of anyone I'd trust sooner than the Farleys,' Matthew went on, and for a second his eyes met Jim's. 'If I had a chance to live with them, I'd think myself dead lucky.'

'Bravo,' said the captain, not too inaudibly. Margaret Wilson blinked. 'Now, what about school?' pursued the captain, covering everyone's embarrassment. 'Mr Davies—perhaps you'd better explain the position?'

Tudor Davies joined battle with alacrity. 'Taking nine subjects for his GCSEs, Matt was expected to get the lot.' He winked at Matthew cheerfully. 'Took seven of 'em—before the fire. Missed two. Never thought to ask about results, did you?'

Matthew looked confused. 'Er—how did I do?'

'One A. Three Bs and three Cs. Not bad, considering.'

'Considering what?' said Matthew, suddenly belligerent.

'Considering the stupidity of the questions and your obstinate mind.' He gave Matthew a mischievous grin. 'Bright the boy is, see? Can't waste talent, can we? A Levels and university, that's what we think.'

'What would you study, Matthew?' the captain asked.

Matthew hesitated, but Tudor did not. 'Maths and computer science,' he interposed swiftly. 'They're his best subjects.'

'Not music?' asked the captain.

This time even Tudor paused, and messages seemed to go to and fro between him and his pupil while he waited for him to answer.

'No,' Matthew said at last. 'I'd like to go on playing. And learn as much as I can. But, you see, music is—' He could not tell them.

'A kind of journey,' said the Welshman softly, the lilt in his voice more pronounced than ever. 'And you go on it alone.'

Matthew nodded. Alone, he thought. A deep, private aloneness which no one can penetrate—no one can spoil.

'We'd like you to come back to school,' Tudor told Matthew. 'And I'd like to go on teaching you—till you outgrow me!' His impish smile rested on Matthew.

'That'll be the day!' murmured Matthew.

'Well then,' concluded the captain. 'Now we come to Mr Harvey. I'd better let him speak for himself.'

John Harvey, the solicitor, had followed the proceedings with discreet interest and not a little secret amusement. Now he spoke in a voice that was almost as neutral and colourless as his long, pale face.

'I have been in touch with the insurance company and have discovered that there was a life assurance policy taken out in your mother's name, presumably by your father. She had cashed as much of it as possible, but there was a small sum—about three hundred pounds—left in trust for you, which she could not touch. With interest, that has increased in value, though it is not a spectacular sum.'

I don't believe it, Matthew thought, and felt suddenly rather sick.

'As to the fire insurance, I'm afraid the premiums weren't paid up. But in view of the circumstances, and the fact that there had been a long-held policy, the insurance company has made a small ex gratia payment of one hundred pounds.'

There was a pause. '*Blood money*,' Matthew muttered at last, and he looked almost contemptuously at the solicitor. 'I can't take it, of course. Can you give it away?'

'Not until you are eighteen. You can give it away yourself then, if you still want to.' John Harvey had the good sense to take Matthew seriously.

The captain looked about to explode, but all at once a strange expression crossed his face—a memory of another time and another anger—and he seemed to change his mind and sigh. Oh, the impractical idealism of youth! he thought, staring back down the years.

Margaret Wilson said quickly, that Social Services could not administer Matthew's private money, and that he ought to appoint someone as trustee, since he was only fifteen.

'Sixteen, actually,' said Matthew.

They all looked at him in surprise. 'When did that happen?' asked Skip, smiling.

'The other day.' He spoke carelessly.

'You didn't tell us!' cried Madge.

'Didn't seem important—then.' He looked round at them warily. 'But now—all these arrangements you're trying to make for me—it's very good of you, but . . .' He hesitated, suddenly embarrassed.

'But what?' demanded the captain.

'I think I'd better leave school altogether and get a job.'

'But what about your A Levels?' Tudor was always a teacher first.

Matthew looked at him sadly. How could he explain that since the fire all his values had changed? And the thought of going back to school with a lot of kids seemed totally irrelevant. Nowadays, he felt twice as old as his contemporaries.

'I'm sorry,' he said, with a small helpless shrug. 'You see . . . since the fire, I've—things are different.'

Tudor nodded. He understood better than Matthew supposed. 'Welcome to the the adult world,' he said, with his wry, lopsided grin. 'Not a particularly pleasing prospect, is it? But maybe this will help.' And he brought out from under the table a brand-new guitar case.

Matthew stared at it, growing slowly pale. 'For me?'

'For you. We had a whip-round, see—your old mates—and this is the result.' He did not say that the captain was one of the old mates involved. 'Happy birthday,' he added with a wink.

Matthew opened the case and lifted out the new guitar. He smoothed the gleaming wood with his hand, and turned it this way and that to look at the fine fretwork round the sound hole and the decoration on the fingerboard. At last, unable to help himself, he curled his hand round the strings and struck one deep singing chord. And he fell in love.

They all watched him, while he tuned it and laid his ear to the soundbox to hear those rich, vibrating overtones, and stroked it and fingered it in awestruck delight. But at last Tudor Davies could bear it no longer. 'Play it,' he said softly. 'It's got a voice. Let it sing!'

So Matthew let it sing. He only played one piece—the deepest and saddest of the Goyescas—to let that wonderful dark bass loose on the listening air. That was enough for the first time. In any case, he felt absurdly near to tears.

THE WEATHER BROKE THE NEXT DAY. It was the end of the holiday season and everyone was packing up to go home. Farewells seemed to hang in the air, and a kind of rain-washed sadness lay on the empty beach.

Madge and her family were packing too, returning with reluctance to their bed-and-breakfast accommodation, with no more substantial promise of better things than Margaret Wilson's cautious support. But Madge got the family and their few possessions together as cheerfully as possible, putting a brave face on it as usual.

She did not have many doubts about leaving Matthew with Skip, but Jampy did. He made an enormous scene, and stamped and roared and clung to Matthew like a small limpet on a rock, crying fiercely, 'I want Matt. Matt come too!'

Matthew did his best to explain between the small boy's roars of rage. 'I'll come soon,' he promised consolingly.

Jampy looked at him sideways out of one tearful eye, while keeping his fist in the other. 'Soon?' The other two children were watching Matthew with the same doubtful mistrust.

'Soon,' repeated Matthew firmly, trying to sound convincing. 'Before you can say—er—floppy disk.'

'Floppy disk, floppy disk,' said Jampy promptly, confounding him. But the laughter relieved the tension, and Matthew hugged them all.

'I'll be in touch,' said Madge fiercely. 'Soon as ever there's somewhere for you to come to—you just come, see?'

'I'll come,' agreed Matthew, and watched them all pile into the campsite minibus that was taking them to the coach station. Hands waved, and the shabby bus moved off in a swirl of rain and blowing sand from the dunes. Matthew watched it go and then turned away with a lump in his throat.

THE PARTING WITH TUDOR EVANS was less emotional but in some ways sadder, for Matthew felt sure now that he would never go back to school, and probably never have another guitar lesson from this generous-hearted teacher.

Tudor had stayed on after the meeting and they had spent a couple of rainy days happily trying out everything they knew on the guitar plus some new pieces Tudor had brought down with him.

'It's a good instrument, mind,' he said, nodding at the rich chords coming out from under Matthew's fingers. 'Lot of heart, isn't it? Give you all you want, it will.'

'I know.' Matthew was smiling, head still bent over the strings. 'All I could possibly want . . . It's a fabulous sound.'

'That's the ticket,' grinned Tudor. 'Keep the fables going.'

They looked at one another with understanding. All the fables? thought Matthew. All that magic waiting for me? What a marvellous thing I've been given—if I can only use it. 'If I can only use it,' he repeated aloud. And it came out like a prayer.

Tudor gave him a brief, admonitory tap on the arm. 'That's it, boy. Use it. God-given, music is. Must be used, or it withers.' Then he got into his battered little car to take the long road home.

'I can't begin to—' Matthew stammered through the car window.

'Don't try,' grinned Tudor. 'Just keep on playing.' He gave Matthew one fierce, challenging glance and added, 'Know where to find me if you need me.' Then he let in the clutch and drove away.

THAT EVENING THE SKY CLEARED and the wind dropped, so Matthew went down on the rocks to play to the seals. Petra had said they would like it, and he was curious to see what would happen. Besides, he hadn't seen Flite for several days, and he missed the dolphin's joyful company. He clambered along the rocks so that he was almost opposite the low offshore island that housed the seal colony, and sat down out of reach of the spray and began to play.

He played anything he could think of, occasionally singing along to keep himself company. At first nothing happened at all, except that an occasional gull swooped down the wind to have a look at him, and flew away again, screeching a protest. Perhaps they don't like my music, he thought wryly, and tried something else. He got so absorbed in the sound that he forgot to look up for a while, and when he did, he was surrounded by curious heads looking at him with alert attention from the water.

'Well, hello,' he said, rounding off a phrase, 'how nice of you to come. I'm glad someone appreciates me.'

The heads came a little nearer. The beautiful, liquid eyes regarded him in wonder, seemingly to implore him to go on.

Matthew went on playing till it was almost dark, and the seals went on listening, fascinated, their round mottled heads thrusting out of the water and turning to him in enraptured stillness. He had never had so attentive an audience.

But Flite did not come.

THERE WAS NO ONE in the kitchen next morning when Matthew came to look for some breakfast, so he helped himself to coffee and a hunk of bread. He had packed up his tent and moved into the clubhouse the night before, sleeping in one of the empty bunk beds in the long dormitory. Most of the aqua-surf club had gone home now, and the few who were left would be leaving at the weekend.

He had just decided to go and search for Flite when Petra came in. Her expression was curiously anxious and hesitant, as if she was not quite sure what to say.

'Matthew?' She paused. 'Would you know Flite? Could you distinguish him from any other dolphin?'

Matthew stared at her. 'I—I think so, yes. Aren't they all different? He's quite a character.'

'Any special identification marks?'

'Um—yes. He has a kind of knotted scar under his jaw, as if he got caught on a hook once—it's a bit like a raised cross, in a sort of

lump.' He looked at her now, with the beginnings of fear stirring inside him. 'Why?'

She returned his look with a grim one of her own. 'There's a dead dolphin reported washed up on the beach, a few miles up the coast.'

Matthew's heart gave a great lurch of terror. 'Oh, my God.'

Petra laid a kind hand on his arm. 'It may not be Flite, you know. Don't let's jump to conclusions. Skip will take us up there in the Jeep.'

Skip was waiting for them with the Jeep already turned round to climb the steep cinder track to the coast road at the top of the cliff. Once there, he drove fast in the direction of St Just and then turned off down another steep, narrow lane that wound down towards a thin headland. The lane finally petered out on a bit of rough, sandy turf, and here they all got out and began to climb down a narrow track to the small cove below.

At last they reached the line of slippery rocks at the edge of the shore, and stood looking down. And there, lying half in and out of the gently lapping waves, was the long, beautiful body of a full-grown dolphin.

Petra and Skip had been in front of Matthew, but now he gave a strange, gasping cry and went stumbling past them down to where the dead dolphin lay. He knelt beside it, struggling frantically to move the huge, heavy head so that he could look under its throat for that telltale scar. But out of the water, the dolphin's body was enormously heavy, lying limp and flaccid under his hands.

'Let me,' said Skip's voice close to him, and two strong brown hands took hold of the dorsal fin and began to roll the body sideways so that the pinkish-white underbelly and long line of throat became visible. Together he and Petra held on, while Matthew ran his hands along the smooth surface of the dolphin's under-jaw and throat down to the limp front flippers.

It was a beautiful, strong young dolphin all right, and very like Flite. But somehow the face was different. Even the shape of the body was different. His fingers explored again, felt, confirmed. There was no scar on the skin, no blemish at all.

Tears stung his eyes as he looked up at Skip and Petra. 'It's not—not Flite,' he said, in a tight, choked voice. 'But it's terrible all the same . . . What do you think killed it?'

Petra shook her head. 'I don't know.'

'Could it be the seal virus?'

She hesitated. 'It could be. Or some other virus. Or simply

pollution. Swimming in polluted waters can lower their resistance to whatever nasty bug is about at the time.'

Matthew looked anxious. 'How will you find out?'

'We'll have to take samples—do a few tests. I think the best thing would be to get it towed round to an easier landing place where a lorry can have access. Then we can take it to the dolphin centre.'

'I'll see to it,' said Skip, speaking gently to them both.

Then Petra said with sudden roughness, 'It's no good being sentimental about *one* dolphin. It's all the others we've got to think about.'

Matthew nodded. He knew this to be true, but even so he could not altogether quench that small flick of joy inside him because Flite, his loving companion, was still alive.

THAT AFTERNOON MATTHEW went away by himself across the rocks and slipped unnoticed into the sea to look for Flite. For a long time he swam alone, and nothing answered his call. At last, almost in despair, he turned back towards the shore, convinced now that Flite would not come. His friendly companion had gone far away, and was lost to him—and the world would never be the same again.

But as he straightened out from his turn and let the sea-swell lift his body and carry it forward, a dark grey shadow knifed through the water and leaped into an arc of gleaming splendour over his head.

What do you mean, I've gone? Flite seemed to say, diving deep and coming up close beside him in a shower of bubbles. *I'm alive! Can't you see I'm alive? Look at me leaping! Look at me laughing in the sun. Why aren't you laughing too?*

So Matthew laughed, or maybe he cried. He wasn't quite sure which, but who could resist that smile? And he clasped the dolphin in his arms and said, 'You see, it might've been you.'

Flite seemed to understand this. He nudged Matthew confidingly with his beak, as if to say: *Well, it wasn't. Here I am, so rejoice!* And the great, powerful body curved into another silvery arch and soared upwards into the sunlight.

Matthew rejoiced. But at the back of his mind lay the shadow of the other dolphin. What did it die of? Was it the seal virus? Or was it the sea itself that was the menace? Were even these clear, translucent waters safe for Flite to swim in?

He decided to tell Flite about it as they swam together, recounting the whole sad tale. His voice rippled and swirled with the moving water, but Flite seemed to hear him. Maybe he just liked the sound of

Matthew's voice, but he seemed to listen attentively—head tilted towards him—just like the seals had listened to his music.

'You see,' he said to Flite, 'it may not be safe for you here any longer. It may be time to go. What do you think?'

But Flite would not tell him what he thought—if he thought at all. He only curved his long body round Matthew, as he came out of another dive, and then rose out of the water in a joyous flash of silver above his head.

Alive! he said, in a cascade of clicks and whistles, gusts of blown air and showers of diamond spray. *I am alive. Today! And so are you. Isn't that enough?* Flite turned a somersault. *Dive deep. Dance and dive. Leap in the air and smile. Today!*

Matthew could not leap. But he could smile.

ALL THE SAME, WHEN HE THOUGHT about the other dolphin, he was still worried, and went in search of Petra.

He found her talking to Skip on the clubhouse verandah, brown limbs spread out in the sun, gold heads close together in earnest discussion, so earnest that he wondered if he ought to disturb them at all.

'—until the results come through,' she was saying. 'I'll need to report on them anyway . . .'

'Gives us a little longer,' murmured Skip.

At that moment Petra looked up. Neither she nor Skip moved, but they both smiled and included Matthew in their closeness. 'Suntrap here,' said Skip lazily. 'Not bad for the time of year. Come and spread out. You're still a bit underdone!'

Petra laughed. 'English summer—what can you expect?'

'It's all very well for you,' said Skip. 'Swanning off to the Caribbean and Mexico every five minutes.' He stretched out an arm that was every bit as brown as hers and gave her a playful push.

Petra clasped his hand and tucked it comfortably under her head.

Matthew sat down beside them awkwardly and tried not to feel superfluous. 'I suppose you haven't had any results on the dolphin yet?'

'Not yet, no.' Petra looked at him kindly. 'We should know by the weekend.'

'What's worrying you?' Skip asked.

'I—if it's the virus—or these waters are polluted, or something—ought I to encourage Flite to come here?' His voice sounded rough with anxiety. 'Oughtn't I to—send him away?'

There was a pause. Then Skip said slowly, 'I doubt if you could. A

187

dolphin is a law unto himself. He decides whether he comes or goes.'

'But he can't know about pollution. How can he decide what is safe?'

'You can't decide for him,' stated Skip.

'No.' Matthew sounded unconvinced.

Petra laid a consoling hand on his arm. 'In any case, I expect he'll be heading south soon. The seas will be getting colder now.'

They all gazed out across the bay, watching the grey-green rollers pile and climb and surge inwards to break on the shore.

Colder, thought Matthew. Colder and lonelier—when Flite goes. What shall I do without him? And in spite of the warmth of the golden autumn day, he shivered.

A FIERCE AND PERSISTENT HAMMERING got Matthew out of his bunk next morning, and he stumbled out into the sunlight to find Skip furiously banging nails into one of the rickety posts on the verandah. He seemed to be driving them in with unnecessary force but, looking at Skip's grim face, Matthew decided to say nothing.

However, Skip saw him there, and attempted a crooked smile. 'Petra's going today.'

Matthew's inside seemed to churn with terror. 'Does that mean she's heard from the dolphin centre?'

'Yes. But she wants to tell you herself.'

'Where is she?'

'Down on the shore.' He didn't explain why he wasn't down there with her, but Matthew was too anxious to notice as he ran across the dunes to the sand below.

Petra was sitting curled up on a rock, looking small and sad. She didn't turn round as Matthew approached. Her sadness hurt him somehow—like Skip's furious hammering—and he had an irrational desire to shake her and say, 'What is it with you two? Why can't you get together?'

Instead he only said, 'Skip says you've got news.'

'Yes, Matthew, I have.' She turned her head a little, and he caught the sheen of tears in her eyes. 'It was certainly a virus—a sort of pneumonia—'

'Like the North Sea virus?'

'Yes. But not necessarily the same one.'

'Where does it come from?'

She shrugged slim brown shoulders. 'Who knows? Other infected animals, of course . . . and pollution may well weaken resistance.'

'Could—could other dolphins get it?'

'Possibly.' She paused and then added, 'I don't think you need worry about Flite. He's strong and healthy by the look of him, and he seems to prefer to be on his own.'

Matthew sighed. 'I hope to God you're right.'

But, all the same, he was afraid. And he knew now, painfully, what he ought to do. He began to turn away from Petra, but then something in her face—a hint of lonely desolation—made him turn back to look at her. The swinging cap of hair seemed to lie flatly against her head, and there was an air of defeat about the set of her shoulders.

'By the way,' he said, lying cheerfully through his teeth, 'Skip's making coffee. He told me to tell you.'

Petra stared at him for a moment in silence. Then a slow smile began in the gold-flecked eyes, and she suddenly reached out and gave Matthew a swift affectionate hug. 'You're a good boy, Matthew,' she said, laughing a little. 'But you're a damn bad liar!'

He watched her go off up the beach, and then began to walk very fast in the opposite direction.

'IT'S NO GOOD,' said Petra. 'I can't stay angry any longer.'

'Nor can I,' admitted Skip, with relief. He dropped the hammer on the floor, and put his arms round her. 'That's better,' he said.

Without hesitation, her arms came up and held him just as hard. 'Matthew said you were making coffee.'

'Oh, did he?' Skip was laughing now.

'Well—aren't you going to?'

'No, I don't think so. I'm much happier like this.'

'I see.'

'Do you?' He framed her face with his two hands and looked at it long and lovingly—as if fixing it in his memory for ever. And she was looking at him with the same loving intensity—held in the same unspoken thrall. The silence continued between them, their gaze locked in startled recognition, and then Skip slowly bent his head and kissed her.

'We won't lose it, you know,' she said, reaching up to clasp the curve of his head beneath the glinting tongues of hair.

'No,' he agreed, kissing her again. 'I know.'

IT WAS MUCH LATER when Matthew came back and found them sitting quite peacefully on the verandah steps, but Petra's bags were packed and lying beside her on the flaky wooden boards.

189

'Are you going right now?' Matthew asked, dismayed.

'In a few minutes.' Petra smiled at his anxious face. 'I'm glad you turned up in time to say goodbye.'

'Where will you be going next?'

Petra's brown shoulders moved in a fluid shrug. 'Somewhere in the Pacific. Wherever the research unit sends me. All I know is, I'll be at the whale-watch in the Laguna Scammon in January, when the grey whales come down.'

'Where's that?'

'In Baja California . . .'

'Mexico,' explained Skip. 'That long thin bit.'

Matthew looked totally bewildered.

'They come over four thousand miles to breed,' Petra told him. 'All the way from the Bering Sea. You can see them coming down the coast of California . . .' She looked at Skip again. 'It's a wonderful sight.'

'Will you come back?' Matthew blurted out suddenly.

'Yes,' said Petra, as if it was a foregone conclusion. 'Of course.'

Skip got to his feet then and picked up her bags. 'We'd better go.'

Petra got up too, and folded Matthew in a warm-hearted embrace. 'Give my love to Flite,' she murmured. 'And be happy.'

Skip said nothing more, and together they climbed into the Jeep and drove away.

Matthew watched them go—feeling surprised at his own sense of loss. But that was nothing to what he was going to face now. It was almost too difficult to contemplate, and he wasn't in the least sure he could do it. But he knew he had to try. Sighing, he went in to fetch his wet suit and snorkel mask and then set off to look for Flite.

THE SEA WAS CALM that day, and blue as lapis lazuli beneath a clear, windswept sky. For a while Matthew swam alone. He did not want to do anything. He wanted to drift in the swell, surrender to its limitless power, and not think.

And then, without any summons from him, the dolphin came. The beautiful, sinuous body appeared silently beside him, weaving effortless circles round him in the translucent water.

Matthew watched enthralled, and his heart seemed to leap with the dolphin in a great surge of joy at its coming. He ought to be stern and decisive, he knew—but he could not. He could only rejoice and greet his smiling companion with open arms. 'Oh Flite,' he said, as the great domed head came near and the powerful beak nudged him with

190

playful insistence. 'Oh Flite, what am I to do with you?'

Do with me? said those bright, intelligent eyes. *Play with me, what else? I've come to play. Aren't you glad to see me?* And the smooth curve of his back arched through another wave, sank deep in the undertow, and then rose in a joyous leap and a swirl of bubbles high over the next wave-crest swelling in from the dark Atlantic.

When Matthew moved rather blindly to follow him, he found that Flite had made a fast turn and had come up behind him. Matthew put his arms round him, laid his head against the dolphin's side, and wept.

'It's not safe for you here,' he told him. 'It's not safe any more. These waters are death to you—do you understand?'

Flite leaned against him, motionless in the quiet sea-swell. Then the powerful body turned with a slow flick of his tail-fluke and the inquisitive head came round to look at Matthew in wonder. *Why are you crying?* he seemed to ask.

So Matthew told him about the virus and the polluted coastal waters, and the threat that hung over him. 'So you see,' said Matthew at last, 'I think it is time for you to go . . . to warmer and clearer seas. Do you understand? It is time to go.'

Whether Flite understood or not, he was not going to let Matthew be sad any longer. He suddenly left his side and went into a series of marvellous convolutions and spectacular leaps and dives, as if trying to distract Matthew from his fears and forebodings. *Look at me!* he seemed to say. *See how high I can fly! Watch me dive! Watch me leap! Isn't life glorious? Now!* And as Flite leaped and dived and swerved through the shimmers of sunlight and cascades of upflung spray, Matthew felt his own spirits rise to meet the dolphin's instant joy.

He had done his best to warn him. How much Flite understood, he could not know. He could only hope that he would be safe—and meanwhile rejoice in his presence.

He had never known Flite quite so playful before—so affectionate, so full of unquenchable delight in the blue and gold world around him. He leaped through the waves, he chased his own tail, he skimmed over the water one minute and dived deep the next to chivvy the shoals of small fish that swam in the shadows. He chased the seals and raced after a fishing boat crossing the bay, and returned like a swift black arrow to Matthew's side.

Matthew did not know what strange communication there was between them, or how the dolphin knew his mind, but he became aware, with a sense of slow wonder, that Flite's spectacular display was a farewell performance. He was going away. Whether it was the normal time for his migration south, Matthew would never know, but it was clear to him that the dolphin's time of departure had come.

'Goodbye then, Lord-a-Leaping Flite,' he murmured, half smiling, and clasped the dolphin in his arms. 'Thank you for everything you've taught me . . . I shall never forget you.'

Flite seemed to shiver a little in his arms and lean against him a little closer. Then he turned in the water so that the great head came near, and for a moment the two of them—dolphin and boy—gazed at one another in love and trust, in perfect understanding.

At last the long, sensitive beak moved gently forward and touched Matthew's face, the wide smile rested on him like a final benediction, and the long, silvery shape of the dolphin turned in an incandescent swirl of bubbles and swam away into the vast jade and indigo depths of the wide Atlantic.

Flite had gone.

PART II

ETERNITY'S SUNRISE?

The captain was looking out of his window. He had been ill and confined to bed, but now at last he was up and sitting in his chair. He always felt better when he could see the sea.

He saw the boy go by, head down, walking fast, and something about the set of his shoulders troubled the old man. He watched him make his way to the far end of the beach, then turn back when he reached the rocks and come steadily towards him with his uneven stride.

He pressed the bell on the wall beside his chair. When the cheerful face of the young chambermaid came round the door he beckoned her over and pointed at the beach below. 'That boy down there, walking alone. I want to see him.'

'Right-o, Captain. See what I can do.'

Presently he saw the girl go out of the hotel gates. She climbed down the steep steps to the beach and ran diagonally across the sand to reach Matthew as he walked by. He saw them meet, and then the two figures turned and climbed up towards the hotel. Soon, there was a knock at his door.

'Come in, Matthew,' the captain called. And when the boy stood there hesitantly in the doorway, he added, 'It's good to see you.'

'They tell me you've been ill.' The grey-green eyes were anxious.

'Ancient history. Better now.' He jerked an imperious thumb at a nearby chair. 'Come and sit down. Could do with some company.'

Matthew obediently sat down and looked at the old man, shocked to see how much older and frailer he looked. 'Won't I tire you?' he blurted out.

The old man laughed. 'Tougher than I look.' He fixed Matthew with a shrewd and penetrating stare. 'So—tell me what's new?'

Matthew sighed. 'New? . . . Well, it all seems to be partings at the moment. First it was Madge and Jim and the kids. And then Tudor Davies. And then today, it was Petra's turn.'

'Who's Petra?'

Matthew paused, surprised. 'Didn't you meet her? Skip's girlfriend? She's a marine biologist or something. Into whales and such.'

The old man nodded. 'Think I did see her with him once—at the club.' He remembered the two heads close together, but she had kept her face hidden. 'And Skip will miss her?'

'A lot, I should think. They were very close.'

The captain was silent for a moment. Then he shot Matthew a hard look. 'Well then, who else has gone?' Something had to account for that air of desolation.

The boy seemed to freeze into himself for a moment. But then he said, 'It's Flite.'

They talked for a long time about the dolphin and then Captain St George said with surprising gentleness, 'You did the right thing, boy. But are you sure he's gone?'

'Oh yes.' Matthew sounded quite certain. 'He said goodbye to me.'

The captain's smile was only faintly quizzical. 'Talked to him, did you?'

Matthew blushed a little. 'Oh yes. At least, we communicated—somehow.' He looked at the captain with honest eyes. 'I mean, words are only one way . . .'

The captain sighed. 'We none of us understand the mind of a dolphin.'

Matthew agreed. 'Of course, he might have been going anyway. It's the time of year for migration, Petra told me. But I'm sure he understood me. And I'm sure he said goodbye—in his own way.' There was a bleakness in Matthew's eyes, but then he said suddenly, 'He'd disapprove of this, though.'

'What?'

'This—regret.' He looked at the old man beside him. 'Flite didn't believe in regret. He believed in *now*—today!'

The old man nodded slowly.

'Instant joy . . .' Matthew murmured. 'That was what *you* said. Instant joy. Don't you remember?'

The captain thought about it. 'Yes. I do. Those children on the beach, and that little fella jumping up and down like a jack-in-the-box.'

Matthew smiled. 'Yes.' Instant joy, he thought. But I don't know how to hold on to it . . . And I suppose I shouldn't try.

'It will come back,' said the captain, as if Matthew had spoken. Then he looked round the room and added abruptly, 'Over there—on my table. Blake. I was reading it this morning.'

Mystified, Matthew fetched the book for him, and waited while he found the place.

'Here,' said the captain. 'Hackneyed, of course, but still true.'

Matthew looked down at the printed words on the page.

> *He who bends to himself a joy*
> *Does the wingèd life destroy;*
> *But he who kisses the joy as it flies*
> *Lives in eternity's sunrise.*

'That's your Flite speaking,' said the captain softly.

But Matthew could not answer. He had a picture in his mind of Flite, leaping through the waves across a gleaming pathway on the sea, swimming away from him and always towards the sunrise . . .

At length the captain said briskly, 'Well, then, Matthew. What now? Will you stay down here?'

The boy seemed to return from a long way off. But he smiled at the old man and said honestly, 'I don't know. The doctors say I'm almost fit now and I ought to get some kind of a job. But I don't suppose it's easy down here in the winter.'

'Not that easy, no. Even the locals find it hard.'

'Maybe I'll have to wait until I get back to London.'

'Will you go back to Madge and Jim Farley?'

Matthew nodded. 'Yes, over Christmas. But to stay—no.' He looked at the captain, willing him to understand. 'I need to be independent.'

The old man understood all too well. 'It won't be easy on your own. You should have accepted that insurance money.'

'I know I should.' He sounded both obstinate and apologetic. 'But it made me feel sick, somehow . . . I'd much rather earn it.'

'I don't blame you.'

Matthew breathed a sigh of relief. It surprised him to find how much he cared what the old captain thought of him.

'Computers,' said the captain suddenly. 'Why didn't I think of it? Good at them, aren't you?'

'Fairly.'

'Well, then.' The old man waved a hand towards a door. 'In there. Have a look.'

Matthew went over and peered inside. It was a small dressing room that had been turned into an office. There was a telex and a fax machine in one corner, and beside them a desk with a computer screen set at one end of it. On closer inspection it seemed a simple enough piece of software, and one he was quite used to handling. He went back to the captain, puzzled.

'Could you handle it?'

'Oh yes. But what for?'

The captain grinned. 'Keep tabs on' em, boy. That's what. Each day. Only way to run a shipping business.' His shrewd glance met Matthew's with amusement. 'Most days, I ring head office in London. They tell me what's going on—any problems—loading and unloading—accidents—strikes—whatever. I feed it all into the computer. That way, I know at once where everything is. But since I was ill, I got behind. Everything's out of date. Understand?'

'Yes.'

'Could you put it right?'

'If you give me the facts—'

'We'll get 'em from head office. Plenty to feed in.' He shot a swift, assessing glance at Matthew's face and added casually, 'Pay you the going rate.'

Matthew protested at once. 'There's no need for that.'

'Rubbish. You'll earn it. I'll see to that.' His glare was very convincing but Matthew didn't believe a word of it.

'Yes, but—'

'But what?' The glare was even fiercer.

Matthew said gently, 'Isn't it time you went south—like Flite?'

The old eyes looked astonished, and then suddenly misted. 'Are you trying to push me out, boy?'

Matthew smiled. 'Only—like I pushed Flite out.'

Captain St George was absurdly touched—and therefore gruffer than ever. 'See here, young man, I've been coming back to this place every summer for years now. Sentimental reasons. Most of the time,

I've been damned lonely. This year for once, I got interested in a couple of things. Decided to stay on a bit, that's all. Anything wrong in that?'

Matthew looked down at him, still half smiling. 'Only if it makes you ill.'

The captain snorted. 'Irrelevant. I've enjoyed myself.' Then, he added slyly, 'But I could do with your help—for a couple of weeks.'

At this, Matthew capitulated. 'All right.'

The captain held out his hand. 'Deal?'

'Deal,' agreed Matthew, and clasped the frail fingers in his own.

THERE WASN'T TIME to think of Flite during the next few days and, in a way, Matthew was glad, Working himself into the ground had always been his way of blocking out unhappiness, even when he was quite a small boy. The more bizarre his mother's lifestyle became, the more he buried himself in books, or his computer, or in the repetitive practice that learning the guitar demanded. If all these activities failed to overcome the unacknowledged ache of loneliness, he would clean the flat. Now, the more he missed Flite, the more chores he would find to do for Skip, before rushing to the hotel to deal with the captain's computer.

This last task he found increasingly fascinating, and his respect for the captain and his enormous business interests grew. He asked the captain whether his shipping empire had got smaller in recent years.

The old man smiled and said, 'Not really, Matthew, because I'm a wily old bird and I knew which lines to get rid of. Big passenger ships are out—their days are over, I'm sorry to say. But the demand for smaller holiday craft keeps increasing.'

Matthew nodded.

'And then there's freight. You can't beat container ships for bulk carrying. Even the biggest planes can't really compete.' He glanced at Matthew, watching the receptive young mind take in the details of his complicated business. The boy really was bright and it was a pleasure to teach him. 'The secret of business success, Matthew,' he told him, 'is to be *flexible*, and a step ahead of your competitors, all the time!'

One way and another Matthew learned an awful lot in a short space of time about how a big shipping empire worked, and he was constantly surprised at how much information the captain kept in his head. In fact he vaguely suspected that the captain scarcely needed his help at all, but he seemed to be glad of Matthew's company and clearly enjoyed explaining things when Matthew failed to understand.

But he also did get very tired suddenly, and Matthew was careful to watch for the signs of fatigue, and to say cheerfully, 'I think we'd better stop now. I'm getting boss-eyed.' The captain usually surrendered with good grace, and Matthew learned how to make him his favourite coffee with a dash of rum.

He wondered sometimes why it was that a man so rich and so powerful was so alone. Didn't he have any family? Any friends? These questions often came into his mind, but he did not ask them. He understood that the captain would talk about almost any topic, except himself. Matthew respected that, but he couldn't help wondering.

He said as much to Skip one evening, when he was busy putting a coat of paint on the bar-room ceiling in the clubhouse.

'Skip, about the captain—'

'What about the captain?' Skip was rubbing down the bar counter.

'Well, why is he here on his own? Doesn't he have any family?'

Skip's face became strangely closed. 'Apparently not.'

Matthew had a sudden desire to drop the paint pot on Skip's head. 'Honestly, Skip, you're as close as a clam.'

'Sorry.' He looked up at Matthew with an apologetic grin. 'What can I tell you? He's been coming down here every summer for—oh, a good many years now. He never has anyone with him—but some of the older villagers say he used to come with his wife long ago. I presume she's dead, but he never talks about it.'

'Didn't he have any children?'

There was a fractional pause, and then Skip said, 'I believe—the villagers say—there was a daughter. But she went off.' He gave a swipe at the bar counter. 'And then, of course, there's Conrad.'

'Who's Conrad?'

'You may well ask. Whether he's a nephew, or just a business manager, we don't know. He comes down sometimes and argues with the old man, and everyone at the hotel gets nervous.'

'Why?'

'Because the old man is frail. A row could kill him. Every time he comes there's an almighty dustup, and the captain is usually ill for days afterwards.'

'Can't he be stopped?'

Skip's eyebrows went sky-high. 'Give orders? You must be joking. Last time Dr Thorpe told the old man he wasn't to let Conrad set foot in the place again, the old captain just laughed and said, "Try and stop him!"'

197

'I don't know what's got into everyone,' grumbled Matthew. 'There's the old captain up there, as lonely as hell and doing nothing about it, and there's you down here, in the same boat and doing likewise. It's so silly, it's such a waste.'

'Yes. It is.' Skip's voice was taut with anger.

Matthew glanced down in surprise and then climbed off his ladder and laid down his brush. 'I'm sorry, Skip. I oughtn't to say anything. But it's just—I'm stuck with being on my own, and I *can't* do anything about it. But you *can!*'

Skip blinked. 'Can I?'

'Well, you could go after her.'

He sighed. 'It's not as simple as that. Petra has a problem that I can't resolve for her. She has'—he hesitated and then went on awkwardly—'divided loyalties. She thinks she's right. I think she's wrong.'

Matthew nodded. 'So?'

The blue eyes widened. 'So—she's got to work things out for herself. I can't interfere.'

Matthew wanted to shake him. 'She's probably dying for you to interfere. Aren't women supposed to like the man-of-action stuff?'

Skip began to laugh.

'Sweep her off her feet, and all that? It seems chicken not to try.'

Skip took a swipe at him, still laughing. 'Chicken, am I?'

Matthew dodged. 'Not in most things,' he admitted, grinning.

'Nor are you, come to that,' Skip acknowledged, aware that Matthew had just dared quite a lot on his behalf. He laid a friendly arm round Matthew's paint-spattered shoulders. 'We've done enough for today, I think. Let's have some coffee.'

WHEN MATTHEW NEXT WENT UP to the hotel, an atmosphere of chaos seemed to have overtaken it. Emma, the chambermaid, was rushing upstairs with a tray of tea, John, the barman, was trying to pour out a stiff whisky for someone and answering the phone as well, and Milly, the proprietress, was literally wringing her hands and saying, 'Oh dearie me, I never should've let him go up.' Upstairs, Matthew could hear raised voices and a stick banging furiously on the floor.

'What is it?' he said. 'Is anything wrong with the captain?'

'It's Conrad,' explained Milly, still wringing her hands. 'He's that persistent. I told him the captain wasn't too well today. But he would go up. And now listen to them! I don't know what to do.'

'I do,' said Matthew. He suddenly felt tall and brave and very angry. No one had the right to make the old captain ill. But no one. 'Give me that drink,' he said.

He stormed up the stairs and paused outside the captain's door, shocked by the anger in those voices behind the door.

'I'll thank you to mind your own business,' said the captain, very clipped and cold. 'When I want any advice from you, I'll ask for it.'

'That's just the trouble,' replied a new voice, 'you never *do* ask.'

'Why the hell should I? This is my company, and I'm not too old to be incapable of running it.'

'I'm beginning to wonder about that,' snapped Conrad. 'Since this merger offer came up, you've done nothing but block it.'

'That's because I don't want it,' barked the captain. 'We are all right as we are. I don't trust those fancy fellas an inch.'

'Just because you are old-fashioned and hidebound,' snarled Conrad, 'doesn't mean the entire company has to be. They are a reputable group, and they offer good terms.'

'They are *not* a reputable group,' countered the captain. 'I have had them investigated. I won't have it, Conrad, and that's final.'

Matthew heard Conrad draw a sharp breath of outrage at this, and thought he had better go in before they actually came to blows. He pushed open the door, and marched up to the captain's chair, brushing past the pink-faced, angry man who was standing over him.

'Captain, I've brought your drink. And it's time to run the evening computer program. Are you ready?'

The captain looked at Matthew in astonishment, and then his eyes began to twinkle. 'Quite ready, Matthew. Are we late?'

'Almost,' said Matthew. 'Head office will be waiting for your call.' He stood beside him, holding the whisky and soda in one hand, and waited for the old man to get to his feet.

Conrad looked at them both open-mouthed, but before he could say any more the old captain simply walked out of the room into his little office, leaving Matthew to get rid of his unwelcome guest.

'Have you far to go?' asked Matthew politely, holding the door open for Conrad. 'I'm sure they'll get you a taxi downstairs.' He had not looked at Conrad very closely yet, but now he saw a big, plumpish man with receding brown hair, a thin, petulant mouth and small, quick-moving blue eyes. 'This way,' he said.

Somehow mesmerised by Matthew's extreme politeness, Conrad began to go out of the door towards the stairs. But at the last moment he called over his shoulder, 'You've not heard the end of this!'

199

'I'm sure I haven't,' agreed the old captain, from the other room. 'Goodbye, Conrad.' The dismissal was final.

There was nothing left for the hapless Conrad to do but go away. He went, giving Matthew an angry glare in passing.

Matthew breathed a sigh of relief as Conrad went downstairs. He turned and walked into the little dressing room. The old captain was sitting in his chair, sipping the stiff whisky he had brought him and looking very tired. 'Are you all right?' asked Matthew.

'Will be in a minute,' said the captain. 'Thanks to you. Ambitious, that one is, d'you see? . . . Makes him aggressive.'

'That doesn't give him the right to wear you out with arguments,' Matthew snorted. Then he looked curiously at the old captain. 'Is he—part of the family?'

'Sort of. Distant.' The captain wasn't giving much away. 'And he's also one of my managing directors. But I hold all the strings—including the purse strings. All he can do is fulminate from time to time. It soon dies down.'

'Well, that's all right then.' Matthew was still looking at him, still assessing that blanched look of strain.

'Godsend,' said the captain. 'D'you know that?'

Matthew smiled. 'I only saw him out.'

'*Only?*' The captain began to laugh again. 'You should've seen his face.'

'I did!'

Suddenly they were both giggling like naughty schoolboys, and Matthew was relieved to see the tension recede from the old man's face, leaving it relaxed and cheerful.

It was later, while Matthew was checking the final day's share prices, that the phone call came.

'Would it be possible to speak to Matthew Ferguson?'

'Er—yes, I mean, speaking . . .' Matthew gulped.

'I tried to reach you at the aqua-surf club,' went on the pleasant voice. 'They told me you might be here. This is your solicitor, John Harvey. I have some unexpected news for you.'

'Yes?' Matthew was still bewildered.

'We have traced a relative of yours—in America. A connection of your father's.'

'My *father's*?' Matthew's voice was faint. 'I never knew anything about his family.'

'So I understand. But Mrs Madeleine Grant was married to your father's brother, which makes her a kind of aunt.'

'*Was* married?'

'He died, I believe, some years ago. She is now married to an American living in San Diego. She wants you to go over and visit her—with a view to offering you a permanent home. She is prepared to pay your fare.'

Matthew's head spun. 'I—are you sure of all this? It isn't a joke?'

John Harvey's voice was firm and reassuring. 'Perhaps you'd better come up to London to see me, and we can discuss it.'

'Yes.' Matthew sounded curiously reluctant. 'I—I was thinking of coming to London for Christmas,' he said. 'To see Madge Farley and the kids. Could I come and see you then?'

'Are you sure you don't want to come right away?'

'There are things I have to do here first. Perhaps—would you like to have a word with Captain St George? He'll explain to you.'

'Very well.' Harvey seemed unperturbed. After all it was the captain who had originally arranged for him to represent Matthew.

'John?' growled the captain. 'What's all this?'

Matthew went into the bedroom to make coffee. When he heard the captain call he came and stood in the doorway, balancing two cups.

'You could go now if you want to. I could manage.'

'No.' Matthew shook his head decisively. He gave his friend a shy, fleeting smile. 'I'll go when you head for the sun.'

They grinned at one another, and the old man turned back to the phone. 'John? He says no. But I'll see that he gets in touch before Christmas.' There was a murmured reply, and the fragile hand put down the phone. Matthew saw that it was trembling very slightly.

'Here,' he said. 'I put in a dash of rum. Thought we might need it.'

The captain laughed. But his eyes were misted with tears.

MATTHEW DID NOT TELL SKIP about the relation in America at first. Nor did he discuss it further with the captain. He did not want to talk about it—in fact, he found himself curiously reluctant even to think about it. A relation? Someone he'd never met . . . who had never got in touch during all these years? And why should they want to do so now? Out of duty? He didn't want to be someone's 'duty'. The whole thing repelled him, and he felt determined not to be taken over by some do-gooding stranger.

It wasn't until several weeks later that the captain tackled him.

'Now then, Matthew, what are you going to do about San Diego?'

Matthew gave him a look of muted anguish. 'I—don't know.'

201

Captain St George's gruff voice was surprisingly gentle. 'What bothers you about it?'

'A lot of things.' Matthew spoke almost reluctantly. How on earth could he explain to a man like the captain, who had anything in the world he wanted, what it was like to be totally dependent on other people's charity? 'I suppose it's—because of how things *were*,' he said. 'I mean, I was never much good at family feeling and all that. In fact, I don't think I like the idea of family ties much at all.' His voice was bleak. 'I mean, my mother couldn't really do with me—I cramped her style. But because she was my mother, she felt *obliged* to do something about me. And I—I didn't get on with her very well, so I mostly opted out. But then I felt guilty.'

The captain made a non-committal noise in his throat. 'So?'

'So this aunt-by-marriage or whatever in San Diego. She's never tried to contact us all these years. So why now? Just because a lawyer told her to? Out of a sense of duty?' He shook his head in fierce denial. 'I don't want it.'

The captain said mildly, 'Well—what *do* you want?'

'To be free,' said Matthew, thinking of Flite. 'To get a job and manage my own life. And not be beholden to anyone.'

'It's a lonely sort of life, with no ties, you know.'

Matthew suddenly smiled. 'I didn't say no ties. I meant no built-in ones. I think—I think you should care about someone because you want to—not because you have to.'

The captain nodded. Then he said suddenly, 'I think you should give San Diego a try. You never know. This aunt or whatever—she may be lonely, too.'

Lonely, too. It was no good trying to fool the captain. He knew very well what it was all about.

'Besides,' he went on, 'it's an excuse to travel. See a bit of the world. San Diego is a lovely place.' He looked searchingly at Matthew. 'Time's getting on, you know. When are you going to London?'

'I thought—the day before Christmas Eve.'

'That's two days from now.'

'Is it?' The expression on Matthew's face became one almost of panic. 'I didn't realise . . .' He met the captain's gaze with painful awareness. 'What will you do?'

The old man shrugged. 'Go south. High time I did, anyway.'

'Alone? At *Christmas*?'

There was a fractional pause, and then Captain St George said neutrally, 'It doesn't make much difference to me, nowadays.'

Well, it should, thought Matthew. And I'm going to do something about it. 'Would you be going through London? Could—would you come and see Madge and the kids on Christmas Day—if asked?'

'I might.'

Matthew laughed. 'It'd be quite a—a—'

'Family occasion?' suggested the captain innocently.

Matthew had the grace to blush. But then he said with sudden belligerence, '*Chosen* family.'

It was the captain's turn to laugh.

SKIP WAS BUSY TURNING the club music-night into a farewell party for Matthew, and had given him strict instructions to be there early.

But Matthew had something else in mind first, and he took his guitar and wandered off to the far edge of the rocks where the seals could hear him—if they were still there. Where Flite could have heard him and come joyously to meet him not so long ago . . .

It was a calm night. The sea was winter dark, and smooth as polished silk. A pale December sun was sliding down into the west, laying bars of white-gold on the inky water. It looked lonely out there—lonely and vast and empty. No Flite anywhere. Matthew shivered a little, and began to play.

After a time he became aware that the darkening water was not empty any more. There were listening heads breaking the surface, staying motionless in the swell to hear Matthew's music.

'Hello,' he said, smiling. 'You've come back, have you?'

He played Granados—de Falla—everything he could remember and then launched into a final piece of Villa-Lobos. The seals stayed upright in the water, their great liquid eyes fixed on the source of this fascinating sound.

'Well, that's all, folks,' said Matthew, somehow curiously cheered by the seals' silent company. 'Have a good winter—and give my love to Flite, if you see him.'

The seals waited till he got to his feet and turned his back on the sea. Then they dived through the twilight ocean and swam away.

SKIP'S MUSIC NIGHTS were famous along the coast. People came from all sorts of small outlying places to join in. The local folk group, which made up in noise for what it lacked in talent, always began the proceedings. They shouted a lot of local songs in a bogus Cornish accent and everyone loved them.

As the folk group thumped its way through the range of good

203

'yelling songs', Matthew found himself strumming along with them. But then, to his surprise, a small visiting jazz group got up onto the clubroom stage and invited Matthew to join them. These were skilled and subtle improvisers, weaving intricate, intoxicating patterns with a piano, a double bass and a clarinet, and Matthew had the time of his life. When they had happily embroidered their way through various numbers the clarinet player paused for breath, loudly demanded beer, and said to Matthew, smiling, 'You're good, kid.'

'Good?' said Skip, coming up with beer all round. 'You should hear him on the classy stuff.'

'Well, why not?' grinned the clarinet player.

'Oh no, not now,' protested Matthew, embarrassed. He looked doubtfully at the sea of cheerful, beer-swilling faces. But, unaccountably, word seemed to have got round and they fell suddenly silent, looking up at him expectantly.

'You better get going, man,' muttered the bass player.

So Matthew got going. It was his farewell to them, after all, and he had become fond of these tough, warm-hearted people. He only played one piece to start with but, when he stopped, they asked for more, and went on asking for more until he had played almost everything he knew, and some he didn't know too well. Then he remembered that he was going away tomorrow, so he began to play *'Sailing, I am sailing . . .'* for them to sing. In a moment or two the jazz group picked it up, and after them the folk group and then everyone who could sing or play anything joined in. And then they progressed from 'Sailing' to 'Rio Grande'. The noise was terrific.

He looked round for Skip, wondering whether this song of parting would upset him, but Skip was singing lustily with the rest of them and waving—of all things—a pair of stiff, brand-new jeans.

'These are for you,' he said, when the singing subsided. 'Because you ruined yours painting my ceiling.'

'And this here is to go with it,' added a group of local boys waving a startlingly bright T-shirt with the words: 'Porthgwillick Aqua-Surf Club' emblazoned across it.

'Well, thanks,' Matthew said, laughing. 'At least you'll see me coming!'

One of them looked at him seriously. 'Will you be coming back?'

The question hung in the air, fraught with extraordinary tension. 'Of course,' said Matthew, glancing swiftly at Skip. 'Of *course* I will.'

'That's all right then,' they cried, and launched drunkenly into *'He'll be coming round the mountain when he comes.'*

Matthew couldn't think of any way to finish the evening adequately, so he went outside and had a fierce argument with himself about getting all worked up about nothing.

Skip came out and found him there, and a different argument began.

'Can you come up to London for Christmas Day, Skip? The captain says he might come.'

'I can't, Matthew. I've got a children's party for the village kids on Boxing Day. I have to get it ready.'

'*Please*, Skip. It'd be—' Well, why not say it out loud? 'It would be like a—a family party of our own.'

Skip hesitated. Then he remembered Matthew's history and he knew suddenly why this mattered. 'OK. But I'll have to get back.'

'Of course,' agreed Matthew, rejoicing.

'The more we are together, *together, TOGETHER*—' shouted the yelling boys.

'Come on,' said Skip. 'They're getting maudlin in there. Time to throw them out.'

ONE WAY AND ANOTHER, it turned out to be a pretty good Christmas, what with Skip coming up for the day, and the old captain being there as well—though he nearly didn't manage it, he told Matthew, because of another row with Conrad who wanted him to go to the South of France. However, he *was* there, laden with presents for them all and smiling quizzically in his usual way.

Madge had cooked a huge Christmas dinner for everyone in her new flat, in spite of the fact that money was tight, as usual. And to add to the general warmth came the surprise of the day: a visit from Matthew's old teacher Tudor Davies, who brought Matthew a new set of guitar strings, two more Granados pieces for him to learn, and stayed to have tea with them all before going down to Wales for the rest of the holiday.

He gave Matthew a beaming smile and said, 'You look a new man. Hundred per cent fit, and raring to go!'

Matthew laughed. But he wasn't raring to go. And that was why there were still tensions, particularly when Madge was so busy showing off her flat, with sidelong grateful glances at the captain who had intervened on her behalf.

'Look, Matt, this is a sofa-bed. You can sleep here any time. And there's a room on the next floor coming up any day now, and the council said you could probably have it if you want it.'

Matthew smiled and nodded, saying nothing yet about America. He didn't want to spoil Christmas, and his eyes met the captain's in silent appeal. Tudor Davies, who was no fool about unspoken tensions innocently interrupted the silence by asking Matthew to play for them.

Matthew looked at his old teacher and smiled. 'I'll play the two new ones you brought me last time—just to show I *have* practised! But then I think it'd better be carols, since it's Christmas.'

Tudor nodded happily—and soon they were all singing together, with even the captain joining in. When someone demanded 'The Twelve Days of Christmas', Matthew agreed without demur, although his hands almost faltered when he got to twelve lords-a-leaping and he thought of Flite leaping through the wild Atlantic as he swam further and further away. But he went on, reminding himself sternly that he was happy *now*, and that Flite would not countenance any looking back.

'I must be on my way now,' said Tudor at last. 'Come and see me off, Matthew?'

Obediently, Matthew followed him down the stairs. At the street door, Tudor said seriously, 'So you are off to America then? The captain told me about your aunt.'

Matthew sighed. 'I don't want to go. But I suppose I've got to give it a whirl.'

'That's it. Never know till you try. I only wanted to say this to you: any kind of trouble, you can always come to me. Haven't got a great deal of cash, but if you need help or anything—you tell me, see?'

Matthew managed a nod.

'And keep playing. That's all I ask.'

'I will,' Matthew promised, and Tudor hurried away.

Then it was Skip's turn. He merely screwed up his eyes in his all-embracing smile and said, 'Remember, the club's always open—and the sea's always there. And maybe Flite will come back in the spring.'

A sudden wild hope stirred Matthew. 'Do you think so?'

'It's possible. They often do return to old haunts.' He hesitated, and then added, 'Particularly if they've got attached to someone.'

Attached to someone, thought Matthew . . . Yes, it's like an umbilical cord, pulling and pulling. Oh Flite, where are you?

But Skip was now holding out something and looking almost shy about it. 'If you go down to the whale-watch in Baja California, you might meet Petra. It's not all that far from San Diego.'

Matthew took the slip of paper. 'Is this her address?'

'Not exactly. But she said she could be reached there.'

'I see.' Matthew looked at him hard. 'Any message from you?'

Skip's sea-blue eyes seemed to cloud with pain, but he only said carelessly, 'Oh, just tell her I'm the same as ever. Nothing's changed.'

'Nothing's changed,' repeated Matthew dutifully. Then some imp of mischief made him ask innocently, 'If I get into a real jam out there, would you come to the rescue?'

'Don't you dare,' growled Skip. Then, surprisingly, he put an arm round Matthew's shoulders and hugged him hard. 'I hope it all works out for you. Let me know how it goes.' Then he went rapidly away down the street without looking back.

And finally, it was the old captain. In the mysterious, quiet way in which his high-powered life was ordered, a chauffeur-driven car had set him down at Madge's door, and now it had returned and stood waiting for him at the kerb. So now he stood leaning on his stick and looking at Matthew with his shrewd, faded eyes.

'Now, listen to me, Matthew. You know how I'm placed—and most of the details of my business. If things don't work out in America, I've no doubt we can find you a job over here. I know you want to be independent, so I'm not offering anything at present. But if the time comes, don't be too proud to ask.'

'Will you—will I see you again?' It suddenly seemed to matter enormously to Matthew that he shouldn't be saying farewell to this fierce, solitary old man.

'I dare say,' murmured the captain, 'if you don't leave it too long.'

'Will you go back to Porthgwillick next year?'

'Do my best,' growled the captain. But there was a hint of uncertainty in his voice that made Matthew afraid. 'You'd better have this,' added the old man. 'I won't guarantee air fares, but this will get you a passage—of a sort—on any of my ships, anywhere.' He held out a small embossed card with ST GEORGE SHIPPING LINES printed on the top and his own name. Underneath, he had written in his fine, spidery hand: *Free passage for Matthew Ferguson to any destination* and had signed it with an indecipherable flourish. 'Might be a tanker, mind,' he added, twinkling at Matthew. 'Or a container ship. Don't get refrigerated.'

Matthew tried to laugh. But it came out like a gulp. 'I—I can't begin—' he tried.

But the old man cut him short. 'Don't. Go and spread your wings, boy. Learn to fly. Come back when you're a true high-flier.'

'I will,' said Matthew, and knew that this was the most serious promise of all.

The old man nodded, tapped him on the shoulder with his stick, and climbed into his car. Matthew watched him go, feeling that some vital part of his own life was slipping away from him in that quiet, fast car. He lifted his hand in farewell, and then the dark Mercedes turned the corner and was gone.

MATTHEW DID NOT TELL Madge about America until after his visit to the solicitor. The arrangements, he discovered, were even more cut-and-dried than he had expected. His air ticket had been bought, money had been sent for 'travelling expenses', and he would be met at the other end.

Then John Harvey handed him a letter from his aunt-by-marriage, Mrs Madeleine (Della) Grant. *Dear Matthew*, said the letter, in a round, rather childish hand. *I hope all the arrangements will be satisfactory, and you will have no difficulty travelling. We are looking forward to seeing you over here. San Diego is a beautiful city, and I hope you will like it. Yours sincerely, Della Grant.*

That was all. No word of family feeling. Just polite and rather distant. Matthew wished with all his heart that he could stay with Madge and Jim and the kids, where at least he knew he was always welcome and could be of some use.

' . . . anything else?' John Harvey was saying. 'Is there anything else you want to know?'

'What happens if we don't get on? If it doesn't work out?'

The solicitor nodded. 'Well, of course, at sixteen you can decide for yourself what you want to do. They have no legal rights over you unless they apply to be appointed your guardians, and they haven't done that yet.'

'Could they?'

'Oh yes. But my guess is, they'll wait and see. After all, they are as much in the dark as you are.'

'Yes, of course.' Matthew saw the justice of that. 'Well, I'll just have to play it by ear. The air ticket is one-way, I suppose?'

'Yes.' But Harvey knew what was bothering Matthew, and went on to reassure him. 'However, I have that money of yours in trust, remember? Maybe you wouldn't refuse to use it if it meant you could get home?'

'Maybe I wouldn't,' Matthew conceded, with a lopsided smile.

'That's all right, then,' said John Harvey briskly. 'Just send an SOS to me, and I'll see that you get it. But—may I suggest that you do give the American visit a fair trial first?'

'Yes,' agreed Matthew. 'I intend to.'

WHEN HE TOLD MADGE and the kids, the expected scene from Jampy came with a vengeance. He stormed and yelled, looking at Matthew with outraged, tear-filled eyes that clearly said: 'Traitor!' and refused to be comforted.

Matthew tried patiently to explain about his aunt, about a new home in America. But that only made it worse. Jampy just yelled louder, stamped his feet and said, '*This* is home!'

Matthew looked helplessly at Madge. He didn't dare say what was in his mind—that he agreed with Jampy. This was home, this small, council flat, bursting with children, toys and washing. No room to turn round, no privacy, and only a sofa-bed to sleep on. But nevertheless, warm, friendly and undemanding—home.

'Never mind, Jampy love,' said Madge, gathering the small boy up and hugging him close so that the wildly flailing arms and legs stuck out round her like a wriggling octopus. 'He'll come back.' She met Matthew's anguished look with perfect understanding. 'He knows this is his home, too.'

'Home-too?' repeated Jampy.

'Home too,' agreed Matthew, and turned away hastily before he howled as loud as Jampy.

Jim Farley watched him in silence, and then added just two words to Madge's statement. '*Don't forget.*'

PART III

HE WHO BENDS TO HIMSELF...

Matthew was dazzled by his first sight of San Diego. It seemed to be all blue sea, white buildings and golden sunlight, the city skyline floating on the bay like a brilliant mirage. He went through customs and immigration in a daze of confused images, nervously clutching his passport in one hand. But at last he heard a voice behind him say in a crisp, English voice, 'Matthew? Matthew Ferguson?'

He turned and found himself looking into the eyes of a tall elegant woman, dressed in a white trouser-suit with lots of gold jewellery glinting in the sunlight. She had a squarish face and grey eyes a bit like his own—and equally anxious. Her hair was ash-blonde tipped with silver and her mouth, which was now attempting to smile at him encouragingly, was guarded.

She, for her part, saw a tall, shy boy with his father's deep grey-green eyes, and the same gold-bronze hair. It was a face just settling into the firm lines of young manhood, already promising good looks and strength, and it was so like his father's—the young man she used to know—that she caught her breath in surprise. 'You *must* be Matthew,' she said, holding out her hand. 'Come along. Is that all the baggage you have?' And she hustled him out into the brilliant sunshine and into a bright green roadster with an open roof.

She drove fast, in a stream of moving traffic. 'You'll have time to explore tomorrow,' she said, waving a dismissive hand at the inviting glimpses of sea, bright yachts in the bay, and tall masts and cranes down by the busy port. 'Right now, I guess you could do with a shower and some English tea.'

He caught her sideways glance at him and grinned. 'You sounded almost American then. But I thought—'

'Oh yes, I'm English. A Londoner, like you. Till I married your father's brother—your Uncle Ned, that was. We went to live in Edinburgh then.' Once again she gave him that half-questioning, sideways glance. 'But I've been out here so long, I almost feel American sometimes.' She waved her hand again at an approaching interchange with wide avenues branching off it, and said briefly, 'Des and I live in a condo—down here.'

They duly arrived at a neat condominium of apartments surrounding a central grassy square flanked by palm trees leaning towards the sun and the flawless blue of the sky above them.

The lift took them to the third floor, where Della opened an outer door into a large, sunny apartment. There was a big living room with windows all along one wall, and a glimpse of the Pacific between two other tall white apartment blocks. Beyond this was an opulent-looking double bedroom with satin covers, and a smaller single bedroom with its own little bathroom. This room was furnished simply with a bed, covered by a bright Indian rug, a built-in wardrobe and a small white-painted desk.

'Yours,' said Della. 'Hope you'll have enough room. I'll let you settle in then come on through when you're ready. Des won't be back till late, so we'll have time for a chat.'

What does 'a chat' mean? thought Matthew. I wonder if she'll talk about my father? A sudden passionate longing to learn more about this unknown figure beset him. He had never known him, never really understood what had happened to him.

Sighing, he stripped off his crumpled, travel-weary clothes and stepped into the shower. Afterwards, he dressed carefully in the only other pair of jeans he possessed and the new 'Porthgwillick Aqua-Surf Club' T-shirt and went to find Della.

She was in the kitchen–diner, frying him eggs, pancakes and hash browns. 'Sit down,' she directed, jerking a thumb at the shiny barstools by the long counter. 'Hope you're hungry.'

Matthew didn't know he was till he began eating. Then he found he couldn't stop till the plate was empty. 'That was smashing,' he said gratefully.

'I'd better explain the set-up here,' Della said at last, smiling at him. 'Des and I are both out all day, at work. I come home around five, Des all hours. He's in insurance, and goes out on calls everywhere under the sun.'

'What do you do?'

'Oh, I work in a downtown boutique. It's OK—not too hard except in a sales rush—and I enjoy meeting folks.'

Matthew nodded.

'We usually eat latish, sometimes out by the beach. Des likes seafood.' She eyed his guitar case a little anxiously. 'Des doesn't like too much noise in the evening, unless he's got his favourite ball game on—then he wouldn't hear an earthquake coming.'

They laughed together, both a little shyly, but Matthew understood that a warning had been given.

'About your schooling,' she went on suddenly. 'Do you want to go on to college?'

'No.' Matthew was quite definite. 'I wouldn't mind doing a computer course at night school or something. But I want a job. I want to be independent.'

There was a gleam of sympathy in her eye. 'You don't like being—beholden is the old-fashioned word, isn't it?'

'No. I don't.' Then he looked confused. 'But that doesn't mean—'

'I know,' she interrupted him. 'But you don't have to feel grateful, Matt. I want to do this. I was—very fond of your father.'

'Can you tell me about him? I know so little,' Matthew asked.

She was staring beyond him, down a long, dark road of memory, and she started when he spoke. 'What? . . . Oh, he was—young and rather handsome when I knew him. I married the older one, Ned—I didn't meet Michael till the wedding.'

'Michael. Was that his name?'

'Didn't you even know that?'

He shook his head. 'My mother never talked about him.' He saw her lips clamp shut at the mention of his mother, and thought desperately, What can I do to make her talk?

'What was his job?'

'He was a civil engineer. Transport. Roads and so on—bridges and things.' She smiled suddenly, a radiance of memory making her look much younger and softer. 'And stars.'

'*Stars?*'

'He loved astronomy. Quasars and light-years. I suppose it goes with engineering.' She looked at him, with a strange light of recognition in her eye. 'You've got it too, haven't you? Computers and such?'

But Matthew was still pursuing a thought, and ignored this. 'Was he a good engineer?'

She laughed. 'Yes. His bridges won prizes, I think.' Her eyes were unwary for once. 'He was always very bright, Ned used to say. We couldn't understand why he—' She stopped, confused.

'Why he married my mother?' He paused. 'She never talked about him. Never told me what happened, really.'

'It didn't work out, Matt. It couldn't have, they were so different.' She glanced at him speculatively again, wondering how much to say. 'You must've realised—?'

'That my mother was a tramp?' His voice was flat. 'Oh yes. There were always boyfriends. There was always someone new. They never lasted long.'

She nodded silently. Then she said abruptly, 'Didn't you mind?'

He shrugged again. 'Not really. I never knew anything else.'

Della Grant shivered at the worldly-wise acceptance in the young voice. What a bleak and loveless life this boy had lived. Could she at least give him some stability and affection here? . . . Or would he refuse to accept it—like his father before him?'

'Well,' she said, trying to be practical and kind, 'no good dwelling on the past. You're here to enjoy yourself. I suggest you spend a few weeks getting to know your way around before you look for a job. There's no hurry.' She ventured another, friendlier smile. 'We're not short of a dollar or two, Des and I, and we'd like to see you have a good time. OK?'

Matthew looked up and answered her smile with a tentative one of his own. 'Why not?' he said.

DES, WHEN HE CAME IN, was large and hot and hearty. He clapped
Matthew on the shoulders, called loudly for a cold beer and flopped
into a chair, seeming to accept his presence with careless unconcern.

By this time, sleep was beginning to catch up on Matthew. He
reckoned vaguely that by English time it was probably four in the
morning—the next morning at that. But here in San Diego it was still
broad daylight.

'Della,' said Des. 'I guess we might eat out at the beach tonight.
Kinda celebrate.'

'I don't know, Des. Matt's probably tired.'

'Sure, he's tired,' agreed Des, laughing hugely. 'Best way to deal
with jet lag is ignore it.' He got heavily to his feet and gave Matthew
another hearty slap on the back. 'Try out some seafood, OK?'

'OK,' agreed Matthew wearily.

MATTHEW REALISED FROM THE FIRST that he would have to make
his own friends. And it wasn't that easy. Della and Des were out all
day, and in the evenings they either stayed in or went out to one of
San Diego's many beachside restaurants and joined other groups of
friends for a meal. But these were mostly people of their own age.
Some of them did have teenage kids, who mostly went off in their
own noisy gangs to their own haunts, but Matthew felt reluctant to
become drawn into their pursuits—their hang-gliding and wind-
surfing, their endless beach games and barbecues. 'I am becoming a
prig,' he said to himself, knowing these careless, golden young people
found him awkward and stiff. But then he remembered to bring his
guitar next time and, from then on, he drew in his own small circle of
devotees, and people forgot about him being strange and prickly.

Des, obviously trying hard to play the benevolent uncle, insisted on
taking him out at weekends to the Zoo and Sea World. San Diego
Zoo was so spacious and well organised that he almost forgave them
for keeping wild animals in captivity, but Sea World was another
matter. He tried to avoid the shows of killer whales and dolphins
jumping through hoops, but Des insisted he would love it. He hated
every minute of it. He wanted to get down into the water and open
the sluice gates and set them all free.

But of course he couldn't. There they were, these tamed, well-
trained, graceful creatures, leaping and diving to order, playing their
appointed games, doing their brilliant acrobatics, and coming up for
applause with their ingratiating smiles fixed on their faces—and he,
watching them, wanted to curl up and die of shame. How could we,

he thought. How could we reduce these glorious creatures to such servility?

'They enjoy it, you know,' said Della, who had seen Matthew's face and knew a little about how he felt.

'Do they?' snapped Matthew. 'How do you know?'

The question hung in the air between them, and Des said cheerfully, 'Oh, they're all clowns at heart. They *love* performing.'

Matthew sighed, and caught the eye of a girl who was standing near the rail next to him, looking as if she was on the point of walking out. She was slim and brown, with a tangled stringy mane of dark hair and a rather angry-looking mouth. Her bright, observant eyes seemed to spark with impatience.

'Pathetic, aren't they?' she murmured. And Matthew didn't know if she meant the dolphins and killer whales, or the audience oohing and aahing at them. Then she jerked her thumb at the exit. 'Coming outside?' she asked, and moved away.

'I'm just going to get some air,' he told Des, and followed the girl out of the noise and heat of the arena.

She was waiting for him outside, and with her were two young men, long-haired and older than Matthew, wearing shorts and sporting the golden, all-over tan that San Diegans all seemed to have. 'I'm Tracey,' she said, and then waved a careless brown hand at her two companions. 'Bud and Spike.'

'Hi,' they responded lazily, crinkling up their eyes against the sun in smiles that were almost real.

Matthew's smile was cautious. 'Matt,' he volunteered.

'Animal Rights,' added Tracey, without any other explanation, and then dismissed her two colleagues with a nod. 'See you tonight then. My place. At eight.'

They nodded cheerfully, grinned at Matthew, and after a brief consultation went off in different directions.

The girl watched them go and then turned to Matthew. 'Didn't like it much, did you?'

Matthew shook his head. 'All that in there? . . . It seems so degrading, somehow. Dolphins are such—such noble creatures.'

She stared at him. 'English, aren't you? How come you know about dolphins?'

He smiled. 'They do come to our cold English waters—sometimes.'

'You seen them?'

He hesitated, wondering how much to say to this blunt, forthright girl. 'I—knew one in the wild once, yes.'

214

She gave a quick nod to herself, as if this confirmed something in her assessment of him. Then she said, even more abruptly, 'You seen the greys going down?'

He looked bewildered. 'The greys?'

'Grey whales. Going down the coast.'

'Oh.' He was still bewildered. 'No.'

'Come with me.'

He paused, wondering what to do about Della and Des. Then he thought, They saw me go out. They won't worry.

Tracey was already climbing onto a small moped. 'This is the Fly,' she announced laconically. 'Get on the back.'

They whizzed out along the coast road to Point Loma, where there were already a small number of visitors looking at the view of San Diego spread out along the bay. But some of them were not looking at the white and gold city on their left. They were looking out to sea where, in the beguiling calm of the blue Pacific, a slow, swirling line of dark grey humps moved steadily down the coast towards Baja California. From time to time they came up to blow, then curved over into a massive, glistening wall of greyish-white bulk, and dived deep, sending a huge shower of spray up with the rising tail-fluke which came out of the water like a vast, branching tree.

Matthew was enthralled. 'Where are they going?' he asked, aware at once that their purpose was fixed, laid down by countless years of custom.

'To Laguna Scammon,' said Tracey. 'And a couple of other places in Baja. To breed. All the way from the Bering Sea, every year.'

'Marvellous,' breathed Matthew.

'Sure is. You oughta go down there, see for yourself.'

'I'd love to.' He sighed. 'But—'

'You're with your folks. I know. Can't you break loose?'

He hesitated. 'It's—not that easy. Things are a bit complicated. Will you be going down?' he asked suddenly, not quite knowing what he was starting.

Her expression changed. 'I might. But I got other things to do first. You into Animal Rights?'

'Not yet. But I'm willing to learn.'

She nodded, then raised a slim hand and pointed down the coast. 'See that line of stuff? Closed area. US Navy. You know what their latest gimmick is? Training dolphins to dive deep and recover bits of nuclear warheads off subs.'

Matthew was horrified. 'What?'

'They buy them from the Japs. Dolphins can go real deep, you know. You can imagine what their life is like.'

Matthew's face was grim. 'So what can we do about it?'

'Protest,' she said at once. 'Carry banners. Get the media in on it. The more noise the better. If you're interested there's a meeting at my place, Friday week, to plan a march. Coming?'

'Yes,' said Matthew decisively.

Satisfied, Tracey gave a little nod and turned back to look at the patient line of grey whales swimming steadily down the sunlit coast of California. Grand and stately, nothing deflected them from their purpose. She wished she was as strong and as single-minded.

DELLA AND DES DID NOT SEEM particularly annoyed that Matthew had walked out of Sea World, assuming that the heat had got to him. But when he mentioned Tracey and her meeting, Des was none too pleased. 'You want to watch it, kid, with that bunch. Trouble-makers, all of 'em.'

'But I—'

'Hoodlums and layabouts. Think they can change the world by violence.' He took another swig of beer—there was always a beer can in his hand—and waved his other hand dismissively. 'Leave it out.'

Matthew glanced at Della in appeal, but she gave him a neutral shrug. 'Their ideals may be OK,' she said, 'but they do get themselves a bad image, cutting fences, opening cages, and even throwing a bomb or two. Des is right. Better steer clear.'

Matthew said nothing. But he made a quiet resolve in his own mind to slip off when the time came.

WHEN HE HAD ENDURED as much idleness and sightseeing as he could bear, he enrolled in a computer course for one night a week, and then went downtown and found himself a job.

Mosky was a shrewd, stringy Jew who ran a café with a bookstore on the side. He looked Matthew up and down and said abruptly, 'Speak.'

Matthew looked bewildered. 'What do you want me to say?'

Mosky grinned. 'You done it, kid. It's the English accent I like. You can read, I take it?'

'Of course.'

'No "of course" about it. Most kids can't these days—or won't.' He waved an expressive brown hand at rows of books on shelves, which Matthew had glimpsed through an archway beyond the café tables. 'Gotta be flexible. They want a burger—you get it. They want Marcel Proust—you find it. Follow me?'

'Yes.'

'But you don't bring the book to the table. Grease-and-tomater all over the dust jacket. You take the guy to the book. See?'

Matthew nodded.

Mosky flashed an impish grin at him. 'When can you start?'

'Today,' said Matthew promptly. He rather liked Mosky. He knew this was the job for him—if he could do it.

Mosky clapped him on the shoulder. 'Come meet the guys,' he said, and led him to the long counter-bar. 'This is Joe—he cooks; and Allie, she waits tables; and Merc, he clears up. But we all do what's needed. OK? Guys, this is Matt.'

The three of them looked up and nodded cheerfully, and went on with their work. Joe was long and thin, and busy turning burgers with a long, flat spoon on the sizzling hotplate. Allie was brown and plump, with long hair tied back in a bright green bow. And Merc, who seemed almost submerged in a mound of washing-up in the double sink, was square and powerful with a sweaty face that managed to flash him a quirky smile.

'Hi.' Matthew sounded shy. 'Can I help?'

Merc stared at him. 'Wow, someone's offerin'.' He reached out one soapy hand and flung Matthew an apron. 'Help yourself.' Matthew's job had begun.

At the end of the first week, he took some of his wages back to Della, and provoked a major row.

'What d'you think I am, a child exploiter?'

'I'm not a child, Della.'

She looked at him, and her smile seemed to change subtly. 'No,' she conceded softly. 'You're not, are you?'

There was a curious little silence. Matthew felt uncomfortable, but he still held the dollar bills out to her. 'Please,' he said.

'I can't take your money, Matt.'

'You can,' he insisted, 'just for my keep. It'd make me feel better.'

'All right,' she said at last. 'I guess you win. But only a small amount, mind. I won't take advantage.'

They glared at each other for a moment, and then began to laugh.

He's a good kid, thought Della, truth to tell he's so like Michael, I find it hard to refuse him anything.

But she didn't tell Des about the money. He might take it amiss, and she didn't want any trouble.

TRACEY'S PAD WAS IN A DOWNTOWN apartment block between a bank and a group of shiny neon-lit bars and restaurants. Its concrete approach was cold and faceless, and clearly none too affluent.

The 'meeting' seemed to spread all over the shabby living room and the half-screened kitchen. There was a haze of smoke and the unmistakable sweet smell of pot in the air, and there were empty glasses and coffee cups strewn all over the place. To Matthew the company all seemed absurdly young and nonchalant, and not in the least like a bunch of ardent activists.

'This is Matt,' said Tracey to the room at large. 'He's English—and into dolphins.' Then she looked at the assembled company through narrowed eyes and then announced, 'Now, listen real good. It's one week from Friday, OK? . . . That's the twelfth. Gives us time to get out the posters and hand out leaflets.' A few heads nodded. 'Assemble at my place and march downtown first.'

'*Only* march?' said one, sounding disappointed. Bud and Spike glanced at one another and then across at Tracey.

'*March*,' she ordered. 'With banners. We got enough?'

'Could make a couple more,' volunteered a thin, mousy girl.

Tracey nodded and turned to Matthew. 'You coming?'

He looked a bit uncertain. He badly wanted to know what else they were planning to do besides march. 'I work till four,' he said.

'Then meet us at Ocean Beach. We'll be about there by then, ready for Point Loma and Fort Rosencranz.' She glanced balefully at the roomful of people. 'That is, if any of you can get yourselves together by then.'

'I'll be there if I can,' Matthew told her.

'OK,' she agreed, and then dismissed him. 'Better spread now. Gotta talk to Spike and Bud—about leaflets.' She grabbed one from a pile and handed it to Matthew. 'See you on the twelfth.'

He knew from the look on her face that she and Spike and Bud were planning something else, but she had made it very plain that he was not wanted on that trip—whatever it was. So he left.

BACK AT DELLA'S APARTMENT, Matthew let himself in and slid unobtrusively off to his own room without saying anything. To his relief, Des appeared to be out and Della was in the kitchen.

He got out his guitar rather guiltily, for he had been neglecting it lately, and began to play a new piece by Rodrigo. It got hold of his fingers, and a sudden wave of dreadful nostalgia swept over him. He longed to be back in grey old London with Madge and the kids, and

Jampy interrupting his practice with endless questions.

There was a tap on the door, and Della's elegant head came round it. 'Can I come in?'

'Of course.' Matthew looked guilty. 'Was I too loud?'

She smiled and strolled over to sit on the edge of his bed, crossing her slim brown legs and leaning back to look up at him. 'No. I like it. It's only Des who—' She did not finish, but instead fished in her jacket pocket and brought out a yellowing envelope. 'I thought you might like to see these.'

Matthew took the envelope from her. Inside it were two faded photographs. One of them showed a young man with curly bronze hair and a curly smile to match, screwing up his eyes against the sun. The second photograph showed the same young man, arm in arm with a slightly older and more serious-looking version of himself on one side, and a young, also smiling woman on the other. He looked at it more closely and recognised Della—a youthful, gentler version, but with the same slightly arrogant tilt of the head.

He looked at her enquiringly. 'Is that—my father?'

She sighed. 'Yes—that's Michael. And that's Ned, my late husband. And me, of course—when young . . .'

Matthew was staring at the stranger in the photograph. There was no stirring of recognition inside him, only a vague feeling of disappointment that it didn't mean more to him. Here was a picture of a man he didn't know, living and working and laughing into cameras before Matthew was even thought of. He looked nice enough, but he was a stranger.

'He looks—a nice guy.' It sounded painfully inadequate.

'Yes,' she said. 'He was. And very like you.'

'Really?' Matthew leaned over to have another look. But I don't have that air of confidence, he thought, that look of belonging in the world. Perhaps I will one day . . . 'It's difficult for me to see it,' he said lamely, and laughed a little. 'I don't really know what I look like.'

Della smiled at him warmly. 'You look pretty good to me.'

Before he could reply there was a sound of a slammed door and a shout from the living room. Des was home. He ambled to the doorway of Matthew's room and stood looking in at them. There was not exactly suspicion in his glance, but a certain watchfulness that made Matthew uneasy.

'Anyone alive round here?'

'Yes, Des, of course. We were just looking at old photos.'

Des snorted contemptuously. 'Not that again? Why don't you

leave the past where it's at, Del. Dead and buried.'

Della looked shocked. 'Des—it is Matt's father.'

Des shrugged massive shoulders. 'So it's Matt's pa, then. But now it's today, and I'm hungry. So get yourselves together, guys, we're goin' out.'

Della put the photographs in her pocket and almost scuttled out of the room to find her handbag. Her face was closed.

Matthew did not look at Des. It was becoming obvious to him that there was something about the past that Des resented—even disliked—and Matthew himself was part of it. 'You and Della go,' he said. 'I've got some work to catch up on for my class.'

'Suit yourself,' shrugged Des.

But when they had gone, Matthew went down to Mosky's and offered to lend a hand on the late shift. He needed the company.

BECAUSE OF HIS HOURS at Mosky's and his evening classes, Matthew had taken to swimming very early in the morning. He preferred the beach then anyway, when it was empty and quiet. It seemed a little nearer to his own windswept Cornish beach where the seals had come to listen to his music, and the gentle presence of Flite the dolphin had filled the day with joy.

Sunrise was nearly always clear and beautiful in these washed Pacific skies, but one morning it was so spectacular that it took his breath away. Great wings of glowing cloud stained the horizon with crimson veils, and even above his head small brush-strokes of pink and scarlet fire were stippled across the robin's-egg bowl of dawn. And as he turned on his back to look up he saw the whole city skyline flushed with a rosy incandescence.

He lay watching it from the lift and fall of the ocean almost with disbelief as the blaze grew in the sky and laid fiery fingers of light on the sea all round him. He seemed to float in sunrise, and the ocean burned with flame. '*Eternity's sunrise . . .*' said the old captain's voice in his mind.

He went to work in a dream, trying vainly to concentrate on serving eggs sunny-side-up, and waffles drowned in maple syrup. When the first rush of breakfasts was over, he drifted into the bookstore side to see whether Mosky had a copy of Blake on his shelves. He had just located it when Mosky's voice spoke behind him.

'Don't tell me I gotta customer?'

Matthew turned, smiling. 'Is it such a shock?'

'Poetry? I might drop dead. You like Blake?'

'I was looking for something about . . . *eternity's sunrise.*'

'Here, I'll show you,' said Mosky promptly. He took the book from Matthew and leafed through the pages until he found the passage. 'This what you want? . . . *Joy as it flies . . .?*'

Matthew looked down at the words, remembering Flite's joyous, unquenchable delight in living as he leaped and dived in the sun. 'That's it,' he murmured, and bent his head swiftly over the page to hide his absurd tears.

Mosky glared at Matthew. 'You workin' today or not?'

Matthew laughed. 'Can I buy this first?'

'Sure can. Discount to staff. But if you read it here, you're fired.'

They were walking back past the tables when a young blond boy looked up and said, 'Matt-the-Whizz. Where's your guitar?'

Mosky stopped. 'You play guitar?'

'*Does* he?' drawled the boy. 'Man, he's class. Beach guru, that's who. Draws 'em in like crazy.'

Mosky glared at Matthew even more fiercely than usual. 'Bring it down tonight—you hear?'

'I—I play classical mostly—not pop,' protested Matthew.

'Who says I want pop?' growled Mosky. 'Just bring it or you're fired, OK?'

'OK,' agreed Matthew, smiling sweetly. 'I will.'

THERE BEGAN FOR MATTHEW a strangely divided existence. In the early mornings when he swam in the ocean, he was himself, full of dreams and the aching pull of longing to find Flite. During the day, working at Mosky's, he was mostly a pair of hands, enjoying occasional sardonic gleams of humour from Mosky and snatched moments of friendly backchat from his overworked companions. One evening a week, he was all head and cool thought over his computer course, and then there were the evenings when he took his guitar down to Mosky's. He was all fingers then—fingers and a head full of sounds and patterns. He played everything he knew and loved, wandering from the early lutanists to calm, measured Bach and on to Spanish fire and back again to tidy Vivaldi.

It didn't leave much time for Della and Des, which in some ways was a relief. The antagonism he had sensed in Des seemed to be growing as he got to know him, and Della was brittle and unpredictable, one moment almost too affectionate and the next offhand and unreachable. He remembered wryly how he had hoped these new relations would give him the family life he had always wanted . . . but then he gave himself a shake and told himself that nothing was ever given to anyone on a plate, it had to be earned.

At the end of the week he suddenly remembered Tracey and the dolphin demo, and knew he would have to join the protest, however little good it did, for Flite's sake. That day he worked his shift at the restaurant and then left his guitar with Mosky for safekeeping. 'I may be late tonight,' he explained. 'Got something to do first.'

Mosky merely raised eloquent eyebrows and stowed the guitar safely away behind the counter in his bookstore. Satisfied, Matthew gave him a lopsided grin of thanks and went off to find the march.

At Ocean Beach, to Matthew's surprise, there was quite a sizable crowd, the different groups marshalled into reasonably manageable marching order. They had already marched through the town and were now reassembling for the more serious march down the coast to the naval base. He found Tracey giving last-minute instructions to Bud and Spike, and to the mouse-brown girl, Stephi, who was adjusting the banners.

'Now, see here, Matt,' Tracey snapped, 'any trouble, you just scram. You get picked up by the Feds, they'll deport you.'

'The Feds?' Matthew was interested.

'Naval establishment. Sensitive area.' Tracey spoke laconically. 'But even the locals would be a drag. You get caught, you don't know *anything*. You're just a dumb student out on a demo. Get it?'

Matthew nodded. 'What about the others?'

Tracey laughed. 'They're just dumb students anyway. Come on, we gotta move.' Someone gave Matthew a banner, and at a signal from Tracey, they all moved off quite slowly and peaceably, chanting 'Save the Dolphins' as they went. Matthew found himself marching beside Stephi and a thin, leggy boy who said he was known as Beaks.

The march progressed cheerfully enough. Some of the students sang the old campus songs, and changed 'Where have all the flowers gone?' to 'Where have all the dolphins gone?' Passers-by and beach parties smiled indulgently at just another student demo, and some of them took leaflets and even stopped to read them. Matthew sang with the rest, and chanted 'Save the Dolphins' along the road to Point Loma.

From there the marchers turned south and went on down the edge of the Cabrillo Highway towards the gate to the naval station. Matthew and his group were fairly near the back, so they could not see what was happening. It was almost dark by now, and several of the stragglers at the rear had switched on torches to warn approaching cars of the marching columns ahead.

Then a commotion seemed to break out in front. People ahead started pushing backwards, and the marchers at the rear went on pushing forwards, so that a heaving scrum began to develop. Shouts were heard, a few strangled oaths, and then the sound of security whistles, alarm bells and police sirens.

'What's happening?' asked Matthew breathlessly, being shoved and pushed from either side.

'Trouble,' said Stephi, and put down her banner. 'We'd better scram.'

'But—' protested Matthew.

'Tracey's orders,' snapped Stephi. She seized Matthew by the hand and yanked him out of the struggling mass of marchers. 'Go, man, go!'

But Matthew stood still, looking down the road to where lights were flashing. 'What were they trying to do?' he asked.

Stephi shrugged. 'Hand in a petition, Tracey *said*. But I guess they tried a break-in somewhere else—that's Tracey's style. Sounds like it failed anyways. Come on, let's go.'

At this point, a police car screamed up alongside the dispersing column and two men leaped out and started running towards the nearest of the protesters. The retreating marchers ran even faster, but two of the stragglers were too slow and were hauled back to the squad car, where they were roughly bundled inside.

'Hey!' said Matthew. 'They haven't done anything—'

'Shuddup!' hissed Stephi. 'They'll grab you too.'

Matthew was outraged. 'They were only *marching*—' But his voice was drowned by the booming voice of a loudhailer which suddenly sprang into life on the roof of the squad car.

'Disperse!' it shouted. 'Disperse quietly. Anyone running will be picked up. Go home.'

The squad car, lights blazing, cruised on down the road. Frightened runners mostly slowed down and tried to walk nonchalantly away. One or two went on running and disappeared in the shadows.

'What will happen to those kids?' Matthew stared after the retreating taillights.

Stephi shrugged. 'They'll just be questioned. Can't hold 'em for marching.'

Matthew stood, irresolute and troubled, on the dark road. 'I must—I must see what's happened to Tracey—'

'*No!*' snarled Stephi, tugging at him again. 'It won't help.'

Beaks also tried to drag him away. 'Too late for heroics now.'

As he spoke, there was another rush of running marchers from ahead. They all surged past, pounding down the road in panic, and after them came another squad car, cruising slowly with a couple of police running in front. Several of the escaping protesters cannoned into one another, and two of them fell over in a struggling heap almost at Matthew's feet. The police were not far behind, but before they could catch the stragglers, Matthew leaped forward, jerked the fallen students to their feet and pushed them on into the darkness.

The police had seen him now and were rapidly closing in on a likely-looking troublemaker, when Stephi's hand came out and yanked him sideways into deeper shadow. 'This way—' she said, and Beaks added from Matthew's other side, 'Beach track not far from here.'

They stumbled along in the dark, through scrubby wasteland and back gardens, for what seemed an achingly long, jolting run, and finally found themselves walking on sand. The shouts and flashing lights still went on behind them and Matthew felt ashamed to be leaving Tracey to face them alone.

'She'll get by,' said Beaks, steadying Matthew as he tripped over a rock. 'Tracey's used to trouble. No big deal.'

'We got transport in Ocean Bay,' urged Stephi, pushing ahead in the dark. 'Better get there fast.'

It seemed a long time to Matthew, but eventually they came out into the wide well-lit streets of Ocean Bay. His two companions made straight for a parking lot where they had left their mopeds.

Beaks laid a friendly hand on his arm as he got onto his moped. 'You go charging off like a white knight, Tracey'd be in more trouble, Matt. She's gotta think of herself as well as you.'

'Yes, of course,' said Matthew, sounding absurdly crestfallen.

'So long, guys,' Beaks called, lifting a hand in mock salute.

Stephi pulled Matthew on behind her and roared off after him.

When Matthew finally got to Mosky's, he was tired, grubby and upset. Mosky did not ask any questions, except after a few minutes of watchful silence. 'You fit to play?'

'I will be in a minute,' said Matthew, gulping coffee.

Mosky slapped him on the back. 'Attaboy!' he grinned.

Matthew had thought he would play badly that night. But in fact the music, as usual, took him away from the frustrating conflicts of the day to a place that was ordered and perfect.

He went home tired but contented and thankfully slid into bed without having met Della or Des on the way.

As he was just drifting into sleep he heard his door open softly, and Della came in and stood looking down at him as he lay. 'Matt?' she whispered. 'You all right?'

'Sure,' he answered, puzzled by the strange look in her eyes. 'Is anything wrong?'

'No,' she sighed. 'Nothing's wrong, Matt.' She came forward and perched herself on the edge of his bed. 'You were late tonight, that's all. I got worried.'

'I went on rather late at Mosky's,' he explained.

She nodded, and fell silent. Finally she said, with a strange note of appeal in her voice, 'Are you—are you happy here, Matt?'

Matthew gulped, trying to get his weary mind into focus. What could he say? 'I—sure,' he said helplessly. 'It's different, of course. Takes some getting used to . . .' He tried a lopsided smile.

'Never mind,' said Della softly, 'I can see you're tired . . .' She leaned forward and kissed him with a curious, lingering sadness. Matthew just managed not to flinch, but somehow he felt frightened.

'Good night,' he said, and turned on his side away from the light filtering in from the hallway.

Della did not say any more. The silence seemed to go on and on, but at last she rose to her feet and went quietly away.

IT WAS A COUPLE OF DAYS later that the stranger came into Mosky's. He stood there quietly looking round for a few minutes, until he spotted Matthew playing the guitar in the corner. Then he sat down at a table to listen. He sat impassively, quietly drinking a cup of coffee, and when Matthew came to the end of his last piece he rose to his feet and went across to the till to speak to Mosky.

Then the stranger strolled across to Matthew and offered him a coffee. 'It's OK, I've squared it with your boss.'

Matthew was startled, but he followed the stranger to an empty table near the bookstore end of the café, away from the main crowd of customers, and sat down. Mosky came over with two cups of coffee, looking at Matthew rather anxiously. After a second's hesitation he turned away.

'Now,' said the stranger, smiling pleasantly, 'let me introduce myself. My name is Morris. Commander Morris. I have an official capacity, but I am here—er—unofficially.'

'I see,' said Matthew, who didn't see at all. He was looking at the stranger attentively now, and he saw a man of middle age with a firm, squarish face and grey intelligent eyes.

'I want to talk to you,' began Morris gently, 'about dolphins. You were, I think, taking part in that abortive march?'

Matthew jumped a mile. He wondered who this man was, and if anything he said now might make things worse for Tracey and her friends.

'Yes,' he said.

'But you weren't involved in the attempted break-in?'

'No.' Matthew was still thinking furiously. 'I didn't even know it was going to take place.'

'Breaking into a military establishment is a serious matter, you know.'

'So is training dolphins to take part in lethal acts of war.'

'Ah.' Morris nodded at him. 'You have strong views.'

'I do, yes.' Matthew took a deep breath. 'Listen,' he said. 'I got to know a wild dolphin once—on the Cornish coast . . .' he stalled there, but then he forced himself to go on. 'He was the gentlest, most loving creature I've ever known. And the noblest.' He glanced rather wildly at Morris. 'He was innocent and powerful and splendid. He used to come through the water to meet me of his own free will. How could anyone want to harness that innocence and turn it into a weapon?'

Morris was silent, obviously impressed.

'There are other arguments,' he said at last. 'The naval authorities would say they are protecting the world against nuclear submarine attack, and any means they use to safeguard their defence is justified.'

Matthew looked obstinate. 'That's their judgment. I don't believe man has the right to order other creatures to do his dirty work. I mean, who are we to tell the dolphins what to do? We aren't God.'

'No,' sighed Morris. 'We aren't God.'

The silence between them was somehow a great deal more friendly, but Morris still had a question to ask. 'You're not a Communist, I take it?'

Matthew looked astonished. 'A *Communist*? I thought all that was exploded with perestroika.'

'Not entirely, Matthew. There's Cuba, remember. And people who break into military bases sometimes have motives other than concern about dolphins.'

'Oh, I see.' Matthew was still mildly astonished but he hastened to add, 'No ulterior motives. And I don't believe the others had, either.'

'You think the girl—Tracey Holland—was sincere?'

Matthew hesitated. He saw the trap Morris had set. If he defended Tracey now, he was admitting that he knew her and that she was the ringleader in this affair. But if he denied all knowledge of her he was quite clearly marking himself as a liar.

Morris did not miss the struggle in Matthew's mind. 'I should be honest, if I were you,' he said in that gentle voice which was somehow more menacing than anger. 'We know quite a lot about Tracey Holland already.'

Matthew sighed. 'Is she in serious trouble?'

Morris picked up the spoon from his coffee cup and looked at it intently. 'That depends on what we think of her motives.'

'I've only met her a few times,' said Matthew slowly. 'But I'd say she was honest about what she believes. She was as concerned as I am about the fate of the dolphins.'

'Did she ever talk to you about—taking violent action?'

'Oh no. She was very careful to keep me out of it. I did feel, once or twice, that she was probably planning something beyond the march, but I don't honestly think she thought about the *military* implications. She's probably as good an American as you are.'

'I'm English, actually,' murmured Morris, and there was a faint smile in those steel-grey eyes. 'But you are a good advocate.'

Matthew shook his head. 'I don't know. The Animal Rights people have been wrong, releasing mink into the wild and letting out infected rats and so on—but at least they make people aware of what's going on. That's what Tracey was trying to do, I think, just make enough fuss to get people talking.'

'You may be right.' Morris had found out what he wanted to know, and Matthew had unconsciously established his own innocence in this affair. But there were warnings that had to be given. 'You could be in trouble with the immigration authorities, you know, if you get mixed up in "subversive activities". How would your parents feel about that?'

'I haven't any parents,' said Matthew flatly. 'I'm just staying over here—for a while.'

Morris looked at him quietly. 'Could you tell me about that?'

There was a moment's hesitation, and then Matthew said in a strange, sharp tone, 'Yes. If you stay neutral.'

'What does that mean?'

'I'm sick of people being sorry for me,' he snapped. Then he added in an apologetic tone, 'Sorry. I know I'm touchy.'

'I promise not to be touched,' said Morris solemnly. 'Go on.'

So Matthew told him the whole of it, including the tensions in the Grant household. 'But I promised the old captain I'd give it a whirl—so I will. Then—who knows?'

'Will you take up Captain St George's offer?' Morris was holding the captain's small card in his hand, looking at it with interest. 'He's a pretty remarkable man.'

Matthew's face lit up in a sudden smile. 'Do you know him?'

'I have met him,' Morris said carefully. 'He is pretty well known in most parts of the world.' He handed Matthew back the precious card and said, 'Take care of that. It may come in very useful.'

Matthew nodded.

Morris got to his feet and held out another card of his own. 'You have been very frank with me, Matthew. I appreciate it. I have to tell you that your movements—and Tracey Holland's—may be watched for a while, but don't let it worry you. In the meantime, if you need any assistance, or advice, you can always contact me here.'

Matthew took the card and looked at it. It said simply: *Commander J.S. Morris, RN* but gave the address of the US naval base at Fort Rosencranz. 'You said you were English,' he said, mystified.

'Let's say—transatlantic,' smiled Morris. 'Liaison.'

Matthew nodded and put the little card in his pocket. 'I don't know why you're taking all this trouble,' he grumbled vaguely.

'Liaison,' repeated Morris, smiling more openly this time. 'Meanwhile, steer clear of trouble!' And he strolled away past the busy tables and into the San Diego streets.

Behind him, Mosky said anxiously, 'OK, Matt?'

Matthew grinned. 'OK,' he agreed. 'By the skin of my teeth!'

BUT WHEN HE GOT HOME that night to Della's apartment, it wasn't OK at all. Des was waiting for him, with a face like thunder.

'What's this about the Animal Rights demo?'

Matthew stood still. 'What about it?'

'Two Feds came looking for you, about the demo, that's what. And I don't like police nosin' about in my apartment.'

'I'm sorry—' began Matthew.

'Sorry!' snarled Des. And then the explosion came.

'Stuck-up, snotty-nosed English kid . . . come swanning out here and think you can do what you please . . . no regard for anyone but yourself . . .' Des's voice raged on. 'And I don't want a hoodlum in my house.'

228

Matthew listened to it in silence. Then he said, 'I'm not a hoodlum, Des. I only went on the march. I wasn't in on the break-in.'

'Just as well,' snapped Des, 'or they'd send you right back home like unwanted baggage—and they'd be right.'

Matthew felt a coldness. 'Is that what you want?'

Des paused in mid-tirade, red-faced and beyond caution. 'You bet it is, kid. Della brought you out here. It was her decision, not mine. I don't go with her still livin' in her past.'

Matthew went pale. 'What do you mean?'

'You're a substitute lover-boy, son. Didn't you know?' The angry little eyes raked him contemptuously. 'She wanted your father, and she couldn't have him. You'll do instead.'

'But that's crazy.' Matthew was so white by now that even Des faltered a little.

'Sure, it's crazy. People do crazy things outa remorse.'

'*Remorse*? Why, Des? Isn't it time you told me what really happened?'

Des looked at him warily and then shrugged his shoulders. 'OK. I'll tell you. Della married your Uncle Ned—the older brother. But she went overboard for Michael as soon as she laid eyes on him. He was having a rough time with your mother.' He glanced at Matthew, then went on, 'So Della invites him up to stay in Edinburgh. I guess she rather threw herself at his head—anyway she got him into bed someways or other. Ned came in and found them. Big scene. So Michael goes off, all uptight and guilty, and drives his car straight into a truck.'

Matthew sighed. It was a long, shaken sound, and a whole lot of vague heroic images of his father seemed to shrivel and die in its wake. 'How awful.'

'Yeah. Della never stopped blaming herself—never stopped trying to make it up to Ned. And never stopped loving the other guy.'

'But surely—?' He did not quite know how to say it.

'Oh, sure, she's happy enough with me, I guess.' He shrugged again, and then went on roughly, 'Leastways, till you came along. That stirred things up all over again, when they were good and buried. And I don't like it.'

'No,' agreed Matthew coldly. 'Nor do I.' Now it was his turn to let private bitterness surface. 'How d'you think it makes me feel? . . . I'm me, not my father. All that old history—I don't want any part of it.' He sighed. 'I'm sorry,' Matthew said, looking directly at Des with troubled eyes. 'It's no good, is it?'

'No, kid,' agreed Des, already regretting his anger, but realising it was too late to take back his words. 'I guess it's no damn good for any of us. I'm sorry too.'

IT WAS VERY LATE when Della came in, and the row between her and Des began. Shut in his room, Matthew could hear every word.

'How *could* you?' screamed Della. 'How could you do this to me? And to him, as well! He's only a kid.'

'He wanted the truth, and he damn well got it.'

'I didn't think you could be so cruel.'

'Time there was some plain sense around here.'

'What will he think of me? How can I face him after this? You fool, you've wrecked the whole thing . . .'

That was it, of course. She couldn't face Matthew. Matthew couldn't face her. It was quite clear what he had to do.

He waited till all the shouting died down and the apartment sank into night-time stillness. Then he got up, packed his few things in his duffle bag, picked up his guitar and crept out into the living room. He paused by Della's desk, picked up a sheet of paper and a pen and wrote her a note.

Thanks for everything. Sorry it didn't work out. Going to visit a friend in Baja. Will contact you before I go home. Matthew. Yes, that sounded reasonable. And it was more or less true, he hoped. He laid the note down on the living-room table and quietly let himself out of the apartment.

It was still dark, and he wasn't sure where he was going. But he knew his way to the beach. He would swim a bit and wait for daylight. Then he could go to work at Mosky's and plan something or other. He reached a quiet stretch of empty beach and laid his duffle bag down with his guitar. For a moment he was frightened to leave that precious guitar unattended, but there was no one about.

Sighing, he went out into the quiet sea, and let its waters lift his tired body, its ceaselessly whispering voice soothe his aching mind . . . Flite, he said, turning under a wave, it doesn't matter where you are. I can still love you . . . No one can take that away, can they? . . . The sea gave him no answer, but it rocked him gently in its arms and demanded nothing.

AT MOSKY'S THE NEXT DAY Matthew suddenly realised that he could not stay. Des and Della knew where he worked, and they would come looking for him. So he did his best to explain the situation to his shrewd old boss, and tried not to see the anxiety in his eyes.

'You in trouble, kid?' said Mosky, ignoring all the stumbling excuses.

Matthew grinned somewhat painfully. 'It's—a family matter.'

Mosky was still looking at him. 'They know you're taking off?'

'I left a note.'

The grizzled head nodded again. 'So where you headin'?'

'Baja California. To see the whales at Laguna Scammon.'

'Well, just you look out for yourself, kid. Wild country that—and hot. Got any dough?'

'Mosky!' Matthew was shocked. 'You pay me plenty. And I've saved some.'

'Huh! That won't go far.' He reached out to his own till and took out a hundred dollars, holding it out in an imperious hand. 'Here. Work it off when you come back.'

'Suppose I don't come back?'

'You will, kid,' said Mosky, suddenly grinning. 'Sure as hell, you will.' He thrust the notes into Matthew's unwilling fingers. 'And meantime keep that guitar by you. It'll always earn you a meal or two.'

'Mosky, I—thanks for everything.' Matthew grasped his hand, suddenly too moved to speak, and went out into the street without looking back.

Outside, Matthew felt isolated and aimless. He paused to take stock of his thoughts, and then went into a travel agent's to get a tourist visa for Baja.

But before he set off he had to find out about Tracey.

He arrived at her apartment and climbed the stairs to Tracey's front door without being challenged by any mysterious observers. Tracey opened the door, and when she saw Matthew she was furious. 'Go away, you mutt. You're not supposed to know me.'

'Sorry,' said Matthew. 'I wanted to know how you were.'

'Well, you can see. I'm OK. Now get going.'

Matthew's mouth set into an obstinate line. 'Not till you tell me what happened to you.'

Tracey raised her eyes to heaven. 'You better come inside.' She pulled him into the narrow passage that led to the living room and slammed the outside door. 'Now,' she said, 'for your info—I got busted and I got fined, and I gotta keep the peace for a year.' She grinned suddenly and added, 'I guess that'll be the hardest.'

Matthew laughed, relieved to find her so relaxed about it.

231

Then Tracey went into the attack. 'How come you're not at work?'

Matthew sighed. 'I left.' He looked at her, not knowing how to explain. 'In fact, I'm leaving San Diego.'

'Why?'

'I—where I was staying didn't work out.'

Tracey nodded, not asking awkward questions. 'Where will you go?'

'Down to Baja, I think, whale-watching . . . I've got a friend who's a marine biologist who said she'd be there—some time about now.'

'Oh. I see.' There was a pause. 'How're you gettin' there?'

Matthew shrugged. 'Trolley to the border. Then hitch, I suppose.'

There was another pause, and then Tracey said cautiously, 'I might come, too.'

Matthew's face lit up. 'That'd be great.'

She shook her head at him. 'It might not be—for you. But I guess if we get together *after* the border, they can't say anything. That guy, Morris, said—'

'Oh. He came to see you too, did he?'

She looked startled. 'Were *you* questioned? I thought I'd kept you out of it.'

'You did,' agreed Matthew. 'He was really quite nice to me. I don't think he'll bother us in Baja. You coming or not?'

Tracey took time to consider, twisting a strand of tangled hair in her fingers as she thought about it. 'I guess it's a good idea to get out of here for a while. I'll meet you the other side of the border—with the Fly. It'll get us there—but it'll be kinda rough.'

'I don't mind.' He sounded quite cheerful. 'When'll we meet?'

'Tomorrow. Got a tourist card, have you?'

He waved it at her. 'All in order. I'll go down to San Ysidro today.'

'Got any dough?'

'Enough. Now stop fussing.'

'There's a youth hostel at Tijuana,' she said, looking at him severely. 'I'll pick you up down there in the morning. You'd better buy a water bottle. Got a sleeping-bag?' She saw him hesitate.

'Take one of mine. I keep several here for the gang.' She yanked one out of a corner and gave it to him. Then, seeing his mutinous face, said, 'You gotta take care, see? You could do without any more trouble right now.'

'So could you,' growled Matthew, and gave her a fleeting grin. 'See you, then.' And he tucked the sleeping-bag under his arm and slipped quietly out of the apartment, carefully not looking back to see if anyone was watching him.

PART IV

THE WINGÈD LIFE DESTROY

Matthew did not linger in San Diego, but made his way straight to the Santa Fe depot and got the trolley to San Ysidro. It was a journey that intrigued him, since the cheap fare brought a mixture of returning Mexicans, day-trippers to the border, impoverished students and a few hardy backpackers.

Matthew listened to the mixture of languages and wished he had learned a bit more Spanish at school. His knowledge so far was mostly connected with Spanish guitar music and its romantic titles and mood directions. Not much use on a trolley-ride, or for buying a meal somewhere. *Andante melancólico, amigos. Con mucha fantasia* . . . No, he didn't think it would help much.

He got off at San Ysidro with a group of chattering Mexicans and followed them through customs where his passport was examined and his tourist card stamped with a valid visa. He checked out the youth hostel, but then decided to go on into Tijuana and head for a beach. He always felt better near the sea. And he was very conscious of his slender resources and he thought sleeping out on the beach would do perfectly well.

He wandered on, getting hotter and thirstier with every step. He found that downtown Tijuana was much like downtown everywhere else—shopping malls and tourist shops and cafés, all looking new and prosperous; and beyond them shantytown squalor.

He walked for a long time, but at last he came to the beach and the Pacific ocean gleamed serenely before him.

He turned southwards along the beach until he had walked quite a distance from the cheerful crowds of Tijuana. At last he paused by a quieter stretch of sand where there was only one beach party of young people enjoying a makeshift barbecue.

He set down his duffle bag and his guitar case, and lay back on the sand to rest his aching legs. They still hurt him sometimes when he walked too far. He badly wanted to swim to get rid of the dust and heat of travel. But if he swam, what about his guitar? His money and passport he kept on him in a waterproof pouch tied into his swimming trunks, but he couldn't swim with a guitar round his neck.

One of the young crowd from the beach barbecue strolled over. 'Going far?'

Matthew shrugged. 'Down to Laguna Scammon—if I can get there. Whale-watching.'

The tall, blond boy nodded. 'You play that thing?'

'Sure.'

The boy considered him, his lazy blue eyes surprisingly alert and sympathetic. 'Hungry?'

Matthew sighed. 'I could do with a swim more.'

'We'll keep an eye on your stuff. Then you can play for your supper.' He held out a sunburnt, sandy hand. 'Deal?'

'Deal,' agreed Matthew, smiling, and grasped the thin brown fingers in his. Then he threw off his dusty jeans and T-shirt, and plunged joyously into the cool Pacific.

He felt better in the sea, less like a rootless stranger. The sea was the sea, anywhere in the world, bluer and warmer here than in the dark Atlantic, but still the same restless, endlessly moving living force. He felt nearer home here and nearer to the far-distant, leaping shadow of a dolphin that came smiling to meet him. There didn't seem to be any place where he felt he truly belonged . . . except in the sea with Flite.

A bigger wave than usual pushed him in the back and shoved him sprawling into the shallows, as if to say, Stop being so sorry for yourself. Get on with living! Obediently, Matthew picked himself up and made his way back to the little party on the beach. The air was still warm even though the sun was going down, and he did not bother to dress. He simply took his guitar out of its case, sat down on a rock, and began to play.

The group of young people had been busy grilling steak, burgers and fish over a smoky fire, but now they turned and forgot to go on talking. They almost forgot to go on cooking, and only just rescued some blackening steaks in time. Matthew ignored them all, oblivious of everything except his own fingers moving on the pulsing strings . . .

He forgot that he was tired and hungry and had nowhere to sleep that night. He forgot everything except the music that flowed out from under his hands into the sunset silence of a Pacific beach.

At last his fingers grew tired, and he looked up to see a ring of faces looking at him in the flickering firelight. 'Wow!' breathed one of the listeners. 'How come you're wandering about loose when you play like that?'

'I like wandering,' answered Matthew, and laid his guitar carefully in its case.

'Have a burger,' said the boy who had first spoken to him, smiling. 'Must be starving after all that,' and busied himself ladling a mixture of fish, steak and half-blackened burgers onto a tin plate. Matthew ate gratefully, and soon they were all plying him with questions about Laguna Scammon and the whale-watch, and where he'd learned to play the guitar.

He played for them again before the party broke up. But at last they began to drift away, some to a caravan park beyond the dunes, and some to parked cars along the edge of the highway. One of them offered to put him up in his tent, but Matthew refused, explaining that he would rather sleep out under the stars. They did not press him, and presently Matthew was alone—absolutely, blessedly alone—on a wide, starlit beach with only the sound of the surf for company. He lay down on the cool sand and turned his face to the sky.

My father had loved stars, he thought. He was glad Della had told him that. It made his father seem more real somehow, it brought him nearer. He, too, had a mathematical mind that wanted to go further than finite thought . . . Up there, among those glittering galaxies, there were huge mysteries to explore.

Patiently, the old Pacific kept breaking gently against the sand, and lulled in its eternal music, Matthew slept.

WHEN DELLA READ MATTHEW'S NOTE, she was distraught. 'Now look what you've done!' she screamed. 'Driven the kid away. What'll become of him?'

'He'll manage.' Des was at bay now, red-faced and angry, too. 'He's been lookin' after himself most of his life.'

'But not in a strange country—with no one to turn to.'

'For Pete's sake, Dell, kids do take off at that age—they do it all the time.'

'We're responsible for him, Des. We agreed to look after him.'

'*You* agreed,' said Des sulkily. 'It was never my idea. I don't like resurrecting the past and I don't want you being reminded of it every day of the week.'

Della looked at him. 'The past is never over, Des. Matthew's alive, isn't he?' Her face paled even further at the next thought. 'At least, I hope to God he is.'

'Sure he is,' said Des comfortably. 'And don't worry, he'll show up one day soon.'

'No thanks to you if he does,' she spat at him. And then, with sudden uncertainty, 'Had I—oughtn't we to tell the police? Or that lawyer in London?'

'No!' bellowed Des. 'He's told us where he's heading. He says he'll contact us again. What more do you want?'

'I want him back here,' cried Della, and burst into tears.

Des patted her awkwardly and let her sob on his shoulder. Then he said, 'Leave it out, Dell. Everything will be fine, you'll see.'

Della sniffed and muttered, 'I hope to God you're right.'

But she did what Des wanted her to do. Nothing at all.

MATTHEW WOKE VERY EARLY, before sunrise, to the sound of surf and the cries of seabirds. He went down to the edge of the water and stood looking out to sea before deciding whether to plunge in for a morning swim or not. That surf looked tricky.

Far out, he could see a long line of dark fins and humps steadily moving south. The grey whales were still swimming patiently onwards to their chosen breeding ground. And then, closer to the shore, he saw a smaller, livelier line of dark fins lifting up into the air.

'Dolphins!' breathed Matthew, watching the gleaming bodies glint in the sun as they leaped and dived. 'A whole school of them!' He left his belongings lying on the sand, guitar and all, and plunged into the smiling Pacific.

He did not dare swim out too far, not knowing the tides and currents on this rocky coast. But he let the big Pacific rollers wash over him and lift him in their arms. Maybe the dolphins would come to have a look at this clumsy invader of their territory. He swam slowly in the translucent water, and waited.

Sure enough, in a little while there was a splash beside him and a puff of air as a sleek body surfaced to have a breather. He turned in the water to look, and another lissom shape curved round a wave, leaped into the air close beside the first one and then cut the water like a gleaming knifeblade. Soon he was surrounded by leaping, diving bodies. Springing into shining arcs, sinking beneath the next crested wave, chasing each other's shadows and racing like dark arrows through the green-gold depths, they turned in swirls of rainbow spume to laugh at Matthew as they flashed by.

Come on, they seemed to call to him, *come and play. The world is all blue and gold, alive with newness, just begun. Rejoice like us. Today!*

Why, thought Matthew, enchanted, they speak the same language as Flite! And, caught up in their joyous celebration, he turned in the water to join in their glorious game. He seemed to be surrounded by smiling faces, as the long, slender bodies wove a charmed circle round him, turning their laughing faces to him for approval after each pirouette, as if to say, *Aren't I clever? Don't you admire my skill?*

Matthew did not try to touch the dolphins as they played round him. Once or twice a sleek body brushed close in a daring swerve, but it swung away again very swiftly and Matthew understood that he must keep his distance. They did not know him as Flite had known him, with that strange unspoken communion. But they leaped in the sun and smiled, and after they had filled Matthew with their joyous delight in living they turned as one and headed out to sea.

The sun had climbed over the brown hills by now, and laid bright bars of gold on the water and on the wet sands as Matthew waded to shore. He felt dazzled and strange—but very happy. Somehow, the dolphins had made him feel closer to Flite.

WHEN HE GOT TO THE YOUTH HOSTEL, the Fly was parked outside near the cafeteria and Tracey was inside drinking coffee. 'Where've you been?' she demanded angrily, as soon as he came in sight.

'Sleeping on the beach,' said Matthew sunnily.

'You're crazy,' she snarled. 'Anything could happen to you out there.'

'Well, nothing did.' He smiled at her.

'You eaten anything since yesterday?'

'Sure. Some folks having a barbecue gave me supper.' His grin got wider at her exasperated expression. 'I did fine.'

'Nothing stolen?'

'No. Everyone was very friendly.'

Tracey relented. 'OK, OK. Get some coffee. We gotta long way to go, and it'll be hot and bumpy inland. Did you get that water bottle?'

'Yes, I did. And I stopped downtown and got some coffee and mugs and a sort of kettle—oh, and some matches.' He grinned at her astonished face. 'Plenty of driftwood on the beach.'

'We're not going on the beach,' she snapped. 'We're going inland.'

Matthew's voice was pleading. 'It'll be much cheaper . . . two of us together will be safe enough. And we've come down here to be near the sea and the whales—haven't we?'

She seemed to hesitate, but there was a gleam of mischief in her eye. 'As a matter of fact, I brought a tent—in case of emergencies. But if there are scorpions or snakes I'll run screaming.'

'There won't be by the shore.' Matthew's tone was confident, but he wasn't a bit sure he was right. He would just have to be extra vigilant, that's all.

'Go get that coffee,' growled Tracey. 'Can't sit here all day.'

Obediently, Matthew did as he was told.

MATTHEW'S FIRST VIEW of the Baja peninsula was somewhat oblique. The Fly buzzed and rattled along the coastal tollroad, which Tracey had grudgingly taken at Matthew's insistence, and the hard little wheels seemed to jar his spine with every pothole, so that he had to cling onto Tracey for fear of falling off. If he turned his head to the right, he caught tantalising glimpses of the blue Pacific, interspersed with sparse headlands, low scrub and cactus. If he turned to the left, the land became rolling and empty and the cactus plants taller and more strange, and beyond this desert-like inland plateau there rose a chunky range of mountains. The few trees—mostly palms—seemed to be concentrated round the shining white restaurants and hotels that lined the beaches wherever they were accessible to the American tourists.

Occasionally, as the road came near to the sea on rugged clifftops, Matthew could look down on surf and gleaming sands, and once he saw a couple of sea lions stretched out on the tawny rocks, sunning themselves.

'Oh, stop!' he called over Tracey's shoulder. 'I want to look.'

She stopped, but grumbled all the same. 'Can't stop for every bit of wildlife in Baja!'

'Just this once,' pleaded Matthew, climbing off the Fly to look over the cliff. 'I've never seen sea lions in the wild before.' He looked down at the gleaming grey-brown bodies below him, and the largest one lifted a languid head and looked back with a surprisingly alert, inquisitive gaze.

'Come on,' said Tracey, ever practical. 'We wanna get some place where we can eat—before we die of exhaustion.'

Matthew laughed. But he climbed back onto the Fly and made no further protest. Tracey was an old campaigner, she knew about distances and limitations. She was also very aware of the ferocious battering the Fly gave to its riders. So she stopped frequently at the small coastal communities on the way to Ensenada, and spent what Matthew privately thought was far too much precious money on tacos and soft drinks.

They did not stay in Ensenada, in spite of its waterfront and elegant fleet of yachts and charter boats. In fact, Tracey seemed to be in more of a hurry than usual, turning her back on the beguiling glitter of white boats and blue water and chugging on down the road to La Bufadora before stopping to rest at all. It was almost sunset by now, and Tracey muttered something about looking for a campsite, although Matthew was happy to stop anywhere.

In the end, they compromised. Tracey insisted on putting up the tent in a small official campsite overlooking the sea. Matthew insisted on sleeping out on the beach.

'There's showers and toilets at the campsite,' pointed out Tracey. 'I like things civilised.'

'And I like stars.'

She shot him a surprised glance at this, but made no further protest, and volunteered cheerfully to share his campfire and try out the new kettle. They sat gazing at a spectacular Pacific sunset, burning away over the sea, and drank their coffee in companionable silence, until Tracey said suddenly, 'What if it rains?'

'Then I'll get wet.'

She snorted. 'Then you'll come in the tent. That's what it's for.'

'All right, all right,' he smiled at her, and poured some more coffee. But he wondered, rather uneasily, what was expected of him on this trip. Sharing a tent in a rainstorm was one thing, but sleeping together was something else again . . .

Tracey was watching him with a sardonic gleam in her eye. 'No strings, Matt. I'm not into casual sex if that's on your mind.'

'No one-night stands?' He hoped he sounded offhand and adult, but he doubted it. You couldn't fool Tracey.

'With Aids where it's at in San Diego? You must be joking.'

Matthew tried not to sigh with relief. He also tried not to blush, but he failed. 'I—er—I'm not into it either.'

She grinned. 'Just as well.'

'Don't you have a boyfriend?'

Tracey's face seemed to close. 'I did, but he—went off.'

'Why?'

'I guess he just loved boats more than me.'

'Boats?' He remembered suddenly how Tracey had turned away from the sunlit harbour at Ensenada with its fleets of yachts and charter boats. 'What kind of boats?'

She shrugged. 'He always wanted to sail—round the world, he said. So when this guy came along and offered him a share in his boat, he couldn't resist it. Why should he?'

'How long was he—were you together?'

'Nearly two years. He helped me get myself together after my parents threw me out.'

Matthew swore softly under his breath. Then he murmured, 'I wondered why we left Ensenada in such a hurry.'

'Lots of ocean-going boats put in there. It's the sort of place Mitch

240

might show up.' Tracey rose to her feet, brushing the sand off her shabby jeans. 'Well—I guess I'm bushed, Matt. I'll leave you to your stars.'

She strolled away then from his bright little fire, and disappeared up the track through the dunes to the campsite beyond.

Matthew sat on alone and watched the starlight glint on the sea. It was dark out there—dark and calm. He hoped the dolphins were safe, swimming quietly in the lightless depths of their own great ocean. Presently he lay down and slept.

This pattern repeated itself for several days. Knowing the short-comings of 'Fly-travel' as she called it, Tracey set the day's mileage limits fairly short, and there was time to swim and to wash off the dust at the end of each bone-shaking stretch of road. Matthew began to realise that travelling down even half of the Baja peninsula was a huge undertaking.

In El Maneadero they stopped at the immigration checkpoint and got their tourist cards stamped before buzzing on through the quail-filled hills. To Matthew's disgust, Highway 1 stayed firmly inland for a long, dusty stretch of passably good road, but eventually even Tracey got tired of endless cactus and headed back towards the sea at Puerto San Isidro—where she bought lobster-filled *burritos* before finding a campsite near the beach.

In San Quintin it rained, a sudden winter storm blocking out the entire landscape with a fierce curtain of stinging fury. Tracey took one look at it and refused to camp anywhere, stamping off to find rooms in a cheap lodging-house and a large, hot Mexican supper, which even Matthew had to admit was worth the three precious dollars he handed over. But he missed the sea and his nightly stargazing and so in the morning, when it was fine again, Tracey relented and bumped on down to Santa Maria beach where they could swim.

'Short run today,' Tracey pronounced later as they climbed back onto the Fly. 'Last chance for sea. Tomorrow we go inland—and it's going to be a long stretch. So today we take it easy just as far as Rosario.'

'OK by me,' agreed Matthew. The Fly coughed and puttered into life, and they bumped back onto the road in a cloud of dry Bajan dust.

That evening, Tracey left Matthew to put up the tent and have his usual swim, while she went back to town to get petrol and supplies for the long trip next day. 'Make the most of it,' she said, waving a hand at the ocean. 'You won't see it again till Guerrero Negro.'

Matthew made the most of it as he collected driftwood, made a fire and watched the lizards on the rocks while he waited for his kettle to boil. He wondered—somewhat guiltily—what to do about postcards home. In San Diego he had sent one to Jampy every week, but if he sent one from Baja, he would have to explain what he was doing. And if he did that, he would have to admit he had left the protection of Della and Des . . . All these explanations were too complicated for a mere postcard—and a card from Baja with no explanation would only worry them. No, better do nothing about it and wait till he was back in San Diego on the way home . . .

At this point in his reflections he became aware that he was looking straight at a scorpion which had come to investigate the food packages lying on the sand. The creature had its tail ominously curled upwards ready to strike, and he wondered how fast it could move when it decided to attack.

He leaped to his feet and seized a solid branch of driftwood in his hand. But the thing was hard to kill, and he was sweating by the time it lay twitching on the sand.

Then he looked up at the darkening sky and began to worry about Tracey. She should have been back long ago. Maybe the Fly had broken down on the way back . . . Perhaps he ought to walk along the track that led back to the town and have a look . . .?

He took the kettle off the fire, piled on a few more bits of fuel to keep it going, and set off with Tracey's torch in his hand. It was a clear night, and by now the moon was rising, climbing up behind the hills to cast bright radiance and sharp shadow on the empty landscape. Even so, he kept the torchbeam moving ahead of him, aware now that there might be unknown hazards in the deep pockets of shadow that lay along the edge of the moonlit track.

He walked on, turning the torchbeam from side to side ahead of him, but in spite of its probing light, he nearly stepped on a snake writhing its way across the path on some purpose of its own. Thin and green, he thought. And deadly?

He had gone about half a mile in this cautious fashion when the track took a sudden bend, and his torchbeam picked up something bright and metallic gleaming in the moonlight. He began to run then, for it was the Fly—lying on its side in the dust, and beyond it, in a patch of deep darkness, lay a crumpled heap that was Tracey.

He bent over her in terror, shaking her by the shoulder. 'Tracey? *Tracey!* Can you hear me?'

242

For answer, she turned slowly on to her back and groaned.

'*Tracey*! Are you hurt?' He tried to feel whether anything was broken or ominously out of place, but her arms and legs seemed intact. Maybe she was just dazed, he told himself, and wondered what to do.

'*Tortillas*,' said Tracey in a blurred voice. 'Find them, will you?'

Matthew put his arm under her shoulders and lifted her head up a little. 'Never mind that. Are you all right?'

She seemed to consider the matter drowsily. 'Yeah,' she said at last. 'Must've hit my head . . .' She leaned tiredly against Matthew's arm for a moment and then began struggling to get up.

'Take it easy,' said Matthew. 'Sit still a minute. What happened?' he asked, hoping to keep her resting for a bit longer.

'Something big ran out across the track, like a dog.'

'Coyote,' nodded Matthew.

'I swerved and the Fly hit a rock and turned over.'

'And you went headfirst into the nearest stone.' Matthew shone the torch on her face for a moment. 'You've got a sizable egg up there.' He reached out a gentle finger and touched her forehead very lightly.

Tracey winced. 'Ouch. Do you mind?' She scrambled to her feet then, and stood weaving slightly in the brilliant moonlight, while Matthew bent over the Fly.

'Doesn't seem to be damaged. Can you manage it?'

Tracey took a couple of unsteady steps forward, and then stopped, shaking her head. 'Too woozy. You'd better put me on the back.'

Matthew was alarmed. He'd never driven the Fly before, but he saw that there was no alternative. Tracey was clearly too shaken to walk. 'OK,' he agreed, with misgiving. 'Just show me.'

'Throttle, gears, brake,' said Tracey laconically. Then she started looking around her on the dusty ground. 'The *tortillas*—'

'Damn the *tortillas*,' he said. 'Come *on*.'

But Tracey was not to be deflected until she found the greasy paper packet. 'Too good to waste,' she muttered. Then she climbed back onto the pillion seat, shaky but triumphant. The Fly came back to life with its usual exasperated cough, and Matthew cautiously set off down the track towards the beach.

The little fire was still burning when they got back, and Matthew set about brewing some strong coffee for Tracey. They ate the squashed *tortillas*, and watched the moonlight cover the sea in peaceful silence. Then Matthew murmured, 'Better get some sleep . . . It's been quite a day.'

Tracey nodded and moved rather stiffly and painfully to get to her feet. But Matthew suddenly leaned forward and hugged her for a moment, muttering into her tangled hair, 'Glad you're safe.' Tracey looked at him in astonishment. But she didn't say a word.

He watched her go into the tent, and then—offering the only comfort he dared—reached for his guitar and played her to sleep. Or he hoped he did. He sat long beside his dying fire in the bright Bajan moonlight, and the sound of his music fell softly and gently on the air, drifting into a fading whisper that merged with the voice of the sea.

IN THE MORNING Matthew left Tracey sleeping and went down to the sea for his morning swim. He remembered to kick out at the sand and tread cautiously in case of stingrays as he waded out, but nothing troubled him except a small silver cloud of little fish that swam round his feet and tickled his toes. Soon he was swimming with them, happily idling in the shallows, and then he began a long slow crawl.

He came out close to a deep inlet by some rocks further down the beach, where a weather-worn fisherman was hauling some green nets and yellow rope into his boat. Matthew stopped to look. Those nets wouldn't hold a dolphin, he was sure, but maybe the fisherman would know where the purse-seine nets were—or where the deadly drift nets hung like invisible deathtraps.

'You want to go shark fishing?' enquired the Mexican, in passable English, and flashed him a crooked, salty smile.

'No-o.' Matthew hesitated, wondering how far out the shark fishers would go. 'The tuna boats—the big ones that use purse-seine nets—how far out would they be?'

'Ah.' The fisherman's cheerful smile turned into a ferocious scowl. 'Those sea-robbers, with their drawstrings and their wheels and winches—' He lapsed into a string of Spanish oaths. 'They take it all,' the fisherman went on. '*All*. They sweep the sea clean, destroy all the fish stocks.'

'And the dolphins.'

The Mexican stopped for a moment in his tirade, and then nodded vigorously. '*Sí*—even *los delfines*. They all die—the big fish, the small fish, they all die.'

Matthew said, persisting, 'How far out? Could you find them?'

The brown, angry eyes glanced at him warily. 'I could find them, God's curse on them, but what could I do? They are too big for me.'

'I want to see for myself,' Matthew said fiercely. 'Then I can—I can tell people about it.' He looked at the seamed Mexican face before

244

him with sudden wild appeal, '*Tell people,*' he repeated, desperate to be understood. 'It's all we can do.'

'I go shark fishing. It is possible my boat might go further out than usual. If you wish to come . . .?'

'How much?' asked Matthew, counting up dollars in his head.

'For *los delfines?* . . . We call them our luck, you know. They lead us to the tuna. We do not like to see them destroyed.' He pondered a little. 'You could haul nets?'

'I could haul,' agreed Matthew.

The fisherman grunted and turned to look out at the blue Pacific, shading his eyes against the sun. 'They are out there somewhere—not far away.'

Matthew was wondering in sudden dismay what to do about Tracey, when her voice spoke behind him.

'What's not far away?'

'The tuna'—Matthew spoke with meaning, knowing Tracey would catch on—'and the dolphins . . .' He looked from Tracey to the fisherman, not knowing what more to say.

'I am Pepito,' announced the fisherman, suddenly holding out a calloused hand. 'And this is my brother, Guillermo. Hey, Guillermo, wake up. There is a lady present.' And he leaned over into the boat and gave something inside a hefty shake.

A large, sleepy head emerged, and two brown eyes looked at Tracey and Matthew with friendly interest. '*Buenos dias*,' he yawned.

'You must forgive,' excused Pepito. 'We have been out all night laying the nets. We only came back for an extra one.' He gave his brother a push and added, 'Hey, Guillermo, I take on another crew since you sleep all day. He will haul nets while you snore.'

Tracey turned to Pepito with her most devastating smile. 'I can haul, too. I am as strong as Matthew.'

'Two crew, Guillermo. You can go back to sleep till tomorrow.'

'*Mañana*,' yawned Guillermo, and climbed out of the boat to shake hands with solemn courtesy 'You wish to see sharks?'

'No,' Matthew answered carefully. 'Dolphins.'

Guillermo's face changed. 'Ah. *La fortuna del pescador* . . .'

'The tuna fleet . . .' Matthew's voice was anxious. 'Can we find it?'

'We can try,' promised Pepito.

ON REFLECTION, MATTHEW THOUGHT, this day out on the sea might be just what Tracey needed after last night's mishap. She was very pale and the bruise below her hairline had turned black overnight. But she was still her brisk, bossy self, insisting on locking their belongings in an empty fishing hut. Then she chattered away to Guillermo while he continued to lay out the nets along the deck of the *Isabella* as she chugged steadily across the bay.

They went first to their own fishing grounds to drop the extra net. Matthew found that the green bundles were laid out in carefully organised swathes so that they fell neatly overboard onto the calm sea, spreading out as each alternate float and weight balanced it in the water. They left a marker float with a small red flag on it that fluttered bravely near the other two nets, and then Pepito turned the *Isabella* towards the open sea and said, 'We will pick up our catch on the way back.' He looked at Matthew and then added carefully, 'This is good net. Not too fine. The driftnet pirates use terrible nets.'

'Terrible?'

His glare was ferocious. 'So fine, so thin it is invisible. Everything gets caught in it—everything dies. *Los ballenas, los delfines*, every-thing . . . They get tangled in the nets, they swim into them because they do not see them—and they drown.' Pepito looked at Matthew hard. 'It is very tough, this net. Sometimes even our boats get tangled in it. A knife will not cut it, so now we always carry these.' He waved a lethal-looking pair of scissor-shears.

'Do they use driftnets round here?' Matthew asked. 'Or the purse seines?'

Pepito shrugged. 'Both. But the driftnets are the worst.' He shrugged his powerful shoulders. 'They are—how do you say? *Illegal* now for most countries, but they are still used, of course—and our own trade is lost as well as the lives of *los delfines*.'

Matthew nodded, and Pepito beckoned him nearer with a salty brown hand. 'I can go near to the big trawlers, the factory ships, but not too close. They are not kind to small boats that interfere with their catch.'

Matthew understood very well that Pepito's boat was his living, and he would not want to risk any trouble. 'Not too near,' Matthew agreed, shouting into the wind. 'I only want to look.'

The sea was still that miraculous Pacific blue, and the sky was clear, but the wind had risen and there was quite a swell. Waves reared up threateningly, as if about to swamp the *Isabella* in tons of surging water, but the sturdy boat ploughed straight through them in cascades of spray, giving herself a little shake of satisfaction as she rode triumphantly out of the next alarming trough.

Then Pepito suddenly pointed forward out to sea. 'They are

246

there—*los delfines*— see? That means the tuna are there, too—the yellow-fins, the skipjacks.'

'And that means—?'

'*Sí*. The pirates—and their nets. Keep watch, Guillermo!' He waved an arm at his brother and pointed towards the horizon.

The *Isabella* took an extra-large sea over her bows, and spray fell in an iridescent shower over everyone. When they had shaken themselves like wet dogs, Guillermo suddenly shouted, 'There!' and pointed. Pepito instantly swung the nose of the *Isabella* away, knowing how lethal these outspread nets could be.

Matthew saw a long line of cork floats stretching as far as his eyes could see, and threading between them a wicked-looking thin wire cable. 'Purse seine,' grunted Pepito. He jerked a thumb ahead, and Matthew saw that there were a number of dolphins leaping in and out of the water. They were clearly excited and distressed, but were keeping their distance from the deadly stretch of netted sea. 'They are the lucky ones,' shouted Pepito. 'They have sense. But their friends have not.' He kept the *Isabella* cruising gently along the edge of the huge nets.

Matthew was watching the dolphins intently. They kept diving and leaping near the nets, thrusting at the cork floats with their beaks and then turning away, only to swim back in a more furious attack.

Their friends are trapped inside, he thought. He leaned over further to have a closer look, and Tracey's hand grabbed his arm.

'Don't do anything crazy, will you?'

Matthew turned his head to look at her fleetingly. 'They're crying in there,' he said. 'I can hear them.'

And he could. He was sure he could. In the midst of the slap of waves and the shriek of the wind, he was sure he could hear the whistles and clicks and calls of communicating dolphins, and beyond them the desperate cries of their trapped companions.

As he watched, he saw the cork floats begin to move, and the drawstring wires at the edges of the floating nets begin to close inwards towards some unseen force that was pulling them away across the water. He could not yet see the trawler—the nets must be enormously wide—but she was there all right, not far away.

'They're pulling in,' shouted Pepito, and turned the *Isabella* away, knowing the turbulence the nets' withdrawal would cause.

The dolphins seemed to get even more agitated, and butted helplessly at the retreating nets in renewed frenzy. Matthew could not bear it. Their voices seemed to be all round him, calling and

247

beseeching, echoing in his head like one long cry of pain. He turned frantically and found himself staring down at the gleaming scissor-shears that Pepito had shown him. Without stopping to think he snatched them in one grasping hand, and leaped overboard into the turbulent sea.

Behind him, the two Mexicans shouted, Tracey made a fruitless grab at him, and then they could only watch in horror.

There followed, for Matthew, a timeless interval of frantic chaos. Waves broke over his head, darkness engulfed him, and blind rage consumed him. He reached the retreating wall of nets and hacked and sawed with furious urgency at the tough nylon fibres. Beside him, he was dimly aware of dark dolphin bodies also butting at the cork floats and the ever-closing curve of the purse seine as it was pulled in. But Matthew's rage seemed to have given his flailing arms extra strength, for all at once a section of the net below the surface parted, and a great gush of fish and trapped dolphin bodies surged out into the water round him, overwhelming him in a tidal wave of wriggling silver, swirling tail-flukes, and thrusting snouts.

The weight of their surge was so great that Matthew sank under it like a stone, and floundered with bursting lungs in the seething water, unable to reach the surface. But, as he struggled painfully towards the light, he felt a firm nudge behind him and another at his side, and two blue-black shapes swam close to him and pushed him steadily upwards till the gold and silver sparkle of sunlight on water was just above him, and his head broke the surface into blessed air. Two great gulps of air Matthew took, and then he sank again among the mass of escaping bodies, and again those two blue-black shapes came close and nudged him upwards towards the light. He thought this time he would never reach it, the pain in his lungs was beyond bearing . . .

Round him the dolphin voices seemed to grow louder and clearer, multitudinous and inescapable—the voices of all the sea creatures in the world, all calling to each other across the water wastes . . . I am dying, thought Matthew. Soon I shall just be part of the ocean . . . then I shall understand their language. I don't feel afraid with all these voices round me . . . Flite, soon I shall find you . . . I will find you when I drown.

But he did not drown. Again, two powerful dark bodies pushed and nudged his half-conscious body, lifting him in the water, forcing him steadily upwards, and this time a hand came down and grabbed him by the hair. He was heaved up and deposited face downwards on the wet planks of the bucking *Isabella*. Then the same hands pushed down on his back and his aching ribs, forcing the water out of his lungs till he lay coughing and retching with returning life. It hurt to come back. He wasn't even sure he wanted to. Out there, somewhere, were the creatures he loved, the voices he knew, and something inside him wept for the understanding he had nearly reached.

Then Tracey's shaking voice, said close to his ear, 'You lunatic!'

And Pepito, sounding equally angry, growled, '*Loco* English!'

'I'm sorry,' choked Matthew. 'They were crying, you see . . .'

They were all looking at him in disbelief. But Pepito suddenly laughed and said, 'I am not sorry. You cut a damn-big hole in their nets!'

Guillermo was still looking curiously at Matthew. '*Los delfines*,' he said. 'They brought you back. You are—*afortunado*.'

'We will not be *afortunado* if they find us here,' rasped Pepito. 'Now we go back to our own nets, pretty damn quick.'

Matthew was too tired to answer. But he managed a watery grin.

Back at their own fishing grounds, the brothers went into action. Matthew insisted on helping to haul in the nets, saying he had promised, and it would warm him up. Tracey silently came up beside him and took her share of the weight. Some of the smaller fish they threw back, but the larger fish and the sharks were soon piling up on the wet floor of the *Isabella*.

'We only take what we need,' Pepito told them, 'not like the pirates who sweep the whole sea clean . . .' He looked down at the silvery harvest at his feet and added, 'This will feed all the village.'

Matthew nodded and leaned over to help Guillermo haul in the last of the nets. 'And now we go home,' Pepito grinned. 'And if anyone asks, we have been here all day.'

THAT EVENING THERE WAS A PARTY in the village. Tracey had already torn Matthew off a strip and told him he was irresponsible, reckless and downright dangerous, but after letting off steam she agreed to go, and Matthew brought his guitar.

While the fish was cooking, someone else brought out a guitar, and the Mexicans, led by Guillermo's strong tenor, began to sing their own songs. Matthew struggled gamely to keep up. He did not know their songs, but he had a good ear and he could mostly guess what was coming next and embroider round it.

Then someone asked Matthew to play for them. So once again it was Granados and de Falla and even Bach, and he did not notice the astonished silence that settled on his listeners. They listened in

249

awestruck attention, and when he paused for breath and to ease his fingers, they passed round the beer and begged for more.

Then everyone was eating lobster and fish and clams, with some spicy *tortillas* that Guillermo had brought to add to the feast. And somehow the singing broke out again, and Matthew found himself both playing and singing as well as laughing in between. He looked round at the smiling faces in the light of the paraffin lamp, and his heart suddenly seemed to clench with unexpected affection. He didn't know how to tell them this, so he simply played his heart out for them on his guitar, the only gift he could give.

At last Tracey murmured something about 'a long trip tomorrow', and they found themselves being escorted back by several companions. The fishermen deposited them safely by their tent, called *buenos noces* across the moonlit sands and departed singing into the night.

Tracey stood looking at Matthew for a moment. 'Matt?' she said hesitantly. 'No more heroics, you hear me?'

Matthew laughed. 'Some chance!' he said, and, greatly surprising himself, leaned closer and kissed her upturned face.

Tracey blinked, glared in fury, and then laughed. 'It's the beer talking,' she said, and turned swiftly away to her tent.

Matthew let her go, and presently lay down in his own sleeping-bag and stared up at the stars. They were very bright tonight, and they reminded him somehow of home—of the Cornish cliffs and pale, washed sands, and the dark spur of rocks where Flite came to greet him. I have to get home somehow, he told himself. I have to go back.

But the stars didn't seem to care much about his problems. They shone on above his head, brilliant and changeless, undisturbed. Smiling a little, Matthew turned over and slept.

BACK HOME IN LONDON, Madge turned over in bed and said to Jim, 'I'm worried about Matt.'

Jim yawned. 'What about him?'

'He hasn't written. Jampy's right upset about it. Every week that postcard came—like clockwork. Matt was that good about it.'

'Maybe he's busy.'

Madge snorted. 'Too busy to write a postcard? I think something's up. I've got a feeling.'

Jim groaned. He was used to Madge's 'feelings'. 'Skip might know.'

Madge agreed. 'I'll ring him in the morning.'

Skip listened to Madge's breathless anxieties about Matthew, and promptly said, 'I'll see what I can find out. Don't worry, Madge. I'm sure he's OK.' And then the pips went and they were cut off.

Skip, meanwhile, simply rang the number the old captain had given him and left a message. The result, very swiftly, was a terse phone call from the captain himself, from somewhere in the South of France.

'What's all this about, Skip?' he rasped, and it was clear from the tone of his voice that he was as anxious about the boy as Madge was.

When Skip explained, he said at once, 'Leave it with me. I'll get the solicitor onto it right away. I'll be in touch,' and rang off.

John Harvey wasted no time either, but rang San Diego in the late afternoon, which was about Della's breakfast time.

'Matt?' she answered blankly. 'Oh—he's not here right now.'

'Not there?' queried Harvey. 'Where is he then?'

'I—' She seemed to hesitate, sounding oddly at bay. 'I don't know exactly. Somewhere in Baja California, I guess.'

Harvey was scandalised. 'You *guess*? Don't you have an address?'

'No. No, I don't,' Della gulped. 'I—there was a bit of a disagreement here—with my husband. Matt just took off.'

'I *see*,' said Harvey. 'And you have no idea where he went?'

'He—he said in his note he was going down to visit a friend in Baja. He said he'd be in touch again before—before he went home.'

'So he mentioned going home, did he?' said Harvey. 'You should have told me.'

'I'm sorry,' wailed Della. 'But—my husband said—boys often take off for a spell and come back, and we'd better wait and see.'

Harvey's disapproval could be felt down the line. 'I shall have to inform the authorities,' he said severely. 'He is a British citizen—and a minor. *Someone* must take responsibility. In the meantime, if you hear anything from him, let me know at once, do you understand?'

Della understood. She understood too that she was in serious trouble. And she was scared.

She was even more scared when later that day a quiet, softly spoken man strolled into the boutique and held out a card to her which said simply: *Commander J. S. Morris, RN.*

'Mrs Della Grant?' he asked, with the utmost politeness. 'Forgive my intrusion. I was wondering if by any chance you had heard from your nephew lately?'

'My—my nephew?' Della squeaked. 'No—er—no, we haven't.'

'Still travelling with his friend, is he?' purred Morris.

She jumped a mile. 'What friend?'

'According to our information,' explained Morris precisely, 'Matthew crossed the Mexican border on his own, and was joined next day by his young friend Tracey Holland on a motor scooter.'

'Tracey Holland? The Animal Rights activist?' Della went visibly pale. 'Are they—is Matt in any kind of trouble?'

'No, as far as our reports go, the two of them have simply been camping on beaches, and going steadily southwards.'

'To the whale-watch,' said Della suddenly. 'I remember him telling me he was interested. Isn't it down there some place?'

'Guerrero Negro, yes. Laguna Scammon. Is that where they're heading?'

'I—I guess so.'

'He didn't tell you his plans?'

'He didn't tell me a thing,' snapped Della. 'He just took off.'

'I see,' murmured Morris. He gave Della one more shrewd and piercing glance and added softly before turning away, 'Well, do let me know if you hear from him, won't you? I shall be most interested to know where he gets to.' And he wandered away out of Della's expensive boutique.

Left behind, Della found she was shaking so much she had to sit down on the only chair in the salon. She felt quite faint.

IT WAS FIERCELY WINDY on the road to Guerrero Negro, with the dust blowing off the desert lands beside the road, and the sun beating down out of a hard blue sky. It was winter, so the temperature was not all that high, but even so Matthew felt parched in the relentless wind.

Tracey allowed them a rest-stop wherever one presented itself. They bought cold drinks and filled up their water bottles, and then pushed on again with grim determination. If anything, the wind seemed to be getting stronger, and by the time they reached their second stop, at Cataviña, it seemed to be blowing a hurricane.

'Come on,' snapped Tracey, pushing Matthew back onto the Fly, 'we can get back to the sea before dark, if we keep going.'

They kept going, grinding along the merciless highway until, towards evening, they turned off the main road for the little fishing village of Santa Rosalia. Here at last they bumped down a track to the beach, and Matthew thankfully fell off the Fly and plunged his aching body into the cool Pacific swell.

He came out to find Tracey standing still, staring curiously at the cluster of boats round the little harbour.

'What is it?' he said, seeing her expression. 'Something wrong?'

'No.' Her voice sounded strained. 'No, I guess not.' She turned away rather abruptly and began to unpack the tent.

'You thought you recognised one of the boats?'

She was shaking out a groundsheet and muttered into the unfolding canvas. 'Guess I was wrong.'

'You're tired,' stated Matthew. 'Why don't we go into the village to see if we can get something to eat?'

'You go,' said Tracey, still keeping her head down. 'Bring back some *tortillas* or something. I'll—I've got things to do here.'

Matthew made no comment. But when he got back from the village, carrying two fish and a handful of spicy *tortillas*, he saw that Tracey was not waiting for him by the tent, but far out along the beach, sitting alone on a rock and gazing out to sea. He busied himself getting a driftwood fire going and setting his two fish to cook over it. He thought Tracey would probably come back when she saw the fire, and sure enough she returned, silent and unsmiling.

When they had finished eating, Tracey suddenly said, 'Play something, Matt. I got shadows.'

Matthew reached for his guitar. He drifted quietly from one piece to another, while the fiery sunset faded in the west, and Tracey sat staring into the fire. They neither of them noticed the tall, fair-haired stranger who came up behind them and stopped to listen, who listened and stared, and stared again, and then spoke when Matthew came to an end.

'Hey, man, you sure can play that thing.'

Tracey, by the fire, seemed to freeze into utter stillness. Matthew saw her face go pale with shock.

'Hi, Trace,' went on the stranger softly, and sat down on the sand beside her. 'What are you doing down in Baja?'

Tracey did not answer, so Matthew replied quietly for her. 'Whale-watching. When we get there.'

'Guerrero Negro? I'm going down there myself. Maybe we could travel together.'

'No, we couldn't,' said Tracey, turning round and glaring. 'Matt and I are on the Fly. No room for anyone else. And anyway, Mitch, if you think you can stroll outa my life one day and stroll into it again another, you got another think coming.'

'No strolling, Trace. Sailing. I was offering you a lift.'

'No thanks,' said Tracey. 'We got other plans.'

Matthew tried to be polite. 'You going down to see the whales, too?'

'Nope.' Mitch shook his head. 'Need a spare part for the engine. They tell me the salt fleet have a maintenance depot, and I might get what I want down there.' He was looking at Tracey in the firelight, and Matthew fancied he was not as confident as he sounded. 'Tracey, couldn't we meet up some place?'

'We could not.' Her voice was flat with suppressed anger. 'Go practise your charm on some other poor mutt.' She moved away to go into her tent, and Mitch got to his feet in one lithe movement and laid a detaining hand on her arm.

Tracey reacted like a spitting cobra. 'Take your hands off me!' she hissed. And she disappeared inside her tent and zipped up the entrance.

Mitch looked shaken by this. He said to Matthew in an apologetic murmur, 'Sorry. I guess I spoke outa turn . . .' and he wandered off down the beach without another word.

In the morning, Tracey was still white-faced and monosyllabic. She got very brisk and businesslike about setting off, and then buzzed angrily down the road at a punishing pace, which made Matthew's bones ache more than usual. She did not let them stop at Santa Rosarito, but forged grimly on down Highway 1 till they reached Guerrero Negro, where she did allow them a pause to ask the way to the whale-watch. But Tracey did not seem inclined to stop for long in the town, tired though she was. She pushed on down to the lagoon and followed the tourist route to the whale-watching area at its southernmost tip. It was a long way down, and both she and Matthew were almost paralysed with weariness and stiffness when they finally arrived among the whale-watchers camping on the shore.

Matthew was amazed by what he saw. The whole lagoon was dotted with whale heads or rising tail-flukes, long, sleek backs and small, accompanying calves. There were boats out on the water, filled with fascinated watchers, and Matthew saw people lean out from their boats and actually touch the huge, barnacle-encrusted flank of a passing whale. The calm, slow-moving creatures seemed totally unafraid.

'Oh,' Matthew breathed, watching in amazement as a mother and baby swam quite close. 'Can we go out in a boat now?'

'You go,' said Tracey. 'I want to get fixed up here.'

Matthew looked at her closed, bleak face, and decided that she still wanted to be left alone. So he went down to the next boatload and paid out some of his precious money to join the party.

The next hour was one of total enchantment for him. There was a curious serenity and patience about the great sea creatures as they lazed and swam and helped their young. Sometimes they came up within feet of the boats and seemed to eye the occupants with mild curiosity, but they seemed unharassed by all the gaping faces, and unbelligerent in the face of all this invasion of their privacy. In the face of such majesty, Matthew felt very small and rather ashamed to be so intrusive.

Humbly, Matthew stretched out a hand and touched one vast, rubbery flank as it came close. I want to tell you, he said, I think you are beautiful and magnificent beyond belief. Please forgive us for being so inquisitive. But the great cetacean sailed quietly past, its huge eye observing him with placid unconcern. And then the mighty tail-fluke came up and gave a gentle twist in the air, and there was nothing left in the water but a swirl of foam and a fading blue-dark shadow.

Matthew was in a daze as his boat turned for home and landed its load of enchanted passengers on the shore.

When he got back to Tracey, he saw that Mitch was there again. His fair sunbleached head was bent close to Tracey's and he was making some kind of impassioned appeal. But Tracey did not seem impressed. All the same, Matthew reflected, she *was* listening—which was more than she had done yesterday.

He skirted the two of them silently and reached for his guitar through the tent flap before sidling off down the crowded shore to join some other American sightseers. He wandered down the shore-line and joined a cheerful group of whale-watchers who were having a barbecue. They were friendly and welcoming, full of talk about the marvels they had seen, and generous with offers of slightly burnt fish and sooty burgers.

The party round the barbecue began to sing, and Matthew strummed along with them happily, abandoning his usual repertoire for their pop songs. The beer got passed round then and the singing went on a long time, till the fire died down and the brilliant stars of Baja garlanded the sky.

The lagoon was shadowy now, lit with faint gleams of phosphorescence where a fish jumped or a whale passed by, pushing a glinting bow-wave before it. Matthew said good night to the singing Americans and wandered off by himself in the direction of Tracey's tent. There was a small dying fire outside it, and beside it was his sleeping-bag, carefully rolled up. There was no sign of Tracey, but a sound from within the tent made him pause. It was the sound of someone crying—and Tracey never cried.

Should he ignore it? Tracey was proud. She wouldn't like him to see her defeated by anything. But it was such a desolate sound that he couldn't just sit there. He decided to make up the fire and brew some coffee in their battered camp kettle. When it was ready, he went over to the tent, pulled the zip down a little and put his head through the gap.

'Tracey? Come on out. I've made coffee.'

There was a moment's silence, and then Tracey's voice, husky and strange, came from the darkness. 'Go away.'

'No,' said Matthew, struggling to sound firm and masterful. 'Not till you've drunk this. I bet you haven't eaten anything either.'

There was a grumbling and heaving from within and then Tracey crawled out, keeping her face hidden in a tangle of hair.

'Here,' said Matthew, handing her a plastic mug full of scalding coffee. 'And I saved you a couple of corn pancakes from the barbecue. I'm afraid they're a bit burnt.'

Matthew waited till she'd begun to eat before he went into the attack. He was suddenly enormously angry with her—and that made the whole thing a lot easier. Here am I, he thought, dying for some roots—some kind of commitment—someone in this empty world to care about—and here's this stupid girl with it all on a plate, and she won't accept it. 'Trace, I don't understand you at all,' he said, stabbing viciously at the fire with a piece of stick. 'What's wrong with second thoughts, anyway?'

Tracey was stunned by his bluntness. 'What?' she said.

'You and Mitch. I don't know what's with you two—but it's obvious you both want to get together—so what's stopping you?'

'He walked out on me, remember? Am I supposed to welcome him back with open arms?'

'Why not?' Matthew flung out a challenge. 'If you want him?'

She was silent, suddenly seeing a different course of action to the cold, barren one of furious pride she had set herself. Mitch? Back again in her life? Would it be possible?

'You haven't even looked at the whales since we came . . . they don't go in for tiny tantrums.'

'Tiny tantrums?'

'On their scale—' He waved a hand at the dark lagoon and the sleeping grey shapes within its quiet waters. 'You were the first to tell me about this. They choose a mate without any fuss. They swim thousands of miles to get here to have their young, and thousands of miles back again to their summer feeding grounds. They don't waste any time arguing about whether to get together or not. Life's too short, and too precarious.'

'I've never heard you talk like that before.'

'No,' agreed Matthew flatly. 'Got carried away. Sorry.'

'It's OK.' Tracey's voice was suddenly soft. 'You kinda made sense.'

Matthew laughed. 'Is he coming back?'

She nodded. 'Tomorrow. He's waiting for that spare part. Then he has to sail back to San Diego.'

'And I suppose he wants you to go too?'

Tracey sighed. 'I guess so.'

'Well, why not? I'll be all right.'

'On your own?' Her tone was sharp with disbelief.

'Petra's place is only a few miles from here.'

'How will you get there?'

He grinned at her outraged face. 'Walk. Take the local bus. Hitch.'

'I suppose you could have the Fly.'

It was his turn to look astounded. 'I could not. No licence, no insurance.' He glanced at her warily. 'Can't you take it on the boat?'

'Oh yes, I guess. But I don't like dumping you.'

'I've told you—I'll be fine. You got me here—now it's your turn to have some fun.'

'I don't know—' She sounded suddenly weary, heavy with doubt.

'Sleep on it,' said Matthew, knowing the battle was won. 'And come whale-watching in the morning. They'll put things back in perspective.'

Tracey actually laughed. 'You're quite a guy, Matt, d'you know that?' And she disappeared inside the tent.

IN THE MORNING Tracey came with Matthew, on the first boat that went out, to look at the whales. She gazed in awe at the huge dark shapes and their smaller offspring swimming close beside them. Like Matthew, she stretched out a hand to stroke one smooth, glistening flank as it swam close, and like Matthew she was utterly enchanted by what she saw.

When they returned to the shore, Mitch was standing there waiting for them. He looked strangely nervous, with his blue eyes screwed up against the sun as he tried to pick out Tracey from the crowd of returning whale-watchers. And Matthew found himself liking Mitch the better for that air of uncertainty.

But Tracey did not immediately go towards him. Instead, she

turned to Matthew and said simply, 'I guess you were right.'

He nodded. 'Cut us down to size, don't they?'

'They sure do.' She was looking at him with anxiety. 'Will you be OK?'

'Sure.'

But she was not convinced. She reached into a pocket in her jeans and brought out some money.

'I'm all right,' protested Matthew. 'I've got enough to get to Petra's.'

'You have to get back somehow, don't you?' And she thrust the notes into his hand, scowling furiously. 'You can always pay it back later.'

Matthew capitulated, and she gave him a brisk, approving nod. Then, seemingly as an afterthought, she put her arms round his neck and kissed him soundly. 'You take care now, you hear?' she told him.

Mitch was regarding all this with some astonishment. But at last he said mildly, 'Do I take it you're coming?'

'You do,' said Tracey shortly. 'The Fly's all loaded. Get on.'

Mitch walked over to inspect the Fly, which had been left in charge of one of the boatmen, and eyed it doubtfully. 'Will it carry us both?'

'It'll get us back to the boat. What more do you want?' She climbed on and gave an imperious jerk of her head at Mitch. 'OK?'

'OK,' agreed Mitch, and somehow folded his long legs on either side of the Fly and clasped Tracey cheerfully round the waist. Tracey kicked the engine into life and they whizzed off in a cloud of dust.

Matthew was left standing by the shore, staring after them. He waited until they were out of sight and the noise of the Fly's engine puttered into the distance, and then he picked up his guitar and his duffle bag, slung his sleeping-bag on his back, and set off to look for a lift to the main road.

Now he was really alone.

THE CARLOAD OF AMERICANS who picked him up were going back to Guerrero Negro, so Matthew went with them. He wanted to buy a few things from the store anyway, and he also wanted to ask how to get to Petra's address. By sheer good luck he discovered a fish truck that was unloading and would be returning to a fish camp near Bahia Tortugas in the afternoon. The driver agreed to take him, and so Matthew climbed on board among the fish crates and boxes of stores and settled down for a long, dusty ride.

The country they went through was extraordinary, desolate and harsh, with strange man-shaped cactus growing among the rocks and sandstrewn arroyos. The journey seemed to go on and on through this dried-up, featureless land, and Matthew began to wonder if it would ever end. But at last the truck pulled up and the driver climbed down and said to Matthew, 'We go to the fish camp from here. The road to Bahia Tortugas is that way.'

'How far?' asked Matthew, also climbing down and looking round at the empty landscape with some misgiving.

'About six kilometres,' said the Mexican, smiling. 'I am sorry we do not go all the way—we have to get the crates to the fish camp.'

'Of course,' agreed Matthew. 'It was very kind of you to bring me all this way.' He began to fumble with his precious moneybag, but the friendly Mexican quickly shook his head. Then, before Matthew could protest, he climbed back into his truck and drove away.

Matthew was alone in the desert with nothing but lizards for company. At least, he hoped it was only lizards. But it was certainly rattlesnake country, and he felt sure there were tarantulas and scorpions or, worse still, black widows behind every stone. He kept to the main track for this reason, but even so he was not vigilant enough. The rattler was lying in the middle of the road and when Matthew came within striking range, it reared up and began hissing and spitting. He sidestepped very smartly, making a swift detour through the nearby scrub and stringy grass, leaving the rattler to hiss and rattle on its own. But, as he hurried to get past, he felt a sharp sting in his right leg, and looked down to find a large yellow scorpion clinging to his calf. He brushed it off in angry haste and put his foot on it. But the damage was done. A scorpion sting, he thought. How bad is it likely to be? Some of them are lethal, some aren't. I must just hope I'm lucky—and get to Petra's place fast.

He went on walking, but his leg was beginning to swell in an ominous fashion, and the pain was shooting further and further up it. The leg seemed to be going numb and he had to drag himself along the road, forcing himself to keep going until the first small houses came in sight.

By the time he got to the little town, he was lurching and weaving on his feet and beginning to see double. He was also beginning to talk to himself. He swayed blearily up to the first person he saw and held out the piece of paper, which said: *Casa Davison, Bahia Tortugas.* He was answered with a flood of incomprehensible Spanish, and seized by the arm and led unprotesting down the road. He scarcely saw the Mexican who was leading him, just a vague brown blur. At the end of the street, the hand was withdrawn from his arm and the brown blur retreated, saying, '*Ahi—La Casa Davison.*'

Matthew took a couple of blundering steps forward and saw a pinkish wall, a dusty courtyard and an open door. 'Petra?' he croaked. 'Petra? Are you there?' And before anyone could answer, he passed out cold on the courtyard floor.

WHEN HARVEY, THE SOLICITOR, reported back the news that Matthew had gone missing, the old captain did not waste time on recriminations. First of all, he rang Skip in Cornwall. 'Have you any idea,' he said, 'who this friend in Baja California might be?'

There was a slight pause at the other end, and then Skip's voice answered cautiously: 'Yes. I think it is probably Petra—Petra Davison, the marine biologist. I gave him her address.'

'*Davison?*' barked the captain. 'Did you say *Davison?*'

There was another pause, and then Skip said mildly, 'It's a common enough name—but she's pretty well known in her field. Her work takes her all over the world, but she has a base in Baja.'

'I see. How did Matthew come to know her?'

'Through me. She was—very kind to him when he was here last summer.'

'What was *she* doing here?' The sharp note was back in his voice.

'She was doing a survey on the seal colonies, and she got interested in Matthew's dolphin.'

'I see,' repeated the captain. 'Skip, how busy are you?'

'Fairly,' Skip answered. 'Nothing that won't keep, though.'

'Could you go out to Baja California?'

Skip's unruly heart did a double flip of hope. *Go and see Petra?* 'I could,' he said cautiously. 'I'd have to make a few arrangements first.'

'All expenses paid,' pursued the captain, pressing it home. 'Heathrow, three days from now?'

'All right.' Skip tried to control his excited breathing.

'I'll get Harvey on to it. He'll be in touch. And Skip—'

'Yes?'

'Bring him back safe. I don't know why but I find I've got mysteriously fond of the boy.'

'Yes,' agreed Skip, smiling over the phone. 'So have I.'

WHEN MATTHEW WOKE, he was lying in a hammock on someone's verandah, and a woman's face was looking down at him. But it wasn't Petra's. It was dark and plumpish and rather pretty. 'I am

260

Mariana,' she said. 'The Flying Sams will be here soon.'

'Flying—?'

'Sams. They are doctors. They will make you well.' Her English was heavily accented, and she seemed determined to keep things simple and direct. 'Was it a snake?' asked the gentle voice.

'No,' he muttered. 'Scorpion.'

There was silence for a moment, and a quiet hand came out and brushed the hair off his forehead. 'Do not worry,' she said. 'They will know what to do. Go back to sleep.'

Matthew did.

THE NEXT TIME HE WOKE, there were voices near him and a tall, bearded man was leaning against a pink-brick pillar, watching him. He reminded Matthew vaguely of someone, but he couldn't think who. There was another, younger man standing beside Matthew's hammock and holding a syringe in his hand.

'Just a little prick,' he said. 'Soon have you right.'

Matthew submitted. He didn't feel right at all at the moment, he had to admit. He tried to smile his thanks. 'Sorry—' he murmured.

'What for?' said the young doctor, smiling back. 'I don't suppose you got stung by a scorpion on purpose.'

'No,' agreed Matthew, and failed to say any more.

The young Flying Sam turned to the bearded man and said cheerfully, 'That'll fix him. Swelling will go down by tomorrow.'

'Any ill effects?'

'No. He'll be fine. He's got the resilience of youth on his side.'

'I wish I had,' said the bearded man, and the young doctor laughed.

The voices receded then, and Matthew fell into a dark hole of sleep.

AFTER THAT THERE WERE several other times when Mariana's face swam into focus, but Matthew couldn't keep track of them. He swallowed cold drinks obediently, and drifted off again while deft hands did soothing things with cool sponges. His leg didn't hurt any more, but he was hot and terribly thirsty.

'Sip it slowly . . .' said Mariana's gentle voice. 'Now you can sleep . . .'

In the morning—he knew it must be morning because the sun was just rising—he woke with a clear head and a thousand questions waiting to be answered. He tried sitting up in the hammock, and found himself looking at the same bearded man, now sitting in a chair on the verandah, watching him with observant, but tired grey eyes.

'Ah,' he said. 'You're awake.'

'Just about,' admitted Matthew, and then added somewhat shyly, 'Sorry to cause so much trouble.'

The man smiled. 'No trouble,' he said. '*De nada*. But perhaps you can tell me why you asked for Petra?'

'D-doesn't she live here?'

'No. I live here. I'm Martin Davison—Petra's father.'

'Oh, I see,' breathed Matthew. 'But—doesn't she come here?'

'Not very often these days,' sighed Davison. 'But as a matter of fact we are expecting her soon. How did you come to know my daughter?'

'It's a long story—'

'We've got all day,' said Davison, smiling. 'But first of all, shouldn't we contact your parents?'

'I haven't got any,' said Matthew coldly. 'They . . . died in a fire.'

Martin made no comment on this, but he did not miss the look of stress in Matthew's eyes. Instead, he pursued essentials. 'Relations?'

Matthew hesitated. 'One—in San Diego. That's why I came out here. But it didn't work out.'

'Wouldn't they want to know you were safe?'

'No.' Matthew's tone was so uncompromising that Martin decided to leave it.

'OK,' he said mildly. 'Now, how does Petra come into it?'

'Well, after the accident—'

'What accident?'

'The fire—I told you.'

'No, you didn't.' Martin was patient. 'But you can tell me now—from the beginning.'

So Matthew told him most of it, including his friendship with Flite the dolphin, and Petra's concern that he shouldn't get too attached to him.

'What was the name of this place in Cornwall?' Martin asked.

'It's only a small place along the coast—but it has a wide sandy bay and wonderful surf. It's called Porthgwillick.'

There was a moment's stunned silence, and then Martin repeated in a shocked voice, *'Porthgwillick Strand?'*

'Yes. D'you know it?' Matthew looked at Martin Davison in surprise. It seemed to him that the friendly, bearded man at his side had gone visibly pale beneath his Mexican tan.

But he did not answer Matthew's question directly. Instead, he went on in a bemused voice, 'And this old captain who befriended you. What was his name?'

262

'St George. Verney St George.'

This time the silence was so long that Matthew was almost scared. 'It can't be,' murmured Martin. He seemed to be in the grip of something like anger, and he turned on Matthew with sudden violence. 'You come here out of the blue, asking for Petra, and you're all mixed up with that—that wicked old man.'

'What is it?' said Matthew. 'What have I said? The old captain isn't wicked. He was very kind to me.'

Martin's mouth was set in a hard thin line. 'He must have changed a lot then.' He still seemed to be seething with anger, but at the sight of Matthew's bewilderment, he softened a little and ran a distracted hand across his face. 'I'm sorry, Matthew. It's an old story. Not your fault.'

'Maybe not,' said Matthew slowly, 'but I think you'd better tell me. It was one of the things I wanted to ask Petra—what to do about the captain.'

'Why Petra?' Martin asked swiftly. 'Did she know him?'

'No,' said Matthew. 'He did come down to the club the night I was playing . . . but Petra and Skip stayed at the back. I remember thinking they were being a bit—unapproachable. And then they went out and walked off down the beach.'

Martin was staring at him. 'Close, were they? Petra and Skip?'

'You could say that,' agreed Matthew, smiling a little.

But Martin was not smiling. 'So they didn't meet?' he persisted. 'Petra and your captain.'

'No. Please,' said Matthew, 'tell me what it's all about.'

There was a long pause, and then Martin made up his mind. 'All right.' He gave Matthew a crooked smile, and then added, almost to himself, 'I don't suppose you were given this address for nothing . . .'

'So what happened?'

Martin took a deep breath. 'When I was young, I was a struggling painter. Well, I still am now, come to that. But now I do a few other things as well.' He took another breath, obviously finding it hard to recount this story. 'I went down to Porthgwillick to paint seascapes for the tourists. I did quite well in the summer—though it was a precarious living. Still, I loved the sea, and I was quite happy to be poor. Then I met this girl.' For a moment he was silent again. 'She was very young, very beautiful—and very headstrong. Needless to say, we fell in love.' He glanced at Matthew half humorously. 'She was a bit of a mystery, young Klytie. Staying at the hotel with her father, but she would never let me meet him. We used to meet on the beach and wander for miles along the sands, and then she would slip off back to the hotel. Almost as if she was afraid of being discovered.' He sighed again. 'It turned out that her father was a rich shipping magnate, and very possessive since her mother's death. He sent all her boyfriends packing, in case they were fortune hunters.'

Matthew grinned. 'So she kept you secret?'

'As long as she could, yes. She told me he had wanted a boy to inherit his shipping empire, and she was a girl, which was a big disappointment to him. She was under a lot of pressure to go into the business, but she hated the wheeling and dealing. She wanted to escape.'

Matthew looked at him sympathetically. 'With you?'

'Just so.' Martin's smile had faded now. 'I was romantic enough to want to see him and ask to marry her. She refused to let me. In the end, of course, he found out and then forbade me to see her, locked Klytie in her room and booked a flight to Paris.'

Matthew whistled. 'What did you do?'

'Eloped,' said Martin, half smiling. 'The real McCoy. She climbed out of her window and we fled. We got married and went to America, where I had an offer of a lectureship at a minor university. It was a living, though not what she was used to. But she never complained.'

'And—and Captain St George?'

'He never forgave her. She wrote to him several times. He never answered. When Petra was born, she wrote again. Still no answer.' Anger had crept back into his voice 'And when she got ill—terminally ill, I mean—I wrote to him, begging him to send her a word, anything, to put her mind at rest. But there was no reply.'

Matthew gave a soft exclamation of disbelief. 'Are you sure it ever reached him? It doesn't sound like the captain, not like he is now.'

Martin shrugged. 'How can I tell? He never forgave her. And I'll never forgive him.'

'It's not like him,' Matthew repeated. 'He's old now, and lonely . . . I should think he regrets what happened as much as you do.'

'Maybe.' Martin's voice was grim. 'But it's too late now.'

'Not for Petra,' said Matthew. 'She's his granddaughter, isn't she?'

Martin frowned. 'I can't understand what she was doing in Porthgwillick. It can't have been by chance.'

'There was the seal colony,' Matthew reminded him. 'She was under orders, I think. And maybe she wanted to see for herself.'

'But you say she didn't meet him.'

'No. Perhaps she thought you'd disapprove.'

264

'Possibly.' He was giving nothing away.

'Feuds are stupid,' muttered Matthew, only half aware that he had spoken aloud. He got to his feet and stood looking out at the sea beyond the pink-washed stones of the little courtyard. 'Where does Mariana come in?' he asked suddenly.

'My second wife? She's been wonderful to me,' smiled Martin, seeming thankful to lighten the mood. 'I came down here to Baja when Klytie died. Petra was away at college, so I was pretty damn lonely . . . I do a bit of painting, and a bit of boat-building. I'm what they call *Presidente* of the inshore fishermen's collective here, which means I argue a bit for them about pirate factory ships, and quotas and so on . . . and Mariana runs the only *tortilleria* hereabouts. She's famous for her lobster *burritos*.'

Matthew looked hopeful. 'I'd like to try one of those.'

'So you shall,' said Martin, easing himself out of his chair. 'Right now. We've talked long enough.'

PETRA LAID DOWN HER CLIPBOARD on the gunwale of the small boat, and signalled to the smiling Mexican to head back to shore. She had almost finished the Guerrero Negro whale count—but this time she had found it curiously disturbing. The great, placid creatures swimming with such calmness and patience beside their growing calves somehow seemed to shame her. I must put my life in order, she thought, and make a few decisions. It is time I stopped being so inadequate.

She put her notes away in her duffle bag, together with her precious camera, and went off to borrow a Jeep from the whale-research team. There was time to drive out through the Vizcaíno Peninsula and visit her father before going on to do the Bahia Magdalena whale count. But a family visit brought its own hazards, and her thoughts drifted to a small bay in Cornwall, and that lonely old man she could not talk to.

Cursing a little at her own weakness, she let in the gear and bumped away down the desert road to Bahia Tortugas. It was a spine-jolting journey, as usual, and she parked the Jeep near the pink wall of the villa and climbed out stiffly. But when she walked into the little courtyard, she found herself staring at a thin brown boy who was smiling at her in extraordinary relief and gladness.

'*Matthew?*' she said, astonished.

'I knew you'd come,' he answered, and came down the steps to meet her in a rush of welcome.

'What are you doing here?' She laid down her bag and returned his impulsive hug.

'Waiting for you, of course.'

She looked at him and smiled. 'I see. Is my father here?'

'Yes.' His expression became apologetic. 'And I think I should tell you—I've rather spilt the beans about the captain—and Skip.'

Petra's expression changed too, but Matthew thought it seemed to reflect relief rather than anger. 'It's about time—' she murmured. 'I should've done it long ago . . .' She rubbed a dusty hand over her face and sat down on the step. 'Come on. Tell me what's been happening. Better know the worst before I see him.'

So Matthew sat down beside her and did his best to explain. But before he could finish Mariana rushed out of the house and embraced Petra and then went running back to fetch Martin, who was in his studio painting, but he wouldn't mind being interrupted for this!

Petra and Matthew looked at one another in some doubt.

'Will he be angry?' asked Matthew.

Petra shrugged. 'He may be. But I'm a big girl now, Matthew. He can't tell me what to do any more. But stay here, I may need you.'

Almost at once, Martin came striding out of the house, wiping his hands on a paint-streaked rag. 'Petra!' He gave her a swift, affectionate hug, and then held her back to look at her. 'You've been holding out on me.'

She sighed and shook her head, so that her blonde hair swung and glinted in the light. 'Not intentionally, Pa. It just—kind of happened.'

'*Happened*? You couldn't have gone to Porthgwillick by accident.'

'No. Of course not. Though, actually, it came up on my schedule several years ago. We do a seal colony count round the coast each year and, when I saw the name, naturally I wanted to go and have a look. You've talked about it so much—the place where you and Ma first met.' She paused, and then added: 'I didn't know the old man still went back there every year. Not till Skip told me.'

'Ah yes. Skip. Where does he come into the picture?'

'Quite a lot,' said Petra, with a smiling, sidelong glance at Matthew. 'Since I've been back to Porthgwillick each year—he's become fairly important.'

'I see I'm way behind the times,' grumbled Martin. 'You didn't actually meet the old man?' he suddenly shot at her.

She stared at him. 'No. No, I didn't. I knew you'd disapprove. But now—'

'Yes? Now?' His voice was harsh.

'He's old, Pa, old and ill.' She turned suddenly to Matthew. 'You told me he was lonely.'

'Yes,' agreed Matthew slowly. 'A lonely, sad old man.'

Martin swore softly. 'You can't sentimentalise over that monster.'

'Why not?' Petra's head went up in a kind of challenge. 'It's all so long ago, Pa. The past is past. Can't you see that?'

'No,' snapped Martin. 'I can only see how much he hurt your mother.'

Petra laid a slim brown hand on his arm. 'She'd forgiven him, years ago. I know, because she used to talk about him to me. She never held grudges.'

Martin was silent, arrested by her words. Had he gone on too long with the old feud, the old pattern of bitterness and useless pride?

'Well,' he said, 'I can't tell you what to do. But I want no part of it. Do you understand?' And he went back into his studio and slammed the door.

Petra looked after him sadly, but Mariana came back, smiling, and said, 'He will come round. I am making lobster soufflé.'

'Anyone would come round for that,' grinned Matthew.

IN THE MORNING, Matthew went down to the beach for a swim. There was quite a swell on the sea, and the surf was pounding in and breaking against the rocks in vast, creamy cascades. I mustn't go out too far, he thought. But I want to see whether the dolphins are there.

He stood for a moment looking out across the tumbling waters of the bay, and sure enough there were the dolphins, leaping and diving round the fishing boats clustered not far out round a shoal of fish that seemed to have been driven inshore by the storm. There was a cloud of sea birds wheeling overhead, and the sea seemed to be alive with glinting fish and the silvery undersides of airborne dolphins.

Matthew plunged beyond the line of surf and swam quietly about in the shallows. And presently, two blue-black shapes left the teeming fishing grounds and cut through the water to inspect this new intruder in their territory. They swam round Matthew in close, inquisitive circles, and then—deciding he was harmless—leaped in the air and laughed at him in the sun.

'Oh,' he murmured aloud. 'Aren't you beautiful! . . . And, yes, I know the world is beautiful today!'

Today—today, echoed the dolphins, diving deep and coming up in smiling arabesques right beside him. *Watch us leap! Watch us fly! Watch us dance with joy!*

'I'm watching,' said Matthew, enchanted. 'I suppose you haven't seen Flite anywhere about?'

But the dolphins did not answer. *Joy, joy!* they repeated to him in silent ecstasy, and leaped in shining arcs out of the water. Then they turned in one fluid movement and headed away out to sea.

Sighing a little, Matthew turned for the shore, but some of their unquenchable joy seemed to cling to him as he swam. When he emerged from the surf and stumbled up the sand, he found Petra waiting for him.

'Did you see them?' He was breathless and glowing.

Petra was smiling. 'I did. Spinners, I think—though there are quite a lot of bottle-nosed dolphins round this coast, too.'

'Like Flite?' He was staring at the Pacific, his expression wistful.

Petra's smile grew gentle. 'D'you still miss him?'

Matthew nodded, sighing. 'Daft, isn't it? . . . I don't suppose I'll ever see him again.'

She was looking at him thoughtfully now. 'They do sometimes go back to old haunts. Will *you* go back?'

He met her challenging glance. This was the crunch, he thought. And he didn't know the answer. 'I don't know . . . As a matter of fact, I came down here to ask you what to do.'

'Why me?' She sounded genuinely surprised.

'Well, I was coming down to see the whales, and Skip had given me your address.' He was floundering. 'And you always seem so certain of your direction . . .'

'Oh, *Matthew!*' She was laughing at him. 'If you only knew!'

He laughed too. 'Aren't you certain?'

'Not any more.' Petra looked at Matthew in friendly sympathy. 'But how can I help?'

'As a matter of fact,' he was a bit wary now, 'I wanted to know what to do about the captain. He's been very good to me, and I owe him a lot. I think he'd like me to go and work for him—he as good as said so. It's a wonderful opportunity, I know. But—'

'But?'

'I don't really want to.' He blushed shyly. 'I want to be a marine biologist—like you.'

She looked at him very straight. 'Why?'

He did not know how to explain to her that it wasn't just a whim, but something real and serious that he had been thinking about ever since he left Cornwall. So he just said, 'Because it's the only way to save them. The dolphins and the whales. It isn't any good just going on demos and shouting. You've got to have—' He was floundering, shaken by her clear, probing gaze.

'Knowledge?' she said gently. 'Authority?'

'Exactly. Then people will listen to you.'

She laughed. 'That's what *you* think! But it will take a long time.'

'I don't care how long it takes.'

'Good. Well then, let's be practical. It'll mean A Levels, university, post-grad research. How will you live?'

Matthew shrugged. 'I haven't a clue. I'd get a full grant, wouldn't I?' He looked rather hesitantly at Petra. 'And the old captain would probably stake me—he's like that. But I'd have to work for him in between to pay it off.'

Petra nodded. 'You don't like charity much, do you?' Then she went on slowly, 'But, as to the captain, do you realise I have the same problem?'

'Why?' Matthew failed to follow.

'If I tell him I'm his granddaughter, it looks as if I'm claiming to be his heir. And he's very rich.'

'You've got to tell him,' Matthew said suddenly. 'You know you have. You can't let him die not knowing.'

She shook her head. 'I don't know . . . It's all so complicated.'

'No, it isn't,' snapped Matthew. 'It's dead simple. You're his family. He needs you.'

He did not say: I wish to God I had some family that needed me. But it was somehow clear to Petra in his accusing glance, and she felt ashamed. This boy, she thought, with no roots and no support from anyone, coming to me for guidance when I can't even guide myself. Oh Skip, I wish you were here to tell me what to do.

A movement on the empty beach caught her eye and she looked up, startled. As if in answer to her thoughts, she saw a tall figure coming towards her over the sand. 'I don't believe it,' Petra murmured. 'It can't be.'

But Matthew had seen it too, and he was on his feet and running. '*Skip!* What on earth are you doing here?'

'I might ask you the same question,' growled Skip, returning Matthew's wild hug with enthusiasm. But his blue eyes, above Matthew's head, went straight to Petra. She had risen too, and was coming more slowly towards him, but there was such a radiance of welcome in her face that he could not mistake its meaning. And then, all of a sudden, she was running too, and they were all embracing and laughing together.

It's all right, thought Skip thankfully. Matthew's safe, and Petra's glad to see me. Mission accomplished.

Matthew, seeing how things were, thought it was time he sloped off somewhere. He disentangled himself from the general embrace and began to stroll off up the beach.

'Hey!' called Skip. 'Don't you dare disappear just when I've found you. The captain will kill me.'

Matthew paused in his stride. 'The captain?'

'Of course.' Skip kept an arm round Petra while he spoke. 'He sent me after you. Who else?'

The captain, thought Petra. I've got to make up my mind. But Skip's here now. It will be all right.

Matthew turned away again and called over his shoulder, 'I'll be up at the house.' Better give them time to sort things out. Skip would know what to do.

'I DON'T KNOW HOW IT IS,' grumbled Martin Davison, glaring cheerfully round at everyone as they all sat over a late breakfast on the verandah, 'but I seem to have gone wrong somewhere in my calculations.'

'Why, Pa?' asked Petra, passing a dish of *chilaquiles* to Matthew.

'I come down here for peace and quiet, and buy the smallest house I could find on the remotest piece of coastline in Baja, and what happens? People descend on me from every side.'

'Sorry,' said Matthew and Skip at the same time, both smiling.

'I hate to add to your tally of uninvited guests,' said a new voice from below the verandah, 'but you're right about it being remote!'

Matthew got swiftly to his feet. 'Commander Morris,' he said, and looked from him to Skip and Petra, then to Martin and Mariana in dismay. What would they think, with him being pursued all the way to Bahia Tortugas by navy security? He turned back to Morris, disbelief clear in his face. 'I can't be that important.'

'Of course not,' agreed Morris smoothly. 'I am on leave at present. Purely unofficial.'

'You can hardly say you were just passing,' retorted Matthew.

'Scarcely,' Morris agreed, smiling. 'Let us say, I had time to spare.' He climbed the verandah steps and held out a friendly hand to Martin. 'I'm sorry to intrude. I was just a bit anxious about our friend, Matthew.'

'Why?' Martin was curious.

Morris grinned. 'Well, look at it from my point of view. After the dolphin demo—no doubt Matthew has told you about that—I go to see his Aunt Della, and she doesn't know where he is. She only knows he has "gone to see a friend in Baja California". The next thing I hear, the Flying Sams report they've just treated a very sick English boy out here for a scorpion sting.' There was a stunned silence round the table. 'You must admit it sounded a bit alarming,' he said mildly, 'so I decided to come and have a look for myself.'

'It was very good of you,' began Matthew, 'but I—'

'Oh, I can see you are all right now,' admitted Morris. 'Now, let me guess. This must be your friend Petra, the marine biologist?'

'It is.' Petra couldn't help smiling this morning anyway, and she turned the full light of her present happiness on him.

Morris blinked. 'And—am I right in thinking this is Skip?'

'You are,' answered Skip, who was just as unable to stop smiling as Petra. The joy that burned between these two was palpable.

'But you—?' He turned back courteously to Martin and Mariana.

'Davison. Petra's father,' said Martin. 'And my wife, Mariana, who, I am sure, is dying to offer you coffee and some fresh *tortillas*.'

It became quite a party then, with everyone explaining things to everyone else, and Mariana in her element dispensing food and coffee.

Finally, Skip said, 'I must telephone England. Can I do that here?'

Martin gave a rather Mexican shrug. 'You'll be lucky. There is a *caseta de telefono* in the village, but international calls are rather beyond it, I fear. The delays are frightful.'

Morris looked at Martin Davison thoughtfully, and wondered why he was being obstructive. 'Maybe the salt-works people in Guerrero Negro would have a decent exchange,' he suggested. 'They were very helpful to me—lent me a four-wheel drive.' He lifted a humorous eyebrow at Skip and added, 'How did you get out here?'

'Jeep-taxi,' answered Skip, blushing a bit at such extravagance. He still didn't like wasting the captain's money, but somehow time had seemed important.

'I could drive you back to Guerrero Negro,' offered Morris.

'No.' Petra got up. 'I've got a borrowed Jeep too, we'll try the *caseta*.' She turned to go, with Skip beside her, and called over her shoulder, 'You coming, Matthew?'

He hesitated, but seeing the summer lightning glancing between those two, he shook his head. 'No. You go. I'll wait here.'

Mariana got up then to clear away the meal, refusing Matthew's offers of help. 'You are still—how do you say?—*convaleciente*,' she told him, in smiling reproof, and went off carrying a pile of dishes.

271

Matthew sighed with frustration. 'No one lets me do anything round here. I owe you all such a lot—and I hate being idle.' He looked at Martin Davison. 'There must be *something* I could do.'

'I suppose you could sweep out my studio.' Martin got up, laughing, and led the way. Matthew followed, and so did Morris.

The studio was at one end of a long, low outbuilding which stood at right angles to the house. It was painted white, and its new tall windows looked out at the blue Pacific. Martin had also let a big skylight into the roof, and the whole area seemed to swim in light, awash with vibrant colour. There were canvases all round the walls, stacked in heaps on the floor, hanging from nails, lying abandoned one on top of another.

The riot of colour held Matthew spellbound. Great sunbursts of red and orange, spirals of singing yellows, fierce blues and startling greens exploded round the walls. White houses in sunlight and sharp shadow, cloudless, burning skies, stark cactus plants and blue, blue seas shouted at him from every side. They were mostly Mexican scenes, street markets, a small boy herding goats on a stony hillside, a group of fishermen hauling in nets, and bright-skirted women haggling over the new-caught fish. And the sea everywhere, in all its moods from storm-dark to guileless Pacific calm.

'Oh!' breathed Matthew, enchanted. 'Aren't they smashing!'

'Beautiful,' agreed Morris.

Martin laughed, but he was clearly pleased. 'Right,' he told Matthew briskly to cover his embarrassment, 'don't touch those, but you can re-stack these.' He glanced at Morris. 'While we two drink some tequila in the sun.'

IT WAS WHILE HE WAS re-stacking a pile of old canvases against the wall that Matthew came across the two small paintings. The colours were so different from the shouting reds and yellows and hot blue skies of Mexico that they caught his eye, and he paused to have a closer look. Cool green sward on top of grey-brown granite cliffs, pale washed sand and black lumps of rock, and beyond them a dark, dark sea . . . He caught his breath, for he knew those rocks at the end of the curving stretch of sand . . .

Yes, he confirmed to himself, turning the little painting towards the light, it was Porthgwillick all right. And there, lovingly and delicately sketched, was a figure of a girl dancing alone on the shore. A nimbus of blonde hair tossing in sunlight, two arms outflung in careless grace, a slender pliant back, and feet poised in a leap of joyous abandon . . .

272

It reminded him of Flite, somehow. And in the second picture the same girl was running towards the painter, her face alight with love.

'Oh, you found those,' said Martin's voice behind him. 'I'd forgotten they were there.'

Matthew looked up, startled.

'That's how I first saw her,' murmured Martin in a slow voice. 'Dancing all by herself on the sands . . .' He paused, and then laughed a little. 'Escaping, she called it.'

'What from?'

'Oh—her father, and the shackles of wealth, I suppose . . . She was always a bit of a rebel, my Klytie.'

Matthew sighed, looking down at the little paintings with a loving recognition. 'I wish I could afford to buy one.'

'Buy one? But you're going back there, aren't you?'

'Oh, it's not for me,' he said carelessly. 'I wanted to give one of them to the old captain.'

There was a long, taut silence. Then Martin spoke in a quite different voice, 'No. Out of the question.'

'Why?' Matthew knew he was issuing a challenge, but he had to try. 'It would be a—a kind of—'

'Peace offering? No!' He was already striding out of the studio.

'A kind of *end*, I was going to say.'

Martin paused in his stride, arrested. 'End?'

'Isn't it time?' Matthew looked down at the lightly sketched dancing figure. 'She looks so happy,' he murmured.

'She was,' said Martin starkly. He did not turn round, but Matthew could tell from the set of his shoulders that his anger was cooling. 'Come on,' he said at last. 'Time for lunch.' And he left the studio without a backward glance.

They were just sitting down when Skip and Petra returned, and Matthew could see by Skip's face that there was something wrong.

'What is it?' he said quickly. 'Couldn't you get through?'

'Oh yes, we got through all right.' Skip's voice was curiously hesitant. 'It's the captain. He's had another heart attack.'

'Is he—?'

'Hanging on, they say, and asking about you. They think we ought to come home at once.'

'Of course.' Matthew got to his feet as if they were going to leave that minute.

'I'm coming, too.' Petra turned to her father and added simply, 'I'm sorry, Pa. I've made up my mind.'

274

Martin shrugged. 'You must do what you think best.' He turned away, then, as if distancing himself from the whole situation, and Matthew felt Petra's disappointment that even in this final crisis he would not relent.

But here Morris stepped in briskly and reduced the tension. 'If you will allow me. I can probably get you all on an early flight. Now, we must make plans.'

THEY FINALLY GOT OFF in a flurry of dust, all crammed into Morris's Land-Rover. At the last moment, Martin thrust a small package into Matthew's hands. 'Here,' he said gruffly. 'Better have this—if it's not too late.'

Matthew did not need to open it to know it was one of the small paintings of Porthgwillick. He smiled at Martin and murmured, 'Thanks.'

Then Mariana flung her arms round his neck and cried, '*Vaya con Dios*,' to them all, and they were away.

PART V
SUNSET?

In San Diego they had a couple of hours before their main flight home, and Matthew insisted on making three hasty visits.

Skip approved of tidying things up with Della Grant, but the other two stop-overs mystified him. 'Why, Matt?' he asked, as the taxi weaved its way through the traffic towards Tracey's apartment block.

'I owe them money.'

'Not a lot, is it? Anyway, we could send it on.'

'No,' growled Matthew. 'My mother owed money all over the place. I never knew who I dared talk to—'

'So you talked to no one,' stated Petra, who was beginning to understand Matthew.

'That's about it.'

Skip was going to protest again, but the taxi arrived outside Tracey's tall, shabby apartment building. All three of them climbed the stairs and stood outside Tracey's door while Matthew rang the bell.

After a pause, a tousled Tracey appeared. 'Yeah?' Then she saw Matthew and her face lit up. 'Matt! You made it. Come on in.'

'No,' said Matthew, smiling. 'No time. Sorry. I brought back your sleeping-bag and the money you lent me.'

She looked incredulous. 'You *what*?' Then, unexpectedly, she came forward and hugged him. 'You're nuts, you know that?'

He laughed, returning the hug with enthusiasm. 'How's Mitch?'

'OK.' Mitch's voice spoke behind Tracey. 'We're both fine.'

'That's good news.' Matthew smiled back, noting that he and Tracey looked almost as absurdly happy as Skip and Petra.

Hastily, he introduced his friends and explained why they were in such a hurry. 'Thanks for everything, Trace,' he added. 'It was a great trip. Especially the whales.'

'They were great, all right,' agreed Tracey. 'You take care now, Matt, you hear me?'

'I will,' promised Matthew, and plunged down the stairs.

Matthew knew Della wouldn't be at home in the daytime, so he took Skip and Petra downtown to the boutique where she worked, and begged them not to leave him alone with her for a single moment. It was going to be difficult enough anyway.

When she saw Matthew, she dropped the elegant black silk dress she was holding and burst into tears. Then she flung her arms round his neck, much to the amazement of the customers in her shop. 'You're safe!' she cried.

'No thanks to you,' muttered Skip, not too inaudibly.

Matthew saw Della wince a little. 'And you are—?'

'Skip. David Alexander to you. Captain St George sent me to bring Matthew home.'

'Oh.'

There was not much more to say after that, but Matthew found himself oddly sorry for Della.

'I have to go home, Aunt Della,' he said, consciously using the hated word 'aunt' and watching her wince again slightly as he spoke. 'The captain is ill, you see.' He paused, and then added more gently, 'But thanks for everything you've done for me. Maybe I'll be able to come back and see you some time,' he went on, and saw the certain knowledge that he never would come back become clear in her eyes. 'I'm sorry,' he said suddenly, and went forward and hugged her.

Skip took over then, and bundled them off with the crisp apology, 'Plane to catch. Not much time.'

So then it was Mosky's turn, and this time Matthew insisted on walking into the café alone while the others stood near the doorway.

Mosky was, as usual, wildly busy and moving from table to table collecting up dirty dishes onto an overloaded tray. Matthew went forward and took it from him without a word and carried it out to the kitchens. At first Mosky didn't even notice who it was, but then the light dawned and a huge smile nearly split his face in two. 'Matt!' he yelled. 'Come back here, you lazy good-for-nothing. You've left some cups behind.'

'Coming!' said Matthew, laughing.

The others came forward then and Matthew handed over money.

'You're crazy,' protested Mosky, scandalised. 'I don't want your dough.'

'Please,' Matthew insisted. 'I can't stay to work it off like I promised.'

'No one wants you to work it off!' Mosky's indignant voice rose in outrage. But then something in Matthew's face seemed to reach him, and he paused in mid-spate. 'OK, OK,' he said, and stuck the dollar bills in the till. 'Square now,' he grinned. 'No obligations.'

When Skip and Petra were introduced, Mosky insisted on giving them all a cup of coffee, smiling his approval at their care for Matthew, and summing it up in the words, 'Worth it. Magic in those fingers.' He glared happily at Matthew. 'You keep it up, you hear?'

'I hear,' agreed Matthew, smiling.

'You still got that book? Joy as it flies?'

Matthew nodded.

'Not only dolphins, kid. Fingers have it, too.'

Time was short and they got up to go, and Mosky stood beside Matthew with an arm round his shoulders. 'So long then, kid. Keep flying!' he said, and rushed away to look after his customers, so that he did not have to watch Matthew go.

THEY GOT BACK TO HEATHROW in a cold grey drizzle, whipped into their faces by a blustery wind. After the warmth and colour of Mexico, England had never seemed more drab or less inviting.

But there was nothing uninviting about the welcome that met them on arrival. Madge and Jim and the entire family were there to greet them, and Jampy was jumping up and down and shouting, 'There he is! That's my Matt. Why were you so long, why were you?'

'How is the captain?' asked Matthew urgently, trying to contain with one hand Jampy's excited leaps and jigs of joy.

'Holding on,' said Madge, dutifully quoting the bulletin at the private clinic. 'Wants to see you tomorrow morning.'

'Not tonight? What if—?' Matthew did not dare put it into words.

'Tomorrow,' said Madge firmly. 'You're staying with us tonight. Captain's orders. Isn't that right, Jim?'

Jim nodded slowly. 'Bullies everyone. Best do as he says.'

'Come on,' urged Jampy, tugging at Matthew's hand. 'Come *on*. I gotta tanker lorry, an' I made a Lego bridge.'

'All right,' smiled Matthew. He fished in his duffle bag and produced a small rolled-up sombrero decorated with vivid red braid. 'Here,' he said, clamping it on Jampy's head. 'Try this for size!'

The whole party moved off then. Skip and Petra went to a nearby hotel. It had been agreed that Matthew should prepare the way for Petra by showing the captain her father's picture and telling him the whole story—that is, if he would listen. He might, of course, refuse to hear any of it, but if he did listen, and was willing to see Petra, then she should come over with Skip to meet him. It sounded a reasonable enough scheme, but Matthew was very doubtful of its success.

HE ARRIVED AT THE PRIVATE CLINIC the next morning to find the place in an uproar. The captain's sleek dark Mercedes stood at the door. The captain's chauffeur, Mackie, stood in the foyer, looking uncomfortable while an irate doctor harangued him about it being 'impossible'. Nurses rushed in and out of the captain's room, looking harassed and disapproving, and from inside came the sound of the captain's voice raised in anger, and another voice answering.

Matthew's heart sank. He knew that voice. It was Conrad. As he hesitated, wondering what to do, the ward sister caught sight of him and came across to say crisply, 'Are you Matthew? For goodness sake see if you can talk some sense into him—and get rid of that nephew of his before he does any more harm.'

Matthew allowed himself to be propelled with great speed into the captain's small, white room. There, Matthew found the old captain sitting up in a chair in his dressing gown, looking frail but belligerent. Beside him, leaning over him in a slightly threatening attitude, stood Conrad.

'It's madness,' he was saying—almost shouting. 'You can't go off on a silly jaunt when you're too ill to stand! Not without making proper arrangements.'

'I *have* made arrangements,' barked the captain. 'There is a perfectly good board of trustees. The firm's interests are all taken care of.'

'But you haven't appointed a successor.'

'You mean, I haven't appointed *you* as my successor.' The

278

old captain's eyes snapped fire. 'You have your place on the board, like everyone else.'

'But—'

'Excuse me,' said Matthew, trying to sound as crisp and formidable as the ward sister behind him. 'I think you are tiring the captain.'

'Visiting has to be strictly limited,' added the sister.

'Is your car outside?' asked Matthew sweetly, taking Conrad by the arm and leading him swiftly away. 'You wouldn't want to cause another heart attack, would you?'

'Of course not,' spluttered the outraged Conrad.

'Come back later,' suggested Matthew. 'When he's rested.' He escorted Conrad to the foyer and watched him leave.

When he returned to the small white room, the captain looked up at him and growled, 'You led us a pretty dance.'

'Sorry,' said Matthew, coming to stand beside him. 'I didn't mean to.' Without shyness he took the old man's transparent hand in his, and added honestly, 'It never occurred to me that anyone would worry where I was.'

'Never did have much opinion of your own worth, stupid boy.'

Matthew laughed. 'Anyway, I thought you were supposed to be at death's door.'

'Shall be if I stay in this place any longer!' He snorted again. 'And if that scheming bastard, Conrad, gets in here again.' Another young nurse came in, looking frightened, and he instantly barked at her, 'I thought I told you to bring me my clothes.'

She glanced despairingly at Matthew and hurried out again.

'What are you trying to do?' asked Matthew.

'Get out of here,' the captain snarled.

'Where to?'

'Porthgwillick, where else?'

Matthew was startled. 'But—Skip's waiting to see you.'

'See me down there. Going home, isn't he? Well, so am I. If I'm going to die,' rasped the obstinate old voice, 'I'll die where I like!'

Matthew nodded slowly. Then he took a calculated risk. 'In that case,' he said, 'it's hardly worth me giving you this.' And he unwrapped the small painting and held it out for the captain to see.

There was a long, tense pause, during which Matthew wondered desperately whether the revelation would kill the old man.

'Where did you get this?' The sharp voice was curiously muted.

'It's a long story—' began Matthew.

'So it *was* that Davison,' murmured the captain, more to himself than to Matthew. 'I thought as much.' He seemed to ponder for a moment. Then he peered at the painting through misted eyes.

'It's her,' said Matthew. 'Your daughter, Klytie. Dancing alone on the sand . . .' He put out a finger to trace the small, ecstatic figure poised against the pale, empty shore. 'Shall I tell you about it?'

'No,' said the captain.

Matthew's hopes fell. It was no use after all. He wasn't going to listen.

'Come with me.' It was a plea, not an order. 'In the car. Tell me on the way.' The old eyes looked into Matthew's with sudden urgency. 'Not much time,' he added, stating bleak truth without self-pity.

Matthew capitulated. 'All right. But are you sure you're up to it?'

'No,' growled the captain. 'Not sure of anything. But I'm going.' He looked up at Matthew again, and a dim echo of his old, impish grin touched his face. 'Escape,' he said. 'Understand?'

Matthew understood.

DURING THE LONG CAR DRIVE down to Cornwall, the old man's heart gave him two small scares and he had to use his angina spray. But he insisted on continuing the journey, and insisted on Matthew continuing his story.

Bit by bit, Matthew told him all of it—his own discovery about Della's motives for offering him a home, his flight to Baja California with Tracey, and his meeting with Martin Davison. He told him about the studio full of vivid paintings, and went on to tell him everything that Martin had said about the past, not leaving out the gentleness of his voice when he spoke of his young wife, Klytie, dancing on the sands.

He did not try to make any judgment and did not allow reproach to creep into his voice, even when he spoke of the many letters written, and the desperate final attempt at reconciliation when Klytie was dying. But there was a vital question to be asked here, and for Petra's sake he knew he must ask it.

'Why didn't you answer the letters?' he said, turning to look into the tired blue eyes beside him.

The old man sighed. 'Never got them. My own fault.'

'Why?'

'Gave orders. In the heat of the moment when I was still angry. Told my staff not to forward anything. They obeyed me.' He sighed again, and rubbed a shaky hand over his eyes. 'Never rescinded the order—forgot I'd made it, really. But I did wonder—convinced myself *they* were the ones who wouldn't communicate.' He shrugged helplessly. 'How stupid can you get?'

And proud, thought Matthew. Stupid and proud. His heart ached for all those years of empty silence. 'Will you see her?' he asked, abruptly coming to essentials.

'Of course,' sighed the captain. 'Of course I will.'

Matthew glanced at him again. 'Before you do,' he began, and this time he sounded shy and awkward again, 'Petra wanted me to tell you something. She doesn't want your money.'

'What?'

'She has her own career. She's independent. It's you she wants—her grandfather—not the St George empire.'

He watched the captain's face as he spoke, but to his surprise the captain laughed. 'Another of 'em!' he said. 'Takes after her mother.'

There was silence for a while as the limousine purred on over Bodmin Moor.

'What about you?' the old captain shot at him suddenly. 'Do you want it?'

'Want what?'

'My money, Matthew. The St George empire. Do you want it?'

Matthew had known this was coming. And he hated to disappoint the old man yet again. But he looked at his old friend out of honest, troubled eyes. 'No,' he said gently.

The captain did not seem surprised. He grunted: 'Thought as much!' and the old gleam of humour was back in his glance. 'What *do* you want?' he asked.

Matthew drew in a slow breath of resolve, and tried to set out his plans in coherent form. 'I want to be a marine biologist—like Petra. That means going back for A Levels. And getting into university.'

'How do you propose to live—and where?'

'I'll get a grant—and I can stay with Madge.' He looked seriously at the captain, and added, with sudden reckless daring, 'I thought—if you'd stake me a little, I could work for you in the vacations.'

'Done!' The captain's smile was positively alight with mischief. 'Stop here a moment, Mackie!' he commanded. 'This calls for a drink.'

The kindly face of the chauffeur turned round, looking concerned. 'Are you sure, sir?'

'Sure I'm sure,' grinned the captain, and watched cheerfully while a small panel was opened in the car, revealing a tiny bar. 'Champagne,' he demanded. When the brimming glass was in his hand, he winked at

Matthew and said, 'Warm and all shook up, but it'll do. What did you say about your dolphins? Today?'

Matthew nodded dumbly, and lifted his own glass. The old eyes and the young ones met in perfect understanding. Then they spoke in unison.

'*Today!*'

WHEN PETRA CAME the next morning, she found the old captain upright in his chair by the window. He looked at her in silence for a while, taking in the smooth, gilded cap of hair and the tawny gold-brown eyes, not missing the proud, faintly challenging set of her head on its slender neck.

'You are very like your mother,' he said at last.

'So they tell me.' Petra smiled at him a little shyly.

'And do you dance on the sand, too?'

To his surprise, she blushed a deep, betraying scarlet, and murmured, 'It has been known to happen!'

He continued to gaze at her, and then spoke with crisp asperity. 'You are a marine biologist, they tell me. In what field?'

'Sea mammals. Cetaceans, mostly.'

His eyes were suddenly piercing. 'And what do *they* tell you?'

She looked at him very straight. 'That family life is important.'

A flicker of surprise crossed his face, and he was silent again for a few seconds. Then he jerked out abruptly, 'What do you want of me?'

Petra came forward, instinctively taking his frail, dry hand in hers. 'Only you, Grandfather. Didn't Matthew tell you?'

The old man nodded, and did not withdraw his hand. 'Family life?' he repeated, trying out the phrase as if it were strange to him.

'Something young Matthew has never really had,' she reminded him.

'He doesn't want my money, either,' he grumbled, sounding a little aggrieved. 'What's to become of him?'

'He'll be all right,' Petra told him. 'He's a survivor.'

'He'll need to be,' barked the captain grimly, 'in this cutthroat world.'

'He's got it all worked out.' She flashed an encouraging grin at him. 'And you know very well we'll keep an eye on him.'

'We?'

'Skip and I.' The blush was back, but fainter this time.

The old captain looked at her sharply. 'Like that, is it?'

Her smile was so radiant and full of certainty that he blinked. 'He's

282

waiting outside,' she added. 'We'd—er—kind of like your blessing.'

The captain snorted. 'What shall I do with my money, then?' he shot at her. 'Give it away?'

'Why not?'

He seemed to consider, but in truth he had already made up his mind what to do. 'How about a marine biology research centre?' he asked, casually.

'Where?'

'Anywhere you like. Maybe, one day, Matthew could work there, too? For those beleaguered dolphins of his.' He interrupted her thanks briskly. 'Fix it with John Harvey. I've given instructions. Might as well do something useful with my money.' An impish grin crossed his face. 'And it'll keep it out of Conrad's hands!'

He began to laugh then, and Petra joined in. Then Skip, who was waiting patiently and in some trepidation outside, heard their laughter and put his head round the door. 'Can I share the joke?'

'Skip, my boy,' the captain commanded, 'I want you to fix one of your music nights.'

Skip looked astounded. 'What, now?'

'Now. And get that boy to play, if he will.'

Skip nodded. 'Oh, he'll play all right. Especially if you are coming.'

The captain smiled. 'Whether I come or not,' he barked. 'That's an order, mind.'

'Ay, ay, Captain,' said Skip, saluting smartly with one brown hand.

The old man looked out at the bay, seeing a figure alone on the pale, tide-washed sands . . . It might have been his young daughter, Klytie, down there—or even his wife who had also had her dancing days on that golden shore . . . But when he shook off the tears of a foolish old man, he saw that it was only Matthew, standing below his window and looking up.

He lifted a hand in greeting, and Matthew waved back and smiled.

'As for "joy as it flies",' he growled, to no one in particular, 'I've had my moments, too.'

Skip had his music night. The various local groups he knew, hastily summoned, descended on the clubhouse with mikes and strobe lights and earsplitting amplifiers. The pop groups and rock groups and folk groups from near and far did their utmost to outclass each other. And in between the items, Matthew played quietly by himself and everyone listened. He played everything he knew, both sorrowful and joyous. But the captain did not come.

'Maybe if we play loud enough, he'll hear us at the hotel,' said one of the boys helpfully.

Skip cast him a baleful look. 'I should think he'd hear you at the Pearly Gates,' he snapped, and then fell silent, realising what he had said.

Matthew intervened then. 'Let's sing,' he suggested. 'The old yelling songs. He liked those.' He struck a chord or two, and soon the room was filled with the sound of young voices until they reached the 'Rio Grande' again.

'*Then away, boys, away—*' they sang, and in the general noise Matthew did not hear the phone ring in Skip's office, or notice Skip slip away to answer it. But when he came back and stood looking across at Petra, Matthew knew.

His fingers faltered for a moment, but then they went on as strongly as before. Sing him home, he thought. Sing with all your might. Oh good old man, we'll make it as loud as we can. As proud as we can.

'*So fare you well, my pretty young girl*'—and Matthew glanced up at Petra then, and smiled—'*For I'm bound for the Rio Grande . . .*'

MUCH LATER, WHEN ALL THE singing was over, Matthew went alone to the far end of the shore and stood on the rocks, looking out at the moonlit sea.

Flite? he said. Are you there, somewhere in this shadowy ocean? The old captain loved the sea, too—though he didn't know you like I did. Will you see him home?

He did not expect an answer. But as he stood there, suddenly there was a swirl of water close to his feet, and a dark, remembered head raised itself above the surface and looked at him.

'Flite?' he whispered incredulously. '*Flite*? Is it you?'

The head drew closer, and a long thin tail-fluke beat the water with an answering slap of recognition.

Unbelieving, almost beside himself with joy, Matthew threw off his clothes and plunged into the sea. 'Flite!' he called, breasting the deep, cold Atlantic swell. 'You came back! You came when I needed you! Oh Flite, you came!' And he flung out his arms to embrace the warm flank of the beautiful creature coming to meet him.

Came back? said Flite, curling round him slowly in a delicate curve, and coming up close with his smiling face near to Matthew's. *Of course I came back. It's nearly spring, isn't it? The seas are getting warmer. Time for rejoicing. Today!*

But something about that slow, curving turn troubled Matthew, and he swam closer to have another look. The movement seemed heavy, somehow, and unlike the effortless glides and swoops he used to know. The dolphin turned again as he came near, and he saw with horror that there was a half-healed gash across the pale belly, and a thin line of strangling net-cord entangled in his dorsal fin and round his neck. The crippled dolphin could still swim and play, but his movements were slow and awkward.

'Oh!' cried Matthew, clasping Flite in his arms for a moment. 'What have they done to you?' For it was clear that Flite had blundered into a net.

Matthew turned wildly for the rocks and his clothes. There was a penknife in his pocket; he could cut that wretched piece of netting away from that vulnerable throat. He collected the knife and swam back, waiting for Flite to circle round him once more. The dolphin seemed to know that he was trying to help, and submitted quite docilely while Matthew sawed away at the tangled netting embedded in the silvery skin. At last he cut through the final thread and the fine green netting fell away. Flite gave an extra pirouette in grateful relief, and then he turned over onto his back and rested quietly in the water.

Matthew's heart ached for him. What could he do? He supposed Flite would just have to take his chance . . . he had to let him go.

But the dolphin seemed to sense his sadness and came close again, resting tranquilly in the dark sea-swell beside him, and nudging him gently from time to time with his beak.

'I don't know how to help you,' groaned Matthew, speaking aloud into the breaking waves. 'But I'm going to try to save all of you,' he said, crooning into Flite's ear. 'One day. Somehow. *I've got to.*' And he clasped the dolphin again in a sudden rush of love and terror.

Flite turned in a lazy circle, with Matthew's arms round him, and began to tow his friend gently out to sea.

Come on, he said. *I am still alive. You are still alive. Life is for living. Now! No time for sadness. I can still rejoice. The sea still holds me. See? I am safe in its arms.*

And he turned again, releasing himself from Matthew's embrace, and circled, sank and rose in the best display he could manage. *After the night, the day!* he said, whistling and clicking confidingly in Matthew's ear. *Beyond the dark is the sunrise! I can still swim . . . There is still joy to catch—if I can fly!*

And he wove one final, loving circle round Matthew and then headed out to sea towards the pale horizon.

Matthew watched him go, his heart lurching with misgiving. For that brave, joyous fin cutting through the water was heading westwards towards the sunset, not towards the sunrise at all.

Matthew swam back to the rocks and began to dress. As he gazed out to sea he became aware that Flite was not alone. There were other dark fins cutting the waves, other heads bobbing, other joyous bodies leaping in the air. A whole school of dolphins had come to meet Flite. They swam towards him, surrounding him in welcoming circles, dancing beside him in plumes of sun-gilded spray.

We are here! they sang to Flite. *We have come to take you home! Dance with us, Flite. The sea is wide, and its gentle arms will heal your pain. Come with us, Flite, and rejoice in being alive. Sunrise or sunset is all one to us, we can still dance!*

Matthew saw Flite reach them, and how they all curled round him protectively, even slowing their ecstatic sea-surge to keep pace with him . . . They will help him, he thought. They will care for him, and guard him from further hurt. They will see him through.

For a long time he stood there, staring out towards the horizon, though his eyes were too misted with tears to see very clearly. Goodbye, Flite, he said, and lifted his hand in a last farewell salute. Goodbye, and Godspeed to you and all your companions. May the wide seas never be empty of you and your kind.

Then he turned and walked away.

ELIZABETH WEBSTER

Elizabeth Webster cares passionately about injustice and her books reflect this. 'My aim is not only to tell a good story but also to make people think again about difficult subjects.' Over the years she has

written novels addressing such issues as wife-battering and deafness—as well as the problem of poverty in South America— and always in a warm and imaginative way, which brings the issues to life.

Dolphin Sunrise evolved out of her concern for the world's endangered species. She chose dolphins, in particular, because her research led her to discover some shocking statistics about their plight. 'It's estimated that over six million dolphins have died in tuna nets since nineteen fifty-nine when counting began. Unless much greater legal pro-

tection is given, many species will not survive. If *Dolphin Sunrise* makes just one person think about dolphin conservation then the book has been worthwhile.' Elizabeth Webster does see hope for the future, mainly through increasing public awareness. 'That's what helped the whales,' she says. 'If people shout loudly enough they do have the strength to change government policy. After all, it was the power of ordinary people that brought down the Berlin Wall.'

Elizabeth Webster has great affection for dolphins and says she has even swum with them off the Cornish coast. 'Somehow it isn't at all frightening, although they are fairly large creatures. They are totally unaggressive.' It was the sighting of a school of dolphins that provided inspiration for the book's ending. Initially, she thought that she would end the book on a pessimistic note with Flite the dolphin badly injured. At the time she was mulling this over, she and a friend went to stay in Cornwall. 'One day we were sitting on the shore staring out at the sea when I saw some dark heads bobbing about. At first I thought they were seals but then, as they leaped out of the water, I realised they were dolphins. Suddenly I knew exactly what would happen to the injured Flite at the end—he would be helped by his fellow dolphins.'

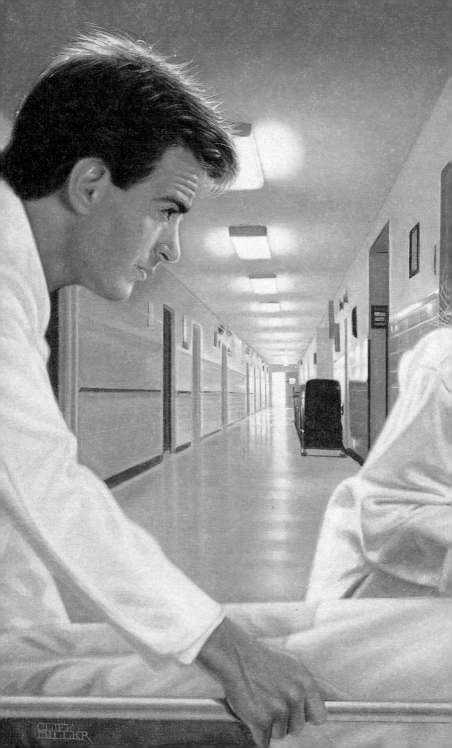

Doctor on Trial

BY HENRY DENKER

ILLUSTRATED BY CLIFF MILLER

Midnight in a New York City hospital emergency room. Trolleys swerve round corners. A heart attack patient needs urgent attention. A gunshot victim has just been admitted. And in the distance, the shriek of an ambulance siren draws ever nearer.

For Dr Kate Forrester, the overworked on-duty resident, it's just another night in the nonstop, high-pressure atmosphere of the emergency room where fast decisions must be made. Kate gives swift, methodical attention to each case, including a young woman complaining of a minor ailment—a patient who will haunt her for the rest of her days . . .

Chapter One

'Get Dr Forrester!' the frantic call rang through the emergency service of City Hospital. 'We got a gunshot wound here! A bleeder!'

Two orderlies rushed the trolley towards the acute-care room at the end of the corridor. One of them called again, 'Dr Forrester!'

In one of the examining rooms, Dr Kate Forrester turned from the patient she had been treating and said to the nurse, 'Take over. Send this blood specimen to the lab. Call me the minute the results get back!'

Kate Forrester raced out of the room and along the corridor. The loose, untended condition of her blonde hair, lack of make-up, and wrinkled lab coat testified to the many hours of continuous service she had already put in on the emergency service. Saturday nights in emergency in this large New York City hospital were always hectic. Tonight was even more so because the doctor scheduled to be on duty with Kate had come down with flu. Kate had been promised help, but, as yet, none had arrived. So she did what young resident doctors always do—the best they can under impossible circumstances.

As she hurried past examining room C, Nurse Adelaide Cronin called, 'Doctor, when you have a moment . . .' But Kate raced on towards acute care, where a young lad of fourteen, who had been caught in the line of fire between two competing drug dealers on a West Side street, lay bleeding from a gunshot wound to the arm.

Aware of the demands on Dr Forrester's time, Nurse Cronin turned back to the patient in room C to begin taking a preliminary history. She would have preferred to carry out this function without interference, but the mother of the patient persisted in hovering over her protectively.

'Tell me,' Cronin addressed the patient, a dark-haired woman of nineteen, 'what brought you here?'

Her mother interrupted. 'I would like you to summon a doctor. I want my daughter to have the best medical attention.'

'I've already notified Dr Forrester,' Cronin said. Then she asked the patient, 'Now then, what brought you in?'

'She was suffering from nausea and vomiting,' her mother replied.

Aware of any mother's natural concern, Cronin took a moment to explain. 'Mrs . . .'

'Stuyvesant,' the woman replied. 'Mrs *Claude* Stuyvesant.'

The name was instantly recognisable to Cronin, but did not alter her routine. 'Mrs Stuyvesant, this information must be entered on the patient's chart. As long as she is able to answer, it is best to have her symptoms in her own words. So please . . .'

'Sorry,' Nora Stuyvesant said, stepping back a bit.

From the manner in which the patient's dark hair was matted to her perspiring forehead, from the spasmodic way in which she was breathing, Cronin could read some of the signs of the young woman's distress. She resumed her questioning, at the same time taking the patient's pulse and blood pressure.

'Now tell me, what brought you in?'

In a voice shaded by pain the young woman replied haltingly, 'It started around six this morning.'

'What started?' Cronin asked.

'The pain. In my stomach. Then I . . . I began to get this nausea,' the patient said, sounding lethargic.

'Vomit?' Cronin asked.

'Yes. That's when I . . . the, the sweating began.'

'Claudia, darling, don't forget about your diarrhoea,' her mother reminded.

'I was getting to that, Mother.'

'Severe?' Cronin asked.

Claudia Stuyvesant made an attempt to recall before she said, 'Not really,' and closed her eyes, as if about to drift off to sleep.

By that time Cronin had determined that the patient had a pulse rate of 110. Tachycardia. Diaphoresis, heavy sweating. Blood pressure 100 over 60. Cronin slipped a fresh antiseptic plastic sleeve over the digital thermometer.

'Under your tongue, please,' she said, then reached into the wall cabinet to assemble the materials for an intravenous (IV) infusion. The combination of diarrhoea and rapid pulse indicated to Cronin that the young woman was suffering from dehydration.

The temperature reading of 100.2 degrees served to reinforce that assumption. Once Cronin affixed the IV, Mrs Stuyvesant asked, 'Aren't you going to give her anything?'

'Only the doctor can prescribe,' Cronin replied.

'Then where is he?' the woman asked. 'We've been here almost half an hour. First at the admitting desk, then with you.'

'Mrs Stuyvesant, in emergency we see each patient just as soon as we can. Dr Forrester will be in very soon.' With that, Cronin left the room.

'Well, I never!' the woman exclaimed.

Despite discomfort, her daughter opened her eyes and pleaded, 'Mother, not one of your scenes, please.'

'Believe me, if Dr Eaves were in town, he'd have been at your apartment in a second. But of all times to get sick—a Saturday night. I don't like to remind you, Claudia, but who said a year ago, "Mother, I'm eighteen and able to take care of myself. I'm going out on my own"? Wasn't me. Wasn't your father.'

At that moment, having clamped off the bleeding artery in the young gunshot victim and sent him up to surgery, Kate Forrester joined Nurse Cronin outside room C. Cronin briefed the doctor on the case. They entered the room.

At a glance Kate took in the relationship: nervous mother, uncomfortable daughter. First put them both at ease. Establish a personal relationship. Kate asked the patient, 'Well now, what's your name?'

Before she could respond, the mother said, 'She's already been questioned by a nurse. We want her to be seen by a doctor.'

'I *am* a doctor,' Kate Forrester replied.

The woman seemed about to dispute that until her eyes fixed on the plastic identification badge on the lapel of Kate's lab coat.

'Oh!' Mrs Stuyvesant said, expressing in a single sound her surprise and her embarrassment. 'I'm quite sure you'll do the best you can.'

Half annoyed, half amused by the woman's reply, Kate turned her attention to the patient. 'Your name?'

'Claudia Stuyvesant,' the patient said with a slight gasp.

Kate observed the patient was having difficulty focusing her eyes. She reached for the patient's pulse, noting: young woman, nineteen, possibly twenty. Generalised symptoms. In pain; at the same time, lethargic. Under considerable emotional tension. Is she tense because of her mother, or from fear of a serious ailment? Surely her mother's presence is not helping.

'All right now, Claudia, tell me why you're here.'

'It should be obvious why she's here,' her mother said.

'Please, Mrs . . .' Kate began.

'Mrs Stuyvesant. Mrs *Claude* Stuyvesant,' the mother replied, expecting Kate would respond with instant recognition.

But the importance of that name was of less consequence to Kate than her patient's condition. So she suggested, 'Mrs Stuyvesant, why not wait out in the reception area?' When the woman gave no indication of moving, Kate asked, 'Please?'

'It's . . . it's all right, Doctor,' the young patient said.

'If you must remain, Mrs Stuyvesant, please allow your daughter to answer my questions.' Kate turned back to her patient. 'Now, Claudia, what brought you here?'

'Stomach pains.'

'When did they start?'

'Early this morning.'

'Have you had such stomach pains before?' Kate asked.

'No. Not like this.'

Kate scanned the sheet on which Cronin had recorded her findings. 'It says here you complain of vomiting. How often? When?'

'Since this morning. Several times.'

'Claudia, when did you eat last?'

She tried to recall. 'Yesterday afternoon.'

The doctor was trying to tie together a group of vaguely defined symptoms and signs to arrive at a tentative diagnosis: this patient is too young to consider a heart attack. The signs and symptoms she presents would likely indicate a stomach virus or some kind of food poisoning. But they could also indicate appendicitis or dozens of other illnesses.

'Claudia, show me exactly where your pain started.'

The woman traced her hand over her abdomen in a general way.

'Not in the centre of the abdomen?' Claudia shook her head. 'And it didn't move down to here?' Kate indicated the lower-right quadrant of the abdomen. Again Claudia shook her head. While that ruled out the likelihood of an inflamed appendix, it brought the doctor no closer to a diagnosis.

With so little to go on, Kate asked Nurse Cronin for a kit to take a blood sample. The nurse had anticipated her. Kate tightened a rubber tube round Claudia's arm above her elbow, causing a vein to protrude. She eased a hypodermic needle in carefully, drew up the plunger until the transparent plastic tube was filled with dark blood. She passed the tube to Cronin.

'Complete blood count and electrolytes. Tell the lab I want them stat! And let's send up a urine specimen. Meantime, we'll keep her on the IV until the results come back.'

Once Cronin hurried out with the blood samples, Kate said, 'Claudia, while we're waiting, I'd like to do a physical. Let's get that shirt off. I want to go over your chest and back.'

As Claudia started to unbutton her blouse, from down the corridor the distress call of a nurse could be heard. 'Dr Forrester!'

The urgency in that voice told Kate that her services were demanded in a life-threatening situation. With a hasty 'I'll be back', she started for the door.

Mrs Stuyvesant stood in the doorway, blocking Kate's path. 'Doctor! You're not leaving my daughter, are you?'

'I'm sorry. They need me,' Kate responded as she gently brushed by Mrs Stuyvesant, barely touching her.

'Well, I never. Deserting a sick patient,' the woman complained.

'Mother, please,' Claudia Stuyvesant said weakly.

KATE FORRESTER RACED down the hall towards the nurse who stood in the doorway of one of the examining rooms. Kate entered to find a man, no more than thirty-three or thirty-four, she judged. Sensors for an electrocardiogram (ECG) had been taped to his chest, arms and legs by the nurse, who reported briskly, 'Severe pain just below the breastbone. Profuse diaphoresis.'

Dr Forrester had already made those observations. The grimace on the man's unshaven face, the sweat that oozed from his brow told her that. Both could be signs of a heart attack.

Kate read the cardiogram tape that revealed the patient's heart action. As the tape continued to flow from the machine the gasping man's eyes pleaded, Tell me, Doctor, am I going to die?

Kate was relieved to tell him, 'Your heart's doing fine. Just fine. You are not going to die.'

'But the pain . . .'

'Your pain will go away very soon,' Kate assured him, then ordered the nurse, 'Demerol. One hundred milligrams. And get a blood sample up to the lab stat. I want a reading on his bilirubin as soon as possible. If I'm right, he's passing a gallstone. Possibly lodged in the bile duct. Meantime, get him to X-ray, and call me when you get the plate.'

She smiled at the patient to reassure him, then left.

Kate started back towards room C to discover Mrs Stuyvesant staring at her from the doorway. When Kate reached her, the woman said, 'I trust that now you will be able to give my daughter your undivided attention.'

Kate did not dignify the remark with even a glance. She approached the examining table. 'Claudia, let's do that chest and back examination now. Off with that blouse. And sit up, please.'

Claudia finished unbuttoning her blouse and wriggled out of it.

'Did you feel feverish earlier today?' Kate asked as she began to stethoscope the patient's chest.

'No,' Claudia said.

'Anyone at home experiencing similar symptoms?'

'Isn't anyone at home. I mean, I . . . I live alone.'

'And you can see what comes of that,' her mother added.

'Mother, please.'

'Have you had any previous stomach problems?' Kate asked.

'No. Nothing like this,' Claudia responded.

'Gall-bladder attack?'

'No.'

Kate knew the lab report on the urine would confirm or refute that. She tried to appear casual and routine as she asked a most significant question.

'Do you regularly use drugs of any kind? Prescribed, over the counter, or any other?'

There was a moment of hesitation before Claudia replied, 'No. No drugs.'

Kate Forrester was forced to think, Is she denying the use of drugs because her mother is in the room?

Rather than press the issue, Kate continued her physical examination. She listened to the patient's lungs, seeking telltale sounds that might indicate bronchitis or pneumonia. She percussed the young woman's back and chest, evoking a drumlike sound, thus ruling out fluid in the lungs.

Kate then directed several light blows to the patient's lower back to see if she flinched in pain. She did not, thereby ruling out the likelihood of a kidney condition. In fact, Kate noticed that the patient was lethargic and hardly reacted at all.

296

Kate examined the young woman's abdomen. It rose and fell with a slight jerkiness that reflected moderate abdominal pain. There were no wounds or evidence of previous surgery, so there was no reason to consider an intestinal obstruction due to resulting adhesions.

Kate applied her stethoscope to the young woman's abdomen, listening for normal stomach sounds. Considering the circumstances, they were not too diminished. She pressed gently along the lower-left quadrant of Claudia's abdomen—the area of the descending colon— suspecting there might be some inflammation and tenderness. Colitis could give rise to the patient's generalised symptoms. But colitis usually presented with a history of chronic symptoms, and this patient said her pain was unprecedented. So that diagnosis seemed unlikely.

With signs and symptoms so vague and nonspecific Kate could not afford to overlook any possible cause. She decided to use the next phase of her examination as a pretext to be free of the nervous mother as well.

'Mrs Stuyvesant, I'm about to do a pelvic examination. I think the patient would appreciate privacy.'

'I'm her mother. There is no need for privacy between us,' Mrs Stuyvesant replied as she remained unmoved.

Kate slipped on transparent plastic gloves and performed a bimanual pelvic examination, at the same time asking questions she had previously delayed because of the mother's presence.

'Claudia, have you been sexually active?'

'No,' the young woman replied.

Kate asked, 'Your last menstrual period—on time?'

'Yes.'

Kate completed her examination. The patient had evidenced no sign of pelvic pain, so pelvic inflammatory disease could be ruled out. While Claudia's uterus felt slightly enlarged, it was not sufficiently so as to indicate an existing pregnancy. In addition, there was no noticeable discoloration of the cervix. And Kate had not discovered any marked swelling in the fallopian tubes, eliminating that area as the cause of Claudia's symptoms.

One thing was apparent: Claudia Stuyvesant was not a surgical emergency. Kate decided that until the results came down from the lab, the most conservative course was to continue the patient on the IV and await developments.

As she was noting her findings and conclusions on the patient's chart, there was a loud call from the admitting desk.

'Dr Forrester! Dr Forrester!'

Kate stopped writing and started for the door.

'You're not leaving my daughter *again*, are you?' Nora Stuyvesant demanded. 'Without *doing* anything?'

'Mrs Stuyvesant, until your daughter's results come down from the lab, there is nothing more to be done for her.'

The woman followed Kate out into the corridor. 'Doctor! I want you to know that my husband is very well connected with important members of the board of trustees of this hospital and . . .'

What had been intended as a warning, if not a threat, was lost on Dr Kate Forrester. She raced down the corridor towards the cardiac treatment room alongside the admitting desk. On the examining table lay a robust man who appeared to be in his late fifties, his sweaty face pale, his huge chest heaving spasmodically. The nurse had already affixed ECG sensors to his chest, arms, and legs. Oxygen tubes had been inserted into his nostrils. The nurse and an attendant were awaiting Kate's diagnosis and orders.

Forrester quickly undid the belt of the patient's trousers, unzipped them, and pulled them down to have access to his abdomen. While he heaved in staccato breaths Kate pushed on his bulging belly to make sure it was not distended and hard. It was not.

Clearly he was not an abdominal case. All his signs pointed to a myocardial infarction. A shot of nitroglycerin was indicated to increase blood flow to his heart and reduce his pain. Kate tested and found that his pressure was high enough.

'Nitro,' she ordered the nurse.

Kate studied the results of the ECG as they rolled out of the machine. Their erratic pattern confirmed that this was indeed a myocardial infarction of life-threatening size. She had to consider administering streptokinase to reopen the clogged arteries to his heart. But she would have to ascertain certain information before she could safely prescribe it.

She stood over the man, whose terror-stricken eyes were pleading for reassurance.

'Ever had an ulcer?' she asked. The man did not seem to understand. 'An ulcer,' Kate repeated. 'Have you ever had—' Kate sensed the trouble. She called out, 'Find Juan Castillo!'

The call went down the corridor. 'Juan! They need you in cardiac.'

A minute later a slim, dark-haired young man came bounding into the room.

'Yes, Doctor?' he asked, his words tinged with a Spanish flavour.

'Juan, ask him, has he ever had an ulcer problem.'

Juan translated. The man responded through spasmodic breathing, 'No.'

'Ever had a stroke?' the doctor asked.

Again Juan translated. Again the man responded, 'No.'

Kate ordered the nurse, 'Get a specimen, and check his stool for blood. I want the results stat.'

'Streptokinase?' the nurse anticipated.

'I'd better check his blood pressure again.' Kate pumped up the pressure cuff attached to his arm. She applied her stethoscope to his arm, listened, then said, 'One forty over ninety. Not high enough to contraindicate strepto. Let me know as soon as those stool results come back. Meantime, give him a shot of morphine for his pain.'

Even before Kate completed her orders to the nurse, a voice from the admitting desk sought her out. 'Dr Forrester! Dr Forrester!' Quickly she started towards the door.

As Dr Forrester reached the admitting desk she was confronted by a man in his seventies who was breathing in a spasmodic, painful manner similar to the cardiac patient she had just left. The grizzled white stubble on his sunken cheeks indicated that he had not shaved in three days or more. His clothes were old and dirty. When Kate took his hand to find his pulse, she noticed that the cuff of his old tweed jacket was frayed beyond mending.

His pulse was slow but regular; still, he complained, 'The pain, Doctor. I need something for the pain.'

She opened his coat and shirt to test his chest and his abdomen. Gingerly she applied her stethoscope, while he continued to repeat, 'The pain. It's the pain.'

'Where?' she asked.

'All over. And it's bad. Very bad.'

In medical school the maxim had been drilled into her: Pain everywhere is pain nowhere. That could well be the case with this old man. But she had also been warned of the folly of jumping to the first and easiest diagnosis.

She tested his back and chest—no signs of fluid. She concentrated on his heart action—regular, steady, slow. She pressed her fingers into his abdomen, listened to his stomach sounds. Aside from indications of lack of a recent meal, she found nothing disturbing. She had barely completed her examination when she noticed Clara Beathard, one of the older nurses, signalling to her.

Kate slipped away from the table.

'Doctor, you're wasting your time,' Beathard whispered. 'I've seen him before. More than once. Always the same symptoms, always on rainy nights. I'll get rid of him for you.'

'Right,' Kate agreed. 'But before you send him out, give him some hot coffee and a sandwich if you can find one.'

'We only encourage him when we do,' Beathard warned.

'I'll take that risk,' Kate said, then returned to her cardiac patient.

Chapter Two

In the cardiac treatment-room, Kate Forrester found her patient less stressed than he had been. Morphine had eased his pain. He no longer seemed so fearful of dying. He did not realise that death was still an imminent threat.

'When the lab results and that blood stool come down,' she told the nurse, 'rush him up to cardiac ICU with orders to put him on streptokinase if the results permit.'

She reached the patient's side. 'You're going to be OK. Just relax,' she said. Even though he did not understand her words, she intended to reassure him by her attitude.

She started out of the treatment room only to be stopped by a woman's shrill cry from the admissions area.

'Somebody! *Por favor! Mi niña!* My baby!'

As Kate Forrester turned in the direction of the outcry she could see Mrs Stuyvesant standing at the open door of emergency room C, glaring in her direction. Kate ignored her and raced to the admitting desk. There she found a young woman of Hispanic origin, clutching to her breast a little girl of three or four, who appeared to be asleep.

Kate eased open the child's eyelids to test her for reflexive responses to a flashlight. Her eyes did not respond in normal fashion. Kate started to remove the child's clothes to make a cursory examination, asking, 'Tell me what happened.'

'Nothing happen,' the mother protested as she twisted a rosary in her fingers. 'Maria she sleepin', and I see she is not breathin' too good. So I think better to see the doctor. I bring her here.'

While the mother was speaking, Kate had placed the child on a trolley and had begun an examination of the child's arms, legs and torso. Sadly she discovered several black and blue haematomas and two other signs, which appeared to be healed burns. Kate suspected a healed fracture in one leg and a swelling in the other.

'Did you ever hit Maria?' Kate asked.

'*Nada! Nunca!* Never hit!' the woman protested.

'Did *anyone* ever hit her?'

'No. *Nadie.* Nobody,' the woman insisted. 'But Maria she fall. She hurt herself.'

Kate was sufficiently disturbed by her findings to decide that a complete set of X-rays of the child's body was mandatory before referring her to paediatric neurology for further evaluation. If her suspicions were confirmed, the neurologist should do an electro-encephalogram and a CAT scan of the child's brain.

'You have to leave her overnight,' Kate said.

'No, no! No can leave her,' the mother protested.

'If you want her to live, you'd better leave her!' Kate ordered.

'No, no . . . I no can leave. No . . .' The woman began to weep, far more fearful and disturbed now.

At that moment the angry, hoarse voice of a man was heard insisting, 'Felicia! *Dónde estás?* Where are you?'

'Please, I got to take Maria. I got to,' the woman said, trembling. 'He will be very bad with me.'

By that time the man had found them. He was short but had a broad and powerful build. His eyes—black and piercing—were hostile and enraged, like a man betrayed.

'Felicia!' he commanded. 'Pick Maria up!'

The woman was torn between obeying the man and Kate's firm, forbidding shake of the head. She was frozen with fear.

'I say, pick her up. We go home.' The woman hesitated. He shouted, *'Rápido!'*

The woman yielded. She moved to sweep up the child in her arms, but Kate intervened, placing herself between the mother and the trolley on which the child lay.

'Maria stays here. She is very sick,' Kate declared.

'I am the father,' the man replied. 'I decide if she is sick.'

'If you move her, she may die,' Kate warned.

The man placed his huge, powerful hands on Kate's shoulders, trying to push her aside. She resisted, not giving an inch.

'Security!' Kate called out loudly as they struggled.

In his anger the man shoved Kate back so fiercely that she was hurled up against the wall, her head striking it sharply. Under other circumstances she might have slumped to the floor from such a blow, but she was determined to keep this child out of hands that would surely end her life. She lunged at the man. Once more he shoved her aside, and this time he was able to sweep the child off the trolley and into his arms just as a uniformed security guard came racing towards them.

'Doctor, you called?'

Even before Kate could answer, the guard sized up the situation. 'You!' he commanded the man. 'Put that child down!'

'She is mine. I have the right!' the man insisted.

'Doctor?' The guard awaited her order.

'This child has been abused. She stays here for as long as we decide is necessary. Use force if you have to,' she ordered.

'OK, mister. Put her down!' the guard commanded. His hand went to his holster. This was no idle gesture, and the father knew it, for slowly he put the child down on the stretcher. 'Now stand back!'

The swarthy man moved back from the trolley.

Dr Kate Forrester approached little Maria and completed her examination. While she was doing so, the man grumbled, 'She fall. She always fallin'. Something wrong with the child.'

'We'll have her X-rayed. Complete body X-rays, then a brain scan.'

'What means that?' the frightened mother asked.

'There could be trouble up here.' Kate pointed to the child's head.

Looking at her husband, the woman crossed herself and mumbled, *'Hombre malo . . . malo . . .'*

Kate took the woman aside. 'Do you want to tell me now?' When the woman did not respond, Kate warned, 'You'll have to tell the authorities later.'

The woman began to weep once more. It was answer enough for Kate. She called, 'Beathard!'

When the nurse appeared, Kate said, 'Take Maria to X-ray. Complete body films of a child who appears to be four years old.'

'Six,' the mother corrected.

It was no surprise to Kate Forrester. Abused children often were stunted, appearing far younger than they actually were. Kate added to her instructions. 'Also, I want an immediate EEG and a brain scan. Ask Dr Golding to take personal charge of this case.'

Beathard started to wheel the trolley towards the swinging double doors that led to the main hospital complex, where the paediatrics service was located.

Throughout, the father had stood silent, glaring. Only the presence of the armed guard kept him from physically interfering. Once the trolley had disappeared, Kate turned to the father and said, 'You will leave now. And you will hear from the authorities very soon.'

302

The man started away. Reluctantly the woman started to follow.

'You don't have to go,' Kate said. Felicia turned to her, eyes filling with tears. 'If you want to stay, we can help you.'

'Felicia!' the man called back angrily.

'Help?' the woman asked. 'He can no hit me any more?'

'I'll call our social services people. They'll take you to a centre where you will be safe. No one will hit you any more.'

The woman considered Kate's offer while the man continued to insist, 'Felicia, *ven aquí!*'

Torn, the woman's eyes appealed to Kate.

'You will be safe, I promise,' Kate reassured.

'I . . . I stay,' the woman finally decided.

Kate turned to the security guard. 'Please take her up to social services.'

'Yes, Doctor. You sure you're OK?' he asked. 'That was quite a blow to the head.'

'I'm fine,' Kate insisted, though her head throbbed.

'If you don't mind my saying so, Doctor, you take too many chances. You could have got hurt real bad.'

'He would have had to kill me to take that child back,' Kate said. She turned away only to discover Mrs Stuyvesant glaring at her.

'Doctor, I insist you take a look at Claudia at once. She's become so restless she's pulled that IV out of her arm.'

Without another word Kate started towards room C with a new concern. A patient who seemed lethargic earlier and was now suddenly overactive might be reflecting the emotional lability associated with barbiturates. Kate now suspected that Claudia had been lying when she denied using drugs.

When Kate reached the door of room C, she found an orderly waiting with reports that had just come down from the lab on patient Stuyvesant, Claudia. Kate studied them at once.

Unfortunately, the findings were not particularly revealing. A haematocrit of thirty-three indicated slight anaemia. A white count of fourteen thousand was on the high side, but neither alarming nor indicative of a serious infection. The urinalysis revealed no trace of blood, no indication of kidney stones.

In the face of such findings the only intelligent and professional course to follow was to keep the patient hydrated, continue to check her vital signs, and do another blood count to see if there was any change. Kate reinserted the IV and taped it to Claudia's arm.

Throughout, Mrs Stuyvesant stood beside her daughter, silently demanding of Kate disclosure of the lab report. When none was forthcoming, the woman left her daughter's side and took the doctor by the arm to guide her to a corner of the room.

'I know it's bad—' the woman began.

Kate Forrester interrupted. 'Mrs Stuyvesant, before you make any assumptions, the lab reports are not definitive.'

'I want a consultation with an older doctor. When my daughter's life is involved, I want the best!'

'At this hour, in this emergency room, in this hospital, I am the best,' Kate replied.

'Then at least—' Mrs Stuyvesant started to say.

'I know. *Do something!*' Kate replied.

'Exactly!' Mrs Stuyvesant said.

'Mrs Stuyvesant, believe me. Until your daughter's symptoms and lab results make it possible for me to arrive at a definitive diagnosis, it is better, safer medicine to do *nothing*.'

'Well, I intend to see if Dr Eaves's service can reach him.'

'You can use the pay phone at the end of the corridor,' Kate said.

'Never mind. We have a phone in the limousine,' Mrs Stuyvesant said, starting towards the street where her car waited.

Anticipating that freed from her mother's surveillance, Claudia might speak more openly, Kate went back to her patient. To make her questions appear casual, Kate completed her entries in the Stuyvesant chart while saying, 'Claudia, I want a few answers from you. I promise that whatever you tell me will not be revealed to your mother.'

Claudia nodded slightly but seemed no more at ease.

'First, *have* you been sexually active recently?'

'No. I told you before, no.'

'And your periods?'

'Regular,' Claudia affirmed.

'Now, about drugs, any kind of drugs—legal, illegal, prescribed, or over the counter. Do you use any regularly?'

'No,' the young patient insisted.

Kate would have persisted in her efforts but a desperate cry for help summoned her to the admitting desk. With a hasty 'I'll be back' to Claudia, Kate started out of the room.

As she hurried towards the admitting desk she could see a team of Emergency Medical Service personnel pushing a stretcher towards her. On it lay a young woman. Hurrying alongside her, holding her hand, was a man in his mid-twenties.

Kate beckoned the EMS officers towards a vacant examining room. When the stretcher was alongside the examining table, the young man and one officer assisted the patient up onto it. From the way she reacted, it was obvious that the woman was too weak and in too much pain to have accomplished it on her own.

Kate made a swift appraisal. The woman was sweating profusely. Her face was pale, her lips colourless. She was breathing with great difficulty, and she was obviously in severe pain.

'Tell me what's wrong. When did this start?'

'I . . . I don't . . . I can't . . . I . . .' She struggled to explain but finally turned her head away, unable to complete the thought.

The man explained. 'She was feeling good until early this morning. Then around noon she started feeling . . . I don't know . . . sort of strange. I mean, she's been sickly before. Lots of times. Even before we got married.'

Kate took the patient's blood pressure. Ninety over fifty. Significantly low. She slipped a fresh plastic cover over the electronic thermometer and eased it into the patient's mouth.

'Under your tongue, please,' Kate said. She watched the temperature register on the dial. One hundred point two. Low-grade fever. 'Sit up, please.' Her husband started to assist her, but Kate countermanded, 'No. Let her do it herself.'

The young man shrank back guiltily. His wife started to raise herself. Kate observed that she evidenced signs of lower back pain. She had barely attained a sitting position when she slumped back, exhausted from effort and pain.

Her husband said, 'She's been that way most of the day. Every time I get her to sit up, she gets nauseous and dizzy. Doctor, please. Can you do something?'

From the manner in which he pleaded, Kate knew he was terrified of losing his wife. And with good reason, Kate thought. While the signs and symptoms the patient presented were not definitive, they were ominous and demanded immediate attention.

She drew a sample of blood and called towards the corridor, 'Juan! Juan Castillo! Room A. Stat!'

The orderly came racing into the room. 'Yes, Dr Forrester?' he asked, breathless.

'Rush this sample to the lab. I want a complete blood count. With electrolytes. And wait for the results!'

'Yes, Doctor,' Juan said, taking the sealed test tube and starting on his way.

'Doctor?' the husband pleaded.

Kate turned back to the patient. While she used her stethoscope to determine the condition of the patient's lungs, heart and chest, she spoke to the husband, who was clinging to his wife's hand.

'You said that she has been sickly lots of times before. What did you mean?'

'She got these attacks. She had trouble breathing.'

Kate turned to the patient's husband. 'This difficulty she had in breathing, what did the doctors call it? Asthma?'

'Yes. Asthma.'

Now the signs and symptoms were beginning to take on the semblance of a syndrome. 'Did her doctor ever prescribe any medication for her asthma?' Kate asked.

'Oh, yes,' the husband assured. 'And it worked fine. Like I said, she was feeling real good. I can't understand what happened.'

'What kind of medication was she taking? Was it steroids?'

'Yes. That's right. That's what the pharmacist called it.'

'You said, "It *worked* fine." Isn't she taking them any more?'

'She didn't have an attack for weeks, so we asked the doctor if she could stop taking the stuff. He said OK.'

'And did she stop taking it all at once?' Kate asked.

'Well, when the doctor said she could stop, she just stopped,' the young husband replied.

Kate reached out to take the woman's hand. Carefully Kate examined every finger, every fold of skin between the fingers. There she discovered what she suspected. Discoloration. Though she had never seen such a case before, she had heard it so accurately described by her professor of internal medicine that she could fit the signs and symptoms together. Low blood pressure. Low-grade fever. Dizziness. Lethargy. Severe pain in lower back and legs. Disorientation. And now the final clue: darkening folds of the skin.

A full-blown case of Addison's disease, brought on by the sudden cessation of the cortisone she had been taking, followed by failure of her own adrenal glands to produce their normal supply of cortisol and corticosterone. To avoid total vascular collapse, two things must be done at once: restore fluids and supply steroids.

Once she had affixed the proper IVs to correct both conditions, Kate turned the patient over to the nurse, with instructions to observe her until the labs came back.

'And when they do, call me,' Kate said, then resumed her rounds of patients already under her care.

Chapter Three

Two hours later. Two hours past midnight. Dr Kate Forrester was becoming very aware of her own fatigue. A cup of black coffee, hot and strong, had not given her the renewed energy she had hoped for. In the last hour she had seen eight cases, treated them and dispatched them to the care of others, and sent seven more home after palliative treatment and much reassurance.

There was still the baffling case of Claudia Stuyvesant, in room C. The results of the second lab tests had not changed sufficiently to lead to a diagnosis. The last two times Kate had looked in, Claudia's pain had appeared somewhat worse. But a third set of lab tests Kate had ordered had not come down, so no further treatment was indicated.

Since the diagnosis still eluded her, she decided to summon the surgical resident for a second opinion. She picked up the phone. 'Page Dr Briscoe. Ask him to come to room C in emergency. Stat!'

As she hung up, she caught the patient's mother staring at her with a look that seemed to say, About time, young woman. About time.

Minutes later Eric Briscoe entered room C, asking, 'Kate, you sent for me?'

'Yes.' She acquainted him with her findings and showed him the lab reports.

With Mrs Stuyvesant hovering close by, Dr Briscoe performed both an abdominal and a pelvic examination on her daughter. Ignoring the woman's enquiring stare, he reported to Kate. 'Abdomen sensitive, but not sufficient to indicate specific treatment.'

'Uterus?' Kate asked.

'Slightly enlarged. No marked discoloration of the cervix.'

'Any cause for surgical intervention?'

'Not at this time,' Briscoe said. 'Repeat the lab tests and let me know—'

Before Kate could explain that she had already done so, Mrs Stuyvesant interrupted. 'Repeat the labs, repeat the labs. Don't you doctors know anything else?' When the young surgeon turned to her, she accused, 'I was expecting an older man with more experience.'

Without replying to her, Briscoe said quietly, 'Dr Forrester, when the next set of reports come down, let me know.'

BY THREE O'CLOCK in the morning Dr Kate Forrester had seen twenty-six new patients. Now she was on her way to see Claudia

Stuyvesant again. Six hours after her admission to emergency her case was still unresolved.

When she entered the room, Mrs Stuyvesant quickly reminded her, 'The lab results have been back for almost half an hour!'

'I've had other patients, Mrs Stuyvesant.' With that, Kate scanned the results of the third set of labs.

This time there were marked changes. Claudia's white count had risen to 21,000. Her haematocrit had fallen to 19. While intravenous rehydration would normally lower the red cell counts, this was too sharp a drop for such a simple answer. To further confuse Kate, the patient seemed less agitated by her pain and more lethargic.

Kate decided to perform another abdominal examination. This time she discovered Claudia Stuyvesant's abdomen was palpably distended, somewhat tense. Her bowel sounds were diminished. Taken together, these signs could indicate a serious abdominal infection. A fleeting suspicion crossed her mind.

'Claudia, I want you to be very honest with me. It's important. *Have* you been sexually active in the past few months?'

'No. Really, no.'

'Did you miss your last period?'

'Regular. I've been very regular,' Claudia insisted.

'She is not pregnant, if that's what you're getting at,' Mrs Stuyvesant said.

Kate decided to do a test that would either corroborate or dispel her suspicion that any infection might be related to a pregnancy, possibly even an ectopic pregnancy. Impatient with the time it might take to coax a urine sample from the patient, Kate resorted to swifter action. She ordered Cronin, 'Scissors.'

Nurse Cronin presented a pair of round-ended surgical scissors. Kate proceeded to cut away the leg of Claudia's jeans.

'What in the world are you doing?' Nora Stuyvesant demanded.

'Securing a urine sample,' Kate responded. She slit the jeans up to the crotch and cut through the patient's underpants. Cronin was ready with a catheter, which Kate inserted. Carefully she drew some urine into the test tube Cronin handed her.

'Assay kit,' Kate requested. Cronin had already opened the kit and reached in for a clear plastic pipette and a round plastic tube. As she was about to remove the rest of the contents and discard the carton Kate said, 'Expiration date?'

Nurse Cronin read the date off the label. 'December thirtieth, nineteen ninety-one.'

Assured that the contents were fresh and potent, Kate dipped the pipette into the test tube to pick up drops of urine. She pressed her thumb over the top of the pipette to hold the urine in place until she could transfer it to the round plastic tube. She removed her thumb, permitting the drops to settle onto a membrane that stretched across the open end of the round tube.

Mrs Stuyvesant asked, 'Doctor, what are you doing?'

'Making an immunoenzymetric assay for the semiquantitative detection of HCG in your daughter's urine.'

'That immuno thing—HCG. What is that for?' the suspicious mother asked.

'HCG is human chorionic gonadotropin. A hormone produced as soon as fertilisation takes place. This test will discover if there is any present in your daughter's urine sample,' Kate explained.

'And if it is, does that tell you what Claudia is suffering from?'

'No. But it will tell me if she's pregnant.'

'My daughter already told you she has not been sexually active!' Nora Stuyvesant protested.

Kate added to the specimen a few drops of the liquid contained in a small vial marked REAGENT A.

'Then there's no harm in verifying it,' Kate said as she added a few drops of reagent B to eliminate any loose HCG molecules from the urine sample, leaving only the HCG that was to be tested by reagent C. Confident the result would corroborate her suspicion, Kate carefully added droplets of reagent C to the urine sample. If her suspicion was correct, the mixture would turn blue, indicating a concentration of HCG in the patient's urine.

Kate studied the contents of the plastic tube, waiting for the mixture to turn an intense blue. It did not turn intense blue. There was not even a trace of blue.

'Well?' Mrs Stuyvesant asked, sensing vindication.

'There are no signs of pregnancy,' Kate was forced to concede.

'Instead of pursuing far-fetched theories, Doctor, *do* something!'

'Yes, Mrs Stuyvesant.' But do what? Kate asked herself.

Something about this case did not ring true. It revived her suspicion that Claudia was on drugs. Many drugs could be masking or diminishing her pain, concealing from both the patient and the doctor the seriousness of the situation.

Kate drew another blood sample and sent it to the lab for a complete toxic screen. A toxic screen, which takes at least twenty-four hours, would be of no help in making an immediate diagnosis, but might prove valuable in the patient's subsequent treatment.

Despite the negative urine pregnancy test, suspicion continued to nag at Kate. She knew from her own examination that Claudia had been sexually active. Whatever the tension between mother and daughter, Kate decided to pursue her suspicion. She picked up the wall phone and punched in a three-digit extension.

'Radiology? Dr Forrester. I need a sonogram on a patient to run down the possibility of an ectopic pregnancy.'

'You've already determined that she's not pregnant,' Mrs Stuyvesant protested.

Kate ignored the interruption. She heard the X-ray technician say, 'I hope this can wait until tomorrow afternoon.'

'Why tomorrow afternoon?' Kate demanded.

'Sonograms are pretty tricky when it comes to ectopics, so only Dr Gladwin does those. She's not on until tomorrow afternoon.'

Aware that even if done under the best of circumstances and by an experienced professional, sonogram findings were not perfect, Kate hung up. She punched in another extension.

'Lab?' Kate asked. 'This is Dr Forrester in emergency. I just sent a blood specimen to you for a toxic screen. In addition, I want a blood serum pregnancy test.'

'I hope you don't want those results stat,' the lab technician replied. 'Serum pregnancies take special equipment and a special technician. We save them up and do them every few days. I'd say you won't be getting those results for at least a day and a half.'

'Put it through anyhow. The results might be helpful.'

Having ordered the tests, Kate repeated the abdominal examination. To her surprise and alarm she discovered Claudia's abdomen was now distended to the point of being rigid. Kate returned to the phone, but then decided to make this call from the nurses' station. No need to add to Mrs Stuyvesant's mounting anxiety.

'Find Dr Briscoe! Stat! Urgent he come to room C in emergency at once. Repeat! At once!'

Kate waited outside room C to intercept Briscoe and privately inform him of her latest findings. In less than five minutes she was relieved to see him barge through the swinging doors that separated emergency from the main hospital complex.

Briscoe absorbed her reports, then said, 'A long surgical needle. I'll go in and see if there is any internal bleeding.'

They entered the room to find Nurse Cronin taking the patient's blood pressure, now a continuing process. Aware of the patient's nervous mother, Cronin reported softly, 'Pressure's dropping.'

'Add another IV. Then get a long needle for Dr Briscoe,' Kate said as she took over monitoring the blood pressure.

At the mention of the word needle Mrs Stuyvesant asked, 'What are you going to do?'

'Madam, please leave,' Briscoe said. The woman's look defied him. 'Please leave!'

Finally Nora Stuyvesant relented, almost colliding with Cronin, who was returning with the long surgical needle and a hypodermic syringe. While Nurse Cronin resumed blood-pressure monitoring, Briscoe prepared to draw any free blood that would have accumulated in her abdominal cavity if indeed there was any internal bleeding.

Just as he began to insert the needle Cronin called suddenly in an agitated whisper, 'No pulse! She has no pulse!'

At once Kate Forrester and Eric Briscoe went into action. They lifted the patient from the table to a trolley nearby.

'CPR!' Kate ordered. Cronin was quick to comply. With Cronin trailing alongside administering CPR, Kate Forrester and Eric Briscoe hurried the trolley out of the room, past the patient's startled mother, down the corridor to the acute-care room where emergency equipment was available. Mrs Stuyvesant trailed behind, pleading, 'What's wrong? What's happening to my daughter?'

No one could stop to inform her. At the door to the acute-care room, Kate prevented Mrs Stuyvesant from entering, despite her plea, 'She's my daughter. I have a right . . .'

'You'd only be in the way,' Kate said, and closed the door.

Inside acute care, the team of two doctors and three nurses went to work simultaneously. Kate ordered, 'Three IVs. Large infusions of saline and Ringer's lactate to replace her electrolytes. Cronin, continue CPR.' Kate turned to one of the acute-care nurses and said, 'ECG leads!' As the nurse began to affix the sensors to the patient's chest Kate ordered, 'One ampoule epinephrine!' The second acute-care nurse provided the ampoule and the hypodermic. Kate tied a rubber tube round the patient's forearm, found the vein, and injected the epinephrine to stimulate heart action.

Meanwhile, Briscoe took a long plastic tube, opened the patient's mouth, eased the tube carefully past her vocal cords, down her throat, and into her trachea. He affixed a pressure bag and ordered the second nurse, 'Force air!' The nurse took the pressure bag in her hands to forcibly drive air into the patient's lungs, careful not to do so while Cronin was pressing on the patient's chest.

Briscoe turned to the door, opened it and called, 'Juan Castillo!'

From down the corridor came a reply, 'Coming, Doctor.'

'Juan! Type O blood! Four pints! Stat!' Briscoe ordered.

At the mention of blood Mrs Stuyvesant fell back against the wall for support. She was now too frightened to ask or to protest.

Inside the acute-care room, Eric Briscoe joined Kate as she frantically took the patient's blood pressure. Soon it became obvious that despite the signs of heart action on the monitor, medication had not restored the patient's pulse or blood pressure.

'EMD,' Kate was forced to admit in a grim whisper.

EMD—electromechanical dissociation. EMD is a condition in which the heart reflexively continues to pump, but there is no pulse, because there is no longer sufficient blood in the arterial system due to internal haemorrhaging.

'Where the hell is that blood?' Briscoe called.

Moments later Juan arrived with four pints of type O blood. At once Kate set up the transfusion, forcing the life-giving blood into Claudia before her system collapsed completely. But even after the infusion of three pints of blood, there was still no pulse. No pressure. It was obvious that the fresh blood could not replace the blood that she was still losing.

'I'm going in,' Briscoe said. 'Got to tie off that haemorrhage.'

He turned to the cabinet that held the surgical instruments. He pulled on a pair of rubber gloves, then selected a scalpel. While Kate continued to infuse blood, with one nurse forcing air into the patient's lungs and Cronin still applying CPR, Briscoe made a large exploratory incision across the patient's abdomen.

A torrent of fresh bright red blood erupted from the incision. Instinctively Briscoe ordered, 'Suction!' to clear away the blood and give him access to the source of the bleeding. But he realised at once that in acute care there was no suction equipment. He would have to work by feel. He inserted his gloved hands into the wound, searching for the source of the haemorrhage.

After a few minutes Kate was forced to announce, 'No pulse. She has no pulse.' Nevertheless, she continued to feed blood while Cronin continued CPR.

It was Cronin who finally said what both doctors had refused to admit. 'Gone. She's gone.'

'She can't be gone!' Kate protested. 'Just keep going. We'll get her back. We'll get her back!'

Briscoe drew away from the table. 'Forget it, Kate. There's no hope.'

As the nurses ceased their ministrations Kate took over the CPR action from Cronin. With sweat dripping from her face and her blonde hair straggling down, she pressed down on the patient's chest in a desperate, if futile, effort to restore her to life.

'Kate!' Briscoe ordered firmly. 'The patient is gone. There is no chance to revive her. So stop. I said, stop!'

But he had to strip off his bloody gloves and take Kate in his arms to force her away from the table. Once the professional part of her mind took over, she asked, 'Did you discover the cause?'

'I didn't even find the source of the bleeding,' Briscoe admitted.

Nine hours after she was admitted to emergency at City Hospital, forty-five minutes after her pulse had failed, and despite all efforts to revive her, Claudia Stuyvesant, aged nineteen, was dead.

Dead from causes unknown, but which would become known once the mandatory autopsy was performed. According to New York State law, whenever a patient is brought into the emergency service of any hospital and dies within twenty-four hours, an autopsy is required.

'I'd better go out and tell her mother,' Briscoe said.

'No,' Kate said. 'That's my responsibility.' She looked at her young patient, from whom the nurses were now removing all the medical devices that had proved so futile.

Outside the door, it was not necessary for Kate to speak the words. The distraught mother read it in her eyes.

'Killed her! You people killed her!'

'Mrs Stuyvesant, we did everything we could.'

'Everything? Examinations, IVs—you call that treatment?' the distraught mother screamed. 'I bring in a healthy nineteen-year-old with a simple stomach upset, and in hours you kill her. Nineteen years old. With her whole life ahead of her. My child, my only child . . . Claudie . . .'

'Please, Mrs Stuyvesant,' Kate said, reaching out to comfort her.

'Don't you touch me! And don't think you'll get away with this! There are laws to punish doctors like you!'

Despite the woman's threats, Kate felt great compassion for her. 'Mrs Stuyvesant, is there anyone you wish to call?'

The woman glared at her through her tears, her eyes accusing and full of hate. It was Dr Briscoe who finally led her down the corridor towards the bright-red neon sign that announced EMERGENCY.

Mrs Stuyvesant went, weeping and moaning, 'He'll blame me ...
He'll blame me.'

As they passed the admitting desk the nurse in charge rose from her
chair to stare at them until they were gone. She started back along the
corridor towards Kate.

'Dr Forrester, do you know who that was?'

'Mrs Stuyvesant,' Kate replied.

'Doctor, that wasn't just "Mrs Stuyvesant". She is Mrs *Claude*
Stuyvesant,' the nurse informed Kate.

'So she said, more than once,' Kate replied. 'He's big in real estate,
isn't he?'

'In New York he *is* real estate,' the nurse said. 'Plus half a dozen
other industries and a power at city hall and Albany.'

'But where was he when his daughter needed him?' Kate asked
without waiting for an answer.

Numb, exhausted, she went back into the acute-care room. On the
trolley lay the body of young Claudia Stuyvesant, draped in a green
sheet. Kate could not resist lifting it to stare down at the pale face, the
closed eyes, the untidy, damp dark hair of the dead patient. *Her*
patient.

She had failed. The patient had been under her care for nine hours.
She had available to her the resources of a large, well-equipped
modern hospital. Yet she had lost a nineteen-year-old young woman
who had everything to live for.

Eric Briscoe returned from escorting Mrs Stuyvesant to her
limousine. He read the defeat and self-reproach in Kate's eyes. 'Katie,
we all lose some. This one wasn't for lack of trying,' he consoled.

She shook her head.

Briscoe could not resist thinking, If she's taking this so badly now,
it's a good thing she didn't hear all the threats that hysterical mother
made before I could get her into her limo. Poor Kate. I don't think
she's heard the last of this case.

Chapter Four

At dawn, when Dr Kate Forrester completed the chart of the
Stuyvesant case and signed the certificate of death, she was free to
leave for the day.

But first there was another case that made persistent demands on
her professional conscience. She passed through the double doors into

314

the main building of the hospital complex and took the lift up to the paediatric wing. She sought out Dr Harve Golding and found him in his darkened office studying a series of X-rays of the entire body of a small child.

'Harve?' Kate asked.

Without turning from the viewing wall on which the X-ray films were mounted, Golding said, 'Kate, come have a look.'

She drew close to the backlighted glass wall.

'Lady, were you right!' Golding exclaimed. 'Look at those two healed fractures on her left leg.'

'This one, on her right leg, is that the fresh one that I suspected?' Kate asked.

'That's it,' Golding confirmed. 'I'm almost afraid of the results of her brain scan. We need a full neurological evaluation to find out how much permanent damage there is, if any.'

'Poor little Maria,' Kate said. 'How could someone do this?'

'Imagine what would have happened if you'd let them take her home,' Golding said. 'You can be proud of yourself, Kate. You saved a life tonight.'

Saved one, lost one, Kate thought. It may balance out mathematically, but it doesn't feel that way.

'So go home, Katie. Get some sleep,' Golding urged cheerfully. 'You earned it.' Expecting some rejoinder from her, he turned to ask, 'Katie, something wrong?'

'Just a bad night,' Kate said as she left.

MOST EARLY MORNINGS, when Kate came off overnight emergency duty, she would take a cab home to the apartment she shared with Rosalind Chung in a block the hospital had taken over to provide decent living conditions for its young residents and interns. This morning, exhausted though she was, Kate chose to walk. The streets of Manhattan's West Side were still wet from the overnight rain. From across the Hudson a wave of fresh, cool morning air rode in on a strong breeze.

Along Ninth Avenue the trucks were making early deliveries to the small neighbourhood grocery stores, modest little restaurants, meat markets and vegetable markets. The West Side of New York was waking up to another day.

Kate made her way among trucks being unloaded by truckers and helpers. The men greeted her with stares of admiration and occasional exclamations of seemingly sexual proposals.

Coming from a small farm in Illinois, Kate had never quite got used to this form of good-natured bantering that passed among truckmen, taxi drivers, and construction workers in New York. At first she was offended. Later she became amused. Today the death of Claudia Stuyvesant was all she was aware of.

Kate arrived at her front door, unlocked both locks and let herself in, calling, 'Rosie?'

There was no response. Rosie, she remembered, was on clinic duty and wouldn't be home till afternoon. Kate went into her own room and started slipping out of her clothes, then realised that she had not yet run her bath. She turned on the steaming water, finished undressing and was about to step into the bath when she became aware that she was weeping. She brushed back the tears, remembering Claudia Stuyvesant, her pale face, her black hair matted to her forehead in her own final death sweat.

Kate determined to put it behind her. These things happen in medicine. No doctor saves all his cases. A hot bath to calm her, a long, long sleep, and by evening she would be fresh and relaxed.

But once in bed, tired though she was, Kate could not fall asleep. Despite her efforts to blot out the disastrous case, she began to relive every moment of it. She reviewed her initial interview and Claudia's responses, so generalised and eventually misleading. She reviewed every procedure, the IVs, the lab results, the pregnancy test that was clearly negative.

Subtly her mind turned from reviewing the events to explaining, arguing, justifying. If Claudia had been as healthy as she first appeared, she would not have died. Why did that violent haemorrhaging remain hidden from detection?

Briscoe had been there. He had concurred with Kate's observations and conclusions. Or was it more correct to say, lack of conclusions, inability to reach a diagnosis?

No, she was forced to admit, it did not relieve the ache to try to put the blame, or even part of it, on Briscoe. Claudia Stuyvesant had been *her* patient from the outset. If anything went wrong, it was a failure on the part of Dr Kate Forrester.

Kate Forrester, who had always been a star pupil, always first in her class. Always first to raise her hand when the teacher called for volunteers. Kate Forrester, who had gone on from the local high school, with honours, to the University of Illinois, where she accelerated her four-year course into three years in order to gain swifter admittance into medical school. During high school she had volunteered at the local hospital. When she applied to medical school, along with her application went the recommendations of three doctors, all chiefs of various services at the hospital.

Medical school had proved tougher than she had anticipated. That only meant she worked even harder, always looking forward to the time when she would begin to put into use all her accumulated knowledge and experience.

Later she had deliberately chosen one of the biggest and best of the big metropolitan hospitals—City Hospital—for her residency. She wanted to learn from the best physicians and surgeons, wanted to compete against the best and the brightest young physicians and surgeons. It was almost as if she were back at school, waving an eager hand in the face of the teacher, begging, Call on me. I know the answer!

Except that this morning, tormented and unable to sleep, Kate Forrester had to admit to herself, No, I don't know all the answers. I didn't know them last night, when for some undetermined reason a young life slipped through my hands.

Kate tried to console herself. I'm too tired even to think straight, too guilt-ridden to be logical. Sleep. I need sleep.

One persistent question refused to permit it. Did I do everything I recall having done?

The more Kate questioned, the more awake she became. Finally she threw back the covers, determined to go back to the hospital and check out Claudia Stuyvesant's chart to see exactly what she had written there.

SHE ENTERED THE EMERGENCY ROOM from the street side, headed straight to the central desk and began searching the charts.

The Stuyvesant chart was not there. Strange.

Charts went with the patient only when that patient was removed to another service. But the Stuyvesant girl had been removed to the medical examiner's office. The chart would not have gone with her body.

When Kate asked about it, the charge nurse explained, 'Oh, that chart. Dr Cummins sent for it early this morning.'

Dr Cummins? Kate considered. Why would the administrator of the entire hospital take time to look into that particular chart? Cummins is always so involved in fund-raising that even the chiefs of the various services have trouble getting enough of his time. But if he's the man who has it, he's the man I am determined to see.

317

WHEN SHE ARRIVED at Cummins's office, she had the uncomfortable feeling that somehow her arrival had been expected. She was immediately shown into the administrator's impressive panelled office. She found him poring over the chart and making notes. Without looking up, he said, 'Sit down, Dr Forrester.'

Cummins continued his study while Kate waited uncomfortably. When Cummins had finished, he spoke with some relief. 'Good.' He turned his attention to her. 'Now then, Forrester, your notes in this chart seem quite adequate. Thorough, in fact. Of course, there is one thing. From what appears here, there is no reason for the patient to have died. But I'm sure that will be cleared up when we receive the medical examiner's report.'

'May I see that chart?' Kate asked.

'Of course. But I can't allow it to leave my office. If you would like to peruse it out in the waiting room . . .' He held out the chart to her. Before releasing it, he added, 'A very well-written chart, which may be helpful under the circumstances.'

While Cummins's words were phrased in complimentary fashion, the look in his eyes hinted at possible trouble. Kate took the chart and started for the door. There she stopped to ask, 'Dr Cummins, may I ask why you called for this chart?'

'Oh,' Cummins replied, 'didn't I tell you? I received a call early this morning from Claude Stuyvesant. At home, in fact.'

Kate was now doubly anxious to read the chart.

SHE REVIEWED EVERY ENTRY in the chart, every lab report. They reminded her not only what she had done, based on the patient's condition, but also her reason for each modality she had adopted. The only lab reports missing were the toxic screen and the serum pregnancy test, but those would be along later.

Kate came away from Cummins's office greatly reassured. She could justify her every action in the case of Claudia Stuyvesant.

She stopped by the paediatric wing to see how little Maria Sanchez was doing. Golding had gone off duty, so Kate looked in on the small room where the child had been installed. Maria was asleep, peacefully asleep, as if she knew she was now safe.

AT THE MOMENT that Kate Forrester was leaving little Maria's room Dr Cummins was in his office, several floors above, bracing himself for the ordeal ahead. He ordered his secretary, 'Get Claude Stuyvesant on the phone.'

Once his secretary buzzed back, Cummins was truly sympathetic. 'Mr Stuyvesant, I can't tell you how sorry I am about the tragedy that struck your daughter.'

'I should think you would be,' came Claude Stuyvesant's flat, curt response. 'But I didn't call you this morning seeking sympathy. I want to know why my daughter died.'

The sharpness and the directness of Stuyvesant's words confirmed Cummins's worst fears. One of the most influential businessmen and behind-the-scenes political powers in New York City, Stuyvesant was at his most vindictive when he adopted that cold, flat tone.

Damage control, Cummins cautioned himself. He responded in his most ingratiating manner, the one he employed when appealing for huge contributions from the wealthy of the city.

'Mr Stuyvesant, I have spent the past few hours meticulously studying every single detail of your daughter's case. At this moment we don't know why she died, aside from a haemorrhage of undetermined origin.'

'Cummins, what the hell kind of hospital are you running? A patient bleeds to death, and nobody knows why!'

'I'm trying to explain, sir. Dr Forrester handled your daughter's case. According to your daughter's chart, she did everything indicated—'

'She? This Forrester is a woman?' Stuyvesant interrupted.

'Yes,' Cummins replied.

'And I suppose she is on your staff so you can comply with all those damn federal and state regulations that say you've got to have so many women on your staff, so many blacks, so many Hispanics. Whatever happened to the days when a person's *ability* counted for something?'

Harvey Cummins felt sufficiently provoked to dispute Stuyvesant directly. 'Mr Stuyvesant, Katherine Forrester is one of the best-trained young doctors on our staff. I'm telling you, nothing that she did caused your daughter's death.'

'Cummins, *I* know that you have to defend your staff, no matter how negligent they are. But as *you* damn well know, I am very close with several members on your board of trustees. You haven't heard the last of this. Nor has your Dr Forrester!'

Before Cummins could reply, Stuyvesant hung up. After a moment of indecision Cummins ordered, 'Miss Hopkins, please get Judge Trumbull for me.'

Though out of deference to his past service on the bench everyone

319

addressed him as Judge, Lionel Trumbull was a senior partner of the eminent Wall Street law firm of Trumbull, Drummond and Baines. He was regarded as one of the shrewdest and least emotional lawyers in the profession.

After he had heard Cummins's report of his conversation with Claude Stuyvesant, Trumbull said, 'Get that young woman in your office as soon as possible to meet with me. With a man like Claude Stuyvesant we've got to be very very careful. We can be facing a malpractice action that could cost millions. Millions!'

'Lionel, I assure you, I went over the entire chart. There was no malpractice—' Cummins tried to explain.

'With juries these days,' Trumbull interrupted, '*everything* is malpractice. Every cough, every sneeze is the basis of a costly lawsuit. To say nothing of the damage Stuyvesant can do to the hospital and its reputation. I want to see that young woman!'

AT TWO O'CLOCK ON MONDAY afternoon, precisely as ordered, Kate Forrester presented herself at Dr Cummins's office. She found the administrator seated at the head of a conference table that occupied one end of the large room. She was surprised to find another man, long past middle age, bald except for a fringe of greying hair. His ruddy face was dour, as if in judgment.

'Forrester, this is Judge Trumbull, counsel to the hospital.'

Mention of the word counsel made Kate aware that this meeting was not the medical consultation she had anticipated. Suddenly Mrs Stuyvesant's threats of two nights ago became more real.

'Sit down, Forrester. Please sit down,' Cummins urged.

'This has to do with the Stuyvesant case, doesn't it?' Kate asked as she slipped into a chair across the table from Trumbull.

'Yes,' Cummins admitted sadly.

'Cummins, I think you ought to acquaint Dr Forrester with the seriousness of the situation,' said Judge Trumbull. 'She might want to take steps.'

'Take steps?' Kate asked, puzzled. 'What kind of steps?'

'Doctor,' Trumbull replied. 'As counsel to the hospital, my firm will undertake your defence. But in a situation like this, some doctors like to retain their own counsel.'

'Defence? Against what?' Kate demanded.

'Dr Forrester, being from the Midwest, the name Stuyvesant may have no particular significance for you,' Cummins said.

'I know he's big in real estate,' Kate replied.

' "Big in real estate" is a very modest way of putting it,' Cummins said. 'The man owns gambling casinos in Atlantic City and Las Vegas, hotels in a dozen cities, enough office buildings here to comprise his own city.'

'What's that to do with me?' Kate asked.

'The man has power—financial, social, especially political. It's been said no man can be elected mayor of this city without the backing of Claude Stuyvesant. If he feels his daughter's case was mishandled, he might retaliate in some way.'

Trumbull added, 'My firm's had dealings with him in the past. Knowing him, a malpractice suit is a certainty.'

'I did everything I could for his daughter,' Kate protested.

'I believe that. Dr Cummins believes that,' Trumbull said. 'But we have to be prepared to prove it to a jury.'

'And we will prove it,' Kate stated indignantly.

'A good reason to consider what I said. While Trumbull, Drummond and Baines stands ready to defend you, you may wish to employ counsel of your own.'

'Lawyers cost money,' Kate replied. 'And I'm still in debt after paying for my med school education.'

'Then depend on my firm,' Trumbull reassured. 'Meantime, do not discuss this case with anyone except the man or woman I appoint to be your lawyer. You never know when you are making some perfectly innocent statement that may one day be used against you.'

'I did nothing wrong,' Kate declared. 'And I can prove it. When do I see that lawyer?'

'My secretary will call you to arrange a time,' Trumbull said.

KATE FORRESTER CAME AWAY from the interview angry but also shaken by the threat that Trumbull had made so plain. All the way back to her apartment her resentment continued to grow. It wasn't fair. Not after all her sacrifices, after how hard she had worked, her years of study. It wasn't fair that some man, of whose existence she had hardly been aware, could suddenly loom up in her life and threaten her.

She thrust open the door to the apartment and heard Rosalind call from the shower, 'That you, Kate?'

'Yes, Rosie,' she replied in a voice so desolate that her room-mate came out of the shower to ask what had happened.

'They're giving me a lawyer,' Kate said. 'They seem sure there'll be a malpractice suit.'

'Malpractice?' Rosie echoed angrily. 'The hours we work. The conditions. *We* should be the ones suing!' Then, realising that solace and encouragement, not anger, would serve Kate best, she embraced her. 'Don't look so down, sweetie. There isn't a resident or a doctor on that staff who won't go to bat for you. We'd love to air our gripes in a courtroom. Look, I just made a fresh batch of coffee. Like some?'

Kate nodded vaguely. What her room-mate had intended as encouragement had become an added burden. Kate did not want her situation to become a cause. She would much prefer the whole thing to blow over quietly, so she could get on with her career.

As Rosie handed her a steaming cup Kate said, 'I keep thinking . . .'

'Stop thinking,' Rosie advised. 'There isn't a doctor alive who hasn't had a case like this. Patients will die. Dying is the price of living. And the way it happens doesn't always make scientific sense, like it does in our medical textbooks.'

Kate tried to sip her coffee but instead shook her head slowly. 'I have to call home and tell them.'

'Can't it wait until things become clarified?' Rosie suggested.

'Do you mean clarified? Or worse?' Kate responded. 'No. I'll call. Dad has a right to know. After all, he sold off part of his acreage to help pay for my tuition.' She glanced at her watch. 'Dad'll be coming in from the fields about now for his dinner.'

Kate moved to the phone, near the end of the couch. She could picture the scene in the Forrester kitchen, back home in southern Illinois: Dad at the head of the table, flanked on each side by his farmhands and her brother, Clint. Mom bringing to the table steaming bowls of stew and two loaves of her own baked bread.

Kate punched in the phone number. She heard the ring. Twice, three times, four. The sixth ring was interrupted.

'Hello?' she heard her mother say.

'Ma, it's me.'

'Katie!' Her mother was delighted to recognise her voice, but was cautious as well. 'Anything wrong, darling?'

'Nothing. Nothing's wrong,' Kate denied. She would have preferred not to start the conversation on this note.

'You, calling long distance when telephone rates are high, and nothing's wrong?' her mother asked.

'Is Dad there? Can I talk to him?'

Now her mother knew there was trouble. It showed in her voice. 'Yes, darling, I'll put him right on.'

Kate waited a moment, then heard her dad clear his throat.

'Dad?'

'Yes, sweetheart. Nice to hear your voice again. Since you got on that emergency service you don't call as often as you should.'

He's making small talk, Kate realised, trying to sound relaxed for my sake. But he senses it's serious. I'd better tell him.

She gave him a brief layman's description of the situation. In the background Kate could hear her mother asking, 'What is it, Ben? What's Katie saying?' She could picture her mother standing beside her dad, just about reaching up to his shoulder when she was on tiptoe. Kate had inherited her dad's blond hair and her mom's tiny frame—the best of both, they used to say.

When Kate finished recounting her situation, Ben Forrester said, 'Would it help if I come east?'

'No, Dad. We're not even sure yet that anything's going to happen. I was just calling to let you know,' Kate explained. 'This Claude Stuyvesant, he's a very important man in New York.'

'You tell that "important" bastard, he does anything to my little girl, I'll come east and put a notch or two in his important hide!'

'Nothing's going to happen to me,' Kate promised. She had not intended to alarm him, but obviously she had. 'Just relax, Dad, and I'll keep you informed.'

'You do that,' he said. Then he added, 'You know, I think about it often—What in the world are you doing in a place like New York anyhow? People hereabout could use a good doctor. And they'd appreciate her a lot more than those savages. Think about coming home, settling down here among your own people.'

'I'm not planning on coming home, Dad,' Kate said. 'I'm staying and fighting.'

'You're forgetting how people around here think of you, Katie. Can't go into town without someone stopping to ask, "And how's our Kate doing?" It's like you belong to the whole town. When I told them you'd been accepted into that City Hospital, they weren't surprised. They just took it naturally that you'd be accepted into the biggest and the best. If you have to, you face up to that bastard Stuyvesant. Let him have both barrels, you hear?'

'Yes, Dad, I hear,' Kate said.

Kate hung up even more depressed than she had been. In his effort to encourage her, her dad had laid on her the added burden of living up to the opinion of her friends and neighbours back home.

That lawyer, got to see that lawyer.

323

Chapter Five

Accustomed as she was to large universities and hospitals, Kate Forrester had never before entered offices as imposing as those of the law firm of Trumbull, Drummond and Baines. The reception room was on the sixth of the eleven floors the firm occupied. Kate asked for Scott Van Cleve, the name she had been given by Judge Trumbull's secretary. The receptionist summoned a page, who led Kate from the sixth floor down to the second floor, past a number of large, well-furnished partners' suites, to a group of smaller, less imposing offices. At the end of a long, carpeted hallway he led her into a small office, then left. The office was in such haphazard condition that she felt sure no one with a sane, orderly mind inhabited it. There were law books scattered across the desk, as well as piled on the floor. There were three yellow legal pads on the desk, with notes scrawled on them. On one corner of the desk was a half-eaten sandwich and a cup of coffee that had gone cold.

Kate suspected now that her case had been handed to one of the less able lawyers in Trumbull's firm. She was debating leaving when suddenly a tall young man burst into the room. He was obviously surprised to find her.

'Oh!' he blurted out with some annoyance, as if she had intruded on his train of thought. 'You're . . . uh . . .' He tried to recall. 'Are you the doctor person?'

Stifling a quick and angry retort, Kate replied, 'Yes. Are you the lawyer "person" I was supposed to see?'

His worried frown relaxed into a smile. 'Sorry. I'm Scott Van Cleve,' he started to say. 'But then you know my name, else you wouldn't have asked for me. And yours is . . .'

Kate realised, He doesn't even know my name, that's how unfamiliar he is with my situation. I ought to leave.

But she decided at least to hear what this harried young man had to say. At the same time, she made her doctor's diagnosis of him. He was lean, in apparently good health. His eating habits were bad, as witness that half-eaten sandwich, but that could also mean he was extremely conscientious about his profession. He was very tall. His hair was dark, not quite black.

She was in the midst of her diagnosis when he caught her off guard with a brisk 'OK, let's get started!' He cleared all books and pads to one side of his desk, then opened a drawer to take out a fresh legal

pad. He fumbled for her name once more. 'Doctor . . . ?'

'Kate Forrester.'

'OK, Dr Forrester, let's get started. First I feel it is my duty to explain your legal situation. We expect that there will be a malpractice action against the hospital. And against you, personally.'

'I thought the hospital's insurance protects all staff doctors,' Kate replied.

'Protects, yes,' Van Cleve said. 'Immunises, no.'

The frown of concern on her face made the young attorney realise that in so far as her legal situation was concerned, Kate Forrester was a complete novice.

'Doctor, if there is a malpractice suit, the attorneys will sue everybody connected with the case. The reason for that is, they don't know how the jury will react. They may hold the hospital liable because of hospital rules and practice. Or they may hold the doctors personally liable—'

'What good is malpractice insurance if it doesn't protect the doctor?' Kate interrupted.

'It does protect the doctor—within limits. It provides your legal defence and pays any verdict for damages within limits. But if the amount of the jury's verdict exceeds the policy coverage, then the hospital and the doctors become liable for the difference.'

'You mean I could be personally liable, that for the rest of my career . . . ?' Kate said while trying to comprehend.

'I thought you should know the potential danger you face in this situation,' Van Cleve said as gently as he could.

'Yes,' Kate said in a soft voice. 'Yes, of course.'

'Now that you do, let's proceed. I would like to hear your version of what happened.'

'My first contact with the patient was at about nine o'clock Saturday night . . .' Kate went on to recount in sequence everything she could recall without having the patient's chart in front of her. Van Cleve listened, from time to time scribbling a note or two on his yellow pad.

Once she had completed her recitation of the events, Van Cleve nodded reflectively. 'Until the patient's collapse, what had been your best diagnosis?'

'A probable stomach virus,' Kate replied.

'If I questioned six doctors, presented them with the same set of symptoms—'

'And signs,' Kate corrected.

326

'Symptoms . . . signs . . . What's the difference?'

'Symptoms are what the patient describes. Signs are what the doctor discovers and observes. Then she puts the two together to arrive at a diagnosis,' Kate explained.

'Thank you, Doctor,' said the young attorney. 'Now let me repeat: if I examined six doctors under oath, presented to them the same symptoms *and signs* as you described, what would their opinions be?'

'The same, I'm sure. Viral stomach disorder,' Kate said.

Van Cleve made a note on his pad. 'Did Dr Briscoe concur?'

'Not in so many words,' Kate said. 'But he didn't find any other cause. Those symptoms—nausea, vomiting, diarrhoea, stomach pain—could signify many conditions. Inflamed appendix. Pregnancy. Ulcers. The process of diagnosis is to test for and exclude each of the possibilities until you arrive at the right one,' Kate said.

'Which, unfortunately, you never did,' Van Cleve pointed out.

'Medicine is not an exact science!' Kate shot back defensively.

'Which is going to be our problem,' Van Cleve said grimly. 'Patients—and juries consist of patients—assume that medicine *is* perfect. That if something goes wrong, it must be the fault of the doctor. We start there and try to fight it. We don't always win.'

Kate nodded gravely.

'That will be all for our first meeting, Doctor.'

Kate rose and turned to the door.

'Oh,' Van Cleve called, 'one further word of warning. Stuyvesant will not only have the best negligence lawyers prosecuting his case, he will also have the sympathetic ear of every judge and every other city or state official who might be helpful.'

'That may be, but I still believe that the truth is my best defence,' Kate insisted.

'Right now, young woman, your best defence is that City Hospital, their insurance company and our law firm are all involved in this case. They'll spend lots of money to defend themselves, which means they'll be defending you. On your own, such a defence would put you in debt for the rest of your life. You'll hear from me, Doctor.'

LATER THAT DAY, after Scott Van Cleve reported on the conference with his new client, Judge Trumbull placed a call to Dr Cummins.

'Harvey,' the lawyer began. 'Just to keep you up to date. One of our junior associates, Van Cleve, met with your Dr Forrester. Nothing unusual turned up.'

'Which doesn't surprise me,' Cummins said.

'However,' Trumbull warned, 'it might be a good idea, for the present, to limit Dr Forrester's activities.'

'Limit her activities?' Cummins said. 'She is a well-qualified resident, and we can use all the staff we have.'

'Harvey, we might at some future time have to justify your hospital's conduct—'

Cummins interrupted. 'There was nothing wrong with this hospital's conduct. Or with Dr Forrester's, as far as we know.'

'Exactly, Harvey. "As far as we know",' Trumbull pointed out.

'I wouldn't want to take any step that might reflect on Dr Forrester's professional competence,' Cummins insisted.

'I'm not advising anything like that. Just remove her from patient contact for the present time, but do it quietly. The one thing we can't risk right now is bad publicity.'

KATE FORRESTER ROSE EARLIER than necessary the next morning. She planned to arrive at the hospital before her scheduled time to report for her new assignment. The sight of little Maria Sanchez, half conscious, bearing the bruised evidence of her suffering, had made a lasting impression on Kate. She was planning to stop by to see if the child was making any progress.

Maria had been consigned to the care of Dr Nate Sperber, a specialist in neonatal and paediatric neurological problems. Though Kate had had no previous contact with him, Sperber had obviously heard of her.

'Do I have the honour of meeting the new lightweight champ of the hospital world?' Sperber asked when she appeared in the doorway of Maria's room during his examination.

'I don't understand.'

'Golding told me about your standing up to this poor kid's old man. Good thing. She's on the borderline. One more episode, and I wouldn't give you a dime for her chances.'

'And now?' Kate asked.

Sperber beckoned Kate into the room. As she drew close to the bed he took Kate's hand and pressed it against the child's face. The child drew back, seeming to shrivel. But slowly she reacted to Kate's soft, warm hand by reaching out to grip her forefinger.

'Forrester, do something for me? Just pick her up and hold her in your arms. We've got to start teaching her that not all adults are dangerous. That it is safe to trust.'

Kate settled onto the bed and lifted the child into her arms. Little

Maria resisted, then gradually gave herself to Kate's embrace. After a time she seemed content to rest against her breast.

'Good,' Sperber said. 'Now do that several times a day, even for a few minutes. Maybe in time we can win her back to a normal life.'

'Her neurological condition?' Kate asked.

'Still in the evaluation process. I see signs of hope. But only signs,' Sperber said.

KATE FORRESTER WAS A LITTLE LATE when she consulted the assignment list on the medical staff bulletin board. She did not find her name assigned to one of the clinics or to patient duties. Instead, she noted that alongside her name—'Forrester, K.'—appeared the words 'Dept. Clinical Effectiveness. Dr Nicholas Troy, Room B-22.' Puzzled as she was, Kate had no choice but to comply with her assignment.

Room B-22 was in the basement of the hospital complex. Though Troy's office was spacious, it impressed Kate as cramped, due to its large old-fashioned computers and the number of tall filing cabinets. Troy himself, who seemed to be in his late sixties or older, was studying a computer printout that started on the far side of his desk and hung down in his lap. His hair was white, wispy and in disarray. He spoke to Kate without looking up.

'Yes?' he asked impatiently.

'I'm Dr Katherine Forrester. I'm assigned to your department for the present.'

'Aha!' he exclaimed in recognition. 'Cummins spoke to me about you. What horrible crime did you commit that they assigned you to Siberia? For a young doctor this department of mine, concerned with mere dry facts and figures, must be exile.'

He looked up from his printout to study Kate. 'H'mm,' he said, greatly impressed. 'If I had met a doctor like you in my youth, I would not now be a crusty old bachelor.'

Troy gestured Kate to be seated, then realised there was no empty chair. He cleared one for her by lifting a pile of printouts off a chair and dropping them onto the floor. 'What do you say to a cup of tea?' he asked. 'I know I could use one.'

Kate nodded.

While waiting for water to boil in the pot on his hot plate, Troy admitted, 'Forrester, I have a confession to make. I heard about your situation.' Then as he dipped a tea bag into the steaming water he continued. 'That's why you are here. Because you might be tainted, they don't want you upstairs in emergency or in clinic or on the wards. After all, if you were to suffer another accident, the insurance company would blame the hospital for keeping you on.'

'Then why don't they let me go?' Kate asked.

'If they let you go now, that *would* be a public admission that you were incompetent. Which could mean they were at fault for hiring you in the first place. So they can't let you go.'

'I'll quit!' Kate threatened, half rising from her chair.

'That really would be an admission of guilt. And you don't look to me like a woman who got this far by quitting. As I understand it, you followed all the correct procedures in your treatment of the Stuyvesant girl.' He stared at her for a moment. 'You *did*, didn't you?'

'Yes, I did. My entries in the patient's chart prove that,' Kate said.

'Stay and fight, then,' Troy said. 'Meantime, work here.' He smiled. 'Look, my dear, what is one week or one month out of your life? Just think what it will mean to an old man to come in here every morning to see your lovely face. Now drink your tea, and let's go to work!'

NEWS OF THE DEATH of Claude Stuyvesant's only child had been featured by all the local newspapers and television news programmes. For two days the switchboard of City Hospital had been flooded with calls from the media.

Public information officer Claire Hockaday responded to all questions with only a single, terse, prepared statement:

This past Saturday night Claudia Stuyvesant was brought to the emergency service of this hospital with an undiagnosed illness. She died Sunday morning from causes unknown at this time.

Left to their own imaginative devices, each local television news department played the story from a different angle. One channel hinted that Claudia's death was due to a drug overdose. Another suggested it was suicide. By the third day, under the relentless torrent of rapes, muggings and murder that is daily fare on New York television, most stations had dropped the story.

Only Hank Daniels, editor of the six-o'clock evening news at Channel 3, regarded it with more than passing interest. For some days Daniels and his investigative reporter, Ramon Gallante, had been accumulating a revealing series of interviews on health care in the New York area.

Gallante had taped conversations with a score of disappointed patients, surviving relatives and disgruntled employees in several city hospitals. He had prodded them to reveal the faults, shortcomings, high costs and wasteful practices in various health institutions. But neither Gallante nor Daniels was satisfied that any of those interviews was strong enough to hold an audience for a week-long series.

'Ray,' Daniels said. 'Do you think we could wangle an interview with Claude Stuyvesant?'

'He's a tough interview unless he's got one of his blockbuster deals to announce. Then *he* sends for *you*.'

'What if we can make *sure* he'll send for you?' Daniels asked.

'Hank, you got an angle?' Gallante asked, tempted.

'Two days ago Channel Two labelled Claudia Stuyvesant's death due to "suspicious circumstances". Which could mean suicide. And Channel Four called her death "sudden and due to circumstances as yet unexplained, which are awaiting further testing". Which hints that she OD'd.'

'Gotcha, Hank,' Gallante said. 'I call Stuyvesant to give him a chance to refute the slanders being cast upon his innocent daughter, who is now unable to defend her reputation.'

'We are serving the highest cause of good journalism by helping to set the record straight,' Daniels agreed.

'I'll get on it right away,' Gallante promised.

'Get that, and I've got a great follow-up.'

'Such as?'

'Nothing like a little controversy to draw a crowd and raise ratings. Once we have Stuyvesant on tape, I call City Hospital and—'

'Give them equal time,' Gallante supplied, smiling broadly. 'Hank, what a kickoff to the series!'

BY QUARTER PAST FOUR on Wednesday afternoon, Ramon Gallante and his crew had returned from Claude Stuyvesant's office to the studios of Channel 3.

'How'd it go, Ray?' Daniels asked.

'Controversy, Hank? Did you say controversy? Well, I've got it. So hot that on the way back I stopped at City Hospital and shot some exterior footage.'

'Can I call City Hospital and ask them to set the record straight?'

'Call them, call them,' Gallante said.

From the excitement in Gallante's voice Daniels knew that the interview with Stuyvesant had more than justified his hunch. With considerable satisfaction he lifted his phone.

'Maggie, get me Dr Cummins at City Hospital.'

THE NEXT MORNING Dr Kate Forrester reported to the basement office of Dr Troy. She found him in his usual condition—desk piled high with computer printouts, wispy hair in disarray.

'Good morning, Doctor,' she said.

The weariness in her voice made him glance at her over the rims of his reading glasses. 'Had a bad night?'

'No, not really,' Kate said, attempting to deny it.

'Insufficient sleep, eh?' Another look, and he changed his diagnosis. 'No sleep at all. Tossing, turning, wondering what they are going to decide at the meeting this morning—'

Kate interrupted. 'Meeting? What meeting?'

'Oh,' Troy replied, flustered, 'I thought you knew. They are holding a special meeting of the medical board of the hospital.'

'To discuss my case?' Kate asked.

He shrugged sadly.

'Without my having a chance to defend myself? We'll see about that!' she declared as she started out of the door.

ROUND THE CONFERENCE TABLE, Dr Harvey Cummins had assembled the chiefs of each department of the medical staff for an emergency meeting. Aware that their decision might involve legal consequences, he had also invited Lionel Trumbull.

With a grave air Cummins opened the meeting. 'Gentlemen and ladies, what I hoped might be contained as an in-house embarrassment threatens now to break into a public scandal. Channel Three is starting a series called *It's Your Life: What Are Your Chances of Survival in a New York City Hospital?*'

Dr Eleanor Knolte, chief of paediatrics, remarked acerbically, 'So they've latched onto the Stuyvesant case, have they?'

'Worse,' Cummins said. 'Yesterday I received a call from the producer. Ramon Gallante has taped an interview with Claude Stuyvesant about his daughter's case. Gallante plans to start his series with that interview this evening on the six-o'clock news. Gallante's producer called only to find out if we wished to respond. That is the decision to be made at this meeting.'

There was an immediate outpouring of opinions for and against responding to whatever charges Stuyvesant might make.

Professor emeritus, Dr Solomon Freund, who had once been chief of neurology and who had recently announced his retirement, waited for Cummins to restore order before he spoke. 'Ladies and gentlemen, let me point out that before we make any decision, we need to discover the cause of the girl's death. There's been no autopsy report yet. I think it would be ill-advised to say anything to anybody until we know the facts.'

'You mean,' Harold Wildman, chief of thoracic surgery, asked, 'you would let a powerful man like Claude Stuyvesant accuse this hospital of whatever he likes and not refute him?'

'I mean,' Freund replied, 'that until we know the facts, we don't embarrass ourselves by making statements that might turn out to be untrue. I say, make no response.'

Lionel Trumbull presented his opinion. 'Doctors, sometimes it does more harm than good to reply to charges of this nature. Replies call forth refutations and endless bad publicity. I suggest we watch Stuyvesant's interview. Then if we do decide to reply, someone goes on television to report on the number of cases we treat each year in emergency—the number of patients who go home cured or helped—so that we present to the television audience a record of good, effective emergency health care.'

Trumbull's advice appeared to go down well with all those round the table.

'Then I take it,' Cummins said, 'the consensus of this meeting is, if we respond, it will be a fact-filled reply, making no attempt to get into a dogfight with Stuyvesant.'

'Do I also take it,' Dr Freund asked, 'that you plan no defence of Dr Forrester at this time?'

Cummins replied at once. 'This hospital stands behind its staff! And it will do so in Dr Forrester's case.'

'In fact,' Trumbull added, 'she has already met with the attorney, in my office, who is preparing her defence.'

'As long as she is being protected,' Freund said with some relief, 'I agree with the consensus here.'

'Good,' Cummins said.

By the time Kate Forrester arrived at Cummins's waiting room, the meeting had broken up. When she asked to see the administrator, she was shown in immediately.

'Dr Cummins, did that meeting you just held have to do with me?'

'In a small way, yes,' Cummins said.

'Then I'd like to know what was decided,' Kate said. 'It's the least I'm entitled to.'

'You are also entitled to know that this evening at six o'clock on Channel Three, Claude Stuyvesant will be interviewed about his daughter's death.'

'Stuyvesant intends to make a public issue of this?'

'You didn't think he'd keep quiet about it, did you? A man with his prestige and power?'

'Do you know if he'll attack me?' Kate asked.

'We have no idea what he'll say, but we'll all be a lot smarter after six tonight.'

Chapter Six

Dr Kate Forrester sat alone before the television set in her apartment watching the local news with impatient anxiety. She endured a weatherman who made bad jokes and a sports reporter who made even worse ones. Finally, the anchorwoman announced, 'And now, *It's Your Life*, the opening segment of Ramon Gallante's investigative series about health care in New York City. Ramon.'

The camera cut to Ramon Gallante, microphone in hand, standing before City Hospital. In the background, nurses and other hospital personnel were leaving and arriving.

'I am standing outside City Hospital, regarded by many as one of the most prestigious providers of health care in the metropolitan area. It contains the best, latest and most expensive equipment, plus a carefully selected staff, supposedly one of the finest available anywhere. And yet, how good is it, really? Good enough for you to entrust *your* life to? Or your child's life?'

While Gallante's voice continued, the TV picture dissolved to Stuyvesant Tower, on Wall Street. The camera moved in on Gallante, who stood before that building.

'Now I stand before another edifice in the Manhattan skyline— mighty Stuyvesant Tower, a landmark in the financial capital of the world. Not many of you will ever enter this enclave of the rich and powerful. I do so now only to meet Claude J. Stuyvesant, the man whose name graces this monument of glass and steel. And to hear the tragic story of one father's experience with City Hospital.'

As Gallante turned and pretended to enter the building the picture dissolved to Claude Stuyvesant, seated behind his huge desk. A tall, muscular man, he had a ruddy complexion that testified to many hours spent on the open sea commanding his yacht in transoceanic races. Behind him was a wall of glass, beyond which stretched the vast harbour of New York City.

'Mr Stuyvesant,' Gallante began. 'Your daughter, Claudia, was not exactly the typical patient who is brought into the emergency service of a city hospital, was she?'

'I suppose people expect that when a Stuyvesant becomes ill, a whole retinue of expensive doctors is available day and night. It just so happens that our family physician was out of town on the night in question. Which is no excuse for what happened to my daughter.' Stuyvesant now spoke with great emotion. 'You bring up a child for nineteen years, and in one night they kill her. Murder! It was no less than murder.'

'Mr Stuyvesant, surely you don't mean that the staff of City Hospital conspired to kill your daughter?'

'Conspired? No. But I do hold them responsible. They put my daughter into the hands of a woman doctor ... a woman named Forrester. Katherine Forrester.' Claude Stuyvesant's tightly muscled jaw, his vengeful grey eyes, his very posture projected hatred.

Alone in her living room, hearing this man denounce her in such vehement terms, Kate Forrester rose from her chair, enraged, but at the same time hurt almost to the point of tears.

'Mr Stuyvesant, have they yet determined the nature of your daughter's death?' Gallante asked.

'No. That must await the autopsy,' Stuyvesant replied. 'You have no idea ... the pain, the grief of a father when his innocent young daughter is lying in a vault at the medical examiner's office, waiting to be cut open to find the cause of her death. And to think it could have been avoided by proper medical treatment.'

'Do you think it's fair to make such a statement, sir, without knowing more about the case?' Gallante prodded.

'Fair?' Stuyvesant countered. 'In this case the facts are apparent. A young woman of nineteen, with a simple pain in the stomach, is treated in a city hospital and dies within a matter of hours.'

'Then I take it, sir, you are suing for malpractice?'

'That's the only way to get the hospitals in this city to toe the mark! Sue them. Let them know there is a price for negligence. And arrogance. That young woman was arrogant as well as negligent,' Stuyvesant accused.

'Then you will be suing her as well?' Gallante asked.

'Suing her will be the least of what I do to her,' Stuyvesant said. 'I want that woman forbidden to practise medicine in this city, in this state, anywhere, ever again!'

'And just how does one do that?' Gallante asked.

'My lawyers told me to make a complaint to the state health

commissioner and have the case reviewed by the state board of professional medical conduct. Once the facts are presented to them, I promise you, they will remove that woman's licence.'

'Thank you, sir,' Gallante said.

The moment the interview was over, Kate turned to the phone and punched in Scott Van Cleve's phone number.

Van Cleve sounded detached as he said, 'Hello?'

'It's me, Dr Kate Forrester. Who goes around killing patients.'

'Oh, you saw it,' Van Cleve said.

'Yes, I saw it. What are we going to do about it?'

'For the time being, nothing,' Van Cleve said.

'But the public should know the truth,' Kate replied. 'I want to tell them. After all, I was the doctor involved.'

'Exactly! And because you were, you're too emotional about it. Gallante's liable to trap you into blurting out something that hurts our case, or worse, something that slanders Stuyvesant. Then Stuyvesant turns round and sues you again. To him that would be an amusing hobby which would cripple you financially for ever.'

Kate had not even begun to consider such consequences. 'But if his charges—' she started to say.

'We will refute his charges in the only two places that count. In a courtroom if there's a malpractice trial. And if you do have a hearing, before the state board. Meantime, let's wait for that autopsy report.'

'All right, then. I'll do it your way,' she conceded reluctantly.

After Kate hung up, she continued to sit in front of the darkened TV, thinking about Stuyvesant's outrageous charges.

Before long she heard the front door being unlocked and heard Rosie Chung call, 'Kate, you here?'

Kate looked up as Rosie came into the living room.

'I saw the whole thing on TV,' Rosie said, 'then got right into a cab and came home.' She embraced Kate. 'Don't you worry, sweetie. The whole staff is outraged. There's talk among the residents of chipping in to hire you a lawyer.'

'I already have a lawyer,' Kate pointed out.

'I mean a lawyer that you pay, who's responsible to you alone,' Rosie said. 'You can sue Stuyvesant for slander and libel.'

'Sure, I sue Stuyvesant. It takes five years for the case to come to court. But no amount of money in this world is going to buy back those five years of my life. Something's got to be done. And I've got to do it. By myself. For myself.'

'Do what, Katie?'

'Tell the whole city what really happened. On television,' Kate said with determination.

'I think you ought to talk to that lawyer first.'

'I already did,' Kate admitted. 'He told me to do nothing.'

'Then maybe that's what you ought to do,' Rosie cautioned.

'Oh, sure,' Kate scoffed, suddenly angry. 'It's very easy for him to give *me* that advice. It's not *his* reputation, not *his* career that's on the line. It's mine! The people of this city should know the truth. And I'm the only one who can tell them.'

Kate looked up the number in the phone book while Rosie warned, 'Katie, you might be making matters worse.'

But Kate was already punching in the number. In moments an operator responded, 'Station WNYO—Channel Three.'

'Ramon Gallante, please.'

'Mr Gallante does not take calls.'

'Then let me talk to the producer of the six-o'clock news.'

In moments a harried, irritable voice came on the line. 'Daniels. Who is this, and what do you want?'

'I'm Dr Katherine Forrester.'

'Look, if you're calling to complain about the Stuyvesant interview, we do not *make* the news. We only report it. The man had a legitimate gripe about a subject on which Gallante is currently doing an investigative series. We thought the interview was pertinent, so we used it. That's it. Now, I've got to go.'

'You mean you won't give me a chance to explain the doctor's side of things?' Kate asked.

Daniels's voice changed from harried and aggressive to interested and alert. 'You mean come on camera and explain?'

'Yes!'

'Let me have your number. I'll have Gallante get back to you.'

It didn't take more than three minutes for Kate's phone to ring.

'Dr Forrester? Gallante here. I understand you'd like to refute the accusations Stuyvesant made against you.'

'Yes, I would.'

'Doctor, in all fairness,' Gallante continued, 'we would like to present you, as we did Mr Stuyvesant, in your normal working background—at the hospital, in emergency preferably.'

'Thanks to your interview with Mr Stuyvesant, I have a feeling the hospital won't allow that.'

'Then what about outside the hospital? I can have a remote truck and crew there tomorrow evening, and we could do it live.'

'As long as I have a chance to respond to that totally unwarranted attack on my reputation,' Kate agreed.

'Good! See you outside City Hospital. Quarter to six.'

'I'll be there,' Kate assured him.

As Kate hung up the phone Rosie said, 'Katie, I hope this isn't a mistake.'

'Somebody has to stop this poison from spreading,' she said.

SEVERAL TIMES during the following day Channel 3 exploited Kate's appearance to the full. It ran teaser promotion announcements promising 'a surprise guest on Ramon Gallante's series on health care in New York City'. Starting at five o'clock, the announcements promised 'a live interview with the doctor whom Claude Stuyvesant has accused of killing his daughter'.

Word filtered through City Hospital quickly. Before six o'clock the news had reached administrator Cummins. Immediately he had his secretary page Kate Forrester to caution her against her appearance, but she had already left the hospital. Cummins was resigned to watching her interview on television.

In other parts of the hospital, those people not actively engaged in patient care were staring down from the windows at Gallante's remote crew, which was setting up across the street. Gallante himself directed the two cameras on the angles he wanted.

'We'll open with the hospital full on camera one. Then cut to camera two for my close-up. I'll do my intro and the lead-in. Then move back enough to include that woman doctor.'

He turned away from the cameramen so quickly that he collided with Kate. Pulling back, he said, 'Look, lady, we're filming here, so please move it!'

'Mr Gallante? I'm Dr Forrester,' Kate said.

'You're the infamous Dr Forrester? I thought lady doctors looked this pretty and this blonde only on TV soap operas. Pleased to meet you.' He shook his head in disbelief. 'Let's go over a few questions so you can be prepared with your answers.'

'Right,' Kate said.

'Mr Stuyvesant came on to complain about his daughter's treatment at this hospital, which resulted in her death. That's the first thing I'll say. Then you are free to respond. After that, I have a few questions about health care at this hospital. Comment on that any way you like. This is a freewheeling interview. But keep talking. One thing we have no time for on TV news is pauses.'

338

'I do not intend to pause,' Kate said, determined to make use of every second of airtime Gallante would grant her.

'OK. Stand by for the news from the studio; then we'll get our cue, and we'll be on.'

Gallante watched the start of the news on the monitor in the back of the truck before he came out to join Kate. He posed her against the background of the hospital. Microphone in hand, he stood braced for his cue. The woman who worked camera one threw him a signal.

'Ramon Gallante here at City Hospital, as we continue our investigative series *It's Your Life*. With me this evening is Dr Kate Forrester, whom Claude Stuyvesant holds responsible for the death of his nineteen-year-old daughter, Claudia, in the emergency room of this very hospital. Dr Forrester is here to respond to Mr Stuyvesant's charges. Doctor?'

'Mr Stuyvesant's charges against me and against this hospital are totally false and groundless. Everything that could be done for his daughter was done, in accordance with the best medical practice.'

'But she did die, didn't she, Doctor?'

'Yes. But no one knows why.'

'She was here for nine hours, treated with the latest medical techniques, but she dies and no one knows why?'

'Claudia Stuyvesant did not present sufficient signs and symptoms to enable a physician to make a definite diagnosis.'

'In this whole large hospital not a single doctor was able to make a diagnosis?' Gallante asked.

'*I* was in charge. *I* was not able to make a diagnosis,' Kate replied. 'And I doubt any other doctor could have done so. There simply weren't enough facts and definitive lab findings.'

'Doctor, you say you couldn't make a diagnosis on the Stuyvesant girl, yet you treated her with the latest medical techniques—'

Kate interjected, 'You said that. I did not!'

'Are you telling our viewers that you didn't even treat her?' Gallante asked.

'We did treat her!' Kate insisted.

'How do you treat an undiagnosed illness? Is there some magic pill that you doctors at City Hospital use in all mystifying cases?' Gallante cast a superior smile in the direction of the camera.

'Until you can make a diagnosis, all you do is try to reduce the patient's fever, feed intravenous fluids to avoid dehydration. And do all the lab tests that you think will help you arrive at a correct diagnosis,' Kate explained firmly.

'That doesn't sound much better than, "Take two aspirin and call me in the morning",' Gallante said. 'But, unfortunately, by morning Claudia Stuyvesant was dead.'

'Everything medically possible under the circumstances was done for her,' Kate protested.

'Then why did she die?' Gallante challenged.

'Unfortunately, nobody knows. But the medical examiner will discover why.'

'Doctor, do you do that often?' Gallante asked.

'Do what often?' Kate asked, puzzled.

'Depend on the medical examiner to make your diagnosis for you?' Gallante asked. Before Kate could respond, he continued. 'This is Ramon Gallante, reporting from City Hospital.'

THE PHONE WAS RINGING when Kate unlocked the door to the apartment. She rushed to answer it, prepared to defend herself against a tirade from Dr Cummins.

'Doctor,' she heard Scott Van Cleve say. 'I have just seen your interview on television and—'

'And you don't approve,' Kate anticipated him.

'If you refuse to follow my advice, I serve no useful purpose,' Van Cleve said. 'Maybe you would be better off with some lawyer whose advice you *do* respect.'

'My decision had nothing to do with you. It had to do with me. I refuse to stand mute in the face of false accusations by a man because he happens to be Claude Stuyvesant!'

Van Cleve knew that to argue with such an angry, principled young woman was futile. He asked instead, 'Doctor, are there times when you tell a patient to avoid certain foods, or not to have any breakfast before taking a blood or urine sample?'

'Of course,' Kate agreed.

'What I am saying is no different. Until we get a clear view of what Stuyvesant is going to do legally, do not make any more public statements. Resent him. Curse him. Make voodoo dolls. But—'

Kate said it for him. 'Not a word about him in public.'

'Yes, Doctor. Now let's try to get on as attorney and client. OK?'

After a long moment of silence Kate conceded, 'OK.'

IN THE WAKE of Kate Forrester's appearance on television Cummins called another meeting of the department chiefs and invited Lionel Trumbull to attend as well.

As soon as opinions were requested, Dr Harold Wildman was first to respond. 'I was all for defending Forrester when this first came up, but by going on television, she's made it seem as if this hospital is a collection of ill-trained, fumbling doctors. Even if she did mishandle the Stuyvesant case, she should have let it just blow over. It would have been forgotten soon enough.'

'I wouldn't be too sanguine about that. Not with Stuyvesant involved,' Dr Eleanor Knolte replied. 'Still, her mistake in judgment does call for steps to minimise the damage.'

Professor emeritus Sol Freund took a different approach. 'We keep talking about "her mistake". I say we are talking about *us*. From what I can make out, what happened to Forrester could have happened to any of us. We must continue to defend her and, by defending her, defend all conscientious doctors.'

'Sol, it's all very well for you to be so understanding,' Wildman countered. 'But those of us facing years of outrageous malpractice premiums have to think of the future. This kind of bad publicity can make our premiums go only one way. Up. I say we take the position that what happened to the Stuyvesant girl was the fault of one doctor being unable to deal with the pressures in emergency.'

Freund stared across the wide conference table at his younger colleague. 'Are you suggesting we throw her to the wolves?'

'I am only saying we consider dissociating ourselves.'

'In my dictionary "dissociate" and "throw her to the wolves" are synonymous. What about a little loyalty to our young doctors?' Freund demanded.

'There are times when we have to choose *between* loyalties,' Wildman shot back. 'Loyalty to Forrester, or loyalty to this hospital? I say we owe our loyalty to this hospital!'

Before the meeting could evolve into a bitter personal battle between Freund and Wildman, Cummins intervened. 'Gentlemen, we have more to consider here than malpractice premiums. We have beds to fill. If we don't, we will have to close our doors. With the kind of bad publicity we've already had, patients will be reluctant to come to us,' Cummins warned dourly.

Wallace Simons, City Hospital's chief of obstetrics and gynaecology, spoke up next. 'I'm afraid I'm forced to agree. Our chief responsibility is to this hospital. Among the four hundred and sixty-three doctors on the staff, only one stands accused. If we have one bad apple, let's terminate her and state the reasons why. Then no patient need fear coming to us for treatment.'

Judge Trumbull said softly but with concern, 'What would happen if Forrester has a hearing before the state board of professional medical conduct, and they exonerate her? She can turn round and sue this hospital and each of you personally.'

'Then how *do* we dissociate ourselves?' Wildman asked.

'Let Claude Stuyvesant condemn her. Let *him* risk a costly suit for libel and slander,' Trumbull advised. 'If the state board finds Dr Forrester guilty of unprofessional conduct, you can get rid of her without fear of reprisals or lawsuits.'

'And in the meantime?' Simons asked.

'Keep her isolated from treating patients, which reduces our risk,' Trumbull said.

'In other words,' Sol Freund interjected, 'we will keep this young woman in solitary confinement before we have the public hanging. And then we are going to do it in a safe, surgical and legally antiseptic manner, so nobody gets sued.'

'I would not classify taking action against a physician that the state board finds incompetent a "public hanging",' Cummins responded.

'Of course not,' Freund replied. 'We mustn't use words that later can be turned against us if there is a lawsuit. I say it is cowardly to abandon a bright young doctor in order to save our own skins.'

From the faces round the table it was clear that very few agreed with him.

THE NEXT AFTERNOON Kate Forrester appeared on the neurology floor of the paediatric wing. Despite her personal problems, she had made it a daily practice to follow up on little Maria Sanchez. On each visit Kate would bring the child a small, inexpensive gift, usually a rag doll or a colouring book.

As she always did, Kate went to the door of Maria's room, peeping in to make sure the child was neither asleep nor being tested by one of the resident doctors. This time Maria was awake, alone, and seemed rather despondent.

'Maria?' Kate called softly.

At once the child turned towards the door and sat up in bed, great expectations brightening her black eyes. The gift hidden behind her back, Kate slipped into the room. With a flourish she presented the brightly wrapped package. The child eagerly tore off the red and gold paper and uncovered a book. Kate had brought it to teach Maria to read.

Excitedly, the child threw her arms round Kate. They were

embracing when Dr Harve Golding came hurriedly into the room. He was visibly embarrassed. 'Kate, can I talk to you?'

'Of course.'

She gently disengaged herself from Maria's embrace and joined him in the corridor. 'OK, Harve, what is it?'

'Cummins has issued an order that you are not to appear in any area of the hospital where patients are involved.'

'He can't do that!' Kate protested. 'I'm not treating anyone. I'm just visiting a lonely child. What harm can that do?'

'He's extremely sensitive to the kind of gossip that your presence might stir up. I'm sorry, Kate, but I have no choice.'

'Of course. I understand,' Kate said. 'I'll just go in and say goodbye.'

She went back in to find Maria rubbing her small hands over the glossy cover of the book. Maria smiled up at Kate. She opened the book, inviting Kate to read to her.

'Maria, this is a special kind of present. It's what grown-ups call a going-away present.'

'Going . . . a . . . way,' the child repeated. 'I going away now?'

'No, Maria. I am going away.'

Tears flooded the child's black eyes. 'You go away?'

The pain on Maria's pinched face, along with her beseeching eyes, caused Kate to make a decision. 'No, I am *not* going away,' she said as she sat on the bed, took the child in her arms, and opened the book. 'Maria, this is an A. Say it. A.'

They had reached the letter E when Kate heard footsteps behind her. She turned to find Harve Golding in the doorway. She braced for a reprimand.

'Katie, at least have the good sense to close the door,' Golding said. He smiled, then drew back, closing the door behind him.

Kate turned back to Maria and said, 'E. This letter is E.'

AT THE SAME TIME Kate Forrester was encouraging little Maria to read, one of the confidential phones on the desk of the mayor's executive secretary was ringing persistently.

'Mayor's office. Madelaine speaking,' she said softly. Only a few people had access to this private unlisted number.

'I have to talk to him,' a masculine voice said.

'Dr Schwartzman?' Madelaine identified.

'Yes,' the medical examiner replied.

'I'll put him right on.'

In a few moments Schwartzman heard the mayor say, 'Ab?'

'Look, holding up the Stuyvesant autopsy report until after the funeral is one thing. That I can do. But I can't change the results,' Schwartzman warned.

'Messy?' the mayor asked.

'Stuyvesant won't like my findings. Cause of death can't be toned down.'

'What was it?'

'Massive haemorrhage due to a ruptured ectopic pregnancy.'

'You're right. Stuyvesant won't like it.' The mayor considered the situation for a moment, then said, 'Ab, when you go before the media, soft-pedal the pregnancy. Emphasise that death was due to massive internal haemorrhage or some such.'

'Right,' Schwartzman agreed. 'Oh, by the way, when you talk to Stuyvesant, suggest that he have the body cremated. If there are legal proceedings, he won't want the body exhumed and tested.'

'Why? What else did you find?' the mayor asked.

'Nothing. But to make sure, I didn't look.'

Chapter Seven

A small detachment of uniformed police had been ordered by the mayor to assure that the funeral of Claudia Stuyvesant was carried out with a minimum of interference from the news media and the curious crowds that were expected to throng round St Thomas's Church on Fifth Avenue.

Half an hour before the appointed time of ten o'clock in the morning, the notables began to take their places in the pews.

The mayor was among the first to arrive. Men and women from the largest companies in the country were well represented among the mourners. But the main group consisted of Stuyvesant's employees and the many members of the civic and charitable organisations that were beholden to him for donations.

Once all of the invited mourners were seated, the church was opened to the public. Among the crowd was Dr Kate Forrester. Along with the others, she entered the lofty church and stared up at the ornate carved altar, before which rested the simple coffin of plain polished dark wood. It was closed.

With the choir humming softly in the background, the minister entered from a door to one side of the altar. Then from the door on the opposite side, an usher preceded the mother and the father of Claudia Stuyvesant. Nora Stuyvesant was dressed in black. Claude Stuyvesant, attired in a black suit, walked beside her.

He assisted his wife to the front pew. Once they were seated, the choir lifted their voices in a hymn. During this, as Kate's eyes drifted over the crowd, she caught sight of one face that startled her.

Scott Van Cleve, her lawyer, sat in the aisle seat some rows ahead of her. What is he doing here? she thought. He's no friend of the Stuyvesants'. Or is he? Her thoughts were interrupted when the hymn came to an end and the minister assumed his place in the pulpit to deliver his eulogy.

He was profuse in his condolences to the Stuyvesants, praising them for their devoted parenthood. He dealt briefly and only in the most general terms with the life of Claudia Stuyvesant, spending more time on what Claudia might have accomplished if only she had lived a normal life span. Kate took that portion of the eulogy to be an accusation against her. She clasped her hands tightly in her lap, determined to fend off any feelings of guilt.

At the end of the service the minister announced that the interment would be private, limited to only the immediate family. The pall-bearers lifted the coffin and started up the aisle towards the huge front doors, followed by Stuyvesant and his wife. They had taken only a dozen steps when Nora Stuyvesant started to totter. Before she could collapse, Stuyvesant caught her by one arm, and from the other side of the aisle Scott Van Cleve leaped forward to seize her other arm. Thus assisted, Nora Stuyvesant made her way up the aisle.

As they approached the pew in which Kate stood in respect, Stuyvesant's sorrowful look suddenly changed to one of anger. Kate realised he had recognised her from her television interview. She stared back at him with the conviction of the innocent.

On the other side of Stuyvesant, Scott Van Cleve gave her a look of rebuke that seemed to ask, Of all the places in the world, Doctor, what are you doing here?

To escape Scott's reproving stare, Kate diverted her eyes to the mourners in the opposite pews. One face she found there intrigued her—that of a young man whose eyes were fixed on the coffin. He was cadaverously thin, in his early twenties, with a dark complexion and longish dark-brown hair pulled back in an untidy ponytail. He wore a faded blue shirt and a western-type denim jacket. Hardly fit attire for such a solemn occasion, Kate thought.

Claude Stuyvesant, his wife and Scott Van Cleve reached the doors

to the street. Kate heard a shout go up from the television crews outside. 'Here they come. Start rolling!'

Kate pushed through the mourners in time to see Ramon Gallante hold up a microphone to Claude Stuyvesant. She could not hear what Gallante asked, but she was chilled to hear Stuyvesant's loud, angry reply. 'I have already started proceedings against her.'

While the coffin was being slid into the hearse Stuyvesant's chauffeur helped him assist his wife into their black stretch limousine. Kate watched as the hearse pulled away, followed only by the Stuyvesant limousine.

As they disappeared from sight Kate saw Scott Van Cleve seize the arm of one of the pallbearers. He exchanged brief words with the man, who appeared puzzled. But evidently Van Cleve discovered what he wanted to know, for he then turned back to mingle with the crowd. He passed the young man with a ponytail whom Kate had noticed inside the church. She watched as the young man looked around furtively, then started quickly down the church steps and along the avenue to lose himself in the street crowd.

Kate was marking his strange conduct when she was turned about by Scott Van Cleve, who asked, 'What are *you* doing here?'

'I could ask you the same thing.'

'I'm here on business. Legal business,' he explained. 'Certain things I wanted to find out.'

'Such as?' Kate asked.

'The coffin, for one.'

'What about it?' Kate asked. 'Polished wood, in simple good taste.'

'Exactly,' Van Cleve said. 'For a Stuyvesant, no metal casket resistant to external deterioration? And why was the body never available for viewing, either at the church or at some funeral home? That started me thinking. I was troubled even more by the way those pallbearers carried that coffin.'

'Is that why you collared one of them?' Kate asked.

'I asked him if the coffin was heavy.'

'What did he say?'

'Interesting reply. "It was a lot lighter than I expected." '

'Mr Van Cleve, what's the significance of all this?'

'You know what I think? There was no body in that coffin.'

'No body?' Kate asked, startled.

'No body. Or else only the ashes left after cremation,' Van Cleve said. 'What's Stuyvesant covering up?'

'Drugs?' Kate suggested.

'You told me you ordered a toxic screen that night. What was the report?'

'I've never seen it. It wasn't in her chart the last time I examined it.'

'Then let's get hold of it. Now!' Van Cleve said.

THOUGH DR CUMMINS WAS GRUDGING about relinquishing the chart to anyone but Lionel Trumbull, he finally gave his permission. Eagerly Kate and Scott leafed through it page by page, but in the end they could find no toxicological report.

'Strange,' Kate said.

Her only recourse was to find Carmelita Espinosa, the technician who had worked on the blood samples she had sent to the lab on Saturday night. Mrs Espinosa answered Kate's questions in brief, accented replies. Did Mrs Espinosa recall doing the Stuyvesant screen? She never recalled specimens by patients' names. Did she recall the night of the Stuyvesant case? Yes. Did she do any toxic screens that night? Yes. She did three. All three came up positive.

'The computer printout, did you send that to emergency?'

'Wherever a request comes from, that's where I direct the printout,' Mrs Espinosa confirmed.

Kate and Van Cleve glanced at each other with the same thought in mind: That tox report should be in Claudia's chart. Where is it?

DR KATE FORRESTER WAS RELIEVED to be summoned from her work in Dr Troy's basement office by a call from Dr Cummins's secretary. She hoped this call meant that Cummins was ready to reinstate her as a resident in general medicine.

When she was shown into Cummins's office, he was on his feet, awaiting her arrival. He greeted her only with a commiserating shake of the head. He held in his hand a thin sheaf of papers. One glimpse, and Kate recognised the seal of the Office of the Medical Examiner of New York County.

'You might want to sit down before you read this,' Cummins suggested.

Kate took the report cautiously, sat down, and began to read. She had not gone beyond the first paragraph when she felt forced to stare up at Cummins. He pointed down at the report, ordering her to continue. ' "Ectopic pregnancy",' Kate read aloud in disbelief, ' "causing rupture of her left fallopian tube—" '

' "Resulting in severe internal haemorrhaging and death", ' Dr Cummins finished the sentence. 'When you go back and check your notes in her chart, her signs and symptoms, you will find they are consistent with such a condition.'

'Her signs and symptoms were consistent with dozens of other conditions as well,' Kate pointed out. 'And twice she denied having had sexual relations.'

'You should at least have suspected she was lying.'

'I did, and I performed a urine pregnancy test. It came up negative!'

'It is obvious that you came up with a wrong result,' Cummins replied. 'If ever we had any hope of avoiding a malpractice suit, this document destroys it. Forrester, I'm sorry about this turn of events. Of course we'll continue to do our best for you.'

But his attitude was so forlorn that Kate was reminded of a college professor who had once told her, 'A man only says he'll do his best when he expects to fail.'

TORMENTED BY THE MEDICAL EXAMINER'S findings, Kate hurried through the underground tunnels of the hospital complex back to her basement office. There she found a note alongside the printout on her worktable: 'Call your lawyer. Urgent.'

Kate was greeted with a harried 'Van Cleve here'. But at the sound of her voice he took command of the conversation. 'Doctor, we have to meet. Tonight. And be prepared for a long session. I have just seen a copy of the medical examiner's report. It is important I see you in my office no later than six this evening.'

Feeling challenged by Van Cleve's brisk attitude, Kate responded in kind. 'Six, Mr Van Cleve. I'll be there!'

BEFORE SCOTT VAN CLEVE began his interrogation, he made sure Kate was comfortably seated opposite his desk.

'OK,' Van Cleve declared as he sank into his chair. 'Everybody who knows Stuyvesant knows there definitely *will* be a lawsuit. And there *will* be charges against you before the state board. Now, we know we can't disprove what the medical examiner found. That puts the onus on us to explain why you didn't find that condition.'

'Ectopics are not always easy to detect,' Kate protested.

Van Cleve brushed aside her interruption. 'Easy to detect or not, we have to prove to the satisfaction of the medical world—and to the public as well—that everything you did was in accord with good medical practice. That's the legal test.'

'And it was,' Kate insisted.

'Then why didn't you detect her condition?' he shot back.

'Eric Briscoe didn't detect it, either,' she countered.

'That's no excuse. Besides, Stuyvesant hasn't charged Briscoe with anything. Stuyvesant is focusing on *you*. So I have to know exactly what you did and why.'

'I don't even know where to start.'

'Start at the beginning. From the moment you first saw her.'

'Actually, I saw her mother before I even saw her.'

'We'll get to her mother later,' Van Cleve said. 'Start with your first look at your patient. Don't omit anything.'

Kate proceeded to recite in as much detail as she could recall the events of that night.

When she finished, Van Cleve remarked, 'At the outset, you said that you saw Mrs Stuyvesant before you saw her daughter. That seemed especially significant to you. Why?'

'It was obvious there was friction between them. Tension of some kind, which I didn't understand until later. Too late.'

'And what was that?' Van Cleve asked.

'After Claudia expired, several people heard her mother say, "He'll blame me . . . He'll blame me." At the time I thought it was strange of her to say that at such a tragic moment. But from what I've since learned about Stuyvesant, I realise now how deeply afraid of him his wife must be.'

'She was fearful he would blame her for his daughter's death?'

'Which could also account for her concern when I first saw her,' Kate explained. 'Her daughter had moved out, was living on her own, most likely in defiance of her father's wishes. I sensed that that conflict prevented Claudia Stuyvesant from feeling free to talk.'

'If she had felt free, what might she have told you?'

'That she had been sexually active. And that she used drugs.'

'Let's accept that she lied to you about drugs. How could that have affected the outcome of her case?' Van Cleve asked.

'This is going to require an understanding of the difference between a normal pregnancy and an ectopic. In a normal pregnancy the uterus is palpably enlarged. But in the case of an ectopic, not nearly so much. In a normal pregnancy the cervix is discoloured. Not necessarily so in an ectopic. And a tender mass may be detected.'

'*May* be detected?' Van Cleve asked.

'It isn't always possible to feel it,' Kate explained. 'In this case it was not apparent to me or to Briscoe.'

'Yet it was there,' Van Cleve considered grimly. 'And the effect of drugs on an ectopic pregnancy?'

'Her pain could have been masked or diminished by drug use.'

'She died of massive internal haemorrhaging. Wouldn't that have presented some important signs?'

'Her haematocrit could have been one sign,' Kate said.

'Haematocrit? What's that?'

'Part of every CBC, or complete blood count,' Kate explained. 'It indicates the percentage of red cells in the blood. Normal for a woman is between thirty-seven and forty-eight per cent.'

'And Claudia's that night?' Van Cleve asked.

'Thirty-eight, as I remember.'

'Then she was certainly within the range of normal.'

'Which proved to be very misleading,' Kate pointed out.

'How?' Van Cleve asked, becoming a bit frustrated.

'Put the whole case together,' Kate said. 'She came in complaining of nausea, vomiting and diarrhoea, which means she was likely dehydrated. Dehydration robs the blood of moisture content. That reduces the amount of plasma, making the red-cell count appear higher than it actually is.'

Beginning to understand, Van Cleve said, 'So that her red-cell count, which would have been low due to her haemorrhaging, actually appeared normal due to her dehydration.'

'Go to the head of the class,' Kate replied tartly.

Van Cleve pushed aside his yellow legal pad and started to pace in his small office. Suddenly he turned to Kate. 'There was one fact that could have put all the others into focus—that pregnancy test. How come your result was negative?'

'No medical test is one hundred per cent perfect,' Kate explained. 'I tried to get a sonogram to confirm the result, but no qualified technician was available. You have to realise the conditions under which we work in emergency. Long stretches without a break. A shortage of examining rooms. Sometimes we have to treat patients on stretchers in the corridors. There are always more patients than the doctor has time for. We give every patient the best care we can.'

'Dr Forrester, do you realise what you have just admitted?' Van Cleve asked with the accusing attitude of an opposing attorney. 'You have virtually said that due to conditions, you did *not* give Claudia Stuyvesant good medical care.'

'I did give her good medical care!' Kate protested.

'You gave her "the best care" that you could,' Van Cleve pointed out. 'Which is not perfect care, not even good care. Just the best you could do under difficult circumstances. Doctor, you can thank your

351

lucky stars that you've got an insurance company defending you on the malpractice end of this.'

'And what about that hearing and my career? I have spent almost half my life preparing to practise medicine. It's all I've ever wanted to do. I won't let them take that away from me!'

'I'll do my best to help you,' Van Cleve assured. Honesty made him add, 'But I can make no promises, Doctor.'

Kate Forrester left the offices of Trumbull, Drummond and Baines feeling far more threatened than when she arrived.

Scott Van Cleve watched her go, feeling even more deeply disturbed than he had admitted to her. More so than the first time he had seen her, he was aware of her strong face, which reflected her determination to devote her life to medicine. But her very determination only served to compound his fears.

I can't let this go to court, he realised. I certainly can't let it get as far as a hearing. There must be some way to prevent both eventualities from coming to pass.

Scott left his office later that night still racking his brains for some solution.

He knew one thing. He would surely have wanted to meet a young woman as attractive and with such convictions as Kate Forrester, in any way except this.

Chapter Eight

The release of the medical examiner's report on the case of Claudia Stuyvesant caused repercussions in other quarters as well.

The following morning there was a full-scale meeting in the conference room at Trumbull, Drummond and Baines. All three senior partners were in attendance, along with Dr Cummins and Marcus Naughton, president of the board of trustees of City Hospital. Scott Van Cleve had also been requested to attend.

Lionel Trumbull opened the meeting with a simple, bald, not particularly legalistic statement. 'Gentlemen, we are in trouble.'

'Don't I know,' Naughton agreed grimly. 'That medical examiner's report leaves us defenceless, utterly defenceless.'

'Let's not panic,' Drummond cautioned. 'I think, with the right approach, Stuyvesant could be induced to settle this thing in a quiet manner. With a couple of million thrown in, of course.'

'How much will the insurance company go for? That's the first

352

thing that we have to find out,' Trumbull declared.

'And the second thing?' Cummins asked.

'Who makes the approach to Stuyvesant,' Trumbull replied. He turned to Naughton. 'Marc, Stuyvesant is a member of your golf club, isn't he?'

'Yes, but I can't say I really know him,' Naughton begged off. 'Besides, golf isn't really his thing. Yachting is.'

'Well, do we know anyone who's close to him in that area?' Trumbull asked.

'We have a man on the hospital board who's quite a yachtsman. Harry Lindsay,' Naughton suggested.

'Contact Lindsay. Find out if he'll talk to Stuyvesant,' Trumbull said. 'Meantime, we have to concoct a scenario that he will buy. I'm open for ideas.'

Scott Van Cleve interjected, 'To a man like Stuyvesant, a couple of million dollars is no real incentive.'

'We already know that,' Trumbull said. He made no secret of his annoyance at young Van Cleve's statement of the obvious.

Nevertheless, Van Cleve pressed on. 'I was about to say that Stuyvesant is jealous of his public image. When Lindsay goes to see him, he should of course commiserate with him. It was a tragedy, what happened to his daughter. But—and here's where Lindsay has to make his point—a great man turns adversity to a benefit.'

'How can a man's losing his daughter be turned to a benefit?' Cummins demanded.

'Dr Cummins, I've heard quite a lot about your emergency service from my client. With all due respect, the place is old, run down and overtaxed.'

'We do the best we can with the funds we have available!' Cummins protested.

'Exactly, Doctor,' Van Cleve continued. 'Now, what if Lindsay said, "CJ, you're an important man in this city. With your millions, money doesn't mean much to you. The way to honour your daughter's memory—and do a public good—is to take the two million dollars from the insurance company and donate it to the Claudia Stuyvesant Memorial Emergency Service, at City Hospital." Of course, Lindsay should subtly point out the acclaim Stuyvesant would receive for such a great public service.'

'Not bad, Van Cleve, not bad,' Trumbull granted.

'Naturally,' Van Cleve concluded, 'he drops all charges against the hospital and everybody involved.'

'Naturally,' Trumbull agreed.

Van Cleve leaned back in his chair, confident he had launched a strategy that would also free his client from the threat of having her licence revoked by the state of New York.

Trumbull addressed Naughton. 'Marc, I'm sure you'll waste no time getting in touch with Lindsay.'

'The moment I get back to my office,' Naughton assured him.

WHEN HARRY LINDSAY CALLED to ask for a meeting with Claude Stuyvesant, the financier assumed this was a move towards forming a syndicate to build a new yacht to defend the America's Cup. So he invited Lindsay to lunch at the New York Yacht Club, on 44th Street. Over lunch the conversation proceeded in the vein Stuyvesant had expected. It was over coffee that Lindsay finally broached his real mission.

'CJ, out of respect for your feelings, I have refrained from dwelling on the painful loss you have suffered. Yet there are times when out of tragedy can come some great public good.'

'You tell me how a man's losing his only child can be a public good, and I'll tell you you're crazy,' Stuyvesant said bitterly.

Not encouraged, but recognising the opportunity he was seeking, Lindsay continued. 'What if there were a way to make people remember the name Claudia Stuyvesant? And bless it as well?'

'How?' Stuyvesant asked grudgingly.

'Have you ever been inside the emergency service of City Hospital?'

'Of course not!'

'You ought to go there one night. See how crowded it is, how overworked the personnel, how old and run down the physical plant. Then imagine what a new emergency service could do for the poor of this city and the other people who depend on it.'

'Harry, if you're trying to hit me up for a donation, you can have a cheque in the morning. Just state a figure.'

Lindsay said softly, 'Two million dollars.'

'Two million . . . !' Stuyvesant repeated, stunned.

'CJ, the insurance company is willing to settle your lawsuit for two million. If you contribute that money to City Hospital for a Claudia Stuyvesant Memorial Emergency Service, your daughter's name would be in people's memories for ever.'

'Claudia Stuyvesant Memorial . . .' Stuyvesant said quietly. He poured himself another cup of coffee.

'CJ, I'm suggesting that you put this whole sad chapter of your life

354

in the past. Let people remember only that Claudia's death resulted in a fine charitable act that benefited this city.'

Stuyvesant drummed his fingers on the stiff white linen tablecloth and finally nodded. 'You've got a deal, Harry.'

'Good!' Lindsay said, feeling his mission accomplished.

'But that woman doctor—' Stuyvesant said.

'She's also covered by the insurance company under the hospital policy. They won't settle just half a claim.'

'I don't mean that. Hell, a malpractice award against her isn't worth the paper it's written on. I want her conduct of my daughter's case judged by a jury of her peers!' Stuyvesant declared.

'You mean before the state board?'

'My lawyers have already filed my complaint. I'll make sure she never practises medicine again!'

'CJ, I don't know how the hospital will react to that.'

'Either they leave that woman to me, or there's no Claudia Stuyvesant Memorial wing!'

Having known Claude Stuyvesant for many years, Harry Lindsay knew that this was the man's final position.

ROUND A SMALL CONFERENCE TABLE in Trumbull's office, Dr Cummins, Scott Van Cleve, and the lawyer for the insurance company were receiving Harry Lindsay's report on his meeting with Claude Stuyvesant.

'So, gentlemen, that's the deal. Two million to City Hospital for a Claudia Stuyvesant Memorial Emergency Service.'

'You did well, Harry,' Trumbull said. He turned to the insurance company lawyer. 'How does that set with your people?'

'We're lucky to get out from under with that figure,' the insurance company lawyer confessed. 'I'll draw the papers.'

Van Cleve interjected, 'That covers Dr Forrester too, doesn't it?'

'In so far as the malpractice suit is concerned,' Lindsay admitted. 'Stuyvesant reserves his right to press for a hearing before the state board. In fact, he's already filed his complaint.'

'He can't settle on one hand and still pursue his vendetta on the other,' Van Cleve protested. 'That's not what I proposed at our last meeting. It was for *everyone* to be free and clear!'

Trumbull felt compelled to take charge. 'Van Cleve, legally all that our client—City Hospital—owes Dr Forrester is to defend her against any malpractice suit. Which we have done.'

'Exactly,' Cummins confirmed. 'We are willing to allow Forrester to serve out the term of her contract, which is another ten months, unless the board decides she is guilty. In which event her contract will automatically terminate.'

'Don't you feel any obligation to her? She is a loyal, devoted, highly capable young doctor who would be a credit to your profession,' Van Cleve insisted.

'I would hardly say she has been a credit to our hospital in this case,' Cummins countered, a flush of anger in his face.

Trumbull came to his aid. 'Van Cleve, you don't have to run City Hospital, Dr Cummins does. So we shall abide by his judgment. Now let's get the paperwork done on that settlement before Stuyvesant has a change of heart.'

After congratulatory handshakes with Lindsay the meeting ended. As the men withdrew from Trumbull's office Trumbull called out, 'Van Cleve, a moment, please?'

'Yes?' Scott asked, returning to the conference table.

'It is obvious that you are very emotional about this Forrester matter. It could be because you're so devoted to fighting for the underdog. *Or*'—he paused before continuing—'*or* could it be because of your personal interest in the doctor *herself*?'

Van Cleve's impulse was to deny it. But there was sufficient truth in Trumbull's observation that he said nothing.

'Now, son, your private life is yours. But I want to talk to you on another level. When I first recruited you for this firm, I listened to your lofty ambitions about doing *pro bono publico* work. And I said to myself, He's one of the new breed, full of lofty idealistic aspirations. But I also thought, Once he's been around this firm and sees other young men devoting themselves to corporate law, earning three, four, and five times what he makes, he'll change. They all do. But you're one who hasn't. I can't tell you how many times in the partners' meetings I have had to defend you.'

'I've lived up to my end of our agreement,' Scott pointed out.

'No one says you haven't. But we expected that you would mellow.' Trumbull shook his head in futility. 'That's why I have to draw the line. As soon as the Stuyvesant settlement goes through, that ends our responsibility to Dr Forrester.'

'Meaning?'

'Her hearing before the state board is a purely personal matter. She must make arrangements to defend herself.'

'And if I insist on continuing?' Van Cleve asked.

'It won't be as a member of this firm,' Trumbull said firmly.

Van Cleve did not respond, merely nodded his head gravely and departed. He returned to his small, cluttered office to ponder the choice Trumbull had posed.

He reached for his phone. He punched in the number, and he said, 'Doctor, we have to meet. This afternoon if possible.'

'This afternoon? What's so urgent?' Kate asked.

'It's not something I can discuss on the phone. I'll pick you up at the hospital at three.'

KATE WAS LATE COMING OUT of the hospital. Scott Van Cleve paced across the street, rehearsing in his mind the least painful way to break the news to her. He was sure that despite her initial shock, she would understand what had happened. It might take her a longer time to understand why he had had to take the course he had chosen. He was prepared for that.

He caught sight of her now. Determined, almost defiant, she raced swiftly across the street against the light. When she reached him, his first sudden and unexpected impulse was to kiss her. But that would defeat what he had come to do.

'What happened?' Kate asked directly.

'Let's go some place where we can talk quietly,' he suggested. 'It's a nice day. Central Park isn't too far.'

THEY WENT INTO THE PARK, away from the sounds of automobile horns, away from the occasional screech of tyres brought to a sudden stop. Deep enough into the park that they could almost forget the city around them.

He led her to a bench shaded from the glare of the sun by a large oak. When she was seated, he began, 'It didn't work.'

'What didn't work?' Kate asked.

He explained his carefully thought-out strategy to defuse Claude Stuyvesant's hostility. How Lindsay had met with Stuyvesant. How Stuyvesant had responded and agreed to donate all monies received to a new emergency service.

'Then it worked very well,' Kate said. 'Why do you say it didn't?'

'The part that didn't work applies to you,' Van Cleve admitted. 'Stuyvesant insists on that hearing before the state board.'

Kate nodded, absorbing the unfortunate fact, then said, 'Of course we'll have to fight him!'

'You'd have been better off if I'd never suggested my plan,' Van Cleve confessed. 'Before there was a community of interest. The

357

insurance company, the hospital, our law firm, all had as much at stake as you did. But now that they're off the hook . . .'

'We're on our own,' Kate said.

'That's not the worst of it. Trumbull has given me an ultimatum.' Scott started to explain, but he didn't have to.

She said it. 'Drop my defence or leave the firm.'

He nodded. Her eyes filmed up. He thought, Please don't cry.

'Is there—Is there another lawyer you might suggest?' Kate asked.

'I hadn't even thought about that yet.'

'Then do think. And let me know.'

'Look, I'm sorry,' he blurted out.

'No need to apologise,' Kate said. 'I'm sure you meant only the best for me. But after all, you have your career to protect, too. No one knows what that means better than I.'

'Look,' Van Cleve pleaded, 'I'll do everything I can. I can advise you, confer with any new lawyer you get. It just can't be official, that's all.'

Kate did not respond, but rose and started away.

'Wait, please!' he called out. She stopped, then turned back to look at him. 'It's not my fault,' he protested. 'Can't I walk you home?'

'I'd rather be alone,' she said, then turned and walked away.

As Scott watched her he wondered, Is this the last time I'll see her?

ROSIE HAD GONE OFF to her night assignment at the hospital. Kate was alone, and had been for some hours. She had made herself a sandwich, but could not eat. She had brewed fresh coffee and had drunk too much. She paced their small living room, considering all her choices, until she felt she would wear out the carpet. A new lawyer? Costly. Likely too costly. Can't let Dad know. First thing he'd do is sell more acreage. But that's Clint's inheritance. I have no right to ask for any more.

Why do I need a lawyer? Why not appear before that board myself? Tell them the truth. They'll believe me. They have to!

But in the end she realised, If it were that simple, why did Scott Van Cleve's law firm think that it was such an involved and time-consuming procedure that he must drop my case?

She knew one thing. She had better try to get some sleep. Lack of sleep could sap her strength at a time when she needed it most.

Getting to bed was one thing; getting some sleep was another. She did doze off several times, but each time awoke shortly thereafter to the grim realisation of her situation.

358

The phone rang. She groped for it in the darkness.

'Hello?' she said.

'Doctor, I've spent a great part of the night thinking over yesterday afternoon,' Scott Van Cleve began.

'And you have the name of a good lawyer for me,' Kate said. 'Wait. I'll get a pencil and pad.'

After a moment he asked, 'Got one?'

'Yes.'

'Write this down carefully. Scott . . . Van . . . Cleve,' he said.

Kate was stunned. 'Are you aware of what this means?'

'I am. In my career this will only be an interruption. But to you it can mean your lifetime, your career. If you'll retain me as your lawyer, I want to go to work. Right now.'

'Right now? It's past midnight,' Kate protested.

'I know. But if I want to get started on your case in the morning, I need to ask some questions now. Can I come up?'

'Why yes, sure,' she said.

'Be there in a minute. I'm in the phone booth down on your corner,' he said, and hung up.

She sprang out of bed and went straight into the bathroom to study her face and her hair in the mirror. No time to put on make-up, but she could make her hair look a bit neater. She had just started to comb it when the doorbell rang. Kate reached for her dressing gown and was still slipping into it when she opened the door.

He stood there for a moment, his eyes fixed on her, before he said, 'Do you always look this good in the morning?'

'Do I have to answer that?' she countered.

'As your lawyer I should know everything about you.'

'Come in and stop making a fool of yourself,' she said, able at last to laugh. 'Have you had supper?'

'Walking around almost all night—how could I?'

'Neither have I. I'll make us something,' she said, heading for her small kitchen.

They talked while she made fresh coffee, scrambled eggs, toast and bacon. He sat on a stool, admiring every simple thing she did.

Scott asked Kate to review the Stuyvesant case in detail, seeking some point at which to begin his investigation. He especially needed witnesses whose testimony would confirm her actions that night. By the time they were through eating, Van Cleve had decided that his best corroborating witness was Eric Briscoe.

It was past four o'clock in the morning when Scott left.

LATER THAT DAY Scott Van Cleve turned off Fifth Avenue and started down Fortieth Street towards Madison. It was a block of undistinguished office buildings—some old, some new. The building Scott was looking for, in which the New York City branch of the board of professional medical conduct had offices, proved to be one of the older buildings.

He consulted the listings in the lobby. Under NEW YORK STATE OFFICE OF PROFESSIONAL MEDICAL CONDUCT he found the name HOSKINS, ALBERT: COUNSEL. Scott knew that Hoskins would serve as prosecutor in the Forrester matter.

Scott made his way into the old lift and pressed the number of the floor. The ancient lift started up with a jerky movement. He stepped out at his floor to find a receptionist typing at a cluttered desk.

'Mr Hoskins, please?' Scott asked.

Without stopping, the receptionist replied, 'He's in conference. Do you have an appointment?'

'No. But I'll wait,' Scott said.

'Your name?'

'Scott Van Cleve. I'm an attorney. I'm here about a matter before the board. The matter of my client, Dr Katherine Forrester.'

The young woman stopped typing at once. 'Oh, *that* one.' Unintentionally she had informed him of the importance the entire staff placed on Claude Stuyvesant's complaint. 'Yes, I think you'd better wait, Mr Van Cleve.'

Minutes later the phone on the receptionist's desk rang. She answered. 'Yes, sir, there is someone waiting. A Mr Van Cleve. Says he represents Dr Forrester.'

She hung up the phone, pointed down the hallway to her left, and said, 'Mr Hoskins's office is at the end.'

Scott found Albert Hoskins sitting behind a large desk stacked with files. A bulky man, Hoskins seemed to move with great effort as he rose to extend his hand across the desk.

'Mr Van Cleve, is it? Well, sit down, sit down. Make yourself comfortable,' Hoskins invited warmly.

A bit too warmly, Scott thought.

'Now then, you want to see me about the Forrester matter?' Hoskins said.

'I know that Claude Stuyvesant has filed a complaint against my client. I also know that before there is any hearing, your first step is to form an investigating committee.'

'For the protection of innocent physicians and their reputations the committee studies all medical records and consults with medical experts. If they find no ground for the complaint, we put an end to the matter right then and there.'

'Exactly why I am here,' Scott replied. 'Dr Forrester has established to my satisfaction that every step she took was in keeping with the highest standards of medical practice. I'm sure Dr Briscoe will corroborate everything Dr Forrester has told me. I want your word that when that happens, the matter will be closed, so no further damage is done to Dr Forrester's reputation and career.'

'You want my word, do you?' Hoskins countered. 'Well, Mr Van Cleve, I'm sorry to say that the patient's chart, the back-up material, and the opinions of several medical experts have already been turned over to an investigating committee.'

'Are you always so quick to act?' Scott demanded.

A slight flush rose into Hoskins's fleshy cheeks. 'We treat all cases with great speed and thoroughness.'

'Even when the complainant is not Claude Stuyvesant?'

The flush in Hoskins's cheeks grew deeper. 'Mr Van Cleve, if you are accusing this office of yielding to political pressure, I may ask to have you barred from representing anyone before this board!'

Scott knew it was useless to pursue the matter. 'I see we have nothing more to discuss.'

'I quite agree,' Hoskins said. 'But as long as you're here, you might do something for me.'

'What?' Scott asked, suspicious.

Hoskins held out a legal document. Scott hesitated, then took it. It was a notice to appear before the state board of professional medical conduct and named Katherine Forrester as the respondent. Appended to it was a statement of charges.

'You can save me the trouble of serving this on your client.'

Chapter Nine

Lionel Trumbull, still nurturing the hope that he could bring his protégé round to his way of thinking, had prevailed on his partners to permit Scott the continued use of his office during his defence of Kate Forrester. However, that did not include the availability of other services, such as the firm's staff of investigators. Scott was thus forced to do his own legwork.

Time was an added pressure. Kate Forrester's hearing was within two weeks, so Scott had little time to interview potential witnesses and to formulate his defence.

His first witness must, by any test, be Dr Eric Briscoe. Scott had been waiting almost an hour in Briscoe's office before the young surgeon raced in, apologising, 'Sorry, but I was assisting at a colon resection.'

As Scott rose to shake hands Briscoe urged, 'Please, no need to disturb yourself.' He took his place behind his desk, then said, 'Whatever I can do for Kate, I want to do. She's an excellent doctor. I hate to see her in this mess. You know, this is the kind of thing that could have happened to any of us.'

'I'm glad to hear you say that, Doctor, because thus far that's the best defence theory I can come up with. That any doctor would have done exactly what Kate Forrester did.'

Briscoe nodded firmly but interposed, 'Van Cleve, I'm due to assist one of the attending surgeons on a complicated exenteration, so I hope this won't take too long.'

'I just need an idea of what you'll testify to at the hearing.'

'Testify? You . . . you want me to testify?' Briscoe asked.

'Dr Forrester's own version will naturally be considered prejudiced, so we'll need corroboration. Who better to give me that? You were there. You examined the patient.'

Briscoe nodded, but was noticeably more reserved this time.

'Dr Briscoe, the crucial question is this. Presented with the lab reports, the patient's symptoms and her signs as observed by Kate Forrester, would you, in your professional opinion, say that the treatment she followed was the proper course indicated in all the circumstances?'

'She did a good job. I mean . . .' Briscoe appeared to be at a loss for words.

'Dr Briscoe, let me put this another way. Did Kate Forrester do a proper professional job in the circumstances?' When Briscoe hesitated, Scott persisted. 'That shouldn't be too tough to answer. Of course, when I put you on the stand, the questions will be phrased more legalistically.'

'Van Cleve, when you called I thought you just wanted information. But being a witness—I've never been a witness before.'

Aware of Briscoe's growing reluctance, Scott was forced to adopt a new approach. 'For the moment let's forget testifying. Just answer some questions.' He took his yellow pad out of his briefcase. 'Now, when Dr Forrester sent for you, did you consider that to be usual,

362

reasonable, precautionary conduct on the part of a medical resident in emergency?'

"Well—uh, yes. I considered that reasonable. With those lab reports, the patient's vital signs, and her being unable to make a specific diagnosis, it would be—uh—usual to call in a surgeon to determine if there was need for surgical intervention,' Briscoe agreed.

'And what was your opinion?' Scott asked directly.

'Well, you have to understand that my opinion was in large measure conditioned by what Dr Forrester had told me. When I am told that a patient is not sexually active, hasn't missed a period, I do not suspect an ectopic pregnancy.'

Scott realised that Eric Briscoe was intent on insulating himself from any involvement. 'Doctor, you did perform an examination on Claudia Stuyvesant that night, didn't you?'

'Yes,' Briscoe replied sharply.

'During the course of that examination, didn't you discover anything to indicate what that young woman's condition was?'

'I was making my examination under a given set of facts. I relied on Dr Forrester's findings.'

'Wasn't Dr Forrester also acting under the same set of facts, so that her professional conclusions and yours were identical?'

Briscoe's concern came to the surface in a rush of colour to his cheeks. 'Look, Van Cleve, *I'm* not charged with anything and I don't intend to be! I am going to finish my residency at City Hospital, leave here with a good reputation and go back to a partnership that's waiting for me in Colorado.'

Scott studied Briscoe for a long moment. 'Did anyone advise you not to cooperate with my investigation?'

Briscoe hesitated. 'No. Nobody.'

Scott knew Briscoe was lying. But to confront him would serve no worthwhile purpose, and to subpoena such a reluctant witness would prove a disaster. Was it possible that by influence or threat Claude Stuyvesant had reached out to silence Briscoe?

Scott slipped his yellow pad back into his briefcase, saying, 'Thank you, Dr Briscoe, for your time.'

FAILING TO SECURE the cooperation and corroboration of Dr Briscoe, Scott Van Cleve decided to consult several doctors who specialised in obstetrics and gynaecology. During each interview Scott assessed the doctor's potential as a defence witness—provided, of course, the doctor proved amenable to testifying.

The first doctor he interviewed was Stephen Willows. He found Willows to be close to sixty, white-haired and bespectacled, with an efficient, capable air. An ideal witness, Scott decided.

Willows looked up from making a note in a patient's chart and said, 'Yes, young man? You're the lawyer who tried to get me on the phone yesterday?'

'Yes, Doctor. This has to do with a hearing before the Office of Professional Medical Conduct.'

'Oh, one of those,' Willows remarked.

'Yes, sir, one of those. And in this case, quite unjustified.'

'That's what lawyers usually say.' Willows then warned, 'I am not a professional witness. In fact, the only time I have testified in a lawsuit was *against* a doctor.'

'I would still like your opinion, sir.'

'Fire away,' Willows said.

Once Scott presented a summary of the events as he had learned them from Kate and from the chart of Claudia Stuyvesant, Willows appeared quite thoughtful.

'Sir, if you were there that night, handling that same case, what would you conclude?' Scott asked.

'I would diagnose run-of-the-mill viral stomach upset.'

'Not an ectopic pregnancy?' Scott asked.

'Ectopics are tricky to diagnose. Very few of them present in the same way,' Willows said.

'So that, in your opinion, what my client did on that night would be considered good medical practice?'

'Now you're talking like a lawyer trying to inveigle me into testifying,' Willows warned. 'I won't take the stand. But, in my opinion, that doctor, whoever she is, did what most good doctors would have done under the circumstances.'

'If the patient were on drugs, would that have made a difference?'

'Oh, indeed!' Willows exclaimed. 'It would certainly have disguised the degree and extent of her condition.'

'Dr Willows, knowing that a young doctor's career depends on it, would you reconsider testifying?' Scott asked.

'In these times the less any doctor has to do with the law, the better. Sorry. Give the young woman my best wishes that she emerge from this with her professional reputation intact.'

SCOTT VAN CLEVE was no more successful in securing the cooperation of the other specialists he interviewed.

364

Of one thing he was now convinced: whether or not Claudia Stuyvesant was a drug user could prove critical to Kate's defence.

WHEN SCOTT APPEARED in the reception room of the medical examiner's office announcing that he wished to see that official about the Stuyvesant case, the receptionist mistook him for a reporter.

'Sorry, sir, but all information on the Stuyvesant case is confidential. Dr Schwartzman sees no one about that case.'

It was only after Scott threatened to resort to a court order for access to the Stuyvesant autopsy that he was admitted to see the chief medical examiner.

Dr Abner Schwartzman was on the phone arguing with some persistent city official when Van Cleve was shown into his office. It gave the young lawyer a chance to study the man. He found him to be short, but stocky enough to fill his creaking swivel chair, and quite aggressive and argumentative.

'You disagree with our findings?' Schwartzman bellowed into the phone as he motioned Scott to a chair. 'Call in your own pathologist!' He listened for a brief instant, then ended the conversation with a sharp 'We'll see you in court!'

He hung up, grumbling. 'Everybody's a forensic expert!' He swung round in his swivel chair to confront Scott Van Cleve. 'So, young man, what's *your* complaint?'

'I'm an attorney, and I'm here to inquire about your findings in the Claudia Stuyvesant case.'

'Our findings have already been made public,' the medical examiner stated bluntly, as if that closed the matter.

'I understand you performed that autopsy yourself.'

'I did. Everything I found is in my report,' the man explained.

'There was nothing in your findings about the results of your toxic screen,' Scott pointed out.

'I did not do a toxic screen,' Schwartzman said. 'Once I found the cause of death, there was no need to pursue the matter.'

'No need? Or against orders?' Scott asked.

'Look, kid, if you are confusing a "courtesy" towards Mr Stuyvesant with a cover-up, you are barking up the wrong tree.'

'Exactly what do you call a courtesy, Doctor?'

'The mayor asked me, and I acceded to Mr Stuyvesant's request that the autopsy be done by me personally and the results not be made available until after the daughter's funeral. Not an unreasonable request, you must admit.'

'Can you at least tell me—if the body were exhumed, could traces of drugs still be detected?' Scott asked.

'Not in this case,' Schwartzman said. 'As soon as my autopsy was completed, the body was picked up by a hearse from a crematorium out on Long Island.'

Scott suddenly remembered that pallbearer's statement when he questioned him about the coffin: 'It was a lot lighter than I expected.'

'THINK,' SCOTT URGED KATE. 'Is there anything a doctor might observe that would be proof of drug abuse without having a tox report or some other laboratory confirmation?'

'Depends on the drug. Or drugs,' Kate said. 'For example, cocaine might induce nausea and vomiting. Also stimulation followed by depression. Sweating. Anxiety.'

'All of which Claudia presented,' Scott reminded her. 'Could you testify that the signs and symptoms Claudia presented were those induced by cocaine?'

Kate hesitated, then shook her head. 'Honestly? No.'

'We need that testimony, and we need it badly,' Scott pointed out. 'One half of our defence is that you were misled by a false pregnancy test. But the other half is that the patient, through her use of drugs, made a proper diagnosis impossible. Now, how do we get that?'

'Her doctor would know,' Kate said. 'That Dr Eaves whom Mrs Stuyvesant mentioned. Of course, he might not want to talk.'

'We'll see,' Scott said. He had a few thoughts of his own.

THE PRACTICE OF DR WILFRED EAVES occupied the entire ground floor of one of the most prestigious buildings on Park Avenue and was run with quiet efficiency by an office manager and a staff of four nurses.

By the time Scott Van Cleve was admitted to Dr Eaves's consultation room, he was duly impressed. Since many of Eaves's new patients were referrals, the doctor immediately asked, 'Did you bring any X-rays, scans, or MRIs with you?'

'I'm not here as a patient. I'm an attorney.'

Eaves pushed back from his desk and rose to his feet. 'If you have any complaints to make, or charges of malpractice, speak to my attorney. Get out!'

Scott remained seated. 'Dr Eaves, I am not here to complain or make charges, but to elicit information on behalf of a young doctor who must defend herself against charges before the state board.'

366

'You are talking about Dr Forrester, I assume.'

'Yes. Since you were Claudia Stuyvesant's doctor for most of her life, you would know. Was she addicted to, or an habitual user of, drugs?'

'I cannot answer any questions that relate to any of my patients,' Eaves responded sharply.

'If I subpoena you, you will have to appear and testify.'

'And I shall stand on a doctor's privilege not to reveal any confidential information about a patient.'

'The patient is dead. The defence of privilege may not pertain any longer,' Scott said.

'I shall leave that decision to the chairman of the hearing,' Eaves retorted. 'Now, Mr Van Cleve, I'm a very busy man.'

'Yes, of course,' Scott said. 'Thank you for your time.'

The moment Scott Van Cleve left his office, Eaves picked up his phone. 'Ms Berk, get me Claude Stuyvesant at once.'

Very soon his phone rang back. Ms Berk reported, 'He's on the line, Doctor.'

'Claude, he was here. That young lawyer, Van Cleve.'

'And?'

'I told him nothing as we agreed. But he strikes me as a digger.'

'Don't worry, Wilfred. He'll get nowhere.'

SCOTT VAN CLEVE was sure of one thing: Eaves had acted like a man with a guilty secret. There was no longer any doubt in his mind about Claudia Stuyvesant's drug habits. What he needed now was the proof. Armed with Claudia's most recent address, Scott searched for her apartment house in the Greenwich Village section of Manhattan.

In the small entryway, Scott consulted the twelve names on the board, each with a bell button alongside. It would probably be futile to ring the bell designated STUYVESANT, C. But neither was there anything to be risked by doing so. To his surprise the buzzer responded. He entered and started up the dark staircase. He had climbed two storeys when he was confronted by a woman leaning over the rail, staring down at him.

Thin, in her late fifties, with dark but greying hair, the woman was obviously on guard and quite suspicious of anyone who would ring the bell of a dead tenant. 'Yes?' she asked.

'My name is Scott Van Cleve.' By now Scott was on the third-floor landing and face to face with her. 'I'm an attorney, and I represent—'

Even before he pronounced the name of his client, the woman said,

'I don't know anything. I am inspecting the apartment to see if it needs a paint job before I rent it out again.'

'Would you mind if I just looked the place over?' Scott asked. 'I promise I won't touch anything.'

'Well,' the woman equivocated, 'if all you do is look around—though there's nothing to look around at.' She gave way to the open door behind her. Her words took on more meaning as Scott stepped into the one-room apartment. It was empty. There was no furniture, no vestige of clothing in the empty cupboard. It was as if no one had lived there for a long time.

'Nothing, nothing at all,' Scott observed softly. 'Usually when someone dies—'

The woman anticipated him. 'In this case nothing was usual. Poor girl died early Sunday morning. Monday afternoon two moving men showed up. Had some legal-looking paper. They cleaned the place out. Everything, including his clothes.'

'Tell me, who is "he"?'

'He was living here with her. She called him Rick. He sure raised hell when he found that they took all his things along with hers.'

'Rick,' Scott repeated. 'No last name?'

'Thomas, I think. Rick Thomas,' the woman said.

'Do you know anything at all about him? What he did for a living? What his habits were?'

'You ask me, he had only one *habit*,' the woman replied, emphasising the last word.

'Doing drugs?' Scott asked.

'I know the signs,' the woman declared.

'What about *her*? Was she on drugs, too?'

'I don't like to talk about tenants,' she replied with such finality that Scott knew he must forego that line of questioning.

'This Rick . . . Can you give me a description?'

'Let me see,' she said. 'He's kind of dark-complexioned. Like maybe Italian. And in his early twenties. Tall. Painfully thin. He wore his hair long, in a ponytail.'

That description fits the guy Dr Forrester spotted at the funeral, Scott thought.

'Does that help?' the woman asked.

'It's better than nothing,' Scott said thoughtfully. 'I'll give you my card. If he should come back, ask him to call me.'

'He won't come back,' the woman said. 'But if he does, I will.'

'It's important. A doctor's career could depend on it,' Scott said.

Chapter Ten

Rosie Chung was getting dressed to go on night duty when Kate returned from her day's stint with Dr Troy. She called from her bedroom. 'Kate, your lawyer called.'

Kate hurried to Rosie's door. 'What did he say?'

'He said to meet him down on Eighth Street and Fifth Avenue at nine tonight,' Rosie replied. 'And he said to wear warm clothes and good, serviceable shoes.'

'I wonder what that means,' Kate said. 'Did Van Cleve say why he wanted me to meet him tonight?'

'No,' Rosie replied. 'But I'll say one thing. He's got a very nice voice. Does he look like he sounds?'

'How does he sound?' Kate asked.

'I picture him to be a good solid citizen. The Spencer Tracy type. Sturdy build. About five ten—'

'Six two,' Kate interrupted. 'And very lean.'

'And blond. A typical American blond male.'

'Brown,' Kate said. 'His hair is brown.'

'Well,' Rosie insisted, 'with a voice like his he's got to be handsome, smooth, and cute.'

'Craggy,' Kate corrected once more.

'Craggy?' Rosie repeated in surprise. 'I had this image of him with a dimple in his chin. A cleft, like Cary Grant.'

'No cleft, but he's nice. And . . . well, devoted.'

'Devoted?' Rosie turned from the mirror, her curiosity aroused. 'You mean there's something going on between you two, aside from legal advice?'

'I mean devoted to his work. To my case.'

'Oh,' Rosie said with obvious disappointment. 'He sounds like the perfect date.' Before Kate could answer, Rosie said, 'Got to rush.' She gave Kate a hug, saying, 'Don't be late. Van Cleve said nine o'clock.' She started for the front door, calling, 'Don't tell him how wrong I was about him.'

DRESSED IN A WARM COAT, wearing a pair of sturdy brown walking shoes, Kate Forrester climbed to the street from the Fourth Street subway station. She started down the dark street, which was still damp from the spring rain that had fallen earlier in the evening, towards the appointed corner.

She spied Van Cleve standing under the streetlamp. Tall as he was, in a double-breasted trench coat he was an intriguing figure, possibly out of some mystery novel or film. He caught sight of her.

As they met, he was so full of his plan that he assumed she knew more than she did. 'Rick. His name is Rick Thomas.'

'Who?' Kate asked.

'The man Claudia lived with. The man you spotted at the funeral. A woman at Claudia's apartment described him exactly as you did. Now the question is, If you saw him again, could you identify him?'

'I think so. *If* I saw him again. Can you arrange that?'

'That's what we'll try to do tonight. Let's go.'

They started along the street as Kate pointed out, 'Ponytail. Wan, thin face. Dark complexion. Wearing jeans. Those are hardly unusual clues to follow in this part of New York.'

'I talked to Dan Farrell, a retired police detective, about that. He handles investigations for the law firm. He gave me advice on how you track down a man with no known address, only a name and a general description.'

'How?'

'No question that Claudia was on drugs. Which means Rick probably was too. Farrell says that on some corner close to where they lived is a dealer who has been selling drugs to Rick and Claudia. With her gone, Rick's source of money is gone. He'll be hitting up the dealers who know him for credit. No strange dealer is going to carry him. Farrell said, "Find that dealer, and you'll find this Thomas guy." '

'And did you?'

'I think so,' Van Cleve said. 'I questioned every dealer for a few blocks around. Of course they all denied knowing anyone named Rick or Thomas. Except for one dealer. Oh, he denied it, but I could tell he was lying. He's the one we watch on the chance that Rick tries to make a buy tonight.'

They arrived at the corner Van Cleve had staked out. He gestured Kate down three steps into the open area outside the basement of a building from which they could keep watch on a man who stood alone, under the light from a streetlamp.

Several times thereafter expensive sports cars drove up, stopping only long enough for the driver to pass money to the dealer and receive a few small envelopes. Many customers approached on foot to effect similar transactions. Whenever the customer was a sole young man, Van Cleve whispered urgently, 'Is he the one?'

Each time Kate stared at the young man in the full glow of the streetlamp. Each time she had to say, 'No.'

After a while Van Cleve whispered, 'When I was in law school, if someone had told me I'd wind up on a stakeout on a misty night in Greenwich Village, I would have said he was crazy. I should have stayed in Shenandoah.'

'Shenandoah?' Kate asked.

'Where I come from. Small town in Pennsylvania. But ever since I was a kid, I had this dream of becoming a lawyer and going to New York. I guess most kids dream of conquering the big city. You, too, evidently.'

'The best medicine in the world is practised here,' Kate said. 'So I came to learn. And wound up feeling betrayed, bruised, hurt.'

'I know how you feel,' Van Cleve said.

'You can't. Nobody can, unless it happens to you.'

'How do you think it feels to go to work for a big law firm, under a specific promise that you'll be allowed to devote part of your time to people who need your help but can't afford it, and then because you live up to your part of the deal, the firm says, in effect, you're fired? Maybe we have more in common than either of us realises.'

It started to rain lightly. Kate had worn a tweed coat, not a raincoat. Van Cleve started to unbelt his trench coat to offer it to her, but she refused.

'It's big enough for two,' he said, opening the coat and surrounding her in its protective overlap. 'Better?'

'Better,' Kate said, though she felt uncomfortable in such close proximity to a man who was still a virtual stranger.

THEY WAITED AND WATCHED for more than three hours. Customers came on foot and by car, made their furtive purchases and left. Some of them resembled Rick Thomas but only in superficial ways, such as dress or hairstyle.

Kate reached out from the protection of Scott's trench coat to appraise the air. 'It's stopped raining,' she said.

Reluctantly Van Cleve opened his coat to allow Kate her freedom. He seemed uncomfortable and needed to talk to cover his embarrassment. 'Your family . . . You mentioned your dad is a farmer. What's he raise?'

'Corn,' Kate explained. 'Soybeans. Some wheat.'

'Difficult way of life?'

'Not easy, but there's great satisfaction in it. To plough, plant, gamble on the weather and see a crop through to harvest, to stand in the middle of a cornfield with the stalks so high they tower over you—that gives a man a real sense of accomplishment.'

'You really love your father.'

'Love. And admire,' Kate confirmed. 'He's a good man. A good father. A good husband. And he serves a purpose in this world. In our money-mad civilisation, that counts with me.'

'How do lawyers count with you?' he asked.

'I guess they're necessary,' Kate admitted.

'Just necessary? The picture of a lawyer standing in a law library with law books towering over him doesn't give you the same sense of satisfaction,' Van Cleve concluded wryly.

She turned to look up into his grey eyes. The twinkle there confirmed her suspicion that he had been teasing.

'Your father,' Kate said. 'You never said what he does.'

'Did,' he corrected.

'Oh, I'm sorry,' Kate said. 'What happened?'

'He was a railroad engineer on the run to the steel mills outside of Pittsburgh. One night, rounding Horseshoe Curve, he derailed. Speeding, the railroad's experts said.'

'Oh, too bad,' Kate commiserated. 'How old were you?'

'Seven.'

'How did your mother make out? What did she do?'

'Thanks to the men on his crew, there was his pension.'

'What do you mean?' Kate asked.

'They kept their mouths shut. My father was drunk that night,' Scott said, hesitating before he could admit, 'He was drunk most nights. If that had come to light, there might have been no pension.'

'You were only seven and you knew,' Kate commented sadly.

'I knew from the earliest time I could remember. The way he treated my mother. Shouting whenever she begged him to drink less. And he hit her. Once, when I tried to stop him, he whacked me so hard I landed across the room against the wall. When I came to, I was in her lap. She was on the floor cradling me, crying.'

'What a tragic memory to have of one's own father,' Kate said softly. 'It still torments you, doesn't it?'

'Yes, especially to talk about for the first time—' But his words were cut off abruptly as he said, 'Look!'

Kate stared across to where the dealer was being approached by another customer. Young man. Unnaturally thin. In jeans. Ponytail. Darkish colouring.

'That him?' Van Cleve whispered.

'I think so,' Kate whispered back.

At once Van Cleve sprang from their hiding place and started across the damp pavement, calling, 'Rick! Rick Thomas!' The suspect wheeled round, caught sight of Van Cleve and fled down the street, with Kate and Scott in pursuit. Finally, the young man's foot caught in a pothole. He tripped and went sprawling in the gutter, his precious glassine envelopes scattering. Before he could regain his feet, Van Cleve was on him, pinning him to the wet street, jacking up his arm behind his back.

'Hey, man, you crazy? I ain't Rick Thomas.'

Van Cleve lifted him and dragged him into the light of the nearest streetlamp so that Kate could get a good look at him.

'OK, Doctor, is this him?'

Kate stared into the face of the terrified young man. She wanted to end their search but was forced to admit, 'No, he isn't.'

Van Cleve released his grip on the man's arm and set him free with a self-conscious and hardly adequate 'Sorry.'

'Man, you are one crazy bastard!' the young man spat out in anger. 'Where are they? Where is my stuff?' He lunged forward, down on all fours, to scour the gutter for the glassine envelopes.

Van Cleve stared at him, shaking his head. 'The stuff's turned him into an animal. Look at him. It makes me sick!'

Disappointed, Van Cleve and Kate started back towards their vantage point. Before they reached it, the dealer blocked their path. Scott was prepared for a physical attack. Kate feared the man was armed and hoped that Scott would not resist.

'You flipped your lid?' the dealer challenged. 'Chasing a guy you don't even know. Down here you get blown away for less than that. Lucky that guy didn't have a piece on him.'

'Thanks for the warning,' Van Cleve replied.

His sarcasm was not lost on the dealer. 'Listen to me, and listen good. Chasing some crackhead down the street and raising a stink is stupid. But worse, you are interfering with my business. And that is a lot more dangerous. Do I make myself clear?'

'I know a warning when I hear one,' Van Cleve admitted.

'OK. I'll tell you what. I don't know what Rick Thomas is to you. And I don't care. I just don't want you hanging around ruining my business. Now, this Rick Thomas, you want him?'

'We need him. Very much,' Van Cleve said.

'OK,' the dealer replied. 'He's one of my regulars. Or was till two weeks ago, when he ran out of money. If I put the word out that because of his being a longtime customer, I am willing to carry him for a while, he'll be back.'

'You could deliver him to us?' Scott said.

'Could. And would. But we got to make a deal. Once you got him, I never see either of you around here again. OK?'

'OK,' Van Cleve said, eager to agree.

'Tomorrow night, between nine and midnight.'

'We'll be here.'

Relieved, Van Cleve and Kate started down the street.

'How's that for loyalty to an old customer?' Kate remarked.

'I don't care how it's done, so long as we get Rick Thomas's testimony.'

THE NEXT NIGHT Kate Forrester and Scott Van Cleve arrived to take up their prearranged vigil. It was another damp and misty night. This time Kate was prepared, wearing a raincoat and rain hat. The brim of the hat was turned up at a jaunty angle, converting her neat and graceful features into such a pleasing sight that Scott resented her wearing her own raincoat. But he warned himself, Never become too personally involved with a client. It can distort your professional perspective. Besides, if you lose her case, you will lose any chance at all with her.

From Kate's point of view she found she no longer thought of him as Van Cleve, but as Scott.

They took up positions behind one of the cars parked across the narrow street from the dealer. They waited. They watched. During the minutes, then the hours, they talked of themselves, of their ambitions.

'Is medicine all you thought it was going to be?' Scott asked.

'Pretty much. After doing volunteer work during high school, I had a pretty good idea,' Kate said.

'Ever get the yen to go back to Illinois and practise?'

'Sometimes. But for me, need is the deciding thing. Practise where the need is greatest,' Kate said with conviction.

'You'd live here? Marry here? Bring up your kids here?'

'I . . . I hadn't thought that far ahead,' she admitted.

'You do intend to marry, don't you?' he asked.

'The right man, the right time, yes, some day. But first I have to become the doctor I know I can be.'

'Ever think about that right man? What he'd—'

374

Before Scott could complete that thought, they both froze. Across the street the dealer had flagged them a signal. They watched as a young man wearing worn jeans and a ponytail came into the light on the corner. He was unnaturally thin.

'Him?' Scott whispered.

'I think so.'

'Rick! Rick Thomas!' Scott called.

The young man turned instinctively, then bolted away. Scott and Kate pursued him. Within half a block they caught up with him. Scott pushed him up against the iron railing in front of a small private house, and held him there despite his struggle to break free. Before long Rick ceased to resist. He breathed in short, quick breaths, trembling from cold or lack of drugs.

'Easy man, easy,' Scott said. 'We don't mean trouble. I'm a lawyer. This is my client. We need your help.'

Rick Thomas studied them both. 'He didn't send you, did he?'

'He?' Scott asked, puzzled.

'He. Him. Her father.'

'Claude Stuyvesant?'

'Yeah. Him,' Rick Thomas said with considerable vehemence. 'Took everything I owned. If I didn't have friends, I'd be sleeping out on the street.'

'Rick, like some coffee, some food, a drink, maybe?'

'Haven't had anything since breakfast,' he admitted.

In a small, inexpensive all-night restaurant on Sixth Avenue, Rick ate so voraciously that it was obvious he had missed many meals in the last few days. At times Rick answered Scott's questions with his mouth full of food.

'Rick, the night that Claudia got sick, where were you?'

'Right there,' he replied. 'I wouldn't leave her when she needed me.'

'But it was her mother who brought her to the hospital,' Kate pointed out.

'She thought it was better, safer, if her mother brought her. Especially since her own doctor wasn't in town.'

'Rick, was Claudia *on* anything that night?' Scott asked.

Rick took a gulp of coffee before he admitted, 'Yeah, we both were. You know, that's the way we met. At a party down here, where there was all kinds of stuff around.'

'Like what?' Scott asked.

'Yellow jackets. Blues. Rainbows. Coke. Angel.'

'She was into it pretty heavy, was she?' Scott asked.

'She always had a dozen prescriptions from different doctors: Valium. Darvon. Barbs. You name it, she had it. Which is also why she didn't want me to take her to the hospital. If they discovered she was on something, she didn't want me to get into trouble. She was very thoughtful that way. A terrific girl, and I loved her.'

'Rick,' Scott asked. 'Did you know that she was pregnant?'

'That was something I heard later. Is it true?'

'Yes,' Kate said.

'She was worried. I mean, she skipped her period. But only once. She was waiting to see what would happen the second month.'

From the look in his eyes both Kate and Scott knew the man was telling the truth.

'Look, how do I know he didn't send you?' Rick said suddenly.

'Rick, we're talking to you because this woman is the doctor who took care of Claudia on the night she died.'

'You?' Rick asked, staring at Kate. 'You're the lady doctor they were talking about on television? What do you want with me?'

Briefly Scott explained the charges that Claude Stuyvesant had lodged against Kate. Thus the desperate need for his testimony on Claudia's drug use.

'All you would be required to do, Rick, is tell an investigating committee the truth. As you told it to us now.'

'Stuyvesant's a powerful man. Once, when I refused to stop seeing Claudia, he had me hassled by the cops.'

'He won't be able to do anything to you now. Just tell the truth, knowing that you're doing it to save the career of the doctor who tried to save Claudia's life.'

When Rick avoided answering, Scott persisted. 'Don't worry about testifying. I'll spend a few hours with you beforehand preparing you on what you'll be asked. Rick, this doctor's career depends on you. You have to tell the truth.'

'I will, I will! Anything to get back at that bastard Stuyvesant.'

'OK! Tell you what, Rick. Since you don't have a room now, why not stay at my place until the hearing?' Scott suggested.

Rick considered Scott's offer, then said, 'I'm crashing with a friend of mine, mister. But if you . . . I mean, I'm a little broke right now.'

'Sure. I understand,' Scott replied. He reached into his pocket and produced two twenty-dollar bills. Before he handed them over, he said, 'Tell me where you're staying, and I'll pick you up on the morning I want you to testify. That should be early next week. The hearing starts on Monday.'

376

'Early next week,' Rick repeated.

'Right. Meantime, I'll check with you every day. Where do I find you?'

'Ninety-seven Charles Street. The apartment is under the name of Marty Lengel. Ring four times—three short ones, then one long ring. That way I'll know it's you and not his gorillas.'

After Scott took down Rick's new phone number, they left the restaurant. At the door Rick made a V for victory sign and walked away. As he turned the corner and disappeared from sight Kate said, 'I'd feel better if he'd taken up your offer to stay at your place.'

'So would I,' Scott said. 'I considered subpoenaing him. But jumpy as he is now, I think a legal paper would scare him into skipping town.'

'You know what's going to happen to those twenties, don't you?'

'I can guess,' Scott agreed. 'Come on. There's something else we have to do.'

As they walked through the streets of the Village, Kate explained those terms Rick had used and with which Scott was not familiar. 'The colours are the colours of the capsules the drugs are contained in. Yellow jackets are pentobarbital. Blues are amobarbital.'

'And rainbows?' Scott asked.

'A combination of amobarbital and secobarbital.'

'All prescription drugs,' Scott concluded.

They reached Charles Street and found number 97. They climbed the stairs and went into the dark entryway. Scott studied the names on the bell panel. He found the name LENGEL, M.

'That's a relief,' Scott said. 'I had to make sure there is such an address and such a person. Without a witness to Claudia's drug habit we wouldn't stand much chance.'

Chapter Eleven

On the same day that board counsel Albert Hoskins had handed Scott Van Cleve the notice to appear and a statement of charges, the three members of the state board of professional medical conduct who would sit in judgment on Dr Katherine Forrester were selected.

According to law, two of the members must be physicians or surgeons chosen from the professional members of the state board. The third committee member must be a lay person selected from the lay members of the board. One of the three members must be designated chairman, to preside over the hearing.

The first professional member appointed was Dr Maurice Truscott, a family practitioner from White Plains. Truscott had already reached the age when he was cutting down on accepting new patients. Thus he had more free time than most doctors.

Because of the cause of Claudia Stuyvesant's death, the second professional member designated was a specialist in obstetrics and gynaecology, Dr Gladys Ward. In her early forties, Dr Ward had already established herself as one of the leading surgeons in the metropolitan area.

When scanning the list of lay members, the chairman of the state board fixed on Clarence Mott, a retired businessman ever since he sold out his real estate holdings to Claude Stuyvesant. The chairman appointed Mott to preside over the Forrester hearing as well.

The final appointment was that of an administrative officer from the legal staff of the state department of health. The administrative officer was expected to rule on questions of procedure or the admissibility of evidence or testimony. Thus he had the powers of a judge, though he did not actually preside or vote.

Once word leaked in Albany that there was to be an appointment to a hearing in which Claude Stuyvesant had such a consuming interest, State Senator Francis Cahill determined to intervene. Using his legislative influence Cahill managed to have his nephew Kevin appointed.

Kevin Cahill, a lawyer in his early thirties, had originally received his position on the legal staff of the state department of health through the intercession of his uncle. Kevin had served faithfully, but with no particular distinction.

At times Uncle Francis felt he had wasted a bit of valuable political muscle in obtaining that job for his nephew. Thus once the senator managed to secure Kevin's appointment to the Forrester hearing, the uncle invited his nephew to lunch.

'Kevin, this is a time for plain talk between men. I used up a big political favour getting you this appointment, so don't blow it. I have word that Stuyvesant himself is determined to sit in on those hearings.'

'I've already seen the report of the initial investigating committee,' Kevin replied. 'This hearing could go either way.'

'It mustn't be *allowed* to go either way!' the senator declared. 'Kevin, listen to me. You want to become head of the legal staff one day? During that hearing you must never never rule against the interests of Claude Stuyvesant. I want him to owe you. In a word, if you want that job, earn it during the hearing. Clear?'

'Clear, Uncle Francis.'

CONFRONTING THE IMPENDING HEARING and representing a client who had never before been involved in any judicial proceedings, Scott Van Cleve felt it vital to educate Kate Forrester in the legal aspects of the case.

To avoid the need for her to come down to the deserted Wall Street area at night, Scott scheduled his meeting with Kate at his apartment. He occupied the entire fourth floor of a brownstone in the East Sixties. That he occupied the entire floor sounded more impressive to Kate than it proved to be. The building was only twenty-one foot wide. The entire floor consisted of a sitting room, a narrow kitchen, one small bedroom and a bathroom.

Scott brought in sandwiches and made quite a ceremony of preparing coffee in an intricate foreign coffee-maker. Then they settled down to work. Soon Scott was on his feet, pacing, lecturing.

'Forget everything you've ever seen on television about courtroom trials. A hearing is not a trial. Lawyers? Yes. Witnesses? Yes. But in place of a judge, a committee chairman, who presides, and an administrative officer, who rules. And in place of a jury, a committee of three members, who will ultimately decide.'

'I'm relieved it's not a trial,' Kate said. 'That's good.'

'No. That's bad,' Scott corrected. 'The rules of evidence are looser. Which means that unfavourable testimony that I might exclude during a trial can be admitted in a hearing. Instead of a jury of average citizens, you will be judged by your peers. And right now your profession is under attack. I hear it everywhere. "Doctors are overcharging." "Doctors don't think of their patients' health, only expensive foreign cars." "Doctors are milking Medicare." '

'That's not true of most doctors,' Kate protested.

'The public thinks it is. Which means doctors have drawn their wagons into a circle to defend their profession. Against the public. Against the media. *And* against any of their colleagues who draw fire on them. Which, unfortunately, now includes—'

'Me,' Kate anticipated.

'Exactly. Have you discovered anything about the background of the two medical committee members?'

Kate nodded. 'Dr Maurice Truscott attended City College and Cornell Medical School. He interned at Bellevue Hospital. Residency at Lenox Hill Hospital. Private practice since nineteen fifty-three. No specialty.'

'Well,' Scott said, 'let's count him as neutral. Now, what did you find out about Dr Gladys Ward?'

'Harvard College, Yale Medical School. Board certified in obstetrics and gynaecology, and also in oncological surgery,' Kate reported. 'Affiliated with Women's Hospital—St Luke's. She has two textbooks and a number of papers to her credit. Very active in women's rights movements.'

'Good, good,' Scott enthused.

'I wouldn't be too sure about that,' Kate warned. 'Rosie went to hear Ward lecture once. Ward made no bones about her loyalty to the women's cause. But she also demands more from a woman than she would from a man in a similar situation.'

'Tough talk,' Scott agreed. He made a large question mark alongside the name Ward, Gladys, MD.

After some instructions to Kate on how to act, what to say, and what not to say during the course of the hearing, he put her in a cab and went back up to his apartment. Free to make his own private assessment of the case, Scott began to lay out all the papers and documents pertinent to the hearing in the order in which he expected Hoskins to introduce them. Photocopies of Kate's notes in the chart of Claudia Stuyvesant. Copies of her entries in the order book noting each step and medication she had prescribed. Lab reports of the various blood tests she had ordered. The actions and medications used in trying to save Claudia Stuyvesant. And finally, the autopsy report that revealed the cause of death.

If only there was support from Kate's medical colleagues. Not from the interns and residents, who all supported her unequivocally, but from older, more prestigious physicians whose endorsement would carry weight with the committee. But none had consented to appear.

The autopsy report was the single most damaging piece of evidence against Kate. Even if Scott had been able to convince several doctors to testify on her behalf, they would not have been able to explain away those findings.

He had one key weapon in his legal arsenal: Rick's testimony on Claudia's drug habit. Still, Scott could not forego that nagging need to find some eminent corroborating physician to testify to the medical correctness of Kate's actions on that night.

The only possible candidate was Sol Freund. Kate had learned that Freund had tried to defend her in the meeting of the chiefs of each department of the medical staff several weeks ago. Recently retired, he had no further obligation to either City Hospital or Dr Cummins. Nor was it likely that he would be beholden to Claude Stuyvesant.

THE NEXT DAY, when Scott found Sol Freund in his office at the hospital, the old man was just taking the last of his many diplomas and certificates off the walls, leaving twenty-six faded rectangles where the framed documents had hung for years.

'Well, young man, what can I do for you?' the old doctor asked.

'I'm an attorney,' Scott began. 'I've come to ask your help in the case of Kate Forrester.'

'My help? What can I do?' Freund asked.

'I've had no success at all in finding any doctor in this hospital who would agree to testify on Dr Forrester's behalf.'

'Of course. Cummins has let it be known that any doctor who defends your client will not be around here very long. And yet who can blame him? He's got a hospital to protect. One of the reasons I decided to retire. Medicine is no longer medicine. In my day you cared about the patients first and business affairs second.'

'Doctor, I need a witness who can testify that what Kate Forrester did in the Stuyvesant case was neither negligent nor a departure from established medical treatment.'

'You understand, I am a neurologist, and far removed from cases like the Stuyvesant girl.'

'I tried a number of specialists in obstetrics and gynaecology and could get no help there,' Scott confessed.

'No surprise. For a doctor to testify for your client is like saying, If I were there, I would have done exactly what she did. Which means, If I did, the Stuyvesant girl would have died under my hand. No doctor is going to admit that.'

'Still, it would help a lot if I had a respected doctor to testify.'

Freund ignored Scott's plea. He started taking medical volumes from his bookshelves, glancing at the titles on the spines, then separating them into different piles. 'This—this hearing . . . When does it take place?'

'Starts Monday,' Scott said, hopeful for the moment.

'Monday . . .' Freund considered. 'Ah, too bad. Monday I will be on my way to frolicking on the beach in Florida. Nettie and I are leaving here Monday morning.'

He picked up another medical tome, glimpsed the title, put it on the smaller of the two stacks. 'You know, being the wife of a doctor is no fun,' Freund said, obviously struggling with his professional conscience. 'In the early years, when I was an intern, then a resident, my Nettie had to get used to waiting, to disappointments. My hours were outlandish. I used to promise her, "Nettie, once I get into practice, things will be different." And they were different. They were worse. A young doctor had to be available at all hours of day and night. Then when you finally become a professor of medicine, do things get better? No! So I had to promise Nettie, "Believe me, darling, once I retire . . ." She laughed and said, "Sol, I'll believe it when we're on the plane and not a moment before." '

'I understand,' Scott said sympathetically.

'You don't understand at all!' Freund exploded, then softened. 'You think I like to say no to Dr Forrester? But I have no choice. I promised myself, this one time Nettie is not going to be disappointed. I'm sorry, young man.'

The meeting was at an end, Scott realised. Though he left his phone number with Freund, he scratched the last possible name off his list of potential medical witnesses.

Scott had only three things to depend on: Kate and how stalwart a witness she would be under cross-examination. His own skill in breaking down the witnesses whom Hoskins would present. And Rick Thomas. His most immediate step was to begin preparing Kate for the fire she would face in the next few days.

ONCE KATE WAS COMFORTABLE in his apartment, Scott said, 'Your function as a witness is to testify to facts. What happened. What you observed. What you did. That's all. Do not volunteer.'

'I understand. Just answer the question.'

'More than that,' Scott warned. 'No matter how Hoskins twists your answers, don't argue. Now let's have a trial run. Start where you called in Briscoe—Doctor, what made you do that?'

Kate replied, 'Since the patient's signs and symptoms were so imprecise, and her abdominal pain could be indicative of an internal infection, I thought a surgeon's opinion was advisable to determine if an exploratory was necessary.'

'Meaning you were uncertain as to the validity of your own judgment, Doctor, is that right?' Scott asked.

'It wasn't a matter of the validity of my opinion. The signs, the lab reports did not add up to a definitive diagnosis. I wanted to make sure that I had not overlooked any possibilities.'

Scott pounced on her unfortunate words. 'So you admit you might have overlooked some possibilities in the case.'

'I admit no such thing!' Kate insisted, her voice rising.

Scott did not respond. After a moment of silence Kate said in a chastened tone, 'I said too much, didn't I?'

'Yes.' He pointed out, 'The proper answer to "Why did you call in Briscoe?" is simply, "To get a second opinion." That's all. A second opinion is a time-honoured practice in medicine. Don't get involved in matters like overlooking any possibilities.'

Kate nodded, resolving not to fall into that trap again.

'Now let's continue,' Scott said. 'Once Dr Briscoe arrived, what happened?'

'I reported to him the patient's vital signs. I showed him the lab results. Then he performed an examination. And he arrived at the same conclusion I did.'

'Which was?'

'Until the patient's condition became more defined, there was nothing to do except continue IVs, repeat the labs and keep checking on her vital signs,' Kate responded. 'Besides—' She stopped abruptly. 'I was about to volunteer, wasn't I?'

'Yes,' Scott said. 'You must learn to overcome that. Now let's go on. Doctor, how long between the time you sent that third blood sample to the lab and the results came back?'

'Two hours, a little more,' Kate said.

'So that for two hours you did nothing for the patient?'

'We did what was indicated for a patient in that condition. Continued the IV. Continued to check her vital signs.'

'That's it. Precise. Correct. Leaving Hoskins no chance targets to pounce on.'

Kate nodded, and smiled. 'At least I'm learning.'

'You are. And forgive me for being so tough on you. You'll appreciate that later,' he was saying when his phone rang. Impatient with any interruption, Scott answered brusquely, 'Van Cleve!'

'Hey, kid,' the gentle voice of Dr Freund said, 'no need to yell. Say hello in a nice gentlemanly way.'

'Hello, Doctor,' Scott said more gently now.

'Listen, I was talking to Nettie. Seems she has been following this Stuyvesant case on television. And she said, "After fifty-one years we could spare another few days for such a nice young woman." Now, if you can guarantee me I will be done testifying on Monday, you got yourself a deal.'

'Oh, terrific, Doctor! I can't thank you enough!'

'Don't thank me. Thank Nettie. Just tell me when you want me. But first let me get a look at that Stuyvesant chart.'

'Will do. And thanks again, Doctor.' Scott hung up. 'Freund. He's coming to testify.'

Relieved and encouraged, Kate said, 'Nice of him to do this for a woman who's a virtual stranger.'

'I don't think he feels that any young doctor is a stranger,' Scott said. 'Well, let's push on. Monday isn't so far away.'

Chapter Twelve

In the same old halting lift that Scott had used once before, he and Kate ascended to the offices of the state board of professional medical conduct. As the lift door opened, Albert Hoskins was passing by on his way to the hearing room.

'Ah, Van Cleve!' Hoskins greeted him effusively. 'And is this Dr Forrester?' He smiled at Kate and gestured for her to precede him towards the hearing room.

Kate had anticipated the room would resemble a courtroom. This room was much smaller and the configuration of the tables and chairs was different. There were three long tables arranged to form a U. The table that served as the base had four chairs—three grouped together and one near the right end of the table. The other two tables formed the legs of the U and faced each other. In the open area between the tables was a single chair for witnesses. Near the wall a stenographer was poised to record the proceedings.

Once Kate was seated, she realised she would be only ten feet from the committee that would judge her. And no more than a dozen feet opposite this man Hoskins, who would prosecute her.

Scott detected her concern. He reached under the table to touch her hand. Cold. Icy cold. He gripped it to give her reassurance.

As she settled in, Kate had the opportunity to study her judges. Clarence Mott—the lay member, who had been appointed to preside—was in the centre, flanked by Dr Maurice Truscott and Dr Gladys Ward. Dr Truscott had a bushy head of silvery hair and a short, plump body. Though the hearing had not yet commenced, he was already busy making notes. Dr Ward was younger-looking than her forty-two years. She was dark-haired and well groomed. Her features were small and precise, but her black eyes were quite sharp, active and penetrating.

Clarence Mott sat back in his chair awaiting impatiently the arrival of Kevin Cahill, the administrative officer. Soon, carrying an over-stuffed briefcase, Cahill came hurrying into the room. 'Sorry, but the plane from Albany was late,' he apologised.

Once Cahill was in his place at the end of the presiding table, Mott commenced. 'I assume we all know why we're here, so there is no need for any introduction from me. Mr Hoskins?'

Hoskins assumed a grave and ponderous attitude. 'Mr Chairman, the matter before us is of great moment in the life of this respondent, and I have enormous sympathy for her during this difficult time. But I trust the members of this committee will keep in mind that our purpose here is not to protect doctors, but to protect the people of this state from physicians who are unqualified to deliver safe health care and thus constitute a danger to the public at large. The testimony we will present will prove that Dr Katherine Forrester is such a person and that this committee should recommend that her licence to practise be revoked.'

'Mr Van Cleve?' Mott enquired.

'Mr Mott, the respondent feels no need to make an opening statement at this time.'

Mott turned to Hoskins. 'Your first witness, sir?'

Instead of announcing the name of his witness, Hoskins strode to the door and had a brief conversation there with a guard. The guard disappeared, returning some moments later with Mrs Claude Stuyvesant. Behind her followed her husband.

Scott rose to his feet. 'Mr Chairman, may I enquire if Mr Hoskins intends to introduce this woman as his first witness?'

'I do indeed,' Hoskins declared, escorting Mrs Stuyvesant to the witness chair.

'In that case,' Scott continued, 'I object to her appearance on the ground that she has nothing of substance or relevance to offer this committee. This woman is not a physician and therefore is not competent to pass judgment on any of the events in question. The only purpose she can serve is to introduce an emotional element into the proceedings.'

'On the contrary,' Hoskins protested. 'While this woman's testimony might not be deemed relevant in a court of law, I am sure that the members of this committee want to understand the conditions surrounding the untimely death of her young daughter. I appeal to Mr Cahill for a ruling.'

All eyes turned in Kevin Cahill's direction. Fully aware of his uncle's instructions, Cahill cleared his throat before pontificating, 'Mr Chairman, the appearance of this witness will bring a strong element of emotion into these proceedings. However, she is an eyewitness to the events in question. If it is clearly understood that Mr Hoskins will not ask her questions of a medical nature, then she is a perfectly qualified witness.'

Clarence Mott gestured Mrs Stuyvesant to take the witness chair. Once she was seated, the stenographer administered the oath and asked for her name and address.

'Mrs Nora Stuyvesant. Nine eighty-seven Park Avenue, New York City,' she replied.

Mott took the moment to comment, 'Mrs Stuyvesant, I want you to know the members of this committee are aware of how difficult this must be for you. So if at any time you feel need of a recess, please do not hesitate to ask.'

'Thank you, Mr Mott,' she replied formally.

Mott indicated that Hoskins was free to begin his examination.

'My dear woman, no one sympathises with you more than I do. It must be the worst nightmare of a mother's life to bring a young daughter, suffering minor symptoms, to a supposedly excellent hospital and watch her die in less than a dozen hours.'

Scott intervened. 'Mr Mott, this is exactly the emotional tone that I objected to. Can we do without these maudlin appeals and get to the so-called evidence Mr Hoskins intends to introduce?'

Mott turned to Scott sharply. 'Mr Van Cleve, I find nothing offensive in Mr Hoskins's expression of sympathy. I will let the statement stand.'

Kate noticed that as Mott finished his brief statement he cast a glance in the direction of Claude Stuyvesant, who sat stony-faced at the foot of Hoskins's table. Stuyvesant, without having spoken a single word, had come to dominate the proceedings.

Hoskins opened with his first question. 'Mrs Stuyvesant, please tell us what preceded your arrival at City Hospital on that unfortunate night.'

'At about eight o'clock that Saturday night my daughter, Claudia, called and asked me to come over. She'd been living on her own for almost a year. She hadn't been feeling well. Nausea, vomiting, slight diarrhoea. Since she'd taken the usual remedies and they didn't work, I called our own doctor. But Dr Eaves was out of town, so I decided to take her to City Hospital.'

'When you arrived, what happened?' Hoskins prodded.

'We were admitted at emergency and then shown to an examining room. Naturally, I asked to see a doctor, but instead they sent in a nurse. She took my daughter's temperature and pulse. When I again asked for a doctor, she told me one would arrive soon. But no doctor came until I protested rather strongly.'

'And when a doctor did arrive . . .' Hoskins urged.

Mrs Stuyvesant glared at the respondent's table. 'It was that woman.'

'And what did she do?'

'Not much more than the nurse did. She started to take Claudia's pulse and ask a few questions. Then she deserted my daughter to see another patient.'

'You mean she did no more than ask a few questions and then leave?' Hoskins pretended this fact was a surprise to him.

'And when I begged her not to go, she assaulted me.'

'Assaulted you?' Hoskins's feigned sense of incredulity invited more detail.

'She rudely shoved me aside and just left.'

'What happened after Dr Forrester assaulted you?'

Scott rose to protest. 'Mr Mott, would you please instruct Mr Hoskins not to characterise my client's conduct! I would like the record to indicate that there is no evidence of violence and I object to such characterisation.'

Impatiently Mott addressed the stenographer. 'See that the record so signifies.' He turned to Hoskins. 'Continue.'

'Mrs Stuyvesant, please, what happened then?'

'The doctor finally came back. She asked more questions. She told the nurse to continue with the IV and to keep on taking Claudia's pulse and blood pressure.'

'Was that all that Dr Forrester did?'

'No. After she came back several times and couldn't make up her mind what to do, she finally sent for another doctor.'

'Mrs Stuyvesant, when was the first time that either doctor actually did anything for your daughter, aside from the IVs?'

'They never did do *anything* for her!' the woman protested. 'The only time they were going to, Dr Briscoe asked for a needle and was about to insert it to see if there was any bleeding. That's when . . . that's when Claudia stopped breathing.'

'And then?'

'They rushed her down the hall to another room. I tried to follow, but that woman shut me out.'

'When was the next time you saw Dr Forrester?'

'She'—the woman pointed at Kate—'she came out of that room. I could tell by the look on her face. She said, "Mrs Stuyvesant, we did all we could." All they could indeed! They did nothing!' The distraught woman began weeping.

Inwardly Scott was seething. He had seen lawyers employ such shabby tactics before—using a witness for purely emotional effect—but rarely had he seen it used so shamelessly. Not only was Hoskins playing on the sympathy of the committee members, but by glancing at Stuyvesant from time to time, he was making sure the tycoon would not forget him when this hearing was ended.

When Mrs Stuyvesant recovered sufficiently to lift her tearful face from her damp handkerchief, Hoskins resumed. 'So they shut you out while your daughter was dying. Then this woman came to tell you— And then?'

'Someone took me out to my limousine in which I had arrived with a daughter who was slightly ill. Now she was dead, and I was left alone.'

Feeling that he had extracted the ultimate in emotional impact from this witness, Hoskins recited the comment he had prepared for exactly this moment. 'Madam, I'm sure the members of this committee sympathise with your feelings at this terrible moment. I have no further questions.'

Relieved of the need to testify further, Nora Stuyvesant gave way to a flood of tears.

'Mr Van Cleve?' Chairman Mott addressed him. 'Do you wish to cross-examine this witness?' But by his attitude Mott was really asking, Do you dare to cross-examine her?

FULLY ALERT TO THE TRAP that always awaited any lawyer who chose to cross-examine a grieving mother, Scott Van Cleve said, 'Mr Mott, I am quite willing to give Mrs Stuyvesant a brief recess before I ask the few questions I have.'

Nora Stuyvesant dabbed at her eyes and sniffed. 'I am ready to continue. I will do my best.'

Hoskins returned to his chair, smug in the knowledge that the more strongly Van Cleve attacked Nora Stuyvesant, the more sympathy she would earn from the committee.

Aware of that danger, Scott approached the witness. 'Now then, Mrs Stuyvesant, when you brought your daughter to City Hospital, were her complaints slight, moderate or severe?'

'I would say . . . sort of moderate,' she replied.

'Not alarming?' Scott sought to narrow her choices.

'Moderate,' she repeated.

'Not life-threatening?' Scott continued.

Hoskins rose to his feet. 'Mr Chairman, how is a mother like Mrs Stuyvesant—unqualified as a medical expert—to respond to a question calling for an opinion of a patient's condition?'

'Exactly the point, Mr Hoskins! Yet only minutes ago she said'—Scott referred to his notes—' "I had arrived with a daughter who was slightly ill." If her opinion was valid five minutes ago, I should think it would be valid now. Mrs Stuyvesant has tried to give this committee the impression that her daughter was only slightly ill, but that as a result of Dr Forrester's actions, she died. The truth is that the patient was severely ill when brought to the hospital, but her condition was concealed from Dr Forrester.'

Kevin Cahill intervened. 'Since the witness is not qualified as an expert, she may not be asked to offer any opinions. She may testify only as to facts.'

'So ruled,' Mott declared. 'Continue, Mr Van Cleve.'

'Mrs Stuyvesant, I understand that at the time in question your daughter was no longer residing under your roof. How long had Claudia been living away from home?'

'Almost a year,' Mrs Stuyvesant replied.

'Had there been any contact between your daughter and you during that time?'

'Claudia called us from time to time.'

'Did she ever mention a person named Rick Thomas?'

'Rick Thomas?' the woman repeated.

'Does that name mean anything to you?'

Nora Stuyvesant paused before responding, 'No, it does not.'

'Would it surprise you to learn that your daughter and Rick Thomas were living together at the time of her—'

Before Scott could complete the question, Claude Stuyvesant was up from his chair, pointing his finger at him while shouting, 'I will not have it! I will not have such cheap shyster tricks used to defame the name of my dead daughter!'

'Mr Stuyvesant, Mr Stuyvesant,' Mott interrupted the outburst. 'Believe me, we are all aware of the strain you are under, but we must conduct this proceeding in an orderly fashion.'

Face flushed, eyes glinting in anger, Stuyvesant slowly sank back into his chair.

Mott signalled Scott to resume.

'Mrs Stuyvesant, I was asking about Rick Thomas.'

Hoskins rose to object. 'Mr Mott, since Mrs Stuyvesant has already said that she knows nothing about a person called Rick Thomas, I do not see how she can be expected to answer any questions about him. If Mr Van Cleve has no further questions, I ask that he conclude what is obviously a painful experience for both the witness and her husband.'

'I have a few more questions, Mr Mott,' Scott replied.

'Proceed,' Clarence Mott said.

'Mrs Stuyvesant, did you have any knowledge of the fact that your daughter was a habitual user of drugs?'

Again Stuyvesant was on his feet. 'Damn it! I insist you stop slandering my daughter!'

'Mr Chairman, I have very substantial reason to believe that my statement is, in fact, true.'

'Then surely the medical examiner's report would have revealed that,' Hoskins argued. 'Yet it contains not a single word to that effect. How do you account for that, Mr Van Cleve?'

'As it was explained to me, once cause of death was established, the medical examiner felt no need to make such a determination,' Scott replied.

'What about a hospital lab report?' Hoskins challenged. 'Surely if there were such a report, Mr Van Cleve would rush to introduce it into the record.'

'My client requested a toxicological screening of the patient's blood, and one was performed. But somehow it is missing from her chart,' Scott replied.

' "Missing from her chart", ' Hoskins mimicked. 'First our Mr Van Cleve treats us to a non-existent person named Rick Thomas. Now he refers to a lab report that is "missing" from the patient's chart. I challenge Mr Van Cleve to introduce this Rick Thomas and to bring us proof of that "missing" lab report.'

'I shall do my best to comply with Mr Hoskins's request,' Scott said. Feeling that he had now set up the situation perfectly for Rick's appearance, he resumed his examination of the witness.

'Mrs Stuyvesant, earlier you charged that Dr Forrester "assaulted" you. Do you know where the doctor was going when that incident occurred?'

'I have no idea.'

'Didn't you hear a nurse summon her to another case?'

'Yes, there was another patient,' Nora Stuyvesant conceded.

'Then is it fair for me to say that she wasn't "deserting" your daughter, but was momentarily leaving her to go to the aid of another patient?'

'I was only interested in my daughter's health and safety.'

'Is that why you took up a position at the door to physically block Dr Forrester from leaving?' Scott asked.

'I could not allow her to leave my daughter, who was even sicker than I'd thought she was,' Mrs Stuyvesant replied.

Encouraged, since the witness was beginning to fight back, Scott continued. 'Mrs Stuyvesant, Dr Forrester was responsible for many lives that night. Since you were standing in her way, she brushed by you to get on with her duties. Would you still call that an assault?'

The witness stared at him and did not reply.

'Mrs Stuyvesant?' Scott prodded. When she did not respond, he continued. 'When Dr Briscoe was assisting you to your limousine, do you recall what you said?'

'I don't recall saying anything,' she denied quickly.

'Strange. Because several people—Dr Briscoe and Dr Forrester among them—heard you say, "He'll blame me . . . He'll blame me." Do you recall that?'

'I've already said I don't recall saying anything!'

'Then am I to believe that Dr Briscoe, Dr Forrester, and others who say they heard you are all lying?'

'Why not?' The woman was half up out of her chair. 'They all had a part in killing my daughter. Now they are all lying to protect themselves. To protect her!' On her feet now, she shouted at Kate, 'You killed her! And now your lawyer is telling a pack of lies to protect you! Well, you won't get away with it!' Her anger spent, Nora Stuyvesant slipped down into the witness chair once more.

Softly Scott Van Cleve asked, 'Mrs Stuyvesant, do you remember Dr Forrester asking your daughter if she had been sexually active?' The woman barely nodded. Scott turned to the chairman. 'Mr Mott, can we have the stenographer record that the witness nodded in reply to my question?'

'Yes, of course. Get on with it, Mr Van Cleve.'

'Mrs Stuyvesant, do you recall your daughter's answer to that question?' Nora Stuyvesant did not respond. 'Your daughter denied that she had been sexually active. Am I correct?'

The woman nodded.

'Did the doctor also ask if she had missed any menstrual periods?'

Mrs Stuyvesant nodded once more. 'And was your daughter's response that she had not?' Again Mrs Stuyvesant nodded.

'Since we now know from the medical examiner's report that both those answers were false, can you offer any reason why your daughter would have lied to the doctor who was treating her?'

'No. I . . . I know no reason,' Mrs Stuyvesant said in a voice barely loud enough for the stenographer to hear.

'Thank you, Mrs Stuyvesant. That is all.' Scott turned away.

Hoskins approached Mrs Stuyvesant and helped her to her feet, at the same time consoling, 'I know this has been an ordeal.' He surrendered her into the hands of her husband. 'You are both free to leave now, sir.'

Stuyvesant nodded grimly. He kissed his wife, indicating that she was free to leave but that he had no such intention.

'I'd rather stay,' she protested meekly.

'You've been through enough for one day, my dear,' Stuyvesant said. 'Go on home and try to recover from this ugly business.'

She lingered for a moment until he said, 'Nora, go!' Obediently she followed her husband's suggestion.

Chapter Thirteen

As agreed in advance with chairman Mott and counsel Hoskins, the hearing procedure was interrupted to allow Dr Sol Freund to testify for the respondent so that he could depart for his retirement in Florida. Freund was bald, except for the slight fringe of white hair that ringed his gleaming rosy scalp. His cheeks were concave but clean-shaven, and the bony structure of his face stood out almost as clearly as it would on an X-ray. He wore a dark blue suit and simple gold-framed glasses.

After Freund was sworn as a witness, Mott nodded his approval to Scott Van Cleve to commence the testimony.

'Sir, how many years have you trained for and practised the profession of medical doctor?'

'Fifty-two years.'

'Doctor, are you familiar with the general procedures and practices in large city hospitals, and in City Hospital in particular?'

'I have served as an intern, a resident, later as a member of the staff of large hospitals in this city for many years, and at City Hospital in particular for the last thirty-four.'

'Dr Freund, have you had time to familiarise yourself with the chart of Claudia Stuyvesant?'

'I studied it with great interest,' Freund replied.

'Did you find it a competently written record?'

'Not only competently written, quite detailed.'

'With that in mind, Doctor, was there anything you would have done differently if you had been the doctor in charge of the Stuyvesant girl on that night?'

'No. There were simply not sufficient findings on which to base a differential diagnosis. Fever, nausea, vomiting, diarrhoea—who of us has not had those symptoms?'

'Would you classify those symptoms as alarming?'

'Oh, no,' Freund responded.

'Since we now know that there actually was extensive internal bleeding,' Scott said, 'how would you account for the fact that the symptoms and signs did *not* reflect that condition?'

'Many factors can distort symptoms and signs. Dehydration, for one. Also the patient's condition may have been affected by the medicines she took before she turned up in emergency.'

Scott Van Cleve took a long pause before saying, 'I have no further questions.'

Hoskins signified he wished to cross-examine. 'Dr Freund, what is your personal association with the respondent?'

'I have no personal association with Dr Forrester. You think I have come to plead for a protégée? No, you are mistaken. I simply hate to see young careers destroyed by baseless accusations.'

'Doctor, when was the last time you served in emergency?'

'Forty-nine years ago,' Freund replied.

'And when was the last time you had to take the initial history of a new patient in emergency or anywhere else, for that matter?'

'Not recently,' Freund conceded. 'For the past thirty-one years as a neurosurgeon, by the time a case reaches my office, that patient has been seen and tested by several doctors, neurologists, even psychiatrists. So the patient comes with a complete history.'

'Doctor, has it been many years since you have had any experience similar to what happened that night in emergency?'

'Of course,' the old doctor said with obvious irritation.

'So that your opinion of what took place that night is not based either on knowledge of Dr Forrester's professional capability or of the situation itself, since you have been far removed from such practice for many years,' Hoskins stated.

'My opinion is based on what is written in that chart.'

'You trust that chart completely?' Hoskins asked.

'It appears to be written in conformity with good medical practice. I have no reason to *distrust* it,' Freund declared.

'Allow me to show you this circled notation on the patient's chart,' Hoskins said, presenting a copy to the doctor.

Freund studied certain lines that were circled in red ink. 'Ah, yes. The negative pregnancy test.'

'Have you also seen a copy of the medical examiner's report?'

'Yes, I have. Ruptured ectopic pregnancy leading to massive internal bleeding,' Freund replied.

'Doctor, aren't we forced to ask ourselves, what did Dr Forrester do which resulted in that false pregnancy report?'

'Don't be too quick to attribute that failure to the doctor,' Freund grumbled. 'No test is perfect.'

'Based on the chart, Doctor, would you say that in your professional opinion the symptoms and signs the patient presented were consistent with an ectopic pregnancy?'

'Yes,' Freund admitted. 'They were.'

'Just one more question. If Dr Forrester *had* come up with the correct diagnosis, would she, or some other doctor, have been able to save Claudia Stuyvesant's life?'

'No one will ever know the answer to that,' Freund replied.

'Can you *deny* the possibility?'

Impatiently Freund exploded, 'I can't deny. No one can!'

Feeling that he had counteracted all the favourable testimony Freund had given, Hoskins was quite pleased as he concluded, 'Thank you, Doctor. That will be all.'

'Oh, will it?' the angered old doctor replied, rising from his chair. 'Well, it is not "all" as far as I'm concerned.'

Hoskins tried to interrupt. 'Doctor, please, your testimony is finished.'

Freund turned on Hoskins. 'You!' he accused, pointing his finger at him. 'You are a lawyer, so stay out of it! This is a problem for doctors.'

He turned to Dr Ward and Dr Truscott. 'Colleagues, in recent years, as a member of the admissions committee of our medical school, I have watched with great concern the applications that have crossed my desk. When I examine them closely, I discover the quality of the students applying is not the same. The best and brightest of our young no longer choose to become doctors. Why? Because other

fields are more attractive. The avalanche of malpractice lawsuits, the rigorous demands of our profession—our best young men and women no longer wish to put up with all that.

'And when they do? Take this young woman. This dedicated, well-trained woman is asked to defend herself for acting as a good doctor should. Yet now she is put in the dock like a criminal, attacked and vilified. Called a murderer, as someone did on television.' He swung about. 'Yes, by you, Mr Stuyvesant!'

Turning back to his colleagues, Freund resumed. 'This persecution, this inquisition must cease. Else all highly intelligent, highly motivated young people like Dr Forrester will take their abilities elsewhere. I warn you, put a stop to this kind of thing!'

With some disdain he glared at Hoskins. 'Now my testimony *is* finished.'

Freund started to leave, stopping to say to Kate, 'My dear, I tried to do you some good, but I don't have the patience for these legal games any longer. I have faith in you and I trust all this will turn out well. Let me know how things end up here.'

Once Freund left the hearing room, chairman Mott asked, 'Ladies, gentlemen, shall we break for lunch now?'

There was general agreement except for Dr Ward, who said, 'I want clarification on one point from Mr Van Cleve.'

'Yes, Doctor?' Scott replied, coming to his feet.

'I was puzzled by the introduction of Dr Freund as a witness. This is not his field of expertise. He is far removed from the usual run of cases in emergency. I am forced to ask why?'

'We could get no other physician to come forward and testify. There is a blackout at City Hospital. The staff is being discouraged to come to Dr Forrester's defence.'

'And were no other doctors willing to come forward?'

'With the hostility and suspicion that doctors now harbour towards the legal system, I could find no specialist in the field who would agree to become involved.'

Kate thought she detected a sympathetic and understanding nod from Dr Truscott. But Dr Ward gave no outward indication of her reaction to Scott's admission.

AFTER THE INTERRUPTION in the proceedings to accommodate Dr Freund, the hearing resumed its prescribed course. Hoskins continued to build his case against Kate Forrester. His next witness was the medical examiner of the city of New York.

Dr Schwartzman's responses to Hoskins's questions were curt and economical. He crisply recited his education and professional background. He then went on to recall the events surrounding the Stuyvesant case. The cadaver was sent down to the medical examiner's building with a special request that he himself perform the autopsy. Since the police and the district attorney had prior call on his services, this autopsy was delayed several days. But the result was definitive. Claudia Stuyvesant had died of an internal haemorrhage due to a ruptured ectopic pregnancy.

'Dr Schwartzman,' Hoskins continued. 'Did you make any other observations in the course of your autopsy?'

'Well,' the medical examiner began, 'with such gross findings I couldn't understand why her condition wasn't diagnosed.'

'Do I understand you to say that in your opinion a competent doctor should have been able to make a correct diagnosis while the patient was still alive?'

'That's exactly what I am saying,' Schwartzman declared, concluding his testimony.

Scott could not allow the medical examiner to escape without being questioned.

'Dr Schwartzman, I accept your findings without reservation. Except for one thing that troubles me.'

'Whatever I can do to enlighten you, Counsellor,' Schwartzman volunteered. 'I am here to help.'

'Doctor, when was the last time you *treated* a patient? Specifically, a young female patient, nineteen years of age.'

Schwartzman glared in resentment. 'Once I entered forensic medicine, I no longer continued to treat patients.'

'And when was that, Doctor?'

'Some . . . some twenty-two or twenty-three years ago.'

Hoskins called from his place at the table, 'Mr Mott, when a man appears here as medical examiner, with a superb professional record, Mr Van Cleve's question does sound ridiculous.'

Scott turned on him. 'No more ridiculous, Mr Hoskins, than asking him whether a doctor dealing with a living patient should have detected a condition that was far from obvious at the time. Especially in a patient who was giving a false history and was, most likely, under the influence of drugs!'

At once Stuyvesant was on his feet, calling, 'Mr Mott! I thought we had agreed—'

Stuyvesant interrupted himself abruptly. Scott turned to stare at him, then at Mott. It had become quite clear that Stuyvesant and Mott had agreed, privately, that there was to be no mention of drugs during the hearing.

Mott flushed slightly. 'Mr Van Cleve, unless you can present proof that drugs played any part in this case, we shall consider any mention of that subject out of order. Do I make myself clear?'

'Yes, sir,' Scott replied.

'Dr Schwartzman, how do you account for the fact that there is no mention in your report of *any* findings related to drugs?'

Mott struck the table with his gavel. 'Mr Van Cleve, I placed limitations on that subject!'

'Mr Mott, you said mention of the *presence* of drugs was off limits. I am enquiring about the *absence* of same from his report.'

On a cue from Mott, Schwartzman addressed the stenographer. 'I wish the record to show that once I established the cause of death, there was no need for further enquiry.'

'Dr Schwartzman, do you recall an occasion when I visited you in your office?' Scott asked.

'Yes.'

'Sir, didn't you admit to me that the mayor himself asked you not to reveal your findings until the funeral of Claudia Stuyvesant was over?'

'A courtesy. An act of consideration to a bereaved family. It didn't change my findings,' Schwartzman protested.

'Dr Schwartzman, is it possible in the course of an autopsy to find residual damage resulting from extensive drug use even if one does not perform a toxic screen?'

'If one were looking for such evidence, yes.'

'Could such evidence be found now if Claudia Stuyvesant's body were exhumed?'

'Young man, I told you in my office that day, the body was cremated as soon as the autopsy was completed.'

'So you did,' Scott agreed. 'Another "courtesy", Doctor? Releasing the body so quickly for cremation? There must be quite a busy hot line between your office and the mayor's office.'

His face red with anger and embarrassment, Schwartzman turned to the chairman. 'Mr Mott, do I have to dignify such sheer speculation with an answer?'

Hoskins was on his feet. 'No, Doctor, you do not!'

Pretending to be defeated, Scott said, 'That is all.'

From her place at the table Kate Forrester studied the faces of the two medical members of the committee. Truscott had been making continuous notes all through the exchange. Gladys Ward, who had been listening throughout the cross-examination with detachment, interrupted as Schwartzman was rising from the witness chair.

'Doctor,' she said sharply. 'In your opinion, if Claudia Stuyvesant had been a casual or even an habitual user of drugs, how would that have affected the outcome in this case?'

'You know, Dr Ward, I've asked myself that same question,' Schwartzman replied. 'The way I see it, drugs could not cause her ectopic pregnancy. I've never heard of such a case.'

'Nor have I,' Ward agreed.

'And ectopics, undetected, *will* rupture and haemorrhage, whether the patient used drugs or not. So I do not see the relevance of all this fuss about drugs,' Schwartzman said.

At that moment Kate Forrester rose to demand, 'Doctor, is it possible for drugs to mask a patient's symptoms and signs and affect lab findings, thus misleading the doctor?'

'Dr Forrester, Dr Forrester,' Mott said as he tried to intervene. But Kate would not be silenced.

'Doctor, could drugs mask pain and other symptoms and signs?' Kate insisted. 'I demand you answer!'

Flustered, his face growing red, Schwartzman glared at her. 'You really want to know what I believe? I believe that since there is no definitive evidence on this matter of drugs, you and your attorney are trying to use it as a smoke screen to divert attention from your medical blunder.'

With that, the medical examiner started from the room, but not without exchanging glances with Claude Stuyvesant.

Once he was gone, Mott turned to Kate Forrester. 'Young woman, we will never again tolerate such unorthodox conduct during this hearing!' Then he addressed the prosecutor. 'Now, Mr Hoskins, your next witness?'

'Mr Chairman, since the hour is late, I ask that this hearing be set over until tomorrow morning.'

'Mr Van Cleve?' Mott asked.

'I have no objection,' Scott replied.

'Then we stand in recess until tomorrow morning at ten,' Mott declared, and banged his gavel.

Quickly Scott took Kate by the hand and led her outside the hearing room. Before he could speak, she did.

'OK, I should have kept my mouth shut. And if I carry on in this way, I will be responsible for losing my case. There! I said it to save you the trouble.'

'Thanks,' Scott said. 'Just one thing,' he added. 'Never do that again. It could be dangerous.'

Chapter Fourteen

Kate had hardly inserted her key into the second lock of the front door when it flew open and Rosie Chung asked anxiously, 'Well? How did it go?'

'Not too well, I'm afraid,' Kate admitted.

Rosie led the way to the living room, insisting, 'Tell me, tell me everything!'

Briefly Scott explained the legal purpose of the testimony Hoskins had introduced today.

'Mrs Stuyvesant's testimony was bad enough,' Kate said. 'But when Dr Ward became involved, things were even worse.'

'Kate!' Scott intervened reprovingly. 'Let's keep things in perspective. Now, did Hoskins score some telling points today? Yes. Mrs Stuyvesant *was* a very sympathetic witness. She *had* lost a teenage daughter. But I'm sure the committee is aware that that colours her version of what happened that night.'

'Not Mr Clarence Mott,' Kate interjected.

'OK, he's in Stuyvesant's pocket. But there *are* two other members of that committee,' Scott pointed out. 'Now as to Schwartzman . . .'

'He had a very convincing response to every question you asked,' Kate reminded. 'That's what led me to question him.'

'You questioned a witness?' Rosie asked. 'Is that allowed?'

'She got away with it this time,' Scott said. 'But she didn't realise I was deliberately sucking Schwartzman in. Giving him every opportunity to insist there was no evidence of Claudia's drug use. Because when I walk Rick Thomas into the hearing room, the committee will not only know we have been telling the truth, they will also realise that there is a conspiracy at work here.'

'And when you do that, that's the ball game,' Rosie concluded.

'I hope so,' Scott said. 'Now, Kate, I'd like a good strong drink to relax. I need it.'

SCOTT AND KATE DROPPED Rosie at the hospital to go on night duty. Then they picked up some sandwiches and went back to Scott's apartment to continue Kate's preparation as a witness.

Scott began, 'Tomorrow, Hoskins will put on his expert witnesses. Then it's our turn. I'll lead off with Nurse Cronin and Nurse Beathard. Not that they can do much besides corroborate some of the things you will say. But I am putting them on to get a clue to Hoskins's plan for cross-examination. Because in the end this hearing comes down to one thing: *You*. On the stand, telling your story, and then being able to withstand Hoskins's cross-examination.'

'And you think I won't hold up.'

'In all honesty I don't know,' Scott admitted. 'I have watched top executives in business, in government, crack under the strain of being cross-examined by a skilful lawyer. Witnesses suddenly go blank. They forget the most obvious facts, or they suddenly offer different versions from those they remembered before.'

'Try me,' Kate challenged.

He gestured her from the couch to the armchair that had become her witness chair during their sessions. Once seated, she was ready for his attack.

For the next three hours Scott pounded her with questions about Mrs Stuyvesant's testimony and the autopsy report. Sometimes his questions flowed in sequence; sometimes he posed deliberate non sequiturs. He went over the same ground again and again until she protested, 'I've already answered that!' She was louder than she wanted to be. Fatigue was taking its toll.

It was past midnight. He could see that Kate was exhausted, but he determined not to let up. Once she took the witness chair, she would be in it all day. To prepare her, Scott decided to push Kate to the limit.

'Doctor,' he continued. 'We've heard a great deal during this hearing about the pregnancy test that you say you performed. You noted it in the patient's chart, along with the result. Negative. Can you explain to the committee why you received a false result?'

'No,' she said. 'I often think—' She broke off. 'No. Beyond the fact that such tests have a recognised failure rate, I can't explain it.'

'Doctor, you said, "I often think—" What is it that you often think?' Scott pursued.

'I often think—I sometimes ask myself—those three simple steps in the test, did I perform them correctly?'

'What do you mean?' Scott pressed.

'After so many continuous hours on duty, I was so exhausted that I might have made a mistake.'

'What kind of mistake?' Scott demanded quickly.

'The three reagents ... Did I apply them incorrectly? Out of sequence, possibly? I was so tired, anything could have happened,' Kate admitted.

'Anything?' Scott demanded. 'Yet you made that entry in the patient's chart stating that you performed the test correctly. Doctor, are you telling us that you wrote down things in that chart that were not true?'

'You're twisting my words,' Kate replied. 'It was days later, when I learned the negative result was wrong, that I began to think back and try to discover why.'

Scott refused to let up. 'So it is possible that when you wrote that note in the chart, it was wrong. Maybe *deliberately* wrong!'

'I have never in my life falsified an entry in a patient's chart!' Kate protested, rising up to confront him. 'Never, do you hear? Never!' By which time she was weeping.

Scott took her in his arms and held her. He led her to the couch and sat her down. He covered her with a rug and said softly, 'You've had a tough night. Just relax.'

Minutes later, when the rhythm of her breathing changed, he realised she had fallen asleep. And why not? She had been under extreme pressure for weeks, and for the past nineteen hours she had virtually been on trial for her life. Let her sleep.

IT WAS EARLY THE NEXT MORNING. Kate woke up slowly, then realised suddenly that she was not in her bed but on a couch. And not her couch. She threw back the rug, looked around and then stood up quickly. Scott must have heard her, for he called, 'Kate, you up?'

'Up,' she replied.

'You'll find a fresh toothbrush in the bathroom,' he said. 'Coffee's ready. Pancakes and bacon, too.'

She freshened up and combed her hair. She longed for her make-up, but it was in her handbag out in the living room. She decided to do without it. When she entered the kitchen, the table was already set. Fragrant steam curled up slowly from her coffee cup. Alongside was a glass of freshly squeezed orange juice. As soon as she finished her juice, Scott whipped away the glass and replaced it with a plate of pancakes, bordered by strips of crisp bacon.

He sat down opposite her. 'Good morning!' he said brightly. She smiled and started to eat. 'You were so beat last night I didn't have the heart to wake you,' he explained.

'I must have been exhausted.'

'How are the pancakes?'

'Excellent,' she replied. 'You're a good cook.'

'Bachelors get lots of practice.' He was smiling. 'More coffee?'

'Please.'

They finished breakfast in silence.

'I'd better get home and change for the hearing,' Kate said.

'I'll take you,' he said. 'Let me clear the table and we can be on our way.'

'I can help,' she offered.

'I'm terrific at clearing dishes,' he said, 'especially breakfast dishes.'

'You evidently associate with the wrong kind of women,' Kate teased. 'I would think that out of sheer appreciation, they would at least offer. But in this era of the liberated woman, they do as men used to—make love and run.'

'Given the chance, I wouldn't run,' he said, no longer bantering.

'We'd better go,' Kate said softly.

ALL THE OTHER PARTICIPANTS, including Claude Stuyvesant, had convened by the time Scott and Kate arrived in the hearing room. Chairman Mott glanced at his gold watch on the table to underscore that they were six minutes late. He rapped his gavel lightly.

'Shall we begin?' He looked in Hoskins's direction.

The portly prosecutor rose from his tight-fitting chair. With a grave air he presented his next witness, Dr John Vinmont, a specialist in obstetrics and gynaecology on the staff of Columbia Presbyterian Medical Center. Citing Vinmont's excellent educational and professional background, Hoskins did not take long to qualify the doctor as an expert.

Slowly Hoskins led him through a recital of his knowledge of the case. Yes, he had studied the chart that Dr Forrester had written up, had studied photocopies of the order book, had carefully studied the medical examiner's report.

Hoskins now came to the question for which all the foregoing had served as prologue. 'Dr Vinmont, in your professional opinion, suppose a doctor had discovered all the findings noted in this chart, and suppose that doctor had instituted all the modalities noted here, and suppose the patient had died of the cause reported by the medical examiner, would you say that the death of such a patient could be considered preventable and hence due to negligence and professional failure on the part of the doctor?'

404

Vinmont's answer was as brief as the question had been long. 'Yes, sir.'

'Dr Vinmont, in your expert opinion, what would have been the outcome if a correct diagnosis had been made in the first few hours of the patient's treatment by Dr Kate Forrester?'

'Routine surgery would surely have had a favourable result,' Vinmont replied.

'Thank you, Doctor.'

Even under Scott's sharp cross-examination Vinmont proved unshakable. He brushed aside questions related to Claudia Stuyvesant's untruthful answers about sexual activity and missed periods. When Scott tried to introduce questions as to the effect of drug use, Hoskins objected on the ground that no such evidence had been introduced. Cahill upheld Hoskins's objection.

Frustrated, Scott returned to the defence table.

He fared no better with Hoskins's next two witnesses, Dr Florence Neary and Dr Harold Bruno. Their expert opinions coincided with Vinmont's. When Scott cross-examined them under the same restrictions, their answers were the same.

Hoskins had skilfully presented an unassailable prima-facie case of medical failure on the part of the doctor leading to the untimely death of a nineteen-year-old woman, which could have been prevented if a proper diagnosis had been made.

'Mr Hoskins, may I assume this concludes the board's case against Dr Forrester?' Scott asked.

'Yes, sir,' Hoskins replied, then continued. 'The board of professional medical conduct, having established the facts in this matter and having presented considerable evidence of Dr Forrester's negligent handling of the case of Claudia Stuyvesant, thereby resulting in her death, rests. And now, we trust that Mr Van Cleve will respond with facts instead of charges. With credible witnesses instead of hints and innuendoes.'

'Mr Van Cleve?' Chairman Mott asked.

'I will need time to assemble my witnesses. May we resume the day after tomorrow?'

'We stand adjourned until then.' Mott rapped his gavel.

Scott Van Cleve went directly from the hearing room to a public phone booth at the end of the corridor. He inserted a coin and dialled the number. He heard three rings, four, five, but no answer. He began to experience a queasy feeling until finally, on the sixth ring, he heard the voice that allowed him to relax.

'Rick? Scott Van Cleve.'

'Oh, yeah. Hi!' Rick Thomas replied.

'Rick, day after tomorrow will probably be the day, so you and I better spend tomorrow together. I'll pick you up at ten tomorrow. OK?'

'You got it, man,' Rick agreed with enthusiasm.

'See you tomorrow. At ten.'

'Oh, by the way,' Rick said, 'I'm broke again.'

'I understand,' Scott said. 'I won't come empty-handed.'

IT WAS TWENTY PAST ONE in the morning. Scott had exhausted himself mapping the precise order of his two crucial witnesses, framing his questions and strategy for maximum impact on the committee.

Which would prove more dramatic and effective? he pondered. Kate's testimony first, followed by the surprise appearance of Rick Thomas? Or Rick Thomas first, to convince the committee that he had been telling them the truth and thus predispose them more favourably to Kate's testimony?

SCOTT WAS STILL DEBATING the most effective way to present his case as he started down Charles Street. He arrived at number 97. He stepped into the small dark entryway and scanned the bell board until he found LENGEL, M. As agreed with Rick, he rang three short rings, paused, then rang one long one. There was no response.

Rick was probably asleep, Scott assumed. He repeated the signal. Again, no response. Scott began to be concerned. He rang once more—three short rings, then one ring so long that his finger was still on the button when the buzzer finally sounded. He raced quickly up the staircase.

Scott became aware of someone leaning over the banister of the fourth-floor landing. He looked up to find a young woman just pulling on a shabby kimono. Her hair was unruly, her eyes blinking, curious and noticeably suspicious.

By now Scott had reached the landing. They were face to face. She stood with her back to the partly opened door.

'I'm looking for apartment four C, Marty Lengel,' Scott said. 'Rick Thomas is crashing with him for a few days.'

'There's no "him", ' the woman said. '*I'm* Marty Lengel.'

'So Rick's staying with you,' Scott said, somewhat taken aback. 'I have a meeting with him at ten.'

'He's not here,' Marty Lengel said.

'He must be here,' Scott insisted. 'I talked with him yesterday. We arranged to meet this morning. He's set to testify tomorrow.'

'Sorry, he's not here,' she repeated.

Scott pushed past her into the small room. It was dark, the shade down. He saw a rumpled bed in one corner. There was a small kitchenette, the sink piled with soiled dishes. He became aware of an odour that hinted that marijuana had been smoked here recently. There was no sign of Rick Thomas.

Resentful at his forcible intrusion, she gloated. 'I told you, he isn't here.'

'Do you have any idea where he went?' Scott asked.

'I wasn't even here,' she said.

'Did Rick say anything the last time you spoke to him?'

'Not about leaving, no,' she replied. 'You're the one called yesterday afternoon. That was you, wasn't it?'

'Yes.'

'I heard him say he was going to meet you,' Marty Lengel said. 'Then later, just before seven o'clock, he gets another call. Said it was this guy he knew promising some very good stuff.'

'Stuff?'

'Coke. Real pure,' she said. 'To Rick coke was like a ring in a bull's nose. You could lead him anywhere with it.'

'And he went for it,' Scott concluded.

'Evidently. And never came back,' Marty Lengel said. 'Last I saw of him was when I went to work. I wait tables all night in this Italian place on Fourth Street. He's probably left town.'

'Have you any idea who the man was who called him?'

'He mentioned a name, but I didn't pay attention,' she said.

Scott nodded grimly. Half his defence—the crucial half—had been shot out from under him. When Hoskins challenged him to produce Rick Thomas, it would certainly appear that he had indeed invented a fictitious witness. His own professional credibility now hung in the balance.

'And he said nothing else,' Scott persisted.

'Oh, yeah, he did say one thing,' she said. 'Something about getting his things back.'

'The things he lost when they cleaned out Claudia's place?'

'He didn't have any other things that I know of.'

'Did you know Claudia?' Scott asked.

'Sort of. Why?' She was defensive again, on guard.

'Did she do drugs?' Scott asked.

'You must be new to this scene,' she observed. 'Otherwise you'd know, if one of them is really into drugs, the other one is, too. That's the way it goes down here.'

'Tell me, Ms Lengel, if you could help a young woman doctor defend herself against Claude Stuyvesant, save her career, would you be willing to testify to what you just told me?'

'Uh-uh,' she refused, shaking her head stolidly. 'Who needs a man like Claude Stuyvesant breathing down your neck?'

'If Rick comes back—' Scott started to suggest.

'He won't,' she interrupted.

'How can you be sure?'

'I didn't like the sound of that call. If someone wanted to get rid of Rick, the easiest way would be to give him all the pure coke he wanted. He'd go anywhere, do anything for that.'

'Ms Lengel, do you think it possible that Claude Stuyvesant had something to do with his disappearance?'

'Why do you ask?'

'It was Stuyvesant's men who cleaned out Claudia's place. If the man who called promised to return Rick's things, there's definitely a connection.'

Though it was clear to Scott what had happened, it was even more clear that he had only one important witness left—Kate.

But how to tell her?

KATE'S FIRST QUESTION when she met Scott was, 'How did it go with Rick Thomas?'

Very simply, as undramatically as he could, he told her.

She was stunned. 'What . . . what does that do? How does it affect . . . Oh, Scott!' She began to tremble. He put his arms round her to lend her the support and courage she needed.

'Rick was the strongest part of our defence,' Kate said.

'Not any more, not any more,' Scott replied, desperately trying to assess his diminished options.

Chapter Fifteen

When the session opened the next morning, Scott introduced as his first witness Nurse Adelaide Cronin. Once she was sworn, Scott established her professional training and background. He then led her through the events of that Saturday night. Cronin established that Mrs Stuyvesant was indeed a hindrance in the examining room and stated that based on her experience, Kate's actions were in accord with usual practice in the emergency service.

When Scott turned Cronin over to Hoskins for cross-examination, the prosecutor said merely, 'No questions.'

Scott realised the prosecutor was saving his attack for Kate and had no intention of hinting what that would be.

After a similar experience with Nurse Beathard, Scott presented his final witness. For the benefit of the stenographer he announced, 'I call Dr Katherine Forrester.'

Once Kate was sworn, Scott's first questions concerned her early life on the family farm, her medical school record, her experience as an intern and as a resident. He presented her as an intelligent, stable, well-trained doctor worthy of the committee's support. Then he proceeded to lead her through some of the cases she had treated on the night in question.

He finally came to the case of Claudia Stuyvesant. Slowly Scott guided Kate through her first meeting with the patient. Assessing the vital signs Cronin found. Taking Claudia's history. Detecting insufficient signs and symptoms to produce an accurate diagnosis.

Scott now arrived at the questions most pertinent to Claudia's eventual death.

'Dr Forrester, did you make any enquiries of the patient concerning her private life, and if so, why?'

'With a young woman her age, it was important to know if she had been sexually active and, if so, had she missed any periods. The answers—the truthful answers—to those questions could play a large part in arriving at a definitive diagnosis,' Kate explained.

'And what did the patient reply?' Scott asked.

'In all cases her answer was negative,' Kate replied.

'Are there any facts about the patient and your observations that are *not* in that history?' Scott continued.

'I did not think my suspicions belonged in the patient's history,' Kate said.

'Suspicions? About what, Doctor?' Scott asked.

'I suspected the patient was afraid of her mother, and therefore might not be telling me the truth.'

'If her mother had not been there and you had received truthful answers, would you have been able to reach a correct diagnosis in time to intervene?'

'Sexual activity, missed periods, all would have been crucial facts in arriving at a correct diagnosis. For that reason I feel the presence of her mother had a critical effect on—'

Claude Stuyvesant rose to his full height to intervene. 'Mr Chairman, I object to your permitting this woman to put the blame on my wife! I will not stand for it!'

'Mr Stuyvesant,' Mott replied. 'Dr Forrester is entitled to present her defence. After which, it will be up to this committee to weigh her testimony and determine if she is worthy of belief.'

Stuyvesant appeared mollified, though he continued to glare at Kate.

Quickly Scott led Kate through the rest of the events of that evening. Taking Claudia's blood sample. Sending it off to the lab. Tending other patients until the results came back. Repeating the procedure two more times when the findings weren't conclusive.

Then Scott asked, 'Dr Forrester, did you at any time decide to send for a second opinion?'

'Acting on my suspicions that the patient might be pregnant, I performed a pelvic examination. But my findings were not conclusive, so I sent for Dr Eric Briscoe.'

'And what did he do?'

'He repeated the examination. With the same result.'

'Doctor, did you perform a pregnancy test?'

'Yes. I catheterised her to obtain a urine sample and carried out the hospital's three-stage urine pregnancy test.'

'And the result?'

'Negative.'

'In view of the medical examiner's later findings, how do you account for that?'

'No medical test is one hundred per cent perfect.'

'Doctor, when was the first time you had any warning of how serious the patient's condition had become?'

'Dr Briscoe was about to go into her abdominal cavity to see if there was occult internal bleeding when Cronin reported the patient had no pulse. We immediately commenced CPR, rushed her to the acute-care room and worked on her with all means available. She eventually died, due to electromechanical dissociation.'

'Doctor, in your review of the chart, in your weeks of reliving this tragic case, have you had any second thoughts?' Scott asked.

'Second thoughts, no. But guilt? Yes.'

Not only Stuyvesant but Hoskins and all three members of the committee reacted with surprise. Truscott interrupted taking his meticulous notes. Gladys Ward stared at Kate for a long moment before making her own note.

In the face of such a startling admission, Scott felt forced to ask, 'Why guilt, Doctor?'

'I hope I never reach a time in my practice of medicine when I will lose a nineteen-year-old patient and not feel a twinge of guilt on behalf of myself and my profession. That despite all our advances, such untimely deaths do occur.'

Scott surrendered Kate Forrester to prosecutor Hoskins for cross-examination.

Hoskins picked up his sheaf of notes and approached the witness, smiling paternally. 'Doctor, let us see if we can help you solve the mystery of what happened on that eventful night in emergency room C. You've described the variety of cases you handled that night. Would you say that it was more hectic than an average night in emergency?'

'It was usual in a place where *every* night is *unusual.*'

Hoskins smiled. 'Nicely put. May I assume that explains why you delayed for so long seeing Claudia Stuyvesant?'

'You assume wrong, sir,' Kate shot back. 'I did not delay!'

'Sorry,' Hoskins said, pretending to apologise. 'Doctor, is it true that even after you finally made the time to examine Claudia Stuyvesant, you really didn't?'

'I performed a complete physical,' Kate protested.

'Doctor, may I refresh your recollection? Based on testimony from a previous witness, you had no sooner started to question her than you left her to go and care for another patient. Isn't that true?'

'There was another case—one with alarming symptoms—that called me away,' Kate explained.

'Alarming symptoms?' Hoskins echoed.

'He had severe pain just below the sternum, was sweating profusely and was in agony,' Kate replied. 'Those symptoms are classic for cardiac cases. Such a case takes precedence over all others.'

'So you left Claudia Stuyvesant to attend this other case. May I ask, What did you find?'

'He turned out to be passing a gallstone,' Kate said.

'And how did you dispose of that case, Doctor?'

'Sent him up to surgery and let them determine whether surgical intervention was indicated,' Kate said.

'Do you know the final outcome of that case, Doctor?'

'Once the case went up to surgery, I had no further contact with the patient. That's one of the unfortunate aspects of serving in emergency. You see patients, treat them, pass them on or send them home, and you seldom see them again. You rarely know the final outcome.'

'Then let me inform you of what did happen to that patient. He was examined in surgery, and it was decided not to operate. He was sent home the next morning,' Hoskins concluded, brandishing a sheaf of records at Kate.

'Now,' Hoskins resumed, 'when you finally found it convenient to return to Claudia Stuyvesant, what did you find?'

Though resentful of Hoskins's use of the word convenient, Kate decided not to take the bait. 'As I testified, Nurse Cronin had already elicited her symptoms, taken her vital signs, and started the patient on an IV.'

'What did you do then, Doctor?'

'I began to take her history.'

'And did the patient respond to your questions?'

'Yes. But, unfortunately, not truthfully. She denied sexual activity, missed periods—'

Midway through Kate's response, Hoskins began to nod. 'Yes, yes, Doctor, I know. We are now about to transfer responsibility for the patient's death from the doctor to her mother.'

Scott came to his feet, calling, 'Mr Chairman, I object!'

Hoskins replied, 'I withdraw the remark. Doctor, did there come a time when Mrs Stuyvesant *did* leave room C?'

'At one point she went out to make a phone call from her limousine,' Kate replied.

'Since you had the patient alone and free of the influence of her mother, did you ask her those highly personal questions?'

'Yes, I did.'

'And what did she answer?' Hoskins asked.

'She . . . she continued to maintain she had not been sexually active, had not missed any periods,' Kate replied.

'Doctor, let us suppose that Claudia had said, "Yes, Doctor, I *have* been sexually active. Yes, I *have* missed my period." What would you have done differently?'

'I would have done a pregnancy test sooner,' Kate replied.

'And if you had?' Hoskins demanded. 'Then what?'

Kate realised that Hoskins had led her into a trap from which she had no logical escape.

'Doctor, what leads you to believe that if you had done that test sooner, you would have come up with a different result?' Hoskins hammered away.

'I . . . I don't know,' Kate was forced to admit.

'Are you telling this committee that if you had done the test an hour or two sooner, you would have been less stressed and thus more capable of doing it correctly?' Hoskins demanded.

'I was perfectly capable and in control when I performed that test!' Kate protested.

He's goading her, and she's taking the bait, Scott observed. He knew he had to intervene. 'Mr Mott, my client has been testifying for several hours. I ask for a short recess.'

Hoskins greeted Scott's request with a slight smile. 'Mr Chairman, I have no objection. This witness obviously needs a break. A recess, I mean.' As he turned away he was rewarded by an approving nod from Claude Stuyvesant.

Mott had already picked up his gavel to declare a recess when Dr Ward raised her hand.

'Yes, Doctor?' Mott asked.

'Before we recess, may I ask the witness a question?'

At once Scott was on his feet. 'Mr Chairman, I object! A member of the committee who will later be called on to judge the respondent should not be permitted to act as prosecutor.'

Mott turned to his administrative officer for a ruling.

'Mr Mott, you may allow the doctor to ask her question,' Cahill ruled.

'Dr Forrester,' Gladys Ward began. 'Knowing the percentage of fallibility of such tests, why were you content to accept that result as final?'

'I wasn't. I ordered a sonogram,' Kate replied.

'Then why is there no reference to the result in the patient's chart?' Gladys Ward demanded.

'Because no sonogram was ever done. Radiology informed me that only Dr Gladwin was authorised to do them, and she would not be on duty until the next afternoon.'

Satisfied as Ward appeared with Kate's explanation, she was not yet done. 'Dr Forrester, since you suspected the patient's answers from the outset—which led you to do the pregnancy test—tell me, if you can, how did the presence of Mrs Stuyvesant actually affect, change, or alter the manner in which you treated this case?'

Kate tried to reply, but her words came haltingly. 'If . . . if I had not had to contend with her, things might have been different.'

'Tell me, Doctor, in your experience as an intern and a resident, have you actually ever treated an ectopic pregnancy?'

'Ectopics are actually unusual, although they are becoming less so in these times—' Kate began.

Ward interrupted, 'Doctor, have you or have you not ever treated such a case?'

'No. No, I have not,' Kate was forced to admit.

'Then you were going purely on book and classroom knowledge,' Ward concluded.

'Yes. But that same night I diagnosed and treated a case of Addison's disease without any previous firsthand experience,' Kate said, fighting back.

Ward did not respond, but merely made a note on her pad. From her crisp attitude and severe frown, both Kate and Scott assumed that note was not favourable.

Mott banged his gavel. 'Five-minute recess!'

As Kate rose from the witness chair she found Claude Stuyvesant on his feet glaring at her with the glint of victory in his eyes.

SCOTT AND KATE HUDDLED outside the hearing room for a few words of advice and caution, lawyer to client.

'Remember what I said—' he began.

Kate interrupted, 'I know. "Don't fight back!" But I can't let Hoskins get away with snide remarks and innuendoes. And nobody can stop me.'

'Now, Kate, hold on. I'm on *your* side,' Scott replied, reaching for her hand. 'Frightened?' he asked softly.

'Scared stiff,' she admitted in a whisper, tears trembling on her eyelids.

'It's not going to get any easier. Hoskins has tasted blood. Just stick to the truth. It's the only chance we have.'

She nodded. With a finger under her chin he lifted her face. He wiped the tears away from her eyes, then kissed her on the lips. She drew back, staring up into his eyes as if to ask, Did that mean what I thought? His eyes responded, Yes, yes, it did.

'Now go in there and face them,' he said.

HOSKINS LED KATE through the steps of the treatment of Claudia Stuyvesant, referring continually to the patient's chart. Try as he did, he failed to catch her in any slips of memory. He then opened a new line of examination. 'Doctor, how much time elapsed between

414

the time of the events and the time you made your notes on Claudia's chart?'

'I entered all orders for her treatment in the order book at once. And all observations about her condition and my plan of treatment in her chart whenever I could,' Kate responded.

'Doctor, do not hospital rules require the doctor to make notes in the patient's chart each time you see her?'

'Yes.'

'Yet now you tell this committee that you did it "whenever" you could,' Hoskins taunted.

'In emergency you do everything "whenever" you can. There never seems enough time, but somehow it all gets done.'

'Is it possible that during that passage of time a doctor would have the opportunity to reconsider what she did and then make her notes in the chart fit with what eventually happened?'

'Your suggestion that I wrote up that chart to justify what I did is a lie!' Kate shot back. 'Everything I wrote in the chart conforms to what I observed, what I did, and why I did it.'

'So that what I hold here in my hand is a copy of the complete and accurate record of the case of Claudia Stuyvesant?'

'Yes,' Kate replied.

Hoskins pretended to study the chart.

Without looking up at Kate, he asked, 'Tell me, would you say that if a doctor received a severe blow to the head, it might incapacitate her?'

'Depending on how severe, it might,' Kate granted, puzzled by the purpose of his question.

'Doctor, isn't it a fact that you engaged in a physical altercation with the outraged father of a patient? Which resulted in your suffering a severe blow to the head?'

'A mother had brought in a child who was almost comatose. I suspected child abuse and decided to keep the child in the hospital. The father appeared determined to take the child back, obviously to conceal his abuse. I refused to surrender her, and he hurled me against the wall. Yes, I did suffer a blow to the head.'

'Severe enough to cause a concussion?' Hoskins asked.

'No,' Kate responded.

'Severe enough to cause dizziness?'

'A moment of dizziness, perhaps,' Kate admitted.

'But you went right on treating patients like Claudia Stuyvesant as if that had never happened,' Hoskins commented.

'If you are implying that I was not capable during the time I treated her, you are wrong!' Kate shot back.

Hoskins nodded sceptically. 'But isn't it a fact, Doctor, that you were so involved with this matter that you deprived Claudia Stuyvesant of the care she needed, with fatal results?'

'That is a lie!' Kate Forrester replied.

'And isn't the real reason you were so intent on removing Mrs Stuyvesant from that room was so she could not be witness to the improper and negligent care you visited on her daughter?'

'She should have been out in the waiting room. Her presence impeded treatment.'

'Yes, yes, we know,' Hoskins said, belittling her. 'I think Dr Ward demolished that argument to the satisfaction of the committee. In fact, I think we've all heard enough.'

'Well, I don't!' Kate protested, rising from the witness chair, despite Scott's frantic gesture to silence her. 'It is all well and good for you to sit in the calm of a hearing room and judge my actions on a night when cases were coming faster than they could be handled. But it is quite another thing to have been there coping with them. Did Claudia Stuyvesant receive all the time and attention that would please her mother? No. Did she receive all the time and attention that her medical condition seemed to demand? Yes!'

Kate turned now to include Claude Stuyvesant in her scope. 'I should have known that night when I heard Mrs Stuyvesant say, "He'll blame me," that it was *him* she was afraid of.'

Claude Stuyvesant's face flushed in anger and indignation.

Mott tried to interrupt, banging his gavel. 'Doctor! Dr Forrester! Mr Van Cleve, please control your client!'

But Scott made no move to intervene.

Kate continued. 'He is who Claudia Stuyvesant was really afraid of—not her mother, but the fact that she would tell *him*. He is why his daughter lied to me. If you wish to blame anyone for her death, blame him!'

Having said all she had intended to say and a bit more, Kate Forrester sank down into the witness chair, trembling in anger.

Dr Truscott shook his head gravely.

Dr Ward remarked, 'Having seen her on television, I am not surprised.'

'Mr Hoskins?' Mott asked. 'Any further questions?'

'I think the respondent has shown us all we need to know. I have no more questions for her.'

Chapter Sixteen

Rosie Chung already had the coffee brewing by the time Kate and Scott returned to the apartment.

'How'd it go?' Rosie sang out from the kitchen.

'Not good, I'm afraid,' Kate replied.

'Not bad, either,' Scott said.

Kate's blue eyes contradicted him so clearly that he was forced to admit, 'No, not good. All the way up here I kept trying to frame my summation. I tried to be as tough on myself as that committee will be. The way I figure, Mott is like a trick you give away in a bridge game. One you know you're sure to lose. So I was banking on Truscott and Ward. But Ward showed her hand today. She is definitely not on our side. Therefore, our chances depend on what I can say to change her mind. Put yourselves in Ward's place. What would convince you?'

Rosie spoke first. 'That pregnancy test.'

'Ward said Kate should not have accepted that as definitive.'

'But she didn't accept it,' Rosie argued. 'She asked for a sonogram. It wasn't available.'

Frustrated, Scott thought aloud as he paced between both women. 'One thing has bothered me from the minute I heard that drugs could have masked Claudia's pain, so that she could bleed to death without enough pain to warn of her condition. She was there for nine hours. Wouldn't the drugs have worn off?'

'You're assuming she took them before she went to the hospital,' Kate pointed out.

'If she took them at all, she had to take them before she went to the hospital,' Scott replied.

'Not necessarily,' Kate disputed. 'Sometimes addicts bring their drugs with them.'

'To the hospital?'

'Oh, yes,' Rosie said. 'I've caught them. So has Kate.'

'Put yourself in Claudia's situation,' Kate suggested to Scott. 'She's terrified enough to call her mother, whom she's been avoiding for months, because she knows she's sick. Maybe she even senses how sick, which only increases her need for drugs. Besides, she is going to a hospital where she has no way of knowing if she'll be given any medication. So she takes an extra-large dose before she goes. For insurance, she conceals more on her person and she sneaks them whenever she gets the chance.'

417

'That might be a reasonable hypothesis on which to argue,' Scott said, 'but without Rick's testimony we can't prove her drug use.'

At the mention of Rick Thomas, Kate recalled, 'Rick said that she always had a dozen prescriptions from different doctors: Valium. Darvon. Barbs. You name it—'

'She had it,' Scott supplied the rest of the sentence.

'Prescriptions!' Rosie blurted out. 'Painkillers, sedatives, barbiturates, drugs like those Claudia was taking—a doctor can only prescribe them by a special prescription form in triplicate.'

'So what?' Scott asked.

'A copy goes to the state department of health in Albany,' Kate explained. 'So the state can check on doctors who give out such prescriptions too freely, or patients who go from doctor to doctor to support their drug habit.'

'So,' Scott said, beginning to fit the pieces together, 'if Claudia did that, there must be a record up in Albany. Let me use your phone!'

Scott spent the next hour and a half on the phone to the state department of health in Albany. He spoke first to the computer section. Then he was transferred to the legal department, then to another office, and to still another. Each time he explained his position as lawyer for Dr Katherine Forrester, respondent in a state board hearing. Each time he was advised to make his request of the next highest official in the chain of command.

Working his way up the hierarchy, Scott was finally connected to the office of the Commissioner of Health himself. Scott experienced his first flicker of encouragement when the commissioner interrupted his presentation by remarking, 'Counsellor, spare me the details. I am quite familiar with the Forrester affair.'

'Then you must be aware, Commissioner, of the vital need for this information in my defence,' Scott stated.

'Oh, I have no doubt that it would be helpful. Unfortunately, the information you seek is of such a highly confidential nature that it cannot be disclosed.'

Before Scott could reply, he heard the phone being cut off. He had no need to report his failure to Kate or Rosie.

'Isn't there anything you can do?' Rosie asked.

'Yes. Think!' he said. 'I need time to think.'

With that, he said goodbye and left.

It wasn't until four o'clock in the morning that Scott finally decided on his strategy. He knew it must succeed before the day appointed for his summation if Kate's career was to be preserved.

SCOTT VAN CLEVE RETURNED to his office to begin making the notes for an ex-parte petition on behalf of Kate Forrester to gain access to state records of all prescriptions made out to Claudia Stuyvesant by any doctor in New York State. It was late afternoon. Since he had been denied use of the secretarial staff, he was forced to do his own two-finger typing on his small computer.

After struggling all night with a document that any legal secretary could have typed in one-tenth the time, Scott was satisfied with his efforts. He watched the pages flow from the printer. When he had them all in hand, he bound them in blue legal backing, then consulted his watch. It was nearly 8am. Kate should be up.

Scott punched in her number. It rang four times. In the middle of the fifth ring she answered.

'Kate, I want you to meet me.'

'This morning? Where?' Kate asked.

'Supreme court, New York County. Take the subway down to the Chambers Street station. Then ask anyone for directions. You'll recognise the building. It's the one with the wide stone steps leading up to the tall pillars at the top and the words "The true administration of justice is the firmest pillar of good government". Well, this morning we're going to find out if those words mean what they say. Meet me before nine thirty.'

AS SCOTT STOOD ON THE TOP STEP of the court building he scanned the street below. He spied Kate and waved to attract her attention. She did not see him. He admired the way she started up the steps—firmly, resolutely. She might seem small and disarmingly feminine, but she was a woman of purpose.

Looking up towards the top steps, Kate caught sight of Scott. As she climbed, she admired his tall, lean frame. She reached the top step asking, 'What are we doing here?'

'Going to see a judge,' Scott said, seizing her hand and starting into the courthouse.

'JUDGE WASSERMAN IS IN CONFERENCE,' the stodgy, bespectacled secretary proclaimed firmly.

'We'll wait,' Scott said.

'He has to go on the bench very soon,' the woman announced.

'We'll wait,' Scott insisted. 'It's important. We're here to present an ex-parte petition for an order to examine certain state records.'

'Leave it, and I will show it to the judge when he comes out.'

'It can't wait that long,' Scott informed her.

'It will have to,' the secretary insisted.

At that moment the door to the judge's inner chambers was thrown open. Two men and two women—obviously clients and lawyers—emerged angrily. The two women marched towards the front door, the two men just behind. As the door closed, from inside chambers came the angry voice of Judge Emile Wasserman.

'Freda, how many times have I told you? No matrimonial property cases first thing in the morning. Ruins my entire day!'

Freda called out loudly, 'Judge, there are two people here to see you with an ex-parte petition, but they have no appointment.'

Before the judge could forbid them entrance, Scott was at the open door. 'Your Honour, a doctor's career is at stake here and time is of the essence. As you will see if you give us the chance to explain.'

Scott beckoned Kate to join him. Together they entered Judge Wasserman's chambers.

Judge Wasserman was dressed in shirtsleeves and an unbuttoned cardigan. But the absence of his formal vestments did nothing to diminish his judicial impatience. 'I've got no time. I'm due on the bench to charge a jury.'

'Your Honour, I represent a physician who is currently facing charges before the state board of professional medical conduct. This is the doctor in question.'

The judge stared at Kate, then turned his full attention to Scott. 'Proceed, Counsellor, but don't take all day.'

As briefly as he could, Scott explained the events leading up to the hearing, then the refusal of state officials to release the confidential data from the State Department of Health. Then he presented for the judge's signature the order that accompanied his petition.

Wasserman scanned the papers, then glanced at Scott. 'You know, Counsellor, one thing puzzles me. Of all the judges in this courthouse, what made you pick me?'

Scott decided to adopt the same advice he always gave Kate: tell the truth. 'Because, Your Honour, you are a maverick. I needed a judge who would be willing to risk being overruled when he ventured beyond precedent and put justice before the law.'

'A nice bit of flattery, young man,' Wasserman said. He turned to Kate. 'Tell me, Dr Forrester, in your own conscience, did you give the Stuyvesant girl the best treatment a doctor could?'

'Under the circumstances, with the information I had available to me, I did what any good doctor would have done.'

'Anything else you'd like to say before I decide?'

'Yes, Your Honour,' Kate replied. 'This isn't merely a court order you are being asked to sign. It's my life. It's what I was born to do—practise medicine, heal the sick.'

Wasserman nodded thoughtfully. He picked up his pen. Before he signed the order, he said, 'Counsellor, you'll never guess what convinced me. Your description of the part Claude Stuyvesant is playing in all this. It's about time someone made him face the unpleasant truths about his own life.'

Having affixed his signature, Wasserman held out the document to Scott. 'Here. Now get the hell up to Albany. Get those records, and rub Stuyvesant's nose in them.'

THE TALL TWIN TOWERS of the Rockefeller Mall dominated the city and the countryside for miles around. Kate and Scott could see them as they emerged from the Albany railway station. The mall contained most of the offices of the state of New York.

They located the offices of the State Department of Health. Scott presented Judge Wasserman's order to the woman in charge of drug records.

After much scrutiny and discussion, a printout of all the drug-related prescriptions issued to Claudia Stuyvesant was in their anxious hands. Scott deferred to Kate's medical expertise.

'Dr Eaves is listed here more than a few times. And doctors named Tompkins, Henderson, Goldenson, Fletcher, Grady, Fusco . . .'

'Poor Claudia, she sure got around,' Scott commented.

'Had to, considering the number and the kinds of drugs,' Kate said. 'It's all there—dalmane, pentobarbital, amobarbital and amobarbital-secorbarbital. Everything Rick said he saw her take. But most significant are these,' Kate added, directing Scott's attention to the last few lines of the printout. He glanced at them.

'What's so significant, or different, about these?' Scott asked.

'These prescriptions are all within the last two weeks of her life. Percodan. Codeine. Valium. She must have been heavily into those just before she was brought to the hospital.'

'And what she likely brought with her to emergency,' Scott added. 'All enough to mask her pain?'

'When you consider the effect of those drugs taken together, they could have masked the most intense pain,' Kate explained.

'Man, she was really hooked,' Scott said with a certain sense of pity for the young woman.

ON THE TRAIN BACK to Manhattan, Scott spent the time studying Claudia's drug history and framing his legal strategy. Even with this new evidence, it might not be easy to convince the two medical members of the committee that the patient was at fault in the matter of Katherine Forrester, MD.

As the train was making the final leg of its run towards Manhattan, Scott looked up from his study of the record to ask, 'Kate, is there any question that a combination of these drugs could have suppressed Claudia's pain sufficiently to make her condition appear far less dangerous than it actually was?'

'None,' Kate said. 'I can testify to that.'

'That won't do,' Scott negated. 'Opinion testimony of that kind must come from an independent expert.'

He was silent the rest of the way, deep in thought. Curious as she was, Kate did not intrude on his meditations. As the train lunged into the tunnel that would bring them to Grand Central Station in a matter of minutes, she detected from the look on his craggy face that he had decided.

When they emerged from Grand Central station onto 42nd Street, Scott said, 'Kate, I need to know everything possible about ectopic pregnancies; about the importance of pain in making such a diagnosis; the effect of drugs on pain, signs, symptoms and lab findings. And I've got to know it all by tomorrow morning!'

For the rest of the evening and into the night, with Rosie's help, Kate instructed Scott as if he were a first-year medical student. The process went on nonstop. When Rosie described pregnancies and ectopics, Kate made the coffee. When Kate looked up references in their textbooks, Rosie made the sandwiches. For more than six hours they kept at it, until Scott leaned back exhausted.

'I haven't had a night like this since I studied for my bar exams,' he said. 'Now I've got to get home and turn all this into legal ammunition.'

He took his notes and the four textbooks Kate and Rosie had used, and left.

Once he was gone, Rosie said, 'I don't know about you, Kate, but I like that man. I have great confidence in him.'

'So do I.'

'Like him? Or have confidence in him?' Rosie asked.

'A whole lot of both. I just hope—almost as much for his sake as for mine—that whatever he has in mind works, because he feels about the law as I do about medicine.'

Chapter Seventeen

As Kate and Scott entered the hearing room the first person they confronted was Claude Stuyvesant, hovering over his wife, who sat at the end of Hoskins's counsel table. While Scott laid out the papers and books he intended to introduce, Mott opened the proceedings.

'Since all testimony has been completed, this committee is ready to hear counsels' summations. Mr Van Cleve, for the respondent, first.'

Scott rose slowly, aware that he was about to cause a furore.

'Mr Chairman, instead of making my summation, I ask to reopen this hearing.'

'Reopen!' Hoskins exclaimed. 'Mr Chairman, I object! Counsel has had ample opportunity to present his case. To reopen now would be irregular. Mr Cahill, I demand a ruling.'

Cahill admonished, 'Mr Van Cleve, a hearing can be reopened at this stage only if there is new evidence.'

'I happen to possess new evidence,' Scott said. 'In addition, I wish to call a new witness.'

'New evidence?' Cahill repeated. '*And* a new witness? I trust we are not back to another invisible man, like Rick Thomas.'

'This time the witness is readily available,' Scott answered.

Mott said gruffly, 'One moment, Mr Van Cleve.'

Then with a brusque, angry gesture Mott summoned Cahill to the corner of the room for a hurried conference. 'Damn it, Cahill, this is a trick. Now rule against him and get this over with!'

'Not so fast,' Cahill said. 'If this were a criminal trial and new evidence came in before the summation, no judge in this state would preclude it. Unless you want this case to be appealed in court, you'd better give him permission.'

Once back in his chair, Mott declared, 'This committee will reopen this hearing to any new evidence or new witness counsel wishes to introduce. Mr Van Cleve?'

Scott rose to his feet to announce, 'Mr Mott, respondent wishes to call Dr Gladys Ward.'

Ward glared at Scott in stunned anger. Dr Truscott slammed down his pencil. Mott glanced anxiously at Cahill.

Hoskins rose to protest. 'Mr Chairman, in all my years of prosecuting hearings I have never seen a member of the hearing committee called as a witness. I object to turning this grave proceeding into a legal circus!'

Scott turned to Hoskins to demand, 'Sir, why was Dr Ward chosen to sit on this particular committee?'

'It is customary to have at least one medical member of the committee be a specialist in the field under scrutiny. Because of her eminence in obstetrics and gynaecology, she was designated.'

'Thank you, Mr Hoskins,' Scott said, 'for qualifying her as an expert. Because it is in that capacity that I call her. Dr Ward, will you take the witness chair?'

Reluctantly Dr Ward took the chair and was sworn in.

Scott approached her. 'Dr Ward, let us proceed directly to what I hope will educate the other members of the committee on the complexities of this case. To start, would you list for them the classic symptoms of an ectopic pregnancy?'

'Counsellor, I'm afraid you have been misinformed. There *are* no classic signs and symptoms of ectopics.'

Scott appeared to be puzzled. 'Since ectopics present no such signs or symptoms, how *does* a doctor arrive at a diagnosis?'

'A combination of findings and observations may be suggestive.'

'What would be "suggestive"?'

Ward started to enumerate impatiently. 'Nausea, vomiting, cramps. Tenderness, especially on movement. Missed periods.'

'Then, Doctor, would I be correct in concluding that very few ectopics evidence themselves in exactly the same way?'

'I would say only ten—possibly fifteen—per cent present a fairly usual picture.'

'Doctor, you mentioned nausea, vomiting and cramps,' Scott remarked. 'Are they generally symptoms of an ectopic?'

'Yes,' Ward replied.

'Doctor, can you name any other conditions that produce those same symptoms?'

'Oh, yes,' Ward agreed quickly. 'Ulcer, gastritis, stomach virus, appendix, kidney stone . . .'

'Now, Doctor, if a physician *is* confronted with signs and symptoms that are "suggestive" of an ectopic pregnancy, what should that doctor do?'

'An immediate bimanual vaginal examination.'

'And that would prove the existence of an ectopic?'

'Not necessarily,' Ward was forced to concede.

'Why not?'

'For one thing, in a normal pregnancy the cervix becomes discoloured. But not necessarily in an ectopic.'

424

'During this bimanual examination, would the physician be able to *feel* the presence of an ectopic?'

'Sometimes, but not always,' Ward said.

'So, Doctor, is it fair to say that there was no negligence on Dr Forrester's part in not detecting a mass on pelvic examination of Claudia Stuyvesant?'

'Yes, that is a fair statement,' Ward conceded.

'Doctor, I would like to read to you from a highly regarded textbook on obstetrics and gynaecology. I quote: "Its frequently vague signs and symptoms, plus the variety of other diseases it mimics, make ectopic pregnancy a puzzling diagnostic challenge. In fact, we might well call tubal pregnancy the disease of surprises." Doctor, would you agree with those statements?'

Ward stared at Scott with a slightly superior smile. 'I not only agree with those statements, Mr Van Cleve, I wrote them. You are quoting from my own text on the subject.'

'Yes, Doctor,' Scott admitted. 'Now that we have established the great difficulty in diagnosing an ectopic pregnancy, may I ask if during your experience as a resident on emergency service, you ever treated patients who were drug addicts?'

Flashes of concern passed between Mott and Hoskins, between Hoskins and Stuyvesant. The prosecutor rose and protested, 'Mr Cahill, such testimony ventures into speculative fields that have no relevance to this proceeding.'

Scott wheeled on him. 'Mr Hoskins, before I am done, I will prove relevance even to the satisfaction of this committee!'

'We will allow Mr Van Cleve to continue, but only subject to connection,' Cahill ruled.

Enraged, Hoskins had no choice but to slip back into his seat, ready to protest again if given a pretext.

Scott continued. 'Dr Ward, may I repeat. Did you ever treat drug-addicted patients during your emergency service?'

'Every doctor has,' Ward replied.

'Have you ever detected or known of patients to take drugs while they were *in* the hospital?' Scott asked.

'I have also seen such cases,' Ward conceded.

'Doctor, if a patient were a heavy user of drugs and were deprived of all drugs for as long as nine hours, might he or she suffer withdrawal symptoms?' Scott asked.

'That many hours would be a long stretch for a real addict.'

'When you add to that a situation in which a patient was suffering heavy internal haemorrhaging but was experiencing only slight pain and discomfort, what conclusions would you draw?'

'That the patient, in some way, had access to drugs *during* those nine hours,' Ward said.

Suddenly Hoskins was on his feet, shouting, 'Mr Chairman! There is no evidence in the record to support such questions. No evidence at all as to drug use by the victim!'

Before Mott could bring down his gavel to close off any further discussion, Scott protested, 'Mr Chairman, since Dr Ward has been qualified as an expert, *she* is permitted to answer hypothetical questions, and *I* am entitled to ask them.'

'Provided,' Hoskins was quick to point out, 'that if counsel cannot provide a factual foundation for his questions, the entire line of testimony is thrown out!'

'Of course,' Scott agreed.

'Then you may proceed, Mr Van Cleve,' Mott ruled.

'Dr Ward,' Scott resumed. 'Suppose a patient had been on high doses of such drugs as Percodan, codeine, Valium, and possibly cocaine as well—'

'All taken concurrently within a relatively short timespan?' Ward asked, betraying considerable concern.

'For the purpose of this question, yes,' Scott confirmed. 'Doctor, could the synergistic effect of such drugs—taken in combination during the crucial last nine hours of a patient's life—have been sufficient to mask the pain of an ectopic pregnancy, no matter how severe it would otherwise have been?'

'There is no doubt that acting together—each heightening the effect of the others—they could easily have concealed such pain from the physician.'

Scott moved back to his counsel table, where Kate was ready with a sheaf of printouts. He turned back to Dr Ward and asked, 'Doctor, would you be good enough to examine these printouts. Especially the last page containing the most recent entries.'

As the document changed hands Hoskins objected, 'I have a right to see that!'

'As soon as Dr Ward is done with it,' Scott replied.

Ward needed only a few moments to study the last page. After which, with a distressed 'Good God, no wonder . . .' she handed the printouts back to Scott.

'Mr Chairman, I offer into evidence this report from the State Department of Health.'

'I insist on seeing that document first!' Hoskins demanded.

'By all means, Mr Hoskins.' Scott held it out to him.

Hoskins snatched it and impatiently began to scan it. Both Mott and Cahill converged on him. Together all three studied the report of Claudia Stuyvesant's drug history.

Claude Stuyvesant started forward to join them, demanding the document. Hoskins had no choice but to surrender it. Stuyvesant examined it long enough for the loathsome facts to burn into his mind. He started back to his wife and said, 'You knew?'

'Yes. So now you can stop pretending.'

Ordinarily his fierce glare would have been enough to silence her, but for the first time in many years Nora Stuyvesant found the strength and the daring to defy him. 'Yes. Stop denying it. Because you knew, too. But instead of trying to help her, you drove her away.'

'*She* left *us*,' Stuyvesant protested.

'So you'd like the world to believe. The truth is, you were glad to be free of her, because she was never the perfect child you always wanted. The perfect son.'

'Damn it, Nora! Be still!' he commanded.

'You never wanted Claudia, so you shut her out, set her adrift. You made her what she became. Once you realised that, you had to hide your ugly truth. So you blamed me, you blamed Dr Forrester, you schemed to destroy records, to prevent testimony.'

Stuyvesant's usually ruddy face, which had always been so strong, seemed ashen-grey and aged. He stood as if stripped naked, his tyranny over his family exposed, his hostility towards Kate Forrester revealed as a shield for his own guilt. Kate felt only pity for him. But even more, she felt great sorrow for Nora Stuyvesant.

Without a word Stuyvesant started for the door. His wife hurried after him, calling, 'Claude ... Claude, wait!' He did not stop to acknowledge her plea. As if to apologise for her abrupt departure, she called back to them, 'He'll need me. . . . He'll need me.'

And she was gone.

Once the door closed, Mott, at a loss for words, weakly gestured Scott Van Cleve to continue.

In subdued manner and voice Scott asked, 'Dr Ward, considering the unusual difficulty in diagnosing an ectopic pregnancy, compounded by the patient's untruthful responses and a faulty test result, plus pain unnaturally suppressed by heavy drug usage, would you say that Dr Forrester's treatment of Claudia Stuyvesant was in keeping with good medical practice?'

'With all the evidence now available, I would have to say her actions that night were beyond reproach,' Ward agreed.

'And as to the charges brought against her?' Scott asked.

'I vote to exonerate her of all charges,' Ward announced.

Hoskins protested, 'A member cannot announce her vote before the summations!'

Dr Maurice Truscott spoke up. 'After hearing Dr Ward's testimony, I don't need to hear any summations. I, too, vote to dismiss all charges.'

Freed from the overbearing presence of Claude Stuyvesant, Hoskins and Cahill agreed that summations now would be meaningless. The votes of Dr Ward and Dr Truscott would be recorded as they appeared in the stenographer's notes. Mott was free to cast his vote by voice as well. After some moments of embarrassment he cast it in favour of vindicating Kate. Then, with one final sharp blow of his gavel, he officially brought to a close the hearing in the matter of Katherine Forrester, MD.

Kate exhaled slowly. She rested her head on the counsel table, exhausted. She did not see Dr Ward approach.

'Dr Forrester,' Ward said crisply. 'You probably think me quite severe. But in my eyes when any woman physician fails, she brings disgrace upon all her sisters in the profession. We must prove ourselves better than any man before they will finally accept us as good enough. Having been through the fire, you measure up now.' Brisk and professional—as was her habit—she strode from the room.

Hoskins approached Kate and Scott. 'The vote of this committee will be transmitted to the State Commissioner of Health. With the record of today's hearing, I do not think you have anything more to fear. I will be in touch with Dr Cummins within the hour. Your reinstatement to full active status should be automatic.'

AS KATE HELPED SCOTT gather up all his papers she remarked, 'At least we know what happened to that missing tox report.'

'And why the medical examiner never did one,' Scott added. 'The S factor. With what we know now, we have grounds for a very strong libel suit against Stuyvesant.'

'No, thanks. I've had enough of the law. Too much. I just want to get on with my career and my life,' Kate replied.

KATE FORRESTER AND SCOTT VAN CLEVE came out of the state board office to find themselves assailed by the bumper-to-bumper, noisy, smelly traffic of 40th Street. Looking up, Kate could see patches of blue sky between the towering buildings.

'In spite of the noise and the fumes, I've never seen a brighter day. It's like starting life all over again. I don't know how to thank you, Scott.'

'One way is not to call me Scott. People who are an important part of my life call me Van.'

Kate tried it out cautiously. 'Van . . . Van . . . That's not bad.'

'The more you use it, the better it sounds,' Scott said. Then he asked, 'I wonder . . . I mean . . . Do you have any plans?'

She smiled up at him. 'No, I have no plans,' Kate said frankly. She knew what he was asking. He knew what she was replying. 'Look,' she said, 'I've got to call home.' She started for a cab that was just discharging its passengers.

He called after her, 'Dinner?'

'OK,' she called back.

'Tonight?'

As she pulled the cab door closed she called back, 'Tonight!'

KATE BURST INTO THE APARTMENT calling, 'Rosie, Rosie!' There was no reply. Then she remembered that Rosie was on clinic duty this week. Kate went to the phone, punched in her parents' number and waited impatiently for it to ring through. She heard the ring interrupted by a pickup on the other end.

'Hello?' she heard her mother say.

'Mama, it's OK, it's OK!' Kate fairly shouted into the phone. 'Everything turned out fine. Just fine!'

'Oh, baby, I'm so glad. So glad.' Her mother began to weep in relief and celebration.

'Dad there?' Kate asked.

'I'll put him on,' her mother said, calling through her tears, 'Ben! Ben! It's Kate. With wonderful news!'

She heard her father clear his throat before he said, 'Katie, that true, what Mother said?'

'True, Dad. Vindicated. Unanimous!'

'Good, darlin', good,' her father said. 'So that young lawyer worked out all right, did he?'

'Better than all right,' Kate said.

'Well, you tell him thanks for us.'

'You may get the chance to do that yourself one day,' Kate said. 'Now I've got to call the hospital and get my new assignment.'

'You do that, sweetheart. Meantime, I've got a call or two to make myself. Lot of folks round here'll want to know.'

She hung up the phone and called the hospital. Before asking for Dr Cummins, she asked for the paediatric ward. Fortunately, Harve Golding was on duty.

'Harve?' Kate asked.

'Kate!' he greeted her enthusiastically. 'The word's already out. Congratulations! The whole staff is elated.'

'How's my little Maria?' Kate asked.

'We held a group consult yesterday. It will be a long, slow process, but she is going to be OK.'

'No residual damage?' Kate asked.

'None,' Golding replied. 'Well, maybe just one.'

'What's that?' Kate asked with considerable alarm.

'Ever since that damned hearing started, she's been asking for you. She's afraid you've deserted her.'

'I'll be there, Harve. I'll be there!' Kate promised. 'I'll stop by on my way to dinner.'

HENRY DENKER

In his superbly researched novels, Henry Denker has made a speciality of exploring medical issues, from ethics to technology. For his latest novel, *Doctor on Trial*, he spent a great deal of time observing the

medical staff who run the emergency service at Mount Sinai Hospital in New York. He was very impressed by their dedication and versatility. 'You can never tell who's going to be rolled in on the next stretcher,' the author says. 'For a young doctor there's no way to prepare for that kind of thing. It just comes to you, and you've got to use all your resources—everything you've ever read or heard—to make a quick and accurate diagnosis.'

Denker's decision to write a book about a good doctor wrongfully accused of negligence stems from his belief that doctors are frequently attacked unfairly, without recognition of the difficulties a physician can face. 'I wanted to pay tribute to any young person who becomes a doctor,' Denker says. 'It's not easy. It entails a lot of sacrifice. I don't think we recognise—and credit—them enough for that.'

Power and money—two other themes at the heart of the novel—also concern the author. He was troubled by a certain breed of 1980s business tycoons who considered themselves above the law. They helped to inspire Denker's creation of his villain, Claude Stuyvesant. 'I wanted to show what these people are capable of doing,' he says.

Like his latest heroine, Kate Forrester, Henry Denker makes his home on the West Side of Manhattan. He has been married for forty-eight years to his wife, Edith, a former nurse.

A CURATE FOR ALL SEASONS

including extracts from *How Green Was My Curate* and *Goodbye Curate*

by FRED SECOMBE

illustrated by Susan Hellard

Fred Secombe was ready for almost anything when he stepped down from the train to begin his new life as a curate in the Welsh village of Pontywen. Under Canon Llewellyn, the local vicar, he would surely be in capable hands.

But nothing could have prepared Fred for the parishioners he was about to meet—people like Full-Back Jones, a gravedigger with an uncanny talent for causing chaos; Bertie Owen, the long-serving, regimental churchwarden; and Mrs Richards, a landlady with a heart of gold and a manner of speech that would outdo Mrs Malaprop. And then there was Charles Wentworth-Baxter, his hopelessly work-shy fellow curate with an infuriating knack of managing to stay out of the pulpit. What's more, and certainly not least, Fred never expected to meet the loveliest doctor in South Wales, the delightful Eleanor Davies . . .

Chapter One

'I hope you have better luck with this parish than you've had in your first one.' My mother's parting words echoed in my head as the train pulled out of High Street Station, Swansea on the first Saturday in June 1945.

Standing in the corridor, jammed between a burly Welsh guardsman and a lanky aircraftsman, my five-foot-seven made me appear like the ungenerous filling in a sandwich. The two servicemen carried on a conversation over my head while I mused on my mother's words.

My first curacy had been a disaster. Burning with enthusiasm I had gone from college to St Matthias, Swansea, only to have the fires quenched by the wettest of vicars, who had never had a curate before. In the eighteen months I wasted there, I learned nothing from a man who was more interested in being outside his parish than inside it. Now I was going to an elderly priest who had trained many curates.

Canon Llewellyn was Vicar of Pontywen (population six thousand) in the Western Valley of Monmouthshire. According to his advertisement in the *Church Times*, there were three churches, two in the town and one in the countryside, recently linked with Pontywen.

My new vicar met me as I got off the train at Pontywen Station, inspecting me as if he were a farmer at a cattle mart, eyeing a possible purchase.

'You don't look well,' he rasped. 'Nothing wrong with your health, I hope.' Obviously he did not wish to 'buy a pig in a poke'.

435

'I'm fine, thank you, Vicar,' I said. 'We tend to be pale as a family.'

He grunted in reply. He was a little man, in his seventies, about five foot two at most and quite unprepossessing. But for a man of his age he was remarkably agile. I found it difficult to keep up with him on our walk up a steep hill to the vicarage.

'I must admit, I feel more than a little excited,' I gasped.

He stared at me.

'I mean about starting my curacy in Pontywen,' I explained.

He grunted for the second time. It was many years since he had been excited about anything or anyone, especially his wife who looked as if she had been born in a refrigerator.

This was evident when she opened the door to us at the vicarage, which was ideally situated between the church and the public cemetery. Mrs Llewellyn's welcoming smile was like a silver plate on a coffin.

The vicar led me to his study, a gloomy vault of a room. I was motioned into a leather armchair, while he sat behind a large desk, almost disappearing from sight.

Silence reigned. I began to feel very uncomfortable. Suddenly he pounced, like a Gestapo officer toying with his prey. 'What prayers do you use at the bedside of the sick?' he demanded.

I was dumbstruck. My previous vicar rarely visited the sick. If he did, he would be more likely to discuss rugby than the state of the invalid's soul. 'I'm afraid I have never said prayers with the sick,' I stammered.

'Never?' he thundered. 'You have been ordained eighteen months and never said prayers with the sick?' He was incredulous.

I thought it advisable to remain silent.

'On Monday afternoon,' he said, 'you will come visiting with me. We shall visit both the sick and the whole.'

There was a further hiatus, until another inquisitional bullet whizzed in my direction.

'Preach from notes or a fully written sermon?'

I was afraid that he was going to ask me that question. Mainly from indolence rather than a desire to communicate with my audience face to face, I had begun to preach without a scrap of paper in front of me. 'I did—er—preach from notes but—er—lately I have been using no notes at all.'

'At your age, no notes at all?' he bawled.

'Of course, Vicar,' I went on quickly, 'if you want me to write out notes or a full sermon, I shall do so.'

'*If* I want you to? Of course I want you to write out your sermon.

However, tomorrow you will have to preach without notes at St Padarn's at eleven o'clock.'

As I was wondering what the next examination question would be, the little man jumped to his feet and said, 'Well, you had better go to your lodgings now. I'll take you along to Mrs Richards.'

We made our way through drab terraces to Mount Pleasant View. Anything less pleasant it would be difficult to imagine. It was a row of brown stone cottages, huddled perilously on a hillside and facing a vista of coal tips on the other side of the valley. Mrs Richards lived in number 13. Ominous, I thought, as the vicar banged imperiously on the knocker.

The elderly, smiling lady who opened the door appeared far from ominous. Dressed in black, in mourning for a husband who had been dead twenty years, she was so short that she made even the vicar look tall. Her white hair was neatly arranged in a large bun which bristled with hairpins. She looked like an amused version of Queen Victoria.

'So this is our new curate.' She smiled with her eyes as well as her mouth, unlike Mrs Llewellyn.

'I won't come in, Mrs Richards,' said the vicar. 'See that he's in church in good time for the eight-thirty service, won't you?'

'Don't worry, Vicar, I'm sure I can cope with this young man.' She smiled at me again.

I was given the front parlour and the little back bedroom as my rooms.

After unpacking my case, I brought my books down to the parlour and arranged them on the bookshelves. Reposing on a crocheted tablecloth was a tray with a cup and saucer and a plate containing two pieces of cake. There was an atmosphere of warmth which compensated for my chilly reception at the vicarage.

A gentle tap on the door announced the presence of Mrs Richards, plus small teapot. 'Are you settling in, Mr Secombe?' she enquired.

'Very well, thank you. I'm sure I shall be very comfortable.'

'That's nice,' she said. 'I've brought you some tea to go with the cake. By the way, don't be put off by the vicar's aptitude. His bark is better than his bite.'

It was evident that conversations with Mrs R. would provide gems of which Mrs Malaprop would be proud.

After tea and the delicious homemade cake, I decided to get on with my sermon for the vicar. Perhaps as time goes on, I thought, he will appreciate my desire to do my best, but at least 13 Mount Pleasant View promised to be a haven of contentment.

NEXT MORNING I FOUND MYSELF in the pulpit of St Padarn's Church surveying the packed congregation who had come to inspect the new curate. The June sunshine poured through the windows and was beginning to roast my audience. Suddenly, during the hymn before the sermon, I became aware of the tall figure of Mr Bertie Owen, churchwarden, who was making signs to me from the back of the church. I decided to look down at the Bible on the lectern with the idea that if I ignored him, he would stop his antics. To no avail. When the congregation was seated and I had launched into my sermon, the strange hand signs continued. I decided to look at him and nod my head. It had the desired effect. A satisfied smile spread across his florid countenance and the semaphore ceased. He sat down on a chair at the back and smiled at me indulgently, nodding his head at the end of every sentence I uttered. This continued for about five minutes before he decided I had gone on long enough. He got up from his seat and went across to a cupboard where he kept the collection plates. Next he proceeded to deliver the four receptacles to various members of the congregation with a whispered instruction to each of them.

By the time he had got to the fourth whisper, my patience was exhausted. I stopped my sermon and glared at him.

'Sorry, Curate,' he boomed, as soon as he became aware that the flow of words from the pulpit had dried up. 'Carry on, we're all with you.'

That was the *coup de grâce* for me. 'And now to God the Father,' I said and announced the collection hymn. The four sidesmen took the collection while I prepared for the next part of the service. I took the alms dish ready to receive the offerings of the congregation. The four men stood to attention at the back, then marched down the aisle. To my astonishment they were followed by Bertie who was bringing up the rear minus a collection plate but with the aplomb and military bearing of a regimental sergeant major.

The sidesmen emptied their takings onto the alms dish in turn. I was about to offer up the money when Bertie took a few quick steps forward. 'You got the number then,' he said.

'What number?' I asked.

'You know—the number of communicants—eighty-seven. I gave you the signals.' His tone was reproachful.

'Oh yes, thank you,' I said and turned to the altar for the presentation of the offerings. It was only much later that I discovered Bertie was Pontywen's unlicensed bookie. As I finished the prayer, Bertie produced a not so *sotto voce* 'Quick turn', and the quartet of

helpers performed a military manoeuvre worthy of the Changing of
the Guard. It was evidently one of the highlights of every service.

The same military precision was present when the time came for
the administration of the consecrated bread and wine. Bertie strode
down the aisle to the front pew and had each benchful of
communicants coming forward by numbers, until it came to the
back pew, when Bertie joined on at the end to make himself the last
communicant.

As I was about to administer the chalice to Bertie, there came
another of his whispers. 'Do you want any help?'

'What help?' I asked.

'I drink what's left of the wine if it's too much for the parson,' he
said eagerly.

'I'll manage, thank you,' I replied, handing him the chalice.

Bertie looked hurt. He could see an end to a much-cherished
perk. However, by the time the service was over he had recovered
his composure.

Leaving him to count the collection I made my way out of the vestry only to be confronted by a bevy of females from the two front rows of the choir, led by the organist's wife, Mrs Collier. They presented a daunting spectacle.

'We've already met, haven't we?' said Mrs Collier. 'Well, here are the rest of the choir ladies. This is Mrs Annie Jones.' The soprano thrust herself forward and revealed a gleaming set of dentures.

'You'll find us a very friendly lot, very homely, if you know what I mean.' Annie Jones purred and fluttered her eyelashes in an effort to do a Mae West. I had difficulty in extricating my hand from hers.

One by one, I was introduced to the other choir ladies but by the time the last introduction was over they were all still there, as noisy as excited schoolgirls. It was becoming claustrophobic.

'Mr Secombe.' A tall, wiry man of about thirty came to my rescue with a powerful basso profundo which drowned the twitterings.

Outside the church, he said, 'I'm Idris the Milk. I thought you was in need of help. I'm not here in the mornings normally, but 'ad time off to come special for this service.' His handshake was a bone-crusher. 'The choir ladies get a bit excited when we get a new curate.'

'Thank you, Idris,' I said. 'I thought I'd still be there at teatime.'

'You must come and meet my wife. She had to leave church early to cook the dinner. Come and have fish and chips with us on Friday night. The last curate, Mr Price, used to make it a date.'

'I'll be pleased to do the same,' I replied. 'Thank you very much.'

When I opened the door of 13 Mount Pleasant View, the aroma of a Sunday roast caressed my nostrils. It smelt like home.

'Do you mind having dinner in the middle room with me?' enquired Mrs Richards nervously.

'Not at all,' I replied. 'I'll be glad of the company.'

She beamed and said, 'I can see we're going to get on with each other—just like a house that's got a fire.'

Chapter Two

'Let us pray for . . .' Before I could say any more of the prayer, I was startled by a loud hiss, like that of an escaped cobra.

It was a few weeks after my arrival in Pontywen and I was standing at the altar in the parish church, with my back to the congregation, conducting the Wednesday morning service. I decided to ignore the interruption. The next few sentences were punctuated by a series of hisses, growing in intensity.

Something serious has happened, I said to myself. I suspended operations and turned round. There was 'Full-Back'. He had once played in that position in a rugby match for Pontywen and had been called Full-Back ever since. Jones the Gravedigger in all his glory. He was now frantically indicating that he wanted to see me in the vestry.

To the consternation of the six godly ladies who formed the congregation, I made a hurried exit and pushed him inside the vestry. 'What's happened?' I asked breathlessly.

A sheepish, toothless grin appeared on his face. 'Can I borrow the church ladder to put some slates on my roof?' he said.

I exploded. 'What do you think you are doing? Can't you see I'm taking a service?'

He looked hurt. 'Sorry, Boss,' he said. 'I thought you was talking to yourself. I didn't know there was anybody in the auditorium.'

'For heaven's sake take the church ladder and go,' I said.

When I came back into church, Mrs Llewellyn and the other five ladies at the service had given up their devotions and were standing in a little gossip circle in the middle of the aisle.

'I must apologise for the interruption,' I announced. The sight of the knot of scandalmongers who should have been on their knees made me add, 'Normal service will now be resumed.'

Mrs Llewellyn's eyebrows shot up to the heavens, and then knitted themselves together. Trouble was brewing, it was plain.

After the service, the vicar's wife stormed into the vestry. 'What was the reason for Jones's disgraceful behaviour?' she demanded.

'He wanted to borrow the ladder to see to some slates on his roof,' I replied. 'Apparently he hadn't realised that a service was going on.'

'Well, that's it,' she decided. 'He's got to go. And as for your flippant remark about "normal service", that was unpardonable.'

The vicar was away for a few days attending committee meetings. In his absence, it was obvious Mrs Llewellyn felt she was in charge of the shop. I was determined to show her that she had no right to be.

'I am sorry you found my remark offensive. It was partly provoked by seeing worshippers standing in the aisle talking, when they should have been on their knees in the pews. As for Jones, surely the vicar is the person to make any decision about him.' Then, picking up my suitcase with a flourish, I said, 'I am going. Good morning, Mrs Llewellyn.'

As I swung the case from the desk, it flew open and my robes were scattered over the floor. I felt an urge to laugh until I saw the scowling face looking down at me as I knelt to recover my belongings.

'Typical,' she said with a sneer and made the grand exit I had planned for myself.

THE NEXT DAY I went to the vicarage for the weekly 'business meeting' the vicar had instituted, expecting to be hauled over the coals. In the event, it turned out quite differently. The vicar met me at the door instead of Mrs Llewellyn. He did not appear to be irate.

'I gather that Jones has been troublesome while I have been away,' he grunted, once he had settled himself behind the desk.

'I'm afraid so,' I said nervously, 'but I think it was a genuine error. He didn't realise he was interrupting a service.'

The vicar put his head on one side and closed his right eye—a sure indication that a pronouncement was to follow. 'All right, I take your word for it that the idiot thought you were on your own.'

Then he frowned. 'There's just one thing, young man. Don't be flippant at the altar.'

That was all—no word about my altercation with Mrs Llewellyn. I began to warm to him . . .

After I mumbled an apology, he continued, 'The bishop has asked me to take another curate. Apparently he is lacking in self-confidence and has only been ordained a few weeks. His vicar asked his lordship if he could get rid of him. I am getting too old for this sort of thing.'

It was the first time he had treated me as a confidant. I felt flattered.

The doorbell rang.

'Will you go to the door, Secombe?' said the vicar. 'Mrs Llewellyn is out. I expect it is the prospective curate.'

When I opened the door, the long-haired figure standing before me was more like a prospective replacement for Jones the gravedigger. He was wearing a brown jacket with holes at the elbow, grey flannel trousers that were in need of a clean, while his red pullover was decorated with the remains of yesterday's dinner. The clerical collar looked out of place as part of the ensemble.

'My name is Wentworth-Baxter,' he announced, with as much aplomb as if he were a member of the House of Lords.

'The vicar is in here,' I said and ushered the hyphenated gentleman into the study. The vicar's eyebrows were raised as high as Mrs Llewellyn's the previous morning.

'Sit down,' ordered the vicar.

442

Wentworth-Baxter dipped into the pocket of his scruffy jacket and produced a packet of Woodbines.

'Do you mind if I smoke?' he asked. It sounded more like a challenge than a polite request.

'Yes I do,' the vicar snapped.

The packet went back hastily into the jacket pocket.

'Now then, the bishop says you are unhappy in your present parish. It seems you would like to come here.'

'I thought it was definite,' replied Wentworth-Baxter.

The vicar's temper shot up to boiling point.

'Bishop or no bishop,' he roared, 'if I think I can do nothing with you, you are *not* coming here.'

The effect on Wentworth-Baxter was electric. 'My apologies,' he stammered, looking like a frightened puppy.

'There are a number of conditions I shall impose if you come here.' The vicar's tone had softened already. 'First, you must get that hair cut. Second, you are not to go around the parish looking like a tramp. Have you a dark suit?'

'Yes, Vicar,' he said meekly. 'That's the only suit I have.'

'Well, keep wearing it until you can get another,' commanded my superior.

'Would you like to come and have a cup of tea at my digs?' I asked my new colleague as we left the vicarage together.

'I'd love to,' he replied, to my surprise. 'By the way, I'm Charles.'

'I'm Fred.' We shook hands for the first time.

He stayed at my digs for a couple of hours. It transpired that he had taken a second at Oxford in theology. His father was an elderly clergyman from Gloucestershire who had settled in the Welsh countryside and had insisted that his son followed in his footsteps. Charles had done so reluctantly.

'He's a nice young man,' was Mrs Richards's judgment after he'd gone, 'but he looks a bit of a crackerbrain.'

ON THE SATURDAY of the following week, he arrived in the parish. The vicar had arranged for him to stay with Mrs Powell, a fierce widow who lived in Melbourne Terrace, one of the more respectable streets in the parish. This was to ensure that he was kept in order.

He managed to last a week with Mrs Powell before he turned up at my rooms in a desperate state. 'I can't stand much more. It's like living in Colditz,' he said. 'Look how lovely your place is. There is a warmth here. That front parlour where she has dumped me is like a morgue, with pictures of her dead husband staring at me every time I sit down.' He launched into a catalogue of complaints.

'She sounds exactly like my college landlady,' I said. 'The only thing you can do is to tell the vicar at our Monday morning get-together that you want to move from there.'

'It's easy to say that,' said Charles, 'but what's the vicar going to think of me? I was only a few weeks in my last parish and now I want to leave my lodgings here after a week.'

'Perhaps he will be more sympathetic than you think,' I said. 'The best plan is to find an alternative place and to suggest that to him. I'll make discreet enquiries at St Padarn's tomorrow while you're keeping the vicar company at the parish church.'

During Sunday supper next day I asked Mrs Richards whether she knew of any likely landlady for my hapless colleague.

'He hasn't been here two shakes of a dead sheep's tail and he wants to move already,' she said severely.

'You must admit, Mrs Richards, that his present landlady is hardly the kind of person to mother a young man who is lacking in confidence.'

'I suppose you're right,' she admitted and paused in thought. 'Moelwyn Howells the fruiterer has got a couple of rooms to spare. Myfanwy, his wife, is very clean, spotless, but quite homely.'

'Perhaps I'll call round there after Sunday School,' I said.

'By the way,' said Mrs Richards, 'I've got a surprise for you. I've given the bathroom a flick of paint. It's really been reformed. So I've got the boiler lit for you to have a bath tonight to celebrate.'

After supper we listened to the nine o'clock news on my newly acquired secondhand wireless. Then, after my landlady had gone to bed, I decided that the time had come to enjoy the comfort of a hot bath in the 'reformed' bathroom.

My landlady had achieved wonders with the hot water, which came boiling out of the tap. I locked the door, hung up my dressing gown on the hook, tested the bath temperature and lowered myself gently into the steaming water. When I went to reach for the soap, which sat on a rack near the taps, I found myself unable to raise my posterior. I was firmly anchored by fresh paint to the bottom of the bath! After several painful attempts to dislodge myself I decided to wait until the water cooled. However, as the water cooled there was no sign that I was becoming unstuck. I began to panic. Although the water was now tepid, I was sweating profusely.

'Mrs Richards,' I yelled. She was somewhat deaf and was probably asleep. 'Mrs Richards!!!' I banged on the side of the bath. The water was getting cold. I began to shiver. 'Help!' I shouted and banged with my fist as hard as I could on the side of the bath.

'Anything wrong?'

'I'm stuck to the bath, Mrs Richards,' I said.

'What?' She sounded bewildered.

'Stuck to the bath!' I was now so desperate that my voice was almost falsetto.

'Must be the paint,' she said.

'I know it's the paint.' I was fighting to retain my sanity. 'I can't move.'

'Don't worry. Keep your chin down. I'll go and get Mr Evans, next door. You'll have to wait till I dress, though,' she added.

I moaned. The thought of waiting another ten minutes while Mrs Richards dressed, impelled me to a final herculean effort to escape from the paint. My numb buttocks strained at their anchorage. The Lord heard my prayer and I shot forward so rapidly that my nose well-nigh jammed itself between the taps. But my bottom, a very painful, paint-anointed bottom, was in the air. I was intoxicated with relief. I jumped out of the bath, grabbed my towel and wrapped it round me. I opened the bathroom door and shouted joyously, 'Mrs Richards—it's all right. I'm free!'

Her bedroom door opened a crack. 'Thank goodness for that,' she beamed. 'You haven't hurt yourself, have you?'

'It's just my posterior. I think I must have left some of my skin in the bath.' My bottom was extremely sore.

'I hope you're all right,' she said. 'That part of your anomaly can be very tender. There's some ointment downstairs. It's for cuts. It's anaesthetic so it will kill any germs. I'll go and get it for you.'

By now, I had begun to shiver again. I disappeared into the bathroom and began to dry myself with some vigorous rubbing. A few minutes later there was a knock on the door.

'Here's the ointment, Mr Secombe.'

I opened the door a few inches and received the precious balm, together with some cotton wool.

When I applied the ointment I was surprised to find a fair amount of blood on the cotton wool. The pain was increasing in intensity. If the ointment was 'anaesthetic' it was completely ineffective. Sleep was impossible. Much of the night, I spent walking round the bedroom. By the time dawn arrived, I knew that I should have to be first in the queue at the doctor's surgery that morning.

I MUST HAVE BEEN a ghastly sight when I came downstairs for breakfast. Mrs Richards stared at me.

'Mr Secombe,' she said, 'you do look dreadful. Is it your posterity?'

'It certainly is,' I moaned. 'I'll have to see the doctor.'

'I'm very sorry indeed,' apologised my landlady. 'You'd better go straight away to the surgery. Then you'll be the first to see Dr Hughes. He's always up to his neck in patients.'

The doctor's surgery was the end house of Melbourne Terrace. At 8.45am I stood outside the door, alone and palely loitering. By 9am I had been joined by a mixed bag of sickly people.

At two minutes past nine the surgery door was opened by the doctor's receptionist. 'I'm afraid Dr Hughes is away today,' she announced. 'There's a locum here instead.'

A number of the elderly went back home to wait for tomorrow. The receptionist looked at me. 'I think you were first, Reverend,' she said and ushered me inside and then through to the inner sanctum.

To my horror, behind the desk was a pretty, dark-haired young lady. She fixed a pair of deliciously brown eyes on me, and said, with a smile, 'Sit down, please.'

'I'm—er—afraid I can't,' I stammered.

'I see,' she replied, 'what's wrong with you?'

I was dying several thousand deaths. 'It's—er—my—er . . .' I didn't know whether to say 'posterior', which sounded coy, or 'buttocks', which sounded clinical. I decided on 'buttocks'.

She burst into peals of laughter which proved contagious. My embarrassment disintegrated and I joined in the amusement.

'I'm sorry,' she said, 'that was very unprofessional. It was the look on your face rather than your buttocks. What's wrong with them?'

'Well,' I replied, 'it started with my landlady deciding to freshen up the bathroom with a "flick of paint", as she put it. In the course of which she painted the stained patches on the bottom of the bath.'

'Upon which you placed your bottom,' she interjected.

'Exactly,' I said. 'I filled the bath with piping-hot water and then sat down on the fresh paint. In wrenching myself from the paint, I think I must have left some of my skin on the bath.'

'Drop your trousers then,' ordered the doctor. 'Don't worry—I have seen men's buttocks before—in the course of my training, I mean.' She stood up, a petite young lady, no more than a few inches over five foot and decidedly attractive.

I fumbled with my braces and my trouser buttons before eventually revealing my smarting bottom.

She whistled quietly. I would have liked to think it was in admiration, but knew that it was in commiseration.

'That looks quite nasty,' she said. She went to the medicine cupboard and produced a bottle.

'This will make you jump when I apply it,' she warned, 'but it will kill any infection that may be there and start the healing process.'

She applied the lotion gently. It was a painful antidote but lost much of its venom due to the compassion of the applier.

'You can make yourself respectable again,' she ordered. 'Come back in a week's time for a checkup. In the meantime, I'll make out a prescription for the lotion.'

As she was writing it out, she said, 'How long have you been in Pontywen?'

'Just over four months,' I replied. 'And if I may ask, how long have you been doing a locum for Dr Hughes?'

She finished her writing with a flourish and looked up at me. My pulse rate accelerated alarmingly.

'This is my first stint. Dr Hughes is a friend of the family and rang me at the weekend to see if I would help out today. But there is a possibility that I might be taken on as junior partner.'

'That would be wonderful,' I enthused. Then, greatly daring, I said, 'You see, I've always thought that the Church and Medicine should work hand in hand. As one junior partner to another perhaps I might suggest we could get together to establish some kind of cooperation.'

'Hand in hand?' she enquired.

'Something like that.'

'Tell me . . .' she paused. 'I don't know your name.'

'I'm Fred Secombe.'

'I'm Eleanor Davies. Tell me, Fred Secombe, are you trying to date me or are your motives purely altruistic?'

'In a word, both. But mainly the first.'

'For a curate, you're a fast worker.' She smiled, and I was already besotted.

'You realise that there is a queue of patients outside while you are indulging in a flirtation with the doctor.' She wrote something quickly on a prescription pad. 'Take this prescription together with the other.'

She stood up and ushered me to the door.

'Next please,' she called.

Within seconds I was out of the surgery and into the street, examining the second 'prescription'. On it was written: *Ring me tonight after 8pm. Llangwyn 292.*

A startled elderly lady stared at a young curate who shouted 'Whoopee!!' as he read his prescription outside the door of the surgery. Pontywen had become the greatest place on earth.

'MY WORD,' SAID MRS RICHARDS when I got back, 'you're a lot better already. When you went out, I was getting ready for your internment. You looked so terrible.'

'It's all down to the doctor,' I replied, and catching hold of the old lady, tried to waltz her round the kitchen.

'Whatever is the matter with you?' she enquired.

'Dr Hughes wasn't there this morning. He had a locum at the surgery and she's the most delicious locum ever invented. What's more, I have to telephone her tonight.'

'So that's it,' said Mrs Richards. 'You've fallen in love by the sound of it. No wonder you've forgotten the pain. What's her name?'

'Her name is Eleanor Davies and she lives in Llangwyn. Her father is a friend of Dr Hughes,' I replied.

'Oh! That's Dr Davies's daughter. Nice little girl. Went to Pontywen Grammar before she went to college.' Mrs Richards was a mine of information.

'So you know her,' I said in reverential tones.

'Well, I haven't seen her since she was at school. Her father used to be the other doctor in Pontywen, till he went to Llangwyn. It's a better class of practising up there.'

At 8pm that evening I joined a queue outside the phone box in the town square and it was 8.45 before I could enter the portals. After two false starts, I got through to Llangwyn 292. The female voice at the other end was calm and self-assured. 'Llangwyn two-nine-two.'

I took a deep breath. 'Could I speak to Dr Eleanor Davies?'

'You're speaking to her, Reverend Fred Secombe.' She was trying to suppress her amusement. 'First of all, how is your bottom?'

'Very painful, I'm afraid.'

'You must get your landlady to dress it tonight and apply the lotion. This is no time for false modesty. Your kindly old landlady will be only too pleased to help, I'm sure. If she were young, I wouldn't suggest it.'

'Now may I make a suggestion,' I said.

'I never thought curates could be suggestive.'

'Well this one is and my suggestion is that we meet somewhere next Tuesday on my day off. The D'Oyly Carte Company are in Cardiff. I thought perhaps we might have a meal and then go to the theatre.'

'I have to take surgery for Dr Hughes that evening. But I could get away afterwards and pick you up at your digs. We could be in Cardiff by seven with a bit of luck.'

'Fantastic. I'll book seats tomorrow morning by phone. By the way,' I asked, 'do you like Gilbert and Sullivan? I should have asked you that first.'

'I have been brought up on them,' she replied. 'My father has most of their operas on records. What's more, I sang quite a few of the soprano leads at college.'

'This is fate,' I burbled. 'For the past few months, I have been thinking of starting a Gilbert and Sullivan group as a church activity in Pontywen, that is, if my lord and master agrees.'

'Which one is that? The one up above or the one in the vicarage?'

'Madame, you are teasing me. Speaking seriously, would you be interested in playing the lead in *The Pirates of Penzance*, for example?'

'I think we had better discuss this next week. My father has emerged from his lair and appears to need the phone. See you next Tuesday. Goodbye.'

AT ST PADARN'S ON SUNDAY I announced that I was forming a Gilbert and Sullivan opera group. Canon Llewellyn had given his permission earlier in the week, after warning me not to let it interfere with my real work—caring for souls. Immediately I put the cat among the nightingales by imposing an age limit for female members of the chorus. I had no desire to have grandmothers masquerading as young ladies.

'No one over the age of thirty need apply,' I said.

The two leading sopranos of the church choir looked at each other with a mixture of astonishment and anger. Annie Jones had just replaced her false teeth after the last hymn. She opened her mouth so wide at the announcement that they were in danger of falling out once again.

'I'll help you out in the men's chorus,' said Bertie Owen. 'I used to be in the Penmawr Male Voice Choir.'

At that moment I wished I had put an age limit on the male chorus.

AT 6.15PM ON TUESDAY evening a dilapidated Morris Minor drew up outside 13 Mount Pleasant View. I had been waiting at the window, and now I ran down the steps clutching a box of chocolates.

I thought Eleanor looked attractive in her white coat in the surgery.

Now, as she stood outside the car, in a navy blue two-piece suit, she looked magnificent—tiny, but magnificent.

'Hop in,' she ordered.

I hopped in and presented her with my month's sweet ration.

'You shouldn't have done that,' she said. 'It must have used up all your sweet coupons.'

'I'm not a great sweet eater,' I lied.

'By the way,' she said, as she threaded her way down the valley, 'have you got anybody in mind as musical director for your G and S?'

'I'm afraid not,' I replied. 'Everything's an act of blind faith. It seems to be working so far.'

'Well, it's going to work again.' She pulled up at a 'halt' sign. 'I think I can get you one. The music master at Pontywen Grammar School is a friend of mine. I'm sure I could persuade him to become your musical director.'

'Thank you very much,' I said, with as much enthusiasm as if she had offered me a Spam sandwich.

'What's happened to your excitement?' she asked.

'Is he a—er—close friend, this music master?' I said.

'Jealousy will get you nowhere,' she replied tartly. 'Mr Aneurin Williams is at least fifty, baldheaded and with a wife and six children. It just happens that he taught me music when I was at school. What's more, young man, it's quite likely that he can get some of his senior pupils to join your society.'

'Isn't life wonderful?' I enthused.

'You are an idiot,' she said and put her foot down hard on the accelerator.

At the theatre, I plucked up enough courage to hold Eleanor's hand halfway through act two of *HMS Pinafore*. It was a small hand but very responsive. By the finale we had established a close relationship and she took my arm as we went back to her car.

By the time we arrived outside my digs, it was pitch dark.

'You may kiss me good night,' she said briskly.

Never was an invitation so eagerly accepted.

'You might let me come up for air,' she exclaimed a minute later. 'In any case, I think I had better be getting back.'

'When do I see you again?' I said. 'I need to know about the music master and G and S.'

'That's your excuse,' she replied. 'Ring me at eight or thereabouts tomorrow night. Now I must go.'

Seconds later the Morris Minor sped away down the street. I stood savouring the delicate perfume that lingered on my coat.

When I got through to Eleanor next day, she was bubbling with enthusiasm. Aneurin Williams would be pleased to act as MD but he could only come on a Wednesday night at this stage.

'Fine by me,' I said.

'And by me,' she replied. 'I shall see that my Wednesday evenings are kept free.'

'Great!' I shouted. 'I'll go ahead and fix a meeting of all interested at St Padarn's for Wednesday of next week.'

'There's one other thing you'll be pleased to know,' said Eleanor.

'You can see me tomorrow?' I enquired.

'No, I can't,' she said firmly. 'It's just that Aneurin has a set of scores of *The Pirates of Penzance* from a school production before the war. He says you can borrow them.'

'Fantastic,' I replied, 'but qualified fantastic. I am grateful, deeply grateful. Honest. It's just that I should love to see you tomorrow.'

'If you can hold your horses until Sunday evening,' she replied, 'perhaps we could meet after you have finished your one working day of the week.'

'I beg your pardon, madam,' I retorted. 'I work six days a week.'

THE FOLLOWING WEDNESDAY Charles and I arrived early at St Padarn's to arrange the benches and bring out the antiquated piano from the vestry.

'This instrument will have to be tuned or, better still, replaced,' pronounced Charles.

A quarter of an hour before the rehearsal was to begin, a dozen schoolgirls arrived, chattering excitedly. Evidently Aneurin, the MD, was persuasive. Bertie Owen arrived with a young man in his late twenties, whom he introduced as 'Iorwerth Ellis who can read music'.

By the time Eleanor came in with Aneurin Williams, the pair of them burdened with a pile of musical scores, there were thirty-six people present. Twelve men, including Idris the Milk and the other basses from the church choir, had turned up. For a society starting from scratch, it was a most encouraging number at a first rehearsal.

Aneurin, baldheaded, bespectacled and bandy-legged, was short in stature but big in personality. His enthusiasm was infectious. After his five-minute talk to the motley band of singers, they felt they were an operatic company already, without a note being sung.

Of the six tenors, only Iorwerth Ellis and myself could read music. The other four included Bertie who sat between Iorwerth and myself.

'We'll try out the tenors first,' said Aneurin. 'With catlike tread! The accompanist will play the tenor line first and then I want all the tenors to come in on the beat.'

Charles hammered out the tenor line on the honky-tonk piano. Aneurin winced. Iorwerth and I hummed the tune while the other four buried their heads in the score, quietly, as if to hide from the conductor. A duet ensued between Iorwerth and myself. The other four sat in silence and wonderment. The MD was destined for a stint of hard labour.

By the end of the rehearsal, it was obvious that the chorus of young ladies was going to be a success. It was equally obvious that the male chorus would have to be augmented, if the production was to be worthwhile.

Eleanor and I stayed behind a moment while the chorus departed and, after the door had closed behind them, Eleanor came up to me and kissed me lightly on the mouth.

'I have news for you,' she said. 'Dr Hughes has asked me to be his junior partner in Pontywen, and I've accepted at once, before he can change his mind. So Church and Medicine can now go hand in hand good and proper.'

I put my arms round her. 'I think I love you,' I said.

'I'm glad,' she murmured, 'because they're my sentiments too.'

We indulged in a protracted embrace.

'I'd better get back home,' she said.

'But what about us?' I enquired.

'We both know about us now, my dear,' replied Eleanor. 'I'll be in touch.' She darted to the door and blew a kiss before disappearing.

My head spun. Events were moving at the speed of an express train. A few weeks ago, I was the junior curate, unattached, a green apprentice in holy orders. Since then, I had become a senior curate with the responsibility of a church, the founder of an operatic group, and now, a lover, passionately attached to his doctor.

When I arrived back at Mount Pleasant View, my thoughts were still in a whirl of happiness. As I closed the front door, Mrs Richards, emerged from the middle room, looking unusually sombre.

'Don't take your coat off,' she said. 'I'm afraid there's some bad news. The vicar's had a heart attack. Mrs Llewellyn phoned up Thomas the Paper Shop to ask if you'll go at once to the vicarage. It sounds as if it's the curtains for him, poor man.'

My landlady was right. By the time I reached the vicarage, 'the curtains' had closed on the life of Canon R. S. T. Llewellyn.

Chapter Three

It was a splendid funeral. Admittedly there were no funeral orations, hymns at the graveside or cold ham, pickles or seed cake to follow. This was a church ceremony, simple, but splendidly simple. The only words spoken were the majestic language of the Book of Common Prayer.

After the funeral was over the bishop, who had said the prayers at the committal, called me aside in the vestry. He was a scholar and a gentleman. Unfortunately for him and the diocese, he had no knowledge of life in a parish. His background was that of the college quadrangle and the bishop's palace. Furthermore, he was inhibited by a painful shyness.

Seated behind the vicar's desk in the windowless vestry, he chose to study what appeared to be at first sight a large picture of penguins. It was a composite of previous incumbents of Pontywen, over the past ninety-nine years, photographed in the black and white of cassock and surplice.

There was the inevitable silence once the door of the vestry was closed upon the two of us.

Boldly I chose to speak first. 'I hope the arrangements for the funeral were satisfactory,' I said.

To my surprise Mrs Llewellyn had asked me to take charge of the service, as well as the preparation of the grave.

Full-Back Jones, the gravedigger, had excelled himself. It was probably the only time he had dug six feet down in the whole of his career in Pontywen. And Mr Matthews the undertaker had conducted proceedings in a manner which rivalled the best of anything which could be offered in Cardiff.

The bishop turned his head away from the clerical penguins and addressed the blotting pad on the vicar's desk. 'I must say, Mr Secombe,' he said, 'that the arrangements were impeccable. So much so that I have no hesitation in asking you to—er, take charge of the parish in the interregnum.'

'How long will the vacancy last, my lord?' I asked.

'The patronage board meets soon to make an appointment. If the man nominated accepts, then it will be another two months or so before he moves in,' replied the bishop. Then he stood up and shook my hand. The interview was over.

As I left the vestry, 'my bosom swelled with pride' in the words of

453

Sir Joseph Porter in *HMS Pinafore*. For two or three months I would be in charge of a parish, after little more than two years in holy orders.

The euphoria vanished some minutes later in the vicarage. I had been invited by Mrs Llewellyn to join the post-funeral tea party. The fare was meagre. No black-market food had ever crossed the vicarage threshold.

I was consuming a tuna sandwich when I was buttonholed by Dr Elias Hughes. 'A most impressive service, young man,' he said, condescendingly. 'It looks as if you are going to have your hands full for the next few months,' he went on. 'You'll be far too busy to indulge in exchanging sweet nothings with my assistant. Just as well. I think you should know that her parents don't approve.'

'This is all I can say to you, Dr Hughes,' I replied in a tone of voice trembling with anger. 'Eleanor and I are responsible adults and we shall decide what is to happen to our relationship.'

I turned away sharply and collided with Charles Wentworth-Baxter who was advancing towards me with a cup of tea.

Cup and saucer went flying and a shower of tepid tea descended on my best clerical-grey suit. 'Ooops!' he exclaimed.

A dozen heads turned in our direction.

'It's quite all right, Mrs Llewellyn,' Charles said reassuringly. 'Your lovely china is intact.'

'What about my carpet?' demanded the widow, her grief in temporary abeyance.

'That's not affected either. Fred's suit took the brunt of it.'

'Oh, you two!' she remonstrated. Then she swooped down on the precious china and carried it to safety in the kitchen.

By now conversation had begun again.

'Sorry, Fred,' murmured my fellow curate.

'So am I,' I replied through clenched teeth.

'I was coming to rescue you from that doctor chap,' he said conspiratorially. 'I could see you were getting annoyed.'

'You can say that again. He was warning me off Eleanor.'

'Never!' gasped Charles. 'What a cheek!'

At that moment Mrs Llewellyn emerged from the kitchen with a tea towel. 'Dry your suit with this,' she commanded. Then she rounded on my hapless colleague. 'Trust you to do something stupid. Heaven help the new vicar when he finds he's got you as his curate.'

So saying she went across the room to talk to her cousin who had travelled from Bournemouth for the funeral.

'Back to normal,' I commented as I applied the towel to my suit.

'All I hope is that the next vicar's wife is not like her,' said Charles, red-faced with embarrassment.

THE FOLLOWING MORNING Charles Wentworth-Baxter arrived at 13 Mount Pleasant View for a parish management meeting I had arranged. With three churches to look after, two in the town and one in the countryside, the months ahead would be busy. Suddenly I was aware that a vicar's lot was not an easy one. With only two curates and a lay reader to perform the duties, making out a rota for Sunday services would be a headache. Baptisms, marriages, Sunday School, sick visiting, pastoral visiting, parish organisations—the list of chores seemed endless.

As we sat in the front room life assumed a very complicated pattern. On the one hand there was my fellow curate who was incapable of taking a service on his own, on the other there was the lay reader, a man called Ezekiel Evans, who thought he was more than capable of taking any service on his own and inflicted inordinately long sermons on his congregations. With helpers like these, the immediate future looked like a disaster area.

'Well, the first thing to do is to put Ezekiel Evans out in the sticks in Llanhyfryd,' I announced. 'The fewer people he can afflict the better. That leaves the parish church of St Mary, and St Padarn's.'

'Can't we stagger the times so that we can take the services together in both churches?' pleaded my fellow curate.

'I'm afraid, Charles, that your hour of destiny has arrived,' I said firmly. 'From now on you will have to stand on your own two feet.'

He stared at me as if I had ordered him to go on a kamikaze mission.

'The best thing,' I continued, 'is to put you down for the Communion service at St Padarn's. Bertie Owen will take care of you, believe me. Then you can come to St Mary's in the evening. It will be Evensong. So you won't have to cope with the Communion service there. I'll go to St Padarn's in the evening.'

'But what about all the other things?' asked Charles in plaintive tones. 'Weddings, baptisms and all that?'

'We'll leave that till next Monday. There's nothing fixed for this weekend as far as I know.'

That afternoon I went to see Mrs Llewellyn at the vicarage. I wanted to go through the list of things the vicar had arranged.

The widow looked genuinely pleased to see me. She showed me into the lounge which reeked of furniture polish and beckoned me into one of the armchairs.

'Would you like a cup of tea, Mr Secombe?' she asked.

While she was in the kitchen I stood up and looked out of the French windows at the lawn. It was a picture of cloisteral calm.

Suddenly the vicarage gate opened and Bertie Owen appeared. Tall and upright, the churchwarden of St Padarn's marched purposefully down the drive. Halfway down he stopped and stared at the side of the house which adjoined the garage. With his head to one side, he walked slowly on tiptoe, pausing occasionally, as if he were a cat stalking its prey. Past the windows he went. Next minute there was one almighty shout, 'Got you!'

There followed a series of muffled expostulations. Into sight hove Bertie, his trilby over his eyes and his arms locked round the throat of a little man, with a cap and muffler surmounting his raincoat.

I ran to the front door and opened it. There was the churchwarden, as pleased as punch. 'A citizen's arrest,' he announced. 'This man was attempting to steal the vicar's car.'

The alleged criminal lifted his head. His bespectacled eyes met mine. They were not those of a criminal caught in the act, but of an innocent, full of righteous indignation. What is more, they belonged to the Vicar of Abertrisant, Father John Whittaker.

'Tell this idiot who I am,' he hissed.

Bertie's hands dropped by his sides.

'This is the Vicar of Abertrisant,' I said. 'What on earth did you think you were doing, Bertie?'

'Well,' he began, 'I thought I'd come and see if there was anything I could do to help Mrs Llewellyn. Then when I was coming down the drive, I saw this man trying to look inside the garage. I knew the vicar's car would be in there and I suspected he was after it.' He turned to the little man who was still purple with anger. 'I'm very sorry, Vicar, but you see, you didn't look like a vicar with that cap and scarf *and* you've got a collar and tie on.'

His explanation did little to soothe Father Whittaker. 'Do I look like a burglar?' he shouted.

'Not now,' replied Bertie. 'But you did then.'

At this stage of the conversation Mrs Llewellyn appeared from the kitchen, alerted by the shouting at the open door.

She stared at the Vicar of Abertrisant. It was one of her hostile specials. It was less than a week since she had told me that she feared he would like to come to Pontywen and that she found him and his

High-Church ways obnoxious. 'What are you doing here?' she demanded.

The purple on Father Whittaker's face was transformed into an off-white. 'I—er—thought I'd come and have a look around as I—er—happened to be passing. I was about to come to the front door when I was apprehended by this idiot.'

Bertie was unabashed. 'Mrs Llewellyn,' he said, 'he was trying to open the garage door and I thought he was a burglar.'

'Well done,' replied the widow. 'Perhaps you'd like to come in and join Mr Secombe for a cup of tea.'

Bertie strutted in, proud as a peacock. The vicar's purple returned.

'As for you, Mr Whittaker, you might have waited another week or so before coming to spy out the land.' With that she closed the door with such a bang that it thundered through the hall.

'Go on into the sitting room with Mr Secombe,' she commanded and went into the kitchen.

'You were lucky it was John Whittaker you got hold of, Bertie,' I told him. 'If it were any other person, Mrs Llewellyn would have treated you to the sharp edge of her tongue instead of a cup of tea. All I hope, for your sake, is that he does not get appointed to this parish.'

'After being a shop steward for the past four years and church-warden at St Padarn's for the past ten years,' said Bertie, 'I think I can deal with him if that happens. He's only five foot nothing anyway.'

'So was Napoleon,' I replied, 'and he conquered half of Europe.'

After a cup of tea and a digestive biscuit Bertie left for home and Mrs Llewellyn allowed me into the vicar's study to rummage through his filing cabinet. The late Canon Llewellyn had been a methodical parish priest. Every street in Pontywen was documented with the names and details of church families.

There were three weddings fixed for November and December and four baptisms for November. I made a note of the dates and arranged with Mrs Llewellyn that all callers at the vicarage should be referred to me at 13 Mount Pleasant View.

Back at my lodgings I told my landlady about Bertie's apprehension of the clerical burglar.

'That vicar shouldn't have been acting like a creeping Tom,' she said. 'It's his own fault.'

'What I'm afraid of,' I replied, 'is that he might be made Vicar of Pontywen.'

'If "ifs" and "ans" were made of pots and pans you'd have to shoot

for bacon,' pronounced Mrs Richards. 'In any case, he won't be coming for a few months. So you make hail while the sun shines.'

Buoyed by my landlady's philosophy, I ventured forth later on to wait for Eleanor outside St Padarn's Church.

Eventually the noise of a large sewing machine signalled the approach of her old Morris Minor. The headlights beamed out from the corner of Taliesin Road adjacent to the church and then swung round to put me in the spotlight.

I hopped into the car and attempted an immediate embrace which was foiled by the handbrake.

'Hold your horses, you impetuous cleric!' she exclaimed. 'We have some important things to discuss, like Dr Hughes, for example.'

'So he's had words with you as well as with me,' I said. 'I told him that our relationship had nothing to do with him. What worries me is that you might lose your post.'

'First of all, well done, you, that you stood up to old Hughes. He needs me too much to get rid of me. I have told him that my private affairs are none of his business. I wanted to see you to stop you worrying. Before long I shall take you to meet my parents. Once they see what a catch you are, that will end any opposition from them.'

'I hardly think I come into the category of a catch,' I said. 'Brought up on a council estate in Swansea, a penniless curate.'

'It isn't a man's background that makes him a catch, it's his character and his abilities.'

'God has been very kind, sending me such a delightful little parcel of happiness.'

'My dear Frederick,' she replied, 'this little parcel had better get home to its dinner because its inside is empty. I'm starving. I'll be seeing you tomorrow evening anyway at the G and S rehearsal.' So saying she kissed me ardently and drove me back to my digs.

THE NEXT MORNING I called in on Mrs Llewellyn again. She greeted me at the vicarage door, her face pale and drawn. It was obvious that events of the past week had taken their toll. She ushered me into the lounge, beckoned me into an armchair and sank down on the settee.

'I'll be so glad to leave this place now,' she said, sighing deeply. 'What with that dreadful man Whittaker snooping around. It's all too much.' She fought back the tears.

Suddenly I felt intensely sorry for the woman. The stony exterior was crumbling and a human being was emerging, lonely and unloved. 'Is there anything I can do, Mrs Llewellyn?' I enquired solicitously.

'Not at the moment but thank you all the same.' Mrs Llewellyn blew her nose. 'I think I've got a cold coming on,' she said. 'Whatever happens, I shall be out of the house as soon as possible.'

That means, I said to myself as I went down the vicarage drive, a new vicar in Pontywen in less than no time. Clergy widows were allowed to stay in a vicarage for a maximum of three months. After that they were expected to leave what had been their home for many years and to find accommodation elsewhere, blessed with a paltry pension and whatever savings had been scraped together. If a vicar's lot was not an easy one a clergy widow's lot was much worse.

To take my mind off Mrs Llewellyn's fate, I decided to spend the afternoon visiting some of the faithful who worshipped at the parish church, using the list I had obtained from the vicarage study. First on my list was Mrs Greenfield, described in the late vicar's words as 'regular churchgoer, neurotic'.

It was a blustery autumn day. The Greenfields lived at Sebastopol Terrace, one of the streets on the top of the hill near the hospital. I knocked at the door of number 10. There was no reply. As I was about to move away, the door slowly opened to reveal a little woman, thin and bespectacled. Her eyes were reddened with weeping. 'Come in quickly, Mr Secombe,' she said, 'before that old dust blows in here.'

I was taken into the front room. Family photographs adorned the mantelpiece. I sat down in the armchair by the window. Suddenly she produced a duster from a pocket in her pinafore and advanced upon the armchair, flicking the dust off the polished Rexine.

'Excuse me,' she breathed. 'I can't stand to see dust.'

Then she retired to the settee where she continued her search for any speck of dust which had dared to defy her. Eventually she turned her attention to me. 'I'm so glad you've called at this moment, Mr Secombe.' Mrs Greenfield paused and produced a handkerchief from the other pocket. Tears began to pour down her face only to be wiped away as quickly as the dust on the furniture.

'Have you had a bereavement? Not Mr Greenfield, surely?'

'No, of course not. He did all he could but it was no use.'

My bewilderment was growing with her every sentence.

'I suppose we have been bereaved in a way,' she went on. 'I know he wasn't a human being but he was dear to us. Billie was a part of the family. And now he's gone.' The tears began to flow again.

'I'm so sorry, Mrs Greenfield,' I murmured. 'I know how attached you can become to a dog.'

'Billie wasn't a dog,' she said indignantly. 'He was our budgie. I used to let him out of his cage to stretch his wings. He'd land on my shoulder and nibble my ear and things. Not any more he won't, and it's my fault. I should have shut the kitchen door.' She wailed loudly and began to sob uncontrollably.

I decided not to venture another comment. So I sat, staring at the carpet. Suddenly the crying ceased. I looked up to see Mrs Greenfield making a determined attempt to keep a rein on herself.

'I'm sorry, Mr Secombe, to go on like this.' She bit her lip and paused. 'He was flying around in the middle room and then came out into the kitchen where I was cooking the chips for my husband's dinner. "Go away Billie," I said and waved my arm. I—I hit him accidentally and he fell into the chip pan. It was awful.' Another bout of tears ensued.

'I can see why you're upset,' I said, fighting hard to contain my inconvenient sense of humour.

'Thank you for your sympathy. But nothing will bring him back. I got him out of the pan with a tablespoon and tried to give him the mouth-to-mouth resuscitation. It was no use, he'd gone—for ever.'

My facial muscles began to ache from an overdose of control.

'When my husband came home for his dinner, I got him to wrap the poor thing in one of my best doylies and bury him at the bottom of the garden. He's at peace there now. Or perhaps he's in heaven. Do you believe there are budgies in heaven, Mr Secombe?'

'Well, Mrs Greenfield,' I said, 'that's something I haven't thought about until now. There's nothing about it in the New Testament, I know that. Still they are God's creatures and you never know.'

This seemed to reassure her. 'It would be nice to think he's up there waiting for me when I go.'

Two cups of tea later, I left 10 Sebastopol Terrace, pleased that I had not been asked to say prayers over the victim's grave.

The rest of the afternoon's visiting was uneventful and after tea I walked to St Padarn's church hall for the second rehearsal of the Gilbert and Sullivan Society's production of *The Pirates of Penzance*.

WHEN I GOT BACK to my digs after that evening Mrs Richards came out of the middle room to greet me, looking flustered.

'Don't take your coat off, Mr Secombe. A man's just come with a message from the hospital. There's a blue baby been born. It's in a tent in the ward and they want you to christen it straight away.'

I grabbed my cassock and surplice and was out through the door in a flash. It was a steep climb to the hospital. By the time I reached the entrance, my heart was pounding and my lungs were bursting.

'This way, Reverend,' said the porter. He led me up a flight of stairs to the maternity ward.

'You look all in,' said the sister after I had been ushered into her office. 'Sit down for a minute and get your breath back. Have you ever baptised a baby in an oxygen tent?'

'I'm afraid not,' I gasped.

'It's quite simple. I'll take the top off the tent and you squeeze a few drops of warm water from a piece of cotton wool onto the baby's forehead. Come and meet the mother. It's her first baby and she's very distressed. Her husband's away in the forces. By the way, the baby's to be christened David William.'

I followed her into a side ward occupied by sleeping babies in their

461

cots. In the corner by the oxygen tent stood a teenage mother in a hospital dressing gown, dabbing her eyes with a handkerchief and staring down at her child.

'This is the clergyman, Mary,' said the sister gently.

The girl raised her eyes to my face.

'I 'ope you can do something.' She spoke in a whisper.

'Let's hope God will,' I managed to say. The sister handed me a beaker half full of warm water and a piece of cotton wool. Then she opened the top of the tent to reveal a tiny naked human being, his blue face contorted.

With a shaking hand I dipped the ball of cotton wool into the beaker. 'David William,' I heard myself say, 'I baptise you in the name of the Father,' I managed to get one small drop of water on the baby's forehead, 'and of the Son,' another drop, 'and of the Holy Ghost. Amen.' I wasn't sure whether a third drop had followed. I knew God would understand if it had not. 'Let us pray,' I went on. 'Our Father . . .' The two women joined me in the Lord's Prayer. Then there was a silence while I collected my thoughts.

'If it be your will, O God,' I extemporised, 'let this child live and give strength to his mother in her time of trial, for Jesus Christ's sake. And the blessing of God Almighty, the Father, the Son and the Holy Ghost be with you both now and always. Amen.'

The sister replaced the cover on the tent as soon as I had finished.

'Thank you, Reverend,' said the baby's mother. 'I feel better now he's been done and you've said a little prayer.'

I passed the porter on the way out.

'You've put the drops of water on the baby then,' he said. 'I don't know what good they think that will do.'

'It's not what they think, you think or I think that matters,' I snapped. 'It's what God thinks and I'm prepared to leave it to Him.'

Before he could say anything else, I had descended the steps in a much more lively fashion than I had climbed them. The night air was cool and pleasant. Pontywen was asleep and I was wide awake, with a mission accomplished. Now it was up to God.

AS SOON AS BREAKFAST WAS OVER the next morning, I made my way to the hospital. The sun was shining low in the sky and not a shred of cloud desecrated the blue expanse. God's in His heaven, all's right with the world, I said to myself as I strolled leisurely up the hill.

A few minutes later I was knocking on the door of the sister's office in the maternity ward.

'Come in,' barked a voice.

Seated at her desk was a stern-faced ogress in sister's uniform. My kind friend had gone off duty.

'I—er—baptised a baby, David William, in an oxygen tent late last night. I've come to see how he is.'

'It's a good thing you've come, Reverend. The baby died an hour ago and the mother's distressed. You'll find her in the ward opposite.'

My heart sank. I had been convinced that the baby would recover and that I would be greeted by a happy and grateful mother.

'Thank you, Sister,' I said and closed the door. It was a minute or two before I could bring myself to knock on the door opposite. When there was no reply, I tapped again and opened the door a few inches. 'May I come in?' I asked.

'Oh it's you, Reverend. Come in, please.'

The young mother was seated on a chair by an empty bed. Her face was tear-stained and her hands were grasped tight together.

She looked up. 'Why did He take him when He'd only just given him to me?' Her voice was hoarse from too much weeping.

I took her hands into mine. Pious platitudes were not going to help. In any case, since I was near to tears myself, I could not have manufactured them. 'To be honest, Mary, I wish I knew.' I stood silent, holding her hands, incapable of any more words.

'Shall we say a prayer together?' I asked after a few minutes.

She nodded without raising her head. I said a homemade prayer for little David William and for herself and then gave her the blessing.

Mary raised her head. 'Thank you,' she said. 'You have been a great help.' She began to weep quietly.

'Come on now,' I said. 'You have been very good.'

She dried her eyes. 'My husband's coming home on leave from the forces today. Compassionate leave. So that will brighten me up.'

As I made my way down the hill, dark clouds were beginning to accumulate. Fine before seven, rain by eleven, I told myself. I should have remembered that. It would have been a useful corrective to my earlier euphoria.

By the time I was turning the corner into Mount Pleasant View, the rain had begun to come down heavily, soaking me right through.

My landlady met me in the hall. 'You'd better dry your hair quick after you've taken your coat off because you've got a visitor in the front room, Idris the Milk.'

In a couple of minutes I had dried my hair and made myself presentable to meet my visitor.

Idris was still wearing his milkman's apron and was seated in my armchair by the fire, his eyes heavy-lidded as if he had been asleep. He had a tendency to drop off once he sat down by a fireside.

'What can I do for you, Idris?' I asked, as I drew up a chair on the opposite side of the fireplace.

'Well, it's more a case of what I can do for you,' he replied.

'That's interesting. Come on, out with it.'

''Ow would you like to come and see a show tonight and come back for fish and chips after?'

'I can't think of anything better. What show is this?' I asked.

'It's the Abergelly Amateur Operatic. They're doing *New Moon*—it's a new company started up. First show in the Valley since the war.'

'I'd love to come. But what about your wife, isn't she coming?'

'Looks like our Elsie's got the measles. We've got two tickets and Gwen thought you'd like to come in 'er place.'

'That's very kind, Idris. I come on one condition—that I pay for my ticket and the bus fares.'

'We'll see about that later. Right then.' He struggled to his feet. 'It's best if we catch the ten past six.'

An evening with Idris was just what I needed to lighten my heart. The show was embarrassingly amateurish, but during the evening I managed to recruit Idris, who had a good bass voice, to accept the role of sergeant of police in *The Pirates of Penzance*, which more than made up for the Abergelly Operatic's limitations.

When we arrived at Idris's house, the plates were warming on the hearth in front of a blazing fire in the grate. After a delicious supper of fish and chips I thanked Idris and Gwen for a nice evening and strode up the street to Mount Pleasant View.

When I arrived at number 13, I found a note on my table. It was from my inept colleague, Charles Wentworth-Baxter: *I think I've got laryngitis. Can you get somebody for St Padarn's tomorrow morning? Charles.*

Chapter Four

I had a sleepless night. At two o'clock in the morning, I made myself a cup of tea, all the time harbouring murderous thoughts about my colleague. My first Sunday of sole charge was off to a disastrous start. I wondered if that was a bad omen for my rendezvous with Eleanor's parents, who had invited me for a drink.

By seven o'clock I was washed and dressed. At half past seven I was hammering on the back door of Moelwyn Howells's greengrocer's shop, where Charles now lodged. A few minutes later, a dishevelled figure in shirt and trousers appeared, bleary-eyed and bewildered.

'You're up early,' croaked Moelwyn. 'Can't you sleep?'

'You've hit the nail on the head,' I said. 'It's your lodger. He left me a note last night saying he had laryngitis and couldn't take the service at St Padarn's.'

'I don't know anything about it, as God is my judge,' replied the greengrocer. 'Why don't you go up to his bedroom and see?'

I ran up the stairs two at a time and banged on Charles's door before throwing it open like a detective on a police raid.

He sat bolt upright in his bed, open-mouthed and staring at the intruder. 'Fred!' he shouted. 'What's the matter?'

'For someone suffering from laryngitis, you've made a quick recovery,' I snarled. 'Come off it, Charles. You get down to St Padarn's for half past nine. If your voice goes, use semaphore.'

He was still staring as I closed the door and went downstairs.

As I made my way to St Mary's Church I felt that the late Vicar of Pontywen would have been proud of me.

Bertie Owen met me at the door of St Padarn's when I arrived for Sunday School at half past two. I could tell by his excited demeanour that he had news to impart about the morning service.

'Come on, Bertie, out with it. What has he done?' I demanded.

'Well, first of all, he was late getting here. Then he couldn't remember the prayer to say in the vestry with the choir. So he mumbled something like "one, two, three, four, Amen". Anyway that's what Idris the Milk thought.'

'A good start,' I said.

'You've heard nothing yet,' he went on. 'When he got up in the pulpit, he pulled out the sermon from his cassock pocket and found it was the one he preached last time he was here. "If you don't mind, I've got to read you the sermon you had at your harvest." You could hear the congregation groan, honest. It went on and on. When it came to getting the wine ready for the Communion, he knocked the chalice over. There was wine everywhere. It was a real picnic.'

'Heaven preserve him when the new vicar comes,' I said.

The next hour dragged by in Sunday School as I waited for half past three to come and Eleanor to arrive for my meeting with her parents. I was dressed in my Burton's best and felt as apprehensive as Charles must have felt earlier about his solo debut.

Prompt on half past three, Eleanor arrived. 'You're looking smart,' she commented. 'Must be going somewhere special.'

'Thanks for the backhanded compliment, but, I must say, it has done my morale a power of good. It needed a boost.'

'Now see here, Secombe.' She stopped the car and switched off the engine. 'I don't want any more defeatism from you. You are coming to meet my parents, not going before a firing squad.'

'Pax,' I said and settled back in my seat.

Some ten miles and fifteen minutes later we were entering the drive leading to the Davies's residence, a large black and white mock-Tudor detached house overlooking an immaculate lawn.

'For heaven's sake, don't look so scared,' said Eleanor. 'Remember that I love you and I want my parents to love you as well.' She squeezed my hand and then opened the car door.

It was with difficulty that my legs transported my body into the entrance hall, where Eleanor announced our arrival in ringing tones. 'Hello, everybody, we're here!' A dog barked and a door opened.

A petite grey-haired replica of Eleanor emerged, her clear blue eyes doing a survey of her daughter's intended.

'Mummy, this is Fred,' came the introduction.

'How do you do, Mr Secombe?' said Mrs Davies in tepid tones as we shook hands.

'His name is Fred.' Eleanor's temper was beginning to rise.

'I am only trying to be polite, Eleanor,' snapped her mother.

It was evident that a tense time lay ahead.

'Where's Daddy, anyway?' asked my beloved.

'He's gone to the village to post some letters. He's due back any time. Would you like to come into the sitting room, Mr Secombe?'

It was a spacious room, with French windows opening onto the lawn. Eleanor took my hand in a fierce grip and led me to the sofa where we sat side by side. Mrs Davies stood by the window. I waited for the interrogation to begin.

'Is this your first parish, Mr Secombe?'

'No, my second. I was a curate in a parish in Swansea before I came here. It was a working-class district, friendly people, but I was unhappy with the training I was getting there. That is why I came to Pontywen—to get the benefit of serving under Canon Llewellyn. It is most unfortunate that my time with him was cut short.'

'That was sad. Do you come from a vicarage background?'

'Not at all, my father is a commercial traveller for a wholesale grocery firm in Swansea. That's my home town and I'm proud of it.'

466

'In that case it was a pity you had to leave it, wasn't it?'

'That's enough of the third degree, Mummy,' said Eleanor. 'Would you like a sherry, Fred?'

'I would indeed, please.'

'Here's your father coming. You'd better pour him one as well. I don't think I'll have one for the moment.' So saying Mrs Davies went out of the room to greet her husband. I could hear a *sotto voce* conversation in the hall. My heart was pounding.

'Keep your end up, Secombe,' whispered Eleanor. 'You're as good as they are, if not better.'

It was the cue for the entry of her father. He was a man of medium height, bespectacled, grey-moustached and of a sallow complexion.

'Daddy, this is Fred,' came introduction number two.

I stood up to shake his hand and collided with a coffee table.

'Don't knock the furniture about, lad,' he said and shook my hand warmly. 'So you are Fred. We've heard a lot about you.'

Thank God for Daddy, was the fervent prayer I sent up.

From that moment I began to relax. When Eleanor disappeared into the kitchen to help her mother, we talked rugby as we sipped our sherry. The Davies's residence began to assume the form of a home instead of an inquisitorial vault.

Half an hour later, Eleanor was driving me back to Pontywen for Evensong. We stopped outside my digs in good time for the service. 'I like your father,' I said.

'But you don't like my mother.'

'I didn't say that.'

'Anyway, you implied it. I can't blame you. She didn't exactly make you feel welcome. In time, she will come to accept you. It's just that she wants the best for her daughter. That's why I say in time she will accept you, once she knows you better.'

She kissed me lightly on the lips and soon the Morris Minor was chugging its way out of Mount Pleasant View.

THE CONGREGATION AND CHOIR at St Padarn's were still recovering from the Charles Wentworth-Baxter show at the Communion service that morning. I made a beeline for the vestry. There I encountered Bertie Owen, who was giving a graphic account of the morning's proceedings to those members of the choir who had been fortunate enough to have been absent. My colleague was making a name for himself in Pontywen. I wondered what impression Charles would make on the new vicar.

I did not have to wait long to find out the identity of the new incumbent. By Tuesday morning Father John Whittaker was knocking on my door, his appearance completely changed since his last foray into Pontywen.

He was clad all in black, black raincoat, black suit and, topping the outfit, a black ten-gallon hat. With his five-foot-five stature and his horn-rimmed spectacles, he looked like a comic advertisement for Sandeman's port.

'After my last experience,' he intoned, 'I thought I had better come here rather than to the vicarage.'

I ushered him into my room. He divested himself of his raincoat and hat and plunged himself into my armchair.

'This morning,' he went on, 'I received a letter from the patronage board offering me the living of Pontywen.' He delivered this information as if he were the winner of a parliamentary election on the steps of the Guildhall.

'Congratulations,' I said halfheartedly.

'I don't know whether it is cause for congratulations or not, until I have surveyed the land, as it were. When you follow an incumbent who has been in a parish for as long as the late Canon Llewellyn, it is no easy task. However, I thrive on a challenge and I shall accept the nomination to the living. By the way, I don't want any changes in the services and so on during the interregnum. The changes will come when I arrive and not before.'

'I have no intention of changing anything, Vicar. The bishop has put me in charge of operations until you arrive and I am answerable to him in the interim period.'

'Well, I can tell you that the interim period will not be long. I understand that Mrs Llewellyn is vacating the vicarage this Saturday. She has been invited to live with relatives in Bournemouth. I hope to be inducted in a couple of months' time. Now, is there anything you want to tell me about the parish?'

'As far as I'm concerned, the parish is in good heart. Canon Llewellyn was a fine priest. He has left you a complete index of all church people in Pontywen with comments on each card.'

'One of my first actions will be to inaugurate a survey of the *whole* of the parish—every house. I want a complete picture of its population. Is there anything else I should know?'

'There is one thing. Some weeks ago I formed a Gilbert and Sullivan Society at St Padarn's and we have begun rehearsals for *The Pirates of Penzance*. I had full permission from the late vicar.'

He stared at me in disbelief. 'Well, if Canon Llewellyn gave you permission I can't very well withdraw it, but if I had been here you wouldn't have got it. A parish priest's concern is for souls not soloists.' He liked that last sentence, so much so that he repeated the words 'souls not soloists'.

He stood up. 'Now,' he said. 'I'd like to visit the three churches. The car's outside. Before that, I wonder if I might wash my hands.'

While Father John Whittaker was 'washing his hands' in the outside lavatory, I looked out of the window at his car. It was an Austin Big Seven, in good condition and gleaming, not like Canon Llewellyn's old Morris. The old order changeth, I said to myself.

Suddenly Charles Wentworth-Baxter appeared outside, looking excited. He ran up the steps and banged on the door.

As I left my room to let him in, the vicar designate came into the hall. I opened the door to my colleague.

'Have you heard the news? That awful Father bloke has been offered the living,' he announced.

'Charles,' I said quickly, 'this is Father Whittaker. He has come to look round the parish.'

The colour left my colleague's face and a sickly smile appeared.

It was a chilly atmosphere in the Austin Big Seven as we made a tour of the three churches. 'I'll be in touch,' promised our vicar-to-be. It sounded more like a threat than a promise.

'WE'VE GOT TO DO SOMETHING special for Christmas,' said Charles Wentworth-Baxter at our Monday morning meeting. 'It's the first Christmas since the war. Can't we have a Christmas tree and dress it up? And have a midnight service?'

'You must be joking. We have been informed by our vicar-to-be that there must be no alteration of the status quo until he arrives. In any case can you imagine the old stick-in-the-muds in the parish church agreeing to it?'

'But you could do it in St Padarn's. You're in charge of it. Besides, if we have a midnight service there then we can be together for St Padarn's and the parish church.'

'I thought there was method in your madness. What you mean is that you will be able to avoid being in sole charge at the big services, you devious curate. In any case, where are we going to get a tree? It has to be a big one if it is going to be in church. Let's think it over.'

After he had gone, I began to warm to the idea. However, if anything was to be done it had to be done as soon as possible.

That afternoon, I was taking a funeral service in the churchyard. After the burial I mentioned to Full-Back Jones that I was thinking of getting a Christmas tree for St Padarn's.

His face lit up. 'I can 'elp you there. I know a dealer up the valley.'

'Will it be expensive?' I asked.

'You can 'ave it for nothing. 'E owes me some favours anyway. Keep it under your 'at, though. It's between you and me.'

I thanked him profusely and he went off like a dog with two tails to his task of filling in the grave.

Later in the week at the Gilbert and Sullivan rehearsal I asked the company if anyone knew of someone who would lend us lights for the Christmas tree. The first hand up belonged to Eleanor. 'Please sir,' she said mockingly, 'I'm sure we can lend ours. I'm getting a bit big for Christmas trees and pillowcases.'

There were three other offers and Bertie Owen said that he knew somebody at work who would lend us a length of cable for the wiring.

After Evensong at St Padarn's I announced that Christmas would be celebrated with a Christmas tree and a midnight service. The idea of a tree met with universal approval. The midnight service was welcomed by the younger members of the congregation but regarded with suspicion by some of the older worshippers.

'I don't like this idea,' objected Mrs Collier, leading soprano. 'It will spoil the seven o'clock service which is always packed. We always have "The Holy City" as an anthem. I've been singing the solo in that for years and years.'

'There's no reason to stop singing "The Holy City" if we do have a service at midnight,' I said. 'Mind, I don't know why you sing it at Christmas. It has nothing to do with the birth of Jesus. Perhaps you would like to sing the solo in a Christmas carol instead.'

'What a good idea,' said Annie Jones. 'We could sing quite a few carols, with other soloists as well.' Annie Jones was Mrs Collier's rival in the soprano stakes.

'This is not the place to be discussing what has to be sung at the service.' I decided to end any further provocation of Mrs Collier. 'I simply wanted to inform you that we're having a midnight service and a Christmas tree. With only two weeks to go we have to move quickly in our preparations to let everybody know.'

'Posters.' Bertie Owen was on his feet again. 'Posters. We'll have 'em in as many houses as we can—and word of mouth, of course.'

'If I were you,' advised Eleanor when we met after the service, 'I should make peace with Madame Collier and let her sing her "Holy City", for this year at any rate. You'll need all the cooperation you can get if you want to make a success of your midnight venture.'

'Your very word is my command, princess,' I replied.

Next morning I called at the Collier abode. The lady of the house appeared at the door wearing a pinafore, with her curlered hair hidden under a turban. A cloud of steam emanated from the open door of the kitchen. It was washing day. Her face, flushed with the heat of her laundering, displayed a mixture of suspicion and surprise.

'I wonder if I might have a word with you, Mrs Collier,' I said.

'I'm hardly in a state to receive visitors.' The tone was acid. 'You'd better come into the front room.' I was ushered in. 'What can I do for you?'

'It's just to say that I would be pleased if you would sing "The Holy City" at the midnight service. Obviously it has been part of Christmas at St Padarn's for some years.'

Her expression changed. The frown gave place to something like a smile. 'Well, when you've been singing that piece every Christmas for years, it becomes part of it, as you say. Anyway, thank you. Would you like a quick cup of tea, Mr Secombe? It won't take a minute.'

'Just a quick one then. I don't want to hold up your work.'

With a smile she went off to make the tea, reappearing a few minutes later with a tray containing two cups of tea, milk jug, sugar bowl and a book of raffle tickets.

'I'm afraid I'm out of biscuits. Would you like to buy a raffle ticket? Threepence each or five for a shilling. Mr Collier's been given a book to sell for the British Legion's Christmas draw. First prize is a bottle of whisky and second prize is a chicken.'

'I wouldn't want the first prize but I would certainly like the second and so would Mrs Richards.'

I bought five tickets, drank my tea and left Mrs Collier a much happier person than when she had opened the door to me.

AS THE DAYS WENT BY, Bertie's homemade posters seemed to be in every other house in the St Padarn's district of Pontywen.

The excitement was not confined to Bertie. It had Charles Wentworth-Baxter in its grip also. After the weekly Gilbert and Sullivan rehearsal he took me aside.

'When is the tree coming? I've got some surprise decorations for it.' He was like a child, wide-eyed in anticipation of Christmas.

'Full-Back Jones tells me it will arrive tomorrow. So we'll put it in position on Christmas Eve and decorate it then.'

'Can't we do it on Saturday? There are only two more days to Christmas after that.'

'Certainly not. Next Sunday is the Fourth Sunday of Advent. You don't celebrate Christmas beforehand even if the shops do.'

When Eleanor drove me back to my digs afterwards, she remarked about Charles's immaturity. 'He's a Peter Pan,' she said. 'I don't think he will ever grow up enough to have charge of a parish.'

'It's amazing what the grace of God can achieve,' I replied.

She looked sceptical. 'By the way, you are invited to tea on Christmas Day. There will be a few family friends as well. It should be a relaxing evening when you won't be grilled by my mother.'

'I was hoping I'd see you on Christmas Day. That's marvellous. Thank you.' I kissed her. 'It's going to be a wonderful Christmas.'

I spoke too soon.

Friday came and by late afternoon there was no sign of the tree. I called round at Jones's hovel. He was not in. His neighbours said that they had not seen him since early afternoon. I began to panic.

When I arrived at my digs, I found Mrs Richards, beaming with delight. 'What do you think?' she said. 'The man from that Foreign Legion club has been here. You've won the chicken in their Christmas drawing. I haven't had chicken since before the war. The man is bringing it here first thing on Christmas Eve.' She looked at me quizzically. 'You don't seem very pleased.'

'Of course I'm pleased we are going to have chicken for our Christmas dinner—but are we going to have a Christmas tree for our Christmas service? It hasn't arrived yet and no one knows where Full-Back Jones is.'

'Don't worry, Mr Secombe,' the old lady said reassuringly. 'I don't think he'll backfire on his promise.'

She was right. At nine o'clock there was a knock on the door. It was the tree provider.

'You'll find the tree, and a barrel to put it in, behind the church.'

He grinned his toothless grin and put a dirty finger to his mouth. 'Keep it under your 'at.' Then he was down the steps and away.

Next morning I went round to the church to inspect the tree. It was enormous. His friend the dealer was indeed generous.

At breakfast on Christmas Eve, Mrs Richards was all agog over the Christmas chicken. 'I hope it's plucked,' she said. 'I can't stand having to withdraw all those feathers. We had one the first Christmas we were married. In the end, Mr Richards had to get his razor to shave off all the rubble.'

We were still at the breakfast table when there was a knock at the door. 'I expect that's the chicken,' I said.

I opened the door to be confronted by a little man wearing a scruffy raincoat. He was holding, by its feet, a live cockerel that appeared to have outlived its normal span. It was too feeble to struggle.

'Your prize, Mr Secombe,' he announced. 'With the compliments of the club.'

'Is it for burial?' I asked.

'Not at all,' he said indignantly. 'We like to bring it fresh, like. Not something that's been killed days ago.' With that he pushed the two ancient feet into my hand and vanished down the street.

I closed the door and stood for a minute in the hall, wondering how I was going to face my landlady. I decided that the only course open to me was to make her laugh. I flung open the middle-room door and exclaimed, 'My prize!'

The suddenness of my attempt at humour produced a resurrection in the fowl. It flapped its wings and managed a few squawks.

Far from laughing, Mrs Richards was petrified. She went for cover in the corner by the dresser. 'Take that out of here,' she shouted, 'before it jumps out of your hand.'

I went out into the back yard at the speed of light.

For safety's sake, I shut it in the late Mr Richards's greenhouse.

When I arrived back in the middle room, the old lady was seated at the table, her face as white as her clean tablecloth.

'I'm sorry, Mrs Richards,' I said. 'I shouldn't have done that. I was just trying to make you laugh at my so-called prize.'

'That Foreign Legion lot and their draw. I was so looking forward to our Christmas dinner.' She was almost in tears.

'Perhaps it won't taste too bad if you cook it a lot,' I suggested.

'Somebody's got to kill it first. I can't, that's certain.'

'Nor me neither. I could shout "boo" behind its back and it might die of fright.'

There was a glimmer of a smile on her face.

'I know what I'll do,' I went on. 'I'll go and see Full-Back Jones. He'll kill it for us, I'm sure.'

'That's a good idea, Mr Secombe. He's a bit of a poaching man. So he's bound to know what to do.'

I called at the gravedigger's on my way to St Padarn's. He said he would be happy to oblige us.

When I arrived at the church there was the usual organised chaos created by Bertie Owen. Ladies were scurrying around the church with holly and Bertie was acting as foreman while some sidesmen he had recruited were attempting to get the tree into the barrel. Eventually the tree was hauled up into position.

'What a massive tree,' exclaimed Eleanor when she arrived with her contribution of fairy lights, to add to the others we'd been lent.

'Full-Back and his friend have done us proud,' I said.

She stared at it for a while and then took me aside.

'I don't want to dampen your enthusiasm,' she whispered, 'but Will Book and Pencil was telling me this morning that the Forestry Commission have reported that some of their trees have been—er—forcibly removed.'

My enthusiasm vanished as light dawned on the darkness of my ignorance—a red light. Will Book and Pencil was the local police constable. 'So that's why the tree was delivered at night.'

'You realise you can be charged with receiving stolen goods.'

I gulped. 'But I didn't know they were stolen.'

'That's what they all say.' The look of mock censure on her face gave way to a smile. 'Don't worry, love. I'm sure Will Book and Pencil won't take away your tree. How many people know it's a "gift" from Full-Back Jones?'

'Only you, Charles and Mrs Richards.'

'In that case you have nothing to fear. Just carry on with the decoration. Speaking of which here comes Peter Pan. I must be off.' She squeezed my hand and went out through the side door.

Charles Wentworth-Baxter was carrying a large suitcase. His face was lit with a seraphic beam of happiness. The surprise was about to be revealed. He sat down in the front pew and opened his case. 'Here we are,' he said proudly. He produced numerous creations made out of cardboard, covered with silver paper. They had no form or comeliness.

'What on earth are these?' I asked.

'They're angels and I've made the Archangel Gabriel to go on the

474

top of the tree.' He extricated a large monstrosity and held it in front of my face as if it were a masterpiece of creative art.

'Well, they will certainly be a talking point,' I said.

'Thank you, Fred,' he replied.

'What are these things?' said Bertie Owen in bewilderment.

'They are angels,' explained Charles, looking at me as if he despaired of the ignorance of the uncultured.

By ten o'clock that night, Bertie Owen was exhausted but triumphant. Hour after hour, perched precariously on a stepladder, he had worked to link up six sets of fairy lights. Eventually, when he switched on the lights, he was overwhelmed with the success of his technical genius. 'They're all on!' he shouted in disbelief.

By eleven thirty, it was standing room only in St Padarn's and the atmosphere was electric. There never was such singing in that church. They raised the roof with 'O Come All Ye Faithful'.

As the prayers began, there was a respectful silence and so it continued until Mrs Collier began her anthem.

'Last night as I was sleeping, I had a dream so fair,' she sang.

We heard no more about her dream because at that moment the lights went out and the organ ceased to function.

There was an eerie silence, only to be shattered by a shout from Bertie, 'Don't panic, it's only a fuse.'

'Nobody's panicking, Mr Owen,' I said quietly. 'If you will go to the vestry and mend the fuse, we'll carry on with the service. In the meantime, we shall sit and sing from memory "Away in a Manger".'

With the aid of somebody's cigarette lighter, Bertie made his way into the vestry.

The unaccompanied singing of the carol was a triumph. Most of the congregation seemed to know the words while the harmonies supplied by the choir gave the necessary depth to the music. As the last notes faded there was a blaze of light.

The rest of the service was uninterrupted and the consensus of opinion was an enthusiastic approval of the midnight venture. Charles was elated. So was Bertie.

I saw Eleanor briefly.

'Did you enjoy the service?' I asked.

'Very much so,' she replied. 'St Padarn's will never be the same again, what with Charles's attempt at modern art and Bertie's attack on the electricity supply.'

'You are mocking me, Eleanor Davies.'

'What makes you think that, Frederick Thomas Secombe?

Honestly, it was a warm, exciting service. Merry Christmas, my dear. I can't kiss you here. I shall do that at three thirty this afternoon when I pick you up.'

'Merry Christmas, my love,' I said.

I went into the vestry to disrobe. Bertie was buzzing around like a demented bumblebee while Charlie Hughes, the other churchwarden, assisted by Idris the Milk, was counting the collection.

Suddenly outside in the chancel I heard the unmistakable tones of Will Book and Pencil. My heart missed several beats. Into the vestry he strode, helmet tucked under his arm.

'Any trouble tonight?' he enquired.

'None at all,' I assured him.

'Good,' he replied. 'I was going to keep an eye on things in case of drunks but I got called to a couple of punch-ups in the town.'

As he went out of the vestry, the constable paused and looked at the tree. 'That's a fine tree, Mr Secombe,' he remarked.

My heart missed several more beats. 'Yes, it was given by a friend of the church who wished to remain anonymous.'

'You must introduce me one day,' said Will Book and Pencil. 'I could do with a friend like that. Merry Christmas.'

'That's the best of knowing the right people,' I replied with my tongue firmly in my cheek. 'Merry Christmas, Constable.'

'What's that you are whistling?' asked Bertie Owen as we walked away from the church a little later on.

'It's called "When You Come to the End of a Perfect Day".'

'That's not a carol.'

'No, but it's often sung at the end of Christmas Eve.'

'Well, I never knew that before,' said Bertie.

Chapter Five

It seemed no time at all after Christmas that the new incumbent was inducted to the living of Pontywen. Despite the sleet and the bitter wind, the parish church was full for the service.

'Before I commend your new vicar as a worthy successor to Canon Llewellyn,' said the bishop in his address, 'I must thank the Reverend Fred Secombe for his care of the parish in the interregnum. He has shown a sense of responsibility beyond his years.'

This episcopal tribute was received with a scowl by Father Whittaker who was anxious to hear his own virtues paraded for the benefit of the congregation, not those of his underling. It boded ill for the Monday morning meeting in the vicarage, at which, Charles and I were informed, the 'pastoral strategy' would be unveiled.

So on Monday it was not without a certain amount of misgiving that Charles and I made our way to the parish church of St Mary's where we were to say Matins together with our overlord, prior to the 'strategy' meeting. He met us at the church clad in cassock and cape.

'Where are your cassocks?' he demanded. 'From now on I want you to wear your cassocks to church for our daily service.'

The mention of cassocks and daily services caused the blood to drain from Charles's cheeks.

Matins over, we went to the vicarage where already there were signs that the old order had given place to the new—for the worse. No longer did the smell of polish predominate as we entered the hall. Instead our nostrils were assaulted by the smell of fish heads being boiled for the housekeeper's two cats. The new vicar was a bachelor, and his housekeeper, Mrs Lilywhite, was named most inappropriately. Her lack of care for her person was on a par with her lack of care for the house.

'Mrs Lilywhite, can we have three coffees in the study?' bawled the vicar on entering his domain.

'You'll have to hold on for a bit. I'm doing the washing,' came the reply from the kitchen. The housekeeper had a strong pair of lungs.

We were ushered into the study where there had been a complete transformation. Gone were the floor-to-ceiling bookshelves, groaning under the weight of indigestible tomes. Now the newly decorated walls were plastered with religious paintings and framed photographs of clerics. One of them seemed to be of the Pope in his white cap.

'Right, now let's get down to business.' He opened a drawer in his desk and produced a file of papers. 'Before we go any further, let's get first things first. Sunday services. I shall be anchored in the parish church. You, Secombe, are anchored already in St Padarn's. That means that you, Wentworth-Baxter, will be anchored in Llanhyfryd.'

'Father!' came a call from the kitchen.

He rose from his chair and stalked out into the hall.

Charles and I looked at each other. 'Who does he think he is?' said Charles. 'Chaplain to the Missions to Seamen?'

Father's head appeared round the door. 'Milk and sugar for both?'

'Please,' we said in unison.

Seconds later he was back at his desk and proceeding to the next item on his agenda. 'Vestments,' he said. 'Before long I shall introduce them in Pontywen as part of a plan to raise the level of worship. Ultimately I should like to see incense and sanctuary bells in all three churches.'

By now Charles had a glazed look in his eyes.

'If you don't mind my saying so, Vicar, I am afraid you will empty all three churches with these changes.' I felt I had to speak my mind before he went any further in disclosing his plans. Vestments and Anglo-Catholic ritual would give the congregation apoplexy.

He glared at me through his horn-rimmed spectacles and quoted the Scriptures. '"He who is not with me is against me."'

'Let me put it this way. Vestments will not worry me but when you begin smells and bells, I shall go elsewhere.'

'Shall we drop this subject for the time being?' he snapped. 'Now then, next week we shall begin a door-to-door visitation of every house in Pontywen. I have prepared forms that will give details of every person in the house, age, denomination and whether baptised or confirmed. When the survey is complete, we shall have an exact picture of the parish and the task that lies ahead of us.'

There was a loud knock on the door. 'Come in,' he shouted.

Mrs Lilywhite entered, carrying a tin tray on which were three cups, generously filled with coffee that was flowing over the brims.

Charles and I sipped our coffee while the vicar proceeded to give us instructions on how we were to conduct our survey.

'We visit everybody,' he said. 'I know Canon Llewellyn had his list but it was incomplete. I want to have full details—age, baptised or confirmed. If they belong to other denominations I want to know what they are. If they are nonbelievers, I want to know that.'

'Don't you think it is rather impolite to ask people their age?'

'If they don't wish to give it, just estimate,' he replied. 'By the way, I shall not be with you when you begin the survey next Monday afternoon. I have a missionary meeting in Cardiff.'

As we left the vicarage, each with a folder full of forms, I said to Charles, 'Thank heaven for the missionary meeting. At least we shall not be under his eagle eye. By the way, as far as I am concerned, everybody's age will be an estimate.'

'Me, too,' replied my colleague.

AT TWO THIRTY the following Monday we met in Thomas Street.

'You take the right-hand side and I'll do the other side,' I suggested. 'Whoever finishes first will come and help the other one.'

'I expect you will be first,' forecast my colleague hopefully.

'"Go to the ant, thou sluggard."' I said.

'What number is she?' he asked facetiously.

'Number one, Thomas Street.' I pointed to the first of the houses across the road. Holding his folder he approached the house and knocked on the door timidly.

A peroxide blonde, in her forties by the look of her, opened the door. The next minute Charles had been invited inside.

I knocked on the door of number 2. Faltering footsteps down the passage heralded the approach of an old lady who opened the door a few inches. 'We're doing a survey of the street,' I said. 'Can you tell me what denomination you are?'

'Labour and proud of it,' she answered and slammed the door.

I opened my folder, and wrote, 'Number two Thomas Street. Name and age not divulged. Age estimated at eighty. Nonbeliever.'

Numbers 4, 6 and 8 were answerless.

Number 10 was Baptist. Number 12 was Welsh Methodist. Number 14 Pentecostal. The old lady at number 16, when asked her denomination, said, 'I listens to the wireless, love.' I decided to write that down on the form to indicate to the vicar how irrelevant most of these answers were.

There was no sign of Charles.

At number 18 I was invited inside by an elderly man, bearing a number of blue scars and coughing intermittently.

'Sorry about the cough. It's the dust, Vicar. Forty years down the mines. Nothing in my pocket, only in my lungs. No, I 'aven't bothered about religion, to tell you the truth. A couple of times down below, I said a prayer when I was trapped by a fall. I suppose it must 'ave worked. Would you like a cup of tea?'

'No, thank you very much. We have to get round all the houses in the street, you see.'

'Well, any time you want to pop in 'ere, you'll be welcome.'

On my form, I put down his name, Edwin Jones, widower, and alongside the remark, 'Nonbeliever. Lonely, sick. Needs a visit.'

Number 22 was 'C of E nonattending' while number 24 housed a full-blooded Communist.

Number 26 was the last of the houses on my side of the street. The lady of the house was a Jehovah's Witness and was intent on teaching me the meaning of the Bible as an Old Moore's Almanac. It took ten minutes to disentangle myself from her attentions.

Still Charles was nowhere to be seen. I went back to number 1 to see if my inept colleague was still incarcerated with the blonde.

I gave the knocker a
hearty thumping. The door
opened. 'Come on in,' said the blonde,
'and join your friend. We're just about to have another cup of tea.'

'If you don't mind, I'd rather not,' I replied, 'and I don't think my
colleague should do so either. We have to complete a survey of this
street by the end of the afternoon.'

With that, Charles emerged from the front room.

'I'm sorry, Mrs Williams. I didn't realise what the time was. I'm
afraid I had better get on with my work.'

'"Get on with my work"!' I exploded. 'You've only just started and I have finished the whole of the other side of the street.'

'It's my fault,' said Mrs Williams. 'I've 'ad such an un'appy life with my 'usband and your friend 'as been very sympathetic.'

'Glad to hear it,' I grunted.

'See you again, Mrs Williams,' were Charles's parting words.

'If you're a wise man you won't,' I warned him as she closed the door. 'Come into my parlour said the spider to the fly. Good heavens, Charles, grow up, will you?'

He dropped his head like a child who had just been scolded.

'Look, Charles. You get down to number twenty-five and work back towards me.' He crawled down the street.

I knocked on the door of number 3. A large unkempt lady who must have been in her fifties appeared.

'All right, Father, I'll go and get the money now,' she said.

'I'm not who you think I am,' I replied. 'I'm the Church of England curate. We are finding out people's denominations. I know what yours is now so I shan't waste any more of your time.'

'Oh, that's all right, love. Don't worry. Anyway, if ever you're collecting for anything, you can always come 'ere. I won't be able to give much but you can 'ave it with pleasure.'

Number 5 produced a thin, tiny little woman with birdlike features, neatly dressed. 'Yes?' she asked sharply.

I launched into my preamble once more.

'C of E 'ere. Always 'ave been.'

'Good. May I have your name, please?'

'Wilkins. Miss.'

'May I ask if you've been baptised?'

'Certainly, and confirmed, too.'

'I don't think I have seen you at Communion.'

'Perhaps I was there when you weren't there. 'Ave you been next door?' She pointed to number 3.

'Yes. I've just called there.'

'She's terrible. Shouts, swears. Spoils the 'ole street. We like to keep ourselves to ourselves 'ere.'

'Christians are not supposed to keep themselves to themselves. Jesus said that at the Day of Judgment He will ask you what you have done for other people. If I were you I shouldn't tell Him you've kept yourself to yourself.'

'You're a cheeky young man,' she snapped and banged the door.

Once again there was no sign of Charles but coming towards me was Will Book and Pencil.

'Just the man I want to see, Reverend.'

'It wasn't me, I swear, Constable.'

'Very funny, Mr Secombe, but it's a serious matter. I've got to go to number fifteen, name of Harrington. The son has been playing truant and was knocked down this afternoon on the main road. He's up the hospital. They're afraid he might not live.'

I was stunned. Barry Harrington was one of the choirboys in the parish church.

'Do you mind coming with me?' asked the policeman.

'Of course not. I know the boy anyway.'

The policeman knocked on the door with such force that the noise echoed round the street. There was a scurry of footsteps down the passage. Mrs Harrington's face lost every vestige of colour when she saw the policeman and the curate on her doorstep. 'There's been an accident at the pit . . .' Her hand clutched her breast.

'No, Mrs Harrington. Can we come in, please?' said Will gently.

We were shown into the front room where on the mantelpiece was a photograph of Barry in his choir robes.

'I'm afraid the accident has happened to your son—down on the main road. He's in the hospital.'

Her eyes opened wide in disbelief.

'He's at school. He couldn't have been on the main road.'

I went and sat beside her on the settee. I put my arm round her shoulders. 'He must have been playing truant,' I said. 'It seems that he was in collision with a car.'

'Oh my God! Don't say that he's—'

'He's alive,' the policeman assured her, 'but he's very ill.'

'If you get your coat and hat on, I'll walk up to the hospital with you. Perhaps the constable will get in touch with your husband at the colliery in the meanwhile.'

She accepted my offer to escort her and we were out of the door in no time. In the street there was still no sign of Charles.

As we walked, the mother talked in gasps about her one and only child, the shock of the news causing this normally reserved lady to chatter incessantly all the way to the hospital.

An elderly doctor was at the boy's bedside when we arrived.

'I'm afraid your son has a suspected fractured skull and a fractured pelvis. The next few days will be critical. I'll leave you with him for a while. He's unconscious and probably will remain so for some time.'

He paused at the door. 'We are doing everything in our power, you can rest assured, Mrs Harrington.'

When he left, the mother sat by her son's bedside and smoothed his cheek. I brought a chair from the corner and sat beside her.

'Would you like me to say a prayer?' I asked.

She nodded. I prayed for the boy's recovery and that his parents would have strength to face the ordeal.

'Thank you,' she whispered, and didn't utter another word until her husband arrived half an hour later. A big, burly man, he burst into tears as soon as he saw his son.

'Come on, Llew,' she said. 'We've got to pull ourselves together for Barry's sake.'

'They're doing all they can for him, Mr Harrington. All we can do is to pray for him.'

So saying I rose and led him to the chair alongside his wife.

'I shall be in touch and we shall be praying for him in church tomorrow morning.' With those words, I left the pair of them. She was comforting her husband and was still tearless.

As I left the hospital, I was praying hard that the outcome for Barry would not be like that for little David William.

I still carried the folder and the forms. I had an urge to scatter them over the hillside as an irrelevance. Instead I walked back to Thomas Street to find out if my colleague had completed his stint. Since I had left him at number 25, the end house, I decided to call at number 7 where he should have made the last of his visits.

The lady of the house claimed to be Welsh Baptist and had not seen Charles. One by one I made my way down the street until I arrived at number 25 in a stage of high dudgeon. My assault on the knocker made that of Will Book and Pencil sound like a mere tap.

Footsteps hurried down the passage. A middle-aged lady appeared. 'He's finishing his tea with my husband. Methodist we are, but always pleased to see the clergy.'

I had no time to say anything because Charles Wentworth-Baxter loomed up behind her. 'I'd better be going now, Mrs Hopkins, and thank you for the tea. Ah, well, on with the work.'

'"On with the work"!' I expostulated when she'd closed the door. 'I have trudged round twenty-four houses, escorted a lady to the hospital to see her badly injured son, and in that time you have called at two houses!' I turned on my heels and marched back to 13 Mount Pleasant View, still seething.

'You've got a face like a thunderstorm,' commented Mrs Richards.

'It's that idiot, Charles. I visited twenty-four houses this afternoon while he managed two. Not only that, I spent an hour in between taking Mrs Harrington to the hospital where Barry is critically ill after an accident on the main road.'

'Oh dear,' said my landlady. 'It's that little boy in the choir, the one who's always making the other boys in stitches.'

'I'm afraid he's the one in stitches now, Mrs Richards. It looks very serious to me. I think I'd better let the vicar know after tea.'

By seven o'clock I felt sufficiently calm to make the journey to the vicarage. Father Whittaker opened the door and when he saw me his face developed one of Mrs Richards's 'thunderstorms'.

'The man I want to see,' he said, through his clenched dentures. 'Come on in. You want to follow St James's advice and keep control of your tongue.'

484

'What do you mean, Vicar?' I said.

'I've just had a lady called Miss Wilkins here from Thomas Street who claimed that you abused her verbally this afternoon.'

'Excuse me, Vicar,' I was fighting hard to keep control, 'that lady verbally abused her Roman Catholic next-door neighbour who was concerned to help my cause, and then she went on to suggest that the great thing in life was to keep yourself to yourself. I told her she should follow the advice of Jesus to do the opposite.'

His mouth opened but no words came forth.

'In any case, I have come here on a matter much more serious than Miss Wilkins's ruffled feelings. One of your choir boys, Barry Harrington, was knocked over on the main road this afternoon and is fighting for his life in hospital.'

Father Whittaker stood up. 'What ward is he in?'

'Ward seven. I expect his mother and father will be with him. I took Mrs Harrington there this afternoon and I've said prayers for him.'

'Thank you,' he said. 'I'll go now to see them. We'll—er—discuss Miss Wilkins some other time.'

With those words, he was out through the door and then drove quickly up the drive, leaving an impressed curate on the doorstep.

'IT'S YOUR TURN NOW,' said Aneurin Williams, the musical director. 'Look at them. They're like a bunch of excited children.'

He and I were standing at the piano, surveying the scene as an eager band of helpers directed by Bertie Owen cleared away chairs at the back of St Padarn's church hall to make floor space. The chorus had been drilled in the music of *The Pirates of Penzance* and now the time for the first stage rehearsal had arrived.

Clutching my prompt copy of the opera I called for order.

'This evening we shall start with the opening chorus of act one with the pirates and Samuel's solo. Then we shall have the entrance of the major general's daughters with the solo from Mabel, if she's here. Now then, everybody off the floor except the pirates.'

The girls, and the men playing the policemen, went to the back chattering like a crowd of ten-year-olds. 'Quiet!' I shouted. 'For heaven's sake let's have silence from those not involved in the action.'

I proceeded to group the nine men who were pirates. According to the score there should have been eighteen pirates to eighteen girls, but as the Pontywen Grammar School hall, booked for our performances, had a stage which could not accommodate a cast that size, it was just as well that male members were below par.

'Now then, before the curtain rises, there is the noise of merriment and some laughter, which gets louder until when the curtain does go up on the fifteenth bar there's a cheer as Samuel comes on with a flagon of wine. He goes round, starting on the right, filling cups, then goes to centre for the solo. We'll do your little dance, Iorwerth, at a principals' rehearsal. Can we have the opening bars, Charles?'

There was no response. When I looked round, I found him engaged in earnest conversation with one of Aneurin's pupils.

'Charles,' I said sharply. 'Can we have the opening bars, please?'

Aneurin tapped his music stand and started to conduct.

A faint murmur was heard from the pirates.

'Stop! Stop!' I shouted. 'Let's have some realism. You're a bunch of pirates getting merry on sherry, like the crowd in the Red Lion half an hour before closing time. Let's start again.'

Once again Charles began to play.

'Rhubarb, rhubarb. Ha! Ha! Ha! Rhubarb.' Bertie Owen was giving a solo performance at the top of his voice, watched in amazement by his fellow pirates.

I went over to Bertie, caught him by the shoulders. 'Rhubarb grows in gardens, Bertie. I asked you to be realistic not horticultural.'

'Excuse me, Mr Secombe. I always thought that everybody in crowd scenes says rhubarb all the time.'

'Somebody's been pulling your leg. So please don't keep repeating the word rhubarb. Talk about anything you like and by the way, when you laugh, sound as if you're enjoying a joke, not forcing it like rhubarb. OK, Aneurin. Straight through this time.'

This time Bertie was too chastened to make himself the focus of attention and the opening chorus started to show signs of promise.

As the last notes died away, Eleanor entered at the back of the hall.

'We'll have a change of face now. Gentlemen, you can give place to the ladies. It's their turn to occupy the stage.'

The men shambled off the floor space and I went down to meet Eleanor. 'I'm shattered,' she said. 'I've just spent two hours delivering a very reluctant baby.'

'You poor thing. Do you think you'll be up to singing "Poor Wandering One"?'

'It won't be brilliant but I'll do my best.'

By now the girls were in a fever of excitement, as noisy as a flock of starlings settling in the branches of a tree.

'Calm down, girls. You are the major general's daughters, not a crowd of factory workers on an outing to Barry Island fair. You are out for the afternoon with a stretch of sand for your private enjoyment. Some of you will have parasols and all of you will be walking daintily on your toes, to avoid damp patches in the sand.'

Charles launched into the music.

'On your toes. Look happy. Smile. Now then, into the lines in which I arranged you. Don't bunch, spread yourselves out.'

Suddenly I was aware of Eleanor standing behind me. 'You're bawling at them like a tinpot dictator. Show them what you want.'

'Stop, stop!' I commanded. Everything ground to a halt. 'Now then girls, Dr Davies will show you how to walk.'

She gave me a long hard look.

'For the purpose of this production, shall we drop the Doctor in front of my name! I'm Eleanor. I had not intended to become part of the production team. However since I have been hijacked into it, here goes. Get off the stage and then watch me.'

For the next five minutes or so in front of an intent audience she gave a perfect lesson in movement. She minced, she tripped along, she gave little gasps of surprise at something apparently discovered in a rock pool. All the time her mobile face indicated pleasure and delight at a seaside outing. I was proud of her.

'Now then, Mr Secombe, they're all yours.'

'Thank you very much. Girls, you couldn't have had a better illustration of what's required than that. So shall we start again.'

What followed was a complete transformation. Most of the girls were between sixteen and eighteen years of age so they looked like daughters of the major general, young and fresh; now they were beginning to move like them. And to top it all Eleanor's solo was received with rapturous applause by the company.

'We'll have a break now,' I announced.

'I'm gasping for a cup of tea, Frederick.' Eleanor was sprawled across a chair. 'If you don't mind, I think I had better go now. I'll pick you up tomorrow evening at seven.'

I went to the door to see her off. She gave me a chaste salute on the doorstep and was away in her chariot in no time.

'All right,' I shouted. 'Back to act one for the capture of the girls by the pirates and then we finish for the evening.'

I positioned the girls around the floor. 'Now then, men, you creep up behind the girls ready to catch them as they turn. They struggle with you then drop on their knees facing you.'

It was obvious that this was going to be the highlight of the evening. The men who were pirates, most of them middle-aged, relished the prospect of grabbing hold of the girls. Those who were police began to feel that they were miscast. The girls became giggly as they contemplated the action involving men.

Bertie Owen was acting like a teenager pretending to struggle with two sixteen-year-olds at the same time. 'Bertie, for heaven's sake, this is not a rugby match. You creep up and grab their waists, not bowl them over. Can we start again, please?'

After a while the rest of the men started to get tired of Bertie's antics and were making it plain. Iorwerth put it succinctly. 'Bertie, you're acting like a bloody two-year-old.' This had the desired effect and a good time was had by all.

'I'M CALLING A PAROCHIAL CHURCH COUNCIL meeting for next week,' announced the vicar at our Monday morning get-together.

'We have only four more streets to survey. These will be done in the next few days. So I shall be able to let the council know the results and enlist their support.'

Next, an update on young Barry Harrington. 'He came out of the coma yesterday and they think his brain will not be affected but his fractured pelvis will keep him in hospital for six months.'

Whatever faults my superior had, I had to admire his pastoral zeal. There were very few days when he was not at the boy's bedside.

'The next news I have to report is that I have ordered a set of vestments to be ready for Easter Day.'

'I hope you will not meet with any great opposition,' I remarked.

'Now look here, Fred, I want support from you and you, too, Wentworth-Baxter.'

Charles sat up as if suffering an electric shock.

'If you don't mind me saying so, Vicar, it is not us you need worry about. Your headache will be supplied by people like Ezekiel Evans and Bertie Owen.'

'My apologies, Fred. I accept that I shall have your support. Any change is bound to be regarded with suspicion. As for Ezekiel Evans and especially Bertie Owen, I can easily deal with those idiots.'

It was with these words ringing in my ears that I walked down the vicarage drive with my colleague. 'I think Father will soon find that Ezekiel and Bertie will not be the walkover he expects. Next week's meeting is going to be very interesting.'

When I told Mrs Richards about the vestments and what the vicar had said about the lay reader and Bertie Owen, she forecast that he would have an unpleasant surprise. 'That Zekiel Evans is a connivling sort of man. He doesn't like it that his nose hasn't got a joint now that this new vicar is here. He'll be round everybody behind the vicar's back, stabbing him all the time, you wait and see.'

AT SEVEN O'CLOCK THAT EVENING Eleanor knocked on the door of 13 Mount Pleasant View.

'I bring you tidings of great joy,' she announced.

'I know you're an angel, love, but would you mind defining the tidings?'

'My employer, Dr Elias Llewellyn Hughes, whom you admire so much, has given me a rise of two hundred and fifty pounds a year.'

'That rise is ten pounds more than my annual pay.'

'If you will choose the wrong profession, my love.'

'Excuse me. I have chosen the right profession but the wrong pay.'

'Perhaps we could discuss this over dinner? I have come to invite you to a meal to celebrate my new-found wealth.'

'I shall be delighted to accept on condition that you will give me time to dash upstairs and put on my best suit.'

Minutes later, she drove us down the valley to the one four-star hotel in the vicinity. There was one table for two left. We were in a corner where we could observe our fellow diners, one of whom I recognised. He was Daniel Fitzgerald, diocesan registrar, who was eating alone and attacking his main course with obvious relish.

'He's eating enough for two,' I said, discreetly indicating his whereabouts. 'That's old Fitzgerald, the diocesan registrar. He's a pompous individual.'

The words were hardly out of my mouth before he was convulsed with a choking fit. His face went purple and he was fighting for breath. Eleanor was away from her chair like a greyhound out of the traps. She put her fingers down his throat, pulling out a piece of meat which had threatened his life. Putting the offending gristle on his side plate she made a quick exit to the ladies' cloakroom.

When she returned, having washed her hands and powdered her nose, the old man came to our table. 'Young lady, I wish to thank you for your prompt action. You have probably saved my life.'

'Mr Fitzgerald, I can vouch for that, as a doctor. A matter of seconds and you could have choked to death.'

'All the more reason to be grateful. By the way how did you know my name? And if I may be so bold, may I know yours?'

'I know your name because my friend here is a curate at Pontywen and apparently you are a diocesan official. My name is Eleanor

Davies and I work with Dr Hughes in Pontywen.'

'Mr Secombe, I don't think we have met.' I stood up and he shook my hand. 'What a fortunate young man you are to have such a charming and resourceful young lady as your friend. May I thank you once more, Dr Davies, for being an angel of mercy?'

As he went back to his table, I said to Eleanor, 'It's not everybody who is called an angel twice in the same day.'

'It's not everybody who has an escort who works for the same firm as the angels.'

'Speaking of that firm and of the low wage it pays its workers, how on earth am I going to keep you in the style to which you are accustomed?'

'My dear Fred, marriage is a union of two equal partners. I am not a shrinking violet to be fed and watered by her lord and master. I have no intention of giving up my profession when I marry you. What I earn will go into the common purse.'

'In that case I must stay with Father Whittaker for three or four years at least. By then I should be in line for a living somewhere not too far from Pontywen if you want to stay with Dr Hughes.'

She took my hand and squeezed it. 'If we are going to get married next year it means we shall have to begin to think of where we are going to live. You know what the housing shortage is like.'

With the men returning from the forces and with no house building during the war years, accommodation was in extremely short supply.

Mr Fitzgerald rose from his table at that moment and waved a goodbye to us before he left.

'There you are,' said Eleanor. 'You called him a pompous individual but he may be the means of you becoming a vicar earlier than you think. Cast your bread upon the water. You never know what a kindness may bring in.'

'I never thought you were so calculating.'

'With a husband-to-be like you, my dear, calculating will be a necessity on my part.'

Chapter Six

It was obvious that the first parochial church council meeting under the chairmanship of the new vicar was going to be a stormy one.

Seated at the table, apparently examining the minutes book with great interest, was the vicar, clad in his cassock and cape. Roving round the various members of the council was Ezekiel Evans indulging in conspiratorial whispers. Since the arrival of Father Whittaker the lay reader was virtually unemployed, apart from reading a lesson occasionally. His heart was bitter within him. Nothing would give him greater pleasure than to see the new incumbent in deep trouble at this meeting.

In the corner of the hall by the door Bertie Owen was in loud and earnest conversation with three members of St Padarn's. One sentence, which reached the ears of Charles and myself at our seats in the front, was ominous. 'I'm not standing for any changes.'

A few minutes later the vicar rapped on the table. 'Will you all take your seats, please?' Bertie and the others who were standing made their way, grim-faced, to the vacant chairs.

The secretary of the council, Sam Thomas, a clerk in the colliery office, joined the vicar who asked everybody to stand for prayers.

In due course Father Whittaker began his address to the meeting. 'Now then, shall we get down to business? We have completed the parish survey and the results show that forty-four-point-seven per cent of the population are Anglican, forty-two-point-five-six are Nonconformist, eight-point-seven per cent are Roman Catholic and the other three-point-seven-four per cent are agnostic.'

'Mr Chairman,' Bertie rose to his feet. 'I don't know what all this has got to do with us. It seems to me you've been wasting your time. Most of us have been born and bred in Pontywen and we know who's who, without having to go round asking.'

'Hear, hear!' chorused a number of voices.

'We have not been wasting our time, Mr Owen. Did you know that at least seventy-five per cent of those who claimed to be Anglican don't come to church?

'I could have told you that without going round with paper and pencil. So what are you going to do about it?'

'That, Mr Owen, is the whole point of this meeting. So would you mind listening to what I have to say?'

Bertie's brain could stand the strain of competition with that of the vicar no longer. He subsided into his chair.

'First of all, baptisms. We will visit all those houses where there are unbaptised children. We hope to arrange a big service when all or most of these infants will be baptised.

'Secondly, I propose to have a series of social gatherings, with a cup of tea and a biscuit, to which we shall invite all the families in a set number of streets who claim to be Anglican but never come.'

491

The vicar leaned back in his chair, looking pleased. There was a pregnant silence in which a batch of objections struggled for birth.

Inevitably it was Bertie's which saw the light of day first. 'Mr Chairman, I think you're in for a big surprise with these baptisms. If they haven't had them done by now, what makes you think they'll bring the kids along simply because you've arranged a service?'

'That's right,' said Jim Evans, a past churchwarden. 'You can take an 'orse to the water but you can't make 'im drink.'

'The same h'applies to your bunfight, Mr Chairman.' Ezekiel joined in the disapproval with relish. 'H'if you think a cup of tea and a biscuit will bring them to the church 'all, h'I'm afraid you're going to 'ave an h'unpleasant surprise.'

Father Whittaker looked a beaten man and as yet he had not broached the subject of vestments.

'I can see that you feel that these two suggestions I have made are doomed to failure. However, we can but try and I hope that you will give us your cooperation despite your misgivings. Now then, I'd like to move on to the next item on the agenda. A person who wishes to be anonymous has given me a generous donation to buy something in memory of the late Canon Llewellyn. With it I have bought a set of vestments for the parish church and for St Padarn's.'

I nudged Charles, as we waited for the reaction. This time it was immediate. A number of members rose to their feet.

'One at a time, please. Mr Vaughan-Jenkins, you were the first to stand.' The vicar's face was ashen.

'Two things, Mr Chairman. The least you could have done was to let us know that you had been given a donation to buy something in memory of the late vicar. That's the first thing. The second is that as Canon Llewellyn never wore vestments, I don't think he would have wanted money wasted on them anyway.'

'I'm next, Mr Chairman.' Bertie was not waiting to be called. 'We don't want this dressing-up in St Padarn's. We've never had it before and I don't see why we should start now. The next thing is we'll be like Our Lady of Lourdes down the road.'

Ezekiel Evans added his contribution. 'Mr Chairman, h'inasmuch h'as I 'ave been lay reader in Pontywen for the past twelve years h'I think h'I know the feeling of the people towards such a big h'alteration in the worship. You'll 'ave an h'empty church.'

The onslaught continued. In the face of this total opposition, the vicar was forced to capitulate. 'I have no wish to foist anything on an unwilling congregation,' he said wearily. 'For the time being the

492

vestments will remain in mothballs. Perhaps attitudes will change. Will you all stand and we shall finish the meeting with the blessing.'

The council members trooped out in jubilant mood with Bertie Owen swelling with pride, almost expecting to be carried shoulder-high like a Welsh captain after a victory at Cardiff Arms Park.

As the last man left, the vicar rose from the table and came across to us. 'I had set my heart on coming to Pontywen,' he said, 'because it was the one parish in the Valley where I thought I could exercise my priestly ministry to the full. Evidently I made a mistake. But I tell you what, we are going to go ahead with the baptisms and we shall have them on the afternoon of Easter Day.'

NEXT MORNING after our daily service we met in the vicarage. By now the vicar had recovered his equilibrium.

'We have three weeks to prepare for the mass baptisms on Easter Day. I propose we begin at once to visit the homes of the unbaptised children to get some idea of how many will respond to our invitation.'

By the end of the week we had learned the lesson which Jim Evans had forecast. 'You can take an 'orse to the water but you can't make 'im drink.' Of the fifty-seven who were to be brought to the water of baptism only eleven children had been booked for the ceremony.

On Sunday morning after the service at St Padarn's, Bertie Owen was jubilant when I told him that the number of children to be baptised was eleven and not fifty-seven.

'I told him he was wasting his time,' he crowed.

'Bertie,' I said, 'you're a fine Christian! You should be sad that so few people want to bring their children to be christened.'

'I thought you were on our side.'

'If by that you mean that I don't want Pontywen to become an Anglo-Catholic centre in the Valleys, you are right. But I'm all for anything which is going to improve church life in Pontywen.'

'Hear, hear!' said Idris from inside the surplice he was taking off. On reappearing, he launched into an attack on Bertie. 'We've had enough warfare to keep us going for donkey's years without starting another war in Pontywen. Now that you've had your little victory, Bertie, there's no need to rub the vicar's nose in it.'

Any further discussion of the subject was cut short by the sudden appearance in the vestry of Eleanor, her face flushed with excitement. 'Do you mind if I kidnap your curate?' she said to Bertie and Idris.

'I'm sure they wouldn't,' I replied, speaking on their behalf and only too pleased to see an end to Bertie's discomfiture.

In no time at all we were in her car.

'Now before you drive off, perhaps you would explain your invasion of my vestry,' I demanded in mock indignation.

'Well, it's like this, your worship.' She touched her imaginary forelock. 'How would you like to marry me within the next six months?'

I stared at her, my mouth agape.

'I know it's not a leap year,' she went on, 'but something has turned up that I don't think we should turn down.'

'Are you being serious?' I managed to say.

'Of course I'm being serious. I've come from the hospital where a Miss Bradshaw has just passed away. Now it so happens that her landlord is a friend of my father's. I'm sure he would let the house to us.'

'Miss Bradshaw's house!' I exploded. 'It's a slum.'

Miss Bradshaw was an eccentric who had lived in a house full of old newspapers and cats.

'Look, my dear. You know what the housing situation is like. If we wait to find somewhere to live we may have to wait for years. There is nothing wrong with the house. When it has been cleaned and redecorated it will be ideal as a first home for us.'

'But it's not just getting a house. It must have furniture. I only have a few pounds in my post-office savings account—'

'Fred!' Her tone was sharp. 'Do you love me?'

'Of course, you know that but—'

'No more buts! At the moment I am in a position to help furnish the house. One day we shall be in a vicarage and your stipend will be much bigger than it is now. Then you can take over. So, please, please, let me do my share while I can.'

By now there were a few interested spectators from the choir standing outside the church gate, pretending to talk to each other.

'I think we had better move,' I suggested.

She turned the ignition key and put her foot down on the accelerator as if a chequered flag had been raised.

'Have you told your parents?' I asked as we headed off.

'That's a pleasant surprise they've got coming to them this afternoon. It wouldn't be a bad idea if you wrote and told your parents as well.'

'And I thought this was going to be just another Sunday,' I said.

ELEANOR'S INVASION of the vestry on Passion Sunday was a watershed in my life in Pontywen. After that morning, events seemed to rush by me as if in a speeded-up film. Both sets of parents

494

acknowledged that in six months or so their children would be wed. Both mothers were concerned that so much had to happen in so short a time. Both fathers were content to let both mothers do the worrying. Meanwhile Easter came and went. The grand baptismal event fizzled out into a ceremony involving nine children. At the Easter vestry meeting Bertie Owen was re-elected once again as people's warden of St Padarn's despite the fervent prayers of the vicar. And the *The Pirates of Penzance* loomed ever closer.

'A fortnight to go, and this production is a shambles,' I moaned to Eleanor. 'Some of the principals still don't know their lines, while the pirates are more like mice than men.'

We were seated in her car after the Thursday night rehearsal at Pontywen Grammar School.

'Nonsense!' said Eleanor. 'You have a delightful chorus of girls. Admittedly the pirates are anaemic, but the police are developing into a force to rival the Keystone Cops.'

'That's the chorus, but what about Trevor Willis? He comes to us recommended by Idris as a seasoned performer. If his voice stays as croaky as it is, he is going to be an inaudible major general. Then there's Islwyn Jenkins who is as nervous as a kitten.'

'Well, my love, once he's got his first performance over, he'll be an excellent pirate king, believe me. Then there's Myfanwy Howells who makes a very good Ruth, Idris a very funny sergeant of police and, of course, the two leads who are absolutely brilliant.'

'Self-praise is no recommendation but I must admit you are right.'

'I thought you would, you bighead. So cheer up, Frederick, and let's go and see if they've started work on our little grey home in the west.'

'It's almost dark. We haven't a key. So how are we going to know if anything is happening there?'

'My dear love, you are about as romantic as a wet lettuce. We'll be able to see something, even if it's nothing. Pardon the paradox, the most ingenious paradox.'

'Excuse me, Mabel,' I said, 'but that's one of my lines, not yours.'

She replied by putting her foot on the accelerator and shooting off down the road. When we arrived outside our future home it was dark but a streetlight opposite illuminated part of the front room.

'The furniture has gone. That's a start.' She squeezed my hand and planted a kiss on my cheek. 'So let's fix a date for our nuptials.'

'First things first, when shall we announce the engagement?'

'Once you have bought me a ring.'

495

'Then I think we should be able to break the news to the breathless public at the same time that we put on *Pirates*.'

'What a good idea. The last-night party can be our engagement party. Frederick gets Mabel in the end.'

THE FOLLOWING SATURDAY Eleanor and I went to Cardiff and returned with a pretty little diamond ring.

'You can save your coppers for the wedding ring till nearer the day,' she said when we arrived back at my digs.

I formally placed the ring on her finger and we went into the middle room to show it to Mrs Richards.

'I think it's a lovely ring. It suits you, dear, nice and not too ostenacious. I hope you'll both be very happy.'

The old lady gave Eleanor a hug and a kiss. Then she turned to me. 'You're a very lucky man to have a fiancée like this and so is she to have you as her future husband. You go together like a horse in a carriage.' And she caught hold of me and planted a kiss on my cheek.

'Mrs Richards, this is so sudden,' I said.

The old lady blushed and then covered her embarrassment with an invitation to drink to our future happiness with the remainder of a bottle of brandy bequeathed her by her late husband.

ON THE MORNING OF THE DRESS REHEARSAL I went down to Cardiff to buy make-up, crepe hair, spirit gum, tins of cream and powder. Eleanor and I had arranged to do the make-up between us, along with Trevor Willis and Iorwerth Ellis, who had claimed to be a master of the art.

Mrs Collier had volunteered to be wardrobe mistress. When I returned from Cardiff she was waiting for me at my digs.

'The costumes haven't come, Mr Secombe. I've phoned the costume people and they said that they had put them on the train first thing this morning. Mr Wilkinson phoned around and discovered that they went to Cardiff General Station by mistake. They say it won't be possible to get the costumes here until tomorrow morning.'

'There's only one thing for it, we'll have to go to Cardiff this afternoon and pick them up.'

'How do you propose doing that, Mr Secombe? You can't go down on the bus and pick them up, that's positive.'

As Mrs Collier and I were leaving my digs we met Mr Matthews the undertaker. 'Busy?' I asked him.

'Very quiet at the moment.'

I offered up what is known as an arrow prayer, and said, 'In that case could you do us a great favour? There are two skips of costumes stranded at Cardiff Station and we must have them for our dress rehearsal tonight. Would it be possible for you to take the hearse and pick them up? I would come with you and pay the petrol.'

'A hearse is not licensed to carry goods, Mr Secombe.'

'I thought you could pull down the blinds and then nobody could see inside. Mr Matthews, this is an emergency.'

The old man looked long at me. 'Be at my house in a quarter of an hour and not a word to anybody.'

Twenty minutes later a cleric and an undertaker were in the front of a hearse with drawn blinds speeding with unseemly haste to Cardiff Station, where two surprised porters found they were loading the skips into a very unlikely vehicle. By the time the cast were arriving at the grammar school the costumes had been unpacked and hung on coat hangers. Mrs Collier was a most systematic wardrobe mistress.

It was a typical dress rehearsal. Lines were fluffed. The orchestra, coming together for the first time, occasionally sounded as if they had never been introduced to each other. The major general's voice was still of the croaking variety but his stage presence was excellent. Islwyn Jenkins's pirate king sang with an uncertain note and his stage presence was nonexistent, but all the other principals were creditable.

After the rehearsal was over, Aneurin, the MD, kept the orchestra back to iron out some of the difficulties encountered during the evening and then pronounced that he was 'reasonably satisfied'. Eleanor's verdict was equally favourable. 'For a company most of whom have never done anything before, they were very good.' Then she added, 'Tomorrow will prove that.'

Tomorrow came. The vicar surprised Charles and myself at Matins by praying for God's blessing on the Pontywen Church Gilbert and Sullivan Society. After the service he told us that he was looking forward to the performance in the evening.

So, too, was Mrs Richards. 'I think it's wonderful what you have done with the Gilbert. It's brought a bit of life to Pontywen. You've been a real shot in the heart for us.'

Gwen, Idris the Milk's wife, was in charge of tickets and had managed to get an almost complete sellout.

At seven o'clock there was only one fly in the ointment and it was a big one. Islwyn Jenkins, our pirate king, had not turned up. Ten past seven came and he was still an absentee. I was about to get somebody to phone his home when he arrived with his wife Rhiannon.

I was amazed to find him smiling and in an expansive mood.

'Hello, everybody,' he announced and quoted a tagline from a radio programme, 'I've arrived and to prove it I'm here.'

'Get dressed,' I ordered him, 'and Trevor will make you up.'

Rhiannon took me aside outside the dressing room.

'I'm sorry, Mr Secombe, but I'm afraid he's had too much to drink. He's been worried stiff about this part for weeks now. When I realised he was tight I got him into the kitchen and gave him a big cup of black coffee. All I hope is that he will sober up before he goes on.'

'Thank you, Rhiannon.' I put my arm round her shoulders. 'Don't worry, I'll get another cup of coffee to him straight away. You go out in the hall and enjoy it.'

'You're being funny, Mr Secombe. The one thing I'll enjoy is the final curtain and to know he's still standing on his feet.'

With that she disappeared and I made my way to the kitchen and got Islwyn another cup of black coffee. Back in the dressing room he was being helped into his costume by a number of volunteers who could tell by the reek of whisky that Islwyn needed assistance.

'Thanks, boys!' he was booming out when I came in with the cup of black coffee. 'I'm going to slay 'em tonight.'

'Coffee for you, Islwyn. Drink this, it will lubricate your throat.' I put the cup in his hand. 'Nothing is better than coffee for your voice.'

'Is that right? Cheers, everybody.' He raised the cup to his lips and downed the liquid as if he were parched with thirst.

There was a silent prayer from all in the dressing room. We sat him in a chair and Trevor Willis worked on his face.

'I feel fine, Mr Secombe, marvellous,' boasted Islwyn.

'Keep quiet. Or I'll shove this stick of greasepaint down your throat,' Trevor threatened. It was effective. For five minutes, there was nothing to be heard from the pirate king.

Aneurin Williams, the MD, entered the dressing room to see if everything was ready for the overture. I took him outside and passed on the information about Islwyn. 'I'm afraid we might be in for some trouble. Islwyn is tight.'

'My God. What are we going to do?'

'He has had two cups of black coffee, and all we can do is to hope that he will sober up, but be prepared.'

'They're not all in their seats yet. So I'll hold fire for another five minutes or so.'

I went back into the dressing room. Trevor was powdering Islwyn's face. 'Would you like one more quick cup of coffee?' I asked.

'Yes, if it's good for the voice.'

I disappeared into the kitchen and came back with the coffee to hear a very loud rendition of 'I Am the Pirate King' coming from the other side of the closed door of the dressing room.

'One more cup and your voice will be in excellent form,' I assured him. The coffee went down in one gulp.

'Ready for anything now,' he informed me.

There was a knock on the door.

I went out to find Aneurin looking apprehensive. 'Is he OK?'

'Well, he's on his feet so I assume he's ready for action.'

He shook my hand. 'Good luck, then.'

'The same to you, Aneurin, or better still. Shall we say it's in the Lord's hands.'

'Very much so,' he said and went out into the hall.

'Every pirate on stage,' I shouted and caught hold of Islwyn's arm. 'What's your first line?' I asked.

' "Yes, Frederick, from today you rank as a full-blown member of our band." '

'Well done,' I said and shook his hand.

'Not only that,' he went on, 'I'll act it as well.'

He did. His first words were accompanied with a heavy slap on my back which sent me reeling.

'Hurrah!' shouted the pirates.

When eventually he reached his set-piece solo, he was the embodiment of the pirate king and his rendition was greeted with rapturous applause. Islwyn Jenkins had arrived.

During the interval, the vicar appeared in the dressing room to say how much he was enjoying the performance. It was amazingly satisfying.

In the second act, the love duet brought the place down, especially since Eleanor and I had to declare our love for each other 'til we are wed and ever after'.

As we sang the Welsh national anthem at the end of the performance, Eleanor and I stood side by side holding hands. When the curtain came down, we kissed each other.

'Now for stage two,' I whispered to her.

'Here endeth the first lesson, you mean,' she said. 'You've learned an awful lot in your first year in Pontywen. You're certainly not as green as you were.'

'More like a man for all seasons.'

'More like a curate for all seasons, with a lot more to be learned.'

Chapter Seven

Eleanor surveyed the newly papered and painted front room of 11 Bevan's Row. 'Now all we need is some furniture, but it's pointless going to the furniture stores, all they have to offer is nineteen forty-six utility rubbish. Auction rooms, here we come!'

'Whatever you say, love. I'm an innocent abroad in these matters.'

'That is an understatement, Frederick. I'm sure you think a Welsh dresser is someone who prepares salads in Aberystwyth. What about a visit to Cardiff tomorrow? There's only six weeks till the big day.'

'If the vicar will let me switch my day off, that will be fine.'

'I'm sure he will when you tell him the reason.'

As Eleanor forecast, the vicar was quite amenable to the change in my day off. 'Certainly, Fred. Have tomorrow off by all means. You can't live in an empty house. It gets most uncomfortable sitting on the floor all the time.' It was one of his rare attempts at humour.

When I arrived back at my lodgings, Mrs Richards greeted me with the news that the Vicar of Abergwynlais was waiting for me.

The Reverend Arthur Bowen was in his early seventies, tall and thin. When I entered my room, he advanced on me with his arm outstretched. 'How are you, Mr Secombe?' he squeaked. 'I hear from John Whittaker that you are getting married.'

'I am indeed, Vicar, in six weeks' time.'

'Well, that's why I'm here. I am retiring in a few months' time. I have laboured long enough in the Lord's vineyard.' He went on to explain that he had some furniture I might like to buy. Moving to a smaller house necessitated a big reduction in his goods and chattels. 'Perhaps you and your young lady would care to come and see.'

'It's very kind of you, Vicar. Would it be convenient if we came to see you tomorrow? We are thinking of going to the auction rooms in Cardiff but it would be a good idea to come to you first.'

'By all means, young man. When would you be arriving?'

'Shall we say about ten thirty?'

As soon as he had left, I went into Mrs Richards's kitchen where she was about to cook our meat ration: a few slices of liver, one rasher of bacon each, with onions, unrationed. A pan of potatoes was boiling away on the gas stove.

'Do you mind if I dash out and phone Eleanor? I won't be long. I'll tell you why when I come back.'

The old lady pushed aside a straggly white hair which had invaded her forehead. 'Don't be too long, Mr Secombe. As you can see, I'm ready for the off.'

Eleanor was most enthusiastic. 'If he has plenty to offer there may be no need to go down to Cardiff,' she said.

WE ARRIVED AT ABERGWYNLAIS VICARAGE prompt at ten thirty.

An aged black and white spaniel ambled towards us from the side of the house and indulged in a couple of wheezy barks. It was just as well that he did so because the doorbell was not working.

As I was about to press the button for the third time, the Reverend Arthur Bowen opened the door.

'I thought I heard the dog bark. Good house dog. Is this the young lady? Pleased to meet you, my dear. Come on in.'

We were ushered into the sitting room where the windows overlooked a lawn of tall waving grass.

'Sit down and make yourselves comfortable. I'll bring my wife to meet you. She's making tea for us in the kitchen.'

As soon as he had gone, I said, 'I think we are wasting our time here. Sorry about that, love.'

'Nothing of the sort,' retorted Eleanor. 'The furniture in this room is good stuff. It's leather. None of your Rexine. This settee is well sprung. So are the armchairs.'

Our conversation was cut short by the entry of the lady of the house bearing a tray full of the best china. Mrs Bowen was short and plump, rosy-cheeked and grey-haired.

By the time we left the house, we had bought bedroom furniture, a dining-room table and chairs and a couple of leather armchairs from the study. During the afternoon in Cardiff, we bought carpets and a leather settee to match the armchairs.

There might still be a thousand and one things to organise before our wedding day, but at least we knew now that we had a bright, clean home and some good, if rather ancient, furniture to put in it.

ON THE MORNING OF THE WEDDING I awoke to find the sun streaming into the bedroom through a gap in the curtains. I looked at the alarm clock. It was seven o'clock. In five hours' time I would be standing by my bride ready to share a new life. I jumped out of bed and opened wide the curtains. The sky was cloudless and the sun was brilliant. This was going to be the happiest day of my life.

My brand-new suit, by courtesy of Montague Burton plus clothing coupons, was suspended on a hanger attached to the door of the wardrobe. On the floor, underneath it, was my suitcase, packed with motherly care by Mrs Richards. 'One of the last things I can do for you,' she had said.

It was a big breakfast of bacon, egg and fried bread which faced me when I had finished my ablutions.

'This looks delicious, Mrs Richards,' I said.

'Well, it is the last meal I'll be cooking for you. Anyway you must have plenty in your stomach for the big day. It will be a long time till you sit down for your wedding festival in the hotel.'

She was forcing herself to look cheerful but it was a hard battle. I felt that at any minute she would burst into tears. The old lady had bought herself a lilac-coloured dress with hat to match—a great change from the black of her widow's weeds. She was doing her very best to be in tune with the occasion.

At eleven o'clock my parents arrived in a car hired by Eleanor's parents to bring them and my sister, Carol, from Cardiff General Station. The driver had taken them first to my fiancée's house where they had had a brief meeting with my future in-laws. Then the car brought them round to Mount Pleasant View. It was the first time that Mrs Richards had met my mother and father. The two women embraced warmly. My mother was more than grateful for the homely atmosphere I had found in 13 Mount Pleasant View.

'Thank you for looking after my boy,' she said.

'I've never had a child,' replied my landlady. 'So I've been very happy to be your subordinate for a year. I must say that he's been the pick in the bunch of all the curates I've had here.'

While my parents were enjoying a cup of tea, Charles came in, looking unusually spruce. I had asked him to be my best man, a decision I might still live to regret.

'I think I've got everything in order,' he said nervously. 'Dr Davies is going to propose the toast to you and Eleanor. Then you reply and propose the toast to the bridesmaids. I reply to that on your behalf. No other speeches, except the one from the vicar.'

'Well done, Charles. You must keep it to that.'

'What about the ring, Fred? I'd better have it now. I'll keep it in the box so that I can't lose it.'

I went upstairs to get it from my bedroom and gave it to my best man for safekeeping.

Charles and I decided to walk to the church. We felt a walk in the sunshine would be good for our morale. The car was due to come at twenty to twelve to pick up the other three.

At St Mary's there were some early arrivals, mainly guests from Eleanor's family connections and friends. Bertie Owen, Idris the Milk, Charlie Hughes and Moelwyn Howells had volunteered to act as ushers. In their best suits with carnation buttonholes provided by Moelwyn, they were a reassuring sight.

'All under control,' said Bertie.

'Famous last words,' added Idris with a wide grin.

Already there were a number of well-wishers occupying some of the rear pews. So far the Swansea contingent of my uncles, aunts and cousins had not arrived. They were coming to Pontywen in a small bus hired for the occasion.

Inside the vestry, the vicar was sitting at his desk filling in the marriage register. He left his seat to greet me as I came through the door. 'What a lovely day you have for your big occasion!' he said as he shook my hand. 'Well, are you nervous?'

'I am petrified. It is one thing to take a wedding. It is another thing to be at the receiving end.'

'That's something which has not happened to me as yet, so I have no idea of how it feels.'

Charles was standing in a corner, looking even more nervous than I felt. Every so often his hand would stray to his inside pocket to check that the box containing the ring was still there.

Suddenly there was a blast from the organ as Mr Greenfield, St Mary's church organist, launched into a murder of Clarke's 'Trumpet Voluntary'. 'Perhaps you had better go out now and sit in the front pew,' said Father Whittaker.

When I opened the door of the vestry, a buzz of conversation met us. Facing me, as I moved with Charles to the front pew, were my mother and father, together with Mrs Richards in her lilac rig-out, and behind them my Swansea relations. We sat down and faced the altar. Charles was so nervous I could feel his body shaking alongside me. It took some of the tension from me as I tried to calm him.

'For heaven's sake,' I whispered to him, 'try to get a grip on yourself. You are worse than I am.'

Before he could reply, Mr Greenfield pulled out all the stops and crashed out Wagner's 'Wedding March'.

We moved quickly from the pew and stood at the chancel steps. Eleanor had given me strict instructions not to turn round to watch her come down the aisle. I stared steadfastly ahead of me until she reached my side.

It seemed an age until the vicar, who had been leading the bride, walked past me to take up his stand at the top of the chancel steps.

A faint breath of fragrance anointed my nostrils. Then the gentle rustle of a bridal gown announced her arrival at my side. I turned to look at the woman who was to be my partner. It was a moment worth waiting for. She was such a beautiful bride that the sight turned my legs to water. A brunette with big expressive brown eyes, set in an oval face, she wore a floor-length bridal gown. It is a picture enshrined in my memory.

'Do I come up to expectations?' she whispered in my ear.

'Five gold stars,' I replied.

The first part of the service passed over my head until I was aware that I was being addressed by the officiant.

'Frederick Thomas, wilt thou have this woman to thy wedded wife?'

'I will.' My voice sounded as if it had come from somewhere else.

'Eleanor Mary?'

'I will.' Her answer was warm and firm.

'Who giveth this woman to this man?'

Eleanor's father stepped forward proudly, took her hand gently and gave it to me. I held it so tightly it must have been painful for her. She showed no sign that it was so but looked at me in such a loving way that my grip slackened as I repeated the marriage vow.

Then it was her turn. She held my hand and squeezed it as she said 'to love and to cherish'.

When she had finished her contribution, the vicar looked at Charles who plunged his hand into his pocket and produced the box. His hands were shaking so badly that when he opened the box the ring dropped out on the floor and rolled towards the heating grating behind me. I made a dive worthy of a Welsh wing scoring a try and caught it before it disappeared into the depths.

'Five gold stars,' whispered Eleanor as I placed the ring on her finger.

The rest of the service seemed to fly past. Soon we were in the vestry shaking hands with the vicar. I sat at the desk and signed the register, as both sets of parents followed the bridesmaids and Charles into the inner sanctum. When I rose from the chair, my father and Eleanor's father were in deep conversation. Both working-class lads in origin, they spoke a common language. Eleanor's mother was adjusting the bridal veil to the obvious annoyance of the bride and my mother was chatting to my sister and Heather, Eleanor's friend, who looked stunning in their rose-pink bridesmaids' outfits.

The vicar called the bride to the desk. My mother embraced me and whispered in my ear that she was proud of me. Then I turned to my mother-in-law who was standing in splendid isolation. I decided that I had better bestow a chaste salute upon her cheeks. There would have been a warmer response from an iceberg. 'Congratulations,' she managed to say, before walking away to talk to Eleanor's friend.

My mother came to my side. 'You are not marrying the mother, love. You are marrying the daughter, thank God,' she said quietly.

Eleanor finished her signing of the register and came straight to my mother. She gave her a hug. 'Hello, Mam,' she proclaimed. 'And what do you think of your new daughter?' They had hit it off from the first time they'd met.

'I don't think my son could have chosen a better partner. You look lovely, my dear, and I'm proud of you both.'

'Now then, let's get everybody in order for the procession out of the vestry.' The vicar had suddenly become parsonical after addressing everybody in conversational tones for the past ten minutes.

Father Whittaker pressed the button which alerted the organist to begin Mendelssohn's 'Wedding March' and we moved out of the vestry to face the world as the Secombes incorporated.

It seemed that half of the town had gathered outside to witness the photography, much to the annoyance of the photographer who had to shout to make himself heard over the hubbub.

Eventually, after several permutations of the happy couple, 'immediate family', vicar, best man, bridesmaids, relatives and friends, the session came to a merciful end.

'It's nice to sit down for five minutes,' I said, as we were driven off to the hotel for the reception.

'As the first words to your bride now that we are alone, I don't think they will rank among romantic gems,' replied Eleanor.

'Actions speak louder than words,' I proclaimed and took her in my arms.

'I hope the driver has his eyes on the road. Otherwise he will have the wrong idea about parsons,' she murmured.

The Tudor Arms was a mock-Tudor hostelry built in the late thirties to cater for the more discriminating clientele of the Valleys. Mrs Davies had booked the Regency Room for the occasion.

As we drew into the car park, the cars bringing Charles, the bridesmaids and the parents pulled in alongside us. Mrs Davies was out of her car and into the reception area before any of us had alighted from our vehicles. Eleanor took my arm and we walked leisurely into the hotel, determined to enjoy the reception.

IT WASN'T UNTIL ELEANOR had gone back to her parents' house to change into her 'going away' outfit that I had an opportunity to have a last word with Mrs Richards who was sitting on a chair looking forlorn. 'Have you enjoyed the reception?' I asked her.

'Oh yes, it was a lovely meal. I thought Eleanor looked very beauteous.' She caught hold of my hands. 'Don't forget to come and see me when you come back. I know you're going to be very industrial doing your parish work and looking after your new wife. If it's only for a few minutes, that's all, but just to know you're all right.' She turned away her head to hide the tears.

I went over to my mother and asked her if she would mind taking Mrs Richards under her wing for the next hour or so. She drew up a chair by my former landlady's side and soon the two were engrossed in conversation.

When Eleanor returned in a lavender-blue twin-set with a toque to match, I felt the same reaction as when she had appeared at my side in her bridal gown. We said our goodbyes in a deluge of confetti and drove off, with the inevitable old shoe tied to the back bumper.

Chapter Eight

'I suppose all good things must come to an end,' sighed a bronzed Eleanor as she packed our suitcases on the last day of our honeymoon in Newquay.

'It's just the beginning, not the end. Ahead of us stretches a lifetime of happiness.' I put my arms round her and drew her to me.

She raised her eyes and fixed a firm gaze into mine.

'What I mean, my dear, is that when we get back there awaits me an inflated list of patients and a tired old partner who can't cope with the demands of the new health service. Add to that the responsibility of being a housewife and these past twelve days of glorious idleness become just a one-off luxury to savour as a memory. I have no doubt that we shall be happy but make no mistake, there will be hiccups in the happiness.'

'All I can say is that I shall do all I can to help in the house, even to the extent of learning to do some cooking.'

'You won't, you know. I like my food. You can lay the table, wash and dry the dishes, make the bed, and perhaps even do a bit of dusting, but I think that you had better leave the cooking to me.'

We set out early on the Saturday morning, and arrived at 11

Bevan's Row at four o'clock. I unloaded the cases as Eleanor advanced on the door, key in hand. She opened up and then stood looking at me. 'Come on, Romeo,' she said. 'You are supposed to carry me over the threshold.'

'With all the food you have consumed on holiday, it's going to be difficult,' I replied.

'You cheeky husband, get on with the gallantry.'

I picked her up. She was as light as a feather. She put her arms round my neck and kissed me. As I advanced down the passage and pushed the half-open door into the middle room with my foot there was a tap on the front door. Standing on the doorstep and grinning like a Cheshire cat at our romantic exercise was Bertie Owen, who had a bottle of milk in one hand and a loaf of bread in the other.

'Welcome home. I thought perhaps you might have forgotten the staff of life, as it were.'

'That's very kind, Bertie. It will save us going to the shops,' I said.

'Well, I won't stop.' He handed me the bread and milk. 'You've got plenty to do, I'm sure. Oh, by the way, Mrs Richards is very ill. She's up in the hospital. I thought you'd better know.'

'When did this happen, Bertie?'

'Not long after you went away. She collapsed in Protheroe the butcher's. Heart, I think.'

'That's a fine welcome home,' I said to Eleanor after he had gone. 'Typical of Bertie. He had to be first with the news, good or bad.'

'It is just as well, love, that he has let you know. I'll run you up to the hospital once we have unpacked. I suggest you ring the vicar and find out exactly what is wrong with Mrs Richards.'

I went into the front room where the brand-new telephone receiver adorned the side table in the far corner. It was the first time that I had used the instrument. As I stood and waited for the vicar to answer, I surveyed our parlour. This was my home. I wallowed in my domestic euphoria until the voice at the other end of the telephone ended the wallow. 'Pontywen Vicarage,' it announced.

'Hello, Vicar, I thought I'd let you know that we are back safely.'

'Good to hear you, Fred. Thank you for your card of Truro Cathedral. I'm afraid I have some bad news for you.'

'If it is about Mrs Richards, Bertie Owen has just been here and told me. How serious is the illness, Vicar?'

'From what I can gather, it's very serious. Her heart is in a bad condition. They hold out little hope for her. It could be a matter of weeks or perhaps even days. She has been asking for you.'

'Eleanor and I will be at the hospital as soon as we can. See you Monday, Vicar.'

An hour later we drove to the hospital where we were greeted by the sister of the Princess Royal Ward.

'Good evening, Dr Secombe, Reverend Secombe. I suppose you have come to see Mrs Richards. She will be very pleased to see you. I'm afraid she's very ill.'

She escorted us down the ward to a bed which was screened off.

'You go in first,' whispered Eleanor. 'I'll have a word with the sister while you speak to Mrs Richards.'

When the old lady saw me, her eyes brimmed over with tears and she could not speak. I bent over and kissed her cheek. 'As soon as my back is turned,' I said, 'what happens? You go and get yourself into trouble. I shall have to keep an eye on you from now on.'

'It's lovely to see you,' she murmured, 'and looking so brown. I have missed you. How is Mrs Secombe? I expect you have had a wonderful honeycombe.'

'She's here. She's coming to see you now once she has had a word with Sister to find out how you are getting on.'

'I feel better than when I came in. So I'll be out before long and back in Mount Pleasant View before you can say John Robinson.'

As she said this, Eleanor entered and kissed her. 'Hello, Mrs Richards. What have you been doing? I was relying on you for a cup of tea when we got back.'

'I only wish I could have done that. You wait, it won't be long before I will be up and out. Look after him, my dear. I can't any more, he's your prodigy now.'

'I'll do that, Mrs Richards. I don't think we should tire you out. We'll come and see you tomorrow.'

We said our goodbyes and left her. As we drove away from the hospital Eleanor told me, 'With her heart condition it could be any time now.'

'In that case, love, all we can do is make her end as peaceful and untroubled as possible.'

NEXT MORNING I WAS UP at seven o'clock, lighting the fire under the boiler and making a cup of tea for us both. By the amount of smoke which invaded the scullery it seemed I had used too much of the *News Chronicle* and not enough firewood to ignite the coal. After a second attempt, the coal began to burn and the water to warm.

Once the kettle had boiled, I made the tea and ascended the stairs with a tray bearing two cups.

'Your morning cuppa, madame,' I announced, 'and your bath-water will be ready in about two hours, I hope. In the meanwhile I shall take tea with you before I leave for eight o'clock Communion.'

'Thank you, Jeeves. Sorry you will not be here to wash my back.'

'I'm sorry too, my sweet, but business is business.'

When I returned from church, I found the tin bath full of soapy water and minus its occupant, who suddenly appeared behind me, clad in her dressing gown.

'It took me about ten minutes at least to fill it via the bucket,' she said, 'but with your help it will take us half a minute to empty it down the drain outside.'

Between us we manoeuvred the receptacle outside and tipped the bathwater down the drain. The glamour of the tin bath had already begun to fade. It would not be too long before it vanished altogether and a bathroom would become a *sine qua non* for our future happiness.

Eleanor drove me to St Padarn's for the Family Communion and afterwards to her parents' for Sunday lunch. Our wedding presents had been taken there ready for collection.

After the meal I had to leave to take Sunday School at St Padarn's. Eleanor dropped me at the church and went on to see what paperwork was waiting for her at the surgery.

At Sunday School there were four teachers missing, leaving Bertie Owen and myself to cope with fifty children. So I decided to do something different.

'We are going to do some acting this afternoon,' I said. There was an excited response from the children. 'I am going to tell you the story of the Good Samaritan. Then you have got to act it in your own words. So sit down quietly, everybody, and listen carefully.'

I launched into the parable, embellishing the story with invented dialogue and extra details not to be found in the Authorised Version.

'Now you are going to act what you have heard. So we want the man who got beaten up, the band of robbers who beat him up, the priest, the Levite, the Good Samaritan, the donkey, and the landlord of the pub where he was taken.'

A forest of hands went up from the boys who all wanted to join the band of robbers hiding up in the hills.

'Hold on, you can't all be robbers. Percy, you can be the man who gets beaten up and robbed. It's a difficult part.'

'In that case, sir, I'll do it.' He slumped forward in his seat, rehearsing his role.

'Sir, can I be the leader of the robbers?' Tommy Harris pleaded.

'All right, Tommy. You've got to plan with your robbers when to come out of the caves and attack the poor old traveller. Four of you boys will be enough.'

I continued casting until finally I came to the principal role. 'Now then, we come to the hero in this wonderful story, the Good Samaritan. For this part I am not going to ask for volunteers. Betty Evans, I am sure you will fill the bill nicely.'

Percy Shoemaker sat up, his face alight with pleasure. Betty was the apple of his eye. To be rescued by her was a fate infinitely more desirable than death.

'Right, Mr Secombe.'

'There is one other part—the donkey. Who is going to be the kind animal who carried the wounded man to safety?'

Silence reigned supreme at the thought of somebody making an ass of himself. 'Come on, one of you,' I said.

No offer was forthcoming.

'It looks as if it will have to be me,' said Bertie Owen.

Cheers mingled with laughter erupted from the children as they relished the thought of tall Bertie Owen on all fours.

'Quiet, please!' I shouted. 'It is very good of Mr Owen to volunteer. Let's get ready for action. Boys, I want you to pile up some chairs on that side of the aisle. They will be the hills where the robbers hide.'

There was a rush of activity as the chairs were carried and formed into two pyramids.

'Betty. There's a bottle in the vestry. It's empty, but you will have to pretend it is full of wine to pour on wounds. Here's my handkerchief. That is the bandage. Use a collection bag for a purse.' She disappeared into the vestry.

'Sir, am I supposed to be tired out, walking?' enquired Percy.

'Yes, you have travelled a long way on foot, but don't forget you are used to walking. Now are we all ready? Action!'

Percy started to plod his way down the aisle, singing 'Roll Out the Barrel'. When he was halfway down the aisle, Tommy gave the thumbs-up sign to his robber band and shouted, 'Get 'im!'

The poor victim was hurled to the ground by five enthusiastic actors, giving war whoops like marauding Red Indians. 'Easy, boys,' I shouted. 'Don't overdo it. Take the purse and go off.'

'Tommy Harris, I'll get you for this,' threatened the 'victim'.

Tommy and his fellow marauders went back behind the chairs. They looked inside the collection bag. 'Twenty-five pounds, thirteen and six,' Tommy shouted. 'We'll be able to go to Barry Island fair with this. We'll have a go on everything and have fish and chips after.'

This was greeted with gales of laughter.

'Calm down, please,' I shouted once more. 'This is not a comedy. Let's have the priest on his way down.'

Bronwen Williams entered from the vestry wearing a boy's cassock and carrying a prayer book, which she was studying intently.

When she came alongside Percy's inert body, she stopped and looked at him. Then she went back to her prayer book. 'Now where was I?' she said and walked on to the sanctuary.

Next came Evelyn Thomas, short and plump, as the Levite. When she reached the unconscious victim, she stopped and had a minute

examination of the body. She looked back towards Tommy and his gang. 'I'm not staying here to be beaten up,' she said and disappeared.

Then came the moment the audience had waited for. Bertie Owen was on his hands and knees ready for his grand entrance. At his side stood Betty Evans, with an empty Communion wine bottle in one hand and my handkerchief in the other. 'Off we go,' said Bertie.

There was much stifled merriment as the 'donkey' made his way down the aisle.

'Whoa!' ordered the Good Samaritan. 'Look at this poor man.' She bent over Percy and raised his head. 'That looks very nasty,' she said and pretended to pour wine from the bottle into the wound in his scalp. She put the bottle down and bound the handkerchief round his head. Percy was savouring every second of this attention. She put her arms round him and lifted him up.

'Stand him against the donkey. Now, Percy, get yourself up on the animal's back, sitting sidesaddle. Fine. Come along then, Good Samaritan, take him to the inn.'

Bertie Owen began to show signs of strain. As he attempted to clamber up the chancel steps on all fours, carrying Percy, he was seized with cramp. He let out a cry of agony, raised himself and dumped Percy who fell against Betty, the two of them landing in a heap on the floor. The children collapsed into hysterical laughter.

'What on earth is going on here?' demanded a voice at the back of the church. It was the vicar and standing at his side was the bishop. There was a deathly silence.

While the children put the chairs back in their places, I went down to join the unexpected visitors.

'Good afternoon, my lord, and good afternoon, Vicar. I know this must have looked like a pantomime, when you came in. If you had arrived earlier you would have seen some impressive acting of the parable of the Good Samaritan by the children. Unfortunately the second before you entered, Mr Owen who had volunteered to play the donkey had an attack of cramp which meant that the three main characters ended up in a tangle.'

There was a faint smile on the bishop's face but the scowl remained upon the vicar's countenance. 'I think there are better ways of teaching parables,' he snapped.

'I don't know about that, Father,' said the bishop. 'It was unfortunate about the—er—accident but play-acting the parables does help them to come alive for the children. However I have not come here to discuss the presentation of the New Testament. I just happened to be passing near Pontywen and decided to make a brief call at the vicarage

where the vicar informed me that you were married recently. I have come to offer you and Mrs Secombe my felicitations. I must meet her one day.'

'Thank you very much, my lord,' I replied.

I EXPECTED A SEVERE reprimand from the vicar when Charles and I were closeted in his study for the Monday morning briefing session. To my surprise he appeared to be in a jovial mood. 'How has your first weekend in your new home gone, Fred?' he asked as we sipped Mrs Lilywhite's execrable coffee.

'Apart from the tin bath, quite well indeed, Vicar,' I replied.

'If ever you need a more relaxing bath, you can bring your towels here,' he said.

'That is very kind of you but Eleanor seems determined to make the best of it at number eleven Bevan's Row.'

'So be it,' he replied, making a triangle of his fingers, his favourite exercise. 'In any case my offer would be for a limited period only. When the bishop and I returned to the vicarage after our—er—visit to St Padarn's yesterday afternoon he asked me if I would consider accepting the living of Abergwylfa. As you know, it is a parish in the Anglo-Catholic tradition and more suited to my churchmanship.'

'Congratulations, Vicar,' I said.

'From me too,' echoed Charles who could not believe his good fortune.

'It will be some months before I go. In the meantime I should like to do something to improve the size of our contribution to the missionary cause. It would make a grand swan song if we could double or perhaps treble the amount sent from Pontywen. So I propose we have a garden fête in the vicarage grounds in late August. I suggest we call a meeting of the PCC representatives from the three churches on Thursday week and get the thing off the ground.'

When I told Eleanor over lunch that Father Whittaker would be departing in a few months' time she said, 'Wouldn't it be wonderful if you could become Vicar of Pontywen?'

'You must be joking,' I replied. 'I have not been ordained long enough for that.'

'Stranger things can happen. I never believed that I could become a partner after just twelve months in practice.'

'You must admit that you did have an advantage by being taken on by an elderly gentleman at the end of his tether, who was also a friend of the family.'

'And I always thought it was because of my brilliance. I tell you something, Frederick, I shall have to be brilliant to cope with a panel of more than two thousand registered customers. I'm afraid I have a lot of calls today, so you will have to see Mrs Richards on your own.'

THE OLD LADY was awake and looked much brighter.

'I'm sure I'm turning the corner. Perhaps they'll let me get out of bed tomorrow. Once I get home, I'll come on like a house on fire.'

'When they are ready, Mrs Richards, they will let you get up and about. Until then, you will have to be a good girl.'

'I've always been a good girl, Mr Secombe. There's too much trouble when you're not. How are you and Mrs Secombe settling up in your new home?'

'Very well indeed. There are just two snags. The first is that I miss having a bath in your bathroom. The other snag is that I miss having you to fuss over me when I come in.'

She glowed with pleasure. 'Your mother thanked me for looking after you at the wedding. I told her that I thought of you as my son. You are the only one of the curates the vicar sent who was close to me.'

Her eyes began to fill with tears.

'I've got to go now, Mrs Richards,' I said gently, 'but I tell you what: you are the nearest pin-up to my mother in my life, that is apart from Eleanor, of course.'

'Of course,' she replied, 'she's a lovely lady. She will take care of you. Are you coming in tomorrow for a few minutes?'

'I'll be here, don't worry.' I kissed her cheek and left her. She was waving goodbye when I turned round at the door of the ward.

Soon after I got back home from a meeting of the deanery chapter in Tremadoc the telephone rang. It was Eleanor ringing up from a call box. 'I'm afraid I shall be late getting back. I am up to my eyes in work. I'll bring some fish and chips on my way home. If you will lay the table, it will be a help. I love you. Ta-ta.'

I sat in one of the armchairs in the front room and switched on the new HMV wireless set which had been given to us as a wedding present by the congregation at St Padarn's. Shortly after that the telephone rang.

This time the vicar's voice was at the other end. 'Fred, I have just heard from the hospital that Mrs Richards has passed away—heart failure. I thought I had better let you know straight away since you two were very close. Is there anyone else I should inform?'

I found it difficult to speak. It was only a few hours ago that she had waved me goodbye and talked about getting up, ready to return to 13 Mount Pleasant View.

'The only person I can think of, Vicar, is Miss Jacobs who was her best friend. If you like I will let her know.'

'Very well then, sorry to have to be the bearer of bad news. We shall have to think about the funeral when we meet tomorrow. See you then. Goodbye.'

When I put the phone down, I began to weep. Perhaps if I had not left her to get married she would still be alive. I switched off the radio and made my way to Miss Jacobs's house in Hill Terrace. I knocked on the door.

'How nice to see you, Mr Secombe,' she said as she opened the door. 'Come on in.'

She ushered me into the front room, and offered me a drink.

'I should love a dry sherry, Miss Jacobs.'

She moved quickly into the middle room and returned with a tray containing a bottle and two sherry glasses.

What can I do for you?' she asked as she poured me a sherry.

'I am afraid I have come to bring you some sad news. Mrs Richards passed away suddenly this afternoon.'

She put down the bottle and handed me the glass of sherry. She poured herself a glass and sat down opposite me. 'Poor old May,' she murmured. 'Well, I am not surprised. When I saw her in hospital on Friday, she looked terrible. She was quite a good age, you know. Looking after you kept her going. I think she thought of you as a son. Drink your sherry. I can see that you are upset.'

As I sipped my drink, she looked at me.

'Now I have some news for you, Mr Secombe. I suppose I should not let you know until after the funeral but I am not a solicitor. She has left the house to you.'

I stared back at her, unable to comprehend.

'Don't look so shocked. Her first will left the house to the church. Then a few months ago when I came round to have tea with her she told me she wanted to leave the house to you. She has no relatives and she wanted to show you how happy the past year had been. So we tore up the will and I drafted the new one for her. We got Mr and Mrs Williams from next door to witness it and I am the sole executor.'

My head was spinning. Tears welled up once again when I thought of the deep regard the old lady had for me.

'You can see the will when the funeral is over. She has some money in a post-office savings account. More than enough to pay for her funeral expenses. She will be buried with her husband, of course. I suppose that as executor I must make all the arrangements for the burial and put the announcement in the paper et cetera.'

She talked in such a calm businesslike manner that I couldn't help but think how typical it was of the old lady that she had chosen Miss Jacobs as her executor, knowing that she would be so competent.

I walked slowly back home, still trying to come to terms with what had happened. As I turned the corner of Bevan's Row I could see Eleanor's car parked outside. I hurried to the house and opened the door to find a somewhat irate wife. 'Where have you been? The fish and chips are getting cold.'

'I'm sorry, love, but so much has happened in the last hour that I don't know whether I am on my head or my feet.'

My expression and my tone of voice were sufficient to dispel any annoyance. 'Would you like me to put the fish and chips in the oven while you tell me all about it?' she said.

'I think that would be a very good idea.'

Ten minutes later, when I finished my recital of the past hour's happenings, she said, 'My apologies for being such a nag. All I can say is God bless Mrs Richards for her kindness and for bequeathing you the bath which brought us together.'

'FOR AS MUCH AS IT HATH PLEASED Almighty God of His great mercy to take unto Himself the soul of our dear sister here departed.' The vicar's voice droned on as I stood at the graveside of my late landlady with Eleanor and Miss Jacobs by my side. The sun shone down on us and on the fifty or so members of the congregation who had come to pay their last respects to a stalwart of St Mary's Church.

I had asked Father Whittaker if I might opt out of taking part in the service to act as chief mourner since the old lady had no relatives. He consented readily to my request, knowing how strong had been the bond between Mrs Richards and myself. In accordance with Miss Jacobs's wishes I had not informed him of the contents of the will.

As the service drew to its close I wondered what his reaction would be when the will was read at the post-funeral repast, a lavish buffet, which Miss Jacobs had arranged at her house. When everybody had been fed and watered by Miss Jacobs's generous hand, she entered the front room where the mourners were assembled and called for silence while she read the will. When she had finished, Miss Jacobs placed the document back into the envelope and handed it to me, amid the shell-shocked hush which had descended on the small gathering.

'It just shows, Mr Secombe, what she thought of you,' said the sole executor. 'You were much more than a lodger. You were the son she never had. The only pity is that you came so late into her life. Still, I suppose that was much better than not knowing you at all.'

The immediate effect of this explanatory postscript to the will was an outpouring of congratulations to me on my good fortune.

Father Whittaker came across to me and shook my hand.

'I must say you kept this a secret. When did you know about this?'

'I hadn't the faintest idea until Miss Jacobs told me just after Mrs Richards had died.'

'Well, what are you going to do with the house now?'

'It's too early to say just yet, especially since we have been in Bevan's Row for only a week. One thing is certain, we shall be coming to Mount Pleasant View for a bath.'

After the last of the mourners had left I went into the kitchen to join Eleanor and Miss Jacobs who were doing the washing-up.

'Thank you for your kind words,' I said to our hostess. 'They certainly helped to cushion the shock of the will.'

'Knowing what people are like,' she replied, 'I thought it was necessary to point out how much she thought of you. It's much better that you have the house rather than St Mary's.'

'Miss Jacobs, you are an angel.' So saying, Eleanor kissed her on the cheek—to her great embarrassment.

Chapter Nine

'Fine before seven, rain by eleven,' said my wife as she pulled aside the bedroom curtains. It was the morning of the Pontywen fête. The sunlight streamed through the window.

I sat up in bed. 'You should have been christened Cassandra not Eleanor. I would prefer that other chestnut, "The sun always shines on the righteous."'

'In that case, Frederick, we are due for a heavy downpour.'

She beat a hasty retreat as I chased her to the bedroom door.

So far all had gone well with the preparations for what was planned to be Father Whittaker's missionary swan song. The three churches in the parish had cooperated without a sign of acrimony. As it was the first big church social function since before the war, much effort had gone into obtaining donations and contributions to the fête.

Minty the Coal's lorry had delivered three tents which Charles had managed to borrow from the local group scoutmaster. This morning the lorry was to be decorated to provide a suitable setting for the carnival queen of Pontywen and her attendants.

When Eleanor and I had finished our breakfast, we went first to the church hall where there we unloaded the scales and various health posters for the baby show, which Eleanor had agreed to judge.

As we came through the vicarage, it seemed as if the whole population of Pontywen was involved in preparing for the fête. Half a dozen cars were parked round the vicarage, with the coal lorry at the side of the house swarming with decorators. On the lawn, trestle tables were being set up and scouts were erecting three tents under the direction of a scoutmaster.

There was just enough room for Eleanor's car to squeeze into a corner. 'Any car from now on will have to park outside,' she said.

'The vicar will be pleased,' I replied. 'Here he comes now, looking like grim death.'

Seated in the back of the vicar's car and holding on to a large ticket drum was Charles, wearing one of his injured, innocent looks.

'There's been trouble,' I murmured to my wife.

As the shiny, clean Austin Big Seven pulled up halfway down the drive, the vicar flung open the front door and then the back door.

'Out you get, Wentworth-Baxter,' he commanded.

'I'm afraid you'll have to help me, Vicar.'

Father Whittaker snorted, and helped to manoeuvre the drum out of the car.

'What a start to the day!' he stormed. 'That idiot was supposed to help me reverse the car out of the welfare-hall car park and only succeeded in jamming the back between a boulder and the concrete gatepost.' He pointed to a buckled wing and a badly dented boot.

'Sorry, Vicar,' said my colleague as he emerged from the car.

'So am I,' said his superior. 'I'm very sorry I inherited you from my predecessor but I'm very glad I'm leaving you behind. Go and make yourself useful, if that is possible.'

Charles sloped off to the secondhand bookstall which Idris the Milk was setting up. He picked up a book and began to read it.

'He's there for the day,' I said to Eleanor, 'if he's sensible!'

'I'd better be off to the church hall to organise things there for the baby show,' Eleanor said.

When Bertie Owen had set up the microphone stand and made sure that the apparatus was in working order I walked with him to the bottle stall, which was another of St Padarn's efforts.

'The secret of this stall,' he told me, 'is to have a bottle of whisky as your big attraction, but you don't put its equivalent ticket number into the box until you have raised a fair amount of money.'

'That's immoral, Bertie,' I said. 'People will be spending money on trying to win the whisky when the tickets they are drawing are worthless.'

'It's not immoral, it's for the missionaries,' he replied. 'I've got the big ticket in my pocket and it's going to stay there for quite a while.'

'I hope you don't get lynched if they find out what you have done.'

As we were talking, a battered old Rover came down the drive towing a trailer in which was a fat piglet. 'Bowling for a pig' was to be one of the big money-spinners for the afternoon. The car was driven by Evan Meredith, a rosy-cheeked chirpy sparrow of a man who owned a piggery in Llanhyfryd. In view of the strict meat-rationing, the prize of a pig, however small, was bound to be a main attraction.

The fête was due to be opened at 2.30pm by Sir David Jones-Williams, Bart, squire of the neighbourhood. At 2.25pm his anti-quated Bentley squeezed its way through the vicarage gates causing considerable peril to the populace of Pontywen, who were making their way into the grounds. It pulled up halfway down the drive and stayed there, effectively blocking any further traffic movement. Sir David considered that all roads, lanes and drives in his bailiwick were subject to his priority.

'Sorry my wife can't come,' he said to the vicar, who had hurried to greet him. 'Touch of the sun, after gardening this morning. Now where do I go for this opening?'

'The microphone is just there, Sir David.'

'Oh, one of those blasted things. Can't stand them. Can't I just shout a few words and get the jamboree started?'

'Well, if you like, Sir David, but if you don't mind we shall have to go to the microphone so that I can introduce you. I trust Lady Jones-Williams will soon recover.'

'Probably be as right as rain as soon as I get back. Her own fault. She should have worn a sun bonnet.'

As they reached the focal point, Bertie Owen arrived on the scene and did a final check by tapping on the microphone.

'There you are, Sir David, it's alive and in good shape.'

'So am I and that means I don't need the bloody thing.'

Father Whittaker moved to take possession of the microphone.

'How encouraging to see so many present here on such a beautiful afternoon to support this very worthy cause. And now I call upon Sir David Jones-Williams to open our fête.'

The vicar moved the microphone away from the squire and began to clap. Few of the crowd felt moved to follow his example.

Undaunted, Sir David began to bellow his few words. 'Well, here you are. Do what you can to help these missionaries in their work with the natives. I declare this fête open.'

There were even fewer claps.

Sir David spent five minutes on a quick tour of the lawn, presented the vicar with a cheque for ten pounds and proceeded to reverse his Bentley erratically back up the drive as incomers scattered in panic. After narrowly missing the gatepost, he disappeared in a cloud of exhaust fumes.

My main task was the selling of raffle tickets for the prize draw. When the vicar came to enquire how the tickets were going, I was able to tell him that six books had already been used up.

'Excellent!' he said. 'My one worry at the moment is to avoid those farmers' wives from Llanhyfryd. I am sorry now that I allowed myself to be drawn into "guessing the weight of the vicar". They keep coming up to me prodding and pinching me as if I were an exhibit in a cattle show. Speaking of that, I understand that there are a large number of entries in the baby show.'

'In that case, I expect Eleanor will be doing more than her share of prodding and viewing. I know one thing, she is only too pleased to have Nurse Thomas with her for protection when the results of the judging are announced.'

As I spoke there was a distant clap of thunder. Creeping into the blue sky from the east was a menacing blue-black accumulation of cloud. The afternoon was hot, sticky and airless. 'Let's hope that storm passes us by,' said Father Whittaker prayerfully.

On the bottle stall, which was heavily patronised, the number of bottles had diminished rapidly and the bottle of whisky was beginning to look lonely. What was more, the buyers of tickets were beginning to look sceptical.

I went to the microphone where Bertie Owen was acting as master of ceremonies. 'Bertie, you are going to be torn limb from limb if you don't put that ticket into the draw,' I warned him.

'It's OK, Mr Secombe, I'm on my way.'

He fished into his pocket for the missing ticket. His face paled even in the heat of the sun. Deeper into his pocket dived his hand, to no avail. He stared at me, wide-eyed and speechless.

'Where did you get the tickets?' I asked, as calmly as I could.

'The newsagents in the square.'

'You had better get down there as quickly as you can and hope that they have another book of green tickets.'

Before I could finish speaking he trotted through the gates watched by bewildered spectators.

By now there was a long queue of miners, steelworkers, farmers and farmers' hands, waiting to bowl for the pig. A skittle score was being kept meticulously by Evan Meredith.

In the meantime the inky clouds encroached further and a clap of thunder echoed round the valley.

The vicar became agitated. 'What are we going to do if there's a downpour?'

'It might be a good idea if we announced that teas and refreshments are being served in the church hall. That will get rid of some of the crowd.'

'Good idea, Fred.'

I went to the microphone and made the announcement. Some of the crowd began moving towards the gates as another clap of thunder shook the ground underneath our feet.

The next minute the heavens opened and emptied themselves copiously upon the earth beneath. The hapless crowd fought for cover in the three tents, which had a capacity to shelter twenty people at most. Meanwhile Father Whittaker ran to the vicarage and opened the front door to allow others to escape the elements. I joined them in the drawing room, all of us uncomfortably wet. Through the window I could see the carnival queen and her attendants perched on the back of Minty's lorry, which was about to enter the drive. As they drew near we could see that they were drenched to the skin with the sodden bunting dripping dye on their faces.

Then through the gate came the lone figure of Bertie Owen, accompanied by a flash of lightning, staggering along like the last exhausted survivor of a marathon race about to collapse at the tape. I went to the door to open it for him.

'I've got it, thank God,' he breathed as he stumbled into the hall.

'That's not the only thing you'll have, Bertie. You might have pneumonia as well, the state you're in. You'd better ask the vicar if you can go up to the bathroom to dry yourself.'

It was half an hour before the storm moved away to plague fêtes and cricket matches in other valleys. As the sun blazed down once again, the vicarage disgorged its sheltered fugitives onto the lawn where the heat began to dry their clothes in a faint aura of steam.

After drying himself in the bathroom, Bertie Owen donned his wet clothes and hurried to the bottle stall to place the number seventy-one green ticket into the box of unsold tickets, more concerned with saving his neck than with the discomfort he felt.

The rest of the day went without incident. Long after the prize draw had been made and the stalls dismantled, the battle for the piglet continued until it was won by Ianto Lewis, Penylan Farm, much to the disgust of the miners and the steelworkers. 'Why does he need a pig?' they said—or words to that effect.

As far as the vicar was concerned, he was quite happy that the fête had raised ninety-eight pounds, eleven shillings and ninepence for the missionary society. 'I'll put in the rest to make it a cheque for a hundred pounds,' he said. 'That's the highest donation they will ever have had from this parish.'

When I went to meet Eleanor in the church hall, she was sitting exhausted in the kitchen and drinking a cup of tea in splendid isolation. 'I don't think I ever want to go through that again,' she complained. 'It was bedlam and mayhem to the nth degree. Was it worth it?'

'The vicar thinks so. The fête has raised a hundred pounds.'

'At the high price of blood, sweat and tears—especially tears.'

'Never mind, love,' I said. 'Let's go to Mount Pleasant View and get the boiler going for a bath *à la* Mrs Richards. I tell you what, she would have loved to hear an account of today's happenings. It never rains except when it's pouring down, she would have said.'

Chapter Ten

'Well, Vicar, it's almost a case of "hello and goodbye", as you might say.' David Vaughan-Jenkins, churchwarden of St Mary's Church, was presiding at a presentation ceremony in the church hall after Father Whittaker's last service in Pontywen.

'We wish you every happiness in your new parish and would like you to accept this cheque as a token of our esteem.' The cheque amounted to twenty-five pounds, collected from the few people who were prepared to give and included ten pounds from Sir David Jones-Williams as a thankyou offering for his departure.

John Whittaker looked round the almost empty hall.

'Thank you, Mr Vaughan-Jenkins, for your words and thank you all for this cheque. One thing I ask is that you give my two colleagues every support until my successor arrives in the parish. Thank you, once again.'

After the brief ceremony Charles came back to Bevan's Row with Eleanor and myself, for a cup of coffee and a chat. He had heard a rumour that Elias Jenkins, an ecclesiastical martinet, was interested in coming to Pontywen.

'He may be interested but there's nothing he can do about it,' I said. 'It is the bishop's turn to appoint and he would not take kindly to Elias putting his oar in. So sleep soundly, Charles. The bogeyman won't get you.'

'Anyway, I wish his lordship would hurry up,' sighed my colleague.

'By the end of this week we shall know who it is. Not that I am in any kind of misery and I can see no reason why you should be. Unless, of course, you are fearful that you might have to work harder.'

'That's not fair, Fred.'

'Only playing, Charles. I know how you like hard work. So would you mind taking Communion to the sick this week? Here's the list. I'll do the hospital visiting. Oh, and there's a funeral on Wednesday at three o'clock. The name is Bevan—Agnes Bevan—an old lady who was living with her daughter at fourteen Balaclava Street. So would you call to see Mrs Smith, the daughter, tomorrow afternoon?'

'Poor old Charles,' said Eleanor, 'and he only came in for a chat!'

Next morning, the day of Father Whittaker's induction to his new parish of St Peter's, Abergwylfa, I received a telephone call from the bishop. 'Mr Secombe, I should like to see you at my residence on Friday at eleven o'clock. There is something I should like to discuss with you. Is the day and time convenient?'

'Certainly, my lord.'

'Good. I look forward to seeing you then.'

Throughout the day my mind kept wandering to the unexpected appointment with the bishop and what it could mean. 'Perhaps he is going to offer you Pontywen,' suggested Eleanor.

'Hardly, my love. After the short time I have been in holy orders. No way. It is probably that he wants to give me the task of looking after the parish until the new man comes, as he did last year.'

On Friday morning, as I made my way down the long drive to the bishop's palace, I could feel my heart begin to beat faster. I was ushered into his lordship's presence by his secretary.

The bishop rose to his feet and left his desk to shake hands with me. 'Good morning, Mr Secombe. Good to see you again. Sit down, will you?' He indicated an armchair near the French windows, which overlooked the lawn, and asked his secretary to bring in coffee.

The bishop was a shy man with whom conversation was always a difficult exercise. I sat down in the comfortable armchair while he resumed his seat behind his desk.

I waited for him to stop looking out through the window and to turn his attention indoors.

'Pontywen,' he said, suddenly, addressing a large blotting pad in front of him. 'Pontywen,' he repeated, this time examining the ceiling. 'Not an easy parish.' He was looking out through the window once again. 'Canon Llewellyn had done wonders with it in his long incumbency, but I am afraid that much was undone in a short time by Father Whittaker, unintentionally, of course.'

He returned his attention to the blotting pad.

'To repair the damage requires another long incumbency to restore trust between priest and people. I have given the situation much thought and prayer since the gift of the living is in my hands.'

Another interminable silence, as he mused on the scene outside, his fingers toying with the pen on his desk.

'Sometimes in life one has to take what is known as a calculated risk. I feel the parish needs someone who knows it and its problems, but one who is young and fresh enough to bring a new and lively approach in these postwar years. That is why, Mr Secombe,' swivelling his head round and looking me full in the face, 'I am offering the living of Pontywen to you.'

There was a knock on the door.

'Come in, Miss James,' called the bishop.

The secretary placed my cup of coffee on a table beside me. Had she put it in my hand, it would have been impossible for me to hold it. When she left the room the bishop continued where he had left off.

'I know it must come as a shock to you as a young man with just a few years in orders. However, I noticed how well you coped in the interregnum before Father Whittaker's induction. He tells me that you were a great help to him during his short incumbency.'

Silence number three arrived while we drank our coffee; my right hand had difficulty holding my cup and required the assistance of my left hand.

'I think that's all. You do not have to give your answer now. You may wish to let me know after you have consulted your wife.'

'If you don't mind, my lord,' I said, swallowing deeply, 'I can give you my answer now and that is I accept your offer of the living. It is a challenge I am prepared to take on. I know the people of Pontywen very well by now and I like them greatly. All I hope is that I can live up to the trust you have placed in me.'

He stood up smiling and held out his hand. 'Thank you, Mr Secombe. I shall be in touch with you about the date of the induction later on. In the meanwhile perhaps you will contact the board of dilapidations and arrange with the diocesan architect to meet you at the vicarage to consider anything that needs doing.'

I walked back down the drive in a daze. Travelling back to Pontywen in the train, I remembered my journey to the station on my first day in the parish. Today there was no Canon Llewellyn to greet me and no Mrs Richards to receive me at my digs. Instead I was the new Canon Llewellyn and my dear wife had taken the place of my old landlady.

It was past one o'clock when I arrived at 11 Bevan's Row. Eleanor's car was outside. Instead of opening the front door with my key, I knocked. My wife's footsteps pattered down the hall. 'Lost your key again, have you?' she said.

'No,' I replied. 'May I introduce the new Vicar of Pontywen?'

She flung her arms round my neck and kissed me until I was breathless. 'I told you so, but you wouldn't believe me,' she said, smiling broadly, and kissed me again.

FRED SECOMBE

The most striking thing about Fred Secombe is his enthusiasm. It bubbles over when he talks about his life's work as an Anglican clergyman and about the pleasure he has had, during retirement, in writing a fictionalised account of his memoirs. 'Suddenly,' he says, 'I had all the time in the world and I wondered what to do with myself. I'd enjoyed writing small bits and pieces over the years so I thought why not try a novel?' Because it was the laughter that he remembered best from his years as a priest in South Wales, he chose to write the books as a humorous recollection of parish life. His depiction of the small Welsh town of Pontywen seems so real that it's hard to believe that it doesn't actually exist. 'Although I have invented it,' he  says, 'it's based on life just after the war in many of the small towns and villages around the Newport area.'

Fred Secombe knew as early as the age of thirteen that he wanted to go into the Church. 'I was always very involved with Church life. By the time I was seventeen I had been accepted as a candidate for the priesthood by the bishop and later won a Welsh church scholarship which helped to pay for my college education.' Now that he's retired he misses his close involvement in parish life, so as well as attending church regularly he enjoys giving occasional sermons as a guest preacher.

Fred Secombe, like his brother Sir Harry Secombe, has a deep love of music, and was involved in staging Gilbert and Sullivan performances for over twenty-seven years. 'I do miss the performances. Altogether I formed three companies and enjoyed myself thoroughly. I would cast the show, produce it, direct it and perform in it. My role could best be described as that of a benevolent dictator!'

He is currently writing the fifth of his novels about clerical life but treats the task as a pleasure rather than burden. He writes regularly but not every day. 'Only when I feel moved,' he says, with a laugh.